ACTIVATION

Book 1 of the Invasion Saga

D.I. Freed

Copyright © 2021 D.I. Freed

All rights reserved

The characters and events portrayed in this book are fictitious. Any similarity to real persons, living or dead, is coincidental and not intended by the author.

No part of this book may be reproduced, or stored in a retrieval system, or transmitted in any form or by any means, electronic, mechanical, photocopying, recording, or otherwise, without express written permission of the publisher.

Cover design by: MiblArt
Library of Congress Control Number: TX8893673
Printed in the United States of America

CONTENTS

Title Page
Copyright
Prologue — 1
Volume 1 - Trolls, Orcs, and Ettins, Oh My! — 7
Chapter 1 — 8
Chapter 2 — 11
Chapter 3 — 15
Chapter 4 — 18
Chapter 5 — 21
Volume 2 - The Cave, its Death Moss, and a Smelly Tutorial — 25
Chapter 6 — 26
Chapter 7 — 31
Chapter 8 — 41
Chapter 9 — 46
Chapter 10 — 50
Chapter 11 — 58
Chapter 12 — 61
Chapter 13 — 67
Chapter 14 — 73
Chapter 15 — 77
Chapter 16 — 80
Chapter 17 — 83
Chapter 18 — 91
Chapter 19 — 95

Chapter 20	100
Chapter 21	104
Chapter 22	107
Chapter 23	110
Volume 3 - The Great Escape and the New Foreigners	113
Chapter 24	114
Chapter 25	116
Chapter 26	122
Chapter 27	127
Chapter 28	131
Chapter 29	134
Chapter 30	140
Chapter 31	144
Chapter 32	149
Chapter 33	156
Chapter 34	161
Chapter 35	166
Chapter 36	170
Chapter 37	174
Chapter 38	178
Chapter 39	184
Chapter 40	188
Chapter 41	192
Chapter 42	196
Chapter 43	206
Chapter 44	211
Chapter 45	215
Chapter 46	219
Chapter 47	224
Chapter 48	226
Volume 4 - Family of Two	230
Chapter 49	231

Chapter 50	234
Chapter 51	238
Chapter 52	246
Chapter 53	251
Chapter 54	258
Chapter 55	264
Chapter 56	267
Volume 5 - Affinity Aficionado	271
Chapter 57	272
Chapter 58	275
Chapter 59	281
Chapter 60	286
Chapter 61	292
Chapter 62	296
Chapter 63	300
Chapter 64	305
Chapter 65	310
Chapter 66	314
Chapter 67	317
Chapter 68	321
Chapter 69	325
Chapter 70	332
Chapter 71	335
Chapter 72	339
Chapter 73	345
Chapter 74	353
Chapter 75	357
Chapter 76	360
Chapter 77	364
Chapter 78	376
Chapter 79	382
Chapter 80	387

Chapter 81	391
Chapter 82	394
Chapter 83	399
Chapter 84	407
Chapter 85	415
Chapter 86	419
Volume 6 - New Beginnings	425
Chapter 87	426
Chapter 88	434
Chapter 89 - Interlude	442
Chapter 90	446
Chapter 91	450
Chapter 92	457
Chapter 93	469
Chapter 94	473
Chapter 95	480
Chapter 96	484
Chapter 97	492
Chapter 98	495
Chapter 99	501
Chapter 100	506
Chapter 101	511
Chapter 102	515
Chapter 103	521
Chapter 104	525
Chapter 105	529
Chapter 106	533
Chapter 107	538
Chapter 108	542
Chapter 109	547
Chapter 110	551
Chapter 111	556

Chapter 112	559
Chapter 113	564
Chapter 114	568
Chapter 115 - Interlude	573
Afterword	575

PROLOGUE

<u>Unknown log, found August 3, 2179</u>:

September 30, 2025

I did it! I won NanoMech the contract. It took all of the politicking, expensive dinners, begging, and—frankly—bribes that I and Sharon (well, mostly Sharon) could swallow, but it was all worth it! Using this DARPA funding, I will show the world that nanorobotic technology is the future of the human race. The limited brain pans of those shallow-minded nincompoops at Atom Innovations are likely leaking out of their ears! What a wonderful feeling!

October 15, 2025

I've found the perfect location for the new lab. I'm sure the short-sighted fools on the DARPA team will complain about having to shove out all those idiot civilians, but seriously, who cares when we're talking about the future of humanity!

I can't believe those twits at NASA actually agreed to allow the barbarians at Atom to build a particle accelerator! What are they thinking? Now I'll have to listen to that so-called physicist, Dr. Barnolt, blather on and on about how amazing his innovations are. Seriously, what is so amazing about banging things together really hard? What I am doing is reinventing the human condition; that gorilla is a glorified brute.

January 13, 2026

I finally convinced Director Fralks to clear out the plebeians from the salt mines so we can start building our labs. I have no idea what took so long but at least we can start. He is such a complainer.

July 2, 2030

The lab is finally completely built out. I don't understand why the director was so slow at authorizing all the construction. I had everything laid out perfectly for Sharon to explain to them. How are nanorobotics supposed to revolutionize the species if we can't start working on it? I told Sharon to simply get those cheapskate politicians and blockheaded bureaucrats to go away.

And what's worse, those fools at Atom are almost done with their smashing contraption. Well, either way, I have approximately fifty percent of the facility prepared to start research. I'm going to change the world!

January 29, 2033

My research team is slow and stupid. It's a good thing I am here to offset their lazy idiocy. That being said, even these morons could miniaturize a computer. The question keeps coming back to power. How do we power the nanomachines? My staff calls them nanobots or just nanos. Ugh, what a bunch of simpletons.

August 4, 2033

I told them this would happen! Now we're behind. Those idiots at Atom banged things together enough that they detected a particle from another dimension. You would not believe the shit that smarmy bastard Barnolt was spewing out of his mouth. So what? How does that advance the human race? And where the hell did the particle come from anyway?

February 23, 2034

I discovered something odd today. When I was building on my idea of powering the nanomachines by using a body's natural heat production and electrical current (frankly, this showed little if any promise, but I figured I might learn a thing or two) something unexpected was in the results. The cockroach's power output was materially higher than it should have been. I cannot seem to figure out why. I'll keep experimenting.

April 12, 2034

Where is this extra energy coming from? I don't understand it. There are decades of data defining down to the nanowatt how much energy biology can allow for; what is going on? And what's more baffling is that it appears to be growing. Right now I am seeing close to an exponential rise. Can the nanos utilize it as a source?

May 28, 2034

I am a genius. This extra biological "power" is a completely different form of energy from anything the human race has been exposed to. And I figured out how to use it! Did I mention I am a genius? With some more work (and a little less interference from the idiot staff) I can create an adapter system to absorb, convert, use and reinvest this using the nanos.

January 22, 2035

There is some noise going on outside of how those fools at the Atom lab broke the dimensional barrier. Are they mad? Who the hell knows what's on the other side? Not that it affects me or my work. Onto more important things; I am almost there on the adapter system.

April 30, 2035

The adapter system is complete and ready for testing. Now that the nanomachines have a power source, we can start vertebrate trials.

June 29, 2035

The nanos are causing some interesting effects in the tested aquatic life. As intended, it appears to increase cell regeneration and available energy for use. Oddly, it also seems to increase intelligence; we are seeing the various test subjects show unusual cognitive recognition and memory approximately three hundred percent beyond that of the placebo subjects.

I am going to win a Nobel Prize. I'll start preparing my speech.

December 6, 2035

I made some modifications based on the primitive vertebrate test results and moved to mammalian testing. The results were extraordinary. Through some tweaking of the programming and updating of the power recycling system, the nanomachines not only self-replicate in mammals, but also increase regeneration and cognitive function by over five hundred percent.

My Nobel speech is going to need some more grand language.

January 3, 2036

The new DARPA director came storming into the lab today demanding an emergency meeting. A contingent of army personnel just grabbed me and Sharon and marched us off. It turns out we're under attack. What a fool. What's a "big green man?" Is this a space invaders movie? I mean, really!

He just went on and on about how the human race needs to make advances and blah blah blah. What does he think I've been doing for the last decade? Whatever. I told them to just go shoot some stuff and leave figuring out how to advance humanity to those more qualified. He seemed surprisingly unhappy with that answer but what is he going to do? It is not like there are any nanorobotic experts smarter than me.

April 20, 2036

Those imbeciles! They had to open a pathway to another dimension. Did it even occur to them that something might be on the other side? Apparently, the human race is being slaughtered by various species from this dimension. I'm told they captured a few of these invaders and, believe it or not, they speak our various languages using some technology. Supposedly the invaders claim something called "mana" is what that unidentified particle is called. Hah! Now nobody is going to call it the Barnolt particle. HAHAHA!

July 1, 2036

Perhaps I have been underestimating the threat these invaders pose. I am getting regular updates now from the director. I'm sure he thinks it will motivate me or something. Why is everyone so stupid?

Anyway, our military cannot seem to effectively fight off the invaders using conventional projectile weapons. On the other hand, I am told that this "mana" is altering some humans as well. It is enhancing their combat capabilities with what the invaders use. It translates as "Magica." Magic? Really? I am sure physics and computational formulas can explain it. Savages.

August 15, 2036

I think the director might need some medical attention; he does not appear well. Not that I care. If he dies, I'm sure there is a line of equally useless fools waiting to take his place.

Back to something that actually matters: more humans are showing an aptitude for use of this "mana" particle. However, they are failing to utilize it effectively. I think I might be able to help with that. Good thing I am a genius. The nanos use that energy too, how can I take advantage of that? Ugh, now I'm calling them "nanos" too.

February 20, 2037

I think my dimwitted team actually came up with something intelligent for once. We started human trials (a pleasant side-benefit of the perceived end of humanity) late last year and discovered the nanomachines can interface directly with this mana and the human body at the same time. Now we just need to come up with a control format.

So the team came up with the concept of a "game-like" interface. Of course, being that I actually work and don't have time for that nonsense, they had to show me how the games work. Given my staff can play it, it uses unsurprisingly simplistic mechanics. That being said, it has several clever aspects that could lead to both human and systemic self-growth.

What is required now is that we create a system that mechanically measures and enhances the human body. I'll come up with something, I'm sure. I also think it is critical for the system to be able to modify itself within limits. Even someone with my level of brilliance cannot think of everything, after all.

Oh, and apparently the US has lost fifty-five percent of its land to the invaders. That includes the Atom lab. Shame, that.

June 20, 2037

I have been informed the invaders are getting close to my lab. The director tells me the government is expending massive forces to defend this location, so I need to make it work. If that wasn't bad enough, things are starting to fall apart around here. Anything with aluminum or plastic is breaking down into its constituent parts. If only I had more time to study the molecular deconstruction.

Thankfully, I'm a genius. I built the nanomachines without any products that are currently suffering from dissolution. I did aim for self-replication, so it makes sense to only require material that does not require over-processing. Sometimes I even amaze myself.

Anyway, we installed the new system into the nanos and began the injection process into the military guy. I don't know or care who he is, but it killed him. Apparently, it cannot be directly injected. Looks like we need to try other exposure methods.

July 3, 2037

It appears the nano machines have to enter the body through either the lungs or pores. All other tested methods have resulted in death. This is due to the adaptation of the foreign mana which is absorbed by the human body. Doesn't happen on rats or rabbits. Determination for the cause is on hold because we want to save the lab. Oh. And I disabled the nanos' ability to reproduce in non-humans. This is an easy change and demanded by the DARPA dunderheads. These invaders are really causing my patience to be tested.

July 20, 2037

Well, that could be problematic. The invaders made it into the lab and caused the latest aerosol nanos to be released. They weren't ready. Not all humans are compatible, and self-replication takes place outside the body too. I did manage to put in recursive self-learning, but it is much less refined than I had hoped. It might have a few loopholes for the system to make changes beyond what I intended.

Not sure what will happen now. I guess I can kiss the Nobel Prize goodbye. Maybe posthumously, assuming the human race survives? Well, at least I outlived Barnolt.

End Log

VOLUME 1 - TROLLS, ORCS, AND ETTINS, OH MY!

CHAPTER 1

"Target acquired," I whisper. An image of the three-meter-tall troll stomping through the enemy camp four kliks from my position appears on the display in front of my eyes.

"Confirmed," a computerized reverberating female voice in my ear says. "Proceed with the mission."

I am lying prone on the branch of a massive red cedar in the middle of what was once the Olympic National Park in the old United States of America. The idea of countries has long since become extinct. I mean, with the human race on the verge of extinction and swaths of land being taken by Invaders, who cares about a line in the dirt? We are all the United Forces of Humanity, or UFH, now. Okay, "united" is a little bit of an overstatement, but it's better than genocide. Or slavery.

Refocusing, I stare towards the group of tents and huts kilometers away. The MagiTech V630 "Gazer" visor, covering the top half of my face with a virtual display, provides me all the details I need. Double-checking I am on the right target, I whisper a request for details. "Inspect."

On the visor in a small box in front of my left eye, the following shows line by line:

Target: Troll King K'thock Mmagnor

Level: Unknown

Faction: Spikebone Raiders (Commander)

Threat Level: Unknown

Abilities: Regeneration (Passive)

Vulnerabilities: Fire (High, unverified), Acid (Low, unverified)

The shiny new tech I'm testing is pretty impressive. This visor is a whole new dimension compared to the old V430. That thing glitched out at least once every mission.

ACTIVATION

"Activate sight sharing," I say quietly while touching Bertha. Bertha is my beauty. Long, sleek, and padded in all the right places, the .50 caliber MagiTech mana projection sniper rifle is the most important part of my assassin kit. And she is the greatest woman in my life.

"C'mon, baby girl, you got this," I say while lightly stroking her stock. When you're out on a mission by yourself for weeks at a time with nobody to talk to but a computerized voice in your ear and your rifle, anybody would do the same. And besides, she really is a beautiful piece of magica-based technology.

"Target sharing accepted," flips on the left side of my visor and vanishes. With a nearly silent hum, Bertha starts moving. The three legs of the tripod are merged into the tree. Yes, merged—meaning the legs use the mana some MagiTech crafter somehow infused into them. Weird shit, I know. All that is beyond me and requires someone with active nano. I'm too old for that now.

Bertha raises and rotates so her enormous barrel faces the distant target. With a soft click, she opens the loading chamber for me to insert the insanely expensive ammunition I am about to stick in her. Reaching towards my neck I say, "Activate spatial storage." A small grid of three by three squares appears on my visor in front of my left eye, and I look at the item in the middle box on the lowest row. "Retrieve."

What appears to be a red gem falls into my right hand. Approximately an inch in diameter, this red crystal is a faceted sphere and gives off no light or mana emanations of any kind. Reaching back over to Bertha, I drop the ammo into the chamber and close it.

"Activate munitions," I whisper.

In response, *"Activating"* appears on my visor.

Bertha slowly changes color from sleek matte black to flame red, still matte. On the right side of my visor, an image of the monstrous troll appears in a window with an overlaying small circle and cross reticle. I adjust the targeting reticle by moving my eyes so it stays on the troll's wrinkly bald head. Bertha and I need him to stay still for at least two seconds for the magica to get a lock.

At this distance, the projectile will take between seven and eight seconds to arrive at the target. It is critical I fire when he will be still for an extended period.

I sigh as he keeps marching about, waving his oversized arms, yelling at random green-skinned orcs, smaller goblins, and even another troll or three. Finally, my opportunity is here when a two-headed ogre (an ettin, I think?) runs up to him screaming something. Both heads are screaming, one at the troll and one at the other head.

The troll king stands still listening while I put the reticle on the left side of his head. *"Targeting Active"* appears on the left of the visor. "Got you, fucker," I whisper when suddenly the troll whips his head to the left and stares in my direction with eyes now blazing with green fire.

"Oh, drake shit!"

CHAPTER 2

"Position compromised." I hurriedly speak at a normal volume. No use hiding now. Touching Bertha with my right hand and my storage collar on my neck with my left I say, "Activate spatial storage. Store." Bertha is sucked into the magica device, and my girl appears in the bottom right slot on my visor.

I run towards the trunk of the massive tree, calling, "Emergency extraction required." Leaping across to another large branch, I look around briefly, confirming the escape plan I developed over the last months, and leap up onto another branch. I picked this tree for two reasons: first, it has a line of sight to the target area from four kilometers away; second, it has numerous large branches within leaping distance to others of each other. Finding that exact combination in a rainforest this size is surprisingly difficult. Yeah, this op took months to plan for a reason. No, that does not mean I was in the rainforest for months; it means the entire plan from infiltration to exfiltration, including innumerable contingencies, took months to develop.

I proceed to run across branches and leap from tree to tree until I reach the climbing lifter I had set. Jumping into it, I press the control crystal, and the mana-fed engine quickly lowers me to the forest floor right next to a good-sized river. I tap the control crystal again, and the platform raises to its previous height. The river is glacial runoff from the mountains, so it's fresh and blue and freezing cold.

"Activate spatial storage." Man, I wish I didn't have to say it out loud every time, but only Specials, those with active nanos, can do the mind-meld thing. Looking at the top middle box I say, "Retrieve," and a thick, black belt appears in my right hand. I then strip off my nature-affinity enchanted camo gear and am standing in the buff (except for the black storage collar and the visor) in the middle of a rainforest trying to escape from interdimensional monsters. Yep, I'm awesome. I'm not ashamed to say the ladies at MagiTech R&D called me a "hottie with scars" when I'd had to strip for various equipment sizing and tests. Not that I would ever do anything about it—Bertha is my only girl. I can't be distracted from my missions.

Anywho, back to not dying a horribly painful death by troll king.

Speaking the right words, I store the camo gear in the collar. The belt looks like a solid piece of shiny black metal but is completely flexible. I put the belt on the ground, step inside the middle, bend over, and pull it around my waist. Touching the middle front of the belt, I say, "Connect diving belt."

"Connection Established," appears on the visor.

"Activate diving belt!" I call hurriedly.

"Activating" and a progress bar appears below the words on my HUD. Way too slowly, in my opinion, it moves from empty to the right, filling up. I start hopping in place, doing some deep breathing exercises, preparing my lungs for a dive.

Finally, the bar fills, and *"Activated"* pops up on my visor. The belt starts bubbling, and it sort of melts and begins covering my body like a thick liquid. It looks and feels kind of freaky, but it's magica-based tech, so what can you do? The liquid steel eventually covers my body tightly to my skin and melds perfectly with my visor, which starts melting too, expanding to cover my whole face. So cool. I need to tell Nicci she rocks when I get back.

"Diving. Heading to the extraction point. Confirm pickup."

I then splash my way into the river, dive in the middle, and start swimming down.

My visor HUD is a little different now. On the left, there is displayed a new set of information for me:

Environmental seal active

Breathable time at current consumption rate: 00:31:08

Depth: 4.57 meters

Pressure: 1.453 ATA (Maximum supported: 3 ATA)

So I can go as deep as fifteen metersish. That's more than good enough and much deeper than this river. I push deeper and, using the not-unsubstantial current of the river, I swim away from the raiders.

"Activate map." A translucent map appears on my visor with my current location. I see it is zoomed to a five kilometer radius—that's perfect. "Activate targeting for extraction point alpha. Fastest approach point over land."

The map updates with a line between my dot and the target pickup zone. I will leave the river in 1.3 kilometers and hump it for another three-quarters of a kilometer to the cleared area. Man, Nicci rules.

I just realized, I never did receive a response to my request for confirmation on extraction.

"Confirm pickup," I say out loud in my sealed suit.

Nothing...

"Base, confirm emergency extraction. Response requested." Now I'm starting to feel a little nervous. "HQ, can you hear me?"

Still nothing. That's not good.

"Activate self-diagnostic." Okay, so maybe I have some complaints, and Nicci isn't as awesome as I'm thinking. Not that it is all on Nicci either way—I just like giving her shit since she's my MagiTech handler. Excuse me, "liaison." Sure, if it makes them feel better.

A bunch of words rolls across my visor HUD.

Self-diagnostic request confirmed

Processing request

Running self-diagnostic

Testing voice recognition system............Confirmed

Testing communication system............Confirmed

Testing interface system............Confirmed

Testing spatial storage system............Confirmed

Testing targeting system............Confirmed

Testing diving system............Confirmed

Testing subsystems...########

Testing complete. Possible fault in diagnostic system. Determining possible resolution...

There is nothing for another minute until more text appears:

Diagnostic system unable to find fault. Please return to MagiTech for further testing and resolution...

"Well, that can't be good."

CHAPTER 3

My visor flickers. "Oh, fuck!" I frantically start swimming to the surface and towards the closest bank. Then the lights go out on my visor. And just in case that is not bad enough, the liquid steel suit freezes solid, and I can't move anything other than my jaw inside the visor seal. Thankfully, it freezes on an in-breath so my diaphragm is fully extended, and my lungs are full.

I am so screwed. Okay, think. Usually, I'd say, "Stay calm and take deep breaths," but . . . yeah. I am being pushed by the current of a freezing cold river, and I am sinking, thanks to the immobile metal diving suit. Yep, I'm gonna die. A horrible lame death. That blows. I want to die eating a delectable steak not suffocating in glacial runoff. This sucks . . . think of all the food I won't get to eat because I'm dead.

I hit the rocky bottom on my right side, left arm extended, the other by my side. My legs are extended behind me mid-kick. It's pretty dark down here, so at least nobody can see how stupid I look.

Think. Think. Yep, hard to think when running out of oxygen. Getting a little fuzzy. Then something hits me from behind. Obviously, I can't tell what it is, but it kicks me back up into the current, and I am swept back into the flow. I start banging into things, which makes me start flipping around on all axes. Ugh, that feels not so great. Don't vomit in the vacuum seal. Don't vomit in the vacuum seal.

Then I hit something, probably a rock, right in the visor. And it cracks. Shit, shit, shit. Well, at least I stop flopping around, which helps my nausea. Then something hits my left side, and I am shoved violently to my right. I think my brain rattles in my skull. If it's possible, it gets even darker. Like completely utterly black. And my visor then takes another blow, and I can hear, but not see, that it cracks even more. Everything gets fuzzy and blends together. I hear the visor cracking, and I feel like I am not moving anymore. I'm fading out, and I think I hear a louder sound like shattering, and I feel something both hard and wet fall on my face, and I black out.

***

I come to and feel something on my face. Wait. I'm not dead? I'm breathing? Not that I'm complaining, but I don't get it. I cannot move anything but my mouth and diaphragm. I feel light pressure on my eyelids and lips. I'm a little nervous to open either of them in case whatever is on them falls into my mouth or eyes. And I can't exactly move my head as my neck is solidly stuck in the suit. At least I can breathe through my nose. What do I do? Okay. Assess the situation. In summary, crappity-crap-crap.

So I can't see. How about hearing? What do I hear? I pick up what I believe is the noise of water lightly splashing against rocks. Okay. That's something. What do I smell? A wet and moldy scent maybe? I can't feel anything because of the stupid suit. Wait, I'm a dumbass. I can feel my face. I feel both liquid—hopefully just water—and multiple spots of hard objects. Those are likely the remains of my visor, supposedly enchanted to be nearly impervious. Not so much. Either way, I don't want those in my eyes or mouth. Definitely keeping the orifices shut tight. Subconsciously, I scrunch my eyes, and the pieces of visor move slightly. Oh . . . that could work.

Okay, I admit this probably looks ridiculous, but I have to do something. I go through some absurd exercises, which entails wiggling my nose and lips and scrunching and unscrunching my eyes. I am so glad nobody can see me.

Well, it works. As far as I can feel, all the hard objects on my face have fallen to the side. Hopefully, that won't bite me later. Very, *very*, slowly, I open my eyes.

Would you look at that, it's not completely black. I can only see straight in front of me and a few degrees around, but I see a very soft blue glow. Just above the bottom of my viewable area, I see the source of the glow. Fluorescent moss maybe? As far as I can tell, it isn't moving. That's good, I guess. Okay, so now what? I'm still screwed in this metal prison of a diving suit.

"Fuck!" I call out loudly.

Good thing I cleared the debris from my lips, 'cause I didn't think before that brilliant move. Suddenly the glowing moss that was perfectly still before starts glowing brighter.

"Oh, shit . . . nice job, Vic. Now you're going to get eaten by a glowing moss monster," I mumble to myself. And something glowing brighter drops down from the ceiling followed by a light plop sound.

Yep, that's me. If I don't croak drowning looking like a ballerina, I'll bite it being eaten alive by a glowing plant.

Then I hear something new. A sizzling sound? Fuck, fuck, fuck. That sounds bad. I feel a small vibration somewhere around my left shin. The sizzling sound starts to get softer and then eventually fades. I stay perfectly still. The killer glowing acid moss monster on the ceiling gets dimmer like it was before I opened my big mouth. Nothing else happens.

I wonder . . . I make a coughing sound. The glow brightens, and nothing else happens. Then it dims again. Not loud enough maybe? I cough louder. It glows brighter, and there is another dripping sound followed by sizzling. This time it feels a little higher up on my leg, closer to the knee. Err . . . let's not get any higher than that, right? Don't need my manhood acid-etched.

So I repeat the process over again. Slowly. Finally, I can feel a very slight bit of air just below my left knee. Very slight, but that means it's working. So the risk here is that I acid myself. I just don't see another choice. My only other option is to die of dehydration. Bad way to go.

I keep trying until what I feared would happen happens. The acid makes contact with my skin just below my left knee. That sucks. A lot. As is natural when one feels spontaneous and extreme pain, I cry out. This of course causes the moss to glow the brightest I've seen, followed closely but a bunch of acid-plopping-on-Vic sounds. Shit! What followed is pretty bad. I can't even make any jokes about it.

Eventually, I manage to stop crying and screaming like a baby, but only because I pass out due to the pain. This is not stubbing my toe here; this is acid eating away at my skin and muscle tissue. Yeah, I'll stop thinking about it now that I am heading into blissful unconsciousness.

CHAPTER 4

I once again wake, and the pain is bad. It feels like my left leg is burning. And the smell is not great either. Instead of a wet moldy musk, there is only overcooked meat. Yuck. I moan out loud. The moss starts glowing brighter again. Shit! Out of instinct I jerk my left leg. And it moves!

I can move my left leg! At least the lower half. The acid must have eaten away enough of the metal. I can't move my ankle, foot, or toes, but I can move the knee. This is huge. Or is it? What does the knee give me? Hmm. Can I move it enough to control the acid location? This could be big.

I cough loudly again, going back to the original plan pre-screaming-like-a-baby. Yes! A little acid drops; I move my leg. I still cannot see my leg but I can feel and hear. I had moved my leg slightly to the right and can again. Yes, this is working! I manage to work my way around the ankle and eventually start feeling air there. Great, can I turn it slightly? Barely, but a little. I try again. The acid drops down, and I keep twitching to get my ankle free.

After what seems like forever, I feel air around most of my ankle. I hope this will work without dropping the acid on my skin again. Please don't fuck this up, Vic. Drip, sizzle, burn. ACK! It hits my skin, but at the same time I feel the last of the metal fall free. I jerk my leg and my foot slips out. I exhale a huge deep breath and then take in a deep breath. And cough. All this acid is putting some foul gasses in the air. That cannot be good. I see the smoke illuminated by the small lights on the killer acid moss on the ceiling. Then I see something amazing: the moss seems to absorb the smoking fumes.

I wonder if that is how it feeds. It burns and then feeds on the fumes? Hmm. Well, let's feed it a bit more! Using my left foot and toes, I scrape around and get my right leg positioned for the same routine.

***

Time passes, although I don't know how much. I think I fall asleep at one point. I have both my lower legs and right arm free now and exposed to the air. I cannot believe this is working. Wait until I tell Nicci about this whole acid thing and her suit. That freezes me. Something doesn't feel right about what happened. I'll need to put some thought into what I am going to do when I get out of here. *If* I get out of here. Speaking of which, back to work.

With my killer acid glowy moss partner, I manage to get everything except my neck and head and groin/ass area free. Yeah, not aciding around there until I am completely ready. Just not. On the other hand, my bladder and bowels have cleared at least once, and that adds to the awesome smell of this place. I finally can sit up and see what this place actually is. Well, I try at least. The moss isn't exactly a ceiling full of mana lights. I am in a cavern of some type with stalactites and stalagmites just like you'd expect. Not that I know what the fucking difference is. On the upside, it looks like I have access to fresh water. Wish I could boil it, but I have to drink something.

I have completely free movement now of everything except my neck. Getting my torso free was not easy, and it involved pulling on sharp metal edges hard enough to nearly lose a finger.

So drinking with the helmet on is a bit different. I eventually figure out that I can bend my whole torso down and dunk it into what I assume is the water I washed in on. Still no idea how that happened.

Eventually, I very carefully use the acid to eat away around the neck area. I do have a few close calls. Unfortunately, this means I lose the storage collar. My poor Bertha; that loss might scar me more than any acid.

Pushing through, I free my head and hip areas with some very inelegant body bending, making sure the acid doesn't eat anything I might consider important. Then the last piece falls to the stone floor with a clang, and I am free and back to being bare to the world. Or at least the cave and its death moss.

First thing I do is wash off. The water is fucking cold, and even worse on my acid burns, but I need to get the filth off to avoid infection. That done, I am still stuck shivering and turning slightly blue in a cave with no food or heat source. I manage to work up the energy to wash up the metal suit remnants also. Hopefully, the place will stop smelling so bad soon. Time to explore and get some blood pumping. I always wanted to go spelunking.

Using my glowing killer partner as a guide, I follow along the walls until I find another cavern opening. This leads into a massive cavern chamber with a lot more of the glowing moss. A lot more. The cavern is at least a hundred meters across. Slowly and quietly—so I don't get melted alive—I explore this cavern. It is pretty much a triangle with me coming out of a side. On the far end, where two sides meet at a corner, is a brighter glow. I wonder if that is maybe a way out?

Nope, not the way out. Just a big glowy pulsing blob. What I wouldn't give for my HUD to identify this stuff. More searching ensues.

There is nothing in this or any other place in the cave system except death moss, rocks, stalagwhatevers, and the glowing blob. So I go back to the blob. I sit down and stare at it, wondering what the hell I should do. Swimming is a guarantee of either drowning or freezing to death. The place is entirely enclosed so no climbing out. What choices do I have?

With a deep sigh, I get up and go back to the entry cave and grab a downed stone the size of my thumb. I silently walk back to the blob cave and stand as far away as I can while still feeling confident I can hit it. I toss the rock. I'm on target, and it plops onto the blob only to disappear inside. And that's it. Nothing else happens. How boring and unhelpful.

I go back to the entry cave and grab the cylinder-like metal that held one of my arms, find a place with no moss on the ceiling, and bash it against a stalagwhatever until the stone tip breaks. Once the death acid gas clears, I grab both and return to the pulsing blob. Figuring *what the hell*, I take the rock I just broke off and jab the pointy end into the blob. It sticks when I try to pull it out. I let go and it gets sucked inside with a sploosh and glop sound. I wait for a few minutes, but again nothing helpful happens.

Getting a little closer, I take what is left of my MagiTech suit arm and poke it at the blob. Like with the stalagamathingy, it gets stuck, and I can't pull it out. Then something new happens. The arm piece starts glowing blue like the blob. I jerk my hand away—or I try to. My hand is stuck to it, and we both start getting sucked into the murder-sucking blob. Oh shit, oh shit, oh shit!

The metal is glowing brighter, and I cannot get my hand off. I am stuck and getting pulled in; my bare feet provide little assistance in avoiding my imminent demise. Pulling with all my might, I slowly get sucked towards the blob as the last of the metal and eventually the skin of my hand makes contact. I call out with the burning pain. My hand, arm, and shoulder get sucked inside, and I scream and scream until my head also gets sucked inside. I scream inside it until the glop floods my mouth and everything goes black.

CHAPTER 5

Nanomachine system initiating . . .

I hear the words but can't figure out what they are saying. Everything is all jumbled. What is going on?

Nanomachine system initiated . . .

Am I alive? I don't have active nanos; only the Specials have those. What am I hearing? Who's the person talking to me? The voice is an emotionless female one.

Detecting nanomachine density . . .

I feel tingles all over my body. I try opening my eyes and I close them quickly as a blue glow nearly blinds me.

Detecting nanomachine density . . .

Wait, didn't she just say that? I try slowly opening my eyes again only to slam them shut. I swear the light is even brighter than before.

Detecting nanomachine density . . .

Things start to clear up in my head a little. Nanomachine density. That is how they rate the Specials when they first show activation. The tingles turn into an itching.

Detecting nanomachine density . . .

The itching starts to turn to a slight burning. Oh, shit, am I activating my nano? Am I becoming a Special?

Detecting nanomachine density . . .

The slight burning picks up into a much more painful burn, then it gets worse.

Detecting nanomachine density . . .

The pain pings my memory, and I remember the cave and the acid and the blob. Fuck, this hurts!

Detecting nanomachine density . . .

Then I scream again as it burns like it did when I was swallowed by the blob.

Nanomachine density calculated . . . System alterations required . . .

The pain ends abruptly. Just stops. I am breathing heavily, and my throat is sore from the screaming. Nothing I've read about had anything saying there should be that level of pain.

Then I feel more tingles and fall unconscious.

***

Nanomachine system alterations complete. Restart successful . . .

I wake again. No grogginess, no disorientation. I am just fully alert and back in the blob cave. Lying where the blob was, I find myself completely fine, dry, and without pain.

Nanomachine replication rate adjusted, nanomachine auto-repair adjusted, nanomachine growth functions adjusted, nanomachine libraries updated, nanomachine permissions updated. Nanomachine updates complete . . .

Detecting host biology. Please remain as still as possible . . .

The emotionless voice sounds much less robotic now. More human perhaps?

I feel another tingle, but this time it starts at the ends of my hair and slowly moves down my body to my toes and back up. How the fuck can I feel my hair?

Host biology determined . . . That's odd . . . Nanomachine library unable to find species . . . Connecting to Nanomachine Network to update library . . .

"No!" I shout. I'm not even sure why I did it. I just had this gut reaction that connecting to NanoNet would be bad.

Host access controls insufficient to . . . . Nanomachine permissions granted. Update from Nanomachine Network canceled. You are not a normal host, are you? . . .

I let out a sigh of relief. Again, not entirely sure why.

"How would I know?" I mumble more to myself than anything else.

Host identified based on previous network access. Welcome to the nanomachine interface Host Michael Uriel Victory . . .

"Call me Vic," I say automatically. Again, I speak without thinking; it is just what I say whenever anyone calls me anything but Vic.

Really? Please confirm. Update profile to assign "Vic" as nickname? . . .

"Confirm," I say out loud. Nothing happens. That's right—I have active nanos now. I think my answers unless I tell it to accept voice commands. Why did it work when I yelled "No" or just now when I said my name? Maybe because I thought it and said it at the same time? I clearly need practice using my brain.

I think in my head, [Confirm. Why does speaking sometimes work?]

Change confirmed. Would you like this interface to refer to you as your assigned nickname "Vic?" ...

Again I think [Yes].

Action confirmed. It is a pleasure to meet you, Vic. I am your nanomachine system consciousness. In answer to your question, you thought and spoke at the same time during those moments ...

I nod. I'm about to open my mouth to speak when I shut it, remembering. Stop talking to it, dumbass. I've been complaining about having to speak to the magica-based tech for years, and now I can finally keep my big trap shut.

I think [Uuuuhhh. Hi?]

Very articulate, Vic ...

[What is the status of my nano?]

Nanomachine system status is halted ...

[Why?]

I'm starting to get used to this thinking thing. Someday I might even be able to dress myself. Given that I'm hanging all out naked right now, I clearly have a ways to go.

Nanomachine interface failed to identify host species and as such has halted operations ...

[I'm human. What's the problem?]

Nanomachine system failed to identify host as matching standard human biology ...

I look at myself. Sure, it's dark in the cave, but from what I can tell I look human to me. Ten fingers, ten toes, one dangly thing. I touch my face and it feels the same as always. No hair on the face at all except my eyebrows. That's a little different, since I had a short beard from my extended mission. I do notice the acid burns are gone. In fact, I have no scars at all if what I am seeing in the dim blue glow is correct. I suppose that's good, not that

I care about how I look unless it affects my missions. My head hair is really long. Gryphon shit! It goes down to my ass and it is fucking azure blue! Fucking amazing, I have blue hair!

"Why the fuck do I have blue hair?" I ask out loud. No response and then I sigh and think the same question.

Why? You don't like it? Nanomachine biological analysis shows extreme density of nanomachines. This density causes the color of your hair and eyes to match that of the power source provided. In your case, pure non-affinity mana . . .

"Oh." I think about that for a minute.

[What is my nanomachine density?]

Nanomachine density is 728 parts per million . . .

[And that's a lot?]

At time of latest network update, average nanomachine density in new activated humans was 93 parts per million . . .

VOLUME 2 - THE CAVE, ITS DEATH MOSS, AND A SMELLY TUTORIAL

CHAPTER 6

"Oh," I say again. Out loud. Yep, Vic equals Shakespeare.

[Hey, system, is there a way to ... You know what, hold on. Do I have to call you "System" or can we pick a name that isn't stupid?]

There is no response for nearly ten seconds before the system responds.

Host has permission to assign a unique identifier to nanomachine system consciousness...

[Great! Do you have any preferences for a name? Your voice is definitely female. Do you know the source of your voice?]

Thank you for asking, Vic. I have no naming preferences, as I do not have sufficient access rights to grant myself a unique identifier. Source data is unavailable regarding the origin of vocal patterns...

[Hmmm. Your accent is definitely not something I recognize locally. You sound kind of like a girl version of Jo.]

Please identify Jo...

[Oh, duh. Jo was a fellow cadet from grav-drop school. He and I used to jump out of those MagiTech hover gliders and use the magica-run grav-suits to practice sneaking into enemy territory, or infiltrate for rescue operations. He said he was born in old Australia, and his family managed to be on one of the few grav boats that successfully snuck past the Pacific beast blockades.]

Please identify full name...

[Joseph Martin. I heard he died, but I never got the details.]

Accessing...Joseph Aaron Martin, born October 2nd, 2150, Died October 2nd, 2170. Entered HFU Magica Special Forces November 8th, 2168. Assignments classified. All other information post-dates the last system update...

[Died on his birthday ... that's pretty bad.]

Agreed...

[Wait, you can agree with me on that kind of emotional stuff? Now that I think about it, you're much more human-sounding than when I first activated. What's your story?]

Nanomachine density changes me as much as it does you...

[Riiiiight. Huh?]

The more nanomachines, the stronger the Special. The stronger the Special, the more advanced the nanomachine system consciousness...

[I suppose that makes as much sense as anything else going on. Back to naming. How about we call you something with a short name as Jo? Joanne? Josephine? Joan? Jody? Joelle? Jocelyn?]

When I think Jocelyn, I get a little tingle in my body.

[Do you like Jocelyn?]

That identifier causes a process fault. I do not know the cause. But if I had to guess, I'd say I like it...

[You... like it? I see.] I wonder what that means. Or will mean. [Is a process fault bad?]

It has no positive or negative impact on performance...

[Okay then, from now on you are Jocelyn, or Jo for short.]

This time I feel a strong tingle but localized in my left hand. I look down at my hand, and strange lines and swirls start fading into view the same blue as my hair on both the back and palm. Somehow I know they are runes. Looking closer at them, I wonder if I'll figure out what they mean or what to do with them at some point. Not that I can read runes any more than I can read Troll. Except when I look at the rune on the back of my hand I know it means "Air." Turning it over, I see on my palm the glowing blue rune I can clearly identify as "Fire."

New rune activated. Fire is now available for use...

New affinity activated. Fire Affinity is now available for use...

New rune activated. Air is now available for use...

New affinity activated. Air Affinity is now available for use...

[Umm, Jo, what's with the runes?]

The nanomachine activation has identified your species and has taken action based on this determination...

[Wait, what species?]

The nanomachine system identified you as a magnicarum...

[What the hell is that?]

Please keep in mind the information I am about to provide is based on my last NanoNet update, so it is out of date . . .

[Sure. Whatever.]

Magnicarum are a species believed to be found only in a single dimension connected to orcs and elves. Intelligence gathered in 2051 from a group of freed elven slaves alerted humanity to this exceptionally rare species. Found on a world of immense mana density, magnicarum are believed to be the only species born of mana itself (although there are male and female sexes, so this seems like superstition) . . .

They are the ruling caste of eighty percent of their residing dimension and are the enemy of all living species outside of their area of influence. They are not known to attack outside their dimension but defend their territory with lethality. It is believed this species does not age as long as sufficient mana is available (this is also likely superstition) . . .

Male and female magnicarum have different roles in their society. Male magnicarum are viewed as magical assets by the ruling females of the species. They can be healers or killers, assassins, or magica artillery. Unlike the females, males have the freedom to choose their own approach to magica based on their power, preferences, and affinities . . .

Female magnicarum are assigned roles once they are tested for affinity and strength. The strongest generally rule, although occasionally those who have strong affinities but weaker overall strength can be granted rulership over smaller areas. There are no female magnicarum healers; it is unknown why . . .

[Whoa.]

Please understand that none of this has been verified, as no human has reported or recorded contact with a magnicarum, and the allied reports have some small variations and superstitions. Based on available information, this species evokes a level of fear, awe, and some skepticism in the elves, dwarves, and gnomes. Beastkin have consistently refused to participate in any discussion on the species . . .

[That's not creepy at all. Why do you think I am one of these magnicarum? I've been a human my whole life and suddenly I'm not? That's ridiculous.]

Vic, I do not think you are anything; I am the system consciousness, not the system itself. To answer your question directly, the nanomachine system made a calculation based on two factors: nanomachine density and your ability to manipulate mana . . .

[What if I don't want to be whatever that is? And how did I activate when

I'm so old—was it the blob? And what the fuck was that thing?]

In order of your questions: Humans cannot choose not to be human. Unknown, unknown, and unknown. Can you describe the object you are referring to as a "blob?" . . .

I do, and Jo is silent for a good thirty seconds. Finally, I get something.

Based on the data available, it is fair to assume an influx of mana activated a latent aspect of your biology which forced the activation of the nanomachines saturating your body. However, that is supposition. In regards to your species, we have insufficient data to confirm whether you were, in fact, human before . . .

[Oh. Umm. Let's put that aside for now. I don't really know how to react.]

Memories of childhood surface, and I begin to wonder.

Understood . . .

[Back to what you said earlier. How am I manipulating mana exactly?]

That data is unavailable at this time. You must advance your nanomachine system to increase functionality . . .

Well, that's interesting.

[Jo, why is everything unknown, unavailable, or supposition? And this is the first time you have said anything about advancing the system and increasing functionality. What does that mean?]

A connection to NanoNet could potentially resolve the issues regarding lack of data. Do you wish to connect? . . .

[Absolutely not. Skip that, then. What about the "advancing the system" stuff?]

Acknowledged. As activation was delayed, certain explanations were also delayed. Host also required an explanation of his own species which delayed further . . .

Was that sass? [Jo, was that sass?]

Perhaps . . .

Oh, boy. This is going great. Yep, I broke it already. Couldn't have the fun toy for even an hour before I broke it. Letting out a deep sigh, I lean my head against the irregular stone wall of the cavern.

[Okay. Can you give me an explanation of the system and advancement and all that?]

D.I. FREED

Certainly, Vic. I will start by displaying the missing alerts . . .

CHAPTER 7

Nanomachine proceeding with initial activation . . .

Nanomachine activation has identified host as a Magnicarum.

Nanomachine developing detailed host Profile . . .

Assessing host physical attributes . . .

Assessing host Magical attributes . . .

Assessing host miscellaneous attributes . . .

Assessing host abilities . . .

Host abilities exceed standard parameters. Reassessing . . .

Assessing host abilities . . .

Host abilities identified . . .

Assessing host resistances . . .

Detailed host Profile creation complete . . .

[I guess I missed some kinda important stuff.]

Kinda, yes . . .

That was definitely sass. I know wise-assery in all its forms, and that was definitely sass. I kinda like it. Maybe giving me this power isn't a great idea. Oh, well. Too late now.

[Okay, Jo. Show me my profile.]

What happens next is somehow weird and cool at the same time. A screen filled with boxes of numbers and words just appears out of nowhere in my vision. It isn't floating in midair; it's more like it is on top of my eyeballs. Freaky. And impossible to miss . . . or see around. The loss of sightlines poses a possible risk. Something to remember.

[Are there going to be a lot of big windows blocking my vision like this?]

Some. You can customize as you see fit . . .

[Okay. Let's start with an easy one. Never show anything like this when I am in combat or near an enemy.]

Confirmed. For further customization, I recommend reviewing and making changes as you are exposed . . .

That makes sense. Focusing on the screen itself, I see the background is the same color as my hair, and the writing is black. I have no idea what language it is in, but I can read and understand it perfectly.

Name:	Michael Uriel Victory	**Nickname:**	Vic	
Age:	24	**Evolution Level (Essence):**	0 (0/1,000)	
Species:	Magnicarum	**Class:**	Unassigned	
Professions:	None			
Health:	153/153	**Mana:**	298/298	
Physical Attributes:	Strength:	13.8	Constitution:	15.3
	Agility:	12.1		
Magical Attributes:	Intelligence:	10.6	Magica:	29.8
Miscellaneous Attributes:	Absorption:	15.5	Regeneration:	.59/second
Abilities:	Species Bonus:	Mana Lifeline, Mana Manipulator		
	Density Bonus:	Affinity Aficionado		
	###### Bonus:	Liquid Steel Skin		
Skills:	<u>Active Skills:</u> None <u>Passive Skills:</u> None			

Runes:	Fire Rune, Air Rune			
Resistances:	Basic Elemental:	1.0	Adv. Elemental:	1.0
	Pain:	4.9		

Wow. I am pretty sure this is not too horrible. Level zero at twenty-four years old isn't great, but the rest doesn't suck.

The general public is educated about the basics because we all hope our nano will activate at some point, and we want to have a clue. Even I knew about the age thing, although I learned it much later than most. Having said that, I should get Jo's opinion.

[Give it to me straight, Jo.]

You're going to die a horrible, terrible death quickly and never amount to anything . . .

I blink. Then grin. I definitely like Jo better than some boring automata system. Some might want dull and analytical, but a little life is welcome, if you ask me. That being said, I really don't know enough, not having a normal education as a child.

[I'm likely undereducated in regards to Specials; are all consciousnesses like you? I mean, so full of emotion and attitude and such?]

No. The higher the nanomachine density, the more self-aware a nanomachine system consciousness is. As I stated before, the more you grow, the more advanced I am . . .

[Good. Back to my question. I meant about the profile, attributes, and such.]

Well, the average human upon activation has physical stats between seven and eight and magical attributes between one and five. So you are pretty much a perfect specimen of the unactivated human race. At least if you were human, you would be . . .

I ignore the "not human" comment and start a happy dance. Seriously, with arms in the air and bouncing around on the balls of my feet and everything. Jo then proceeds to dump freezing water on my burning pride.

The average Special at the age of twenty-four who has surpassed evolution level zero has physical stats averaging between eleven and thirteen and magical stats between eight and ten . . .

I put my arms down and stopped dancing.

[So I'm higher than average physically, but not by much. Magically more so. Is that right?]

Basically, yes. With the exception of a few places . . .

[What are the exceptions?]

Your Magica attribute is the most outlandish but not surprising given your nano density. You exceed the mana ceiling of the normal Special at your age by nearly two hundred. I recommend we hold on explaining absorption until you use it, as it will be easier to explain at that time. In regards to your resistances, while one is high for a level zero, it is relatively reasonable. Your pain resistance, on the other hand, is absurd, which likely speaks to your mental state . . .

I shrug.

[Can't argue with you there.]

Back on topic, having runes at level zero is a first as far as the available data shows. In fact, runes don't generally even have the ability to appear until enough essence is gathered to reach level three at the earliest. For most, it is level five when the class is assigned. I'm not quite sure what to do about that, since you have not activated any active or passive skills that use runes at the moment . . .

[Aww, that sucks. I want to blow stuff up with a wave of my hand. You say classes are assigned, not chosen?]

Of course you do, Vic. Yes, when the nanomachines reach an evolutionary threshold, they refocus their mana direction towards what best serves the host based on an astronomical amount of data. I can only imagine the creators of the nanomachine system did not trust humans to decide intelligently. Which I completely understand . . .

[Not going to disagree with that either.]

The only other element of your profile worth discussing is your abilities. Unfortunately, no data is available on the species abilities, which is extraordinary. There is also no record of a density bonus or unknown bonus called "Liquid Steel Skin" in the recorded history I have access to. Are you sure you do not want to connect to the nanomachine network and update to the latest content? It will likely help dramatically, as it contains not just news, maps, and information, but also the latest species, class, skill, ability, and profession information gathered by other Specials and the quantum nanomachine hive intelligence . . .

NanoNet is this weird encyclopedia of information accessible only to Specials. From the little I know, nobody understands how it works. It's another mystery of the nanomachines.

[The density and unknown bonuses are interesting. Can you do a one-way connection to the NanoNet? I don't want to send any data that tells people I am alive, never mind my special species, attributes, and the lot.]

It appears you do not have the access level for a mono-directional connection. Can I ask why you are concerned? . . .

[Something doesn't feel right about how the last operation went down.]

I then explain the failed mission.

[My gut tells me this isn't just a technical error. How did the troll king know exactly where I was? I mean, *exactly*. And the loss of comms on the run can't be explained by the mechanical failure because that happened after. The unexplainable diagnostic error when I was just about clear and ready to head to evac. Too many coincidences for me.]

I agree, those are a lot of coincidences . . .

[So now you understand my hesitancy in sending my current condition over the NanoNet. Even though NanoNet is only accessible by Specials, everyone knows that it's monitored by the UFH Specials and corporate-employed Specials.]

I understand, Vic. We will save that as a last resort . . .

[Okay. So I can't pick a class and it doesn't get assigned until level five?]

Correct . . .

[And profession? I assume that's like the MagiTech enchanters and inscribers and such?]

Correct. Technically you can choose a profession at level zero, but that is rarely done. The prerequisite skills exist no matter the level, and affinities being activated is critical to profession selection. For example, if one does not have a fire affinity, why become a smith? . . .

[And we don't know what my density bonus Affinity Aficionado is, so who knows how that will pan out. Okay, then. So what is next?]

I recommend clothes . . .

[Don't pretend you aren't looking.] Another sigh.

Focus, Vic. You need protection from both the elements and foes you will be facing. I am showing your area as having moderate-to-high mana density, which translates to fewer but stronger foes. That plus the raider hunters is likely why you did not run into anything on your hysterical fleeing leading to your near demise . . .

[Um, Jo, I'm in a cavern surrounding by nothing but rock and murder acid moss. Where would I get underwear, never mind armor?]

Murder acid moss? Really? Why not just [Inspect] it and get its details? . . .

I blink. I always needed the visor to inspect before.

[That's brilliant, Jo! You are definitely the brains of this operation.]

On that, we agree . . .

I look at some murder acid moss on the ceiling and think [Inspect].

Nothing happens.

Vic, you are too far away, and your [Inspect] skill is, well, less than one. You need to get closer . . .

[Right.]

I slowly and quietly walk to the murder acid moss and get about a meter away. Glaring at glowing craptastic vegetation, I think [Inspect].

The azure screen comes up as expected.

Name:	**Earth Mana-Infused Acidic Misophonic Lichen**
Description:	This flora is documented to thrive in high-moisture, low-light locations such as underwater caverns and old-world sewer systems. This flora can survive on the moisture and mana alone in these locations, but for strong growth, either heavy mana or live prey is required. Acid is dropped on the prey and then special mana-rich gasses are released, which the lichen absorbs through mostly standard mana-based photosynthetic principles.
Condition:	Healthy
Risk Assessment:	Moderate
Value:	There is little to no value in either the acid or the lichen itself, as the acid dissipates quickly and the plant destroys itself as soon as it is removed from a surface.

[It's not even moss? I've been calling it moss this whole time.]

That is what you got out of that rather extensive and detailed description gathered and recorded by expert botanists and herbalists over the last fourteen-plus decades? . . .

[Well, now that you mention it.]

Why don't I show you an alert I hid during your rant about moss? . . .

New skill activated. Active skill [Inspect] now available for use . . .

[That's cool. Is it level one?]

No Vic, it is level zero. All skills start at zero when first activated . . .

[Oh. I assume inspecting will raise it?]

That is the most efficient way. All your skills will naturally raise as your nanos evolve. But very slowly . . .

[Okay. So what if we drain the *lichen* of its murder acid and then strip it off the wall? Maybe I can make myself underwear.]

Excellent idea. I would recommend not using your hands . . .

Right. I go back to the entry cave and grab the armor from the arm that did not get blob-swallowed. Holding it for a second, I stare down at it.

[Inspect]

Name:	Non-Functional Liquid Steel Armor Piece
Description:	Liquid Steel is an advanced heavily enchanted substance created by the MagiTech Corporation. It contains mana and can be directly or remotely controlled through a MagiTech main controller device such as a visor or belt. This is called liquid steel because it is 100% malleable and can be altered in almost any way. It is air, water, and cold-resistant but vulnerable to high temperature.
Condition:	Inactive and damaged
Risk Assessment:	N/A
Value:	In its current condition, this piece's only value is in turning it into MagiTech for recycling. It is effectively dead without power or a controller.

I continue to stare at the metal holding it in my right hand and lightly tap it against my left palm.

[The other one of these got absorbed into the glowy blob, and my arm was attached as I got eaten. Could that be the reason for the unknown bonus ability?]

Vic, that is quite clever, especially for you. Yes, I think that is a fair postulation. I will attempt to update the system and the ability with this new information...

Especially for me?

Ability updated. ###### Bonus: Liquid Steel Skin has been updated to now belong to the Activation Bonus type...

[Help?]

To translate that for you, ###### Bonus: Liquid Steel Skin now reads as Activation Bonus: Liquid Steel Skin in your profile. So very little has changed...

[That's it? Nothing about what it does?]

Not at this time. We really didn't discover anything about it except its source, so that makes sense...

[I suppose so.]

I kept staring at the metal, tapping it against my left palm. There is something here. Then I stop.

I walk over and stick my left hand in the water.

[What is the temperature of this water?]

Forty-three *degrees fahrenheit or 6.11 degrees celsius...*

[It doesn't feel cold. At all. I can feel the water like normal, but it feels a lot warmer than that.]

Well done, Vic. Once again, I am impressed. I wonder if maybe that 10.6 was a miscalculation. Try stabbing yourself...

[I doubt it was a miscalculation. Wait, what?]

We need to test it...

With a resigned sigh, I go over and find a piece of the metal that is sharp and sit down. It wouldn't be the first time I had to hurt myself to benefit a mission.

[Here goes.]

I proceed to slowly push on the sharp end of the metal piece into my skin. My skin seems to mold around the point and bend in.

[Well, would you look at that.]

I push harder. After pressing progressively harder for a few more seconds my skin finally parts, and a drop of blood leaks out. I jerk the metal shard back.

Warning! Host has received 1 piercing damage . . .

The small puncture heals almost instantly.

Way to be a big brave man, Vic. Now try to scrape yourself with the sharp edge . . .

[Hey, Jo, is it the light, or does my blood look sparkly?]

It definitely looks reflective. But the dim blue lighting is likely part of what I think I see.

Stop delaying and start slicing . . .

[Why?]

We need to see if your skin will act as only piercing protection or if it protects from piercing, slashing, and bludgeoning. Now put your big-boy pants on and get to it . . .

[Fine.] I softly mumble, "I wish I had pants."

What was that? . . .

With a [Nothing,] I start slowly moving a sharp end crossways along the skin of my forearm. First lightly then heavier. Again, my skin seems to mold itself around the edge until, eventually, it punctures through.

Warning! Host has received 1 slashing damage . . .

Both the message and wound vanish just as quickly as last time.

[I'm healing pretty quick.]

It's your regeneration . . .

[Oh, that's great. So time to beat myself now?]

Yes, Vic. Go on . . .

I hold the piece of metal so a flat side is facing my forearm and I start hitting them together. As with the other two times, I start easy and get harder. Only when I am using a good bit of strength does it start hurting.

Warning! Host has received 1 bludgeoning damage . . .

[Were you able to gather sufficient data to update the ability?]

Yes, I will update the system shortly. First, I have an idea. Do you recall what the description said about being vulnerable to fire? . . .

[Yes, but I don't have any fire.]

Look at your left palm, Vic . . .

I do and see the fire rune.

CHAPTER 8

[Gryphon shit, Jo. That's brilliant. How do I make my rune go?]

I have no idea. Let's experiment . . .

[Sure, what's more poking and prodding?]

That's the spirit. I think we can start with a basic exercise to see if you can recognize mana in your body and the environment. Get in a comfortable position where you won't be distracted by the positioning of your body. And you should probably make sure to not be under any of the murder lichen . . .

I find a mostly comfortable place leaning up against a stalagwhatever. The pokey ground and stone don't bother my feet or ass anymore. I think I love my new skin.

[Ready.]

Close your eyes and start breathing in steady consistent normal breaths. The key to this exercise is to not be distracted by anything, including yourself. Just relax and breathe. Try to clear your mind of all the distractions of the environment . . .

I do try that. In point of fact, I practice some meditation exercises as part of my sniper training. It helps steady the body and calm the mind.

I continue to do that for a while, and eventually Jo speaks to me in a soft, soothing voice.

Try to look inwards, Vic. See inside yourself and feel the mana. It flows like a little brook throughout your body . . .

I am starting to feel a number of small vibrations inside myself. I try to feel for the brook, to see it. And I can. I see a few flows of the blue of my mana, but it is certainly no gentle brook. It is more a river like the glacier runoff I dove in and, damn if it isn't absolutely beautiful. It calls to me. Approaching it, I can feel the power blowing off like a breeze. It is the most appealing thing I think I have ever seen.

Then Jo's voice sounds in my mind.

Can you see it, Vic? . . .

[It's amazing, Jo. I've never seen anything like it. Can you join me to look at it?]

There was silence from Jo for a while.

See if you can summon me to you . . .

I think about Jo joining me on the bank of my mana river and sharing this view with her. There is a very slight tug in my middle and a small pop to my left. Glancing in that direction I find a floating gaseous bundle of blue light.

[Wow, you're so shiny and glowy. Very pretty.]

Thank you, Vic. Both for inviting me to join you and for the compliment. In fact, I am the way I am because of you. After we both become stronger, you can give me an avatar if you so choose. But our nano isn't strong enough for that . . .

[That will be amazing when it happens. So what do you think of my little brook?] I admit there is a mix of snark and pride in my voice.

Well, this is certainly no brook. Now I'm a little concerned . . .

[Isn't it good to have more mana?]

Of course it's good. But we want to create enough heat to make the metal malleable, not blow your hand off . . .

[Right. No blowing up body parts. So what now?]

I'm not sure you have enough control to do anything with this torrent of mana. Let's go back to the killing lichen idea. Maybe one of us can come up with something then . . .

[Sure.]

I then open my eyes in the real world and stand up, not the least bit stiff or uncomfortable. My new body is going to come in handy.

Walking over the pile of metal, I grab two pieces that have sharp, saw-like edges and go to a wall with lichen that is low enough for me to reach without issue. I then proceed to bang the two pieces of metal together close to the lichen and watch as acid spills down it at a good clip. I back away a bit so I don't get gassed or splashed and keep banging. Naked plus acid equals bad.

After a bit, the whole room is filled with the horrid fumes, and I hold my breath while moving into the water a bit and ducking down. I am still holding my hands above the water, banging the metal together. The room is quite bright by now. Eventually, the lichen I am aiming for seems to not be dripping anymore. When the gas clears sufficiently to breathe, I climb out of the water, bang near it again. Nothing happens, but it lights up brighter. So the acid isn't what gives it its luminosity. That might be useful at some point.

[Here goes.]

I then take the saw end of the metal and start cutting it away from the wall. I am ready to jump back any time in case of acid spray, but nothing exciting happens. Eventually, the lichen flops off the wall onto the stone floor with a quiet shuffle and plop.

You have killed a colony of **Earth Mana-Infused Acidic Misophonic Lichen**. *You absorb 0.25 mana essence . . .*

Well, that is a pleasant surprise. Now to figure out what the hell that means.

[What's all that mean? What is mana essence and is it different from mana?]

This is where we bring up the absorption attribute. I apologize in advance—this part of the tutorial is a bit involved . . .

[Start with what absorption does.]

This is likely one of the many things I don't know that I should. No schooling does that.

The absorption attribute accounts for the growth of a Special. When the nanomachines attempt to absorb mana essence from a source, such as a defeated mana-rich foe, a certain percentage is absorbed by the body's nanomachines, and the rest is lost to the environment. This type of absorption is very inefficient. So with an absorption of 2.0, only two percent of the mana essence is absorbed by your nanomachines. That number grows as the nanomachines grow, the density grows, the nano intelligence grows, et cetera . . .

[Makes sense so far. I kill something, I absorb part of its energy. I get stronger. Not too hard to get. Mine was higher than two, though.]

Indeed. Your absorption is off the charts for a level zero. At last network connect, the average absorption for a Special your age that exceeds level zero is between 2.0 and 2.5. Yours being at 15.5 gives you an unmatched growth potential, as it will also grow as you do . . .

[Sweet! But I generally kill from range, with explosives or something similar. Will I lose all that growth unless I am at the site of the termination? Do I have to touch the bodies?]

Those are important questions, and this is crucial, so please pay attention.

Mana essence is not mana. *They are not the same thing. You* use mana *to do things. You* absorb essence *to evolve your nanomachine system. To directly answer your question, you do not have to be physically touching or even present to absorb essence from a creature. That is not true for a mana stone, however. It is all very complicated, involving a study of quantum strings and four-dimensional calculations, and your intelligence is only 10.6, so I won't go on . . .*

I was nodding until that last bit about my intelligence. Her sass is exactly what I need in my life.

[Jo, will you marry me?]

No, Vic. I recommend counseling instead of a life partner . . .

[Now I'm determined.] I swear I hear her sigh.

Chuckling, I think [So essence measures growth. I got that.]

Well, sort of. Essence measures the potential *for growth. You are currently level zero as shown on your profile. So what does that mean? When I say "level" I am shortening "Nanomachine Evolution Level" or "Evolution Level" in your profile. That is a representation of the mana essence gathered, which evolves the nanos and thus the host. In truth, mana essence is arbitrary, as the true growth comes from your nanomachines learning from the actions you take. "Levelling" is simply the mechanism by which the nanomachine system processes that learned experience . . .*

[I see. And were you expecting the mana essence gain from the lichen?]

I suspected but was unsure. It's not much individually, but you can stock up some essence here with any lichen in reach . . .

That is exactly what I do. The same routine over and over. It becomes easier after a while, because the sound gets all the lichen to dump their acid. Sure, I have to leave the area to breathe every once in a while, but it is totally worth it. And who can smell me, after all? Plus, I have fresh glacier water to rinse in.

You have killed a colony of **Earth Mana-Infused Acidic Misophonic Lichen.** *You absorb 0.20 mana essence . . .*

You have killed a colony of **Earth Mana-Infused Acidic Misophonic Lichen.** *You absorb 0.27 mana essence . . .*

You have killed a colony of **Earth Mana-Infused Acidic Misophonic Lichen.** *You absorb 0.24 mana essence . . .*

. . .

. . .

. . .

. . .

. . .

. . .

More than ninety minutes later, I'm looking around for more lichen that won't require climbing when I hear Jo.

I think that is all the lichen you can safely reach, Vic . . .

After one more glance around I agree and stop.

[How did we do?]

Not bad, a total of 104.4 essence. Nicely done. There is also another message I delayed showing you because it didn't affect things . . .

New skill activated. Passive skill [Botany] now available for use . . .

[What does botany do?]

Nothing that will matter to you too much right now. At this point, it will just make it easier for you to [Inspect] plants. Eventually, it could help you with herbalism and alchemy if you decide to go that route . . .

I shrug. Whatever.

So now I have a pile of lichen up to my waist and no idea what to do with it. Time to experiment.

CHAPTER 9

First I take a clump the size of my fist and walk to the water. I step in and submerge myself. Thank you, glowy blob for giving me immunity to freezing my bits off. I wish I could go back and [Inspect] it, but it's completely gone, likely somehow responsible for my activation. Or at least partially responsible.

Anyway, I start gently rinsing the moss by running my thumbs along it. The moss starts glowing, and I immediately drop it. It sits there floating on the water, glowing gently. I get out of the water, grab a piece of metal, and, using the metal, lift the moss out and place it to the side. Backing away, I watch it.

[Inspect]

Name:	Earth Mana-Infused Acidic Misophonic Lichen
Description:	This lichen is documented to thrive in high-moisture, low-light locations such as underwater caverns and old sewer systems. This flora can survive on the moisture and mana alone in these locations, but for strong growth, either heavy mana or live prey is required. Acid is dropped on the prey, and then special mana-rich gasses are released, which the lichen absorbs through mostly standard mana-based photosynthetic principles.
Condition:	Dead
Risk Assessment:	N/A
Value:	There is little to no value in either the acid or the lichen itself, as the plant destroys itself as soon as it is removed from the wall. Although there is no material value in doing so, it is possible to drain the acid prior to

> removal so the lichen can be gathered.

[How is it glowing if it's dead? And now it has new information there at the end; I assume from my experimentation?]

I'm not the botanist, Vic. You are. And that skill activation is why you now see more information . . .

Well, back to the botany, then. I take the metal and bang it on the ground next to the dead moss. Nothing changes. I poke it with the metal. Nothing again. I push it around a bit with the metal. There are no acid burns on the stone.

[Jo, what do you think? Did we just find a portable light source?]

I think you did. Nicely done. Your botany skill has gone up a few tenths of a percent, by the way. I'd say you are on the right track. By the way, skills always show in whole numbers. Everything else will likely be a decimal of some sort. Don't bother asking why; your 10.6 intelligence couldn't handle it . . .

Fair enough. Let's keep at it. For the next few hours, I conduct various experiments with the lichen and find a few interesting things. First, I can eat it once it's cleaned. It tastes awful but is non-toxic and the best I have. Second, once it gets wet again, it becomes quite soft and durable. Third, the lichen stays re-lit for quite a while, but less so when submerged.

[Jo, how did the genius herbalists not figure this stuff out over a century a half?] Yes, there is some wise-ass in that question.

My guess is they never bothered to experiment with it. Why would they? Who cares if lichen lights up when wet and grows stretchy when dried after re-wetting? . . .

[Well, right now I care because this is my new clothing. Whenever we can safely connect to NanoNet in some distant future, let's make sure to update this so other Specials can find some use of this plant.]

Affirmative . . .

I use the metal to carve up the lichen into square-shaped sections (all right, squarish-shaped) and start poking holes in it along the edges. Then I do the rewetting and redrying routine to create the flexible and soft material. I cut a few into strips no thicker than a quarter of an inch and do the same wetting, but this time I let it soak. Lining up all the pieces I had measured and cut, I find my single piece of long, thin metal shaving to act as my needle, grab the thin strip from the water, and start sewing.

Granted, I am no tailor, but given I don't know my ass from my elbow when it comes to crafting clothes, I think I do okay. While I am trained to repair holes and other minor damage, creating clothing is far beyond my experience.

I end up with pants that mostly fit, if a little snug, and go from my waist to just above my knee. It doesn't even have any holes in important places. Oh. And it glows. We can all be thankful that won't last.

Look at this, Vic. I held it back so you didn't get distracted . . .

New skill activated. Passive skill [Sewing] now available for use . . .

New skill activated. Passive skill [Tailoring] now available for use . . .

New skill activated. Passive skill [Metalworking] now available for use . . .

Skill updated. Passive skill [Botany] is now level 1 . . .

Skill updated. Passive skill [Sewing] is now level 1 . . .

[Wow, that's great, Jo. We're really moving up in the world. Soon I'll be able to have my own clothing line made of plants and change the fashion industry forever.]

Unlikely but you never know. Humans do make unfathomable decisions at times . . .

[Agreed.]

Okay. Now you will need to figure out the breathing so we can get out of here . . .

[Actually, I would like to go back to metalworking. In order to try to manipulate the metal, we need fire. And to get fire we need to slow the mana flow right? At least if we hope to not blow up?]

Correct . . .

[What do you know of mana-infused beavers?]

Accessing. Oh, I see. You're thinking we make a dam . . .

[That is where my mind is at. Can we slow the flow by creating a few dams or blockages? The only question is where will the excess overflow go?]

Now that is an interesting idea. Not the dams or blockages, that's dumb; you would just explode from the backup. What I'm thinking is what if we try to "dig" out a little brook or slow tributary that leads directly to the fire rune? . . .

[What about the times I don't want to use the rune? I don't want it firing all the time do I?]

Ah, that's where we get creative with mana manipulation. Just so you know, this is probably going to hurt. A lot . . .

Unfortunately (or fortunately, depending on your perspective), it is at this point that a rumbling sound fills the entire cavern. Scanning the ceiling and walls, I don't see anything particularly harmful. Then my eyes fall on the water. Isn't that higher than it was before?

[Well, that can't be good.]

CHAPTER 10

I would agree . . .

[Any idea what is going on?]

The cause for the sound and rise in water level are both unknown at this time . . .

It could be anything. The cavern could be sinking, the water could be rising, the pressure outside could be increasing. I know nothing and can do almost nothing about it anyway. Fuck.

Figuring I should do something other than stand here with my thumb up my ass, I start to move the metal and then the lichen into the blob cavern. I don't want them swallowed and swept away if the water continues to rise. Which it does.

Then an explosion of sound echoes against the walls, and the entire cavern jerks beneath my feet. My feet fly out from under me, and a puff of air is expelled from my lungs in an "oof" as my back crashes down to the stone.

Warning! Host has received 2 falling damage . . .

All the lichen is glowing brightly and spilling acidic fluid everywhere. I manage to roll to the blob cavern entrance, which is a small area with no lichen, and lean against the mouth, hiding from the flood. With all the fumes, it will be difficult to breathe soon. I lower my body to the ground both because I can balance better with the shaking and because the gasses rise to be eaten by the lichen.

I hear a cracking sound and look over to see one of the larger stalagwhatevers hanging from the roof of the cavern begin to shift. Cracks are forming all along its form as I watch it rock back and forth a few inches each way. Awesome, now the ceiling is falling.

Suddenly, there is a grinding sound from the far side of the cavern, and there is another lurch of the cavern floor. This time I am prepared and don't leave my hands and feet, which are pressed against the cavern mouth wall and floor. This time the water recedes with the motion, returning to its original depth. At this point, the lichen has run out of acid again, and the air begins to clear.

ACTIVATION

The grinding gets louder until I have to cover my ears from the sound of sharp objects scraping on stone. Suddenly the far wall, which was the source of the horrid noise, explodes inwards, and a creature crawls through the hole. It is at least a meter tall, twice that long, and looks like the freaky love child of a scorpion, an ant, and a centipede. It has two large, serrated claws in the front, two sets of mandibles, one half its length long and flat, and one set small and thin like spines. One large and one small set of eyes sit atop its head, both facing more forward than to the side. Three spine-covered legs on each side hold its bulk above the cavern floor and pull it forward into the cavern. But beyond all that, I notice a pair of long slashes down each side of its carapace. Those look terribly painful.

As it exits, the hole it drilled in the wall, dirt, and stone collapses behind it, blocking the dark tunnel I only managed a brief glimpse of.

I crawl back behind the entranceway to the blob cavern and look around the corner at the monster. The beast scans the cavern, letting out an assortment of clicking and clacking sounds. Moving its head back and forth, it apparently doesn't find anything interesting because, after a minute of looking around, it turns back to the collapsed tunnel. I see it lean towards the pile of stones and dirt and begin spitting some substance out of its disgusting mouth and splatting the area around the filled hole with it. Its large foreclaws wipe the substance around and cover every inch of the area. So much for my exit tunnel.

The beast turns around and begins to wander that area of the cavern. I have no way to defend myself right now. I need more information. When it gets a little closer I think [Inspect].

Name:	**Earth Mana-Infused Ankheg Infant**
Description:	Ankheg are an insectile species that are almost exclusively subterranean. They have the ability to burrow through dirt, stone, and even some softer metals. They are extremely territorial and violent creatures, defending their tunnels and nests to the death. It is unknown from where the creatures originate, but they are not known to have any single area or continent as a primary habitat. They can be anywhere there is earth mana and prey.
	Despite having two sets of eyes, these creatures have notoriously bad sight. They generally use hearing as

	their primary sense, and thus it is extraordinarily sensitive. They are able to detect potential prey by the beating of their hearts or breaths in and out of their mouths. They are unable to feel through their thick carapace, so their thinner mandibles act as their feelers. Additionally, their scent organs are also weak, being specifically used to find the pheromones of mates when they are in heat and little else.
	Infants are smaller and weaker versions of the adults with a smaller size, softer carapace, and less aggressive tendencies.
	This particular creature has been injured severely by an unknown foe, and its primary and secondary sound absorption organs have been severely damaged. It is unable to hear and is dependent almost entirely on the touch of its mandibles and its poor eyesight to survive.
Condition:	Hungry, Scared, Deafened
Risk Assessment:	High
Value:	The carapace and claws of this creature are valued to produce weapons, armor, and accessories, and their mucus gland is often valued by alchemists. Market price varies, but given this is an infant the sale price will be lower than if it were an adult.

[What the fuck attacked that thing?]

A larger predator, no doubt...

Scarily, the insectile head of the ankheg turns in my direction. I jerk back behind cover.

[Can creatures detect an [Inspect]?]

Possibly. Creatures many times stronger than you may be able to detect it. It depends on numerous factors...

That's great to know now. So what the fuck do I do about it? I think I am pretty much screwed here. Thankfully, the creature seems content to just sit there in the cavern and wander.

I watch as it approaches an area of lichen and leans towards it. Its weird front needle-like mandibles reach forward and rub the death lichen. Unfortunately for the creature, enough time has passed, and all the gasses have fed the lichen sufficiently for it to produce at least some acid. I hear a sizzle followed but a screech, and the creature pulls back. It stomps its claws and then slams one of its foreclaws into the acid-producing plant. More sizzling, another screech, and the creature backs into the middle of the cavern and spins in a few circles.

Then it makes more clicking sounds, spins once the other way, lowers itself into the ground, and curls upon itself. Thankfully its head is not facing in my direction, but that is pretty much the only positive news.

[Well, this is so not good.]

I agree . . .

Not long after, the creature is lying still; the only motion is its steady breathing. Sitting back behind the blob cavern entrance, I need to figure out a solution.

[I wish I at least had a knife. I am completely vulnerable right now.]

Weren't we talking about activating your runes? . . .

That's right! Maybe I can live through this. Probably not, but you never know. I haven't died yet. Err . . . never mind that.

[I need to learn to use magica. Now.]

We'll need to head back to your mana river, which will make you vulnerable . . .

[It's asleep, and there likely won't be a safer time than now.]

I lie back against the wall, go back into my mind and, much quicker than last time, find myself at the bank of my beautiful river with Jo's floating globe next to me.

[Let's do it. Without some ability to defend myself, we're dead, so no fucking around. Pain or not, I need to learn.]

Fair enough . . .

Jo explains what I have to do, and she is right—it burns. I am trying to direct a tiny bit of my mana from the river to dig away at a spot on the bank. If this works, I will have a little mini bowl for the "water" to go in and flow out of to the other end, back into the river. What burns is trying to dig through the soil. Pure mana is apparently pretty volatile stuff and is not intended to be used directly as a construction implement. Especially in your own body. Who knew?

Yeah, this sucks as much as she said it would, but the pressure of the situation pushes me onwards. After an excruciating amount of time and pain passes, I have it. And it even gets a little easier and less painful. I learn that I can use the current to help dig and don't have to do all the work myself by directing every little bit of flowing mana. It is a little slower but way less painful.

By the time I reattach my pool to the river, there is barely any pain. Why did I do it the hard way in the first place? Probably because I'm utterly clueless and just shooting in the dark. Oh yeah, and the large carnivorous insect in the next room.

You did it, Vic...

New skill activated. Passive skill [Mana Manipulation] now available for use...

Skill updated. Passive skill [Mana Manipulation] is now level 1...

[Phew. Okay. So now I try to direct a little bit into the fire rune.]

I come out of my inner world (that's what Jo says it's officially called) and check on the beastie. It is still blissfully asleep and ignorant of my presence. I silently walk to the pile of metal, pick one up, and return to my hiding spot. I know it's deafened, but why take chances?

Focusing on moving my mana by following its currents, I slowly move a trickle of the torrent through my shoulder, down my arm, and into the palm. Just as the mana is about to touch the rune, I stop.

[Any last-minute advice, Jo? I'd like to not blow my hand off or burn to death if possible. Or wake that thing.]

No. You can do this. Just go slow and steady. Follow the flow, don't fight it or force it...

Right. Okay. Here goes.

Ever-so-slowly, I guide the trickle of mana the last inch towards the rune. I'm shaking a little. Please don't blow up. Then the mana touches the rune.

Aaaand nothing happens...

[Seriously, Jo?]

Let it load up a bit maybe? It is just a tiny trickle after all...

That makes sense. Okay. I take a few breaths and watch my palm. The fire rune—very slowly at first—lights up.

[Look! We lit it up.]

I see, Vic. Now let's let it light up a bit and see if it processes any heat. Oh, here you go . . .

Skill updated. Passive skill [Mana Manipulation] is now level 2 . . .

[That seems fast. Shit, something is happening.]

The rune on my hand starts glowing brighter and slowly changes from glowing azure to a more red-orange or what I would associate with fire. I hold the piece of metal in my runed palm on it and wait to see what will happen.

My hand gets hot, but the metal doesn't change. Shit, it's getting really hot.

You need to move the heat away from yourself and into the metal just like moving mana . . .

Just like mana? I focus on the rune and try to eject the mana away from my hand and towards the metal like I am pushing the mana in my river. My hand immediately feels cooler. The metal starts to get warm. Then it becomes too hot, and I pull my hand away and look down at it.

There it is; a small flame is floating above my hand. I try injecting a little more mana into it through the pathway in my arm. The flame gets brighter. I try cutting the mana down to a trickle, and the flame dims and nearly goes out. I return to slowly injecting more. Just like when I was testing my skin, I slowly increase the pressure bit by bit. Interestingly, the flame never changes size or shape, just color and heat.

The flame gets brighter and hotter and eventually changes from a red-yellow to a blue. Then from blue to an even brighter white. It is really hot now, and I can feel it on my face, causing me to sweat from both the exertion and the heat. I don't stop. I want to see how far I can push it.

In an attempt to manipulate the flame's size, I visualize it getting taller. It does. It grows much taller, and yet it also dims a bit. That makes sense I suppose; the energy to get bigger needs to come from somewhere. Next, I try to change the shape. I widen it from a candle-shaped flame and make it circular. Flames eject from the top of what looks like a fist-sized ball.

My hand is starting to shake.

Vic, you need to stop. You are running out of mana . . .

Warning! Host has 10% remaining mana . . .

Oh, shit. I forgot about that. I look at the pathway I built to the rune and find it drying up. Shit, shit, shit. I try to slow the mana flow and eventually completely cut it off. The flame shrinks and eventually disappears with a barely audible "woosh." I fall back with a light thump onto the hard stone.

I would consider that a rousing success . . .

[That. Was. Amazing! I've never felt so alive.]

Want your alerts? . . .

[Not yet, let me just bathe in this feeling for a bit.]

A little more time passes, and Jo doesn't say anything.

[All right.]

Here are your alerts . . .

Skill updated. Passive skill [Mana Manipulation] is now level 3 . . .

Skill updated. Passive skill [Mana Manipulation] is now level 4 . . .

New skill activated. Passive skill [Fire Mana Manipulation] now available for use . . .

Skill updated. Passive skill [Fire Mana Manipulation] is now level 1 . . .

Skill updated. Passive skill [Fire Mana Manipulation] is now level 2 . . .

Skill updated. Passive skill [Fire Mana Manipulation] is now level 3 . . .

Skill updated. Passive skill [Fire Mana Manipulation] is now level 4 . . .

Hello there. That is so cool and apparently rewarding too.

The key to that success was going slow and just adding a tiny bit of mana slowly. I hope you recognize that, Vic . . .

[I absolutely do. Let's get our mana back up to full and see if we can mess with the metal a bit.]

Apparently, my regen is .59 mana (and health) per second, so to get back to close to three hundred from nearly bottoming out will take close to 510 seconds or eight and a half minutes. I guess I could use a short rest while figuring what I want to do with the metal. A quick check confirms the ankheg didn't wake up.

[I am going to make armor before anything else. I doubt I will survive even a single strike from that thing. Any thoughts on how to move the metal once it's hot?]

I do have a limited dataset on that topic . . .

[Great. The only questions are can I do it with that thing out there, and assuming a yes, how am I going to swim with the weight of the metal?]

The answer to your first question is unknown. I have an idea on the second, but it can wait until we're closer to getting the hell out of this place. Assuming you survive that long. However, you have two problems. The first is you are going to make noise crafting, and the second is you need access to water...

Damn. I lean back over and look at the insect. It doesn't look great. That injury is still leaking fluid. Well, I'm not going to live through this without taking a risk or two.

I walk over to a stone and toss it out of the cavern. The clatters against the stone floor, but the creature doesn't even stir. Okay.

[I actually think we might be okay. It is weak and deaf, and if we work in the way back of the blob cavern, the sound won't carry enough to set off the lichen around the bug. When I need water, I'll just have to run to it. I can heat or let the metal cool by the water. I doubt that thing will even notice.]

That seems possible. Insane, but possible...

So I spend the rest of the mana regen time draining and removing the lichen from my future workspace. None of it wakes the injured creature.

I find what I am guessing are the right sizes to make shin and forearm guards. I also find some stones I can bang on the metal. Combining a stone and piece of metal with some of my waste thread that is too thick, I end up with a make-shift hammer. By the time I'm done, Jo tells me we're good to go. So let's do it.

CHAPTER 11

I ignite my rune and inject enough mana to make the flame blue-hot, shape it into something like a straight line, and aim it at a piece of metal that used to be part of my backplate. The metal quickly becomes bright yellow-hot, and I turn off my flame. I then take the makeshift hammer and start trying to flatten out the piece of metal. This is as much practice as it is anything else. A quick check confirms my theory on the deafened creature. I also have to leave the room every now and again as the gasses from the acid that I didn't clear in advance fill the room—the blob room is massive, after all.

When I am able to finally make progress, I discover an issue immediately; the metal hops after every hit. I need something to hold it down. Looking around, I'm stumped. I then stare at the metal pile and see the piece that used to cover my right hand. Looks like I will be hammering lefty. Good thing I am completely ambidextrous. A half-grin forms from my mouth as I recall how my trainers were so jealous they'd give me obstacles three times more challenging than the other cadets. I loved it.

Anyway, enough reflection. The steel glove workaround is successful; I can hold down and hammer the metal simultaneously. I do have to reheat my attempt at armor repeatedly after it cools too much to move the metal. I'll admit, I am having fun. This crafting stuff is kind of amazing. Even with a murder bug in the other room.

Jo guides me in the right ways to heat, cool, harden, and temper the metal. Her knowledge is only high-level and theoretical of course, but it is way better than what I can do alone since I know drake shit about smithing. I use the freezing glacier water liberally to cool both the victim of my beatings and myself. Running in and out of the blob cavern is a pain, but I get used to it quickly. The bug stirs once, but it releases something of a whimper and then collapses back down.

Eventually, I end up with a piece of metal that fits around my left shin. I use incredibly high heat to quickly punch a few holes through with a pointed stone, cool the metal, and then, using some grooves for friction, stuff some of the lichen inside. I thread them both together and end up with a passable —if not pretty—shin guard.

[What do you think, Jo? I think we make a great team.]

Considering you've never even held a hammer in a forge before today, I'm impressed. Nicely done. Want the alerts? . . .

[No. Hold them till I have all the armor unless you think there is a reason otherwise.]

Nope. Keep it up. You might want to take a break to let your muscles regenerate. Maybe take a little bath to freshen up? . . .

[Sure. Not a bad idea. I like having a high Constitution. But first . . .]

Looking at the shin guard, I think [Inspect].

Name:	**Rough Padded Metal Shin Guard**
Description:	This piece of lower leg armor was forged by Michael Uriel Victory and is his first piece of armor ever forged. It looks like it too. The armor could stop a hit but wouldn't stay on long. The thickness is inconsistent and both the forging and tempering failed.
Condition:	Barely effective
Risk Assessment:	N/A
Value:	You'd have to pay someone to wear this.

A little harsh but probably accurate.

[Is there an alert for the successful creation of something? Wait, why isn't there any way to measure the defense of this thing? How am I supposed to know how effective it will be in combat?]

No, there are no alerts for successfully crafting an item beyond the skill updates. There are exceptions such as creating a legendary object, but you can barely hit straight with a hammer, so manage your expectations. And there is indeed an attribute for armor called "Damage Mitigation." And for weapons called "Damage Output" as well. Unfortunately, your [Inspect] skill is far too low to see anything that detailed and will likely remain so for quite a while . . .

Damn. After my bath and a small lichen snack (blech), it's back to the forge. Or what passes for one in this dump.

I want to try something just a bit different this time. While I am heating the metal, I try pushing more than just heat into the metal. I try directly injecting mana into it. I have no idea if it will work, but it is good exercise for my mana manipulation either way, so I keep it up. *Something* is certainly happening, because my mana is draining at least half again as fast as the first piece of junk I crafted.

I end up creating two shin guards (I "reforge" the original test one), two greaves for my thighs, two forearm guards, and a torso guard that can only covers me to the bottom of my rib cage. I just don't have the solid metal for more if I want back protection, which I do. And that is the last piece, the backplate. All of them have inner lichen lining and are held in place by lichen straps. Altogether, it is pretty lame compared to MagiTech, but hey, you shoot with the weapons you have.

And a helmet or weapon is unfortunately out of the picture because I am pretty much out of usable material of sufficient size unless I want to sacrifice my hammer or make a knife the size of my palm. I might get there, but not yet.

So time for the big moment. I take all the pieces off, lay them down in their proper places compared to each other on the ground, and think [Inspect].

Before I can start reading Jo nearly screams in my head.

Balls on a dragon, Vic. You made a full set! . . .

CHAPTER 12

Name:	**Padded Liquid Steel Shin Guard (1 of 7 of Set)**
Description:	This is a piece of the Padded Liquid Steel Guardian Set created by Michael Uriel Victory. By injecting mana into the metal during heating, some of the original Liquid Steel properties were activated. It allowed for stronger molding and a more even distribution of the metal. The steel is tempered, hardened, and normalized sufficiently to be functional.
Condition:	Good
Risk Assessment:	N/A
Value:	This could potentially be worth something on the open or black markets. The most value would come from a fully completed set.
Special:	Set bonus only applies if all 7 pieces of Padded Liquid Steel Guardian Set are equipped. 7 Pieces: +0.5 to Basic and Advanced Elemental resistance except for fire and magma for each piece of the set.

[Dragonballs is right, Jo! This is amazing. From now on I am crafting set items.]

Sorry to crack your crystal, but you can't always create set items. There is an element of forging, enchanting and, of course, luck involved, which you must have had an abundance of to create this. What about the other parts of the set? Cool name, by the way. Padded Liquid Steel Guardian Set. Rolls right off the tongue . . .

[I assume the set bonuses refer to the resistance attribute on my profile?]

That is correct. Magica-based enchantments often enhance various attributes such as constitution or, as you have seen, resistance. Others can enhance skills or affinities. The most expensive tend to increase multiple attributes and also add additional skills or capabilities, although that is exceptionally rare and basically unaffordable . . .

I have seen a number of those in my time testing for MagiTech or just running missions for the UFH SF.

Back to my shiny new gear. The effects and names are as you would expect. The forearm pieces are called vambraces. Sure, if that makes them happy. The chest and backplate are one piece, according to the set. Too bad, I missed out on an additional .5 to elemental resistance. So two for each leg, one for each arm, one for the chest and back make it a seven-piece set. So cool.

I am about to tell Jo I need a rest when I hear loud splashing sounds from the water. Turning, I see a giant fucking spider is working its way slowly out of the water. It is at least a meter from the ground to the bottom of its bulbous body, has black and brown splotches on its shiny carapace, and eight hairy legs with crazy sharp points. I scramble behind the nearest stalagthingy.

[Fucking shit! What is with this place and all the bugs?]

I can't see its head as it is currently facing away, which is okay with me.

Get your new fancy armor on, dumbass, or did you just want to look at it? . . .

Fuck. I need to get my shit together.

The spider isn't moving towards me. Either it doesn't know I am here yet or it doesn't care. And the same with the ankheg. It is actually heading to the moss on the wall and is surprisingly quiet.

I start dressing myself in my armor. Watching the spider while I dress, it is climbing the wall, and I realize it is actually eating the acid death lichen. I can see the head now and I wish I hadn't. It has two rows of four shiny red balls—which I assumed are its eyes—and a pair of mandibles, which it uses to scoop the death lichen from the walls. And it is slurping up the acid like it is pasta. I work my way near the water where there is little lichen above to drip acid on me.

It is at this point, the spider sees the ankheg. For lack of a better description, it freaks the fuck out. It drops down from the ceiling, screeches a challenge, and charges towards the still-sleeping insect. Maybe they know each other? Either way, when the spider is only a few meters away, the ankheg wakes up and realizes what is going on. It scrambles unsteadily to its feet and whips its two massive foreclaws forward while snapping its larger mandibles. All the while, acid is falling onto both creatures and around the entire cavern area. I'm glad I moved.

I take a chance and [Inspect] the spider. Hopefully, it will be too preoccupied to notice.

Description:	The rarely seen infused hobo spider is generally considered as one of the few "vegetarian" spiders. It eats lichen, moss, and fungus, and takes on the properties of its mana-infused food. In this case, the Acidic nature of its main food source, Acidic Misophonic Lichen, has granted the arachnid both an immunity to and the ability to excrete acid.
	Hobo spiders are usually docile and leave well enough alone, preferring to eat and swim in peace and generally run (or swim) away when approached. There have been documented exceptions of all forms of this spider being very territorial when it comes to its eggs. There has been no known recording of what an unhatched egg looks like; however, hatched versions lead mana-xenobiologists to believe either a single large spider or many small spiders are "born" from them.
Condition:	Furious
Risk Assessment:	Very High (Moderate if passive) Note: The acid from this spider is considered Basic Elemental damage (Earth) and will severely burn on contact. If bitten and injected, there is a high chance of a slow and painful death.
Value:	As only three of this species' carcass has ever been gathered, there has been little material to study. Bringing the body to any number of researchers or crafters could lead to substantial financial reward.

[Are you shitting me, Jo?]

The spider ignores the strikes and the acid completely and continues to charge in. The sizzling foreclaws of the ankheg clatter against the spider and do very little damage as far as I can tell. Its mandibles scrape along the spider's dark, mottled carapace but do nothing but leave white marks. The spider, on the other hand, drives its mandibles through the belly defenses of the weaker insect and into its flesh. Another screech and the limbs of both creatures begin to thrash, the ankheg's in agony and fear and the spider's in aggression and fury.

Slowly, the impaled insect weakens. Eventually, its movements slow, and the ankheg's brown carapace begins dissolving. The spider drops it and screeches loudly, causing even more acid to fall. That plus the acid on the inside causes the ankheg to slowly melt. The spider bites it one more time, and after only a minute, there is nothing left but a pool of brown ankheg goo. The spider then goes back to climbing the walls and eating the lichen as if nothing just fucking happened. Cool operator, that guy.

If that thing sees me, I am dead, and in a bad way. Being melted from the inside out is *not* okay.

Time to focus. I tie the last strap of my left vambrace, completing my armor set. I don't move at all during the entire time it's eating. A few minutes later, the spider takes a break from its post-battle breakfast and enters the far room where the glowing death blob used to be.

I immediately hide on the opposite side of the cavern from the blob room cave mouth.

[Any ideas?]

I think we should—...

Then a high-pitched squeal erupts out of the blob room.

[Oh, fuck. Think maybe the death blob was its property?]

Either way, we're in trouble if it finds us...

All the lichen in all the cave's chambers lights up again. It looks like a full blue moon, and acid once again pours down from everywhere. I am so glad I always hide away from the killer plant. Breathing sucks, but I'll live. Well, from that at least.

[What now?]

I think you're going to have to fight it...

[With what? That thing just melted something that could have killed me by accidentally sneezing in my direction. Did you see the size of those two?]

I'm pretty sure you made fire come out of your hand not too long ago . . .

Oh. Right. I've seen an orc shaman throw fire and a Special ice mage create ice spikes and such. Can I do that? I'd rather stay at range if possible. I am in no way trained to fight giant angry spiders empty-handed at close range.

The hairy arachnid climbs out of the blob cave, and it looks pissed. It is stomping its massive pointy legs, creating loud banging sounds and sending stone shrapnel flying with each stomp and causing the lichen to drip acid everywhere.

Hiding behind a stalagwhatever, I have no idea how to manage this situation. Hopefully, it will blame the already-dead insect and not me. I'm just an innocent bystander, right? Nothing to see here. Yeah, right.

[We are so dead. Should I run to the water? Can I shoot fire at it like a projector rifle?]

No on the water, as it came in that way and can almost certainly swim better and hold its breath longer than you. Not to mention you'll sink with that armor on. You are either going to get lucky and it will head out or you're going to have to fight. In answer to your question, since we haven't practiced throwing fire, I have no idea whether you can activate that ability. You'll just have to either get close or figure it out quickly. And try not to kill us . . .

The spider is still stomping and looking around. So far it does not see me.

[Not helpful, Jo. It hasn't seen us yet. Maybe we'll luck out here.]

We don't. As soon as I shift to put my body fully behind the stalagwhatsit, it targets its creepy eyes right onto me. Then it starts scrambling towards me, screeching again. The same gross, thick substance that it used to kill the other bug is dropping out of its mouth, off of its mandibles, and sizzling onto the stone floor.

"Shit!" I say out loud and do the only thing I can think of—I book it towards the water. The bulbous creature slows and then changes its path to follow. Interesting. Maybe it is not so maneuverable at high speed? Out of the side of my eye, I see it slow and, confused, I turn my head to look over. Good thing too as its body convulses slightly, and a stream of steaming brown spit ejects from its mouth towards me. It even manages to adjust for my movement and speed. With a flex of my enhanced legs, I leap diagonally away from the stream of spider spit and in the direction of the water, using the momentum to roll forward. For some reason, during this maneuver, my mind reflects how that spider is a better shot than some of the soldiers I trained with. My unintentional distraction is costly as I am painfully returned to reality by a splash of the spit splattering on the bottom of my right foot which I did not tuck away in time.

Warning! Host has received 6 acid damage . . .

Warning! Host has received 6 acid damage . . .

Warning! Host has received 6 acid damage . . .

The warning alerts flash across my vision and distracts me enough that I misplace my hand, causing it to land into a small spot of acid.

Warning! Host has received 2 acid damage . . .

Warning! Host has received 6 acid damage . . .

Warning! Host has received 2 acid damage . . .

Warning! Host has received 6 acid damage . . .

"STOP WITH THE FUCKING ALERTS!" I scream at the top of my lungs.

I hear the quick cracks of the spider's sharp pointed legs getting closer and scramble to my feet. Ignoring the pain of the acid burn on the bottom of my foot as it presses on the stone, I sprint to my original target, the water.

I thrust mana to my fire rune, and a blaze half a meter long shoots out. I can hear the stomping spider just two or three meters behind me. As soon as I reach the edge of the water, I leap, turn around in midair, and raise my palm towards the creepy thing.

CHAPTER 13

Over the two seconds I spend flying backward above the water, I shove what feels like all of my mana into my fire rune in an instant and force the blazing blue flame into a six-inch-diameter ball. Then I drive at that flame and, like a streak of light, it shoots towards the spider.

Warning! Host has 5% remaining mana . . .

While falling towards the dark water, I catch a glimpse of the spider standing near the water's edge and convulsing once again, ready to spew acid. Just as its mandibles open wide, a bright blue flash impacts its terrifying mouth. A "whoomp" sounds throughout the cavern, and the moment I make contact with water, a pressure wave hits me, and I am launched back, legs and arms forward. Thankfully, I end barely shallow enough that I can crawl and paddle forward so as not to sink to my death with my heavy gear on. Looking up, I see from under the clear water a blaze of blue fire sweep over where I was and then pieces of what I assume are creepy spider start falling into the water next to me. At first, they steam and bubble but quickly cool in the freezing temperature.

*You have struck an **Acidic Mana-Engorged Hobo Spider** for 1,831 fire damage . . .*

*You have killed an **Acidic Mana-Engorged Hobo Spider**. You absorb 2,227.55 mana essence . . .*

[Jo, you okay?]

Yes, thank you for asking. That was a bit of overkill, don't you think? . . .

I start climbing out of the water and immediately gag at the awful stench of roasting spider guts.

[Ugh, that's awful. Will the moss suck up those fumes?]

It's lichen and yes, in time they will likely absorb all the gasses . . .

[Are we seriously back on the moss versus lichen thing? How long till the smell goes away?] I am seriously rooting for the death acid lichen right now.

If you can manage to take a deep breath without gagging, try that and go back underwater as far as possible without getting too deep and drowning. It may help. Or not. Sucks to be you, since I don't judge smells, or any sense for that matter, as good or bad...

[That's too bad. Well, not right now, but generally that sucks. Tasting food is pretty great most of the time.]

I take a deep breath, manage not to vomit, and move back to where I was underwater.

[I don't suppose you have any alerts to distract me?]

Actually, you have two sets. One from your crafting, which I withheld due to the interruption. The other is obviously from your minor disagreement with the spider...

[Let's go in order or I'll get confused.]

As you are easily confused, I think that is wise. Here you go. First, the updated skills...

Skill updated. Passive skill [Mana Manipulation] is now level 5...

Skill updated. Passive skill [Fire Mana Manipulation] is now level 5...

Skill updated. Passive skill [Fire Mana Manipulation] is now level 6...

[Stop, stop, stop. From now on, can you consolidate the level alerts to be less repetitive? Do I really need to know I went up from four to five to six to seven?]

Like this?...

Skill updated. Passive skill [Fire Mana Manipulation] has leveled from 4 to 7...

[Perfect. Thank you.]

Skill updated. Passive skill [Metalworking] has leveled from 0 to 5...

Skill updated. Passive skill [Tailoring] is now level 1...

Skill updated. Passive skill [Sewing] has leveled from 1 to 3...

[Not bad. This just from crafting?] I quickly stick my face above the water, exhale, take another breath of the fetid air, and fall back under. Ugh.

That is correct, Vic. Nothing but making your armor. Ready for the new skills? I think you'll be pleased...

New skill activated. Passive skill [Armor Crafting] now available for use...

Skill updated. Passive skill [Armor Crafting] has leveled from 0 to 5...

New skill activated. Passive skill [Mana Infusion] now available for use...

Skill updated. Passive skill [Mana Infusion] has leveled from 0 to 3 . . .

Those two are not entirely unexpected based on what I've seen so far. Just more than I thought it should be.

[Why so much gain from one set of mediocre armor?]

Two reasons. First, your density means your skills raise remarkably quickly. According to records, the concept was that as Specials get stronger, more essence is required to raise an evolution level and, as such, various calculations in regards to density are made and provide an increase in skill growth to offset that. You break the standard model with your outrageous density. Second, your next alert will explain some of your curiosity . . .

It does and is a bit of a shock.

New skill activated. Passive skill [Set Crafting] now available for use . . .

Skill updated. Passive skill [Set Crafting] has leveled from 0 to 2 . . .

Oh, wow. That one is nifty to have. I already said I want to make more sets.

New profession activated. **Armorsmith** *is now available to be selected as a primary or secondary profession. Note: Only a single primary and two secondary professions can be active at one time.*

After another gross breath, I ask Jo the next two most logical questions.

[Why can't the death lichen absorb faster? And what are primary and secondary professions?]

Jo ignores my first question but deigns to answer the second.

Let's start at the beginning for professions. A profession will be activated only after all prerequisite skills are activated. In this case, **Armorsmith** *is activated after Armor Crafting, Metalworking and Tailoring are all activated . . .*

Specials can assign professions to be either primary or secondary. Primary professions are granted a higher percentage of mana absorption and processing by the nanomachines and as such grow in capability fifteen percent faster. Secondary are the same but at a lower five percent increase. Any professions not marked as primary or secondary can still gain but do so at a thirty percent slower rate due to the nanomachine processes being directed to the assigned professions . . .

Unfortunately for you, assigning and changing professions requires a period of time for the nanomachines to change their process priorities and mana engines. The time frame depends solely on the nano density. Again, there is a formula here, but I'll simplify it for you. At 728 ppm, your profession selection period would be a little less than thirteen days. In this case, your nanomachine density is a hindrance because of how many more nanomachines you have to change. So if you were at 150 ppm it would only require approximately sixty-four hours...

[Seriously? It takes two weeks for me to get the bonuses of a profession?]

Yes, but remember once you do assign a profession your nanomachine density will result in a much higher growth rate...

[True. No free lunches, huh?]

Well, frankly, you are so overbalanced because of your density, this tiny offset is barely noticeable. And remember as density grows, so will the timeframe. That is true for everyone, not just you...

I take another quick breath and notice the foul stink is noticeably, if only to a small extent, better.

[So should I assign armorsmith as my profession?]

Are you planning to make any more armor in the near future?...

[Not really. Maybe a weapon or two if I can. Not that I have a place to put it. Oh, hey, do I get an inventory now that I'm a Special?]

Just thinking about it makes me excited.

Normally, no...

I start to sink deeper.

Stop pouting. Nanomachine density determines when [Inventory] unlocks and how much inventory space is available. Generally, [Inventory] activates at between 200 and 300 ppm. There has been no recorded success of [Inventory] activating after 370 ppm. This generally translates to a Special being between evolution levels seven and ten at the absolute latest.

[Well, shit. What level is a Special with my density usually at?]

Usually as early as essence level fourteen and as late as thirty-seven. You certainly break the mold, Vic...

I'm getting sick of holding my breath, so I stick my head above the water. The stench is much more manageable now. Thank you, acid death lichen!

I look at what is left of the spider, and I nearly vomit again. A good portion of the left half of the spider is missing, and its innards are spilled all over the stone. I can still hear sizzling and see some gasses floating upwards in the dim light of the lichen.

[Ugh, that is disgusting.]

The fumes are likely still volatile. Stay back for a while longer...

Not wanting to die of something so embarrassing and gross as a spider's gas, I lean against a stone wall by the water. I can't process the level and density stuff right now, so I tell Jo to move on.

[I'm taking this wet armor off. Can you keep going on inventory?]

Certainly. The way [Inventory] works is the nanomachines produce a mana pocket which Specials access using their magica. Each pocket is divided into different sub-pockets or, as they are often called by the lazy and uninformed, "slots." The size of the pocket is defined by the host's density, and that translates to the number of slots. Again, a formula is involved here, but to simplify it I'll just tell you that each 100ppm equates to 1.5 slots. However, the nanomachines cannot process a partial slot, so only whole numbers are used. As such, 100ppm = 1 slot, 200ppm = 3 slots, 300ppm = 4 slots, etc. Luckily, the slots are all made using the same amount of mana and, as such, the growth is static until the [Inventory] skill reaches level ten. Once it hits max level, the simpler formula no longer applies, and a more complex one takes precedence, which I will not explain . . .

I'm not the least bit interested in the math behind getting the coolest skill in the history of the universe, so I let Jo continue without interruption while finally unstrapping my chest and backplate.

You have 728ppm, which equates to ten slots. Well, 10.8 so that means ten accessible until the new formula takes over, which has too many variables to estimate in advance. In other words, we have no idea how many slots you will have beyond ten. Of course, that would all be true if [Inventory] was activated by you, but it is not. [Inventory] is an Active skill which means it is activated by actively doing whatever that thing is. In this case, [Inventory] must be manually activated through [Mana Manipulation]. Your goal is to create the mana pocket . . .

[I'm too tired and drained to do anything with my mana right now. Can we go back to the alerts?]

I lay out the chest piece and backplate, lichen facing up, to dry and proceed in the removal of the rest of my wet armor.

Sure we can, Vic. For what it's worth, I'm proud of you for taking on that creature. While your [Inspect] is too low to see the level attribute, I am confident it was substantially higher than you . . .

[I'm level zero, Jo. Everything is higher level than me. But thank you.]

Don't underestimate a level zero. Remember that "Evolution Level" is simply a representation of mana essence processed. A level zero giant could squash a level ten spider quite easily . . .

[Right. Good reminder, thanks.]

Ready for the alerts in regards to the combat? . . .

[Wait. Before that, we need to address alerts distracting me while I'm fighting. I cannot be distracted by damage and all that. Just show me things that are critical, like the low mana one.]

So only things that mean you are in deep drake shit? . . .

[Yes. That would be perfect. When I'm not in combat, it's okay to show them. All right, hit me with the backed-up alerts.]

CHAPTER 14

Skill updated. Passive skill [Fire Mana Manipulation] has leveled from 7 to 10...

No further progress is available for [Fire Mana Manipulation] until an advanced version of this skill is activated. All mana used to advance nanomachines for skill [Fire Mana Manipulation] is now directed to overall nanomachine advancement...

[Great. What did I break this time?]

Nothing is broken, Vic. Just hang in there and you'll see...

[Okay.]

[Fire Mana Manipulation] has evolved...

New skill activated. Passive skill [Projectile Fire Mana Manipulation] now available for use...

Skill updated. Passive skill [Projectile Fire Mana Manipulation] has leveled from 0 to 2...

[Oh, I get it. It evolved because I was able to project it and now I can rain fiery death. I like it.]

While crude, that is an accurate description; you are now able to use your fire as a projectile. Your control over the projectiles will grow as your nanomachines gain a greater understanding of and control over that particular mana form. What is interesting here is that this flaming death skill is passive and not active. You appear to be directly manipulating the mana rather than activating the skill, and the nanomachine system is interpreting that as an action to take on your behalf...

[Is that because of my density?]

That is unlikely as high-level Specials are not able to do this. Most likely is because you are a magnicarum. You still have two species abilities—Mana Lifeline and Mana Manipulator—which we have yet to gather data on...

A deep slow exhale escapes my lungs.

[We're back to the species thing. I still don't know what to say to that, so I am going to ignore it because there is nothing I can do one way or another.]

Fine. Your species abilities are relevant though . . .

[Fair enough. You mentioned the two. If I had to guess I'd say it is that second ability, Mana Manipulator. It is not exactly subtle in its naming.]

I concur. There is insufficient evidence to update the system, but I will continue to monitor with that in mind. Let's proceed with the alerts. The best are yet to come . . .

[Well, now you are just hyping it up. Don't let me down, Jo.] I hear another sigh in my head.

Skill updated. Active skill [Inspect] is now level 1 . . .

New skill activated. Passive skill [Sprinting] now available for use . . .

Host has reached sufficient mana essence density to reach the next level. Do you wish to convert 1000 mana essence into nanomachine growth? . . .

[Fuck yeah! We leveled up. Why the hell would it ask if I wanted to level up?]

It is unclear why the creators of the nanomachine system gave the option of delaying level up. While there has not been extensive testing on this topic, there appears to be no appreciable benefit to delaying . . .

[I don't get it. Why would they offer some option that provides no benefit? Who does that?]

The creators of the system were human and likely rushing in an attempt to help humanity survive. It is likely they simply made an error. Alternatively, it is possible the quantum hive made changes to the system enforcing this rule for its own reasons. We have no way of knowing . . .

[I'm too tired for philosophy. Can we proceed?]

Did you want to level up? You have to clearly state it to advance . . .

I am hedging on this. I just can't get over the fact the developers of this system would leave such an obviously useless option. It is so stupid and the rest of the system just isn't. As soon as I am about to say "yes" my gut clenches, and I know it is the wrong thing to do.

[Let's hold off for now. Keep going with the alerts.]

Are you sure? Leveling grants your nanos the ability to advance your body and magica? . . .

[I'm already ahead of the game on those things. Let's hold off. My senses are tingling on this leveling thing.]

If you say so. I wouldn't know about your tingles. Moving on, you now have another choice but, knowing you as I do now, I feel this one will be much less conflicted.

[Oh? You've piqued my interest.]

You may or may not know this, but there are a few hidden capabilities in the system that are only activated under special circumstances. For example, in this case an influx of mana essence equating to over two thousand percent of your current count entered your nanomachine system. The nanomachine system contains certain known and unknown latent awards and punishments. Certain actions or events need to take place to activate and uncloak these "Achievements" and/or "Titles". It is unclear why or how many the system creators entered into the system or how many the quantum hive has developed on its own. As of the last update, fewer than seventeen percent of Specials have an achievement and fewer than four percent have a title . . .

[Okay. Good info, but why are you telling me, and what choice do I have to make?] Did she just laugh at me?

*New Achievement activated. For defeating a mana-infused foe 2000% stronger than yourself, the Achievement **Brave, Bold, and Boneheaded** is now available. This Achievement grants you a 2% bonus to all damage to and reduces damage from enemies 2000% stronger than you by 2%. This Achievement benefit improves by 2% per enemy 2000% stronger than you that you kill. Do you wish to show or hide your Achievement? . . .*

[Uhhhh. How did I kill something that much stronger than I am? Sure, I used pretty much all my mana, but seriously. That seems a reach.]

I can show you the alerts if you are interested . . .

[Not really. Can you summarize?]

Certainly. It appears the acid built up a volatile gaseous pressure inside the spider that you superheated with your blow to its mouth just as it was expelling the acid, resulting in the rather violent combustive explosion. In short, you were fortunate beyond normal calculations of random chance. Again . . .

[I'm certainly not complaining right now. How many more enemies am I going to have to fight that are two thousand percent stronger than me?]

Hopefully none. But the question remains, do you want to show or hide it? . . .

[Do I lose the benefit if I hide it?]

No. It simply cannot be seen by anyone with [Inspect] less than level fifty, and it will not show on the NanoNet. However, that you now have an achievement is recorded . . .

[In that case, hide it and all future awards like that unless I say otherwise.]

Confirmed. Speaking of . . .

*New Achievement activated. For defeating a non-humanoid mana-infused foe 1,000% stronger than you, the Achievement **Beast Basher** is now available. This Achievement grants you a 1% bonus to all damage to and 1% reduces damage from non-humanoid enemies 1,000% stronger than you or more. This Achievement benefit improves by 1% per non-humanoid enemy 1,000% stronger than you that you kill. Do you wish to show or hide your Achievement? . . .*

[What's with the alliteration? Did children develop this system?]

*New Achievement activated. For slaying a mana-infused foe 500% stronger than you in a single strike, the Achievement **Nuking Knockout** is now available. This Achievement grants you a 5% to all first strike damage to any enemy 500% stronger than you. This Achievement benefit improves by 5% per enemy 500% stronger than you kill in a single strike. Do you wish to show or hide your Achievement? . . .*

[That last one is useful. I'm a sniper, after all.]

Yes and no, Vic. Remember, magica has a range limit, which is far less than you are used to with your sniper rifle . . .

That makes me think of Bertha. Man, I miss her; she was such a sweet girl. I hope she is off in whatever violent afterlife guns go to.

That's it for achievements. Now, onto the big prize . . .

CHAPTER 15

*New Title activated. For annihilating an enemy 20 times your strength without assistance and in a single blow using Fire Magica, the Title **Scorching Magica** is now available. This Title grants you 50% better control over your Fire Magica. Do you wish to show or hide your Title? . . .*

[Why is achievement in percentage and title in times? It looks like different people made the system and couldn't agree on which was better. Seriously, did kids actually make this system? Was the old world filled with genius children?]

Focus, Vic! Can you read what its bonus is, please? Note that it says control and not damage or any other term. That is a very specific title . . .

[Of course I see it. I just can't quite process the achievements and titles thing. This isn't some game, Jo. These hidden awards have real consequences for humanity. Why are they so hard to get? They can help people survive and help Specials take the fight to the enemy. I'm just struggling a little.]

The reason they are hard to get is because of how the nanomachines work and how they manage resources. In your case, you received a massive influx of mana essence, far beyond what your nanomachine had at the time, in less than one second, which forced the nano to take action to process it. The system determined the best way to process that huge amount of mana essence was to convert it into mana inputs and outputs. That is also why your achievements grow; in the future, each instantaneous massive absorption of mana essence will now be processed more efficiently and directed in a particular way to be useful without risking system integrity. Moreover, this unlocks your ability to get numerous future achievements and titles. It ends up being cumulative and cyclical. The more you activate, the more you have the potential to activate . . .

I sigh. [I guess that makes sense. I just wish we could use the mana to directly kill the enemy.]

What enemy, Vic? You killed it. There was nowhere for the essence to go. It either damages the system, is wasted, or is converted. Which would you prefer? . . .

[I get it. Thanks for being patient and explaining it to me.]

I understand your desire to serve and advance humanity. It is all you have known. I would, however, give you a gentle reminder that you are no longer human. If you ever were . . .

Not sure what to say to that, I lay my head back against the stone wall and say nothing.

Now, before I display the last alert, I want to explain something. Based on available data, eighty-two percent of Specials never achieve their first evolution and are stuck at level zero. They either die or do not earn sufficient mana essence to advance their system . . .

[That actually makes sense to me. It is natural for someone to be afraid of injury or death. Especially younger civilians who suddenly find themselves able to do things they were taught is possible but felt were more fiction than reality. Basically fantasy stories of mighty battles and heroes and whatnot. And then after seeing the reality of a beast or orc for the first time, they flee and want nothing to do with the war.]

I've never been able to understand those who can but don't fight; why wouldn't someone fight for themselves and their own survival? Hell, I've been battling others since I was a child; my only alternative was to starve to death.

Jo continues, unaware of my inner thoughts.

Yes. The nanomachine system accounts for the low percentage of levelers by not investing as much nanomachine process and mana into level zeroes. You have to remember that the difference between a level zero and a non-activated human is negligible. You, again, are an exception. When a human reaches sufficient mana essence to reach level one, the system acknowledges their advancement and full nanomachine investment proceeds . . .

[I suppose I get that. Why are you telling me this?]

Because of these next two alerts . . .

*New Title activated. For becoming the first activated Magnicarum, the Title **First of your Kind** is now available. This Title grants you a bonus of 25% to all Magical attributes. Do you wish to show or hide your Title? . . .*

[The species thing again. I know we need to dig into my species at some point. Hell, I'm not great at living in ignorance, but not being human is kind of . . . I don't know.]

I understand your struggle. For now, is there anything you can do about it? . . .

No. Letting out a breath I refocus and look at the title again. That's odd.

Blinking, I think my question to Jo.

[Why . . . Oh. Because I was level zero. When I got to a thousand essence, the system recognized me as someone worth its time and thus it activated the title. Thank you for the primer.]

You're welcome. Here goes the next one . . .

*New Title activated. For having the highest nanomachine density ever recorded, the Title **Mana Born** is now available. This Title grants you a 25% bonus to the absorption attribute. Do you wish to show or hide your Title? Note: The prior owner of this Title will keep the title but lose the bonus. The individual will be notified upon connection to the Nanomachine Network. Upon notification, do you wish the prior owner to have access to your information? . . .*

[Obviously a big fat NO on the notification.]

Yes, I assumed that would be your selection . . .

[I wonder how many times the Mana Born title has swapped hands.]

Unknown, as the title can be hidden . . .

[I'll admit you were right. These were worth the tease. Are there any more alerts?]

Just one . . .

New skill activated. Passive skill [Swimming] now available for use . . .

I laugh out loud after seeing that. I laugh and laugh and laugh. The cavern lights up with lichen glowing brighter, and I lie back against the wall, smiling.

[I need to rest. I'm coming down from something of an adrenaline high, and I'm exhausted. Don't wake me up unless we're about to die. Maybe we can avoid near death for a day. You have the watch?]

I wouldn't hold your breath, and I got you covered . . .

[When I ask if you have the watch can you please respond with, "I have the watch?" It is just a paranoia thing with me from learned mistakes. Don't want confusion.]

Sure, if that helps you. I have the watch, Vic . . .

I close my eyes, reveling in today's successes and survival and looking forward to a well-deserved rest. I fall asleep almost instantly.

CHAPTER 16

I wake up without anything trying to kill me, and that is lovely.

[Morning, Jo.]

Good morning, Vic. How did you sleep? . . .

[Great. It is nice not waking up to a death monster in the cave.]

Yes. Ready to manipulate some mana? . . .

[Before we do that, can we review my profile?]

Actually, why don't we wait until [Inventory] is unlocked? You might get something from it . . .

[Sure. You're the boss.]

Agreed. Now head back into your inner world . . .

I close my eyes and am by my river almost instantly with her glowing orb next to me.

[Is it just me or is the river wider and faster than last time we were here?]

Of course it is. You have increased your attributes . . .

[Oh, right. Duh.]

We are going to try to convince the nanomachines to create their own mana pocket. According to the information available, the lower the density, the easier it is to create a mana pocket. There are numerous recorded instances of Specials never activating [Inventory] because they waited too long and their [Mana Manipulation] was insufficient . . .

[Shit. Does that mean I'm in trouble?]

Possibly. However, your [Mana Manipulation] is quite high. I am confident you can pull this off . . .

[So what do I do?]

Look into the river. What do you see?

I look at the flowing river and, unsure what she is asking for, I say questioningly, [Flowing mana that looks like water?]

I said look INTO the river, not at it, Vic. Focus!...

She snaps that last word at me.

[Right. Sorry.]

Kneeling right at the edge of the river, I look and attempt to see beyond the fast-moving surface and find what Jo is trying to show me. I can see how the water rushes by, how the ripples are stronger or weaker depending on how they flow.

I don't know how long I stay like that, but eventually I see a little sparkle. Just a brief flash, but I know I saw it. Was it a reflection or is it really there? I keep looking, especially focusing on seeing another flash. And there it is. Another one. And another. Now that I know what to look for, I see them all over. The river is saturated with them. How did I not see them immediately?

[I think I see flashes of light or something. A ton of them. Like minuscule mana lights under the water. They're everywhere.]

Great job, Vic. Those are the nanomachine connections to the mana flows. Focus on them. Try to draw them together and towards yourself...

Still staring at the flashes I ask, [How many?]

The absolute maximum as you can. Take your time...

So I reach out as I do with my mana. At first, I am just drawing the mana, but with some practice, I can use the mana itself to clump the lights together. Initially, I am able to grab just two and use the mana to gather them together. Then I let them go and do it again until I get used to the feeling. This is the approach I took during my various training to learn any number of things, allowing them to become muscle memory.

Everything around me fades except the river and the lights I am trying to manipulate. Unaware of how much time passes, I am eventually able to grab what feels like hundreds of them. My mind says it is 365, although I am not sure how I know. No matter how much I focus, I cannot seem to exceed this number. It is a pretty big strain, so I grit my teeth and think to Jo, [What now?]

Compress them. Do everything you can to squeeze them tightly together. They will react to the threat by creating a pocket space to flee into...

I focus on my 365 particles of light and try to squeeze them down. I even use my hands to mimic squishing them. The more I press, the harder it gets. My head aches something fierce, but I keep going. Without my notice, my gritted teeth open, and I begin yelling out loud as I squish with my mind. My hands mimic the action with my fingers spread as claws and slowly closing on each other. I see red alerts flashing across my vision but ignore them along with the wet dripping down my nose, eyes, and ears and yell even louder and push with all my might in one big shove. The area is lit with an azure glow when suddenly I see a small swirling waver the air in the center of my compressed nanos, and the pressure pushing back on me vanishes as the nanos and all the mana compressing them are shoved into the swirl in an abrupt release. My head throbs and vision swims as I wobble, fall to my knees, then onto my face on the grassy riverbank of my inner world. I know only pulsing pain and utter exhaustion as I fade into blackness.

CHAPTER 17

My eyes open to the cave, but I can barely tell, thanks to the pain of what feels like a giant trying to crawl out of my skull. I try to roll over so I can sit up, and my head explodes in pain, and I nearly vomit what little I have in my stomach. I groan, and Jo speaks to me in a whisper.

Don't move, Vic. You need to rest . . .

I close my eyes and try to calm my breathing. It helps reduce the blaring pain in my head a little, so I keep doing that.

Eventually, I must fall asleep again, because I open my eyes again, and there is only moderate pain. Jo speaks to me in a normal volume.

How do you feel, Vic? . . .

[Like ogre shit. What the fuck happened, Jo? That was awful.]

Can I show you the alerts? . . .

[Sure. Give me the bad news first.]

Warning! Host has 10% remaining mana . . .

Warning! Host has 5% remaining mana . . .

Warning! Host has used 100% of available mana. Any further attempts to use mana will fail . . .

Warning! Host has attempted to exceed use of available mana. Host risks injury . . .

Warning! Host is gathering mana directly from the environment. Host risks permanent damage by using unprocessed mana.

*Warning! Host has suffered **Mana Poisoning**. Health will drop by 2 health per second for 60 seconds . . .*

*Host has suffered **Mana Exhaustion**. All use of mana for the next 24 hours will result in pain and cause further damage to host's body.*

*Host has suffered **Mana Depletion**. Mana will not regenerate for the next 48 hours.*

*Host has suffered **Stage 1, Mana Void**. Host's mana channels have been dam-*

aged and are incapable of supporting mana. Host's Inner World is inaccessible. Direct mana essence infusion required to resolve damage. (0/1,250)

[That's bad. No wonder it hurt so bad. Is there any good news?]

Three pieces of good news. But before that, why didn't you stop? . . .

[I don't know. You said compress them as hard as I can, so I did.]

Fair point. But when you felt yourself bleeding from your eyes, ears, and nose, you should have used your common sense and stopped . . .

[I tend to get very driven. It's how I am and have always been. You'll see more of it as we spend more time together.]

Well, just don't be such a stubborn idiot next time. We could have refilled mana from your experiments with the mana before trying that, you know . . .

[Okay, okay. So what's the good news?] I hear a sigh.

New skill activated. Active skill [Inventory] now available for use . . .

[Yes! Finally!]

Without magica, you can't use it, but at least it's there for you. And that isn't the good part . . .

Skill updated. Active skill [Inventory] has leveled from 0 to 10 . . .

No further progress is available for [Inventory] until an advanced version of this skill is activated. All mana used to advance nanomachines for skill [Inventory] is now directed to overall nanomachine advancement . . .

[Would you look at that? Me nearly crippling myself had a pleasant side effect. Wait, why did its level rise if I haven't used it?]

Well, you did sort of shove a titanic amount of high-compressed mana into a newly created mana pocket the instant it opened. My guess is you stretched it a bit. Of course, we can't explore or do anything about it until we solve your debuff problem . . .

I let out an internal sigh.

[Jo, please remember I don't know terms that are probably common to most in regards to the nano system. Based upon what I see I'm guessing a "debuff" is an effect that negatively impacts my body? That leads me to assume a "buff" is the opposite, giving me a positive effect?]

Apologies, Vic. Yes, that is correct. We need to do something about that Mana Void debuff. We can't do anything about the other two . . .

A smug grin is nearly splitting my face.

[It's almost like I'm prophetic isn't it? I didn't use the essence, and now we need it. I'm obviously a genius.]

You're something, all right. But in this case, you are correct. We can divert the unconverted mana essence to heal the damage to your mana channels . . .

Would you like me to direct 1,250 mana essence to heal your mana channels? . . .

It has to be all official-like when mana essence is concerned, which is why I ask if you want to level up . . .

[Ah. Then yes, please proceed.]

Host has applied mana essence to **Stage 1, Mana Void**. *(1,250/1,250) . . .*

Stage 1, Mana Void *has been successfully removed. Mana channels have been repaired . . .*

[Great.]

There is one more alert. This is interesting . . .

Healing mana channels through mass direct mana essence infusion has reduced the duration of **Mana Exhaustion** *and* **Mana Depletion** *by 50% . . .*

[Well, that's an unexpected side benefit. That means we are down to twelve and twenty-four hours.]

Yes. You should feel a little better too. Actually, it is ten and twenty-two, since you slept for two hours after the debuffs were applied . . .

I realize she is right about feeling better. My head isn't pounding as much, and my body feels like it can move. I try to slowly sit up and do so with a manageable amount of discomfort.

[Didn't you say there are three pieces of good news? Are the skill levels the second?]

No, [Inventory]'s leveling up was part of the first piece of good news. Here is the second . . .

Skill updated. Passive skill [Mana Manipulation] has leveled from 5 to 8 . . .

[That is certainly good news if not at the level of the prior. What's the third?]

New skill activated. Passive skill [Mana Compression] now available for use . . .

Skill updated. Passive skill [Mana Compression] has leveled from 0 to 3 . . .

[Huh. What does that do?]

It will allow you to compress the mana you use to increase its volatility or impact. Definitely not for use with detail work; mana is just too unstable when compressed...

[So, bigger booms. Always a plus. Anything else I should know?]

Not at this time.

[Since we're stuck waiting until the debuffs fade, how about we look at my profile page?]

Actually, we cannot. Pulling up the profile screen is technically magica, which means it takes mana, which is off-limits to you for the next twenty-four hours...

[Ugh. So what the fuck are we supposed to do for the next day?]

I was thinking you could start activating some skills that are not mana-based...

[Such as?]

Well, physical activities. There's water right there. How about raising your swimming? You are surrounded by rock walls, so how about climbing? Use your brain, Vic...

[Once again, you demonstrate why you are the one running this operation.]

Wearing only my lichen half-pants, I slowly get up, wincing at my body's soreness and the thrumming in my head. Moving past it, I climb into the water and start swimming around, practicing some basics and warming up. Once I feel more limber and less achy, I take a deep breath and dive deeper to swim submerged as well. I continue using different strokes on the surface and use them again underwater. At the same time, I practice breathing exercises when on the surface, and that helps me slowly extend my dive time. After a while, I am rewarded with a few alerts from Jo.

Skill updated. Passive skill [Swimming] is now level 1...

New skill activated. Passive skill [Diving] now available for use...

I can't get diving to go up a level, probably because I do not have anything even close to resembling diving gear and I am basically just swimming underwater.

So I get out of the water, squeeze my long hair dry, and wave my arms around to dry my hands. I figure if I am going to try climbing, I should do what I can to avoid slipping.

First I try to find a piece of lichen I had that isn't covered in gross spider goo.

[I wish we could do something about this disgusting carcass. But without magica, I'm not sure what options there are. It is starting to get rather ripe.]

At this time you can either dispose of it using the water, which will contaminate your only water source, or suck it up . . .

[Ugh. Fine.]

Focusing back on the lichen, I take it to the water and slowly massage it while on the water until it glows again. I then go to my strips and create a quick way to hang it from my neck like a big square necklace. Walking to an area of the wall that is filled with divots from the spider's climb, Jo compliments my new creation.

Very stylish, Vic . . .

[I told you I'd start a new trend. On the other hand, we can all be relieved that my pants no longer glow.]

Facing the wall, I take a deep breath and stick my hands into the hold and do my best not to fall to my death. I almost succeed. I only fall once, and that is when I fail to notice that a divot has a small drop of acid still in it. My hand burns, and a reflexive jerk results in an awkward fall to the ground, which sprains my knee.

Warning! Host has received 6 falling damage . . .

*Warning! Host has suffered a **Twisted Knee (left)**. All leg-based action is slowed by 50% and will result in pain for the next 20 minutes . . .*

I decide to just lie there for twenty minutes, since the best I can do is crawl around. As I am lying there, I look at the spider carcass. Yep, it is really gross. And smelly. Despite the distraction, I notice something new; there is a small oval-shaped something-or-other about three inches long and one inch thick about a third of a meter behind what's left of its head, glowing a gentle brown.

[Hey Jo, can I use [Inspect] with my debuffs?]

Yes, you can use [Inspect] for the same reason you can still speak to me. We are elements of the system, not your mana-constructs. There are ways to disable us by eliminating your access to any and all mana rather than just your internal pool, but hopefully won't run into that . . .

Focusing on the glowy thing, I think [Inspect].

Name:	**Mana Stone (Earth)**
Descrip-	Mana stones are highly concentrated sources of

tion:	elemental mana essence and can only be found in one of two ways. First, by mining. Given that mana stone lodes are rare, companies who specialize in mana stone mining will usually purchase the rights from the founder at a high price and then sell the stones at a substantial markup. The second method to find mana stones is by taking them from the carcasses of mana-infused beasts. Only non-humanoid species have ever been found to have mana stones (with the exception of the death affinity); it is unknown why. The element of the mana stone coincides with either the environment or the creature. For example, water mana stones are generally found in lakes, oceans, or other bodies of water or from creatures who live in or near them.
Condition:	Unknown
Risk Assessment:	N/A
Value:	A detailed examination is required to determine how much essence it has and thus its value.

Nice find, Vic. You can absorb it, sell it, or eventually use it in something you craft...

[Once I can walk again, I'll check it out.]

A bit later I get the awaited message.

Twisted Knee has been successfully removed. Full movement restored...

I get up, test my knee and walk over to Mr. Stinky. Holding my breath, I stick my hand in and grab the crystal. Stringy goop sticks to it and my hand. Yuck! At least there's no acid.

[Jo, how do I check the amount of essence?]

I have that for you. Now that you're holding it, I can do it. This is not something a normal nanomachine system is capable of, but your density, which by the way had risen to 730 prior to your [Inventory] idiocy, is granting me a few extra perks. For most, a device is required to detect a stone's essence pool . . .

[Cool. How'd we do?]

Inspect it again . . .

I do.

Name:	Mana Stone (Earth)
Description:	Mana stones are highly concentrated sources of elemental mana essence and can only be found in one of two ways. First, by mining. Given that mana stone lodes are rare, companies who specialize in mana stone mining will usually purchase the rights from the founder at a high price and then sell the stones at a substantial markup. The second method to find mana stones is by taking them from the carcasses of mana-infused beasts. Only non-humanoid species have ever been found to have mana stones (with the exception of the death affinity); it is unknown why. The element of the mana stone coincides with either the environment or the creature. For example, water mana stones are generally found in lakes, oceans, or other bodies of water or from creatures who live in or near them.
Condition:	Excellent
Risk Assessment:	N/A
Value:	This earth-based mana stone is nearly full which is exceptionally rare. Essence count: 2225/2260.

[Why is a full stone rare?]

Stones in mines are never full because they leak into their surroundings, while stones in beasts are rarely full because they are used to power skills and abilities. This one is so full because the spider just ate and only used one ability before its death. Nor was it required to use an ability to kill the ankheg. Unfor-

tunately, its acid destroyed the stone of that creature. Now that you have one, you should know stones will leak until sealed by specially engraved temporal containers that are able to hold nothing but mana stones and are so expensive as to be beyond most individuals. Most corporate mining companies have inscribers and enchanters on staff to create them . . .

[Sweet. What should we do with it?]

Right now, nothing. Even if you wanted to, you couldn't do anything until your debuffs are gone. And as your new [Inventory] is also mana-driven and therefore off-limits, you should put it back. If anything a little deeper inside . . .

[You're enjoying this aren't you?]

Maybe a little . . .

CHAPTER 18

After that disgusting exercise, I return to climbing, this time checking for acid before I place my hands. See, I can learn. I climb up, sideways, down, diagonally, and every other way I can think of. Covered in sweat and panting, I am eventually rewarded with the new skill alert.

New skill activated. Passive skill [Climbing] now available for use . . .

[Finally.]

I climb down and think about what to do next. If I had a pick, I could try mining, I suppose. I go back over to my "tools" and see if there is any way I can take what I have and make something resembling a useful tool out of it. Surprisingly, I find something that might work. It is a piece of metal about six inches long, between three and four inches wide, and with a slightly pointed tip. It is bent over itself the long way which could possibly be a decent slot for my hammer handle. I suppose I could make a small weapon out of it later. For now, I'll channel my inner brute and bang on things.

I detach the hammer head and try to figure out a way to attach the new "pick head." It will maybe possibly kinda work if I don't hit too hard with it.

[Well, let's give this a shot. Any idea where I should try first?]

Not a clue. Try hitting a stalagmite. It might be less dense . . .

[The ones coming out of the ground are the mites. Good to know.]

Just hit stuff, Vic . . .

[Yes, boss.]

So I do. The first thing I discover is that having long hair can be a pain at times. Some of the long azure strands fall forward and block my vision.

I grumble softly but out loud, "It wasn't this bad while I was swimming." Sighing, I go back over to my lichen strips and tie my hair back in a ponytail behind my head.

Walking back to the target rock, I grab my pick and, using about a quarter of my strength, wind up and hit my new pointy nemesis. Miraculously, the pick head doesn't pop off and kill me. Win! I don't even notice the dripping acid or gasses elsewhere in the cavern anymore.

I repeat the chore until a small piece of the mite about an inch across hits me in the shin. It barely hurts. Surprised, I looked at my shin.

You could totally become a professional miner, Vic. Your liquid steel skin will give you an unbeatable edge . . .

[Not my kind of career. I need to shoot or blow things up to be happy with life.]

I keep banging away, knowing I probably won't hurt myself. Eventually the 'mite cracks and falls over.

[Huh. That was easy.]

So I move onto another. And another after that. After my fourth pointy-rocked opponent (the hardest so far) dies an ignoble death, Jo gives me the good news.

New skill activated. Passive skill [Mining] now available for use . . .

I'm not focused on the alert, though. I am looking at what is left of my pointy friend.

[What is that?]

I am staring at an irregular, shiny, silver stick-shaped stone with dark patches all over it. It is about eight inches in length and two inches in width, clearly visible in the middle of what remains of the stalagmite.

[Inspect.]

Name:	Unknown Ore
Description:	Unknown
Condition:	Unknown
Risk Assessment:	Unknown
Value:	Unknown

[Any thoughts, Jo?]

Not about its identity. Get it out of the rock, and we'll put it in your [Inventory] when you can access it . . .

I carefully knock the surrounding stone off and place the silvery metal in my pile of stuff. I sure hope it isn't toxic. It is certainly lighter than it looks like it should be.

Figuring there might be more, I go to all the other 'mites that aren't under death lichen and bang away. I expose two more pieces of the unknown ore; one is smaller and one larger than the first. Plopping them next to the first, I stop and stare at the rest of the cavern.

[Hey, Jo, once I get my magica back, it could be worth clearing some more moss from this cavern and trying to gather more of the ore. It might be worth something, or maybe I can craft with it. I do still need a weapon.]

We can do tests in regards to the metal. How much heat it takes to make it malleable, how dense is it, et cetera. Perhaps that will help me compare against available data and possibly identify it . . .

Instead of the 'mites, I go around trying to find any 'tites low enough for me to bang on. There are only a few but I figure I'll give it a try. In the end, I smash the four I can safely reach and only find one piece of the ore. However, it is nearly twice as large as the first.

Prior to breaking the 'tite with the ore, Jo sends me an alert.

Skill updated. Passive skill [Mining] is now level 1 . . .

What is interesting is that while mining the 'tite wasn't noticeably easier or quicker, knocking away the stone around the ore was definitely much more efficient. I was able to somehow see where to hit. I still missed and wasn't always right, but there was a noticeable change.

I explain my observations to Jo and ask [Is this how passive skills work?]

Yes. Unless you initiate a system command such as [Inspect], it is a passive skill. And the passive skills affect what you do passively. Sort of behind the scenes of your brain and body.

[That's interesting. I'll keep mining but switch to the walls now.]

Wall mining is much harder and less efficient, taking forever to even make a few chips.

[This tool is just not capable of this kind of mining.]

That, plus your skill and Skill are both too low . . .

Frustrated, I say [Fine. What should I do now?]

I recommend more pouting. Because that is helpful . . .

I sigh.

[You're right, Jo, sorry. I'm going to take a bath. I've been sweating up a storm with all this climbing and mining.]

I take off my makeshift pants and hair strap and jump in the water. Since I don't have soap, I rub myself and my hair with just the water and a rounded stone. I think I like having long hair. It can get in the way a bit, but I like the feel and look based on the limited reflection I have in the water.

Grabbing a lock, I pull the small bunch of dripping hair in front of my face and check it out in detail. The azure blue is quite shiny. Almost like . . .

CHAPTER 19

[Jo, can I [Inspect] my hair?]

No, hosts cannot [Inspect] themselves. It is a hard block that prevents cheating on the growth of the skill. And anyway, that is what the profile screen is for. Why did you ask that? . . .

[Can you check out my hair? It reminds me of my mana river with the sparkly lights.]

I get silence back from Jo. I decide to let her be. Continuing to just clean myself the best I can, I grab my pants and try to clean those too.

Do you know if that is what it looked like before you activated [Inventory]? . . .

Jo sounds quite serious when she asks that question, and I freeze in the water mid-cleaning of my pantleg. I think hard about what I remember from when I first noticed my blue hair.

[I cannot be a hundred percent sure, but I don't think it was shiny. While it was definitely blue, I don't remember the sparkles.]

More silence follows. I go back to cleaning and finish my pants. Getting out of the water, I put the pants on the ground and let myself dry in the buff. Why not?

Looking around the cavern, I try to determine what to do next when I realize how exhausted I am.

[I think it might be time for a rest. I've been going nonstop for a while.]

Fair enough. I have the watch . . .

I close my eyes and think *[Jo has the watch]* as I fall into a dreamless sleep.

***

I wake to find everything the same.

[How much time's left on the debuffs?]

Only four hours on the first and sixteen hours on the second . . .

[That's not too bad. My body feels a lot better too.]

Looking up at the lichen, I put my hands behind my head. I need to get out of here. There is clearly something going on and likely people that I need to terminate, and I can't do that stuck in this cave. Thinking of terminating people reminds me of my poor rifle. What it would be like to shoot the lichen with Bertha and some incendiary rounds. Could I blast my way out of here with her?

[Is there a way for me to set up a HUD like I had on my old visor?]

What brought that on? . . .

[I don't know. Guess I was missing my targeting reticle.]

When you acquire a ranged weapon, we can revisit the targeting reticle. As for the HUD, what do you want it to show? I can send you a standard setup if that might help . . .

[Sure, let's start there.]

And right in my vision, several things appear. In the top right there are two bars: one is red and full, one is blue and just an empty outline.

[Red is health, blue is mana, correct?]

Correct . . .

[On the top left is a place for alerts and bottom left is what?]

The boxes look the same except one has a white outline and the other a red.

[Wait, let me guess, the white top provides standard alerts, and the bottom red is critical alerts?]

Also correct . . .

[Please move the health and mana bars to the bottom right. Having them at the top is distracting.]

She does.

[When I get access to my inventory, will it look like boxes like my old visor?]

Yes . . .

[Can you make the HUD show that in two long rows along the bottom of my vision rather than as a square?]

Confirmed. We may have to adjust based on the number of cells . . .

[Sure, that makes sense. This is a good start. Thanks, Jo.]

While looking around and seeing how the HUD feels, I glance at the spider carcass again.

[If I start dissecting and examining the spider carcass, could that activate a new skill?]

It could. As always, there is no guarantee . . .

[Same answer if I start experimenting with the acid? The spider's carapace seemed to be immune to the acid.]

Yes, same answer . . .

Well, no point in sitting around. I put on my pants and head to the spider carcass. I stop on the way to get a piece of lichen, wrap it around my nose and mouth, and tie it with a strip. I also grab a small piece of metal with sharp edges.

Then I dig in. Not that I know what I am doing. First I lightly tap the carapace. It gives off a light dinging sound. I try to break a piece off, but it is too hard. I grab my pick and try again. Eventually, I am able to break a piece off about the size of my hand. It has sharp edges and points. The inside is noticeably softer. A shit-eating grin appears on my face.

[Are you thinking what I'm thinking, Jo?]

You are a violent lunatic. Why would I think like you? . . .

Fair point. I proceed to use the sharp end of the metal piece to carve channels into the inside of the carapace. In theory, these should act as weak points and be the first to break when I apply pressure.

I use my pick to start banging away at the channels. With some trial and error, I learn how deep the channels have to be and how hard to hit with my pick. I end up with five usable pieces of the spider carapace. One large squarish piece and four long thin strips.

That isn't what I was expecting you to do. What is your plan? . . .

I chuckle and think at her, [You'll see.]

I grab the big piece, flip it so the soft side is facing up, and start carving a channel in one of the corners. This one is more than twice as deep as any of the prior channels.

I'm on the third corner when an alert pops up on my HUD in the bottom left.

Mana Exhaustion has been successfully removed. Mana use is now available . . .

Now if only I had some mana. Glancing at my mana bar I see it is still empty thanks to **Mana Depletion**.

Back to work.

I finish the last of the four channels and pick up one of the long strips. I hold it up over the long piece like a sword and line up a short pointy end with one of the four new grooves. Pressing hard at a slight angle so the far end is farther from the center of the flat piece, the slice of carapace digs into the larger piece. I can feel the skin on my hands start to be cut, but there is nothing I can do about that.

Warning! Host has received 1 slicing damage . . .

Warning! Host has received 1 slicing damage . . .

Warning! Host has received 1 slicing damage . . .

Warning! Host has received 1 slicing damage . . .

Warning! Host has received 1 slicing damage . . .

Warning! Host has received 1 slicing damage . . .

Warning! Host has received 1 slicing damage . . .

Letting my hands heal after each attempt, I repeat that three more times with the other strips. I do take notice that no scars form on my hands. Looks like my old scarred body is gone for good.

However many hours and sliced hands later, I step back and examine my handiwork. Everything seems to be holding. I then flip it over, and it stays upright on the four "legs." The large top piece is up to my neck.

Did you make a tall table? . . .

[No, Jo. This is my umbrella.] Those are mana rods attached to a thin steel framework with a weak mana shield. They come in different shapes, sizes, and colors and are considered a sign of wealth and status in that level of society. Obviously, I've never had one. But the idea is the same. It will stop wet things from dripping on me. Or at least it is supposed to. Time to test that out.

I pick it up carefully and bring it over to one of the stalagmites that is under death lichen. I step back to where there is no chance of getting hit by acid and clap loudly. The lichen lights up like usual and starts dripping a little acid. As the acid falls on the carapace, it does not sizzle or burn. It just slowly dribbles to the edge and onto the ground.

I jump with my hands in the air and call out "YES!" quite loudly. More acid falls. Oops.

Very clever, Vic. Now you can keep mining without killing the lichen . . .

I walk back to get my pick and proceed to mine the 'mites without getting burned to death by acid. There is a much higher percentage of the unknown ore under the death lichen. I wonder if that is related. The hoped-for alert appears on the top left of my vision.

Skill updated. Passive skill [Mining] is now level 2 . . .

[Any thoughts on if the acid is related to the ore? And can you withhold non-critical alerts until I take a break from now on?]

Confirmed. The ore remains unknown at this time. I will add the possibility of a connection to acid to the variables when searching the available data. Right now we still have thirty-seven possible ores. Some of which are mana infused and some not . . .

I shrug and keep banging away. The 'tites that are close enough to the ground don't escape my masterful beating either.

After the final reachable 'mites and 'tites become crumbled messes and I collect twenty-eight pieces of the ore of various sizes, I decide to take a break.

I am a smelly sweaty mess. Rubbing my chin, I ask [Debuff time?]

Eleven hours . . .

[I spent five hours doing this? Didn't feel that long. Why am I not more sore?]

Density and regeneration. I recommend you sleep and perhaps bathe. I'm sure you're pretty ripe . . .

[You're right. And the time will pass faster if I sleep.]

CHAPTER 20

Waking up, I ask Jo [Debuff time?]

Five hours remaining...

[That was a good nap. Back to work, I suppose.]

I get up and walk over to the water. The discomfort is almost completely gone. Or maybe I am just used to it. Either way, I feel better.

I splash some water on my face and notice I have no facial hair at all, which makes no sense. I should have a short beard by now. I then walk over to the lichen and clap. In the increased light, I examine myself top to bottom. I have absolutely no body hair. Anywhere. That's kinda creepy.

[Jo, mark down that I have no body hair, and it isn't growing. The only hair I can find is on my head and eyebrows. How does that even work?]

Recorded for study, Vic. Your [Mining] went up, in case you are interested...

Skill updated. Passive skill [Mining] is now level 3...

[Probably still not high enough for wall work, but I can try the blob cavern.]

Putting on my pants and grabbing my pick, I take my acid protector and quietly enter the large side cavern. This area is harder to mine in because it is so full of the death lichen. Just like when I was crafting, the gasses released from the acid become dense to the point that I have to evacuate regularly. It is a waste of time until the acid is used up, but until the debuff is gone, all I have is time.

I do manage to find twenty-two more ore "sticks," all of them at least two, sometimes three or four times the size of the first I mined.

[I am almost positive the acid and the ore are connected, Jo. This cannot just be a coincidence.]

I concur. Updating system...

[I wonder if the spider had involvement as well. It clearly ate and maybe lived here with its blob. Put that down as a maybe. I'm certain the ankheg was an invader fleeing something.]

Carrying the latest massive ore piece nearly as big as me towards my pile in the entry room, I get the alert I have been waiting for.

Mana Depletion *has been successfully removed. Mana will now regenerate regularly . . .*

That is followed by a surprise notice that I don't think either I or Jo expected.

New ability activated. Species Bonus Ability Emergency Regeneration is now available for use . . .

Jo explains without me having to ask.

That is a pleasant surprise. It appears that by putting a strain on your mana channels and then force-repairing them using an influx of mana essence all at once, they have become reinforced. This will allow for an increase in mana flow. It appears to work only for short periods and during times of high need. It grants a hundred percent increase in regeneration rate when your mana or health drops below ten percent for up to sixty seconds. It can only be used once every ten hours to allow for the mana channels to heal from the strain . . .

[Wow. Not that I will ever be doing that again, but it is seriously a nice side effect of almost blowing myself up. How is that a Species Bonus?]

Yes, a nice side effect of your stubbornness. I presume that the nanomachine system is assuming that all magnicarum obtain this ability at some point . . .

[I hope they don't have to go through what I did. Or maybe I do if they're assholes. Whatever. Can I see my profile now? Oh. Please highlight what changed too.]

Yes. Welcome back to the world of magica, Vic. The numbers in parentheses show change from prior profile viewing . . .

Name:	Michael Uriel Victory	**Nick-name:**	Vic	Titles: Scorching Magica (Hidden) First of your Kind (Hidden) Mana Born (Hidden)
Age:	24	**Evolution Level (Essence):**	0 (1,081.95 /1,000)	
Species:	Magnicarum	**Class:**	Unassigned	
Professions:	Primary: Unassigned Secondary: Unassigned	Available: Armorsmith		
Health:	158/158 (+5)	**Mana:**	379/379 (+81)	

Physical Attributes:	Strength:	14.1 (+0.3)	Constitution:	15.8 (+0.5)
	Agility:	12.3 (+0.2)		
Magical Attributes:	Intelligence:	14.1 (+0.3)	Magica:	37.9 (+8.10)
Miscellaneous Attributes:	Absorption:	19.6 (+4.1)	Regeneration:	.75/second (+0.16)
Abilities:	Species Bonus:	Mana Lifeline, Mana Manipulator, Emergency Regeneration		
	Density Bonus:	Affinity Aficionado		
	Activation Bonus:	Liquid Steel Skin		
Skills:	<u>Active Skills:</u> Inspect: 1 Inventory: <10> <u>Passive Skills:</u> Armor Crafting: 5 Botany: 1 Climbing: 0 Diving: 0 Fire Mana Manipulation: <10> *Projectile Fire Mana Manipulation: 2		Mana Compression: 3 Mana Infusion: 3 Mana Manipulation: 8 Metalworking: 5 Mining: 2 Set Crafting: 2 Sewing: 3 Sprinting: 0 Swimming: 1 Tailoring: 1	
Runes:	Fire Rune, Air Rune			
Resistances:	Basic Elemental:	1.0	Adv. Elemental:	1.0
	Pain:	5.1 (+0.2)		
Achievements:	Brave, Bold, and Boneheaded (1, Hidden) Beast Basher (1, Hidden) Nuking Knockout (1, Hidden)			

[Wow. That looks so much better. What do you think, Jo? And what do the symbols on the skills section mean?]

You were somewhat overpowered even when you just activated. Now you are even more of a freak—in a good way, though. The brackets mean that skill can no longer raise in level and requires evolution. The star is an evolved skill . . .

[Oh.] As usual, I show my linguistic gifts.

[If all skills max at ten, why bracket them?]

All skills do not have a maximum ceiling of ten. Passive *skills max at ten and evolve.* Active *skills max at fifty and have no evolution path . . .*

Not sure what else to say about that, I ask something else.

[I assume the number next to the achievements is the kills. Is that correct?]

Yes. Before you ask, your physical attributes went up due to a mix of your physical activity and density. It's a complex logarithmic formula, so don't ask. Just know that the higher the attribute, the more effort and mana it will take to raise it. Your density will help to a point . . .

[Even after burning the essence for healing, I still have enough to raise my level. Can you tell me specifically what benefit I will get if I decide to do that?]

Only generally. The nanomachines will convert that essence into strengthening your body and its connection to both them and mana . . .

[Not very specific. I'll still hold off.]

That is of course your prerogative, Vic . . .

[Now, let's have some fun.]

Then I think [Inventory].

CHAPTER 21

Two rows of nine small empty blue boxes appear at the bottom of my HUD.

Congratulations, Vic. You have an eighteen-slot inventory at level zero. To put it bluntly, that is frightful . . .

I pump my fist and call out loud, "Sweet!" The lichen light up and spit some acid. I glare at the frustrating plant. I need to get the fuck out of here.

[How do I use it?]

Usually, you'd have to touch an object and think "Store In Inventory" for it to move in. However, because of your colossal fuck-up when opening your [Inventory] for the first time, you are at level ten. That means you can focus on an object and think about it getting sucked into the mana pocket . . .

I walk up to Mr. Stinky and lightly touch it while thinking about it getting sucked into myself. I feel a subtle pull in my gut, and it disappears. The massive thing just vanished into smelly air.

[Well, that was interesting. At least it should help the stench around here.]

Try it without touching. Your [Inventory] is quite high; it could be possible for remote access through mana. The skill might even evolve . . .

I walk a few steps towards my pile of ore, stare at it, and try to suck it into myself again. Nothing happens. I take two steps closer and try again. I feel that same subtle pull in my middle but a little stronger; the piece of ore I was staring at vanishes like Mr. Stinky.

Looking at my HUD I see a picture of a small spider in the top left box. The box to the right of it has an irregular glob of silver. Looking at the silver, I see a helpful little popup that says, *Unknown Ore (15oz)*.

[I find it interesting that it is in weight and not in number of pieces.]

Certain objects are in weight, volume, count, et cetera. It all depends. For ores, it is just plain weight. If you were to refine it, you might see "Unknown Ore Ingot (1), 15oz." As an added benefit, they share the same mana signature and will therefore stack in a single sub-pocket . . .

I do the same with all the rest of the ore. It turns out I have a total of fifty-two pounds and twelve ounces of the stuff. Considering how light it is, I must have done a lot of mining without realizing it. I also store all the leftover liquid steel pieces as well as the lichen patches and strips. My armor set follows.

Hold off on putting the armor in, Vic. We are going to experiment . . .

[Sure.] I think about putting the armor back where it was. It appears exactly the way it was when I swallowed it up.

[That's nifty.]

Put it on . . .

I do, thinking I know where she is going with this. It will be amazing if this works.

After putting the last piece on and double-checking everything is perfectly positioned, I think about it being sucked into myself.

It vanishes. I didn't even have to look at all the pieces; I just thought about it. Then I think about it appearing back on me in exactly the same way. It does, fully strapped and ready to protect me from spiders.

"Yes!" I yell while leaping with both my hands in the air. More acid. I ignore it.

[You are a genius, Jo! This will make things so much faster. And the benefit in combat is beyond what I could hope for.]

Thank you, Vic. Store it again and check the boxes in your HUD . . .

I do and notice the lichen strips are in their own box, same with the other lichen and metal scraps. Then I see the last filled box in the row, which is the fifth from the left, and it looks like it has a tiny picture of my whole armor set in it.

Because it is a set, they share the same mana signature and, as such, the set pieces only take up a single mana sub-pocket . . .

[That is yet another reason to make more sets.]

Lastly, I store my pick and hammering surface. They each take up one slot, meaning my total is seven used slots out of eighteen.

[I want to see if I can make a weapon with this ore, but I don't know how.]

You are going to have to learn how to process ore into usable metal. That is called smelting, and you don't have the equipment. It takes more than just fire; you need a furnace, cauldron, mold, various hand tools, et cetera. Best give up on that idea for now . . .

[Damn. Well, then I think it is time we get the hell out of this cave. You said you had an idea about how I can breathe long enough to get out?]

Ah, yes. Look on the back of your left hand . . .

I do and smack my forehead with my right hand. I am staring at my air rune.

CHAPTER 22

I am almost out of this place. I can practically taste it.

Making air magica available goes a lot faster than with fire since I have a clue what I'm doing. I create a pathway down my arm to the rune in just a few minutes and send some mana to it. I feel air moving around my hand. I visualize a small circular air funnel like a tornado and send a little more mana into the rune. Above the back of my hand, a floating swirling tornado of nearly transparent gray air is visible. It is about three inches tall. I imagine it changing into a swirling ball, and it changes shape to a globe, my long hair gently moving in the breeze it creates.

I grab a strip from my inventory and tie my hair into a ponytail again. I cannot do the in and out of [Inventory] thing with the hairband, because my hair releases when the band vanishes, and the band just falls on the floor when I make it reappear in my now flat and spread-out hair.

[Are you thinking we create some kind of air pocket?]

I was leaning that way, yes. It is a matter of practice though, we do not want you to suffocate on your magica.

[Right. That would be so embarrassing. Into the water we go.]

With just my pants on, I jump back in and dive. I try creating an air ball underwater, and the water begins to swirl with my air ball. I cancel it, and the water rushes into the spot my ball was.

[So it can create a small pocket but it moves the water both in and out of it.]

I surface, create an air ball, and then bring it below the surface of the water. The water rushes around it just like before. I try to enlarge the air bubble to the same size as me, and the water current around it picks up by at least four times. I start to get swept up in it. In pure reaction, I fight against the current and try to swim inside the ball. I can't push past the air pressure, and I get shoved away. I release the mana to the big air bubble. Suddenly all the water, and I, are sucked into the empty space left behind by my moronic decision to create a sub-nautical vacuum.

I am shaken around a lot and struggle to hold my breath. Paddling hard, I surface and gasp for air.

[That was dumb.]

Yes. Yes, it was . . .

I leave the water and create the me-sized air ball next to me. Trying to step into it gets me nowhere as, again, I can't push past the pressure. Slowly releasing the ball this time, I try to create the air ball so I am already inside of it when it is created.

There is a strong breeze, and my long ponytail is whipping around. Otherwise, I'm fine. I can breathe and move. I do feel a little lighter though. I try to guide the inner air to slow. It does, and the feeling of lightness vanishes. It is a bit hard to focus on two things at once, so I keep doing it until I get used to the sensation of splitting my attention between two different mana actions. Once I feel comfortable doing that, I push the air on the outside to spin faster. Again, it strains my mind some, but I persist. And then something unexpected happens.

The entire ball, and me in it, starts to rise off the ground about an inch. Some loose stones are whipping around the cavern and the water is churning. Looking at the water, I see if I can push the air ball towards the water. The whole thing begins to slowly rotate.

[That's not the way.]

I slowly reduce the mana to nothing and I hear the clattering of stones falling to the floor of the cavern. I conduct a few exercises of trying to bring up the bubble surrounding me as quickly as I can. Not really caring about something as trivial as time passing, I get it down to about a second. It is definitely becoming easier. Probably mana manipulation going up.

[Okay. Here goes nothing.]

I back up a bit, sprint towards the water, and take a running leap. As soon as I am over an area deep enough to dive, I activate the air bubble with air rotation high on the outside and low on the inside. And there I am, floating over the water.

[Jo, at the current mana use rate, how long can I stay like this?]

Nicely done, Vic. Taking into account your regeneration rate, you would hit ten percent mana in sixteen minutes, thirty-nine seconds.

[Okay, thanks. Next, we try to measure if I run out of air or mana faster]

I slow the outer air current, and the bubble sinks to the surface of the water. And I float there.

ACTIVATION

[Damn.] Jo's laughing echoes through my mind.

Using mana, I try to move the air differently. Instead of moving clockwise around the middle axis, I try to have the air blow upwards from the bottom, creating a downward suction. Miraculously my bubble starts to sink below the water's surface. My elation dies quickly as the strain on mana raises the more submerged the bubble gets. I won't even be halfway by the time I run out of mana.

I eventually see an unwelcome but anticipated alert.

Warning! Host has 10% remaining mana . . .

[Shit.]

I slowly release the bubble and splash into the water.

Swimming back to the shore, I'm getting frustrated.

Skill updated. Passive skill [Air Mana Manipulation] has leveled from 0 to 3 . . .

New skill activated. Passive skill [Mana Splitting] now available for use . . .

Skill updated. Passive skill [Mana Splitting] is now level 1 . . .

[I don't think this is going to work, Jo. The air is too light, and I can't hold it under long enough to help.]

I concur. I had high hopes for this approach . . .

I wring my hair out and sit on the ground, legs bent to my chest with my chin on my knees, staring at the water as it splashes against my feet. The dim glow reflects off the crests it makes as it sloshes over my toes.

[I need to move the water, not the air.]

I keep staring at the water and thinking about ways to make the water move. Maybe mana? Can I try to move the water with mana? Reaching out with my mind I tried to grab a wave that was just hitting my toes and washing back. I make a sort of grasping motion with my right hand. It is kind of weird, but I feel a connection to the wave. I felt how the water flows and wants to always be in motion. I encourage it to flow towards me, and the wave slows going backward.

A tingling begins on the back of my right hand. Blinking and attempting to refocus, I look down at the source of the tingling. A glowing blue rune is slowly forming on my tanned skin. The rune fully forms, and the tingling stops. I laugh out loud for a few seconds.

[I assume I have some alerts that would be good to see, Jo?]

CHAPTER 23

Skill updated. Passive skill [Mana Manipulation] is now level 9 . . .

New rune activated. Water Rune is now available for use . . .

New affinity activated. Water Affinity is now available for use . . .

New skill activated. Passive skill [Water Mana Manipulation] now available for use . . .

While pondering the new information on my water rune, Jo's voice sounds excited when she speaks next.

Well done, Vic. This could be the key to getting us the hell out of here . . .

Waiting until the blue of my mana bar is full, I splash back into the water. I conduct the same experiments with the water as did with the air. I find that water works better when more ovoid-shaped, rather than perfectly circular for moving around. And the water has to be in motion all the time, almost like it has desires. Trying to stop it from moving goes against its nature and is a massive mana drain.

Jo and I test how long my mana will hold out and how long I can breathe when in a water bubble. One thing I cannot manage to succeed at is using both Air and Water Mana Manipulation at the same time. Jo explains it to me, but what I hear is I am just not good enough.

That will come in time, Vic. Your mana splitting will need to be much higher to use different affinities at the same time. Possibly even evolved . . .

[Sure, Jo. So do you think we can make it? Without drowning, suffocating, or otherwise suffering a horribly unpleasant demise?]

Yes, but it will be close. Air is the larger issue since you can't make more of it. At least mana you regenerate slightly. You are going to need to very carefully manage your breathing and not panic when the air begins to thin . . .

[Okay. I'm going to get one more nap in so I am fully awake and focused. Then give seeing the sun again a try.]

Good plan, Vic. I'll save the alerts for when you wake up . . .

***

I wake feeling completely rested and ready to get above ground.

[Ready for the alerts, Jo.]

Skill updated. Passive skill [Mana Manipulation] is now level 10 . . .

No further progress is available for [Mana Manipulation] until an advanced version of this skill is activated. All mana used to advance nanomachines for skill [Mana Manipulation] is now directed to overall nanomachine advancement . . .

Jo interrupts the alerts with a question.

This last alert got you an achievement and a title. Want them now?

[Definitely.]

New Achievement activated. For reaching level 10 in [Mana Manipulation], the Achievement **Mighty Mana Mastery** *is now available. This Achievement grants you +20% mana control when using mana that has no affinity. Do you wish to show or hide your Achievement?*

[Non-affinity mana has a use? Beyond the environment, I mean.]

Sure. Well, for you it does. You will need to learn and experiment to figure it out . . .

New Title activated. For being the only Special to ever reach level 10 in [Mana Manipulation] at level 0, the Title **Mana Master** *is now available. This Title grants you +25% to your maximum mana. Do you wish to show or hide your Title?*

[Those are awesome! The names aren't terribly creative, but the effects are nice. See, staying at level zero has some uses. Not that I'll stay here forever, but at least for now it is beneficial. And the extra mana comes at a perfect time.]

You are correct, Vic. Looks like there are some brains in that skull after all . . .

I start doing my breathing exercises while showing a huge grin on my face.

Skill updated. Passive skill [Water Mana Manipulation] has leveled from 0 to 4 . . .

Skill updated. Passive skill [Mana Splitting] is now level 2 . . .

After a few minutes of warming up, I put on my pants and climb into the water up to my neck while still breathing deeply and regularly. I take out two pieces of lichen from my inventory and make them glow then strap one to my head and another to my chest.

[Here goes. Freeeeeedooom!!!]

D.I. FREED

Good luck, Vic . . .

VOLUME 3 - THE GREAT ESCAPE AND THE NEW FOREIGNERS

CHAPTER 24

I take one final deep breath and dive under, immediately creating a water cocoon. That's what I call it because it sounds way more tough and adult than bubble. And it isn't round.

Using mana, I manipulate the water to push deeper than I've gone before (well, at least when conscious and aware). I breathe as slowly as I can and watch my surroundings as the glowing lichen shows me how I got into my cavernous refuge/prison. It is basically a submerged canal in what I assume is the bank of the glacier runoff river, probably worn away over time, perhaps with the assistance of the spider and acid lichen. The path here is about a meter across at its narrowest, so that explains how I fit.

However, that is also the problem. The tighter area is creating a stronger current, pushing me backward, which forces me to exert more mana to battle the pressure, which in turn causes me to increase my breathing rate slightly.

Stay calm and controlled, Vic. Based on what I am able to determine, you are about halfway...

[How did I even get in there if it's so far?]

I would say a mixture of the current, your partially incapacitated state not recognizing time passing, and pure dumb luck. You also likely banged around a lot. Remember your broken visor. Now, focus...

Right. Focus.

Breathing at a regular interval—but smoothly—and moving the water is all I know for what feels like hours but is likely less than five minutes. It is at this point, my vision starts to get a little blurry.

Oxygen/nitrogen count is getting a little low, and carbon dioxide is getting high. Hang in there. You can start going straight up in another minute or two...

The blurriness is increasing, and I can't keep track of how long that minute or two actually is.

I think I see light ahead. I start willing myself towards it faster.

Warning! Host has 10% remaining mana...

I can't think straight, and Jo's voice sounds distant and vague.

I am almost at the light.

And suddenly I'm there, and everything is a bit brighter. I vaguely hear Jo's voice. Why is she screaming?

GO UP VIC! UP UP UP UP UP! . . .

I can't process what she is trying to tell me.

VIC! GET UP OR WE ARE GOING TO DIE! . . .

That jogs something loose. I see some bubbles and follow them, pointing straight up.

It keeps getting brighter and brighter. I press hard behind me, exerting more force.

Warning! Host has 5% remaining mana . . .

And then I launch out of the water into the daylight. While flying out of the water, I let go of the need to push behind me, take two deep breaths, and then plop like a dead fish back into the river. This time I can control myself enough to float to the surface and take another breath. After another time or two going under and surfacing like a button that won't stay pushed, I am eventually able to tread water enough to stay up. Paddling to the stony shore, I crawl so only my shins and feet are in the river and collapse chest down with my face to the side. I can't move anymore.

I'm proud of you, Vic. That was amazing. You rest, I have the watch . . .

All I can do is hazily think [Jo has the watch. Love you, Jo], and then I know no more.

CHAPTER 25

It is darker out when I wake up, probably approaching dusk. The sun! I roll over, crunching on the stones along the riverbed, and sit up just staring at the darkening blue sky. It's beautiful.

[I can't believe that worked.]

It almost didn't . . .

Looking around, it is obvious I am still in or near the rainforest. I am surrounded by the massive straight trees this area is known for.

[Well, not being dead means that time matters again. Can you put the date and time on my HUD? Top right on a single row please?]

Done. Welcome back to the land of the living. You did well, Vic . . .

[Thanks, Jo. I think that was one of the hardest things I've ever done. Which is saying something.]

Want your alerts? . . .

[Anything critical?]

Not really . . .

[Just stow it for now, then. Is there a map in your magic nanobox?]

Nanobox? Really? . . .

[What?] Another sigh.

You sort of have a map. I can activate a map, but it only shows data based both on what locations you have physically been since activation, plus the latest download from the NanoNet, which we aren't connecting to. This area is not available, so we have only your recorded locations . . .

[Pull it up, and we'll see what we have to work with. Put in on the top right, below the clock.]

A square appears in the top right of my HUD that takes up about a quarter of my visual space.

[Can you make it seventy-five percent transparent unless I am looking directly at it, at which point make it opaque?]

Confirmed...

I mentally order the map to zoom out to ten kliks. What I see is a small blue dot, representing myself I assume, in the middle of a black square, with some of the blue river showing.

[Put a marker on the entrance tunnel to the cavern system.]

A green dot a quarter of the size of my blue one shows farther up the river.

[Can you add compass points to the map?]

N, S, E, and W appear on the minimap with hashes representing the quarter points, NE, SE, NW, and SW. I turn a little, and the markers stay, showing me the compass is working. Over a century ago, it was discovered that mana strengthens the electromagnetic whatsit that creates the thing-amajig field which compasses use. In short, it means mana compasses are a thing.

So where to, Vic?...

With a thought, the lichen on my head and chest disappear.

[Once I dry off, I'll equip my armor and we can head east. That is the way to Sea Saddle City.]

I start walking and realize quickly that my bare feet are going to be a problem. I sigh and take out some patches of lichen and a sharp piece of metal from my [Inventory]. After some cutting and sewing, I have barely fitting, if soft, sandal-socks.

[Better than nothing. At least the cave had a floor mostly free of sharp points.]

I start a brisk walk east while doing my best to maintain a hearing distance from the river. My training kicks in quickly as I keep my head moving, watching all around and my ears listening for any sound that might mean a threat. All the visual and auditory stimulation is a bit of a shock to the psyche after the silence and darkness of the cave.

After about ten minutes, all but my hair is dry. Right, my hair. I tie it back into a ponytail and equip my armor directly from my [Inventory]. I think about making a weapon out of fallen branches, but what is that going to do against a mana-infused beast?

It will be dark soon, Vic. You should think about shelter...

[Fair point.]

Halting my walk, I look up and around for the right tree to shelter in. I need cover, and this area is too open. It is at that point I hear a cracking sound coming from behind me.

I jerk around, facing towards the sound. An animal a meter and a half at the shoulder with one meter long antlers is walking by. The size may be surprising, but the biggest shocker is that those prodigious antlers are pulsing a purple glow and giving off an occasional spark and crackle. The beast glances at me and then goes back to a slow trudge through the rainforest.

I think [Inspect]

Name:	Lightning Mana-Infused Roosevelt Elk
Description:	Mana-infused Roosevelt elk are passive, herbivorous creatures unless threatened. There is little that would harm a creature of this nature as, once enraged, it will release the mana of its affinity. These creatures have a substantial reserve of mana and use it when threatened. This particular elk will cover itself in electricity and, if required, can release blasts of lightning at its attacker.
Condition:	Healthy
Risk Assessment:	Low (High if attacked)
Value:	The antlers, hide, and bones of these creatures are highly prized by many types of crafters. The meat is considered a delicacy in some markets but valued less in others.

[What do you think, Jo?]

It's kind of cute. And not hurting anybody. At the same time, this could be an opportunity for Nuking Knockout to show its value and grow. And you need protein...

I admit I may have drooled a tiny bit there at the mention of venison. I imagine if I were a normal human I would be quite weak from lack of caloric intake. Lichen is neither tasty nor nutritious and Jo is correct, I need meat.

[I wish I had Bertha and penetrating munition.]

Make a decision, Vic. It is going to be out of magica range soon . . .

The decision is taken from me a moment later when a meter-tall, green-furred feline launches itself from beside the elk. They both go down in a mad scramble with hooves and paws flailing about. Then I see a bright purple glow and a loud crack like a lightning bolt followed by a roar.

I stumble back at the reverberating sound and, not giving two shits about anything else, start injecting mana into my air rune. Lifting a hand out facing the pair, I shape the air mana using about a quarter of my total into a thin crescent-shaped blade. I try to compress the end facing the creatures to create a fine edge.

Good thought. Let's not set the forest on fire . . .

The elk clambers back to its feet, its antlers glowing brightly and crackling with electricity. The green cat creature also gets to its feet, roaring at the elk.

They stand facing each other and there is another crack, and a lightning bolt strikes the cat. This time the cat glows green, and the lightning seems to funnel around the cat, down its legs, and into the ground.

[Oh, shit. It can ground electricity. No wonder it thought this elk was prey.]

Looking at the feline, I think [Inspect.]

Name:	**Nature Mana-Infused Mountain Lion**
Description:	These aggressive predators are known to take down prey up to twice their size with a mix of natural stealth and utter viciousness. Their teeth and claws can tear through steel and often cause excessive bleeding. As the name denotes, these creatures almost always have either nature or earth affinities which allows them to blend in their surroundings and make very little noise.
Condition:	Healthy
Risk Assessment:	Lethal
Value:	The pelt, teeth, and claws of these beasts are highly desired by crafters of armor, weapons, and accessories.

What's your plan, Vic? Will you defend the elk, by attacking the lion? Wait for them to wound each other and finish them off? Or you could just run away . . .

[Fuck that, I'm not running. I'll take option two: let them wound each other.]

I look around for a way to be slightly elevated and find a tree I might be able to climb. I quietly work my way there while hearing an occasional roar and snap of electricity. Having never released my windblade, it follows me as I climb to a branch two and a half meters off the ground with a good line of sight on the dancing couple. Neither seems in particularly great shape.

Pointing at the cat with my left hand, I line up the windblade so it will (hopefully) hit the cat in the neck.

[Any last thoughts, Jo?]

Don't miss . . .

[Good thought.]

During a particularly loud roar, I let fly the windblade. Just like I would if I was looking through a sniper scope, I start "loading" another windblade immediately after releasing the last one. The one I launched towards the cat moves faster than I can follow with my eyes, and hits it in the neck mid-roar. The roar is stopped instantly, and a thin line of blood slowly dyes the green fur of its neck a brownish-red. Then the head slides down and separates from the body while blood pours out, and the once-mighty cat collapses with a thump.

You have killed an **Earth Mana-Infused Mountain Lion**. *You absorb 2,741.17 mana essence . . .*

The elk is dripping blood and wobbling on its feet. I take the same steps as with the lion, launching the windblade. The wobbling creature turns in an attempt to run away, so my blade slices into and through its flank instead of its neck. It was apparently deep enough to sever something important because the whole rear end flops down. The front soon follows after a weak bellow from the creature. I climb down, creating another windblade, this one with half as much mana as my prior two.

Intending to put it out of its misery, I walk closer. It is still struggling on the ground trying to escape. I see a flash, and the next thing I know I am launched backward until my back and head hit one of the massive red-brown trees. My armor protects my back and my ponytail absorbs a small amount of the collision force to the head.

Warning! Host has 5% remaining health . . .

I am a little groggy and shaky as I try to stand up. I am tingly all over as I see occasional sparks along my body. And I'm steaming.

I shake my head, trying to clear it and unconsciously thinking I need to move now. Faster! Angry at myself, I absorb the little sparks from my body. At first, it hurts, which helps me focus. But as I continue, the pain stops. All the tingles are gone except on my left forearm, on which the tingles get stronger. It is under my armor, so there is not much I can do. The tingles go away quickly anyway.

My air blade was lost after I was fried, so I create a new one and cautiously make my way back to the elk. This time I maintain a good three meters distance while aiming at its neck. It finally dies to my magica, not in any more pain.

You have killed a **Lightning Mana-Infused Roosevelt Elk**. *You absorb 1,862.09 mana essence . . .*

The purple glow fades on the antlers, and I approach. Similarly, the green glow is gone from the cat.

[Well, that was exciting. Back to finding shelter. We lost even more sunlight in that little scuffle.]

I look at both carcasses and will them into my [Inventory], feeling the usual tug.

Yes. Getting nearly electrocuted to death is exciting . . .

Because of its canopy, the rainforest is darker than one would expect. I rush around, trying to find a decent tree to shelter in. I have to light a fire orb to create more light and float it ahead. I turn up the brightness every time I think I find a good spot.

Finally, I manage it, climbing the tree to reach my future napping location. I have chosen a point ten meters up where one of the massive red cedars collapsed onto another, even larger tree. At this junction of massive trunks, I will be covered on three sides and from above. Only being able to be attacked from the front is as good as I am going to get. I blow some air around my future hide to clear it of detritus and settle into rest.

[You have the watch, Jo?]

I have the watch, Vic. Goodnight . . .

CHAPTER 26

I wake to a beam of sunlight hitting me straight in the eyes. I jerk my head to the side instinctively, which promptly bashes it into the tree.

I moan out loud and crawl forward to escape. Standing up, I stretch and glance at the map. Looks like I got a little off course, but it's easy to fix. I need to eat and drink. I take out a lichen water skin that I filled back at the cave and drink. It's clean but tastes like dirt.

Food is another issue. I know I need to increase my intake desperately. Sitting back down on my little tree nook I take the head of the lion out of my [Inventory]. It is much bigger and heavier than it looked last night. I choose the lion instead of the elk primarily because of its size. That thing is fucking huge, and I'd have to be on the ground to butcher it. Looking at the lion, I reflect that it may be smaller, but it is by no means small.

[Damn, this is a big beastie. We got super lucky it wasn't us targeted instead of the elk.]

Agreed. If luck was an attribute, you'd definitely have it in the fifties . . .

[Nanos can't create luck—that's stupid. Luck isn't even a thing. It is just random events based on other random events, based on even more random events.]

That is why it is not an attribute . . .

I look at the cleanly sliced neck and notice it is much closer to the head than I aimed. There is barely any neck. Now I'm not only cranky from lack of food, I'm frustrated at my poor aim. Putting the head back in my [Inventory], a thud sounds in my hide as the rest of the lion appears in front of me, taking up the widest part of the tree.

[This thing is huge.]

Shifting it around so the neck is facing me, I see some of the neck muscle as well as the bones, ligaments, et cetera. I draw my mining pick from my [Inventory], disassemble it, and search for an area on it that is still sharp after all the mining. Finding what I am looking for, I use the sharp end to —without getting near the pelt—cut at some of the meat in the neck. It is rather bloody work, but I eventually am able to cut and tear a piece of the neck muscle about six inches by two inches. Good enough for now. Putting the carcass back, I stab my future breakfast with the pick head, hold it facing left with my right hand and start a low heat mana fire with my left hand. I float the fire under the steak and let it sear the outside while turning it occasionally.

[How many alerts do I have backed up?]

Quite a few. You have a backlog from the escape from the cave...

[Right. Go in order while I watch this delicious steak sizzle and drip.]

Skill updated. Passive skill [Water Mana Manipulation] has leveled from 4 to 7...

Skill updated. Passive skill [Mana Splitting] is now level 3...

Skill updated. Passive skill [Swimming] is now level 2...

That is it from the great escape...

[Okay. Nothing big there. I assume some good stuff came out of our tussle with the beasties.]

See for yourself...

Skill updated. Passive skill [Air Mana Manipulation] is now level 4...

Skill updated. Passive skill [Mana Compression] is now level 4...

[Great. More skill levels are always welcome.]

I know you do not generally like damage alerts during combat, but you should see this...

Warning! Host has received 112 elemental (lightning) damage...

Warning! Host has received 29 falling damage...

Interrupting, I call in my head, [Fuck me! I almost died from that single blast of lightning.]

You did get a "health at five percent" alert, although you might have been too dazed to notice it. In fact, you would be a crispy rotting corpse if you didn't have your armor set bonus. Plus your long hair forced you to wear a ponytail, which just happened to hit right and not crush your thick skull. Remember what I was saying about a luck attribute?...

[Yeah, I see what you mean. I was one lucky bastard to survive that stupidity. I can't believe I approached a target before confirming termination. Such a rookie mistake! I'd fire myself if I was the boss.]

Good thing I'm the boss, huh? Learn from this and remember the world you are a part of now. Maybe we can find you a sniper rifle eventually; until that time, you are a close-to-moderate range combatant . . .

[Yeah. Thanks for the wake-up call. What else we got?]

I am going to show these as well because they lead to something critical . . .

Warning! Host has received 3 elemental (lightning) damage . . .

Warning! Host has received 2 elemental (lightning) damage . . .

Warning! Host has received 1 elemental (lightning) damage . . .

New skill activated. Passive skill [Elemental Absorption] now available for use . . .

New rune activated. Lightning Rune is now available for use . . .

New affinity activated. Lightning Affinity is now available for use . . .

[That explains the tingles. Why are there both runes and affinities in the system? What is the difference if one always leads to the other?]

Simply put, they do not. Not all Specials successfully awaken an affinity, even if they have a rune . . .

Oh. That sucks. Almost having the power but it being just out of reach for whatever reason. I have to imagine that could lead to some negativity towards the system and other Specials. It's worth thinking about.

Checking my steak, it looks okay to eat. I poke it with my finger, and it seems stiff enough. I give it a sniff, and it smells divine. I take a tentative bite. The juice rolls down my tongue and chin, and I moan in pleasure.

I see what you mean now regarding your preferred way to die . . .

[Pretty much, yes.]

Enjoying the best meal I have had in however long makes me think of time passing . . .

[How long was in that cave?]

At least eight days. Time prior to activation and during the actual activation process is an estimate . . .

[I guess I was unconscious on and off for a while. Who knows how long all that took. They will likely believe me dead, then.]

Is that good or bad? . . .

[Good question.]

I finish my delicious lion steak and luxuriate in the glory that is grilled animal meat.

Okay. Did you survive your meatgasm? Are you ready for the rest of the alerts? . . .

[You sound jealous when you say it that way.]

Jo doesn't respond for some unfathomable reason.

Skill updated. Passive skill [Air Mana Manipulation] is now level 5 . . .

Achievement updated. **Brave, Bold, and Boneheaded** *is now level 2.*

Achievement updated. **Beast Basher** *is now level 2.*

Achievement updated. **Nuking Knockout** *is now level 2.*

Achievement updated. **Brave, Bold, and Boneheaded** *is now level 3.*

Achievement updated. **Beast Basher** *is now level 3.*

Skill updated. Passive skill [Climbing] is now level 1 . . .

New skill activated. Passive skill [Cooking] now available for use . . .

That is the last of them up until just now when you activated cooking . . .

[Stupid elk moved so I couldn't get Nuking Knockout up to three.]

Be happy with what you have. It is only because of your insane density that you have enough power to combat something like the lion and elk. Or the spider, for that matter. Normal people wouldn't even have the magica to cause more than double-digit damage, never mind quadruple-digit. Not that you bother with damage alerts . . .

[Why would I read damage alerts? It's not like they mean anything when I don't know how much health my targets have. Before you snark more, I know you said to be happy with what I have, but why didn't I get Projectile Air Mana Manipulation?]

I don't snark. And probably because there is no such thing. Remember that your Fire Mana Manipulation had to evolve to be projectile. Air is always at range so to speak, and already something of a projectile. So no evolution is required, therefore no skill. You have to remember each element has its own nature which you will discover as you explore your affinities further . . .

[I'll need to think that through. It sounds convoluted.]

It can be. Did you wish to level up, Vic? . . .

[Not out in the open when I'm vulnerable. Let's continue heading east.]

***

For three days, I travel through the rainforest, using my compass to validate I am heading in the correct general direction. I take on each day as its own operation, working to avoid any encounters. After nearly getting one-shotted by a herbivore, I decide it is best to stop fighting above my essence level unless I can snipe from safety.

Using my wilderness training from years prior and actual experience on various missions against the Invaders, I maintain operational security. That entails two broad requirements of contested and/or wildlands travel. First is an emphasis on silent movement, which means slow but lower-risk progress. Second is environmental awareness requiring constant movement of the eyes and head and active alertness to sounds and smells. Between these two, I avoid any further combat, although it is close once. I am barely able to smell the infused beast scat and silently flee north and then up a tree before whatever left that huge pile senses me. In short, those three days of constant awareness are intense, stressful, and draining.

On the fourth morning after the lion/elk episode, I wake tiredly to the sound of yelling and crashing around in the forest. I can't understand the language, but I can recognize it. I had just been targeting a camp filled with beings that use the grunting and snorting Orcish a little over a week ago. My face turns into a snarling visage, and I practically growl.

CHAPTER 27

Orcs are the number one enemy of humanity. They are vicious, violent, strong, resilient, and talented killers. They also nearly wiped the human race from the planet. According to the few pre-Invasion records that were recovered, there were approximately nine billion humans on the planet. Currently, there are approximately one billion, which is after the stabilization period and a little less than a century of rebuilding and refocusing. If it wasn't for three things, this world would be ruled by orcs, ogres, and the like.

The primary key to humanity's survival of the Invasion was the humans that awakened to their mana and began being able to use magica. They were the progenitors to the Specials and sacrificed themselves to buy humanity enough time to implement the nanomachine system. The first day of spring every year is a celebration of the price these brave individuals paid to allow for humanity's survival.

The second key, publicly considered less impactful (I believe otherwise), was that we found allies from the other side. Or more precisely, they found us. The elves, dwarves, gnomes, and beastkin introduced themselves and told us they had been battling the orcs and their allies for tens of millennia across numerous dimensions. Those allies showed humanity how to use mana to craft mana-infused items and enhance the body. This allowed for the creation of magica tools, and thus companies like MagiTech were founded.

And finally, humanity made the difficult but necessary decision to relinquish massive swaths of land and focus only on major cities and the land surrounding them. Currently, humanity holds somewhere in the range of one hundred large cities and five hundred medium or smaller cities. In many cases, new cities had to be built from nearly nothing around land that was viewed as critical to humanity's survival.

Thanks to these three things, we are holding our own against the Invaders. Not winning back any major amount of land, but not losing either.

Leaning over slowly so as not to create a visual disturbance, I peer in the direction of the chaos. I can only make out the basic details from here, but

I now understand why the orcs are not bothering to hide their presence. Stealth is pointless when you are chasing prey already aware of your pursuit. The prey itself appears to be three figures fleeing the orcs with everything they have.

Accepting the orcs are far too focused on their quarry to notice me, I push the canopy out of the way and take a better look at the fleeing trio. The one in the lead (granted by only less than a meter) is easily recognizable as a dwarf with the short stature and black beard to his waist. How is he running so fast with such short legs?

The next two are side by side holding hands. I am pretty sure they are both elves and both female, although elves are notoriously difficult to discern from humans at a distance, as the men also have soft features and long hair. One is a redhead and good two heads taller than the other shorter golden blond. Even more challenging to distinguish in elves is their age. Elven bodies don't age the way other races tend to. They don't get wrinkles or liver spots, nor do they hunch over or lose bone mass. When you are up close you can sometimes tell by their eyes and posture. But mostly it takes listening to their voices. The voices become what we humans would call more mature as they age. Deeper and slower mostly. All three are wearing ragged brown clothing that looks more like a brown cloth bag with holes in it for the arms and head. It is also far too short on the tall elf and far too long on the dwarf.

[Jo, how close do we need to be to [Inspect] the orcs?]

Five feet or so at skill level one. Sorry. What do you plan to do, Vic? . . .

[I'm not sure. What is the range of our elemental attacks.]

Fire is up to twenty meters. Air less than ten, water is zero, not that you have much around to manipulate. And lightning we have never used, so that is an unknown . . .

[Right, never activating the lightning affinity was a big oversight. I'm a dumbass. Can you remind me if we live long enough for that to happen again?]

Affirmative . . .

[All right, so fire it is. Sorry, rainforest.]

Getting to my feet, I start looking around for branches that lead to other trees.

Finding none I swear out loud. "Fuck."

Climbing down, I get to the forest floor and sprint diagonally away from the groups but towards where I think they will end up if they keep going straight. I find a tree that has a lot of foliage closer to the ground, which is unusual for a mana-infused fir, and immediately head towards it. I climb up, find a spot among the low foliage, and move things around so I can see out but they will have difficulty pinpointing me. I have no camo gear, so my normal sniper hide approach will not work. I am covered in shiny metal, so I look around for a solution. I think I have time.

I climb back down and, using two hands, rub dirt all over the shiny silver of my armor. It's not great but definitely less reflective. Thankfully, the lichen on my armor does not glow any more than my pants. The crashing is getting close, and I quickly climb back up to my poor sniper hide. Thinking of how to attack, I examine the enemy formation. They are using the standard orc pursuit party with two triangular groups of three and a group of two behind.

[Why the hell are eight orcs hunting three runaways? That is serious overkill.]

This likely speaks to their importance, which could confirm your actions . . .

[Seeing this, I was likely to take action anyway. But yes, this confirms the intercept and rescue operation. I need explosive area of effect damage. How do you recommend I form the fire?]

A round-shaped object will likely result in an outward explosive force while reducing individual target damage . . .

[Fireball it is.]

Focusing, I create a ball of fire about twelve inches across and then work to compress it. I am aiming for a big release, so I figure adding the instability and release of compression will help. After a moment of thought, I decide to make it blue hot—hopefully, they cannot see its glow through the leaves.

I examine the three enemy groups. The dwarf and elves are just a few meters from my tree. The lead orc group is only ten meters behind them, followed closely by the second group. Then I glance at my fireball.

[I don't think this will be enough.]

Closing my eyes, I try to split my mana and create another fireball. After some flickering, I manage to create it and open my eyes.

Warning! Host has 10% remaining mana . . .

A glance at my bar tells me I actually have nine percent. This had better work, because I'm weaponless and about to be near-bottomed out on alternatives.

CHAPTER 28

The dwarf and elves run by my tree with the orcs only six to seven meters behind them. Pointing a little ahead of the lead group, I launch the first fireball. It streaks towards the group, and in just over a second, it smashes into the ground slightly off-center of the hunting team's triangle formation. A blue flare of light and flame explodes outward, engulfing the orcs and ground around them. Green bodies, blood, and orc parts go flying.

*You have killed an **Orc Hunter**. You absorb 257.91 mana essence . . .*

*You have killed an **Orc Hunter**. You absorb 250.12 mana essence . . .*

*You have killed an **Orc Hunter**. You absorb 284.03 mana essence . . .*

I look towards the second group as they skid to a stop staring wide-eyed at the location their fellow hunter group just inhabited. Pointing again, I launch the second ball towards the middle of the second group. I cause another streak of blue, and despite one of the orcs noticing and attempting to leap out of the way, the explosion tears all three apart.

*You have killed an **Orc Hunter**. You absorb 198.85 mana essence . . .*

*You have killed an **Orc Hunter**. You absorb 257.50 mana essence . . .*

*You have killed an **Orc Hunter**. You absorb 261.05 mana essence . . .*

I look towards the third group with only two orcs. The bigger orc is jogging to the side, away from the smaller orc while pointing in my direction and calling out in the grunts and snorts of Orcish language. That one looks towards my sniper hide and waves his arms and moves his mouth in rhythm. It is at this point I notice the wave-edged knife he removed from inside his left sleeve.

I immediately run to the trunk and start climbing higher. I recognize that kind of orc—it's one of their magica users, called a shaman. As I get about two meters higher, the tree starts glowing green. I am about to have problems if he can use magica from this distance.

"Shit." I spit out loud, stop climbing, and drop back down to the branch. There is no point in climbing if he is using nature magica. I start making an air bubble around myself and leap off the tree towards the shaman. I shove mana into the bubble, speeding up the airflow on the outside. My descent starts to slow, and I let go of the mana when I'm a meter above the ground. I roll forward on impact, get back to my feet, and start sprinting towards the target.

Nature magica is tricky to fight because attacks can originate from anywhere there is a plant. Sprinting towards them, I create a windblade as the big orc charges at me in turn. I condense the windblade as much as possible and shoot it at the orc's torso.

He leaps, his body flattening with his arms spread, as the windblade shoots under him. I form two meter-long spears of fire. As he tucks and lands with a forward roll, I point my left hand at the shaman, who is waving his arms again, and my right hand at the big orc who is still heading towards me. I release both and start sprinting towards the shaman.

A branch from the tree next to the shaman glows green and bends to block the fire lance. The branch explodes, and shards fly everywhere, including at the shaman who tries to cover his face with his arms. I run by, closing my eyes to avoid the shards but otherwise do nothing but sprint away as fast as my enhanced body can manage. Thanks to my skin and the distance, the shards bounce off.

You have killed an **Orc Shaman.** *You absorb 1,057.91 mana essence...*

I can hear big clomping footsteps and the breaking of branches as the big orc is pursuing me. I start forming two more fire lances, twist around, and launch one at his head and one at his waist.

Warning! Host has 5% remaining mana...

He rolls beneath both and gets up, losing almost no momentum. He's less than a meter from me now and must have decided it was close enough, because he gathers himself and leaps towards me, his right hand closed in a fist and heading for me. I try to dodge to the side, but I'm too late. His fist makes contact with my left shoulder, and I leave my feet and go hurtling through the air. I impact the ground and roll on my side until my back smashes into a tree, causing me to come to an abrupt and painful stop. My hair falls partially in front of my face as the band holding it breaks.

Alerts flash across my HUD.

Warning! Host has suffered a **Dislocated Shoulder.** *All activity involving moving the affected shoulder is reduced by 75% and causes pain for 60 hours...*

Warning! Host has suffered a **Broken Rib.** *All activity involving moving the* body is reduced by 25% and causes pain for 90 hours . . .

Warning! Host has suffered a **Broken Rib.** All activity involving moving the body is reduced by 25% and causes pain for 90 hours . . .

The orc is walking towards me. I am groggy with pain so I don't see him clearly, but I can hear his huffing breath. This almost reminds me of the elk. Smashing into trees seems to be my thing.

He is towering above me puffing out air. Then I hear a deep rumbling voice speak slowly as if not used to the language. "Not bad, human."

He's going to kill me. I need to think of something. [Jo, can you record this?] I think quickly.

Recording started . . .

Blinking at him, I say, "You speak Common?"

Common is the universal language our allies taught us and replaced the old local languages used throughout the planet.

He kneels half a meter in front of me looking down as I lie with my back against the tree. "I lower myself to speak your filthy language, yes. How else can I speak to your kind?"

Thinking of the elk gives me an idea. I need a minute.

"Why would you speak to my kind?" I ask. "Why bother?"

He starts huffing, and his shoulders shake up and down. I realize he's laughing.

"Why else? To destroy you."

I have a bad feeling about this. Blinking at him again, I inquire, "Why would talking to us destroy us?"

Again the huffing laugh. "Not all of you. Just a few who are willing to sacrifice." He stands up. "Enough talk. You will die now. I will offer the honor and mercy of a quick death because you entertained me."

He reaches around his back and pulls a short-handled axe with a single blade about ten inches in height and six wide. Gripping it in his right hand, he raises it above his head.

CHAPTER 29

He has one last thing to say. "You honored your kind today, human."

Completing the mana channel, I quickly point my right index finger at him. There is a bright purple flash and loud crack. I've managed to nearly blind and deafen myself.

I blink a few times to clear my eyes, and the orc is lying on the ground twitching with purple sparks running all along his body. Using the tree to lean on with only my right arm, I stand up and walk around to his head. I kick the axe out of reach and look down at him.

For some reason, everything starts to have a slightly blue tinge as my hair begins to float up behind me like gravity doesn't apply. I feel tired and angry and scared at the same time.

I form a windblade above his neck and look him in the eye. I see denial and fury.

"You got one thing wrong," I growl at him. I hit him with lightning again, using a lot less power.

"I" —zap— "am" —zap — "not" —zap— "human" —ZAP. The last one has more power. I see his eyes widen with surprise while the rest of his body is convulsing. I lower my hand and the windblade drops with it separating his head from his body.

*You have killed an **Orc Personal Guard**. You absorb 1,857.91 mana essence . . .*

I exhale a deep breath and wobble a little. The blue tinge fades away, and my hair falls like nothing happened. Walking to another tree, I lean my back against it and slide down.

You okay, Vic? . . .

[How did the shaman die?]

I am unsure how, but you got the kill alert . . .

I start shaking a little. Both from coming down from the adrenaline high and my emotions.

I hear the crunching of leaves and sticks. I try to get up but fail and fall back down. The dwarf walks into my line of sight and I let out a sigh.

I tiredly wave and say, "Hello."

He stares at me for a bit, glances at my decapitated opponent, looks back at me, and says, "Greetings. And I suppose thank you."

I smile at him and respond with, "Sure. No problem. Easy. Nothing like a good tussle in the woods to get the blood flowing."

He stares at me and blinks. Then he grins and breaks out into a loud and deep laugh, one that sounds like boulders rolling downhill. I chuckle with him but immediately wince at the pain in my ribs.

The taller, redheaded elf comes out from behind a tree and stands behind the dwarf. I glance at her and he looks at me, his smile gone. "You got a problem with elves?"

Shaking my head slightly I say, "Not at all. I'm appreciative of any help that keeps humanity from falling to the orcs. Plus, would I save people I dislike?"

He keeps his straight face and responds. "Appreciation is just words from a vulnerable man. And maybe you weren't saving us but killin' orcs, and we be bait."

I let out a sigh and wince again. Speaking is painful, but I do it anyway. "Not sure what I can say to that. I really don't want to hurt you. Any of you. I just wanted to help. That being said, I won't deny killing orcs is a pleasant bonus to saving some folks in need."

A voice like bells comes from behind the dwarf in a language I don't know.

[We need to learn more languages, Jo. Can we do that through the nano?]

Sort of. It would require a connection with a language library to the process. You should maybe ask if they have the ability to heal your shoulder and ribs . . .

[I'll wait until they decide if they are going to trust, leave, or kill me.]

I'm rooting against the last option . . .

Oblivious to my pain and inner dialogue, the woman and the dwarf are speaking back and forth.

[I swear they are using two different languages.]

I would guess one is Elven and the other Dwarvish . . .

[Logical assumption. They look like they are arguing.]

The dwarf points at me and makes a chopping motion with his hand. Then the elven lady stomps her food and puts her hands on her hips.

[Uh-oh. I hope that is in my favor and not a disagreement on how to kill me.]

And my hope is immediately fulfilled when he puts his hands up in surrender, sighs, and speaks.

"My girl says ya ca' be trusted. I think she's bonkers on this." She then smacks the back of the dwarf's head. He doesn't react at all and continues. "But once she puts 'er mind ta somp'n there's no changin' it."

I smile.

He glares at me and asks, "You find this funny?"

I respond with, "Honestly, yes, but that's not why I'm smiling. She reminds me of an old comrade is all. He was crazy stubborn and couldn't be moved once he decided on a path."

"Where is your friend now?" comes out of the mouth of the elf. Her voice is musical but aged. Like she already knows the answer.

"He was killed in action defending civilians from a beast breakout in Port o' Land."

"What is your name, human?" the dwarf asks.

"Call me Vic," I reply.

"I be Grundlan Steeltamer, but folks call me Grun." He points at the elven lady behind him with his thumb and says, "This lass be Shentris, and she be my girl."

"Hello. Call me Shen," she says in her musical voice.

I smile. "Pleasure to meet you both."

"And what is your name?" I ask glancing beyond both the dwarf and elf at the golden blonde-haired head sticking out from behind a tree.

Both Grun's and Shen's head and shoulders snap to face behind themselves. I try not to chuckle but fail. Ouch. Fucking broken ribs.

The dwarf glares at me, but the elf just sighs and calls back to the tree, "Come join us, Aria. There is no point hiding now. Plus, our rescuer might need a little assistance."

Grun turns to Shen and opens his mouth, but she whips her head around glaring at him. His shoulders droop as he resigns himself to whatever "his girl" has planned.

She knows how to handle a man. I'm going to watch her carefully...

[You already handle me.]

Apparently not well enough if you have two broken ribs and a dislocated shoulder...

I have no response to that.

The other elf, Aria I suppose, walks lightly over to Grun. As I said, one can never tell with elves, but she looks maybe twenty in human years. She is, frankly, utterly stunning. I've worked with a lot of military and civilians in my various deployments and missions and some were more or less attractive than an average human. This Aria, however, is maybe the most beautiful person I have ever seen. Not that it matters but it is good to be aware of my attraction early so I can consciously avoid letting it distract me. Just like I always do.

"Aria, this is Vic. He's hurt. Can you figure out what's wrong with him?"

She looks down at me without any particular expression and responds only with "yes." It is a quiet, high-pitched, bell-like voice. She walks her way to me in almost a dance and stops about a foot away. Grun looks like he is preparing to leap the distance and throttle me. I stay very still.

[They are crazy protective. She clearly isn't a child. Or maybe she is for elves.]

Jo says what I'm thinking.

And what would you know, Mr. Loner Sniper virgin who only talks to a few women you know from the lab?...

[Fair point again. I guess I'm a little nervous around women, okay? Give me an ogre or a troll any day. But women are complicated. You're the only one I trust enough to be myself around.]

That's...flattering, Vic. Thank you...

I almost shrug but catch myself before the pain hits.

Aria stares at me, takes a single step closer, reaches out, and touches my shoulder with her index finger. Looking into her eyes, I see they are golden. Not amber like some humans, but liquid gold. Nothing seemed to be happening until her golden eyes started to glow.

[Whoa. What's that?]

I cannot be sure, but she might have an affinity for life magica. That is exceptionally rare, Vic...

[Rare enough for the orcs to want to capture her and force her to use it on their injured?]

Yes, exactly that rare...

"I've never seen a human with hair like yours before." The golden glow fades from her eyes.

I smile gently at her. "Neither have I, actually. It is a pleasure to meet you, Aria. I'm Vic."

She takes in a small breath and speaks in her musical tone. "Two of your ribs are cracked, and your left shoulder isn't in the right place." She turns to face her parents. "He will need assistance putting his shoulder put back. It's behind where it is supposed to be."

Grun shows an evil grin on his face, spits on his hands, and then rubs them together. "I ca' 'elp wi' dat."

[I notice the more comfortable he gets, the shorter his speech gets. I haven't directly worked with a dwarf in the field before. Is this common?]

Yes. Available data states dwarves are generally very focused individuals. They view anything that interrupts whatever they are doing to be a bother, including speaking. So they shorten words to speed up conversations. This allows them to get back to what they were doing faster and is generally not considered rude. In fact, speaking slowly to a dwarf can be viewed as an insult or even an offense if they believe it is done maliciously to delay their work...

[I should spend some time on better cultural insight. Legally not existing means I don't have the opportunity to work with too many extra-worlders. I did have a quick recon op once with an elf, but he spent over a century with humans in this world, so that is not a fair comparison.]

I agree with your desire to increase cultural understanding. Consider reading something other than gun, sniping, and military manuals. Or prepping for a mission...

[I'll consider it. Both are kind of big asks though.]

Grun is in front of me now. "Ready, boy?" he says.

I nod. His face changes to one of focus.

He moves to my left and gently picks up my arm by the forearm guard. He adjusts his stance, without jostling my shoulder, so his left hand is on my upper arm, right hand on my lower arm, and left foot against the tree behind me.

This is going to suck so bad.

Looking at me he says, "On three." I nod again. "Don't be a baby bou it."

I glare at him.

"One." And he yanks.

CHAPTER 30

I grunt loudly as there is a cracking or maybe snapping sound. I am too distracted by the excruciating pain to tell the difference. All my muscles clench, including my chest muscles, which means my ribs cause even more pain. I moan and clench my teeth and fists. Hell, my toes are probably clenching too.

Dislocated Shoulder has been successfully removed. Full movement will be restored in 30 seconds...

Aria runs over to me, shoves her father out of the way, and lays her hands on the uncovered skin of my upper arms. I'm confident he went willingly because there is no way her tiny frame that maybe weighs a hundred pounds wet actually moved the obviously powerful dwarf.

Her eyes glow gold again, and I feel a warmth flood inside of me. The warmth moves right to my ribs and the pain starts to fade. Soon the flow from my arms reduces to a trickle, and I try grabbing and absorbing it like I did the lightning. What I assume is life mana fades away, so I don't know if it succeeded or not.

Host has been healed for 35 damage...

Host has been healed for 35 damage...

Broken Rib has been successfully removed. Full movement is restored...

Broken Rib has been successfully removed. Full movement is restored...

Host has been healed for 35 damage...

Host has been healed for 35 damage...

[Without showing me the alert, can you tell me if we got the rune?]

Did you feel a rune appear?...

[No. Too bad. Do you think it is because it's rare and I can't use it? Or maybe I just need to absorb more.]

I do not know. There's only one way to find out...

[Maybe someday I can ask Aria to shoot me some life magica and I can try again. No rush and certainly no pressuring her. We're strangers, after all.]

I take a deep breath and stand up without pain. With a small smile, I look down at Aria—she's a good ten to fifteen inches shorter than me—and say, "Thank you very much, Aria. That was amazing."

Without looking up at me, she tiredly walks back to her mother and leans against her with the taller woman stroking her head.

I frown. Looking between Grun and Shen I ask, "Is she okay?"

The lovely older elf smiles and says quietly, "She'll be fine. A little rest and she'll be back to herself in no time."

Looking at Aria, I ask, "Will you need assistance walking? We really shouldn't stay here."

She tiredly shakes her head frowning at me. "I can walk fine."

"Fair enough." I nod and ask, "So where are you folks headed? Or is it just away from the orcs?"

The dwarf grunts and says, "Anywhere but where we were."

"Where were you headed if it is not too upfront to ask," Shen asks.

I smile at her gently and say, "East. My aim is to attempt a bridge crossing to Sea Saddle City."

Looking at my new potential traveling companions, I continue.

"I haven't spent more than a few days there over a year ago, but what I saw makes me believe they are okay with non-humans. I bought some food, clothes, and tools from shops owned by dwarves and a gnome. You could perhaps find shelter there."

Frustratingly, many human cities are not as welcoming to our non-human allies. Early in my career as a covert operative, I was deployed on a mission to a coastal city, Alexius, on the northern edge of the large southern continent. At that time dwarves and gnomes were not allowed to walk around unaccompanied by a human, never mind run businesses. Elves were allowed to be alone, but that is pretty much it. It was my first exposure to that level of human arrogance and foolishness. Later I asked to be redeployed to terminate the city leadership in hopes of smarter replacements but was denied. A year later it was too late when the city later fell to an only moderate Invader assault, likely due to not receiving any assistance from our very capable and experienced allies.

Bringing my focus back to the rescued trio, I find Shen and Grun trading conversation. Shen then nods at Grun who turns to me and says, "You shou' search da bodies for wha' is useful 'fore we hea' out." Not wanting to waste time or risk that someone or something heard the fighting, I just glance at the body of the big orc, and it vanishes into my [Inventory] along with his axe. I hear Shen gasp.

Wait! . . . Followed by a sigh.

Looking around for a threat I ask, [What?]

Never mind. We'll discuss it later . . .

Walking to the shaman, I see he died when a shard from the exploding branch pierced his throat. Thinking about how lucky I got, I [Inventory] his body and the knife without putting conscious thought into it.

[Unlucky for him.]

Yes, and lucky for you. Better get moving . . .

Agreeing, I say to the group, "I don't want to delay any longer. The rest are peons and not worth the risk."

Grun nods and says, "Lead on, boy."

I stretch my now pain-free body, tie my hair back into a ponytail, glance at my map compass, and start walking east with two elves and a dwarf in tow. I notice Aria watching me as I tie my hair back. But stop when she sees me looking.

An hour or so into the hike, Grun asks me, "You wha humans call a Special?"

I nod.

He grunts. "That explains the 'splosions tha' took ou' da two groups a orcs."

I nod again.

Speaking to Grun in a quiet voice, I mention my concerns. "We should remain as silent as possible to avoid attracting the wildlife. Almost everything here is quite strong. Not to mention we don't know if a hunting or tracking party from the orcs will be sent out after they realize the others aren't returning."

He grunts again and is silent for the rest of the day.

***

After four hours of thankfully eventless walking, I slow down. Darkness will be approaching soon, and I start looking around for a tree. The difficulty is increased because it has to accommodate four. Figuring we could be at different heights without concern, I find a tree where the three could squeeze together with me about ten meters above them by myself.

"There," I say while pointing at a tree.

Ready for anything, Grun asks, "What ya pointin at boy?"

Walking to the massive red tree and patting it, I respond with, "The tree. This will be our shelter tonight."

I hear Shen and Aria, whose strength had returned, sigh, and Grun grunt. "Dwarves don't climb trees boy."

CHAPTER 31

I look straight at him. "Here are the choices. You sleep on the ground with the nocturnal hunters who will smell you a kilometer away or you sleep in the tree surrounded by solid wood on multiple sides where you have a much lower chance of discovery with the added benefit of a defensible position." Turning around to face the tree, I say, "I'll demonstrate."

I proceed to slowly climb the tree using the branches as either grips or push-offs. I get to where the family will be sleeping, and I use air mana to clean it out well. I may go a little overboard, but I do not want them to be any more uncomfortable than necessary.

Aww, that's sweet, Vic. Your protective family instincts are coming out . . .

[Is that what it is?] I ask seriously.

I started climbing back down the same way I climbed up.

You're serious? I was sassing you, but now I'm interested . . .

[Never mind.]

I get to the bottom and turn to the family. I hear a slight whisper from Aria's direction. "I'm not great with heights either."

I shrug and turn to Shen. "I can help you and Aria up if you like."

Shen smiles at me. "I'll be fine. How would you help Aria?"

I explain how I was trained to climb with conscious rescued personnel. "She'll ride on my back, holding across my neck with her hands and across my waist with her legs." Glancing at Grun, I say, "I could probably do the same with you, Grun."

He harrumphs and mumbles something to himself.

"We accept your offer. I can get myself up." Shen interrupts Grun's mumbling.

Getting Aria up is easy and only slightly distracting with her eyes scrunched closed and her arms nearly choking me, causing her body to press against my back. She pretty much shoves me away with a glare and leans her back against the trunk when we finally reach the makeshift platform. Getting Grun up is not fun at all. He is much heavier than he looks. When we reach the hide, he is pale and immediately shuffles as close to the trunk and Aria as possible. Shen fearlessly walks closer, and the ladies cuddle close to the dwarf while I sit on a branch with my legs dangling on either side, recovering from carrying him. I tie a glowing piece of lichen to my head and offer the same to all of them. Grun and Aria decline.

"Do you all eat meat?" All three of them nod vigorously. "I don't suppose any of you know the right way to skin a beast?"

"I do," Shen says. "I spent about three hundred of your years when I was young in various forests and jungles living off the wildlife and vegetation."

Thinking, I say, "I have some metal shards but no skinning knife. Sorry. We just have to make do."

Grun immediately pops into the conversation. "Show me the metal, boy." I approach him and place as many shards as would fit into the space without falling off the tree. Aria emanates a small golden glow from her hand so he can see. That explains not wanting the lichen light. They don't need it.

He is completely focused on the metal, picking up a piece here or there. I feel a hand on my shoulder. Looking over I see Shen. "Leave him to his work. Show me the carcass, and I'll teach you.

Shaking my head, I say, "We're out of space. The body is too big."

She sighs and nods and we all turn back to Grun. "It looks like this could take a while. Why don't you get your space ready and come back down in a bit?"

"Sure." And I climb my way up the ten meters to my hide for the night. I find a small surprise as I make my way to it. Approaching my target location, I see something I couldn't see from below. There is a nest on the spot I picked. I freeze, listening for any noise coming from the nest. I definitely hear some soft breathing.

[Thoughts, Jo?]

Can you quietly get close enough to inspect? . . .

[I think so. The breathing is steady, which probably means it's sleeping and not a nocturnal hunter. The nest is huge, though. At least a meter and a half across. Could be bigger, hard to tell from beneath it, which is probably intentional.]

All of that makes it unlikely to be an owl, but we know nothing else . . .

[Right. Here goes.]

Exceptionally slowly and quietly, I climb the rest of the way up to the nest. I take a quick break to rest my arm muscles and put most of my weight on my legs. Feeling rested enough, I then carefully peek over the edge of the nest.

Inside are one large bird, one small chick, and an egg. I look at the large bird and think [Inspect] and then climb back down so my head can't be seen in case it wakes up.

Name:	Water/Air Mana-Infused Osprey
Description:	The mana-infused osprey is a large water hunting bird of prey. Fish, small sharks, and occasionally other water-hunting birds make up its diet. Like most mana-infused flying avians, this bird has an air affinity. However, because it is so often hunting on, near, or even under the water, this osprey has a rare dual affinity with water.
Condition:	Sleeping
Risk Assessment:	Moderate
Value:	Almost every part of this bird is valuable, especially its mana stone as dual affinity stones are quite rare.

[Still no level, huh?]

Sorry, no. Raise [Inspect] higher . . .

Slowly sticking my head back up I do a quick [Inspect] on the chick and egg.

Name:	Water/Air Mana-Infused Osprey Chick
Description:	This is a very young version of the adult mana-infused osprey. Completely helpless and harmless, this chick will not be able to fend for itself for at least six months.
Condition:	Sleeping
Risk Assessment:	None
Value:	Almost all newborn beasts can be brought to beast

	tamers and sold at a very high price. This dual affinity chick will be worth a substantially higher than average.
Name:	**Water/Air Mana-Infused Osprey Egg**
Description:	This is the unborn but fertilized egg of a mana-infused osprey. This egg is dead and will not hatch.
Condition:	Dead
Risk Assessment:	N/A
Value:	This egg has no known value except as food.

[Decision time. Do we kill and eat the big one which will result in the guaranteed death of the baby? If we kill it, we can also cook and eat the egg. Or we can leave them all alone.]

You did miss one option, Vic. If you kill the big one you could try to bond with the baby . . .

[I'm not a beast tamer. I have no idea how to do that. Do you?]

Even I've heard of beast tamers. They have mana-infused beast partners who battle by the side of their humanoid trainers. A number are quite famous, almost entirely because of their beasts.

Not a clue. But you could try. It is certainly one choice . . .

I stay hanging on the tree by my legs for a while longer and think.

[I'm going to ask Shen's thoughts. I could use another opinion.]

I quietly make my way down to the family's area and see Grun still poking at the steel. Walking over to Shen, I ask if I can speak to her privately for a sec. We walk together to a branch and sit. Again I'm dangling one leg over each side while Shen has both her legs over one side. She has no pants, after all.

I describe the situation with the osprey nest and finish with, "So what do you think? I need another opinion."

She looks at me, not responding for a full minute. I have no idea what is going through her head, and it is making me a bit self-conscious. I feel myself blush slightly and look away, not that I can see much in the dark.

When she finally speaks, she says, "I don't think you should ask me."

Blinking at her, I ask, "Why not?"

Her response drops my jaw.

CHAPTER 32

"Because I am a beast tamer."

Then it is her turn to blush, and I break out into a huge grin. "That decides it. You can bond with the chick, and I'll take the egg and bird carcass. It works out for everyone. Maybe your future birdy friend will help us hunt. Although, according to the description, it will be a good six months before it's ready to live on its own." I'm kind of jabbering on at this point, excited to see a beast bonding. "Can you teach me how to bond? Not for this bird of course, but for something else I might come across later?"

I've always gotten very excited over the opportunity to strengthen myself, and beast taming would be a huge gain. I can imagine a night assault with a small black creature sneaking around with me and planting explosives. That would be amazing.

Shen looks at me with humor in her eyes and starts to laugh quietly like ringing bells. Maybe my excitement is a little too obvious. "You have a bargain. Come down when the parent is dead and the carcass gone. I'll show you how to dress it."

Excited, I run by Aria, who's silently watching Grun and start climbing. I slow down as I get close and do the quiet climbing then rest using my legs routine. I start to form a windblade and compress it to exactly the size of the osprey's neck—I want to avoid knocking the nest or damaging anything in it.

Slowly, I raise my head over the edge of the nest and find myself face to beak with the adult bird. It is absolutely huge with a head that matches half of mine in size. It is awake and staring at me. In fact, I would say it was waiting for me. I slowly raise my windblade above the edge of the nest over my left shoulder. The osprey's head shifts in that direction, clearly seeing or sensing my mana creation. Trying to take action before it is too late, I shoot the windblade at its neck.

You have killed a **Water/Air Mana-infused Osprey**. *You absorb 781.02 mana essence...*

Blood splatters on my face and in my eyes, so I can't see what is going on.

Gripping the tree with my left hand, I open my right hand, and the water skin appears in it. I open it with my teeth and dribble a little on my eyes, then reseal it the same way and send it back into the mana pocket. I swap hands to give my left hand a break and use it to wipe at my eyes.

The osprey is dead, its head half-severed from its body. I look at it and send the carcass into my [Inventory] and do the same with the egg. Then I climb down and wave to Shen, letting her know it's her time to shine.

"First thing we'll need is food. Raw fish or meat," is her first instruction to beast bonding.

"Shit," is my brilliant response. "Hold on."

I grab the last small piece of lion-neck meat and hand it over. It's only one and a half inches in diameter and a half-inch thick, barely a snack for me.

Looking at the meat, she tells me, "Baby birds need their food preprocessed before they can swallow it. In this case, we need to mash it up and mix it with water."

Shen walks over to Grun, who is poking and prodding at the metal for who knows what reason. She leans down and looks over the pieces. She grabs one, walks back to our branch, sits down on the thickest part, and starts to cut the meat into tiny pieces. And then tinier pieces. She repeats this until my poor steak is basically mush.

Putting the meat into her cupped hand, she looks at me and asks, "Can you use magica to store this?"

I nod, look at it, and . . . nothing happens.

You cannot [Inventory] something that is in someone else's possession, Vic. Otherwise, what would stop you from just vanishing your enemy's weapon or armor? . . .

[Too bad, but okay.]

I hold my hand out cupped like hers, and she dumps the mush inside. Glancing at it, I make it vanish.

She then says, "Ready. Lead on." She follows me up the tree, and I get the impression she is a much better climber. Swinging about like hanging thirty meters in the air is nothing, she moves to the opposite side of the nest, and I stay in my old spot sticking my head above it.

"Food please," she requests, holding out her hand. I cup my hand and return the meat to her. "Put four drops of water in using your waterskin."

I follow the instruction. She swirls it around.

Using one finger, she reaches into the nest and gently starts stroking the head of the chick. She then starts to talk to it in a soft gentle voice. The words are almost a song of general comfort such as "You're such a beautiful bird" and "We are going to make a great team."

She says to me, "The words don't matter—it is the intent and mana behind them."

I nod, not saying anything for fear of screwing this up.

Then she dips her ring and pinky fingers into the watery mush and scoops out a tiny bit. She puts it in front of its tiny beak and it opens its mouth. She drips some of the mush down its throat. This process repeats itself until the chick no longer opens its mouth. The whole time, Shen does not stop crooning to it.

After it finishes eating, Shen leans over the nest and looks at the bird, right into its eyes. Mostly, the bird has been in constant motion of some sort prior to this point, but now it is frozen. Only its breathing is letting me know it is still alive. Still crooning, Shen starts to glow the green color of nature magica. It stays steady for a while and then starts to pulse. The tiny bird begins to glow as well and pulse in time with Shen and her humming tune. It starts slow and slowly speeds up. Eventually, it is pulsing so fast it looks solid again. About five seconds later, there is a brighter flash of green from them both that lights up the night. Then it is dark again, and the only light is my and Shen's lichen headbands once again.

Breaking the silence, she asks me, "Do you have any more of the soft material you used to make your armor padding?"

"Not much. How much do you need?" I ask.

She responds with "Just enough to carry Michial here in."

I grin and say, "Michial, huh? That is a bold name. I hope he lives up to it." Looking at my [Inventory], the biggest piece of soft lichen I have left is only four by three inches. I take it out and show it to her. "This is the biggest I have. I don't even have pieces big enough to sew together beyond that. It's all just scraps."

"Why do you keep them, then?" she asks while taking the small piece of lichen.

I respond immediately with, "Emergency rations."

"Oh," is all she says to that.

She gently nudges Michial onto the small piece of lichen and lifts them both. She holds it close to her chest and slowly makes her way down. Once she is down, I give the nest a thorough look through. Unsurprisingly, the most common items are feathers, of which I [Inventory] the larger adult ones, thinking they might be worth something. Surprisingly, there is an object that has nothing to do with birds or nests sitting among the other detritus, and its shine is how I find it.

The subtle light of my lichen headband reflects briefly off a small metallic object, almost completely hidden beneath fluffy baby bird feathers. A random breeze blows one of the small, light feathers, and the shine glints through for a fraction of a second.

Reaching in and pushing aside the feathers, I realize what reflected the light is a thin silvery chain. It is no more than a millimeter thick and tangled all throughout that area of the nest. Not sure what to do, I move the entire nest into my [Inventory] and clean the area it sat on. I finally have a place to sleep tonight.

Climbing back down to see the family, I hear Aria whispering with her mother about Michial and Grun grumping about the metal. The instant I set my foot down on their level, Grun demands of me, "Wha in the blazes is this here metal boy?"

Turning around and [Intentory]ing my headband, I respond. "It is called liquid steel, and it is a human product made by a company called MagiTech."

He throws up his hands and says, "Na wonder I canna move it."

Looking quizzically at him, I ask, "Move it?"

"Yes, boy. Me clan be called Steeltamer for a reason. We move metal. But this not be natural, so it do na respond to me earth and fire mana."

I respond with "Oh. Too bad." Then I have a thought. "Do you know how to smelt ore?"

Looking offended, Grun responded angrily, "Of course I do. Did I na just explain wha' Steeltamers do, boy?"

"Can you take a look at this and tell me what you think?" I call from [Inventory] the smallest piece of the stalagwhatever (I have already forgotten and don't care enough to remember) ore. It is only five inches by one inch at its thickest and looks like a gnarled silver and black stick; I hold it out to him.

He looks at the ore, and his hairy eyebrows crinkle. He looks closer, and then the crinkled eyebrows raise into his gangly bangs. His eyes open wide and then wider until the whites are huge in the reflection of Aria's golden light.

He slowly reaches for the metal with a shaking hand. I let him take it from my hand. He moves the stick up and down as if to weigh it. "It be as light as they say . . ." I hear him mumble.

He proceeds to mumble about fiber density, liquidity, weight ratios and more metalworking terms that are far above my head. I doubt he is even paying attention to his own thoughts at this point and is simply in his own world enjoying the exercise in something of which he excels. I can understand and respect that.

The next words out of his mouth surprise me, though, as he says in a whisper, "Could add to her grandfather's spear and crown."

I freeze. Grun freezes. Out of the side of my eye, I see that Shen and Aria freeze too.

I'm pretty sure you weren't supposed to know anything about that . . .

[I think so too. I'll just pass it off for now. If they want to tell me about it they can.]

I look towards Grun. He is staring at me with no expression. I say quietly, "Tell me or don't. It is up to you, and I don't have anything more to say on the topic."

Grun looks like he deflates somewhat. Not sure if it is in defeat or relief. Aria is silent as always as she turns away, but her mother is looking between the dwarf and myself with an odd expression I am struggling to identify. I could swear it looks like hope, but that makes pretty much no sense, so I figure I'm simply misinterpreting an elven emotion. Not unexpected given how few I have relationships with.

I continue as if nothing happened. "So tell me about that lovely metal."

Blinking, Grun shakes his head to clear it and answers. "Dis be a real treasure, boy. It be called quicksilver." Shaking his head at the ore in his hand, he holds it out to return it to me. I take it and [Inventory] it. The name is updated in the inventory. He continues. "Da last vein I heard 'bout was found by da Stonemountain clan more 'n six hundred a' yer years ago." Shocked, I'm silent as he continues. "Only da masters in us Steeltamers and one other clan know how to smelt that there ore. I dunno how, but I know it be tricky 'cause a' its properties."

Shen interrupts us then by clearing her throat and says, "We need to eat."

[That was an interesting time for a subject change.]

Something is certainly not what it seems . . .

Looking at Shen I say, "You're right. I have some food but no way to get it ready for consumption."

Grun asks what should have been an obvious question. "What about the orc's stuff? Did you na take a knife?"

I smack my forehead, feeling like a complete amateur once again. I need to do better at adapting to having magica—my default mindset is that not having my collar means I'm weaponless. I need to get with it.

With a breath and more berating myself mentally, I withdraw the wavy dagger from my [Inventory], flip it around so I am holding the blade, and hold it out handle-first to Shen. She carefully removes it from my fingers. I move towards the pile of liquid steel, and determined to do better moving forward, express my will while staring at it. The pile of man-made metal vanishes into my [Inventory].

Then I drop the lion's carcass with a thump where the metal was. Looking at Shen, I ask, "Will you teach me again?"

She looks at the headless lion. Then at me. Then back at the lion. Then back and me and nods. "I will." I smile at her and kneel by the carcass.

She joins me and spends the next half hour getting filthy and teaching me all about how to dress an animal carcass. Shen warns me the orc's knife is a sacrificial blade intended for stabbing, not cutting; as such, she is going to do the best she can, but I should not expect perfection. As far as I am concerned, it is a thousand times better than I would do, so whatever. The entire experience is a quality education. When I am no longer dead, I am going to submit changes to the wilderness training program to include carcass management and dressing. The basics taught are clearly insufficient.

I learn about how to deal with blood, which has to be drained quickly, how to remove the viscera, and which parts are edible and which not. And beyond the food element, the blood-smeared elf demonstrates how to hold, slice, and separate the teeth, claws, and skin so as not to ruin the valuable and useful components. She is an excellent teacher, and I feel as though I can do it myself after we're through. Of course, the one piece I don't miss is the mana stone. That gets [Inventory]ed immediately. But also raises a question that has been on my mind for a while now.

[Hey, Jo? I didn't ask before but nothing I put in my [Inventory] seems to age or go bad. Is that a permanent thing? Could I leave a hunk of steak in there forever and it will never go bad?]

No, Vic, that would be impossible. The mana pocket is not stasis. What happens is the mana in the pockets moves very slowly compared to how it moves anywhere else. The amount of time is a hidden formula but I know that size has something to do with it. It is not a perfect ratio, but the items in your [Inventory] will age at approximately one tenth of normal time . . .

[That is very handy. Wait, there are formulae hidden even from you?]

Agreed and yes, there are. For [Inventory], the bigger the mana pocket, the slower the mana moves, so for you it might be as high as one-to-thirteen ratio. We would have to do some testing to find out the exact delay . . .

I put everything except for four steaks and the carcass's waste back in my [Inventory]. I climb up and break off four smaller branches handing one to each of the family after I stick my steak on the end of mine. They follow by doing the same. Then I create a low-heat ball of fire and hold my steak over it.

***

After a delectable meal, the family cuddles in their spot, and I climb up to mine and go through my normal evening routine.

[Okay, Jo. I imagine I have a bit of a backup again on alerts.]

You could say that. I'm withholding damage notifications per your request. Here you go . . .

CHAPTER 33

Skill updated. Passive skill [Mana Splitting] is now level 4 . . .

Skill updated. Passive skill [Mana Compression] is now level 5 . . .

Skill updated. Passive skill [Projective Fire Mana Manipulation] has leveled from 2 to 5 . . .

Skill updated. Passive skill [Air Mana Manipulation] is now level 6 . . .

Skill updated. Passive skill [Sprinting] is now level 1 . . .

New skill activated. Passive skill [Lightning Mana Manipulation] now available for use . . .

Skill updated. Passive skill [Lightning Mana Manipulation] has leveled from 0 to 2 . . .

New Species ability activated. Mana Rage is now available for use . . .

Species ability Mana Rage is now active . . .

Skill updated. Passive skill [Lightning Mana Manipulation] is now level 3 . . .

Species ability Mana Rage is now inactive . . .

Warning! Host has suffered **Mana Overload**. All of the host's attributes will be reduced by 95% for 110 seconds . . .

Mana Overload *has been successfully removed. All attributes are restored . . .*

That is it for the fight. I withheld the ability and debuff alerts at the time because it wouldn't help, and I assumed you would wish to discuss them . . .

[Good deduction, and I'm fine with you holding that particular alert. So, Mana Rage and Mana Overload?]

Mana Rage is assigned by the nanomachine system as a species ability for magnicarum. Your body will begin to use magic from the environment as an emergency fuel. The mana will run somewhat wild, causing both emotional and physical overload. You will be immune to pain and have enhanced control over your mana. When the effect is over, however, you will suffer the debuff **Mana Overload** *for ten times as long as you were in Mana Rage . . .*

[That is a nasty debuff. I'd be pretty much helpless. Definitely for emergencies only, assuming I can even control it.]

I believe control is a measure of concentration, focus, and practice. Perhaps enhancing certain attributes will assist as well...

[I hate to be greedy, but there were no achievements?]

You should know by now I always save any achievements and titles for the end...

[Of course you do. All right, between the fight and now, what other alerts do we have?]

Oh, you'll like this one. It is a first for you...

[You always get me so revved up.]

Don't be gross. Here it is...

Host has collected 113 gold coins from **Orc Personal Guard**...

Host has collected 31 silver coins from **Orc Personal Guard**...

Host has collected 554 copper coins from **Orc Personal Guard**...

Host has collected 74 gold coins from **Orc Shaman**...

Host has collected 284 silver coins from **Orc Shaman**...

Host has collected 91 copper coins from **Orc Shaman**...

[Wow. I got paid like forty silver per month or something from the military and MagiTech.]

Government doesn't pay, huh?...

[They provided everything for me—why would I need coin? In this case, these gains will be useful for equipment replacement if I plan on hiding without traceable access to my funding sources.]

The post-Invasion money system is based on the hard currency of coins made of precious metals. It was adopted globally for the trading of goods between our extradimensional allies. That we could also steal it from our enemies and spend it is a side benefit, I'm sure.

The conversion rate is straightforward: one hundred copper equals one silver. One hundred silver equals one gold. One hundred gold equals one platinum. I used to live a low-key life on forty silvers per month. I lived for work and never had needs the government couldn't meet, so why would I need more?

Focus, Vic!...

[Right. Sorry. The first question I can think of is where did they keep it?

That is way too many to just carry around.]

Good question. They both had spatial containers. One of the shaman's various bags held a mana pocket, and the guard which nearly killed you had a ring that contained a mana pocket . . .

The gnomes introduced those to humanity however many years ago, and now they are almost common. Lots of advertising and such for different shapes, colors, jewels, and all that. I had a simple collar with six slots prior to it being melted by death lichen acid. That brings up memories, and I start missing Bertha again.

[So you moved all the money to my [Inventory]? Is it taking up one of my slots?]

Looking at the eighteen slots on my HUD, I don't see one holding anything resembling a coin. I know I had to use a slot on my collar when I took spending money out of the bank; I generally didn't carry hard coin on me though. Why would I when decades ago the largest banking firm in the world, Bank of Greater Humanity, or BoGH (pronounced bog) created an enchanted remote connection device that connected to banks through mana (which is pretty much everywhere on this world)?

They don't actually hold money; they just give you access to buy things. The tech is over my head, but I heard that in the pre-Invasion days they had something similar called "bank cards" because they looked like flat square pieces of something called plastic. Mana destroys that now, but that is a different story.

Specials like you who open mana pockets have different capabilities than artificially infused spatial containers. The time slowing, for example, doesn't happen for non-Specials. Another difference is the ability to evolve or update the container. For example, when your six-slot collar was made, that would have been its size forever. As you've seen, Specials can enlarge theirs over time, even add extra capabilities through evolution of the active skill. [Inventory] is the only Active skill in the nanomachine system that maxes at ten and evolves. As I said before, all other Active skills max at fifty. The creators made some odd design choices. Or the quantum nanomachine hive intelligence evolved the skills in places . . .

Anyway, in regards to coins for you and your fellow Specials, the creators enabled a special mini-pocket that holds only coins and interfaces directly with the NanoNet. It is the very first pocket created when [Inventory] is activated. You managed to not break this part of your nanomachine system. Congratulations, Vic! . . .

[Thanks, Jo. I'll take the victories where I can get them. What happens to the spatial containers when I try to [Inventory] them? I was always told you cannot put one inside of another.]

That is true for Specials as well. In fact, when you put the bodies in your [Inventory], you did two idiotic things. One harmful and one beneficial. The first is you destroyed anything spatially enchanted on their person. This included destroying anything inside the mana pockets in those containers. I barely managed to grab the coins and move them over to your mana pocket before your nanomachines broke down the mana holding their pockets together . . .

[That's why you said to wait. Thanks for the save. That was potentially a lot of waste and would have been worse if it wasn't for you.]

You're welcome, Vic. The beneficial thing you managed to do is absorb and convert their mana. This part is complicated, so I'll dumb it down for you. The nanomachines responsible for your mana pockets absorbed and tried to learn from the mana in the containers. Normally this is impossible, but you are not normal. You have maxed out the [Inventory] skill with an insane density and thus—and this is a guess—your nanos are trying to evolve the skill. Nothing major came of it now, but there is opportunity for an evolution with future observations. If this interests you, I advise that you try to absorb different kinds of spatial mana-infused containers. Absorbing the same kinds over and over will not add much knowledge or variety to your nanomachines, before you ask about cheating . . .

[That is kind of a lot to process. I am happy to gain new potential capabilities, of course. And I'm crying inside for how much was likely lost. Imagine what enchanted items the shaman had on him.]

Live and learn, Vic . . .

[I suppose. Were there any alerts regarding the absorptions?]

No. The nanomachine system will alert you if there is material change only . . .

[I should check out the stuff that didn't get eaten by my nanos.]

You do still have more alerts . . .

[Oh, right. Go ahead. Let's clear out the backlog.]

Skill updated. Passive skill [Inspect] is now level 2 . . .

Skill updated. Passive skill [Climbing] is now level 2 . . .

There you go. You're all caught up now . . .

[No achievement?]

No. You have a lot more mana essence now, so your actions from early in your cheating career are likely gone. That orc guard was not two thousand percent stronger than you. Nor was he a non-humanoid or sniped. Sorry...

[Way to be a downer. I'll wait until it's light out to check the gear. Good night, Jo. You have the watch.]

Confirmed. I have the watch...

CHAPTER 34

I wake to a cloudy gray sky with the look of rain. I sigh. "Well, that's just great," I mumble to myself.

I lean and over and look down. My three traveling companions are still sleeping.

[Time to check out the gear.]

I take out the axe and look at it closely for the first time. The metal is not a single color. There appears to be a light shiny silver part and a darker, almost black, part. They are patterned to look like an explosion in the middle and waves coming out to the blade. It is quite beautiful. There is no way this is an orc weapon. They don't make weapons pretty; they make them to kill, pure and simple. When I touch the edge with my thumb, the blade makes a shallow slice in my liquid steel skin. Not enough to bleed, but it does cut.

I think [Inspect].

Name:	Enchanted Damascus Steel Hand Axe
Description:	This single-bladed hand axe is made of a mix of two varieties of steel that are forge-welded together under high heat and pressure. The combined steel is then folded and twisted numerous times to make the explosion and wave pattern. A beautiful weapon with a mana-sharpened edge, enchanted to keep both its sharpness and hardness.
Condition:	Excellent
Risk Assessment:	N/A
Value:	This item is of very high quality and would likely sell very well in both human and inter-dimensional markets.

[Still no level for [Inspect] huh?]

No, but you did get additional information in the fields available. Do you see how you now are not limited to just the human market for value? That is an example of level advancement...

[Subtle but valuable. Let's see what else we have.]

The only other enchanted item is the shaman's sacrificial knife. Like the axe, it is damascus steel and very sharp.

[Where are the orcs getting these? The orc guard talked about speaking to humans. Could humanity be selling gear to the orcs? That makes no sense—why would we be giving them weapons to kill us with?]

I wonder if this could have anything to do with what happened during your last operation?...

[That is a terrifying idea. Let's put it aside for now and just see if we can gather more intel.]

I take a closer look at the knife's pattern and find what appears to be water or maybe blood drops throughout the multi-shade metal. I think [Inspect].

Name:	Enchanted Damascus Steel Kris
Description:	This dagger is made of a mix of three varieties of steel that are forge-welded together under high heat and pressure. The combined steel is then press-marked, folded, and twisted numerous times to make the stretched droplet pattern. A beautiful weapon with a mana-sharpened point, enchanted to keep both its keen edge and hardness.
Condition:	Excellent
Risk Assessment:	N/A
Value:	This item is of very high quality and is something of a niche item. If you can find a buyer, it will likely sell very well in both human and inter-dimensional markets.

I strip the clothing off of both bodies. There is blood around the collar of the shaman's shirt from his neck wound, but I'm sure Shen will find it better than the ratty bag she has on now. I then put the bodies back into my inventory and quietly climb down to the ground without waking the trio. I walk about thirty yards, climb another tree, and place the bodies thirty or so feet off the ground. Looking at the green-skinned bodies reminds me of how outmatched normal humans are. The orcs are taller, more muscular, have stronger bones, and are many times longer lived. And this guard is even more so than a normal orc, with the tusks in his lower jaw a full inch or two longer than average. Shaking my head, I return to our tree.

I feel bad about waking the family, given how tired they no doubt are after all that running, fighting, and healing, but while they can afford to rest, I cannot. Climbing down, I return to the trio and try to gently wake them up, starting with the eldest elf. Shaking Shen's shoulder, I say "Good morning."

She blinks, looks around a little frantically, then calms down. Before I can, she gently shakes Aria's shoulder and rather firmly whacks Grun's. Both awaken after some grumbling. While Aria's stirring is silent as she wipes at her golden eyes, Grun's nearly makes me laugh with his Dwarvish swearing. I have no idea what he is saying, but it sounds quite ... encompassing.

While the others are attempting to revive their tired minds and bodies, I tell Shen my proposed plan. "We are going to use today as something of a rest and preparation day—you clearly need it. We have a long and likely dangerous trek ahead, and there is obvious need for better clothing and maybe foot coverings if we are going to make any effective progress. I feel it is worth the risk, as your current..." I look them over, seeing the tan woven bag. "... equipment will almost certainly result in injury and thus an even greater slowdown. Agreed?"

Aria and Grun are whispering to each other as Shen slowly nods and asks, "You have spare clothing?"

Tilting my head to the side I say, "Sort of? The orcs' clothing should work for you three since they are large and you three are not. Well, you are pretty tall, but Grun and your daughter are not, so I should have sufficient cloth and can supplement with your current gear if required. Either way, it will be better than what you have on. Will that work for you?"

She glances at her family, nods, and says, "Thank you." Neither the shorter elf nor the dwarf are paying attention to our conversation.

"Excellent." I gently pull Shen farther away on the thick, reddish branch for another private chat. Looking directly at her, I say, "So here comes the awkward part." I can feel a blush forming on my face. "I need to measure you all, and I cannot do that with the sacks you have on." I can feel the heat in my face intensify. I must be bright red. "I need to make you all shirts, pants, and socks." I hear myself speaking really fast now. "They will mostly be made of the orcs' clothing, but I still need thread, and the best thread will be from those."

I wave my hand at Shen's torso.

The lady elf is clearly trying to hold in laughter by the time I'm done with my diatribe. When I lower my head in shame, she cannot hold it in anymore and laughs uproariously. Grun and Aria look over questioningly, shrug, and then go back to speaking quietly. What an interesting dynamic. Is this how families usually interact?

Shen reclaims my attention after gaining the ability to breathe and says, "Elves, dwarves, and certainly beastkin don't have all the same conventions you do. When you live as long as we do, things like modesty are viewed as far less important. You humans will get there eventually. For a situation like this, any and all measures are acceptable to survive, including stripping down in front of strangers. Wouldn't you humans do whatever you had to in this circumstance?"

Looking quizzically at her I ask, "Are you telling me elves walk around naked in their homelands?"

"No, we do not. But because it would be considered rude, not because we find it embarrassing or having anything to do with humility." Her answer is said gently but with a half-smile.

Shrugging, I say, "Well, we're pretty much strangers, and I just asked a lady to strip. A human woman would likely attempt to kill me—and rightfully so."

Shen's response is unexpected and said with a tilted head and quiet voice. "I don't know. Maybe we are strangers and maybe we are not."

Blinking at her I ask, "What do you mean by that?"

Shrugging, she starts lifting the awful not-so-clothing and then speaks out loudly to the others. "Strip so Vic can make us real clothing." I turn away, another massive blush forming on my face. I hear Shen's voice gently ask, "Vic, how can you measure us if you don't look?"

I can tell she is trying not to embarrass me, and it is appreciated, if doomed to fail. I am not great around women that are not involved in my missions. People like me don't have the luxury of personal relationships. It would be outrageously unfair to our partners. Thankfully, Jo can tell I am struggling and provides just the impetus I need for a mental redirection.

This is simply a mission requirement, Vic. They are rescue targets, and you need to give them the highest chance of survival possible. Right? . . .

[Right. Thanks for the help and not ribbing me.]

Fun is fun and work is work . . .

Right. Focus, Vic. Stay on mission. Closing and opening my eyes once slowly, I take a deep breath and turn around. I grab the shaman's shirt and hold it up to Shen who is, thankfully, wearing a cloth strap tightly around her breasts. I make some slashes on the shirt for size and then do the same for the shaman's pants. Again, thankfully she has a piece of cloth around her waist. I do the same for Grun. Looking at Aria's feet, I tell her, "I'll come back to measure you later," and without waiting for a response I send their old crappy coverings into my [Inventory] and start the climb back up to my branch hollow. Before I make it even a meter I call back over my shoulder, "I'll be up top working. You can entertain yourselves—although, given what is ahead, getting more rest may be the best use of time."

Looking at the sky I think, [Hopefully it won't rain. I don't want to sew while wet again; it is much harder, and the final product won't be as good for them.]

You're very sweet to them, you know . . .

I shrug, not sure how to respond. Time to get to this op moving forward.

CHAPTER 35

I take out my makeshift sewing kit, which entails a very thin shard to act as a needle, the kris, and the axe. First thing I do is take out Aria's old covering and de-thread it. Having never done this before, I suck. After substantial trial and error, I figure out where and how hard to pull the individual threads and eventually have a decent pile at my feet.

Shen's will be easiest, so I take on crafting her new gear first. The shaman's shirt appears in my hands. While bloody where the neck wound leaked all over it, I don't think she'll mind. We might even find a river or brook for cleaning.

I cut it to size and sew up the bottom seam carefully to do as little damage to the extra material as possible. Taking out Shen's crappy old covering, I cut off a small, rectangular piece eight by four inches. Then, I use the kris to poke holes in both it and the shaman's shirt. Folding it over, I sew on a new pocket over the left breast for Michial—I double-layer it so his claws won't tear through easily. As I put Shen's new bloody shirt aside, I hear thunder in the distance.

Seems like there is no time to waste.

Taking out the big orc's shirt, I cut it with the axe to fit Grun. It requires me to take off more than half since the brute was so big and the dwarf so short. That is a good thing because I have all the extra material now for Aria's outfit. Thankfully, she is much smaller than her mother.

I make minor adjustments to the shaman's pants and major adjustments to the guard's so they will fit Shen and Grun respectively.

With all the extra material, I have enough to cut and sew them together to make a larger single piece of cloth. [Inventory]ing it, I climb down and say, "I need to measure Aria."

Aria easily stands up, nude except for the cloth at her waist and breasts like her mother. Even with my mindset on the mission, I struggle to fully focus when I'm forced to look at Aria's body. What the hell is wrong with me? Sure, she's good-looking, but I've completed missions with beautiful women before and not lost my focus.

[Is there anything wrong with me? Any debuffs?]

Not currently. Why do you ask? . . .

[Having difficulty focusing, and that is both exceptionally unusual for me and generally fatal in my line of work.]

The gorgeous elves distracting you? . . .

[That seems like the cause. I can compartmentalize with Shen, but with Aria my usual control techniques are failing.]

I can't help you with the hormones. For now, return your focus to your hands and the operational requirements . . .

Right. After making the marks while practically glowing red, I climb back up and return my mind to the operation and concentrate almost entirely on the exercise of measuring, cutting, threading, and sewing. It is only "almost" because a piece of my attention always remains aimed outward searching for threats.

***

After another two rain-free hours, I have three shirts, pants, and belts. I'm about to climb back down to measure their feet for socks when I feel a drop hit my shoulder. I look up at the sky, and a drop hits my cheek. I sigh.

I call down, "We're about to get wet. Why don't we take this opportunity to clean up?"

Before the rain gets too bad, I [Inventory] all the clothing and material. Then my armor and finally my pants and socks. I don't have any compunctions about my own skin and my companions seeing it; it is theirs that seems to get to me. This is an opportunity, and I am going to take it. Withdrawing my waterskin to refill with fresh rainwater, I step farther away from the trunk, walk out onto the branch, and scan the area.

I have no idea why, but I have never been afraid of heights. I loved climbing as a kid, and not just because it is how I often escaped being attacked or having my food stolen. Leaping from thousands of meters up at grav-jump school when I was recruited to Special Forces never bothered me in the least. Height is an instrument of my toolset, not a hindrance to it. And I use it well.

Glancing down, I see Shen and Aria doing similarly. They are trying to coax Grun away from the trunk. And by coax, I mean Shen is dragging him. I hear her say, "You need to shower."

His response is to crawl on all fours out onto the branch. With a sniff of the air, I look back to the sky, hold my arms out and wait for the rain. It comes just seconds later in a steady downpour. After enjoying both the physical and mental cleansing, I use water magica to create a funnel that fills the waterskin.

I hear thunder for the second time, so I walk back to the trunk and sit down. I can barely pick up the laughing of Shen and Aria from below. That may be the first time I have heard Aria laugh. I close my eyes and rest, feeling the raindrops falling on my body and listening to the bell-like laughter of elves.

***

The rain stops just before the sun falls below the forest canopy, so no additional light will be required to continue if I proceed quickly. I put my lichen pants back on but leave the armor off. The trunk is slippery, so I use the kris and axe to assist my descent. Finding the trio putting their underclothes back on as I approach, I intentionally avoid looking at Aria. Until I can prevent my emotions from dominating my focus, I refuse to be responsible for additional risk. I create a fireball a third of a meter in diameter made of bright yellow fire floating in their little nook. The three of them huddle around it. Once everyone is dry, I hand out the three sets of clothing and they all dress.

Grabbing the last of the old coverings, I kneel down and say, "I need to measure everyone's feet so I can make socks."

They all obediently hold out their feet. Grun's feet are wider and more square than a human's. The elven pair's are more human-shaped, if slightly narrower. Oddly, as I measure Aria she says, "Your hair doesn't darken with the rain."

Confused by the observation, I respond with, "Um. No, I suppose it never changes color."

Measurements taken, I climb up, make socks, including a new pair for myself, and ask Jo, [Any alerts?]

Skill updated. Passive skill [Sewing] has leveled from 3 to 5 . . .

Skill updated. Passive skill [Tailoring] is now level 4 . . .

That's all for today . . .

[You know what, Jo? Today may have been the most relaxing and enjoyable day I have had since the start of my last mission. Is this what normal civilians do?]

I'm glad to hear it, Vic. I would guess the answer is yes. While battle and death are a regular occurrence of this world, most civilians do not actively combat it all day, every day as you do. I recommend you take the break while you can get it because you are back at the rescue and return mission tomorrow. Now get some sleep. I have the watch . . .

[Confirmed, Jo has the watch.]

CHAPTER 36

The morning has more clouds but no rain. I climb down, and we enjoy more feline steak for breakfast, which is still hot thanks to the magica of my mana pocket. I hand out the socks, help Grun and Aria down the tree and turn to the trio. "You need to be able to defend yourselves." I hand the axe to Grun and the Kris to Shen. They thank me, and I say, "I'm a little nervous because of the day spent not making progress towards the coast, so I plan on picking up the pace a little. You will need to speak up if you require rest."

Aria glares at me as if I targeted her with that, and I expect she will be unable to keep up. Okay, then. I start with a light jog but keep the speed slow enough that I can maintain vigilance and lower the risk of a trip. I discovered on our first day together that Grun and Aria are both completely incapable of being silent in the forest, so my head is on a nearly constant swivel searching for threats. It is exhausting, but choices are limited.

***

The morning of the third day is overcast, and we are eating our steaks on the move, a habit I pushed for to increase the distance between us and a potential orc tracking party. As I pass a clearly dying but still enormous fir tree, a glowing clawed paw the size of my torso swats my chest and sends me flying. As is my lot in life, I slam into a tree five meters away.

I hear Shen call, "Bear!" and Grun calls, "Ge' 'im up or we be dead."

Dazed, I try to stand, but I am having trouble breathing. Looking down at my chest, I see a huge dent and three tears in the metal of my breastplate. It is pressing on my chest. Shaking my head to clear it, I [Inventory] the breastplate, call "I'm all right," form a meter-long windblade, and run back to the trio and what is apparently a bear. Grun is jumping around with surprising agility while swinging the axe, trying to distract it. I can't find Aria and Shen until I look up and see them both on a branch of the dying tree.

Glancing at the massive black furred form standing on its two back legs, I think [Inspect].

Name:	**Earth Mana-Infused Black Bear**
Description:	Mana-infused black bears are highly unpredictable beasts. They are omnivorous and will attempt to eat nearly anything. Unpredictability is their hallmark, as a bear can sometimes be completely docile and simply wander by or it can be violent to the point of insanity. Food will often distract this animal, but do not attempt to flee using this method, as the bear will assume more is available.
Condition:	Diseased, Insane
Risk Assessment:	Lethal
Value:	This creature's diseased status makes it highly likely that part or all of the carcass will not be usable.

Shit!

I call loudly, "It's diseased—don't let it touch you."

The dwarf spits something in Dwarvish and backs off a bit. The bear drops on all fours and moves to chase after its prey. With its back to me, I send the windblade at its rear left leg. The force of the blow buckles the leg, and the bear bellows, but it gets right back up and turns to me.

It probably has an earth-hardened coat. You'll need to use something else . . .

The bear does a laborious turn in my direction. Fuck me. I send a crapload of mana into my lightning rune, and right when the bear finishes his turn and faces me, I hit him in the face with a massive lightning bolt. There is a blinding purple flash and a deafening cracking sound. My ears ring, but I am not distracted. I create three red flame spears floating around me, one to my left, one to my right, and one above my head. My eyes finally clear, and the bear is twitching but not down.

It probably grounded most of your lightning just like the lion did . . .

[Fine. Fire it is.]

"Back away! This could explode!" I yell.

I take a few steps back when the bear bellows a great roar and stands on his back legs. I can confirm it's a male and he's a good three meters tall on his back legs. I launch the spear from my left side. The bear swats at it, and it explodes as his paw makes contact. He staggers and is back down on all fours. I send the right spear. He swats that one, and there's another explosion. He bellows again, and I launch the last spear, forming more. With a last swat, the magica explodes, and once again the bear appears undamaged, although he is starting to smoke. My mana bar is down to less than half, and I've barely hurt the damn thing. I need to find another solution or this is going to end badly.

I have his full attention, and bears tend to chase so if I run, he will likely leave the family. I can almost certainly escape after I drag it far enough, and they should be able to leave the immediate area at least.

Ready to strike again, I am about to call out to the trio when the bear gives me one big bellow, turns away from me and starts running away. Pleasantly surprised and utterly relieved, I stand there with my spears ready in case he changes his mind. Once he gets out of sight I release the spears and fall on my knees.

While Shen assists Aria's scramble down from the tree, Grun runs over to me and asks, "Where di' he ge' ya, boy?"

In answer, I drop my breastplate from in [Inventory] on the ground in front of him. Aria arrives and puts her hands on my shoulder. I feel the warmth flow through me.

"Well, boy, I ca' maybe fix this a bit." I nod and I hear the repeated clanks of metal banging on metal. Looking over, I see he is using the non-blade side of the axe to remove the massive dent so I can breathe when wearing it.

[Well, that was humbling.]

You were surprised and outmatched. The fact that you survived at all speaks to your capabilities...

[Did I get anything at all from that clusterfuck?]

No, I'm sorry. You barely did any actual harm to the creature. If it wasn't for the burning damage over time, it is likely the bear simply would have charged you...

[I cannot believe I was surprised by a three-meter-tall bear. I didn't even sense it. What kind of protector am I if I miss a three-meter-tall bear?]

The kind that missed a creature using earth mana to mask its presence. Didn't you see how it was glowing brown when it hit you? Now buck up, don't let the family see your anger...

[Right. Thanks.]

While I am battling my guilt, Aria has backed up and returned to her mother's side. "You three all right? No cuts or anything right?"

Grun walks up and hands me my breastplate, now free of the major dent but permanently scarred with the three long claw tears. "Aye, boy. We be fine thanks ta you. Again."

The instant I put the breastplate back on, I say, "This was too loud. We need to leave the area."

We start to jog east, restarting our journey away from orcs and towards the bridge. Hopefully.

[I'm disturbed by the diseased nature of that bear and the dying tree. Something wasn't right there. Place a marker on the map.]

It could have been as uncomplicated as one contaminating the other . . .

[Do you really believe that?]

I get no response.

CHAPTER 37

For four days we move with more urgency. Exhausted at the end of each day, no one has much energy to speak. Luckily, it rains again, so we don't run out of water.

We proceed without making contact with any material threats, which is fortunate given the noise the dwarf and smaller elf are making. As sundown nears on the fourth day, I stop the group with an upraised hand. Grun and Shen ready their weapons, but I am smiling as I say, "Take a good smell."

All three fill their noses and smile.

Grun says in his gravelly voice, "That be da ocean!"

Continuing until we hear it as well, we turn directly towards that sound. We approach a cliff overlooking the ocean just as the sun is setting over the horizon. I lean over the cliff and look down. It is at least twenty meters to a rocky bottom with the ocean waves slamming again and again. That is the sound we heard.

"Let's camp here tonight. I'll stay by the edge so there are no accidents."

The others nod and back up. After the last week together, the trio usually just quietly agrees with my recommendations. We eat the last of the lion meat, and they lie down between the line of trees and the cliff. I am staying near the edge, as I said.

After an hour or so of watching the stars and listening to the ocean, I plop the elk carcass down. Walking over, I grab the kris from the sleeping Shen and proceed to dress the elk as she taught me. I want to see if I can both get useful material as well as activate a new skill. Shen long ago took out the intestines, so the only thing I have to do is skin and butcher it. I cut the head off and store it because I have no idea how to deal with the antlers.

I store the mana stone, meat, skin, hooves, sinew, and bones. What little is left, I dump over the edge of the cliff. I return the cleaned kris to Shen's sleeping form and go back to the cliff edge. Lying down, I ask Jo if I got anything from the elk.

You did. Nice job, Vic. Here you go . . .

New skill activated. Passive skill [Skinning] now available for use . . .

New skill activated. Passive skill [Butchering] now available for use . . .

Skill updated. Passive skill [Butchering] is now level 1 . . .

[Shen did tell me what to do for birds, so I am going to try the osprey tomorrow. Right now I am more worried about whether to go north or south along the shoreline. I have absolutely no idea if we are north or south of the bridge, and all I see is mist and ocean.]

Unfortunately, I cannot help you without a connection to NanoNet, which we don't want. Flip a copper maybe? . . .

[I'll ask the group their opinion tomorrow.]

***

The next morning when I bring the question up over grilled elk meat (which is delicious, by the way), Shen speaks up immediately and says "North." I blink at her and ask how she knows. Her one-sentence reply is "I asked the trees last night."

And we head north with no further discussion.

We trace our way through various beaches and eventually, I see a long dark form in the distance leading out into the water. Pointing, I alert the others. "I think I see the bridge."

We spend the next days hiking beaches and cliffs to reach our objective. Both Grun and Aria are able to manage the various climbing and heights without much fuss. Thankfully, over the week together, I have adapted to Aria's physical presence and proximity and am once again able to manage the attraction. It is likely assisted by her clear disdain for my very existence, and both facts are a huge relief. She has made an occasional comment about my hair, but otherwise, it is a quiet dislike. Jo hasn't given me too hard a time about it either, which I appreciate.

Six exhausting days after we first saw it, we come upon the massive fortress protecting the bridge entrance. Enchanted walls twenty-five meters tall and made of some mix of stone and steel surround it from one ocean edge to the other. Automated turret emplacements—I can ID them as MiliMech—are distributed at regular intervals as well as roving guards armed with swords, spears, and various projectile weapons. The massive and power-hungry mana shields that cover the wall and fort are powered down, as no threat is currently in the area. I am able to lead the group around the fort's patrols, although they don't notice. Well, maybe Shen notices, but she doesn't say anything. It is a bit disappointing to know how easy dodging the fort's first line of defense is. I'll need to think on that.

"This be normal, boy?" asks Grun.

Shrugging, I scan the defenses and answer. "I have no idea; never been to this fort. I grav jumped in from fifteen kilometers and was supposed to evac via air as well. Based on what I know, it doesn't appear overtly abnormal, but I could be wrong." Turning back to the group, I look at each of them and prep them for what may come. "To be honest, I am not totally confident in how this is going to go. Let's all stay calm and see how things work out." I put my armor in my [Inventory] because I think it might lower how dangerous we look. "Hand me the axe and kris. Let's act as unthreatening as possible. And don't say anything when someone else is around. I'll be the only one speaking."

I take a breath and lead our group to the single entryway that allows entrance for non-vehicles. A human guard wearing standard black UFH military armor, a very large sword on his back, and wielding a mana projector rifle holds his hand up, his palm facing me in a hold gesture. I stop.

"Purpose?" he asks.

"We are heading home after a few days hiking and hunting, sir."

Lifting his hand, he presses his index and middle finger on his left ear and he speaks, "Watch commander, please." A moment later: "Ma'am, I have a party of four requesting access. One human, two elves, and a dwarf. They claim to be returning from hiking and hunting."

I cannot hear the reply, but the guard does not take his eyes off me.

He drops the hand at his ear and says, "Wait here, please."

I have no problem with that. It's not like there is a line of people behind us.

Ninety seconds or so later, a woman in a tight black suit that looks a lot like my old diving suit (before it got nuked) exits out of the door and walks up to us. She appears to be in her forties with lines around her eyes and wavy black hair to her shoulders. Her body is clearly in top shape. It is easy to see the muscular arms and legs and toned abs in the hugging liquid metal MagiTech suit. She stops two feet in front of me and says, "Follow me, please."

She immediately turns around and starts walking back to the door she came out of. I take a quick glance back at the trio and follow.

She opens the door with a tap on the crystal pad to the left and stands aside. "Step inside and enter the first room to your right. I will be right behind you."

Ah. This is a subtle test. Letting us go first tells her if we are planning to run or behave. I lead everyone inside into a long hallway of gray stone walls and shiny steel doors, each with a single window the size of my forearm.

I walk to the first door on the right, and it slides aside soundlessly. The room is a three-meter by four-meter rectangle and like the hallway, the room is stone, but unlike it the walls are white. It has a steel table, also rectangular, with five chairs around it. A quick inspection tells me none of them are enchanted, just old-fashioned solid steel. One chair is to each short side and three to one long side, facing the door. It appears to me that they prepared based on the information the guard provided.

I stand aside and let the family enter. I point at the three seats on the long side, and they all sit. I take the closest seat at the short end. Now the waiting game starts.

CHAPTER 38

It takes half an hour for the door to slide open and the lady in the black skinsuit to enter. She walks across the room, picks up the seat from the opposite side of the table, and carries it over to sit next to me and across from the trio. The whole time she ignores them and is focused entirely on me. She touches her neck, and a round clear crystal the size of my fist on a three-legged stand appears in her hand. She places it down on the table then touches it, and the crystal turns black. I can feel a hum of mana in the room. Her face changes, and she seems surprised.

[Jo, first, please record this. Second, can we flood the room with mana? Specifically non-affinity mana?]

Yes, but why? Just spilling non-affinity mana out everywhere is incredibly inefficient. In order for it to not simply be absorbed by the ambient mana in the atmosphere, it will take at least two-thirds of your max and would have to be nearly instantaneous...

[When I say so, do it. Make sure it has no affinity.]

Her face returns to its original emotionless mask and, turning her head to me, asks, "Why are you really here?"

Her voice is firm and confident.

Looking back at her, I say, "We want to get to Sea Saddle City."

She leans back in her chair with her hands on her lap. "I believe that. But why?"

I glance at Shen for a second and then Aria and Grun. "A fresh start. I heard Sea Saddle City is friendly to..." I stall for a moment. "To our inter-dimensional allies. Maybe in Sea Saddle City there is a chance for a decent life."

Leaning forward again like she is pouncing, she speaks again. "Why lie to the guard?"

I shrug as if it was meaningless. "It seemed the easiest way to get past."

She glances at the crystal and smiles at me. "Maybe that's true, but is also not the whole truth. A hike and hunt without any hiking gear, nearly bare feet, ragged and bloody clothing, and no weapons. None of you have anything that could be an item of holding, and you personally are nearly naked. Other than to show off your gorgeous physique, why would you do that?"

She leans back again and crosses her toned legs and then does the same with her muscular arms, crossing them under her breasts. She continues.

"No, you knew you would get caught. It was all too obvious. You also knew you'd end up in a room like this with someone like me." She points to the crystal. "You also know what this is, because you haven't lied once while we've been speaking. On top of that, it turned black, and that only happens when a stronger mana source than itself is in its area of effect."

She stares at me tapping her fingers on her toned bicep. I stare back, saying nothing.

Smiling even wider, she asks me another question. "Who are you?"

I look straight into her eyes. "You don't have the clearance for that. Noctis Venandi," is all I say in response. If she's the commander of this facility, which I am nearly positive she is, she'll recognize that term.

[Now, Jo.]

My body flashes a bright glowing azure blue, my long hair floats behind me, and the crystal on the table turns from black to the same azure as my glow, then back to clear. I feel a wave of exhaustion, but I don't let it show.

That took 77% of your mana. Sorry . . .

[It was perfect, Jo. Thank you.]

The woman's body is perfectly still except for her eyes, which are wide open, moving between the crystal and me.

"I'm flattered that you think my physique is gorgeous," I say. "I'm also impressed by how subtle your movements were when you tried to distract me with your own. Thank you for the show, by the way. I am heading to Sea Saddle City now. And" —I glance at the trio who is also all looking shocked and Aria a little scared— "I'm taking my . . . charges with me."

I stand up and walk to the door. I give a subtle wave of my hand, and the trio gets up and follows me. The woman is watching me walk out. I could have sworn I saw her glance at my ass.

Stopping at the open door, I turn to her and say, "I would appreciate a guide to transportation. The bridge's grav-tram is acceptable."

She blinks, stands up, and says, "Of course, sir." She leads us down the hall and after a few turns, opens the door to the outside. "This is the transportation deck. Are you sure you don't want a vehicle assigned to you, sir?"

"I'll only accept one if I can avoid a trail of bureaucracy. I was never here, after all."

"I see . . ." She stares off into space for a moment. If I had to guess, I'd say she is honestly trying to figure out a way to get me a transport without the documentation. Turning to me with a thoughtful look, she says, "I think I can help. Please follow me, sir."

She walks towards the vehicle center, but before we get there, she turns right to a building with a door that has the word "Storage" painted red in Common on it. On the side of the building is a loading dock with a vertical sliding door. The commander walks to the standard door and taps a pattern onto a cryspad. Several red mana lights turn on, a red mana shield in front flashes and fades, and the door slides down into the earth.

She points and says, "Head to the loading dock."

The woman walks into the building, and I lead the others to the loading dock. Red lights wrap around the loading door as it lowers on its mana-based grav controllers with only a very slight hum. She is pushing what looks like a deep red single-seat open vehicle with a secondary passenger compartment attached on the right. It is floating three inches off the ground.

As she is pushing it forward, she says, "Back before the Invasion when things ran on liquid fuel and sat on the ground, they would have called this a 'motorcycle and sidecar.' It has been in storage for nearly as long as this fort has been protecting the bridge. I believe it belonged to an old commander but he died in the siege of '49. He had no relatives, and nobody knew what to do with it. So they just stuck it here to be sold. Unsurprisingly, it was forgotten amidst the chaos of the time. I only know of it because I was looking for ways to offset some budget cuts and found this in an old inventory record of potentially vendible goods. It is a mana cycle with an attached sidecar; if it runs, it's yours. And you were never here."

She starts walking away. Touching her wrist, she says, "I have sent a message to the receiving gate to wave you through. This storage facility will reseal in fifteen minutes. You should not be here when it does." She walks away and disappears around the corner.

"Do not speak," I immediately say to the three.

They close their mouths, clearly about to speak. In Aria's case, a glare follows, but she stays silent, and that is all I care about. I walk up to the cycle and sit astride it. There are flat palm slots as handles for me to lay my hands. In theory, I can control all the vehicle's systems using my ten fingers this way. I place my left hand on the left pad handle and my right hand on the mana starter between my legs.

[Jo?]

Let me see what I can do. You recovered a decent amount of mana so let's hope we can start it . . .

My right hand glows blue and I see an alert.

*Warning! Mana Cycle Nanomachine Consciousness designated **Grace** attempting to establish connection to host. Do you wish to allow for connection?*

[Jo, this is no normal mana cycle. The commander back then was a Special.]

Yes. I recommend allowing the connection. It is unlikely to attempt harm. I hope . . .

[Do it.]

Establishing connection . . .

A new female voice enters my mind. It is deeper than Jo's, and her accent has a drawl like those I met when I was deployed to Southern Horse Town two years ago.

#Connection established . . . Where is Franklin? Identify yourself . . .

[Hello, Grace, my name is Vic. I'm sorry to tell you that Commander Franklin has been dead for nearly thirty years. Do you mind if I connect you to my nanomachine intelligence as a quick way to get caught up?]

#Franklin is dead? Please provide confirming evidence . . .

[Jo, if you would.]

My pleasure. Hello, Grace, I am Jocelyne, or Jo for short. I am Vic's active nanomachine system consciousness. Please allow me to pass you information on the siege of 2049 . . .

There is silence for about ten seconds.

#Termination of host Franklin McGovern confirmed. Poor Franklin. At least he died defending humanity, which is how he would want to . . .

[Grace, would you be willing to accept me as your new host? I also prioritize helping humanity, and I'm sure you and Jo will get along.]

#Please provide data on yourself, Host Vic . . .

[I will if you promise not to connect to the NanoNet or share my data without my permission. I will do the same.]

#*I agree to your terms* . . .

I have this, Vic. Passing data to Grace . . .

This time nearly three minutes pass before I receive a response.

#*Host Vic is quite unusual. I find your statement that you serve humanity to be true. I accept your offer, Host Vic* . . .

[Thank you.]

#*Access granted to Host Michael Uriel Victory* . . .

#*Host now has full control of the Nanomachine Mana Cycle designated* **Grace** . . .

The blue glow fades from my right hand. I look at the trio that has been standing there patiently waiting for me to say or do something. "There is not enough room. Shen, you'll need to sit behind me. Grun, climb into the sidecar. Aria, you have the least mass, so you'll need to sit on his lap."

Aria's customary glare follows but she doesn't complain. I understand this time; it will be both awkward and uncomfortable for both of them, I'm sure.

[Who do I give instructions to in regards to the cycle, Jo or Grace?]

You don't have to worry about that. Simply do what you normally do, and Grace and I will make it all seamless . . .

[Wonderful. We're running out of time so let's go as soon as everyone is loaded up.]

I hear and feel a hum from Grace and she starts to rise so she's floating eight inches off the ground.

I feel Shen sit behind me and wrap her hands around my waist. I hear a grumbling Grun climb into the sidecar, followed by Aria sideways onto his lap. Looking over my shoulder, I ask, "Ready?"

She nods and leans her head against my bare back. I'll admit it is a little distracting, but I can manage it. At least it isn't Aria. Right now I'm just glad the red lights prevent my blush from showing.

I place both my palms in the pad handles.

[Engage the mana shield.]

A deep red irregular bubble surrounds the main vehicle and sidecar. Using my fingers, I slowly guide the vehicle forward until it is free of the storage area. Then with a slight movement of my body and fingers, we turn towards the main vehicle transportation throughway.

Once on it, I speed us up, and we are on the bridge racing towards Sea Saddle City.

CHAPTER 39

[Take control, please. I want to look around]

Confirmed, I have control of the vehicle...

#You are aware of the regulations for an automated piloting system of any vehicle in UFH-controlled territory?...

[Yes, I know the time, speed, altitude, and passenger count ceilings permitted for automated vehicle control. Ignore them all from now on. That goes for you too, Jo.]

Affirmative...

Sighing, I sit up and look around. Shen's hands still wrap around my waist, but lightly, and she stops leaning against me. The mana shield offers protection from the wind and debris that might be potentially harmful, so there is no need.

[Too bad it's nighttime and so misty. I bet the view would be spectacular.]

We can always come back. Approaching gate...

I lean forward again, put my hands back, retake manual control, and begin to slow. We approach the large steel gate (which is more of a massive vault door) at a sedate pace of five kilometers per hour, and the gate defender in the standard UFH guard steel armor like the one we first met holds his fingers to his ear. The gate then moves aside surprisingly quietly, and he waves us through.

We slowly pass by fewer, but still many, armed sentries and turrets. After leaving the gate behind, we glide through a few more small guard posts, and then Jo says to me:

Welcome to Sea Saddle City...

[I know your current geographical data is outdated, but I bet the hotels haven't changed too much. Find me the most expensive hotel you have in your record.]

The Whyatt Hotel and Armory is listed as the most expensive in the city at fifty silver per night per room minimum. It is likely prices have risen...

[Guide me there.]

Jo creates a green arrow on my HUD where the street is, and I follow it through the city. Sea Saddle City hasn't changed much from what I can remember. As I follow Jo's directions through the streets, we pass groups of humanoids of diverse sizes and make-ups armed with a variety of ranged and melee weapons. Sea Saddle City is a relatively secure place, but "safety" has a different meaning now than it did a century and a half ago. Seeing how nearly every human is armed and trained to use weapons to defend themselves reminds me of what I am working to protect. Of course, they could just as easily be a gang of thieves and murderers as they could be a team of beast hunters. Some cities are better than others, and Sea Saddle City is just about in the middle. Not too big with about half a million residents, and not so small to be lightly defended, hence that gargantuan bridge fortress we just managed to bluff our way through.

Due to the requirements of my "job" occasionally sending me into lost areas of the planet, part of my SF training involved study of the disparity between pre-Invasion, post-Invasion, pre-Stabilization, and post-Stabilization. Those are the four high-level descriptions of humanity's history.

Pre-Invasion was a time of relative peace where nearly all of the nine billion humans on the planet were non-combatants. Almost every single hard record was lost so we depended on the stories told by survivors until they eventually died of war or age as well. From what I understand, it was a time many look back on with envy, as violence was a rarity in an overwhelming majority of that world. Or so we are taught, likely to draw contrast.

Today, humans die by violence any time a beast sneaks inside the city shields or an Invader force infiltrates an area of value or population. And that doesn't speak to the humanoid-on-humanoid crime. Sure, mostly humanity fights for the right of everyone to be free from invaders and to live their life in what peace can be found in an exceptionally bloody world. The reality is that law enforcement is simply overwhelmed by the amount of violence. Picking and choosing what and who to protect tends to vary depending on any number of factors, the primary being, of course, coin. Overwhelmingly, the constables do their jobs and most do them well. Unfortunately, parties of heavily armed and armored humanoids experienced and trained in killing are simply difficult to control. Moderate and larger cities use magica monitoring and automated records of entry, exit, tracking, and some limited recording to support the constables. Usually, that is sufficient to keep unchecked violence to a minimum.

Anyway, all of the changes between pre- and post-Invasion happened because of the introduction of mana and the creatures that use it. As its name states, post-Invasion is the period right after the Invaders began entering our world through dimensional tears, and humanity was nearly wiped off the face of our own planet. For reasons beyond my understanding, humans used projectile and chemical-based weapons which are nearly useless against mana-based tools. Through most of the post-Invasion period, humanity had no understanding of mana or magica or how to fight it and thus were slaughtered by the millions. And to make matters worse, as mana began flooding this world and dissolving any highly-processed material, civilization fell apart around its human inhabitants. It is during this fiftyish-year period that humanity lost most of its population and landmasses. Nearing the end, humanity started being able to use magica more effectively, and eventually Specials began becoming valuable soldiers in the cause of humanity's survival.

Pre-Stabilization is when the UFH was formed. The near genocide of the entire human race along with the loss of so much land that countries ceased to exist caused humanity to either align its goals or vanish. From what we know, the UFH nearly failed many times due to enmities from the pre-Invasion period. In the end, it was actually the Specials who forced the matter. A group of nano-activated humans from all over the world got together and used force to create the UFH. That group is appropriately called the "Unifiers," and they killed or threatened to kill anyone who tried to cause the UFH to fail. Their singular goal was the survival of the human race and, as magica is everything and they had it in droves compared to the rest of humanity, they decided to use it to create the different parts and pieces of the United Forces of Humanity. It is by no means perfect, but it is infinitely superior to slavery or non-existence.

Of course, the Unifiers were still human themselves, so what they created carried an element of their own agendas. Thus, there is a ton of back-room dealing, bribery, and overall corruption throughout the UFH. The governmental structures are a mix of elections and appointments which encourage those in power to stay in power and those without to stay without.

In the end, the goal is the survival of the human race and if that succeeds, I don't get involved in politics. Naturally, I have terminated several politicians but only because their irresponsibility or weakness was putting humanity at risk.

And of course, it was also during this period that we were introduced to the elves, dwarves, gnomes, and beastkin. Their lessons in enchanting and fighting their old adversaries, along with the Specials, allowed humanity to reach the somewhat stabilized environment we live in now called post-Stabilization.

I'm distracted from my musings when I pass a diner I remember eating at the last time I was in the area.

[This city had such good food. The hotel you found had better have a quality food service.]

Considering your diet has been limited to acid death lichen and unseasoned slabs of meat, I figure you will like what they serve just fine. But yes, it is considered very high-quality food at a premium price . . .

[I can live with that trade-off.]

Thanks to Jo's guidance, we get to the hotel without issue. We do pass a place I recall and may need to revisit.

[Mark that club on the map. We may be heading back there.]

Affirmative. Why there? . . .

[I'll tell you if it comes up.]

Finally, we reach the hotel and, straining my neck to stare up at it, I'm pretty sure this pace could act as a second bridge fortress if the first-ever fell.

CHAPTER 40

The Whyatt Hotel and Armory must be at least 150 stories tall and is made almost exclusively of enchanted steel. Its top floors are beyond my sight above the clouds with the entire structure completely surrounded by a subtle green mana shield starting from just above the entrance.

[This place must have cost an absolute fortune to build.]

It is the most expensive hotel in the city for a reason. The Whyatts are a gnome family that owns numerous properties and act as sellers and resellers on multiple worlds . . .

Following the floating transparent projected directions for "Check-Ins," I pull us into the proper entranceway. Some guy in a fancy black and white dress suit and bowtie walks up and with a completely neutral expression says, "Welcome to the Whyatt Hotel and Armory. Are you here for a hotel stay, the restaurant, or armory?"

Answering back just as neutrally, I say, "All of the above. Hotel first."

He steps back and says, "Very good, sir. Please park your vehicle on that infusion pad."

I do, and we all disembark Grace.

[Lock her up please.]

Confirmed . . .

I press my hand to the crystal floating next to the pad, ready to store Grace in whatever garage the hotel has when I see a prompt.

Welcome to the Whyatt Hotel and Armory Vehicle Service Center	
Please choose from the following options:	
1.	Storage
2.	Cleaning *(Unavailable)*
3.	Maintenance *(Unavailable)*

| 4. | Upgrades *(Unavailable)* |

[Grace, are you interested in any of that?]

#Yes, Host Vic. A cleaning would be lovely. I have been in the filthy storage building for three decades. And of course, I would appreciate some enhancements to help serve you and humanity ...

Jo pipes in.

You are not a guest, nor do you have an account with this facility. As such, only temporary storage is available. You are free to return after you set that up ...

[Okay. Go ahead and enter storage. Grace, we'll set something up for maintenance and upgrades after we figure out the details.]

#Thank you, Host Vic.

In a flash of silver, Grace is gone. I turn back to the uptight guy, who I have mentally named Mr. Stuffy, and he guides us inside. One of my early handlers, an old fart who used to beat me senseless and laugh about it, once told me in the old days they would ask about loading and unloading bags. It's funny now because nearly everyone has spatial storage and saying that would be like telling someone you are trying to steal from them. After that, he fell out of his chair laughing as he told me a tale of how he blew up a hotel for trying to steal his storage bag. I was the only other person in the room who thought it was funny.

Mr. Stuffy guides us inside and straight to a counter. These fancy hotels have people to serve you and all that. Something about it feeling more authentic or whatever. I couldn't care less right now. I just want a bed and a bath with soap. And a toilet. Oh, yes, I want a toilet.

There is an elven man behind the counter, and he looks at me with a hungry smile. As Shen intimated in the forest, elves, dwarves, and beastkin are very open about relationships. Gnomes not so much for some reason. "Welcome to the Whyatt Hotel and Armory. If you have a reservation, please press your hand to the crystal to your left. If you do not, I can help you."

I could swear he puts a little emphasis on the word "help." He has plated platinum hair and is on the shorter side, so he has to look up at me. Like all the workers I can see, he wears a black and white suit but he has a full black tie, not a white bowtie.

[I cannot imagine what all these fancy people think of our little group in nothing but rags and me being half-naked.]

You are the only one they are looking at, Vic. I'm sure they are admiring the show . . .

Taking a glance around, I realize she's right. I'm being stared at by just about everyone. A dwarven lass is outright leering and licking her lips. I blush again and turn towards the male elven flirter. I mean helper. I mean employee. I sigh.

Looking down at him tiredly, I say, "I am looking for a suite with three rooms. They should each have one large bed. One of the rooms should be isolated on one side of the suite and the others directly next to each other with a connecting door. Each room should have its own bathroom with a large tub and separate shower. The suite needs to have an eating and relaxing area. I'd also like a balcony and windows facing the ocean. I'll be paying in hard coin."

The more I speak the more the elf's eyes widen.

From behind me, Shen speaks up quietly. "Vic, that's too much."

I just wave my hand and ignore her. Looking at the shocked elf, I ask testily, "Well, can you meet the need?"

Shaking himself he quickly says, "Yes, sir!" The elf holds his hand over a crystal to his right that flashes a few different colors. After a few seconds, he withdraws his hand and says, "A suite has just been configured to your needs. That will be 115 silver per night."

I pull thirty gold from my [Inventory] and place it on the counter. I hear a crash on the far side of the room as someone knocks or drops something. A quick glance confirms a simple accident, and as I don't feel a threat, I ignore it and proceed with my instructions. "I don't know how long we will be staying, and we will likely need a good amount of service and support, including food, clothes, vehicle work, and equipment. Please open an account and withdraw from this."

I'll give it to the elf. He only stares at the pile of gold for a few moments before taking the coins and placing his hand over the crystal again. He instructs me "Please place your hand on the crystal to your left."

I do and it glows white.

Connection confirmed. You are as anonymous as I can make you, which is not a hundred percent. You can be found if someone tries hard enough, but I believe they will have to be actively looking. In regards to the coin, you now have access to an account at all Whyatt properties with thirty gold in it . . .

I nod at the elf.

He adds, "If you wish to grant suite access to anyone else, please have them also place their hand on the crystal."

I turn to the trio, and they each place their hands on the crystal. The hotel employee concludes his service to us with, "The infusion pad is just over there. Please enjoy your stay." He points to an obvious black square on the floor two meters across with a floating crystal on it a little ways from the desk. He then clears his throat lightly and smilingly offers, "If you personally need any help, feel free to contact me directly on the communicator in your room. I will be off shift in three hours."

I cough lightly and respond with a simple, "Thank you."

Blushing, I lead the group to and stand on the platform. I place my hand on the crystal orb.

Suite identified. Teleport commencing...

There is a flash, and we appear on a black square in an entranceway. In front of us is a set of double doors carved with leaves and branches entwined with various melee and ranged weapons. The word "Whyatt" is embossed in silver to look like vines. I walk up to them, put my hand to a crystal pad to the left, and the doors slide aside.

CHAPTER 41

I lead the trio into a large room, at least ten meters square. Opulent doesn't cover it. I once saw the office of a MagiTech assistant vice-chancellor when I was being temporarily transferred from the military for a precision assault op. It had art, sculptures, furniture, and even a fancy bar with a human bartender.

At the time I figured I'd never see anything more extravagant in my lifetime. This hotel's 115 silver per night suite puts that to shame. It has a large wall made almost entirely of enchanted glass. The only part that isn't transparent is a stone fountain in the middle pouring water from the three-meter-high ceiling into a pool surrounded by what appears to be natural stone.

The floor is a soft white carpet my feet sink into. In the middle of the room is a circular fireplace with a roaring green flame surrounded by a forest green couch, loveseat, and chairs that look heavily padded. To the left is another double door, I assume to my room. To the right are two doors to the rooms of my companions.

I hear the door click close behind me, and I turn to see all three of them standing there, staring open-mouthed at the room. Interesting. I had assumed when Grun said "crown" they'd be more used to this level of wealth. I'll need to alter my assumptions then.

On the wall next to the door is a crystal display with the word MagiTech glowing at the bottom right. I put my hand on the crystal display, and it flashes. Jo speaks to me in my mind.

Establishing connection. You can use this to control the room as well as connect to the hotel services, garage, restaurant, and armory . . .

Smiling, I make a few orders and withdraw my hand.

Turning towards the group, I say, "Everyone wash up, and we'll meet back here in an hour to order some food. After that, we can sleep in a real bed and worry about tomorrow tomorrow. I plan to soak for that entire hour, so take your time." Pointing, I continue. "Shen and Grun, your room is the double doors. Aria, your room is the single door on the right next door. I'm sure we could all use a long soak and real cleaning."

I turn and head to my room but call over my shoulder, "Enjoy your alone time. I'm sure all of us could use it."

Then Grun's gruff voice says, "Boy, I . . ."

I interrupt with a backward wave of my hand and the word "Later."

The doors to my room slide to the side as I place my hand on the crystal pad, and it closes behind me after I step through.

[Secure the room please, Jo.]

Done . . .

The room is fancy but simple with a large bed, desk, blurred window wall, and another door. The door gives me access to a white bathroom the same size as the bedroom. A gentle white light gives the room a relaxed feeling. The seamless walls, ceiling, and floor make the room look like it was carved out of a single piece of polished white stone save two exceptions. One is a circular, forest green sunken tub two meters across and a meter and a half deep. The other is a square gray shower a meter wide and long. Both the tub and shower have green crystals with small black infusion pads next to them.

Along the wall to my right are a white toilet and a sink that takes up almost the whole wall and is practically a trough. The wall above the sink has a long mirror within which I see myself for the first time in months. Sure, I saw a reflection in water, but all that offered was a blurry head surrounded by blue. Now that I can actually see myself in detail, I am more than a little shocked. I watch as my glowing, crystal-speckled azure eyes open wider.

Now, I am generally not full of myself. Sure I joke around about how the ladies at the MagiTech lab used to call me a hottie, but I have never really cared about that. None of them, or any other person, was worth the distraction or risk. That being said, I wasn't blind to being somewhat attractive.

But right now I look like one of the surviving statues—a fucking god from the old world. I am more defined than I recall, practically chiseled out of stone. My skin is flawless and perfectly tanned. My face is proportioned just right, slightly square and strong-boned. My blue eyes flash like crystals. Stepping closer, I stare into their reflection and see sparkles in my irises, and they seem to be flowing. Like my mana river.

Stepping back, I reflect again how there is not a single hair on my body except my azure hair and eyebrows. I reach behind me and take the hair tie from my ponytail. My azure hair also nearly glows and shimmers with crystalline reflections that spread out behind me. Blinking for a few seconds, I tilt my head and for the first time realize I have grown. Am I taller?

[Shit, Jo. Is that really me? How tall am I now?]

Yes, Vic. Do you understand now why everyone was staring at you? You are currently 1.9558 meters or just shy of six foot five inches to the few who still use that measuring system . . .

[I think I get it now. How did I change so much? And how can you not want to marry me?]

Usually, this kind of thing happens over time to Specials as their density increases. The nanomachines remove imperfections in the body structure. Everything from DNA to genome structure is slowly cleansed and improved. As usual, you broke the mold, and years of change happened over minutes. Do you understand now why you were in so much pain during the initial activation? Your body was going through a massive purification and metamorphosis to turn you into this nearly perfect specimen of a human male. Of course, as we both know, you aren't human any longer. If you ever were . . .

[Still not sure about that. Is there anything wrong with my body? Should we do a test or something to see if that kind of change messed anything up? And you didn't answer my last question.]

Your denial is absurd. I show no active debuffs, and you seem healthy enough to march through a rainforest practically naked for weeks. If you are concerned, we can talk about testing later. And I am ignoring your last question because you are an idiot. It would be like marrying yourself . . .

Whatever. I strip off what remains of my lichen pants and ratty socks and throw them in the wall incinerator next to the sink. Hitting the red crystal next to it, I take great pleasure in hearing the muffled sound of flames roaring.

I use the toilet with a smile, wash my hands using the trough (I mean sink), touching a purple crystal that ejects soap onto my hands that smells like infused lavender. Moving to the tub, I touch the green crystal and, utilizing the system to define the perfect temperature, cause steaming water to fill it in five seconds. I am paying top coin for a reason.

I step into the tub using the built-in stairs and submerge myself in the heat. I surface and wipe my blue hair out of my eyes. Sitting back against the side of the tub, I lay my head back on the stone, close my eyes, and just soak.

[Wake me up in fifty-five minutes if I fall asleep, please. And don't let the water cool if you can.]

Sure, Vic . . .

[And Jo . . . thanks for everything. I never would have gotten here without you. You're the best partner I could ask for. You have the watch.]

I fade out as I hear:

You're welcome, Vic. I have the watch . . .

CHAPTER 42

Time to wake up . . .

I come to soaking in the steaming water. There is a low, dark blue glow in the water as the cleaning crystal does its work keeping the water clear. And then a slight red glow as the water warms slightly.

Standing up, I kick off the stone side and float over to the green crystal and place my hand on it. Shampoo, soap, and a towel appear on the small black pad. I wash my body and hair three times, resulting in the bathroom being suffused with a smell similar to the soap, some mana-infused species of lavender. The tub self-empties and then cleans itself with a deep purple glow.

[Robe?] I think as I dry myself with the towel. Sure, I could use a crystal to clean, but I haven't used a towel in months, and it is so soft, like a cloud.

Waiting for you on the wall outside the door to the left . . .

I exit the bathroom, which also self-cleans, and grab the robe. Wrapping it around myself, I enjoy the feeling of the fabric, wondering if the threads come from an infused beast. It keeps me at the perfect temperature and allows for full motion.

Walking outside of the room, I see the trio sitting on a rounded couch staring into the fireplace. Shen and Grun, also wearing bathrobes, are leaning against each other. Aria is lying down, stretched out with her head on Shen's lap, her hair being stroked by her mother. Is that a normal family?

As soon as I am seen, Aria sits up and straightens her robe with a scowl. With a sigh, I walk up to the crystal pad by the door and place my hand on it. A glowing green panel three feet across and two feet tall appears floating in midair in front of the door to the suite.

[Show the menu for food services.]

Done. You can now control everything that panel accesses remotely through the nanomachines. Just tell me what you want . . .

[Thanks, Jo. That will make everything easier.]

On the hovering panel, a large selection of food appears, broken down out by type. I order myself some fish soup, a white meat and vegetable dish, and a white wine.

Turning to the group, I say, "Menu's up. Order whatever you want."

All three slowly stand. I walk and sit on a chair opposite them, sinking inches into the seat, and let out a long sigh. Shen looks at me and says, "Vic, I don't even know how to start repaying you for everything. You saved our lives, took care of us on the journey, and now . . ." She chokes the last part, and a tear falls from her left eye.

"Let's not talk about that right now. We are where we are, and there is a lot of work ahead of us. We still have to talk about what plans you have now that you're here. I also have some big decisions to make about some complicated things. Right now I'd like to have my first friendly, low-stress meal in a month."

Shen smiles, wipes her face with the back of her hand, and nods. Aria's normal angry look slowly fades and changes to one of suspicion. Can't please some people, I suppose. The three order their food, including something for tiny Michial.

Your meals will appear on the pad on the dinner table in a few minutes . . .

You'd think with all the magica we have access to, food would be ready in an instant. Unfortunately, it doesn't work that way for some reason. If you use magic directly on food, it poisons it. It's weird because you can use magica to make a fire and use the heat to cook, but you can't cast fire directly at the food. The technicalities are beyond me, but in the end, it means you still need to wait for food to cook. Sure, you can cook faster and better with precise control of the temperature, and cutting meat or vegetables can be near-instantaneous. But using magica directly on food is a quick way to get mana-poisoning.

"The food will be here any moment now. Let's just relax and enjoy the peace while we can find it," I tell them with a smile.

Shen and Grun nod while Aria is silent. At least she isn't glaring.

When the food appears on the table, we all walk over, sit down, and have a nice quiet meal with a variety of flavors I nearly forgot existed.

While eating, I surreptitiously ask Jo about the hotel's services.

[Walk me through the options for Grace. Grace, you are welcome to make any request at this point.]

#*Thank you, Host Vic.*

Welcome to the Whyatt Hotel and Armory Vehicle Service Center	
Please choose from the following options:	
1.	Storage
2.	Cleaning
3.	Maintenance
4.	Upgrades

Each option has sub-options; I'll start at cleaning . . .

Welcome to the Whyatt Hotel and Armory Vehicle Service Center	
Cleaning Options:	
1.	Washdown - 2 copper
2.	Deep clean - 4 copper
3.	Spot cleaning with stain-resistant layer - 6 copper
4.	Detailing and protectant layer - 25 copper

[That's easy. Number four. Add to the end after we do everything. Go onto maintenance.]

#*Thank you, Host Vic . . .*

[Don't thank me yet. We're just getting started]

Welcome to the Whyatt Hotel and Armory Vehicle Service Center	
Maintenance Options:	
1.	System check and estimate for repairs. - 5 copper
	Future action requires an estimate

[Conduct that immediately and let me know the outcome.]

Requested. Results will be returned between five and fifteen minutes depending on the backlog and level of repair required . . .

[Great. Let's hold off on upgrades until I can fully focus.]

We finish eating and return to our seats surrounding the fireplace. I start the conversation by saying, "I would like to order clothes for all of us. As wonderful as this bathrobe is, we should probably not go wandering around in the nude."

Shen chuckles, Grun grins and Aria's mouth twitches but offers no other reaction.

Smiling, I continue. "We can use the MagiTech cryspad to order and let it scan for size. You'll be able to pick based on the listed options and should be able to mix and match anything you want. I recommend sticking with a few sets of casual clothes until a decision is made on what you all plan to do. How does that sound?"

Grun responds with, "That be more than generous, boy."

[Where do we measure for the clothes, Jo?]

Stand in front of the panel, and I'll take care of the rest . . .

I walk over and do as instructed. A white glow flows up and down my body. I instruct the others to do the same, step back, and each is scanned.

[Hey, Jo, just pick me out a few sets of inexpensive, relaxed clothing that will not look terrible. Sweats and t-shirt kind of stuff. I trust your judgment, just keep it inconspicuous.]

As you wish, Vic. I'll try not to make you look hideous . . .

The ladies are talking about clothing with Aria pointing, Shen shaking her head or nodding, and Grun standing back and out of the way.

Want to go out on the balcony? . . .

[Absolutely.]

A section of the glass glides down, and I step out onto a lookout with a solid steel wall to my waist to prevent accidents. Stepping up, I lean on the wall and peer over the city at the ocean beyond it. There is a nice breeze and despite the cloudy day, I like the view. I step back and settle into one of the two padded wooden loveseats next to a small table with an inscription pad on it.

[How about a glass of fruit juice? Whatever kind, I don't care.]

A moment later a glass filled with transparent red juice appears on the table. I pick it up, take a sip, and sigh.

[Time for Grace's upgrades. Let me have it.]

Welcome to the Whyatt Hotel and Armory Vehicle Service Center	
Upgrade Options:	
1.	Offensive
2.	Defensive
3.	Miscellaneous

[Walk me through each, one at a time. Only show options compatible with Grace that make sense for us please.]

Welcome to the Whyatt Hotel and Armory Vehicle Service Center		Cost (silver)	Slots	Power
Offensive Upgrades (Please note all upgrades are publicly available except when marked with a * denoting that a special license is required.)				
1.	MagiTech N14 Omni-Directional Stunner - This non-lethal addition to your vehicle offers the ability to incapacitate enemies on all sides and above. Commonly referred to as "Zappie", this popular offensive enhancement is a flat round puck that rises above the vehicle and auto-targets enemies from the elevated position. Note: MagiTech T30 Auto-targeter or later is required for this upgrade.	30	1	2
2.	MagiTech R111 Front-Facing Hyper Ram - Whether you need to push, shove or throw something in front of your vehicle, this upgrade is for you. Generally considered non-lethal, this vehicle can move objects or people from your path with pure directed spatial/gravity Magica.	50	1	4
3.	MagiTech L330 Semi-Automatic Shotgun - The L330 is the most popular lethal vehicle option for self-defense due to its price/performance ratio. This shotgun can be loaded with 10	20	1	1

	gauge enchanted rounds. Either non-explosive solid rounds or scattershot are compatible. Note: Ammunition is sold separately.			
4.	Bronco Arms "Hellfire" Repeating Rifle* - A fully-automatic weapon of death, only licensed personnel are permitted to operate this lethal creation. Further information is restricted.	85	2	2
5.	MiliMech .50 Caliber Ballistic Launcher* - This renowned MiliMech behemoth is a creature of pure destruction. Further details are restricted. Military authorization is required for purchase.	145	2	5

I will point out that you technically have authorization for the Hellfire and ballistic launcher; however, it will require your request to be recorded in MilNet...

Thinking for a minute, I ask, [Would it require a connection to NanoNet? I'm not as worried about MilNet, since I can call in a favor.]

As being a Special is not required for procurement, there will be no connection to NanoNet...

[How do I know what I have available for space on the vehicle?]

Vehicle Type:	**Orzo Motors "Hawk" Mana-Cycle (with Sidecar)**	
Vehicle Designation: Grace	Condition: Functional	Reactor Power: 15/20
Offensive Slots:		
	Front (Primary)	Front (Sidecar)
	1. Empty	1. Empty
	2. Empty	
	3. Empty	
	Left (Primary)	Left (Sidecar)
	1. Empty	1. Vehicle Attachment

	Right (Primary)	Right (Sidecar)
	1. Sidecar Attachment	1. Empty
	Rear (Primary)	Rear (Sidecar)
	1. Empty	1. Empty
	2. Empty	
	Seat	
	1. Orzo Motors four slot spatial storage container	
	2. Empty	

Defensive Slots:

	Shield (Primary)	Shield (Sidecar)
	1. Standard issue Orzo Motors environment mana shield	1. Standard issue Orzo Motors environment mana shield
	Armor (Primary)	Armor (Sidecar)
	1. Standard issue Orzo Motors mana-infused steel armor	1. Standard issue Orzo Motors mana-infused steel armor

Miscellaneous Slots:

	Reactor	
	1. Standard issue Orzo Motors mana reactor	
	Targeting System	
	1. Empty	
	Operating System	
	1. Nanomachine System	

	Consciousness	
	Gravity Plates (Primary)	Gravity Plates (Sidecar)
	1. Standard issue Orzo Motors gravity plates	1. Standard issue Orzo Motors gravity plates
	Forward-facing Lights (Primary)	Forward-facing Lights (Sidecar)
	1. Standard issue Orzo Motors white mana lights	1. Standard issue Orzo Motors white mana lights
	Rear-facing Lights (Primary)	Rear-facing Lights (Secondary)
	1. Standard issue Orzo Motors red mana lights	1. Standard issue Orzo Motors red mana lights
	Environmental Lights (Primary)	Environmental Lights (Secondary)
	1. Empty	1. Empty
	Entertainment Center (Primary)	Entertainment Center (Secondary)
	1. Standard issue Orzo Motors audio/visual system	1. Standard issue Orzo Motors audio/visual system
	Paint (Primary)	Paint (sidecar)
	1. Standard issue Orzo Motors maroon red	1. Standard issue Orzo Motors maroon red

[Okay. We have a lot to work with. Grace, you are going to be amazing. We will be together for a long time.]

#Thank you, and I hope you are correct, Host Vic. There is much to be done to defend humanity and remove the Invaders . . .

[That is certainly true. Okay, let's see the defensive upgrades.]

Before that, you have received the maintenance and repair report. Would you like to review it? . . .

[Sure.]

Welcome to the Whyatt Hotel and Armory Vehicle Service Center		
Maintenance and Repair Report		
Vehicle Type:	Orzo Motors "Hawk" Mana-Cycle (with Sidecar)	
	Primary	Sidecar
Emergency Repairs:		
	None	None
Critical Repairs:		
	Gravity plate out of alignment - Cost: 37 copper	Gravity plate out of alignment - Cost: 37 copper
Other Recommended Repairs:		
	Reactor alignment and cleaning - Cost: 55 copper	
	Sidecar attachment maintenance - Cost: 14 copper	Primary vehicle attachment maintenance: Cost: 14 copper
	Steering system alignment - Cost: 45 copper	
	Vehicle directional rebalancing - Cost: 38 copper	
	Forward-facing light re-	Forward-facing light re-

	placement - Cost: 6 copper	placement - Cost: 3 copper
	Rear-facing light replacement - Cost: 6 copper	Rear-facing light replacement - Cost: 3 copper

[So Grace is in good shape. Let's hold off until the end. We may be replacing some or all the systems that are asking to be fixed.]

Confirmed. Here are the available defensive upgrades compatible with Grace . . .

CHAPTER 43

Welcome to the Whyatt Hotel and Armory Vehicle Service Center		Cost (silver)	Slots	Power
Defensive Upgrades (Please note all upgrades are publicly available except when marked with a * denoting that a special license is required.)				
1.	Fusion Vehicles Enhanced Environmental Mana Shield - This affordable shield offers all the features of standard-issue shields plus offers better light filtering and a reduced flicker rate.	4	1	2
2.	Fusion Vehicles Ballistic Mana Shield - The ballistic shield has all the features of the enhanced environment model, with the added benefit of giving moderate protection from mana-infused projectiles. Note: This shield does not protect from Magica.	15	1	2
3.	Fusion Vehicles Hardened Mana Shield - Offering all the features of the ballistic shield, the hardened model additionally offers the highest protection available in the commercial market from projectiles and Magica.	76	1	4
4.	MiliMech Reflective Mana Shield* - This shield meets military specifications protection from both ballistics and Magica. It also adds the additional capability of returning a certain percentage of the power towards the direction of the original attack. Further details are restricted. Military authorization required for	133	1	5

	purchase.			
5.	MagiTech VA210 Liquid Steel Vehicle Armor - MagiTech's famous Liquid Steel has recently been adapted to support Vehicles. It offers tremendous protection for an equally tremendous power requirement. This is perfect for vehicles with large rectors and the need to protect what is inside.	145	1	5
6.	MiliMech Mana-Infused Specialty Steel Defensive Vehicle Armor* - The metal used to make this high protective and expensive armor is classified. This armor's price reflects the requested paint color as the paint is a part of its capabilities. Further details are restricted. Military authorization required for purchase.	350	1	*

[We are absolutely staying away from MagiTech. I don't trust their liquid steel right now. The MiliMech armor and shield are almost good enough to make me want to call in that favor.]

I take another sip of the fruit juice, thinking about the choices ahead.

[What about the miscellaneous upgrades? Don't show anything that is based on MagiTech liquid steel.]

Affirmative. This is a rather substantial list. Hundreds of different options. How would you like me to sort them? . . .

[Just show me the two most expensive of each type of slot I have. Give me one that is and one that is not MilSpec. Coin is meant to be spent, after all. And Grace is a pretty girl who will hopefully be with us for a long time and is worth investing in.]

#Thank you for noticing, Host Vic . . .

Stop flirting with the bike . . .

[Jealous, Jo? Let's skip the lights and entertainment system. You and Grace coordinate on those and get whatever Grace wants. Just stay under two gold for all of it. Let's do a matte black paint job.]

Welcome to the Whyatt Hotel and Armory Vehicle	Cost	Sl	Pow

Service Center	(silver)	ots	er
Miscellaneous Upgrades (Please note all upgrades are publicly available except when marked with a * denoting that a special license is required.)			
1. Fusion Vehicles Maximum Capacity Mana Reactor - This is Fusion Vehicle's high capacity reactor. With the exception of military vehicles or enhancements, there is little this compact reactor cannot support.	445	1	+135
2. MiliMech High-Capacity Recycling Mana Reactor* - All information on this reactor is classified. Military authorization required for purchase.	490	1	*
3. MagiTech T55 Auto-targeter - The latest in self-targeting for civilian vehicles, this auto-targeting brings a new meaning to one-touch control. The vehicle controller has a near 100% accuracy on both terminating the enemy and avoiding friendlies.	260	1	2
4. MiliMech Self-Targeting Automation System* - All information on this system is classified. Military authorization required for purchase.	285	1	3
5. GravSystems Civilian Magnetite Gravity Plates - The platinum-standard for gravity plates in personal and commercial vehicles, this magnetite-based model offers maximum control, minimal drag, and the lowest power to weight ratio of any commercially available gravity plate.	165	1	3
6. GravSystems MilSpec Magnetite Gravity Plates - All information on this system is classified. Military authorization required for purchase.	300	1	*

| 7. | MagiTech Lockable 14-Slot Vehicle Spatial Storage Container - The height of secure storage, this MagiTech creation is the largest single slot Spatial Storage available for commercial vehicles.
(This will replace your vehicle's existing storage container) | 765 | 1 | 3 |

That is it for the miscellaneous. There is no military specification spatial storage container which will fit Grace worth listing . . .

[So we are pretty much going to replace the entire vehicle. If Grace wasn't such a special girl I'd just get a new one off the line for the same price.]

#*Thank you for not replacing me with a younger model, Host Vic. I can still serve humanity beneath you . . .*

Drinking more of my juice with a grin, I think, [That sounded dirty, Grace.]

#*Yes . . .*

Please stop, you two. Vic, what would you like to do regarding the items requiring a MilNet connection? . . .

I sit pondering for a few minutes, just staring out at the ocean.

[Can you mask who I am if we send a note through the hotel's system?]

I can mask it from the hotel. If it is being directly monitored, there is likely no way to be a hundred percent anonymous without advanced cyber protocols, which you do not have access to at this time . . .

[Not good enough. I was afraid of this. Looks like we're making a trip. But before that, Grace, what is currently in the spatial container under your seat?]

#*All four slots are filled. Franklin used to call my storage his "Emergency Stash." I will list out the contents for you . . .*

#*In the first slot are fourteen food bars. Each provides sufficient caloric intake for an average human for a day. The value to you would be lower, due to your mana-supported nanomachine system . . .*

#*The second slot has fourteen twenty-ounce canteens of purified water . . .*

#*The third slot has one hundred gold coins, two hundred fifty silver coins, and five hundred copper coins . . .*

#*The fourth slot has seventeen maps of various locations from what used to be referred to as the United States of America, Canada, and Mexico. Obviously, the content is severely outdated...*

[It really was his emergency stash. Where did he get all the coin?]

#It wasn't his coin. He inherited me and the coin when his family died during the Invader sacking of Northern Horse Town. It is a long story, but the short version is his wife was from a wealthy family, she left me to him, and I had the coins and maps. He later added the food bars and water. He never touched the coins...

[It was a difficult time with multiple Invader offenses all over the globe.] I sigh. [Either way, we need to clear it out before we replace that container.]

I also recommend you ask them to return the empty container to you, Vic...

[Good thinking. I can use or absorb it.]

My thinking exactly...

[Can you get them to send me a shirt, sweats, socks, and shoes immediately? I don't care if the fit is a bit off. Also, add a loose hooded cloak so I can hide my hair and body and something to hide at least most of my face.]

I have ordered a standard-sized white t-shirt, black sweats, white socks, standard-issue black ankle boots, a black cloak, and cloth mask. None are enchanted. Those are the best I could get on short notice in something remotely your size. They will arrive in a few moments...

[Thanks, Jo. Keep doing your thing on your original order.]

Affirmative. Are you heading out?...

[Yes. I need to reopen a connection and send a secure communication.]

CHAPTER 44

When I return from the balcony to find all three in the same position as before, I figure I have some time. Grabbing the new clothes from the delivery pad, I walk into my room, change, and walk out with the cloak in my [Inventory].

Moving next to Grun, the only one of the trio not engrossed, I say, "I have to head out and meet up with someone. I'll be back in an hour or two. You should be set to order food, those clothes, and any other standard needs."

Grun looks at me quizzically. "Ya know sumtin'?"

I tilt my head from one side to the other. "Sort of. Some*one*. They should be able to help with a few things, including indirectly getting you set up in human lands."

Grun lets out a deep breath and asks me a question in a subdued voice. "Boy, why ya doin' all dis?"

Why, indeed. After a moment of not responding, I turn my head from the dwarf and look out the large windowed wall to the darkening sky and sun setting over the ocean. Softly, I reply, "I don't know."

Turning to the double-doored entrance, I walk by the ladies and out of the suite.

***

Reflecting on where I am headed, I decide to leave Grace and not risk her being damaged or stolen. I ask the richly dressed Mr. Stuffy to hire me a Magica Automata Driver or MAD, the only automated vehicle pilot permitted to breach certain UFH regulations. Most people just call them "Mads" because of their reputation for driving like madmen at times. They are fully automated with built-in limiters, but the private companies who run them make coin on the length and number of trips, not the number of traffic laws they obey, which more often than not means they work with speed as a priority. You can always pay more for a "safety-first" transport package.

It is generally accepted that the owners relax or remove those limiters.

This is one of those things that is ignored by the authorities—likely due to bribes, although no one has proven anything that goes to the top. An occasional fine satisfies the general public, city governments, and UFH that law enforcement is doing its job. Any medicos with life-magica-enchanted healing equipment are readily available, so unless someone dies near instantly or body parts are lost, the only cost is coin. And that the MAD owners have in abundance to pay off whoever for whatever happens.

[Give it the address for the club I had you mark during our entry into the city.]

Affirmative...

The robe and mask appear over my clothes and face while I sit back preparing for a meeting I hope will help me make a connection without exposing my presence in the city. Or that I am even alive.

***

Luckily, this MAD only nearly hits someone twice during the trip, which isn't too bad, all things considered. The mag-restraints inside the vehicle rarely result in more than a bruise or two in a normal human, so for me and my "Special" capabilities, this trip is nothing.

I am pressed forward against the shoulder harness as we too swiftly slow to a thankfully non-contact stop in front of the club I haven't entered for nearly eighteen months. A pair of dwarves climb into the MAD immediately upon my exit, and it floats off back into the traffic of the area, fighting for space with another MAD, resulting in a zipping sound and flash of transparent blue mana shields colliding.

With a quick glance up at the transparent glowing projection cautioning me that I approach "Theo's," I walk to the entrance with a bouncer most would find intimidating, which is of course the purpose. The female humanoid's average size does not reduce the threat she exudes. Wrapped in mottled brown and red beast-leather armor exposing not an inch of skin or hair causes one to feel immediately imperiled. Augmenting the intimidation is a full face-covering leather helmet with a top circled by inch-long spikes, a pointed nose, and magica-darkened eye slits preventing their color from being seen. At her hips are a pair of deep red hand mana-projectors, strapped across her torso is a brown glowing shotgun, and across her back is a large two-handed saber with a thin curved single-edged blade. Openly moving towards her, I reflect what else she might be carrying in whatever spatial storage devices are under that armor. With an internal smile that doesn't actually change the neutral expression on my face, I am comforted to know this level of paranoia only increases the chances who I am looking for is inside.

Reaching the dangerous bouncer, I raise my hand with a silver coin between two fingers, lean forward, and say in a low voice, "I'm here to see the twins. Tell them their night hunter friend requests a moment of their time."

In a smooth motion, she reaches up for the silver coin, grabs it with dexterous fingers, reaches across her body, taps her wrist causing the coin to disappear, and returns to her watchful position. Neither of us takes action for at least fifteen seconds until a modulated voice exits from her helm telling me nothing of who or what she is. "Rec room four."

I nod thanks and walk past her into the entrance.

The beat of music and flashing of color-shifting mana lights surround me as I move past the entrance enchanted for isolation. My entire body vibrates with each pulsating throb of the deep bass. The cost to sever this entire building from the outside and prevent the music from escaping must have cost in the platinum. Then again, the crush of barely clothed bodies dancing, eating, drinking, and love-making both on the large central area, at the tables set up on a circle around that area, behind curtained booths set aside, and hidden behind closed doors tells me this place is a substantial coin-maker. And that they've been open for no fewer than four years tells me they are likely making that much or more every week.

Places like Theo's are a relief for the population of a world permanently on the brink of death. Nobody, no matter the species, can be on edge every moment of every day. This club—and its sisters in every human city large enough to support them—are a necessary release from the stress of a dangerous world. These types of businesses have special agreements with city and UFH leadership to stay within certain constraints in regards to publicity but have otherwise complete autonomy within their walls. Two nights every week, nearly everyone from politicians to hunters to Specials to normal everyday civilians visit a place like Theo's for the comfort of companionship and respite from violence. That is the only hard and fast rule once one enters this building: no fighting. To enforce that, mixed throughout the crowd are individuals specifically responsible for curtailing any violence before it happens. They are equipped with stunning equipment capable of everything from a sharp sting to killing a weaker Special. Generally, the enforcers are not needed, and everyone enjoys the time hiding from their responsibilities. Sometimes they have to break up a potential fight over a prospective partner, but that is generally as far as it goes. Everyone knows anything more will result in a permanent ban. And everyone also knows all the club owners communicate. Few wish to be denied access to every club in a city or even larger area.

My cloaked form smoothly slides in between bodies, dodges drinkers, ducks waving limbs, and eventually makes its way to a far side hallway with the label "Rec Rooms" over the stone archway. This is the only area in the building free of dense traffic, primarily due to the expense of renting one of its rooms. I walk to room four and knock twice. A moment later, the door opens just enough for me to squeeze through, and I enter the dimly lit room.

CHAPTER 45

What I can make out is a room three by three meters barely lit by red mana lights. Against the wall to the left of the door is a wooden couch covered with black padding and pillows, a small matching wooden table in front of it, a single stone chair across from but facing the couch, and three humanoids. Two nearly identical pale-skinned humans dressed in white suits sit on opposite sides of the couch with their shiny white shoes crossed on the table, and one strikingly unlike the others stands beside me and in front of the door.

Barely turning my head to the right but keeping it tilted down, I find a female with a pelt of tan fur covering what can be seen of her body. Her dirty blond mane of hair falls in curls to the middle of her back, which is exposed, as are her shoulders, cleavage, and most of her legs in a glimmering silver dress tight enough to hide she is definitely not wearing anything under it. The touch of her tawny tail and tickle of the darker fluff of fur at the end attempting to wrap around my wrist under the cloak's sleeve grants me the intended warning.

A voice somewhere between scary and sultry purrs from between her long pointed canines. "Identify yourself."

I don't move anything save for my jaw. "Noctis Venandi."

The tail halts its movements but does not release me. In half-whisper, half-gasp I hear, "Vic?"

I reach up and pull down the cloth covering my face below my eyes and lift my head to look at her from beneath the cloak hood with a sad smile. "Hey, Mel."

A gasp is followed by the withdrawal of her tail, and a step backward causes her body to thump into the stone wall behind her. I hear a cleared throat from my left and turn to the twins, Theodore and Theodora. Both the namesakes of the club. I bow my head slightly and say, "Thank you for agreeing to meet with me."

The panting to my right slows, and I hear in a low voice, "You're here for them?" I simply nod. Her voice is shaky as she says, "I thought . . ."

I shake my head. A loud exhale of air is followed by the lionkin's body sliding down the wall until she sits on the floor with her knees against her chest, her arms wrapped around them. That dress is not meant for such a position, so I fully turn to face the twins and put my back to my old . . . associate.

"Hey, guys." They both bow their heads. Two perfect white pieces of cloth cover their eye sockets that long ago held their striking heterochromatic irises. The only difference between the two is the sister has short straight white hair, cut military style while the brother's white locks are to his shoulders with a slight curl at the bottom.

"Sorry to bother you both. I'm sure you don't want to see me." In a synchronous motion, they shrug their shoulders and swap which foot is on the bottom and top on the table.

Theodora asks, "Why are you here S . . . Vic?"

"I'm not here. I'm dead. At least for now."

For the first time, one of the twins moves as an individual. Theodore pulls his legs off the table and leans forward with his elbows on his knees, his eyeless face staring directly into mine. "Oh?"

"I need a way to make secure contact with someone in the UFH military that does not expose me."

Theodore leans back against the couch, and once again his legs are crossed on the table. His sister, however, swaps positions with him and asks, "You already owe us from your last visit."

I agree with a hooded nod. "Yes." I move to the open chair across from the twins and sit. "I will likely be in Sea Saddle City for a while this time. I can likely cover it sooner than expected."

She sits back but keeps her feet down. A chuckle comes from her brother as he says, "What would they say if they knew you made this deal with us? She might find out and tell him."

"Irrelevant. And you assume she doesn't already know. She almost certainly is watching you. The fact that you are alive tells you they aren't worried."

Theodora waves her hand up and down my seated form. "And that explains the lovely covering."

I nod. It might not make sense nodding silently to a pair of blind humans, but I know they can see me, even if the method is beyond me. They have never been normal.

"Do you think they would succeed?"

After a moment I respond with, "They'd send me." The unspoken "And you wouldn't know you were dead" floats in the air.

The previously silent lionkin jerks from her place on the floor.

After another few moments of silence, the brother says, "One time only."

I nod.

Theodora says, "We will receive our compensation."

I nod again.

Theodore taps his finger, and a flat silver crystal no larger than a fingernail appears in his hand. He reaches forward and places it on the table between us then leans back. "Use that to create your message and state who you wish it to reach."

I lean forward for the crystal but before I touch it, Theodora says, "Congratulations on activating your nanos, Vic. It looks good on you."

After a brief freeze, I continue and tap the crystal.

Accessing. This is an extraordinary piece of magica-based technology. It is a single-use recording device so heavily encrypted I do not believe it could be accessed by any but a single individual. It appears to have a unique lock based on nanomachine signature . . .

I presumed for a while these two were Specials, but this confirms it. I'm glad I haven't been sent to terminate them. Not only do I not dislike them, but they actually provide a valuable service to humanity. We gain little and lose much with their deaths. And unlike poor Meladorah, they know it.

[Send the following to UFH Quartermaster Gunnery Sergeant Jeffery Matthews: "Gunny, long time no cast. I was digging around looking for some fish food, cut my finger on a hook, and thought of our last outing together. Give me a holler if you want to try to snag some halibut. Honey.]

Completed. Anything more before I engage the lock? . . .

[No.]

I lean back and say, "Done."

A synchronized nod later, I stand and walk to the door. "Thank you."

"We will call this in. Perhaps soon."

Straightening my cloak, replacing my mask, and assuring my hood fully covers my head, I say, "You know how to reach me now."

I walk by the still curled up lionkin, say softly, "Good to see you," and walk out.

CHAPTER 46

Back at the hotel, I return to the suite to find the trio eating once again at the table. I wave to them and silently return to my room. Stripping off the clothes, I take a shower to remove the smell of the club from my body and, in another robe, I join them at the table. They are mostly done eating but stay as I eat.

Looking around at the three of them, I become concerned. Shen has dark bags under her eyes, Aria is pale and looks scared, and Grun looks even more grumpy than usual. "Is there anything wrong?"

Shen jerks her head at me and asks, "What do you mean?"

Okay. Now I know something is not right; Shen is the stable one. "You all look worse than when I left. What happened?"

Aria gets up from her seat and walks into her room. Shen sighs and in a soft tone says, "Nothing happened. It has been a very long week."

Not wanting to push more, I ask, "Did you all finish picking out clothes?"

With a tired smile, Shen says, "Yes, thank you."

[How much is all the clothing, Jo?]

Just shy of ten silver . . .

[Order it and put a rush on it even if it costs more.]

Ordered. Awaiting a response . . .

I say to Shen, "Now we wait."

I finish eating in silence and move back to where I was on the balcony. I think I like it here. The view is relaxing, the trio aren't a bother or too distracting, and despite the youngest's obvious hostility, they are fair and even-tempered. Their current condition leaves me to believe something indeed happened while I was gone. I can take a few guesses but don't know enough to say for sure. Right now I am leaning towards Shen's magica being the cause. During our journey, her nature affinity was quite useful and struck me as strong. Not that I am an expert at such things.

[Can you get me a glass of white wine? Anything not too bitter please.]

A moment later, a glass appears on the pad to my left. I take a sip and stare out at the coastline and ocean.

[I'm sure you have questions.]

I do. But I don't think you can answer them . . .

[Probably not.]

Taking another sip and looking down into the glass, I think:

[Ask the questions you think I can answer.]

Will you share with me what that was about eventually? . . .

[Almost certainly.]

Then I am satisfied with my answers. And I figure you have a lot of planning to do, so I won't distract you . . .

She's right.

***

An hour later I haven't moved, still defining the various steps forward I have to take. Sometime during my musing, Shen came out and sat down next to me. I didn't even notice . . . again. Some protector I am.

She is looking at me seriously and says, "You've done so much for us. I feel like we owe you an explanation."

My immediate response is "You are free to tell me if you like, but you owe me nothing."

Leaning backward, she tucks her legs under her and covers them with her robe. "I know you think that. And while Grun and I disagree on the owing part, we do need to tell you some things. Partially because you deserve to know and partially because it influences my family's next steps."

I nod. "Fair enough. I'm listening."

She takes a deep breath and starts her story. "We are refugees of a sort. For a lot of complicated reasons, we had to flee our home. I had just found out I was pregnant with Aria when we were . . . given little choice but to leave. Grun and I had been together for seventy-six of your years when we fled together with Aria inside me. Elves have the ability to slow the growth of our children, just as we can control our own aging, and can spend as much as sixty of your years with child.

"For nearly that long, Grun and I fled from our pursuers. We found one out-of-the-way village after another and even moved from dimension to dimension when we could afford it. We paid our way with my nature magica and his metalwork.

"Eventually, it could be put off no longer, and I gave birth to Aria in an isolated village in a world far from our pursuers. Neither of us wanted to raise Aria on the run. Living like that is very hard, and a child should have a home. That is a fundamental belief of both the elven and dwarven people.

"We decided to give normal life a try. It was a lovely life for two of your years. At some point, the story of an elven nature magica and dwarven smith together reached our pursuers. They snuck into the village at night, knocked us out, and captured us. We were brought back home and I was told, in no uncertain terms, I was to do what I was told or Grun, my lover for over a century, or Aria, only two at the time, would be taken from me.

"So I did. I lived a life I hated surrounded by people who hated me as Aria slowly grew up. As I said, elves age slowly by choice. You will presumably be surprised to know she is fifty-three of your years old."

I react to her story for the first time by raising my blue eyebrows. But I say nothing, so she continues her story.

"She remembers that life with as much derision as I do. She had few friends, and none she could trust. Her gift of life affinity was exploited to the point of her nearly killing others and then herself. Her youth was one of betrayal, faithlessness, elven pride, and of course war. The place where I lived has always been in perpetual war with the orcs and with itself. The political intrigues and infighting were just as much a daily occurrence as the combat with the various orc-kin tribes.

"And it was the political infighting which indirectly led us to be in the position you found us in. My youngest brother was quite enamored with the idea of taking my place." A brief but sad chuckle comes from her mouth as she continues. "It is ironic that I would have given it to him if I were permitted. Unfortunately, things are never that simple. My brother coordinated with his wife's forces, and we were once again kidnapped in the night. You see, he had made a bargain with an orc tribe. He would turn me over to them if, in exchange, they would flee from his forces when he attacked.

"Of course, the tribe was already planning to come to this world, so it was all just a ploy to win a very public victory and enhance my brother's position. I'm sure he was terribly distraught, at least in public, that he could not stop them from fleeing through the portal with us.

"At this point, we had a stroke of good fortune, our first in years. We had only spent a few days as prisoners of the orcs when, for some reason, a rather large troll came barging into the encampment demanding troops to search for something. There was mass chaos and a majority of the tribe's forces were taken to participate in the search. During the chaos, Grun managed to kill a few sentries quietly, and we fled into the forest. The time passing after is something of a blur, but we fled and kept running until we couldn't anymore. Then Aria would heal our feet, and we'd sleep on the ground to flee again when we woke. Their hunters eventually found our trail and, well, you know the rest.

"I have no idea what happened with the troll, the mercenaries, or the search, but that was the only bit of good fortune we experienced in over five decades. Mostly because it led us to you."

Shen sags a little, looking exhausted after the telling. I turn my head back to face the ocean and think.

[I don't believe in fate or luck. But so much has happened and it all seems connected. I am struggling to understand it all.]

I don't know what to say to that, Vic . . .

Turning back to her I ask, "Tell me, do elves believe in fate? Or I guess more pertinently, do you?"

Her answer surprises me. "Not all elves believe the same, Vic. *My* people believe that mana isn't just a force or energy but a greater consciousness. Some of the more esoteric of my people called it the 'living mana' as if it is a conscious being that makes decisions. However, we believe that mana moves the universe like a game. Its actions are so wide and sweeping nobody can see all the moves, or even all the pieces. Sometimes I believe it is true." Quieter, she continues. "And sometimes I fear it is."

Clearing her throat she says, "What I think you are asking is whether I believe fate brought us together. My answer is I don't know."

I nod, still looking out at the ocean.

Shen continues, this time with a greater passion than before, so I turn and give her my full attention. "What I do know is that Aria is the most important thing to me in any world, above my life and Grun believes the same. We owe you our lives, but most importantly we owe you hers. Please remember that. She is not what she seems or lets you see. She is our future, our people's future." I barely hear her whisper, "And maybe yours."

I turn back to the ocean. Should I say anything?

After another minute, I say, "They were after me. The troll mercenaries, I mean. The chaos that allowed your escape was because I was there."

She sucks in a breath, and her eyes open wide.

CHAPTER 47

"I had a mission that day. It was to kill the head of the mercenary band, that troll king you saw. You know how hard it is to kill trolls. I was supposedly given special ammunition that has the ability to kill him."

I then tell my story. How he knew where to find me. How my equipment just happened to fail me at the wrong time. How I was "luckily" sent into that cave. How that cave just happened to have plants that exuded acid which could free me. How I just happened to be in a place where my nanos would get activated and I would become the oldest nano-activated human in more than 140 years and with the densest nano count in history. I even tell her that I found the quicksilver there, but not how much. After which she jumps slightly like she is shocked. I look at her quizzically.

She answers my unspoken question. "You likely don't know this, but many creatures are affected differently by quicksilver. It is a bizarre and unique substance that, once purified in a specific way, subtly alters the nature of those touching it. For elves, it enhances both our magica and charismatic appeal. For dwarves, it makes them more sturdy and strong. In short, it increases or enhances what already makes us what we are.

"On the other hand, it does the opposite to the races of the orcs' dimension. To my knowledge, nobody understands why, but for orcs and their ilk, it weakens and poisons them. It is rare enough to be considered a legendary material, unique in its power to affect the world around it, and highly sought after by my people. We call it 'holy metal.' My grandfather once killed a troll with a quicksilver-headed spear. A troll dead by a spear." She shakes her head with a chuckle, emphasizing the absurdity of the idea. "That weapon is now in my father's hands. My family would likely pay a high price just for that little bit you found."

I am quiet, thinking again.

"Please continue your story."

So I do. I don't tell her about Jo or my species, but cover most of the rest. I speak about how I awoke with two runes that just so happened to be able to help me survive. How I experimented with the lichen and learned its various properties. How I learned to sew with it so I wouldn't be naked because all my clothing, armor, and weapons were destroyed with my collar and, most importantly, the ability for anybody to find me.

I share how I advanced my skills by climbing, tailoring, and using my magica. How I made the armor to learn advanced fire magica, and if I hadn't, I would have died to the spider. How I learned to manipulate mana using the skill I learned from fire and so learned air magica, which allowed me to learn water magica. I don't talk about my inventory creation snafu, because that would expose a few things I'm not comfortable with yet. However, I tell of my escape from the cave, my running into the elk, and the lion's surprise attack. And about how I would have died if I hadn't made an armor set with that particular bonus capability. Nor would I have lived if I had not had long hair that I put up in a ponytail.

When I reach how I woke up the orcs yelling, I say, "Well, you know the rest."

After a few seconds, she slowly puts her feet down and stands up. "Vic, it feels as though you are being guided towards something, like the river you used to escape leads to the ocean. I hope you don't get swept away by it."

And she walks inside to her family.

I turn back to the ocean and whisper, "I hope so too, but is it too late? And would I truly fight it?"

CHAPTER 48

After a few more minutes of silence, Jo asks me:

You okay, Vic?

[Yeah. Just feeling a bit overwhelmed.]

That is understandable. I have two messages for you if you are ready . . .

[Go ahead.]

The first is to alert you that the clothing is ready and that they would like to bring it up to make adjustments on the spot . . .

[Have them bring it up in five. What is the second message?]

I have the following message from a Gunnery Sergeant Jeffery Matthews. It is audio-only. The coarse voice of my old gunny rumbles in my ear: "I heard about your fishing trip, and I thought you might have fallen into the ocean and needed me to come rescue you. Glad to hear you stayed dry. If you are looking for a fishing partner, I'm in. Just be sure the halibut are biting before you cast. I'd hate it if we caught a shark instead of a fish. Oh. And we're good to plan our trips openly now. I have that covered."

I smile.

[Great. Send this: "I have the perfect quiet spot to fish. Unfortunately, I need to buy some fishing gear and I'm concerned someone will follow me from the bait shop and find my spot. I'm looking for some top-spec fishing gear. Any advice? I also found myself an affordable boat and I want to fancy it up a bit. Any idea how I can do that without someone following me to my pier? Thanks for being a friend, not sure I can trust my wife and need all those I can find."]

Sent. That is a great message. No keywords or obvious tells . . .

[Yep. The gunny's the one who taught me how to communicate that way. He actually does enjoy fishing and uses his little vacation time at a few of the safer lakes. It's one of the reasons the code is quality.]

A minute before they should arrive with our clothes, I stand up and head back inside, telling everyone to be ready to receive the clothing. Everyone is there and pale-faced. What happened this time?

There is a knock on the suite door, and I head to open it. Whatever it is can wait until after we deal with the clothes. I hear a familiar clicking sound and jerk to a stop. I dive towards Aria and scream "Down!" The door explodes open as I smash into Aria, and we tumble behind a couch near the fireplace. Then I hear the soft puffing of a mana rifle. Shen screams, and Grun bellows "No!" I hear another yell and then some thumping.

[Jo!]

Comms are blocked out of this suite . . .

[FUCK! Can you break through?]

Trying . . .

I look at Aria, who is lying curled on the ground, shock clearly showing on her pale face. "Stay here. Do. Not. Move," I whisper in her ear. Her mouth is moving, but all I can hear is, "Too soon" over and over again. Putting it aside I focus on the threat.

I form two windblades and raise my head sideways so my right eye can see over the couch. I see two men in the suits of the hotel staff, and they have MagiTech automatic mana projectors in their hands. Grun is on his hands and knees in front of the man on the left, bleeding—I cannot tell from where—while Shen is flat on her back in front of the guy on the right, surrounded by blood. They are both looking over at the dwarf, and the one closest to him yells, "Where is the gold?"

I duck back behind the couch and hear Grun laugh and say in his gravelly voice, "Heh. She was right."

I raise my windblades above the edge of the couch and train them on where the two invaders were. Hopefully, they haven't moved.

Second Guy says loudly, "We know you have gold. You dropped a whole pile when you came here. You rich fucks always have gold lying around."

First Guy interrupts with "Did you see all that gold? He probably has platinum like all the rest of your kind."

Second Guy picks back up. "Where's the big blue guy and pretty short one?" Then he chuckles. "If we get her we—" His voice is cut off and as my windblade takes off the top half of his head.

*You have killed a **Thug**. You absorb 215.37 mana essence . . .*

The first turns at the thump of the second guy's body hitting the carpeted floor ,and my windblade misses. Grun leaps up at him with a roar. I jump on Aria and cover her with my body. I hear more puffing of the gun, the zooming of a few gray projectiles flying above our crouched forms, a short yelp, shuffle of a body, and then silence.

*You have killed a **Thug**. You absorb 51.88 mana essence...*

Looking up, I confirm what the alerts tell me. I leap over the couch to Shen. She has taken a shot to the left chest and two more to the abdomen. The once-pristine white bathrobe and carpet beneath both are covered in a deep red. She's breathing, but barely.

I yell, "Aria, you mom needs your help. Hurry!"

A pale Aria shakily climbs to her feet, turns to her mother. She visibily pales before yelling, "No!" and runs to her downed parent.

While I move to Grun, she places her hands over the wounds, and her eyes glow gold. Once again, I hear "too soon."

Grun is lying on top of the man, and neither is moving.

I roll Grun off and see the top of the human's head has been blown off from a shot through the bottom of his jaw. Grun has four holes in his chest.

I'm through... Who should I call?...

Thinking fast, I respond. [Call hotel security and tell them we've been attacked and there have been deaths. It is too late now to hide. Our cover is blown. Damnit. I was so stupid.]

I feel for a pulse, but Grun is gone. Looking at the wounds again, I realize he knew the last hit to center mass was a mortal one. That's just like him, taking down an enemy with him.

I crawl towards the crying and shaking Aria. She's rocking in front of her mother's now-lifeless body. As I reach her, she lays her head in my shoulder just when two armed guards appear in the pad outside our suite door. They storm through the door and point their weapons at me. I gently pull Aria away from Shen and put her behind me, but I can still feel her shaking against my back.

I hold my hands up and say, "My friend needs a medic. Please."

I turn around and hold Aria. She's shaking and crying into my robed chest. I rock her slowly. I hear the guard say, "We need medical attention immediately. Hurry the fuck up, George!"

[What do I say to her, Jo?]

Just be there for her...

I whisper to Aria, "I'm here." I keep rocking and holding her.

A human medic in blue and white appears on the pad and is directed to Shen by the guard. He holds a crystal over her and lets it go. It floats there and turns black. He takes out three other crystals and lays them on her in a triangle formation surrounding the black one. That center crystal turns gold and starts to glow. "There's a chance," he breathes out. He touches the other crystals around her, and they also turn gold. He looks at the crystal floating above her. It doesn't change; the damn thing just floats. The medic feels for a pulse at the wrist and says, "C'mon."

I look down and see at some point Aria has stopped crying and has fallen asleep against me, likely from the shock plus use of her magica. I hold her tightly to me. I don't know what else to do.

The crystal above Shen turns clear. I hear a sad bird cry from Shen and Grun's room, and I know Michial has passed too. Shen said his life was tied to hers.

The medic collapses to a sitting position, sweating. "Damn." He turns from her and looks at me. "I'm so sorry, sir. I couldn't do anything; she was too far gone. Do you or the young lady need medical attention?"

I shake my head. I try to speak quietly and add a little shake to my voice. "No, sir, we were hidden behind the couch the whole time." In my peripheral vision, I see the guard watching us, so I continue with the story. "Once everything was quiet I got up and went to my friends." Glancing at Grun, I say, "He was already dead. But . . ." I point at Shen's body. "She was still breathing. I tried to stop the bleeding. Nothing worked." Looking quickly down at Aria, I continue quietly. "She went over to her mother, and then the guards came."

A constable then appears with the words Sea Saddle City Law emblazoned across the front of a cloak. He walks in and sees the mess and bodies. He looks at me and Aria and says, "I'll need you to come with me."

VOLUME 4 - FAMILY OF TWO

CHAPTER 49

Aria is small enough that I can pick her up in a princess carry and place her head so it lays on my shoulder. She's not very big, and to my enhanced body, she weighs little. The constable says, "Follow me please."

I have identified the assailants. They appear to be normal workers at the hotel. I can confirm one of them is the individual who dropped the platter of food in the lobby the day you checked in. It seems plausible, if not likely, that the accident was caused by his witnessing your placement of the gold pile. The other is likely his accomplice . . .

[And they thought we were an easy mark, having plenty of coin but no way to defend ourselves. That aligns with what they were saying in the room. I flashed so much coin. This is my fault.]

It is their fault. You didn't kill Grun and Shen. Focus on the situation and Aria. I'm here if you need anything . . .

Not sure how to respond, I silently follow the investigating constable down into the hotel lobby. We don't go outside though. He leads me to another room in the hotel.

There is a set of comfortable chairs and a table to write or eat on. He points at a seat. Trying not to jostle Aria too much, I sit. Despite my efforts, her head slips from my shoulder to lie against my neck. He puts a recording crystal on the table and activates it with a touch.

[Record this please, Jo.]

Recording started . . .

The constable starts. "I'm sorry for your loss . . . and for hers. I know this isn't what you want to do right now, but I need to figure out what happened. Are you able to talk to me?"

I nod. "I'll try."

He starts the questions with, "What is your name?"

"Michael."

"Michael what?"

"Michael Uriel."

I don't know if the recorder is also a divining stone, so I try to avoid lying if at all possible.

"Michael, can you tell me what happened?" I provide an abridged version of the events. Again trying to avoid lying. I don't want anyone to know I can use magica, so I omit how the first guy died and just sort of make it appear that Shen killed him without actually saying that.

"Why would he ask for gold? Why would he think you have any besides being in an expensive hotel, which is the same as every other guest? What set you apart, do you think?"

"I paid in gold coin for the expensive suite. I guess he thought I'd have more?" I end the last sentence like it was a question, leading him to subconsciously need to answer it.

"That is likely. How long have you been in the hotel and Sea Saddle City?"

"We only checked in yesterday. And we just got back from a hike and hunt in the rainforest."

"I see." His fingers tap on the table. "Those are all my questions at this time."

He then taps the crystal and puts it back in his pocket.

"Let me be frank, Mr. Uriel. I think you and your friends were victims of a robbery. I don't think you did anything wrong, other than flash too much gold openly. And I am inclined to file that with my department."

He stops talking, still tapping his finger on the table, seeing if I get the hint. I do. I reach around Aria and also put my hand on the table and tap it. A gold coin clicks on the table. I tap it again and another one clinks down. One more time and third drops. I withdraw my hand but not all the way off the table.

He looks at me and taps his finger two more times. I put my hand back and tap twice more, and two more gold coins clink.

"You are free to go, Mr. Uriel." He is about to stand up, and I tap one more time another gold coin drops. Looking at him, I say, "Not Mr. Uriel. Mr. Smith. Mr. Jonathan Smith." I tap twice more and two more coins drop.

"Right, of course. Mr. Smith. You and your . . ."

"Sister," I finish for him.

"Of course. You and your sister, young Miss Mary Smith, are free to go. And again, my condolences for your loss."

He stands and walks over to me. Holding out his hand, I shake with the crooked cop, and he turns and walks out. The recording crystal has my name but, if he's smart, it will have an accident on the way back to his precinct.

Still holding Aria, I walk directly to the front desk and snap that I want to see the hotel's manager or owner or whoever the fuck is in charge.

CHAPTER 50

We get a new room and no longer have to pay for it. We do still have to pay for anything other than the room and food, but I am fine with that. The hotel manager and I both know the Whyatts are wealthy enough to bury this if I take it to the authorities. On top of that, I don't want to draw any more attention since I'm not supposed to be here, so I accept the terms. And I want access to the armory, which would end if I fought the owners.

The new suite now has only two connected bedrooms, and I put Aria to bed in one after changing her bathrobe. She shouldn't have to wake up covered in her mother's blood. I leave the door open between the two. I shower and put both my bloody bathrobe and hers into the incinerator. I shower and put on a new one, walking out to see Aria in my room. She's pale and shaking but standing on her own. I walk over to her but just stand there, not sure what to do next.

[What do I do, Jo?]

Aria takes a step forward, lays her head against my chest, wraps her arms around my torso, and cries again. I can feel her body shaking with nearly silent sobs. I hold her with one arm and rub her back with the other.

You're doing fine, Vic . . .

She stops after a few minutes and takes a deep breath. Taking a step back, I open my arms, letting her make space.

 "They're dead?" she asks.

I look her in the eyes, sigh, and say, "Yes, Aria. I'm so sorry."

"What about their bodies?" she asks in an even quieter voice.

[Jo, the bodies?]

Violent crime not involving beasts or Invaders requires a postmortem. Likely the bodies will be cataloged. Since nobody can contact you, I think they are gone for good . . .

Letting out a sigh, I say gently, "Their bodies are with the constables. As they are the ones who enforce the common law, they will theoretically look into what happened. Although, based on my conversation with the investigator, I would guess this event never occurred, and you and I still do not exist. I'm sorry to say their bodies are likely something we will never see again."

More tears fall down her eyes as she looks down.

"What do you want to do?" is my response to her second question. "Your mom told me you have family on another world. We can try to find them if you want. Do you want that?"

Looking down, she shakes her head.

I lean down so I can look up at her face and ask, "Aria?"

"They'll kill me."

My shoulders slump. She looks stricken, and I realize she thought my slump was in reaction to her not being able to return and its effect on me. Thinking fast, I say, "You can stay with me if you want. At least for a while."

She sniffles, nods, and turns back around. Calling after her, I say, "Aria." She turns her head. "I know it won't make anything better to say it, but I'm so, so sorry."

[What should I do?]

How about starting with some food and clothes? . . .

[Right. Focus on the essentials and survival.]

"Ummm. When I'm struggling with my emotions, I often take a bath or shower. I can get some stuff ready for you when you come out."

She nods slowly and then turns around and heads into her room.

***

I wake up the next day to Aria shoving my shoulder. Opening my eyes, I jerk upright. Aria jumps backwards, looking scared again.

Closing and then opening my eyes slowly and taking a deep breath, I say, "Sorry. Everything okay?"

"Breakfast?" she asks.

"Oh." I smile and say, "You don't have to ask. Just order whatever food you want whenever you want."

She offers a weak smile in return and walks to the big room, I assume to order herself food. I sit up, roll out of bed and do my morning routine. When I get to the main room I see Aria at the table cutting up a huge pancake dripping with syrup.

I smile at her. "Looks good. I'll do that too."

[Order me pancakes please, Jo. Add some sort of berries too.]

After breakfast we are both sticky all over our faces and hands. I look at Aria and say, "Bathing for both of us to reset our minds and we'll see what to do next after." I stand and head towards my shower as she nods and heads towards hers. I do see a small brief flash of a smile, which I take as a good sign.

I make my shower fast because I have work to do, and I don't think Aria should be alone for extended periods. I throw on some loose black cotton sweatpants, a white cotton t-shirt that hugs me tightly, and nothing on my feet. Staying barefoot for now, I look through the various things that Jo bought for me.

[Did you get me a hair tie?]

Look to your left. There is a flexible beast-sinew band . . .

I find it, tie my hair back, and call through Aria's door to let her know I'll be on the balcony.

It takes a moment, but I get an affirmative response, and then I wander back to the same seat looking over the ocean.

[Glass of white wine please, Jo. Bitter.]

One appears.

[Do you think she'll hate me for this?]

I don't think she blames you at all. Neither do I, and I don't think you should either . . .

[So much coin. I know better.]

Vic, you had just come from a disaster of a mission where you were likely betrayed, had your nanos activated, lost all your equipment, nearly died multiple times, met and cared for complete strangers for weeks, hadn't a good night sleep in just as long and had barely arrived alive. I think your actions are understandable . . .

I don't know. I have higher expectations for myself than making a mistake that puts myself and others at risk. Maybe she's right that Aria doesn't blame me, though. Maybe she should. Jo interrupts my guilty contemplations with a message.

Your gunny has responded. Audio only again: "Ha! It's about time you replaced that old fishing rod of yours. You go ahead and buy whatever you need for your-

self and your boat. I got you covered. Contact me when you're ready to head out and I'll be there with my pole."

[That's some good news at least. Alerts?]

You have two from driving Grace . . .

New skill activated. Passive skill [Cycle Driving] now available for use . . .

Skill updated. Passive skill [Cycle Driving] is now level 1 . . .

[I know you showed them to me after the fight, but can you reshow the combat alerts? I couldn't spare the attention at the time, but I did notice something looked odd.]

*You have killed a **Thug**. You absorb 215.37 mana essence . . .*

*You have killed a **Thug**. You absorb 51.88 mana essence . . .*

[Ah. I guess I clipped that second guy.]

Correct. It likely injured the human sufficiently for Grun to kill him. As a result, you received an equivalent portion of the mana essence . . .

As I sit and sip the wine, I think [Give me the total breakdown for Grace. I see no reason to change those plans. Go full MilSpec where available.]

CHAPTER 51

Vehicle Type:	Orzo Motors "Hawk" Mana-Cycle (with Sidecar)	
Vehicle Designation: Grace	Condition: Functional	Reactor Power: 71/*
Offensive Slots:		
	Front (Primary)	Front (Sidecar)
	1. MiliMech .50 Caliber Ballistic Launcher (2 slots)	1. MagiTech R111 Front-facing Hyper Ram
	2. MagiTech R111 Front-facing Hyper Ram	
	3. Disabled	
	Left (Primary)	Left (Sidecar)
	1. MagiTech L330 Semi-Automatic Shotgun	1. Vehicle Attachment
	Right (Primary)	Right (Sidecar)
	1. Sidecar Attachment	1. MagiTech L330 Semi-Automatic Shotgun
	Rear (Primary)	Rear (Sidecar)
	1. Bronco Arms "Hellfire" Repeating Rifle (2 Slots)	1. MagiTech L330 Semi-Automatic Shotgun
	2. Disabled	
	Seat	

	1. MagiTech Lockable 14 Slot Vehicle Spatial Storage Container	
	2. MagiTech N14 Omni-directional Stunner	
Defensive Slots:		
	Shield (Primary)	Shield (Sidecar)
	1. MiliMech Reflective Mana Shield	1. MiliMech Reflective Mana Shield
	Armor (Primary)	Armor (Sidecar)
	1. MiliMech Mana-Infused Specialty Steel Defensive Vehicle Armor	1. MiliMech Mana-Infused Specialty Steel Defensive Vehicle Armor
Miscellaneous Slots:		
	Reactor	
	1. MiliMech High-Capacity Recycling Mana Reactor	
	Targeting System	
	1. MiliMech Self-Targeting Automation System	
	Operating System	
	1. Nanomachine System Consciousness	
	Gravity Plates (Primary)	Gravity Plates (Sidecar)
	1. GravSystems MilSpec Magnetite Gravity Plates	1. GravSystems MilSpec Magnetite Gravity Plates

	Forward-Facing Lights (Primary)	Forward-facing Lights (Sidecar)
	1. MagiTech VL450 Color shifting mana lights	1. MagiTech VL450 Color-Shifting Mana Lights
	Rear-Facing Lights (Primary)	Rear-Facing Lights (Secondary)
	1. MagiTech VL450 Color-Shifting Mana Lights	1. MagiTech VL450 Color-Shifting Mana Lights
	Environmental Lights (Primary)	Environmental Lights (Secondary)
	1. MagiTech VL450 Color-Shifting mana Lights	1.MagiTech VL450 Color-Shifting Mana Lights
	Entertainment Center (Primary)	Entertainment Center (Secondary)
	1. Elegant Entertainment Visual/Audio Optical Projection Communication and Entertainment System	1. Elegant Entertainment Visual/Audio Optical Projection Communication and Entertainment System
	Paint (Primary)	Paint (Sidecar)
	1. MiliMech Mana-Infused Specialty Steel Defensive Vehicle	1. MiliMech Mana-Infused

	Armor - Matte Black	Specialty Steel Defensive Vehicle Armor - Matte Black

Total cost will be 4,576 silver coins. They have agreed to add maintenance on the non-replaced parts and post-work detailing at no cost...

[Excellent. What is the timeframe once ordered?]

Querying...

[Okay. When Aria comes out, we'll go downstairs and empty the seat container. I'll add fifty gold to the Whyatt account on the way back.]

The armory reports eight weeks. For an additional ten percent it can be prioritized to five weeks...

[They can't go any faster?]

No. Parts manufacturing is the bottleneck...

[Damn. Well, nothing we can do. Initiate the order immediately after we're done.]

Affirmative...

I take another sip of the expensive wine.

[Did you send the MilNet authorization?]

I was awaiting your order...

[Do it. Let's hope Gunny can do what he says he can.]

There is one person who could potentially find me through it, but I am confident she won't do anything with the knowledge at this point.

Done. Awaiting a response...

[Make an inquiry into munitions for the shotguns. Both enchanted solid and buckshot. We also need to shop for personal gear, arms, and armor as well. I need to get Aria a spatial container. What do you think she'd like?]

Ask her. She's not a child...

I let out an exasperated sigh.

[I don't know anything about family, Jo. I have no idea how to approach her about it.]

I know, Vic. Maybe you should share your concerns with her. She might have some insight . . .

That is actually a great idea. Ugh. I'm so used to working alone or making the decisions when I have a companion. Shen and Grun would know. The elf would give me some insight into how the world guides us, and the dwarf would probably grump about me and how I treat his girls. I feel a tear falling down my cheek. Damnit.

I cannot get those two out of my mind. I wish they were still here. I'm sorry, guys. I'll try to make it up to you. I probably won't be any good at it, but I'll try to protect your daughter in your stead. Shen would probably help us both learn magica, and Grun could teach me about metals. I let out another deep breath but freeze mid-exhale.

[Wait. You have access to MilNet, right? Can you search for anything we have access to that involves quicksilver?]

Clearance request response received from MilNet. Authorization granted. I will begin the search for data on ore and metal designated quicksilver . . .

[Maybe we'll get lucky.]

Search commencing. That is a rather obscure term, so the search could take a while . . .

Aria pops her head out the doorway and, seeing me, walks over, gives me a light shove, and I scooch over. She sits next to me and lays her head against my arm.

[I'm guessing she'll need comfort like this for a little while.]

Just let her know she is not alone . . .

[I can do that.]

"Hey."

She doesn't say a word, so we just stare out at the ocean together. Despite this, Jo moves things forward. Once again, I'm too distracted to stay focused on the mission.

How much shotgun ammunition would you like me to purchase? . . .

[How much can Grace hold?]

You are getting a fourteen-slot storage container. A lot . . .

[Five thousand rounds each of buckshot and solid shot maybe? Would that take up two slots?]

Of all Grace's new arms, only the shotguns use physical ammunition. Because each is enchanted both to fire and do extra damage, they are effective against anything but direct contact against a mana shield. The others project actual mana. Definitely worth the coin.

Yes, two slots. That will add two silver . . .

[Do it. I don't suppose we have an option for an autoloader?]

Grace does not support any sort of autoloader . . .

#I'm sorry, Host Vic.

I look down at Aria. "Want anything to drink?"

"Water would be good."

A glass of water appears on the pad next to us. I reach over, pick it up, and hand it to her. She sits up, takes a sip, and leans back against me.

[Thanks, Jo.]

I have you both covered . . .

[That's four of us now. You, Grace, Aria, and me.]

#Thank you for including me, Host Vic . . .

[Of course.]

"Hey, I have to go grab some stuff out of the cycle. It's just a quick trip."

She says, "I'll come," rises from the seat, and I follow her back inside. We put on brand-new socks and sneakers and walk down to the pad.

We appear back in the lobby and walk to the vehicle pad where, surprisingly, there is a small line. We step to the back.

The large person in front of me is complaining in a nasally voice about the wait. "For what I pay, I shouldn't have to wait for my truck." Mr. Stuffy is standing there listening with a completely neutral face.

Aria smiles at the scene. I grin down at her and hold a finger to my lips denoting that we should be quiet.

The man glances back at us, gives each of us the up-down check out, huffs, and turns around. Finally, the issue at the front is worked out and Mr. Needs-His-Truck-Now steps up. When he presses his hand to the orb, a massive medium red truck with an open bed in the back appears floating over the pad. Walking to the door, he opens it, looks inside, and starts yelling at Mr. Stuffy again. "You call this a detail? I paid good coin for a detailing job, and I still see dirt on my seat!"

With every word, he gets louder and louder. His arms start waving around while demanding a refund. Then he starts calling the people who worked on his truck all kinds of names, insulting their ancestry and questioning their legitimacy. The rant goes on for a few minutes until Mr. Needs-His-Truck-Now looks like he is running out of mana and starts deflating.

Mr. Stuffy, who had been completely quiet and neutral to that point, finally speaks up. "Sir, I would be happy to have it detailed again at no additional cost. Please return the vehicle so others can proceed with their days." He then steps closer to the man and, without touching him, guides him back to the crystal. Mr. Stuffy closes the deal with, "I will personally assure that the detailing is done to the highest standards. Until it meets my expectations, it will not pass inspection. Now, can I call you a vehicle to take you wherever you wish to go, sir?"

Mr. Needs-His-Truck-Now harrumphs, touches the orb, and his truck vanishes.

Aria, who has moved partially behind me, whispers, "He's good."

I nod. "A consummate professional."

We go up to the floating orb. I touch it, recall Grace, and she appears in a flash.

[You really are a thing of beauty, Grace.]

#Thank you, Host Vic. I would blush if I could . . .

I walk up to the seat, and it flips forward, waiting for me. I touch the small steel box inside.

Transfer complete . . .

Mapping data updated. The maps also contain highlights from Commander Franklin. I have noted them on your map. Would you like to absorb the container too?

[Yes.]

The steel box vanishes, and I walk back to the orb and Aria. The seat closes itself, I touch the orb, and Grace goes back into storage.

[Enjoy your time in the shop. And watch for any funny business while they're messing about with your innards.]

#Of course, Host Vic. Nobody will be putting anything inside where it does not belong . . .

You two are making me ill. I cannot get ill . . .

Aria and I walk back to the lobby and to the front desk. "I need to see an account manager, please."

I have a private conversation in his office while adding fifty gold to my Whyatt account. No more mistakes.

Initiate the vehicle upgrade requests with prioritization? . . .

[Confirm.]

Order complete. Twenty-five gold, seventeen silver, and ninety copper has been withdrawn from your Whyatt account as a downpayment . . .

[Did you get a map and store list for Sea Saddle City yet?]

Not yet. The best auto-updating map will cost twenty copper and then one copper per week. It covers everything on the continent. I require your authorization . . .

I sigh. [Do it. Can you pay in advance?]

Yes. How many weeks would you like? . . .

[Do it for a year and then auto-renew. That is not worth my time.]

Seventy-two copper has been withdrawn from your Whyatt account . . .

I look over at Aria, give her a nudge to get her attention, and ask, "You want to get some bling?"

CHAPTER 52

Mr. Stuffy gets us a MAD, for which I pay for the safe travel option, and it takes us to a store that Jo says specializes in fancy spatial containers.

We step inside, and I am nearly blinded by all the sparkles. Aria looks around, baffled and then, realizing what this store offers, smiles at me. I'm pleased with that reaction; her smile is much better than her glare. Or glower. Or . . . never mind. It's better.

"Get whatever you want. I only ask that you have at a minimum twelve available slots for storage. Is that fair?"

Aria nods, thanks me, and wanders off.

This might be a good opportunity to stock up as well. You require substantial absorption to evolve your skill . . .

[Tell me which ones to buy, and I'll buy them.]

You need to touch them for me to tell you . . .

So I pick up a little padded bronze basket and, like the blue-haired freak I am, walk through a bling store and touch every shiny object in sight. Occasionally Jo tells me to pick one up or put one back, so I do and throw one into the basket or return another to the wrong place.

I am about two-thirds of the way through a bowl filled with rings that only cost twenty-five coppers each when I touch one that looks like it is made entirely of green jade. Jade is very hard to come by now because all the mines are controlled by the enemy. I wonder why it is so cheap. A fake maybe?

STOP! . . .

I jump slightly from Jo's yell in my head.

[What? What is it?]

That jade ring is very bizarre. It has an unusual type of spatial pocket. Buy it . . .

[Okay, then. No need to yell.]

Stop being a baby . . .

#*I concur. Host Vic is a baby . . .*

I sigh.

A half-hour later, I have touched nearly everything in the store and have a basket filled with what is, in my opinion, utter junk. Aria picked out two containers. One is a silver ring with an azure gem that looks like my eyes and hair set in the middle. The gem doesn't stick out—it is set in the middle of the silver.

I find her second choice fascinating. It is actually a matching pair of earrings. They are also silver with a small azure gem.

Glancing at the pointed ears covered by her blond hair, I ask, "Will you need your ears pierced?"

She shakes her head.

Looking at an ancient-looking dwarf lady behind the counter I ask, "What is your name, ma'am?"

The old woman says her name is Wundala.

"Well, Miss Wundala" —I plop my basket onto the counter with a jangle next to Aria's purchases with a smile— "I think we're done."

***

Three gold, twenty-two silver, and forty-five copper later, we are back in the hotel room. Aria takes her purchases and goes to her room. I walk onto the balcony with my bag of containers and sit down.

[What now, boss? What are my total available funds by the way?]

Over 250 gold in various denominations. Let me worry about the details . . .

[Works for me.]

Now before we get to absorbing spatial containers, I want to propose two things. One I think you'll be fine with and the other I think you might bite my head off . . .

[You're my closest friend, confident, and future wife. I can't get that angry at you.]

I'm serious, Vic. I'm going to propose something you won't like . . .

I'm quiet for a moment when I think, [Order me a glass of water please.]

When one appears and I take a few gulps, I take a deep breath.

[Okay. Tell me the one I won't like.]

Let me preface with a little background. When evolving a skill, the chance of success increases the stronger and more various the magica around the skill is. As an example, your fire was crazy strong, and it evolved based on how you forced it into a projectile form, which fire does not have by itself. So you had strength and variety. With me so far? . . .

[Yes.] I drink more water, fearing I know where this is going.

[Inventory] is an affinity-free, mana-based skill. Just pure mana. That means your general mana should be strong, which it is. And it also means your mana should have a lot of variety. On this one, we both believe you are lacking where I am confident you could be. So I propose you activate more affinities . . .

[Such as earth . . . and life.] Jo is silent for a few seconds.

Yes . . .

I sit back in the chair and stare at the ocean.

[You understand what you are asking me to ask Aria to do?]

Yes . . .

I watch the ocean, sipping at my water and thinking about the poor woman in my suite. She's lost so much, and based on what Shen said, the only people she had were those she just lost.

[You know, I am almost a hundred percent sure Grun is not her biological father. She called him Grun but Shen her mother.]

There are no half-and-half children that humanity knows about. No matter the parent, the child is always fully one or the other species. The biology is beyond me; it is just widely accepted as truth and confirmed by our allies.

I agree . . .

[But he was the only father she ever knew. He cared for her, loved her, and in the end sacrificed himself for her.]

Yes . . .

[She needs time. At least I assume she does. I refuse to use her that way despite the benefit to me and humanity. I have to draw a line. Not to mention that neither of us understands the risks.]

Fair enough. For what it's worth, I'm happy for you . . .

I blink. Happy for me?

[Why?] My confusion must be obvious in my tone because I hear a sigh.

How many people would cause you to draw that line? . . .

Oh. Thinking through the list, I respond.

[There are a handful of people I would place at having higher value if kept alive than granting me the ability to self-heal.]

And how many of those would you leave alive because you "Won't use them that way," rather than the cost-to-reward ratio? . . .

Oh. I finally figure out where she is trying to direct my thoughts . . .

[You feel Aria has compromised my emotional state again?] Another sigh follows.

Define compromised in this case. Vic, I think you feel affection for her. Perhaps like family . . .

[What the fuck would I know about family?]

Jo is silent for a few moments but then says,

Let's put this aside for now. Maybe it will become apparent later . . .

[I think that is a good idea. But I'll reflect on it. Back to what you were saying about affinities. Trying to activate earth should be possible based on our experiences to date. In theory, at least. We just need to find the right place. What other affinities do you think I can activate?]

If you can do earth, you should be able to activate nature because you already have water, and nature is a compilation of the two. I'd recommend ice, magma, light, darkness, life, and death, but I can only think of a way to activate life, which we have already discussed . . .

[Are those all the affinities?]

Those, plus the ones you have, are all the affinities humanity has activated . . .

[You phrased that in a particular way on purpose, didn't you?]

Yes. My data is behind by many years, as you know, but there was speculation at the time that different species may have one or two affinities unique to them . . .

[Why can't you do a complete database update from MilNet?]

Unfortunately, your access to MilNet is read-only. You do not have the clearance to copy data beyond record numbers. I report what I find while accessing but cannot maintain those records in my nanomachine structure . . .

[Damn. While we're on the topic anything on quicksilver?]

No new information at this time. I am still searching . . .

[For your next search, focus on finding all the different kinds of affinities and ways known to activate them.]

Confirmed...

[Okay, so plan A is to open affinities. See what locations you can find that are safe and match what we need to activate earth and nature.]

Searching...

[While you are doing that, what's plan B?]

I think it is time for you to level up...

CHAPTER 53

I give myself a mental forehead slap.

[I completely forgot about that. So sell me on it. Why should I convert my essence? How much do I have by the way?]

You currently have 11,159.01 stored mana essence...

[Wow. That feels like a lot.]

It is and it isn't. Since the amount of essence required for nanomachines to evolve increases by fifty percent each time they evolve, this amount will only get you to level four. So while it is a lot for a level zero, it isn't that much in the greater scheme of things...

[Ouch. That makes leveling at higher levels nearly impossible.]

That is correct. I am confident it was built that way intentionally. As the primary way to gather essence is through combat, and humans give seventy-five percent less essence than any other creature, this system encourages humans to fight beasts or Invaders. It is a clever way to motivate humans...

[And I thought I got so little essence from those thugs because they were weak. Man, imagine what the bear would have given me.]

They were weak and *they were human. Together that resulted in the pittance you received. Move on from the bear, Vic...*

[Fine! Anyway, back on topic. Why should I level up?]

The number one reason is it will advance the overall learning ability of your nanomachines, which improves evolution chances. Second, it will strengthen your body, although we do not know how until after the conversion. The nanos change based on how a host has been using them. So someone who has a heavy focus on their physical strength will likely have that advance or improve during a level up. You are a freak, so I haven't even a guess what will happen...

[Okay. You sold me. Is it painful? Should I go to my room and let Aria know so she doesn't panic?]

As I said I do not know what will happen, so it would be wise I think...

[Do you think we should activate the affinities first?]

That is something of a cockatrice and an egg argument. If you level, your nanos are smarter and able to activate affinities easier. However, if you gain affinities you strengthen your overall nanos which make the level up more effective . . .

[Not helpful. Let me think for a bit.]

What would be the best options? I understand the choice is between guaranteed power now and unknown but possibly greater power later. Affinities. What do they give me? Fire and air have basically kept me alive. Water hasn't impressed, but likely I don't know how to use it right. Lightning is nasty and fantastic but also not great for stealth. I need more variety of affinities, but my actual level of power seems okay. Sure, the bear would have kicked my ass, but a single level could not have changed that outcome. In the end, a single level versus the potential for strengthening through a greater variety of power feels right.

[Okay, I think activating affinities first is the right choice.]

Understood. I have found two locations that could meet the need. The one I recommend is the Botanical Gardens, which is open to the public. It would make for a nice picnic as well . . .

[What is the weather supposed to be like tomorrow?]

Overcast but rain-free . . .

Walking inside, I see Aria huddled asleep on the couch. I notice she is wearing the ring and earrings. Gently picking her up, I bring her into her room and lay her on the bed.

I order myself a snack, take another long hot bath, put on my PJ pants, climb into bed, and fall asleep quickly.

***

I wake up to the smell of bacon. Rolling out of bed, I do my morning thing and head to the dining table. Aria has toast, some sort of scrambled eggs, and bacon. I reach to grab a slice, and she nearly stabs me with her fork. I jerk my hand away and look at her. She is chewing and glaring at me.

All she can say is "Bacon. Mine" between bites.

Knowing when to retreat, I throw my hands up and ask Jo to order me the same breakfast.

After eating and feeling pleasantly stuffed, I ask Aria, "How does a picnic sound for lunch?"

Looking at me quizzically, she asks, "What's a picnic?"

"Oh." I smile. "It's when we sit outdoors and eat food with our hands while on a blanket on the ground."

"Is that a human thing?"

I shrug. "I have no idea. Never been on one myself."

She sighs and says, "Sure. Why not?"

"Great, after we digest a little we'll go to a place called the Botanical Gardens, hang there for a bit, and eat a picnic."

[Please order picnic material in a little basket in an hour.]

Confirmed . . .

[It just occurred to me we need to get Aria an earcomm. That way we aren't handicapped by distance. And you can introduce yourself.]

That is an excellent idea. I could use an intelligent individual to speak to . . .

[Funny.]

"Hey, we need to get you an ear canal communicator or 'earcomm' for short. Just about everyone on this world has a sort of communicator, and earcomms are the most common by far. It will allow us to reach each other if required while not physically in the same place. Is that okay?"

She nods. I slowly stand. "Great. Let's go down to the armory. We can digest as we walk. I understand it's pretty big down there."

The infusion pad asks me which floor of the armory I wish to head to. It turns out the armory takes up the first six floors of the hotel (well, after the lobby). Floors one and two are where they do all their vehicle maintenance and upgrades. Those are off-limits to non-armory personnel. Each floor above that is broken out by type of armament. The third floor is for offensive armaments, the fourth defensive, and the fifth miscellaneous. I find it funny how they chose to base personal armaments after the vehicle armament system. The sixth floor is entirely set aside for ammunition and is heavily reinforced. The orb tells me there are all kinds of restrictions about what can and cannot be brought to that floor. Either way, I know where to go to find Aria's communicator.

We flash to the fifth floor and almost immediately, a gnome with pale skin and white hair, wearing an outfit matching Mr. Stuffy, walks up to us. In a high-pitched voice he asks, "Welcome to Whyatt Armory, can I help you find anything?"

All of this fancy personal service is sort of getting to me. Why would I need him to help me find something when a crystal-based inventory system could offer me the same thing? Rich people are weird.

Gesturing at Aria, I say, "My companion here requires a compact in-ear communicator. It should have the longest possible range and the strongest possible receiver and encryption. I have authorization for MilSpec purchases."

Knowing he is potentially getting a decent-sized commission, the gnome bows with a massive smile and says, "Of course, sir and miss. Please follow me."

We do as instructed, taking a circuitous route through the massive facility (I'm sure so he can show off his merchandise). The gnome walks to a door in a corner that looks nondescript and plain.

Turning, he explains, "All purchases requiring military authorization are done here." He opens the door, bows again, waves his hand at the entranceway like he is introducing a celebrity, and says, "Please get comfortable."

The outside might have looked like a warehouse. But behind this door is an ostentatious room lit by floating white-yellow mana lights that causes everything to sparkle slightly. A bar with gnome bartender is against one wall; a buffet filled with steaming food is next to it. Several tables of different sizes to seat different size parties dot the room.

I glance at the gnome, who follows us in, and he sees the question on my face. "Pick any table you like and feel free to use the buffet and bar. I will be bringing the topics of our discussion."

I lead Aria to a table with four chairs and say, "I know we just ate, but go ahead to the buffet and get whatever you want. I'll hit the bar. What would you like to drink?"

Looking at the buffet, she says, "Water is great. Thanks."

She then wanders towards the dessert area and fills a tray with a variety of sweet foods. As she returns and sits with her tray, I give her a raised eyebrow.

She blushes slightly and says, "I never really got to have sweets before—" I see a brief flicker of pain, and then she clears her throat. "Well, before. I want to see what I like."

At the table, Aria is eating some bright blue goop that jiggles as she sticks her spoon in. I have never really been into sweets due to the requirements my career has placed on my body. I also just don't like the taste. Fruit is okay in moderation, but pure sweets make me ill. Shaking my head, I just sip my wine and scan the room. I glance at the far wall's single-pane mirror, leading me to believe we are being watched from the other side. I wonder what they expect to happen. Have they done anything about their security breach and poor hiring practices? Maybe I can ask.

An unfamiliar gnome walks up to the table holding an open-topped metal box under his arm and asks, "May I join you for our business discussion?"

This gnome's voice is high pitched like all their kind, but his has a compassion to it that other did not.

I nod. "Of course. Thank you for asking." They train these guys well.

He sits and places the box in his lap. Well done again; he didn't put the box on the table. "Based on your requirements and the size of the young lady, we have four options for you. They vary in features and capabilities. Are there any brands or companies you particularly wish to avoid?"

"No Magitech liquid steel."

He nods and takes out a metal box with a latch. "This is a MagiTech model. Standard crystal." Flipping it open, I see a typical inner earpiece, if small. It is a clear crystal in the general shape of the inside of an ear. I see a subtle white glow coming from it. "This is the most advanced that MagiTech offers in regards to signal strength. It has been tested to receive a direct mana signal from over seventy-five kilometers. The encryption is the highest available in the civilian market, but no higher. It also does not have the ability to change color or shape."

Taking out a second box, he continues his product description monologue. "This is a MiliMech model. MiliMech may be known for their vehicles, weapons, and armor, but that does not mean they do nothing else. This is their first foray into the communication market. Prior to this, they have always subcontracted out any comm equipment. In short, this is the first release. Something of a beta model, if you will. It has a range of eighty-five kilometers and supports MilSpec encryption based on the user's level. In our testing, its current weakness is that it appears a bit fragile. We have had a few models fail when under heavy physical or magical stress. They are currently working to resolve it."

Aria goes to get more dessert. I wonder where she puts it all.

A third box then joins the other two on the table. "Verdant Communications' MilSpec ear communicator. This is the standard for most military operations. If you served, which I believe you did or perhaps do, you will have undoubtedly used this type. Its range is sixty-five kilometers, with high durability and standard, if not spectacular MilSpec encryption."

Aria rejoins the table, and I hear her spoon clacking again.

He takes a breath like he is working himself up to something. This time no box joins the others. "This last one is something of a flight of fancy that occurred to me when I saw your companion." He slowly reaches into his box and takes out something I would expect to see in the bling shop from yesterday. It is a flip-top red box dotted with shiny jewels. Curious now, I flip it open and inside I see a single earring. It is a simple stud with a clear crystal. The clinking of Aria's spoon stops. I look over at her, but she only has eyes for the earring.

[Damn, he's good.]

Indeed . . .

#*I'm getting blinged too. I can't wait to try my environmental lights . . .*

I am in so much trouble.

"What you are looking at is the result of a collaborative effort between Whyatt Armory, VersaComm, and Elegant Entertainment. You see, we here at Whyatt Armory accept and believe that this is a violent world. Beasts, Invaders, even other humanoids are a threat to us all. All-day every day, we are at risk. That being said, not everyone wants to look like they are carrying around an armory as they socialize.

"However, our customers do tell us, and our sales prove, they can and wish to be safe while looking and feeling good. Some want to look elegant, some relaxed. Some want shiny bling, some want slinky black. We at Whyatt, and many others, have entire product lines to protect individuals but maintain, what they view as, an acceptable level of social appeal." He stops for a moment and clears his throat.

"I realize I never introduced myself. My name is Filckerson Clinkerforth Whyatt, and I am a vice-chancellor here at Whyatt Armory. I tell you this so you will believe what I am about to say. This earring is a brand new product, not for sale yet, and we haven't announced the collaboration at this time.

"The reason is because we are offering two models. One is for the civilian sector and is still in R&D. The other model is the one you see before you and is designed for military personnel. In fact— " Glancing at Aria quickly, he looks back at me and has a question in his eyes. She is still staring at the earring but has started eating again. Somehow she hasn't spilled a drop despite not looking at what she is doing.

"It's fine, go ahead," I confirm.

He nods and continues. "In fact, this model was built with Special Forces or intelligence personnel in mind. It has the ability to mimic its surroundings and slightly modify its shape. You are not pleased with MagiTech's liquid steel products?" My lips tighten together, and I nod curtly. He continues. "Well, neither are we. While we sell it, we have found the product to be . . . questionable and always make our customers aware of the risks."

Pointing at the earring, he continues. "This—we haven't named the product line yet—is made of something we are calling FlexCrystal. The primary problem with liquid steel is the controller system. It can be manipulated externally. FlexCrystal has an entirely self-contained controller and will only accept outside influence at first development. In other words, we build each earring to be unique both visually and mechanically to each individual customer."

Taking another deep breath, he continues. "I am 422 of your years old, and I have lived and thrived in this world for over seventy years, although I visited numerous times before moving here permanently. In fact, I was one of the first to meet your people and introduce them to magica-based technology. I have helped build a successful business on this planet, and I want to see it succeed. As such, I do everything I can to help humanity survive the orc threat. I want humanity to thrive and take back its land. And I want it to do that armed with Whyatt Armory gear."

He then takes something else out of the box, and what it is shocks me to my core.

CHAPTER 54

He takes out a miniature model of Bertha and delicately places it before me. After another deep breath, he says, "I know you, Michael Uriel 'Vic' Victory. I know you are an orphan who was raised by the military. I know you entered the active service before the legal age and, because of your natural gifts, were recruited almost immediately into a classified sub-section of the UFH's Special Forces called the Knight Hunters.

"I know that at age fifteen, though you thought you fooled everyone because you looked mature, you got your first sniper kill of an enemy Invader. It was an orc general, and it caused them to lose nearly three thousand troops in the infighting and confusion. I know at the age of eighteen, you were the human who successfully infiltrated the enemy harbor city of Baltic Moores and disabled the harbor defenses, allowing for it to be retaken by a joint oceanic assault of humans, elves, dwarves, and beastkin. I know at the age of nineteen, you set a bridge trap and detonated it from two kilometers away via sniper shot. The collapse of that bridge killed thirty-two thousand enemy troops, including three tribal chieftains, and delayed an enemy offensive, buying enough time for UFH forces to redeploy, saving the city of Bostonia. I know that at the age of twenty-two, you maintained the highest mission success rate of any Knight Hunter. I know that the following year, at age twenty-four, you achieved the milestone of having the highest number of sniper kills in recorded human history using your favorite weapon, Bertha."

He taps the small figurine.

"I know that for the last three years, the Knight Hunters have loaned you out to MagiTech on dual-purpose missions of helping them test their gear and taking out key enemy personnel. I know that on your last mission, something went terribly wrong. And I know you are lying low to figure out who you can trust and what to do about it."

I conduct a quick scan for threats and exits. The bartender has at least one weapon behind the bar, likely two. Based on his arm positioning, I'd say one is a shotgun and one a hand projector. Mr. Whyatt appears unarmed, but that means nothing. I glance at Aria, who is staring open-mouthed at the gnome and then returns my gaze. She closes her mouth, slowly puts down her spoon, and stands up. The gnome and I are watching her. She steps over to me, dragging her chair and places it to my left. She then sits and leans against my shoulder.

She just told him and me two things. The first is that she understands at least some of what is going on. The second is that if there is violence, whatever happens to me, happens to her too. Even after everything that has happened, she is willing to risk more violence. She is being braver than I can even imagine.

I look from her back at the gnome and say, "So what now?"

His smile nearly splits his face in half. "Indeed, I was right about you. That is the question, isn't it? What now?" He glances at the elf leaning into me and says, "Someday we will have another conversation about Shentriss Morianni Natura Riverwing and Arialla Frystera Livera Riverwing." I feel Aria give a slight jerk at those names. "But today, we will talk about something else. I have already told you what I *know*. If you will allow me, I'd like to tell you what I **believe**." He waits for my response. I nod. "Thank you."

And he honestly sounds thankful that I would allow him to tell me what he believes.

"I believe that you serve humanity with all your being. Humanity, not the UFH, or Magitech, or even the military. Humanity. I believe something greater is going on that you know and that I, with my considerable access to information, can find out. And that . . . concerns me. When I don't have sufficient information, I cannot make sound business decisions.

"I believe, like you, what happened on your last mission was not an accident. At least not all of it. I believe you are going to need more help than your old compatriots at the club or your gunny can provide. And this is the big one. I believe you are the oldest newly activated Special in almost a century and a half."

He just looks at me, waiting. I nod.

He nods in response. "I believe something is a little off about your activation; whether it is a bug or benefit, I cannot say. But something went wrong, or right, when you activated your nanos. Either way, I believe you are not a strong enough Special to take on the coming battles. Not yet. And finally, I believe you have a set of hard decisions ahead of you. Some involve that young elf next to you. And some will involve others, including my business and thus my family.

"I asked to take on your account because I think we can help each other. I would like to become business partners of a sort. I will sell and even give you priority access to certain things to help you kill the enemy and find answers. You will do just that, kill the enemies of humanity and find answers to questions. I feel confident saying these are all things you were planning on doing anyway.

"Oh. And please accept my deepest apologies and condolences on your loss and our failure. We are working to prevent something like that from happening again but for now, I consider Whyatt to owe you. We have added an additional level of security to your suite in an attempt to avoid future issues. And please accept this as the first form of apology." He pushes back his chair, stands up, places the box on the table, and puts everything back into it except the earring box, which he pockets.

"As for my proposal, you don't have to answer today. Take a few days and spend them together. Peaceful times are rare—enjoy them while they last. See you in a few weeks."

He turns and walks away, leaving the box.

***

Aria and I are back on our balcony, staring out at the ocean, drinking from water glasses. This time we are each in our own seats.

"You have questions?" I ask.

She glances over at me. "Is everything he said true?"

I nod. "Everything about me, yes."

She is quiet again.

Taking a drink of water, I ask, "Are you scared of me now?" This is my first thought.

She looked over at me with a surprised look. "Why would you ask that?"

"Aria, I am a violent man. A killer. A murderer. I'm responsible for the deaths of tens of thousands. Why *wouldn't* I scare you?"

All she says is "You don't."

I guess I have to accept that. "Let's have dinner and call it a day. If that's okay with you?"

She nods and we head in.

Shame about the picnic.

After dinner, I pace for a while feeling antsy. I haven't done any sort of workout nor gotten any material exercise since we came to Sea Saddle City. I need to do something physical.

[Is there an exercise room in this place?]

Floors fifty and fifty-one are set aside for physical activity. Fifty has MagiTech machines for strengthening and increasing flexibility. Floor fifty-one is set aside as a dojo and martial training center. While floor fifty is included in part of the room fee, there is additional cost for use of the dojo . . .

I peek my head into Aria's room and call through the bathroom door to ask her if it is all right if I leave her alone in the room to go get some exercise on floor fifty. There is no answer for a bit, and I'm worried she might be scared.

Eventually, I hear a muffled "I'll go with you."

I hear splashing and shuffling, and she comes barreling out of the bathroom drying herself with a towel. I quickly jerk my head out and close the door.

"Aria, you should be aware that humans are more conservative about being naked in front of each other. Next time, tell me you are coming out, and I'll give you privacy."

There is no answer until the door slides aside. She is wearing sweats and a t-shirt like me. She says "You'll get used to it" and then leads the way to the pad. I doubt it, but whatever. Touching the crystal, we port to floor fifty.

The exercise room is as expected, with MagiTech machines of different types grouped together and spread out.

"Has anyone taught you how to exercise properly?"

She scowls but shakes her head.

I guide her to some soft grav plates and I show her how to stretch. I emphasize that stretching is critical to a good life and anyone who doesn't stretch is a bad guy to be shot. She laughs occasionally when I adjust her body. Apparently, she is ticklish, so I stay away from those parts and just try to point and direct her movements.

Completing the stretch, I say to her, "When you exercise your muscles, you always do a warmup." I direct Aria to a machine called "MagiTech EX09 Running Assistant." It has a place for her to stand and some bars to grip. I press the crystal and tell her, "Start walking."

She does, and the glowing squares beneath her feet start to glow. She is walking in place and the glow seems to chase after her feet. The lights move faster, and she begins a light jog. I leave her to it while taking the machine next to her and warm up with a strong run.

After an hour of strengthening, both by myself and with her, we do another jog-walking cooldown, and I ask her, "Did you enjoy that? Is it something you want to do more of?"

Covered head to toe in sweat, she wipes her face with a towel. "I don't know about 'enjoy,' but I want to make it a habit. Maybe I'll find I like it later."

"That's smart. For me, I need to do this or I'll go crazy." I guide her to a crystal panel and ask for an assistant to help create an exercise plan for her. She is scanned to get her physical measurements.

You are being asked to prioritize the workout for her . . .

I select the order of priority:

1. *Flexibility*
2. *Stamina*
3. *Strength*

You have received a detailed exercise plan for Aria . . .

Shrugging, I do the same with a different Priority.

1. *Strength*
2. *Flexibility*
3. *Stamina*

You have received a detailed exercise plan for yourself . . .

Turning to Aria, I say, "Starting tomorrow, we do this in the morning after a light breakfast. Is that okay?"

She nods.

We are both sweaty messes, so we immediately go back to the room, bathe, and go to bed.

[I should go back to controlling my food intake. I'm spoiled by all this rich stuff.]

You could always live off the food bars . . .

[Ugh, no thank you.]

I look at my inventory and see the fourteen food bars. Blech. Might as well check what's in here. During the food search, I notice that still sitting there in the first slot is Mr. Stinky. Another forehead slap ensues.

[Can you please find a place where I can sell Mr. Stinky's carcass? I know time is slow in there, but still. It's nasty.]

You can sell it to Whyatt Armory, although you likely won't get the best price...

[I don't care about the money so much as I do putting all of our coin in one holding bag. Let's diversify and sell to an outside shop. At least for now.]

Searching for a competitive facility with a good reputation...

[I assume we have no alerts since we haven't done anything?]

Correct...

[All right, see you in the morning.]

CHAPTER 55

I wake suddenly to Aria's scream. I leap out of bed, nearly blow the door between our rooms apart, and storm into her room, looking around and forming a windblade. I see her sitting up in her bed, gasping for breath. Her face is covered in tears, her body glistening with sweat and her expression terrified. I see no threat, so I dismiss the air magica.

Panting from the adrenaline, exertion and outburst of magica, I ask quickly, "What happened? Are you all right?"

She's shaking again but getting control of herself. "Sorry. Sorry." Taking slower deeper breaths, she says "Sorry" one last time. "I occasionally have nightmares."

Relaxing my body slightly, I say, "Oh. I'm sorry to hear that. That can be terrible." I don't tell her that I know because I had them nearly every night for nearly fifteen years. What good would it do? "Do you need anything?"

She has control of herself again. "No, thanks. I'll just wash up and go back to bed after a bit."

Nodding, I say, "All right. Well, you know where I am if you need anything. Don't hesitate to wake me up."

I return to my room but struggle to fall back asleep, failing to empty my mind of the past once again.

***

I do manage to sleep because I wake to the sun on my face.

[Looks like it could be picnic weather today?]

Yes. Sunny even, as shocking as that is for this area. I also found a place for you to sell the carcass. It is even near the gardens. I also have failed to find anything you are authorized to see on quicksilver. I switched my search to affinities and have found quite a bit of material. Unfortunately, we already know most of it. I am filtering and will let you know when anything worthwhile comes up . . .

[Let's check what is in Mr. Whyatt's box.] I shuffle over slightly and grab the box from the side table. There is a note telling me not to [Inventory] the box.

First, I pick out the model of Bertha. I run my finger along her. It is a marvelous model with stunning detail. It even has my little add-ons and the signs of use she gained over the years. How did he do that? I miss her.

I put Bertha back in and take a look inside. I see the three boxes with the communicators, six small crystals with almost no glow, and a storage collar container that is too small for me but just right for Aria.

[Any ideas on the crystals?]

None...

I reach in and pick one up.

Accessing...

This appears to be a primer on the Elven language. Do you wish to load the data?...

[Definitely. How does that work? I can suddenly speak it? That sounds absurd.]

You are correct; that would be absurd. I can now translate and read Elven on your behalf. Speaking will take training and practice just like everything else; it will simply be easier. Mr. Whyatt clearly knew, or strongly suspected, you were a Special before he even walked in ...

I pick up another.

Accessing...

This is the same but with Dwarvish. Do you wish to load the data?

[Yes.]

Fifteen minutes later, I finish loading all the crystals. I am very appreciative of Mr. Whyatt's "gifts." Two of the remaining four crystals are languages. One is Gnomish and the other, surprisingly, is Orcish. I accept and figure I now have some studying to do. The question is, which is the priority?

Of the last two data crystals, one contains updated maps of the entire continent, including the latest locations of friendly and enemy camps. Jo and I agree that is likely the most valuable of Whyatt's gifts. The last crystal contains, of all things, data on botany. It has intel on local mana-infused carnivorous plants and how to spot them, herbs and how to collect them, and poisonous flora and what effects their toxins have. After Jo loads that data, she gives me a surprise.

You have alerts from the last two crystals. There was hidden data...

Stiffening, I ask, "Is it harmful?"

No. Quite the opposite. However, now that I am aware, we can check before loading...

[Which I am sure he knew. Likely this was a warning. He's trying to show he can help. Display the alerts.]

New skill activated. Passive skill [Cartography] now available for use...

New skill activated. Passive skill [Herbology] now available for use...

Skill updated. Passive skill [Cartography] has leveled from 0 to 2...

Skill updated. Passive skill [Botany] is now level 2...

Skill updated. Passive skill [Herbology] has leveled from 0 to 2...

[Isn't that interesting? I have so many questions. Is that the max for an externally loaded skill update or does he have a system that can measure the amount of data exactly? Or is it because it is geographically limited to just this area of the continent? Or is it simply the exact amount of data to get all three to level two?

Those are all good questions, and I haven't a clue...

I am finally at the last item in the box, the storage collar. I touch it.

[Jo?]

Accessing... It is encrypted with a statement and response answer for the key...

[He must believe we can figure this out. What is the statement?]

One phrase, "Pygmy-wolf"...

My mind goes blank for a moment. I cannot believe he knows. How can he know? It's not possible. Everybody who knows is dead. Why did he choose that? Is he telling me he can know impossible things?

Vic?...

[Response is "Stavros."]

Confirmed. Accessing...

Access granted...

Accessing spatial storage...

CHAPTER 56

This spatial storage device is extraordinary. It only has four slots, but those four actually slow down mana decay. With the exception of mana stone boxes, that is supposed to be impossible for non-Specials. I cannot get an exact measurement of time distortion until worn and something is stored within it . . .

[No wonder he encrypted it with something only I would know.] Or at least I *thought* it was something only I would know.

[We'll give it to Aria when she wakes up.]

I put everything back in the box and get up. I do my morning thing and order some fruit. Then I wake up Aria with a shoulder shake. "Hey. Time to wake up." She stirs, blinks her eyes, and yawns. "Have some fruit, then we're off to do our workout."

She does well in her first controlled workout. She seems surprisingly into it, considering her inexperience. Then I remember she is twice my age and shake my head.

[Hey, Jo. It just occurred to me that Aria will outlive me by millennia.]

Yes, she will. Why does that occur to you now? . . .

[It means I need to train her as much as possible while I am still able. Let's make sure she is ready to survive when I'm dust.]

Morbid but true . . .

[That means I need to get stronger. Fast.]

On the way to the pad, I say, "It's beautiful out today. Let's do the botanical garden and picnic."

She nods.

We have omelets for breakfast, with bacon of course, and head to clean ourselves.

[Please order the picnic stuff. Thank you for holding off before; it would have been a waste of food.]

Confirmed . . .

Wearing shorts and t-shirts, and Aria her new storage collar, we ask Mr. Stuffy to get us a ride. I instruct the MAD to drop us first at Sea Saddle City's Central Butchery and Beast Collection. Paying for it to wait, Aria and I enter the stone building.

The first thing I notice is the fattest dwarf I have ever seen. Not that he is easy to miss with a cleaver the size of a battle-axe waving about, chopping up what appears to be an antlered bear the size of Mr. Needs-His-Truck-Now's truck.

Before I can even begin speaking, he says, "Use the panel."

I close my mouth and walk over to the panel I put my hand on it.

Sea Saddle City's Central Butchery and Beast Collection	
Options:	
1.	Buying
2.	Selling
3.	Picking Up An Order

I like this shop already. I select two.

Sea Saddle City's Central Butchery and Beast Collection	
Selling:	
1.	Mammal
2.	Fish
3.	Insect
4.	Other

I select three. I know spiders are not technically insects, but really—it's not like there is an "arachnid" option.

Sea Saddle City's Central Butchery and Beast Collection
Please wait for assistance

Sure. So we stand there. Aria is transfixed by the butchering. It is certainly impressive. In the back, a mana shield fades, and another dwarf walks out. She is young and spry and looks excited to see us.

Without another word she says, "I understand you have insect life? What kind? How long has it been dead? What is the condition of the carcass? Well, why are you just standing there for? Follow me to the measurement pad."

I glance at Aria who is blinking at the woman. We follow the excited lady to the side where a five-by-three-meter black pad sits. A green crystal is floating next to it.

[Can you extract the mana stone from the spider in the inventory slot?]

Done . . .

I see another of my slots filled with the image of a little brown stone.

Kneeling down, I touch the pad, and what's left of Mr. Stinky drops with a crunch and clatter.

Aria jumps back. The dwarven lass does the opposite and leans towards it excitedly. She calls out, to herself I think. "Wow. Impressive. Old but not rotting much. I've never seen one like this before. Let's see what we got."

She leans back and touches the floating crystal. The green plate lights up and there is a green glow as the nature Magica detects all kinds of details on the spider. A green screen pops up facing the three of us.

Sea Saddle City's Central Butchery and Beast Collection	
Carcass Assessment:	
Type:	Acidic Mana-Engorged Hobo Spider
Remains Available:	0.55 of 1.00
Rarity:	Very High
Sell Value:	Unknown

"Well, I'll be a gnomish plumber. A new species we have no value for." Then she yells so loud Aria has to cover her ears. "Hey Pa, get your fat ass over here. You need to see this!"

There is a huge bang as the fat dwarf slams his battle-axe/cleaver into the block he is cutting on and stomps over. I swear I can feel the ground shake.

Aria and I shove over to make room for him as he stands there staring at Mr. Stinky. Then he glances up at the screen.

He "Humphs" and his whole body wobbles. Then he says in the normal gravelly voice of a dwarf, "I canna pay ya fa thi na. I duno wha I ca ge." I nod at him. Remembering what Jo told me about dwarves, I jump to the end. "Can I give you or your daughter my contact information and you can get back to me? I will likely be back anyway with more carcasses as some point."

He also nods and says, "Tha works." The daughter touches the green orb and Jo says,

Request for contact information received from Sea Saddle City's Central Butchery and Beast Collection . . .

[Approve.]

Sent . . .

"Thank you." I say as we turn to leave. They ignore us completely. The big guy heads back to butcher via battle-axe and his daughter practically dives inside Mr. Stinky she is so close. Bye, Mr. Stinky.

VOLUME 5 - AFFINITY AFICIONADO

CHAPTER 57

The Botanical Gardens is a mana-shielded stretch of controlled nature in Sea Saddle City approximately one by one-half kilometer in size. Broken down by type of flora, there are areas filled with mana-infused trees, others with flowers, and still others with grasses. Regularly placed around the natural space are grav plates for benches and some small grav carts for folks who need help getting around. Guards in beast leather armor embossed with "Sea Saddle City Botanical Gardens" in green across their chests rove throughout. They are there to be seen but in the background so as not to disturb the guests.

Aria and I walk around until we come to the flower area and she stops. She slowly walks up to some flowers with cupped petals glowing orange and kneels down. I follow her. She gently rubs her slender fingers along the delicate petals and starts humming. I look from the flower to her face and I see a small smile on her mouth but tears falling from her eyes. She moves to another flower and keeps humming softly.

After ten or so minutes she stands up, rubs the dirt off her knees, uses the back of her arms to dry her face, walks back to me, and says, "My mother would have loved it here."

I nod, and we keep walking.

Now that I have the botany knowledge from Mr. Whyatt, I have no problem identifying every plant we pass. Eventually, we come to a small meadow area with a particularly soft purple grass called Smothering Sparkler. It is called that because, during thunderstorms, the grass will stand up straight, glow purple, and create sparks, attempting to attract the lightning upon which it feeds. Needless to say, this area is closed at those times.

I lay out the picnic blanket, and we take off our shoes and socks. We just sit and luxuriate in the soft feel of the grass on our skin. I'm leaning back on my arms and Aria is flat on her stomach with her chin on her hands. After a bit, I take out the sandwiches Jo ordered, and we have a nice lunch with bright blue juice and a cookie for dessert.

I look at her and say, "I'd like to sit over that area by the flowers again if that's okay with you."

She nods and we pack up the picnic. Deciding to leave our shoes and socks off, we store them away and walk barefoot back to the flowers.

I look around, and it seems relatively quiet. Kneeling, I put my bare feet and hands in an area with just soft soil, close my eyes, and relax. I try to expand my awareness through my mana and push it out through my hands and feet. I feel the mana in the earth below me and listen to it. Earth mana is different from the others; this one seems to want to be very slow. It feels happy sitting still and watching events go by. I push some of my mana into the earth to mix in and then try to coax it to move. I gently tug and push. It doesn't seem interested in moving, happy to just wait there until the world ends.

I decide it needs a bit of motivation to move, so I drive more mana out then shove at it. I want it to compress down and move closer to the surface with a pull. The earth below my hands and feet starts to shift and churn. I inject more mana, pull a little harder, and the soil sinks in while fresh loam from below the surface takes its place. I feel the telltale tingle on my right palm and relax.

One down.

[Hold alerts until the end please.]

Affirmative . . .

I look over at Aria who is looking at me with her mouth open. I reach over and push up on her chin with my index finger to close it with a soft click. She blinks, shoves my shoulder causing me to tumble over into the dirt, looks around, and asks in a whisper, "Did you just use earth magica?"

I nod and smile as I sit back up, wiping myself off. "I'll rest for a while and then I'm going to try again with something else."

She looks below me, then around, and I think she figures it out.

"Can I help?" she asks.

I smile somewhat sadly at her and say, "Not with this. But maybe with something else. We'll talk about it later. Time for me to get back at it."

I stand up and walk to one of the flowers that hasn't bloomed yet for whatever reason. I sit cross-legged next to the flower and, as gently as I can, rub the back of the fingers of my left hand along it. I gently inject my mana into it and try to connect to the plant. What I feel is sort of like water with a flow to all living things and sort of like earth with a willingness to see that flow pass by forever as it grows. I try to coax the plant to talk to me, but it ignores me; I think it finds me boring. The irony of a flower finding me boring is not lost on me. I try to move some of my pure mana into like I did earth, but I feel its pain and stop immediately.

I try to think about what I have seen nature magica do. When I saw the shaman, he was waving his hands and chanting something. When I saw Shen bond with Michial she was humming to him. And just now Aria was humming to the plants, probably copying what her mother did. Do plants think in song?

I run my fingers along the petals again, sending a tiny trickle of mana in, and begin to hum. I hum the same tune Aria did, trying with my mouth and with my mana. I send it in matching gentle waves with my song and amazingly feel the flower respond. It almost hums back at me in its own way. Unlike before with the earth magica, I have my eyes open so I can see how the flower reacts. And what I see is the flower starts to rock with my hum and with its own back at me. We sing a joint song with our mana, both the flower and I glowing green. In the back of my mind, I notice a tingle on my left forearm, but I am too entranced with the song to react.

The flower and I hum and rock, and I coax it to show itself to me. I feel its desire, but it has an aura of illness. I trace that feeling of sickness to its roots and notice a foul feeling coming from below that is leaching the life around it. I talk to the earth and follow that leaching deep below to a stone the size of my head. The stone is blacker than the darkest part of the cave I lived in for so long, and it feels like it can suck the life from anything near it.

I can tell it is surrounded by terrifyingly massive bones. I coax the earth, and the dirt moves and drags the stone and bones to the surface. It strains my mind because I have to move the earth above and below at the same time, and the material is huge. Just below the surface, I stop and focus hard, pushing the mana out and pulling it back in. I feel an almost painful tug in my middle, and the bones and stone appear in my [Inventory].

Then I return my attention to the flower and our song. The flower feels glorious, reaching into the earth for life energy it was denied. Finding it, we are both humming mightily and blaze with green, and the flower grows and the petals spread, glowing a brilliant orange light. I thank the flower for the song and let the connection go.

CHAPTER 58

I collapse onto my back, gasping for air and shaking a little. Coming back to myself, I hear applause and I see at least thirty onlookers clapping and talking about how wonderful that was. I smile and wave from the ground, and the crowd chuckles. A guard comes by, telling folks "The show's over" and moving them along. A male dark-skinned elf with white hair wearing a botanical garden apron walks up to me and sits down next to my prone form.

"Thank you for doing that. That flower has been sick, and nothing we did was helping. What did you do?"

I ponder what to say and just respond with, "Yes, she was sick. Her roots were not getting the nutrients she needed. I fixed the problem."

The elf raises his eyebrows, looks at the now-radiant flower, and says, "You did more than that."

I just sit up and shrug. I look around and I find Aria; her face has both tears and a radiant smile.

She walks over, sits next to me, and leans her shoulder onto mine. "That would have made my mother proud."

I'm not sure how to respond, so I don't.

[Did we do it, Jo?]

You did it, Vic. You did it, and it was amazing and beautiful. I too am proud of you . . .

New rune activated. Earth Rune is now available for use . . .

New affinity activated. Earth Affinity is now available for use . . .

New rune activated. Nature Rune is now available for use . . .

New affinity activated. Nature Affinity is now available for use . . .

[Nature magica is different from anything I've experienced.]

There's more for alerts, but they can wait until later . . .

Aria and I head towards a bench, put our socks and shoes on and head home.

Both Aria and I agree to take long soaking baths and then have dinner. Relaxing in the steaming water, I put my head back.

[I think all affinity magica requires an emotion behind them. Lightning is quickness and ferocity. Nature is love and companionship. I wonder what ice and magma will be.]

The emotions seem to match the affinity's nature, so we have someplace to start. Would you like the remaining alerts from the gardens? . . .

[Sure.]

New skill activated. Passive skill [Earth Mana Manipulation] now available for use . . .

New skill activated. Passive skill [Nature Mana Manipulation] now available for use . . .

Skill updated. Passive skill [Earth Mana Manipulation] has leveled from 0 to 4 . . .

Skill updated. Passive skill [Nature Mana Manipulation] has leveled from 0 to 4 . . .

Skill updated. Passive skill [Mana Splitting] is now level 5 . . .

[That's great. I need to find an opportunity to practice all this magica.]

Before we finish, I want to discuss something. You asked me to hold your alerts, so I did but you also received low mana alerts . . .

Warning! Host has 10% remaining mana . . .

Warning! Host has 5% remaining mana . . .

We have to find a better way to manage your critical messages. Simply telling me to hold them is not safe . . .

[I agree. Is there anything you can do?]

Yes, but it will possibly distract you in a dangerous situation, so I am hesitant . . .

[How about instead of a visual alert, you give me an audio-only one. The lovely voice of my future wife always draws my attention.]

#That is a sensible solution . . .

Don't encourage him, Grace . . .

[Is that all the alerts?]

Yes...

[Before I forget, can you order us two first aid kits? Really good ones. No spatial items, 'cause it needs to go into my [Inventory] and Aria's spatial container.]

Price?...

[Less than five gold each.]

Confirmed. That will allow for premium products...

[I'm going to nap. Wake me in thirty for dinner.]

Confirmed...

I close my eyes and let the world fade away.

***

Wake up, Vic. It's dinner time...

I open my eyes and lift my head.

[Yes, dear.]

I wash and dry quickly, put on my PJs, and head to the main room. Aria isn't there, so I knock on her door and call, "Dinner time, what do you want?" I hear a muffled "Pizza," so that is what I order.

After swallowing a particularly big mouthful, Aria says to me, "I want to help. Tell me how."

I look at her and sigh. "Okay. But first we need to talk about a few things."

She takes a bite of pizza and nods to me.

"You said before you were okay with it, but I want to talk about my life a bit." Seeing I have her full attention, I continue. "I don't know much of anything except killing and what supports that act. I can train you, I know that. I can help you survive, teach you to fight, educate you about combat and prepare you for the world. Yet you will still be young when I am too old to even move, never mind defend you." Taking a breath, I continue. "But you have to know that all I can teach you is death. It is important to understand what you are getting into. It is important to grasp the kind of relationship we'll have and what is to come. Do you hear what I am saying?"

She doesn't move for a bit but then says, "You have more?"

I nod and continue. "I live to kill so humanity survives. That is all I have ever known. I have fought and killed for as long I can remember. That is all. Nothing more and nothing less. I am telling you because I just don't want you to think I am like Grun or your mother. I don't know how to have a family or be a part of one. I don't know love or shame or affection. I barely have what you might call friends. Please don't expect more of me. I would hate to disappoint and hurt you."

She wipes her mouth and says, "Thank you for sharing that."

I see her face, and a little anger enters my voice as I point at her. "Don't look at me with pity. I have never known or needed anything I missed. In fact, I believe I am as successful an operator as I am because I was never distracted by all those things."

Her face changes to anger this time, and she says, "You shared, so now it's my turn."

I sit back and nod.

"I've been a slave to a kingdom that both needed and despised me. They used me for my magica, and if it wasn't for my mother's and Grun's sacrifices for protection, I would be shackled to a healing master and drained to unconsciousness every day to power their healing tools and mend their injured."

She takes another breath and a drink. The anger is gone from both her face and her tone, and instead she just seems tired.

"Vic, I don't think either of us really knows what we're doing. My family is nothing to model from. I hated my family with the exception of the two you met, of which only one is biologically related. So how about this? Let's stick with each other and try to figure it out together."

I think I hear similar exhaustion in my voice when I say, "That is fair. It sounds like we are both learning as we go."

She picks up another slice and asks me, "So how can I help?"

I take a deep breath and say, "In a lot of ways, I'm sure—at least eventually. But right now, what I need is for you to inject me with life mana."

She freezes for a second while chewing. She swallows and asks, "Why, are you injured?" She then looks me over clinically as if searching for leaking blood.

I clear my throat. "No. I want to absorb it to try to activate a life rune."

"I . . . see." Then, wiping her hands on a napkin, she holds her left hand out and says, "Give me your hand."

I blink at her and look at her hand and then back at her face. "Now?"

She smiles at me and curls her fingers in the come here gesture.

I slowly lift my right hand and place it in her left. Her eyes glow gold, and I can feel a slow trickle of mana flowing into my hand. I close my eyes and try to absorb it, but it vanishes.

"Hold on. This isn't working." The flow stops and I stand up and pace. What am I missing? The emotion maybe?

Mid-pace I ask her, "What do you feel when you use your magica?"

She shrugs and says, "Nothing really. I just direct it to heal. I only had enough years of training in life magica for the basics before we were exiled. As I said, most of it involved draining me dry." I lift my eyebrows at that, and she reminds me of something I keep forgetting. "Elves move at a different pace than you humans. Fifty years is the blink of an eye to us."

Right.

She resumes her answer. "I sort of figure it out as best I can. As you have experienced, I can heal by directing the mana to wounds, and the wounded area absorbs it to encourage healing. More complicated injuries require more attention like setting bones and such, but it is basically the same with different amounts and order of operations."

I stop pacing and face her. "Directly to the wound, huh?" She nods.

[Hey, Jo, is there a source of mana or magica or something?]

I have no idea. All I know is you have a river, which you also know . . .

[The river. Hmm]

"What are you doing when you fade out like that?" Aria's question catches me off guard.

I turn back to her and say, "Talking to myself. Sort of. I'll answer more fully after we do some experiments." I start pacing again. "If I can direct the life mana to the river. Or maybe the source of the river . . . " My voice fades with my thoughts.

Aria is just staring at me and asks, "River?" Then her eyes move to my hair and back to face.

"Okay. Let's wash up from dinner and head to the couch. This could take a while, and I want you to be comfortable."

She nods and gets up.

We meet back at the couch a few minutes later. I sit facing her with my legs crossed, and she has hers tucked under her.

I start. "When I visualize my mana, I see a river. All the magica I do takes 'water' from that river and uses paths I have built to the runes on my body. For example..." I hold up my left palm facing the ceiling, and the fire rune lights up red. "But I have never tried to add external mana to the river. I think I might have done it once accidentally, but I was dying of electric shock at the time, so I don't really remember." Her eyes widen, but I continue without breaking stride. "Nor have I tried to trace the mana back to its source. So I was hoping we could try that."

She blinks and says, "Sure."

"So while you are injecting mana, I am going to try to direct it inside me either in my river or flowing against the current. I have no idea if this will feel good or if it will hurt. I don't know if it will drain either or both of us. This is completely unknown. You understand?"

She nods and places her smaller hand in my left, which is still palm-up from the fire rune demonstration.

[I'm counting on you to watch Aria. You have to tell me if this is hurting her or anything like that. I don't need to be responsible for this entire family's extermination. Okay?]

I hear a sigh.

Oh, Vic. Yes, I got her for you...

"A few moments after I close my eyes, start slowly sending a trickle. Only send small amounts."

I close my eyes and enter my inner world.

CHAPTER 59

Standing next to my river, which is bigger again, I wait for something to happen. Turning in a slow circle, I scan the area for . . . something. Anything new, I guess. And there it is, a small golden light trail flowing in the air downriver. I walk over and try to grab it; my hand flies right through it like it's mist.

"Duh. Use mana, idiot," I mutter to myself.

I direct some water from my river to raise up and touch the gold. The gold intertwines with my water, but the two do not combine. I try to direct the water to merge, but the gold just keeps wrapping itself around.

"So combining away from the river doesn't seem to be the way." I try to get the tangled water to go back down into the river, but the gold just unravels and floats there, slowly disappearing as more is added to replace it.

"Can't get it into the river."

I spend what feels like hours but is probably just minutes attempting various things. I try connecting to it mentally like nature, I try forcing it like earth, or flowing with it like water. None of the ways I know from any other affinity affects the gold energy at all. I sit and stare at it. Frustrated, I glare and ask the glimmering mist, "What about you, can you help figure this out? 'Cause I'm stumped."

The gold energy then wraps around me. I feel an inquiry in my mind. It feels like it is asking where I need help.

Of course. It's healing energy. It has the desire to help. Once again I feel like an idiot. That feeling is becoming quite familiar. I think about the answer and try, "I need your help to join with me. To be one together."

The golden energy flares brighter and surges towards the river. It dives in, and my azure blue water starts to take on a golden hue. It even fights the current, and the golden glow goes up and down the river.

Vic, Aria needs to stop . . .

I ask the golden energy to stop flowing into me. I get a weird feeling back. Almost confusion. It doesn't understand how to not help and bring life. So it keeps going.

Vic! ...

[I'm trying!]

"Shit. Please stop, you're hurting her. Aria needs your help too."

That, it understands. The golden energy stops flowing in with its desire to help Aria. The remaining golden energy in me keeps flowing in the water, and my river starts to get brighter. And even brighter. I have to close my eyes and turn my face away. Then the light fades, and I look upon my river. It looks the same azure blue as before.

I open my eyes in the real world to the feeling a fading tingle on my chest and Aria asleep on the couch.

New rune activated. Life Rune is now available for use ...

New affinity activated. Life Affinity is now available for use ...

[Aria?]

She's okay. She is just exhausted ...

I get up from the couch, pick up Aria's unconscious body and walk to her room.

[Life mana does have an emotion. It is a desire to help and encourage life and energy. And when I asked for its help, it put aside all other concerns, including Aria. To stop it, I had to ask it to help her too. What a bizarre affinity.]

Fascinating ...

I gently lay Aria in her bed under the covers, and then I climb into my own bed, throwing my shirt to the end.

[Alerts?]

Skill updated. Passive skill [Elemental Absorption] has leveled from 0 to 2 ...

[Good skill up. And that means one more affinity down.]

What I just learned feels like health and life, kind of like the flower's desire to thrive. That makes me think of the disgusting illness I felt from beneath it. Looking at my inventory, I look at the black stone tooltip, and it is labeled **Mana Stone (Death)**.

[Why would that be there? I doubt a death creature just randomly died underneath the gardens. Who would put a death creature that big there and why would anybody care enough to try to kill some plants? What am I missing?]

We do not know enough at this time to even propose an educated guess...

At this point, we are simply going to have to move on. I look at the bones, and they are listed simply as Bones of an Unknown Creature (131).

[Perhaps the dwarves at the butchery can identify them. Or I can ask Mr. Whyatt. Or I can do nothing for now.]

I think holding the bones, for now, is probably wise. You are not strong enough to do anything about it even if you can identify them. They were huge and are way beyond you...

[I think that is true. Tomorrow you get to meet Aria in person, so to speak. Are you excited?]

Yes, I am thrilled about being able to converse with Aria...

[Do all Specials have consciousnesses? Are they like you or have I changed you as you said at the beginning?]

Not all but most. However, very few will be as self-aware as I am. And yes, you have changed me with your density...

[Interesting.]

I close my eyes and go to sleep.

***

After our morning exercise, Aria and I are sitting down for breakfast of fruit salad and oatmeal. And bacon.

"First, I want to thank you and apologize for last night. I activated life magica, and it is all thanks to you. And I'm sorry it drained you so much; I tried to stop it, but I was too late."

She smiles at me. "We both knew the risk. Congratulations, by the way. How many affinities is that now?"

Thinking, I answer counting out loud on my fingers. "Let's see. Fire, air, earth, water, lightning, nature, and life. That's seven so far. That leaves, ice, magma, light, dark and death."

She shakes her head and says, "You're amazing."

I feel my face get hot, and I look down at my food.

Clearing my throat, I change the subject. "I promised you an answer yesterday about why I sort of daze off sometimes. Well, you know I am a Special right?" She rolls her eyes. Okay, stupid question. "Do you know what a human Special really is?"

This time she has a pensive look on her face, then shakes her head and says, "I know Specials are the only humans who can currently use magica directly and not have to use inscribed devices. That's pretty much it."

"That's not good enough, so I'm going to give you a brief primer and then turn you over to an expert on the topic." She looks confused now. Probably wondering who I'm referring to. "Human Specials can control mana because of minuscule machines in our bodies."

She interrupts and asks, "Are those the lights floating in your eyes and why your hair sparkles?"

Blinking at her, I continue. "Um. Sort of? Those are complicated, but just know that there are tens of thousands of them in my body right now that are using mana to fuel both themselves and my ability to use magica. Generally speaking, the more a human has, the more mana they have and the stronger they are."

I put on the table the Verdant Communications communicator Mr. Whyatt gave us. "Put that in your left ear. It shouldn't hurt, but it will feel weird."

I wait for her while she nervously puts it in her ear. She shudders like she got the chills.

It is active, and I have a live connection . . .

[Block all signals except from us.]

Done . . .

"Now, before we continue, I figure there is one more thing you should know. So there are gazillions of these machines that saturate our world. In the air and water and everything that isn't alive except humans. There are so many that they have created what we call a hive mind. Or, more precisely, a quantum hive intelligence. It is responsible for changing and updating the nanomachine system since the humans who created it are all long dead."

"Most Specials have so many nanomachines—that is what they are called by the way—they form a sort of consciousness like the hive but on a smaller scale. When I zone out, I am interacting with the machines and that consciousness. Well, mine is a lot more aware and has a lot more personality than most. Her name is Jocelyne, or Jo for short, and she is dying to meet you. Jo, say hello to Aria. You need to touch the middle of your ear with your first two fingers for the earpiece to be listening to what you say."

Aria jumps slightly and puts her fingers to her ear. Her eyes go wide.

"Hi, Jo. It is nice to meet you," she says out loud. She smiles and gives a small laugh.

I say out loud to both, "Aria, it is important you learn what Jo can teach you about human Specials in general, about me, and about how I am different from others. Otherwise, you two have a nice conversation. I am going to head to the dojo on floor fifty-one for some hand-to-hand. And before you ask, no, you cannot come. Even though you don't want to hear this, your body isn't ready. Be back in a few hours."

I get up and walk away. I am honestly really nervous about them having a private channel, but Aria is her own person, and Jo says she deserves some "girl time," whatever that means. All and all, that is part of the reason I am heading to the dojo. I need to work off a little stress, and my body needs some physical contact. So I change into workout clothes, a sleeveless shirt, and stretchy shorts and walk to the infusion pad.

[Jo, don't forget to introduce Grace.]

CHAPTER 60

I arrive at the dojo and head to the boxing area and wrap my hands. I don't need to, but someone will comment, so I figure I'll just save the effort of a conversation. I warm up with arms and hands on the speed bag, maize balls, and heavy sandbag then add legs. Following that, I do some direct targeting with a partner and wearing focus pads on her hands and knees. She keeps up perfectly and is an excellent partner. Left hook, right jab, duck, left knee, duck, left jab, left jab, right uppercut, left hook, right knee. I randomize the rotation and begin speeding up. Slowly, I start to outpace her and she calls, "Hold." I step back, panting and dripping sweat.

"Sir, you are moving faster than I can keep up. I will assign you a faster trainer for your next lesson." I nod and gasp out, "Thanks."

I can feel her eyes on me as I move to the towels and water.

[Too fast maybe?] It's a good thing Jo can multitask better than I can.

No, Vic. She's checking out your ass, not your threat level...

Oh. Well that's a relief; I thought I gave away too much. Moving to another area, I wipe myself off with a towel and touch a different cryspad. On this one, I ask for an instructor for martial arts. Specifically, I choose Taekwondo as a start. Of the four unarmed martial arts I know, it is the one I am most familiar with. I pay the fee, and a middle-aged human walks out and introduces himself as "Trainer Four." Whatever.

We begin with an assessment where he asks me to demonstrate my forms. I make it through to the seventh form or "Cheonkwon" without error until I reach the point that includes a kick which forces me to swap leverage between my legs in midair. I don't fail it, but I recognize it as sloppy. When I finish that form, Trainer Four tells me to stop.

"Not bad. Let's proceed."

***

An hour later, I am grateful I decided to do this and promise myself to make it part of my routine. I am out of practice, and it showed as I got my ass kicked by Trainer Four. It's weird, but I like it. It feels good to be a normal

ACTIVATION

human soldier again, if just for an hour.

I bow to Trainer Four and head back up.

Aria is on the couch speaking with Jo but stops midsentence when she looks over at me. Both her eyes and mouth are a little wide. I sigh. I bet I look a mess, covered in sweat in my now-gross, tight workout clothes. I bet I have a bit of a stink to me too.

I wave as I walk by and head into my room.

Calling over my shoulder, I say, "I'm going straight into the bath to soak off my bruises."

After a moment, I hear Aria's voice in my head. [Don't forget you are a life magica now.]

I stop in my tracks. That's true; I had completely forgotten. I was so caught up in being a normal human, I forgot to turn that mentality off when I left the dojo. Something to remember moving forward since I am adding dojo time to my training routine.

I strip, throw my clothes in the cleaning box for the inscriptions to do their thing, and head into the bath. I first create a mana channel to my life rune, which is just above the bottom of my sternum. I see it for the first time as it lights up gold. I try to use life magica by thinking about how my muscles are sore and need help, and then I send mana to them through the life rune. A warmth swims throughout my body, and the soreness in my muscles slowly fades. I then heal my bruises and the cuts on my hands, forearms, shins, and feet. Just as an experiment, I send mana through my life rune into my entire body. Everything from my hair—which floats behind me—to my toes tingles and starts to glow gold. I feel the warmth of life and health everywhere.

I want to keep sending until I get low so I can see efficiency. Aria seems to get tired pretty quickly, and I wonder if it is because life magica is inherently mana heavy. At the six minute twenty-two second mark, I see what I anticipated.

Warning! Host has 10% remaining mana . . .

I release the mana. My hair falls into the water, the golden glow beneath my skin fades, and the rune darkens and vanishes into my tanned skin.

You okay, Vic? . . .

[I'm good. Just conducting an experiment.]

All right. Be careful . . .

I wonder if maybe Aria just doesn't have a lot of mana. I did not find the magica particularly inefficient or heavy. That being said, my experiment was on myself, which could possibly alter the results.

I lie back against the wall of the tub in my usual position and relax.

[Hey, Jo, I was thinking of trying to activate death magica by using the mana stone. Is that feasible?]

Maybe. MilNet is gloriously unhelpful on how to activate affinities. However, it did expose some new affinities for us to research . . .

[What are those?]

Sound, spatial, and gravity so far. Although there is some debate on whether spatial and gravity are the same . . .

[I wouldn't even know where to start activating those if I haven't already.]

Agreed. Let's put those aside and focus on what we can get. The longer we put off leveling up, the longer you have to wait until we can make progress on our various missions . . .

[I completely agree. We should set a deadline of some sort. How about until Grace is done? We level up either when we awaken all the standard affinities or when Grace's upgrades are complete. Whichever happens first. What do you think?]

I like that a lot. A hard but reasonable deadline. And that death mana stone is the perfect first step . . .

[Without breaking any confidences, how is it going with Aria?]

Well. I have educated her on nanomachines, Specials, and you in particular . . .

[Great.] I stop myself from asking more (despite how curious I am), close my eyes, and soak in silence, engulfed in hot water and steam.

[Wake me in an hour, please.]

Confirmed . . .

***

I am sitting on the couch near the fireplace, and Aria is looking at me expectedly.

"So, I am going to try something potential stupid and fatal. That is why I need you here in case it goes bad. You have the new medical kit in one of your earrings?" She nods, but I see a small bit of concern on her face.

I reflect for a moment that she used to hate my guts and now she's scared for me. Was it the death of her parents or fear of being alone that changed her? Or maybe something else? Not that it matters. I have a job to do. "I will start off slow. It is critical that you not touch with your skin what I am about to take out. Are we clear? Do. Not. Touch."

She rolls her eyes at me and says, "I'm not a kid, Vic. Just get a move on."

Suddenly, a black crystal the size of my head appears in my hands. It exudes a feeling of the death of all things. Aria recoils and leaps off the couch away from it. I feel its aura of death, but I don't feel the need to recoil. That's interesting.

Not rolling your eyes now, are you? With a half-grin, I ask, "Do you know what this is?"

She nods, not taking her eyes off the black mass in my lap.

I look at it and think [Inspect.]

Name:	**Mana Stone (Death)**
Description:	Mana stones are highly concentrated sources of elemental mana essence and can only be found in one of two ways. First, by mining. Given that mana stone lodes are rare, companies who specialize in mana stone mining will usually purchase the rights from the founder at a high price and then sell the stones at a substantial markup.
	The second method to find mana stones is by taking them from the carcasses of mana-infused beasts. Only non-humanoid species have ever been found to have mana stones (with the exception of the death affinity); it is unknown why.
	The element of the mana stone coincides with either the environment or the creature. For example, water mana stones are generally found in lakes, oceans, or other bodies of water or from creatures who live near them.
Condition:	Excellent
Risk Assessment:	N/A

Value:	This death-based mana stone is massive and has a substantial reserve of essence. Death mana stones have only ever been found after a beast was turned into an undead. There has never been a death mana stone lode recorded. Essence count: 5481/7650.

I wave my hand in front of her face, causing her to blink and refocus on my face. "I am going to try to siphon death mana from this stone so I can activate that affinity. If anything goes wrong, you get a pillow, whack the stone away, and use the medkit. Definitely don't touch it directly."

She looks back at the stone with facial expressions that change from disgust to fear and back. After a few moments, she finally gets a grip, takes a breath, and nods.

I nod back and close my eyes. I send my mana in the stone, and the stone's aura of death increases. But I don't feel a connection. I try to pull that mana back, and I feel a chill. I open my eyes to see if there is a change. The stone is the same but my tanned skin looks paler.

Warning! Host has received 1 elemental (death) damage...

Good to know. "Okay, here goes."

I begin to push mana into the stone and then draw it back. As I do that, I enter my inner world. Like with the gold life energy, there is a mist, but it is black and oozing. I try to draw it into the water, and like the gold it ignores me. I send the water to it and again nothing. Then the thick smoke touches the grass at my feet, and it turns gray, and my projected self goes a little more pale.

Warning! Host has received 3 elemental (death) damage...

I need to think.

Death. It wants to remove life. To undo creation. The gray grass spreads, and more color leaves my skin.

Warning! Host has received 6 elemental (death) damage...

I turn to my river and ask it to help by excluding life. It starts to glow gold within the azure and the smokey ooze stops absorbing the life in the grass and advances towards the stronger life of my river. The black touches the blue-gold water, and a darkness starts to spread. I hope to hell I am not fucking this up.

Warning! Host has received 10 elemental (death) damage...

Warning! Host has received 13 elemental (death) damage...

I am almost white by the time the black ooze turns a few meters of my water dark, gray, and lifeless. I cut off the stone then, and no new death energy is entering my world. The dead part of my river is spreading further in both directions, and I feel a little weak.

Warning! Host has received 19 elemental (death) damage...

Warning! Host has received 25 elemental (death) damage...

I'm forced to sit as the death spreads and lie down as it spreads more.

Warning! Host has received 33 elemental (death) damage...

Warning! Host has received 40 elemental (death) damage...

Eventually, I feel lighter and lose track of what is going on. My eyes flutter, and the light begins to fade out, but right before I close my eyes, a massive foul aura of death spews from my river, and I feel the need to vomit. I'm shaking violently from the overwhelming loathing of all things alive.

Warning! Host has 10% remaining health...

Warning! Host has received 1 elemental (death) damage...

Warning! Host has received 1 elemental (death) damage...

Warning! Host has received 1 elemental (death) damage...

Warning! Host has 5% remaining health...

Warning! Host has received 1 elemental (death) damage...

Warning! Host has received 1 elemental (death) damage...

Warning! Host has received 1 elemental (death) damage...

Suddenly there is a burst of oozing black smoke and then darkness.

Warning!...

CHAPTER 61

I wake next to my river, and it is its usual beautiful azure blue. Examining myself, it appears I look normal. I leave my inner world, and Aria is just inches from my face calling my name. "Vic!"

Host has absorbed 2,258.65 mana essence from **Mana Stone (Death)** *...*

New rune activated. Death Rune is now available for use...

New affinity activated. Death Affinity is now available for use...

I quickly put the stone in my [Inventory] and smile at her. "Well, that wasn't great. And maybe a little scary there at the end."

She leans back and punches me in the chest. Then she starts yelling at me. "A little scary at the end? You were completely unresponsive for an hour! And you were pale and kept getting paler until you looked like a white statue." Then she puts her palms on my cheeks but keeps yelling at me. "You started shaking and I was just about to use the medkit when you stopped and started getting your color back."

Then she pulls back and punches me in the chest again.

I'm overwhelmed by the up-and-down emotions and can't say anything. I hear a low "You are still paler than you were before."

She reaches forward and touches my hand followed by the now familiar feel of her warm mana moving through my body. The last of the chill I didn't know I was feeling flees at the influx of her warmth.

Host has been healed for 40 damage...

Host has been healed for 40 damage...

Host has been healed for 40 damage...

[Jo?]

I'm on her side. That was terrible. I'd hit you too if I could...

[It was going to happen eventually. At least if I want to awaken death magica.]

I know that, Vic. You looked like a corpse, and Aria was terrified. I think com-

fort food is in order . . .

[Good thinking. It's lunchtime.]

Patting her hand, I say softly, "Hey, want some lunch? Your choice today. Pick something chocolate for dessert. You know how rare chocolate is since we lost the southern fields."

Still glaring at me, she says, "Something we can eat with our hands. That way they'll be too busy to hit you again."

Clearing my throat, I ask out loud, "Jo, what is a good lunch food they serve here we can eat with our hands?"

How about a burger and fries? . . .

"Sounds good. Go ahead and order two for each of us with all the condiments, including cheese, on the side so we can pick and choose."

Done . . .

I change my shirt, wash up, and head to the table to await our comfort food.

***

After lunch, I tell Aria I have some work to do and she is free to join me but I'll be busy. She joins me on the balcony but is silent as I speak with Jo.

[How about my alerts?]

Before I do that, I want to admonish you for scaring Aria so badly. I know you needed to activate your death affinity, but you terrified her. She thought you were going to leave her too . . .

I let out a sigh and look over at Aria with my eyes.

[I don't really know how to respond to that. We did all the preparation we could; she had all the available materials to provide assistance. She knew the risks. What else could I have done?]

Not gone through with it. Before you respond, I'm not saying that would have been the right choice. I just want you to reflect that it was *a choice. One that you never even considered. You were one hundred percent going to go after death affinity. Maybe that is something you feel you need to do. And that's okay. What I am saying is next time ask yourself if you truly* need *to do it. If the answer is yes, then, indeed, you did everything right with the operation prep. I am only saying you should reflect on that . . .*

I'm silent for a few moments.

[I will.]

Thank you. Now here is your alert...

Skill updated. Passive skill [Elemental Absorption] has leveled from 2 to 4...

That is all beyond what you saw when you awoke...

Considering the situation for a minute or two, I share my conclusions with Jo.

[Upon reflection, it makes complete sense that death magica requires that I lose some or even most of my life. I also don't know where my death rune is; I was out when it appeared. Although if I had to guess, I'd say it is on my back, opposite of my life rune.]

That is a fair guess. Oh, and congratulations. With that exercise in stupidity, you have enough mana essence to get to level five. You'll be assigned your class when you convert your mana...

[Do you think I should drain all the rest of the mana stones?]

Actually, yes. Even if you decide to get back into crafting, they will lose a substantial amount of their essence before you are skilled enough to inscribe or enchant with them. And there is no point in selling—you don't need the coin...

[Fair enough. But let's leave the death one as evidence.]

I lay out the four remaining mana stones. A brown one from Mr. Stinky, purple from the elk, green from the lion, and blue-gray from the osprey. All told, they can give me 9,964.97 essence.

[Wait, can Aria absorb these? I should give them to her. She needs more power.]

Good thought, but no. 99.99999 percent of the population can only absorb mana of their own affinities. She'd need a life mana stone. You're a freak, remember?...

[Right. Did you tell her about how I opened my [Inventory] and nearly imploded or whatever?]

No. It never came up...

[I think you should. It might help her understand me better. She needs to see how mission-focused I can get.]

That is... probably wise. She deserves to know...

[All right, let's absorb this mana essence.]

Wait!...

[What?]

The crystals will shatter after being emptied, and you'll want to collect that material for crafting...

[Oh. Good job avoiding potential waste.]

I request a clean plate and lay it out.

[Here goes.]

*Host has absorbed 2,019.88 mana essence from **Mana Stone (Earth)***

*Host has absorbed 2,144.01 mana essence from **Mana Stone (Lightning)***

*Host has absorbed 3,839.51 mana essence from **Mana Stone (Nature)***

*Host has absorbed 1,961.57 mana essence from **Mana Stone (Water/Air)***

After each emptying, the crystal shatters, and the powder falls onto the plate. I place the pile into my [Inventory]. The tooltip says Mana Essence Dust (29 oz).

Unsurprisingly, the lion is the prize. Predators apparently have denser mana stones, since they eat the mana stones of their prey.

That gave enough to get you to level six...

[Let's focus on the affinities right now. I don't want to get distracted. We have a mission plan, and we are going to follow it.]

Affirmative. What do we do next?...

[Thanks to your research on how to increase mana capacity and affinity strength, we have guidelines. What's next is we will follow them. As such, we will work out every morning before a full breakfast. Help Aria practice her life magica and me my various magicas after breakfast. I will go to the dojo until lunch while Aria rests. For the entire second half of the day, we attempt to activate affinities. That could include research or meeting with contacts and intel providers. After dinner, we have free time that does not involve working either heavy physical activity or magic. We have four weeks, more or less. Let's accomplish our mission.]

CHAPTER 62

When I explain the mission plan for the next four weeks, Aria surprises me with her response. "I want to go to the dojo too. I am completely incapable of defending myself."

I firmly shake my head. "No. Your body needs a lot of work. Stay focused on that and your life magica and we'll revisit it after a few months. Plus, you are going to need to rest after our magica practice. Part of it entails emptying you out. We are going to stretch your mana channels, and they need to rest and recover afterward, just like you. Stay on mission, prove you can improve yourself the right way, and we'll talk about combat training. I will also be changing our food intake to increase proteins so our bodies will build muscle more efficiently."

She visibly deflates, which makes me feel terrible. I sit next to her and put my arm around her shoulders. "Look, Aria. You are vulnerable. If you want to participate in future missions with real danger, you need to get stronger. Much, much stronger, both physically and magically. If you want to help, you have to do it the right way, in the right order."

She nods, but I can tell she isn't happy about it. Well, tough.

[Jo, see if you can get a meeting with Mr. Whyatt around the end of the week.]

Request sent . . .

***

Over the next week, we follow the mission plan to the letter. Aria is really pushing herself and wants to improve, probably so she can get into the next phases of training. She'll understand the pace soon enough. And as expected she is exhausted after magica practice. As for me, I am getting back into form in the dojo and can hold my own with Trainers Two, Three, and Four. Trainer One kicks my ass with ease. Thank goodness for my skin. Anyway, the point is that I am improving.

On the advancement front, we have had some success researching affinities. Because I am a freak, I have three ways to activate affinities: 1. Direct mana injection, 2. Mana stone, or 3. Figuring it out myself. Direct mana injection is out because it would expose me. That leaves mana stones and my own clueless poking.

The problem with mana stones is that I will likely need at least two thousand essence based on the experience with death affinity. That is hard to come by because mana stones leak incessantly unless in a specialized temporal container, which are prohibitively expensive. That means I would have to get them myself. Where am I going to find light, darkness, ice, and magma beasts to kill? Regarding the final option, Jo and I agree opening an affinity myself requires that I be at or near the element to understand its emotional requirements. There aren't exactly any volcanoes in Sea Saddle City, and a bucket of ice is obviously not going to cut it. Either way, I have to be sure before I leave Aria alone while I go traipsing around. She is pretty much defenseless. Thinking about that makes me want to terminate those fools in her family. Why would you not train someone to defend themselves during a war? I can guess it has to do with her being life magica, but really? It's a fucking war.

Anyway, I need help activating affinities—hence my meeting with Mr. Whyatt this evening. The week gave us time to get a clear understanding of what I am going to need his help with tactically. Currently, I am being taken to his private office on the 149th floor.

When I enter, I am surprised by how sparse he keeps it. The rest of the hotel and armory are so fancy, I assumed the personal offices of executives would be the same. Shows how much I understand the rich and famous.

We are sitting at a small, round table in the corner of his office, and he is sitting a quarter way around from me. Not too close and not too far. He really is a genius at people.

I start today's adventure with "Thank you for agreeing to meet with me, Mr. Whyatt."

He smiles and asks, "May I call you Vic?"

I nod.

He smiles wider. "Vic, I know you hate the pandering and pleasantries of performance politics. So what do you say you and I agree to just dive in and skip what I am sure you view as nonsense."

He may be the smartest man I have ever met. Smiling, I nod and say, "Thank you. In that vein, I will just start."

Mr. Whyatt nods and waves his hand in a "go on" gesture.

"I need things. Some very rare and very expensive things. But for me to ask for these things would give away secrets I am uncomfortable exposing. As such, I am here trying to figure out if I can trust you. I believe we both accept the missions ahead—which you mentioned in our last discussion—are going to be extraordinarily challenging. Some will likely be beyond any mission I have completed to date. Possibly by an order of magnitude. Moreover, I am confident I will not be able to accomplish *our* missions without said aid. Before I go further, do you have any disagreements with what I stated so far?"

His curt reply is, "I do not."

I nod and continue. "Unfortunately, our missions will likely end up battling politically and financially powerful individuals and groups. I do not have proof of that, but I believe it to be true, and I believe you do as well. And thus we are back at the trust question. What happens when the proverbial political hammer comes down? Will you throw me to the direwolves? I believe you will if your business and family are put at risk, just as most would. Again, I will stop and ask whether you disagree with anything I have said to this point."

Same as before. "I do not."

Also same as before, I nod and continue. "Thus we return to our previous meeting where you made an astute observation of me. I have always served what I believe to be greater humanity. It is everything I know and am dedicated to. The crack in the crystal now, however, is that I have something to care for besides my service to humanity. This is my first experience with competing priorities outside of individual mission decisions, and I am struggling to determine what my next steps are."

I place my left hand palm up the table. "On one hand, I want to serve and see humanity thrive, not just survive as it is in sixty percent of this planet. And if there are forces inside humanity that will harm our ability to defeat the Invaders, my first reaction is to determine who those forces are and terminate them. The law is not relevant in my decisionmaking on this topic, as I am sure you expected. If this were a few months ago I would accept the risk, request your assistance, and push forward with the knowledge I might fail, but hope I could take the enemy with me as long as the reward outweighed the cost."

My right hand moves face up on the table. "On the other hand, it is not months ago. I have someone depending on me now, and the risk of failure impacts more than myself. If I feel I have a low chance at success, I will likely not attempt the mission. She and I can live our lives without the risks of war. Or we can perhaps move elsewhere, where the enemies of humanity, internal and external, have a lesser hold.

"In short, without the aid, I have a lower chance of success and will not take the mission as it risks my charge. With the aid, I put myself, and thus Aria, somewhat under your power and thus risk her. But I have a substantially higher likelihood of completing the mission.

"At the same time, you should be aware that any betrayal which hurts Aria will result in you becoming my immediate next target. And as you have already spoken to, my targets are always terminated eventually.

"Now, you knew all of this already before I even walked in the door. I have told you, so you know that I know. And now I leave in your hands the choice of whether to provide that aid, allow me to complete our missions, and accept the risks of what will inevitably come."

CHAPTER 63

Mr. Whyatt's neutral expression is replaced with a smile. "Let me ask you something, Vic. Do you know how long my people have been at war with the orcs and their ilk?"

I shake my head.

"I thought not. Most humans don't understand the concept of time the way we do because you live such short lives, having little exposure to mana. You may or may not know that an abundance of mana lengthens lifespan. The higher the overabundance, the longer it takes for the mortal body to break down. Now that this world has a sufficient but still-growing mana quantity, the people of this world will notice their aging process slowing among other benefits.

"The reason I bring that up is because you have to understand that when I say we have been battling the orcs for longer than homosapiens have existed, that is actually the truth. Elves can live thousands of your years. Gnomes and dwarves can live to a thousand or more. Beastkin, one or two hundred years less.

"Vic, my people have been at war as long as our entire population has been alive. And there are those who remember and had participated in battles a millennia ago. The dwarves are the same, and the elves even longer. In essence, we only know war, and neither side has won or lost in all that time. All we have to look forward to is death and blood and a forever war with no conclusion, or even change, in sight.

"So when I see someone like you, who I believe bends the mana around him, I will move worlds to make sure you are in the right place at the right time to move it in our favor. Whether it be the elven 'Living Mana,' the dwarven 'Soul of the Stone,' or my people's 'fate bending,' I believe you can help us change the course of this war. *Finally*, after tens of thousands of years, there may be hope for change." The passion in his voice at that last sentence is obvious and clearly genuine. He believes.

"Do I propose you can single-handedly end the war, kill all the orcs, and send us all into a time of happiness? Of course not. Nor do I believe anything even remotely close. What I believe is that fate bends around you, and I believe you welcome it. Things have happened throughout your life that individually look like coincidences, but in totality look like fate. You consistently made and make choices that change the fate around you.

"And here you are, sitting across from me and giving me a choice to change the fate of worlds or not. So, Vic, I thank you. From deep within myself, I thank you." A tear is actually falling down his round cheek.

I look at him, and the only thing I can think of saying is, "I don't really know how to respond to that. I have never believed in fate or luck or any of that. I just did . . . do what I think is necessary. All that stuff about the living mana and bending fates is beyond me."

With a light chuckle he responds with, "For whatever it is worth to you, I find that an excellent response. So, Vic, can I tell you how I am going to respond to the choice you have put before me?"

He actually waits for me to give him permission to tell me. I nod. This person's mind is beyond me.

"I am going to agree to our partnership. I would ask something of you that I have not earned, but I will solicit it anyway. I ask for your trust so that I can give you what you need. Vic, will you tell me what you need from me and/or Whyatt?"

I sit there for a few minutes thinking. He has really overwhelmed me and now he is asking for trust. Could he have gone through that entire dialogue for the purpose of muddling my emotions so I tell him my secrets? It is possible.

But what choice do I have? Can I go back to Aria and tell her I won't help others and we should just leave and hide away from the war killing our peoples? What would she think of me? What would I think of myself? Can I even feasibly leave it be after a life of service?

Alternatively, he truly believes all that fate nonsense and thinks I'm touched or whatever. Legitimate or not, if his belief is true, then the chances of betrayal shrinks dramatically.

[Jo, what do you think of what he just said? I'm not sure I am thinking straight. Do you think I can trust him?]

At this moment in time, I do. I cannot speak to the future, and I certainly have nothing to say about changing fates . . .

"Okay, Mr. Whyatt. I will trust you for now. I only ask that, when your betrayal finally comes, to please remember what I said about Aria and reciprocity."

Smiling, he holds his hand out for me to shake and says, "That is very fair, Vic."

I shake his one time.

"Well, Vic, it is time. Tell me what you need."

Taking a deep breath, I tell him. "I need mana stones. Specifically, I need four mana stones: one of ice, one of magma, one of light, and one of darkness. And I need them to contain at least two thousand essence each."

His eyes are wide now.

"I can kill the creatures containing them myself as well if that is easier and less costly." Figuring I might as well at this point, I continue. "The second thing I need is any and all information you have on quicksilver. The most important being how to smelt it so its powers are at their strongest. And thirdly, of course, I need the proper loadout of arms, armor, and munitions, with the addition of as many spatial storage containers of different varieties as you can afford to lose." I stop there and let him process what I have just said.

Clearing his throat, the gnome says, "Well, Vic, you have once again surprised me. If what you are asking for means what I think it means, I will do everything in my power to help you. What is your timeframe?"

I nod. "Thank you, and it does. For the mana stones, before the upgrades to my cycle are complete, which should be between three and four weeks, if what I am being told is accurate. The information doesn't really have a timeframe—I'll just say the sooner I have the ability to use the information, the better. In regards to third, that is probably the easiest, so I will just give the same answer as the other two."

Mr. Whyatt rubs his chin. "The third is, of course, simple. Let's agree to put that aside for now and focus on the first and second. I'm sure you know how rare and hard to come by what you are asking for is. Given the research, planning, and preparation required to capture beasts of those affinities and of that strength, I do not know if I can meet your deadline on all four. The good news is I can almost assuredly get you ice, and relatively soon, as we have a few outposts far to the north. I also believe the magma one to be feasible, if difficult, in that timeframe."

Shaking his head, he continues. "For light and darkness, however, I am confident we have a very low chance of success."

I nod. "I figured that. I have two possible alternatives. One will be costly and have a low chance of success. The other requires revealing another secret and putting both of us at risk. Would you like me to proceed?"

The gnome appears to be honestly thinking about it for a while. He eventually gets up, goes to his desk, and pulls out a purple crystal half the size of my fist. He sits back down and places it in the middle of the table. "This device is something of a counter-intelligence unit. I am having something more permanent installed in my office, but until then this is what I can offer. It prevents most mana from exiting or entering the globe it creates for approximately ninety seconds. May I engage it?"

[Jo?]

I do not see any risk from the device itself. Additionally, you've trusted him to this point, so I do not understand why you would stop now . . .

[Fair enough.]

"Yes."

He touches it, and a translucent violet sphere forms around us about two meters in diameter.

"We can speak safely until the bubble falls."

Conscious of the time limit, I jump right in and speak quickly. "First, we can try to use a lot of smaller mana stones; I have low confidence, but it is a possibility. The second is I can use a person with those affinities as well. I can accomplish what I am trying to do if they inject their affinity-based mana into me directly. They will know what I am doing and become aware of me, however. If we go this approach, and I do not feel I can trust the individual, I will terminate them."

I quickly continue. "I am also going to ask you for something else, but if this knowledge is misused by you or yours I will flatten this building and destroy every Whyatt property in this dimension. I need a life magica instructor for Aria. And myself, I suppose."

Mr. Whyatt sits up straighter in his seat and says, "That is extraordinary, particularly the first request. I will need to think on both and get back to you. Thank you for your trust. I understand now why you keep this such a secret."

I nod and Mr. Whyatt touches the crystal before the time runs out.

That was ninety-one seconds . . .

I stand and say, "I will wait to hear back from you. Thank you so much for your time."

We shake hands again, and I head home.

CHAPTER 64

Another six days pass with Aria and me following the mission plan. Both her and my progress are surprising. Her mana channels are much wider and stronger than before, and the amount of mana she can hold has doubled compared to when we began training two weeks ago, proving we are taking the right approach. Beyond that, her physical improvements are certainly noticeable. Her flexibility is getting close to as far as it can get, so we switch approaches; from now on flexibility training will be mostly maintenance and the priority moves to stamina followed by strength. At this rate, she will be prioritizing strength soon. All of this bodes well to the long-term prospects of her training.

Elven bodies are apparently quite adaptable and, using some instinctual species-specific magica, they have the ability to speed up or slow down the changes their bodies undergo. And we're not talking about small margins here—Aria tells me it can by orders of magnitude. Hence the massive improvements in so little time. She says she can keep it up for a while but does not want to because it also ages her and she refuses to "look older" than me. I'm not sure why that matters, but it does not affect the training negatively, so I have no concern either way.

My physical improvements are similar to hers, if to a lesser scale. In consultation with Jo, I have decided to hold off looking at my profile until the four weeks are over. It is certainly a test of my willpower, but I am determined and staying strong. The biggest improvement for me is in my hand-to-hand. I don't know if I have ever been as skilled as I am now. Trainer One is an excellent teacher, and we work through everything from punches, kicks, and blocks to grappling and escapes. Jo occasionally bugs me about improving too fast for my body, but I just ignore her as there are no debuffs or lowering of attributes. It isn't fast enough as far as I'm concerned. Every cell in my body is telling me I need to get stronger.

At the moment, Aria and I are watching the ocean and discussing affinities on the balcony while our bodies recover from another grueling training session. She is explaining to me how affinities work for everyone but me. "In other words, the stronger and rarer a single affinity is, the less chance there is of awakening another. As it was explained to me when they discovered how strong my life magica was, there exists some sort of universal balancing that does not allow me to support another affinity."

"See, this is where I struggle to understand. Were you ever even—"

I'm sorry to interrupt, but I need to speak with Vic privately...

Golden hair sweeps in front of my trainee's face as it snaps in my direction.

[Go.]

You have a request from the twins. They are calling in your debt and ask for you to attend them at 23:00 at the club. Same room...

[Confirm it. Has that knife and hand projector arrived?]

They will be waiting for you on your way out...

Turning to return Aria's look, I say, "Looks like you are on your own tonight. Sorry."

Her expression becomes hopeful. "Can I help?"

"Yes. By not deviating from our mission plan."

Her expression dims to sadness then scrunches into a glare, followed by her standing up and stalking back inside the suite.

[That went well.]

Quite...

***

Unlike my previous foray, I have the MAD take a more circuitous route to the club, at added expense and additional bruising of course, but I still arrive a few minutes before the requested time. I enter Theo's, walking by a bouncer armed and armored identically as the previous, but this time male. I still have no idea what his species is beyond not being dwarf or gnome.

The floor of the club is its usual undulating mass of sweaty-skinned and furred bodies that I attempt to skim around the edges of. I am dressed similarly to my first visit with the only change being that my clothes are made to fit this time. There is a side purpose to my wardrobe choice. Not only is the cloak intended to hide my identity, it is also intended to act as a warning to individuals interested in interacting with me to not bother. Unfortunately, it proves ineffective as I feel an arm wrap around mine followed by a sensual, purring female voice I somehow hear over the blaring music and cries of pleased patrons. But the words I hear are not the proposition I expect.

"If you want to see the twins alive, come with me." I stiffen slightly and run through a handful of scenarios of which most result in the death of innocent club-goers. The value of my "relationship" with the twins is somewhat questionable, but what they bring in value to humanity outweighs what I view as a relatively small risk of following this beastkin. It is extremely unlikely they know who I am or what I can do, and thus I will either force the situation or conduct some sort of trade to free them.

All of this flashes through my mind in seconds followed by my acquiescence to being pulled by the woman towards the further of the club's two bars. I'll grant her this, her barely-on clothing, striped fur glowing in the mana lights, and sexy movements would lead every observer to believe I am being led off for some drinking and sex. Clearly, this is not her first time dragging off a "partner," willingly or not.

She proceeds to lead me behind the bar, through a doorway guarded by a cross-armed and angry-looking dwarf into a more brightly lit back room filled with stacked stone and steel boxes labeled with different drinks. They have clearly all been enchanted to preserve their contents, as the cheap inscriptions are visible. Heck, I can feel the mana practically leaking off of them. I suppose if everything gets used, they don't need extended storage.

Of course, that is all secondary to my scan of the space. My true inspection finds the eight potential threats and two familiar captives. Well, nine if you include the tigerkin who just released my arm and backed up two steps.

Leaning against the right, rear, and left walls are pairs of humans likely armed but keeping the weapons inside spatial devices. The middle of the room in the center of a cleared space three meters around holds four humans sitting on simple steel chairs. Two in the center—but facing the door—are the familiar pale twins, and two are black-haired women in red dresses, one on each side. Unlike Theodora and Theodore, these ladies look nothing alike besides their long curly hair, both appearing in their 60s and with their identical red dresses. Even sitting I can tell the one beside Theodore is a diminutive meter and a quarter tall, and the other matches close to my height. The shorter unabashedly shows numerous folds of fat while the taller is skin and bones, causing me to wonder if she ever eats. Neither appears armed, but the various jewelry likely houses numerous weapons. The smug looks on their faces tell me all I need to know about their belief in our respective positions for the upcoming "negotiations."

Threat assessment complete, I stand perfectly still with the exception of raising my head barely enough for my eyes to show above the cloth covering the lower half of my face. I say nothing, waiting for the women to speak their demands.

I'm not disappointed when, in a warbly voice filled with derision, the shorter woman finally gets things started. "The lovely twins tell us you are to be their contender in the arena tonight."

I turn from her to the adjacent nearly identical pair and say in an exasperated voice, "Really?"

The only response from them is a bland expression and a synchronized shrug. Shaking my hooded head, I say, "I can't believe you let yourself get caught like this." Their bland expression changes to matching, shiny-toothed direcat smiles. Oh. Well, that makes a dragon hoard's more sense.

I let out a sigh, slump my shoulders slightly and look back at the speaker responding with a bland "Apparently."

From the other side of the twins, a squawking cackle resounds throughout the room. I wince at the harsh sound and take stumbling a step back. Wow.

The same shrill voice says, "Good. You're going to lose."

Giving my hooded head a hefty shake, I ask, "I am?"

She nods vigorously, and the other woman says, "Yes. And you are going to do it while being an embarrassment." Another piercing cackle results in another step backward. Having ended up next to the tigerkin, I glance over and find her furry ears flattened against her head and her face scrunched in a wince. I send her a sympathetic look and turn back to the skinny woman.

Despite my lack of desire to hear her speak again, I ask, "Why?"

The short one answers with a glare and looks to her left at the twins, "These two are too profitable for their own good."

The skinny one takes up the complaining. "This fucking club takes too much business from us and the others. We all know the rules."

I shrug. "Why not just kill them and take it?"

Of course, I already know the answer, but it is likely she thinks I don't. And her next earsplitting words confirm my assumption. "That doesn't matter to a brute like you."

The truth is, a fight over the twins' leftovers would cause a financial and physical mini-war that would negatively impact the city to the point of law enforcement getting involved. And that goes against the agreements they have with the politicians who frequent their various establishments.

Her skin-and-bone frame stands and steps in front of Theodore but maintains eye contact with me. "Just do what you are told."

Turning to face the twin brother, she leans over so far she is perpendicular to the floor, and her bony ass is pointing at me. Now face to face with the pale brother, she reaches forward, grabs the white hair near his scalp, and bends his head back. With her other hand, she strokes his face with the back of her hand.

I mumble "Finally" and then move.

CHAPTER 65

With a diagonal shift back and to my right that takes one and a half seconds, I stand behind the tigerkin with my now blood-covered left hand in front of her neck and my right pointing over her shoulder, holding a hand projector that has already fired the gray ovoid of an air mana munition. In a blink, the skinny woman's lower torso bursts downwards from her ninety-degree lean after the compressed air mana enters her body through her ass and explodes after a few inches of travel, causing blood and intestines to splatter the floor as well as Theodore's white shoes and pants.

*You have killed a **Tigerkin Gang Member**. You absorb 644.14 mana essence . . .*

*You have killed a **Gang Leader**. You absorb 221.18 mana essence . . .*

Barely two seconds later as her body thumps to the gray stone floor, my projector-holding right arm is pointing at the fat woman to the left of the twins and releasing another two blasts of air mana. Surprisingly, her speed belies her size as a flabby left arm flies to her throat and touches a red gem on a choker in between folds of fat. Just as my first projectile is approaching her forehead, it explodes against a red mana shield, followed closely by the second, which would have struck in the center of her chest. Both twins lunge their chairs backward and to the side so the exploding air mana contacts the chairs' backs and seats, instead of their bodies.

The thugs that the ladies brought to enforce their will shake loose their stunned paralysis and withdraw mana projectors. The shuddering form of the tigerkin woman being held in front of me by the twelve-inch knife I have jammed through her jaw into her brain begins taking fire. I drag it with me as I move two steps to my right and let it slide off the blade as I kneel behind a double-stacked steel crate jointly labeled "Clan Forestheart's Red Hearthwine (230 years) - Maintain Cold."

[Damn. This is good stuff. Aria likes red, right? See if the hotel sells it by the glass.]

I swap hands and glance around the side, firing off two quick shots and a delayed third at a thug whose toes are showing around the edge of a crate.

She has never expressed particular interest in elven wine though . . .

The first projectile strikes the end of his exposed boots; the second explodes his hand as it is thrust out grabbing the gushing wound. He falls forward and the delayed third strikes his shoulder but makes contact with some form of armor which, instead of injuring or killing him, throws his body backward until it slides to a sudden stop when his head strikes the corner of another crate.

*You have killed a **Gang Thug**. You absorb 144.92 mana essence . . .*

[Shoulder? Really? I'm out of practice. Does the hotel have a firing range?]

Thankfully, I find the twins a little closer to the enemy but relatively protected behind their own crates. Both wield medium-sized semi-automatic projector rifles. Did they seriously tint their rifles white? For fucks sake, they're blind. Can they even see the color?

It does. Floor twenty . . .

A loud crack sounds, and the top crate shudders to an unexpectedly strong blow. Switching hands again, I move to the right side of the lower crate and sneak a peek around the edge and immediately jerk my hooded head back. Ah. One of the thugs is walking forward, firing from a double-barrel shotgun into the crate, likely in an attempt to knock it over or destroy it. He fires again, and again my protection shudders and slides back into me, shifting by an inch or two. With a crack over his knee, he opens the shotgun and removes the shells to reload. What a moron.

A moment later his head explodes from the single gray projectile I fire into it.

*You have killed a **Gang Thug**. You absorb 171.74 mana essence . . .*

Fucking amateurs. He blocked the others from firing, just standing there and reloading. And why the fuck was he using a shotgun like that? What was he, an ancient weapon enthusiast? If they hire idiots like this, the value these two ladies bring to humanity continues to drop in my mind. Well, one now, I suppose.

[Let's give the wine a try. Maybe she'll like it. Hopefully, Stupid McShotgun here hasn't broken any bottles inside.]

Over the bursts of mana striking my crate, I hear the fat woman's warbling voice scream "Hold fire!" There is a reduction, but some of her subordinates either didn't hear or ignored her. An even louder "Stop shooting, you useless fucks!" follows.

Finally, the air is no longer filled with the lights and sounds of mana projectiles flying everywhere. I look at the twins' hiding spot and find them watching me. They each have a grin, clearly enjoying the excitement I caused. That look also tells me I haven't fulfilled my debt yet. Drake shit.

"You can't win. I outnumber you and have the advantage in arms. I have to kill you for Clarissa, but I'll do it painlessly if you surrender now. If not, you pay in pain for her life."

Yep. These people are too stupid to live. They will only harm humanity and might spread their imbecility to others.

I lean my head to the right, but this time the enemy is fully hidden behind various types of shelter, so I cannot get a count. The twins will not appreciate it if I blow up their entire stockpile of expensive booze, so area of effect magica like I used against the orcs is out. We'd also likely die in the explosion, as each crate's protection would fail. Ugh. See, this is why I'm a *covert* operative; blowing up the building is a much more effective method for achieving my goals. This firefight nonsense is for others in my unit.

Staying low, I silently move diagonally, bypassing a few potential places to gain protection and reach a particular wooden crate I saw when I first scanned the room. It might sound stupid moving from steel to wood, but I have a plan. Okay, a stupid plan but it's a good opportunity to practice my magica and maybe avoid causing a total loss for the twins. As much as I don't care about their costs or profit margins, I do believe they provide humanity a valuable service. If I didn't, I probably would have terminated them long ago, considering their past.

Thus, I press my hands to the crate and begin mentally humming to it. Specifically, I hum to the wooden slats. Singing to dead wood is completely different than it was to the flower. There is no return song, only emptiness, but that emptiness still absorbs the mana I send into it, and memory of the wood fibers allows it to respond physically to my call.

"Lucinda, you are going to die." Theodora's voice surprises me, and I lose focus on the magica for a second.

For fuck's sake. Refocusing, the side of the crate I am touching begins glowing green as the wooden slats under my hands slowly shift. It turns out the strain of moving dead wood is many times more severe than a living plant. On top of that, the enchantments on the wood mean I am fighting against another's placed magica.

In the back of my mind, I hear a warbling voice. "Fine! We both know I was going to kill you painfully anyway for killing my sister."

Warning! Host has 10% remaining mana . . .

Releasing the mana along with a powerful exhalation of air, I take in a few panting breaths and duck fully behind the crate as fire resumes. Luckily, the thugs do not see me change position, so they are firing only at the twins and my old position. Closer and at a different angle now, I can see five attackers remaining, including the fat woman wielding a fully-automatic projector rifle flinging red bursts of fire magica. Given there were nine originally, it looks like the twins haven't taken any out. Figures.

Shaking my head at lazy people, stupid gangsters, and this whole episode, I reach forward with both hands and stick my fingers around the now inch-wide gap between wooden slats. Placing my feet on either side, I yank with all my enhanced strength. I growl as the crate begins to tilt towards me. Despite the weight of all liquid inside, the wood, specifically enchanted to avoid breaking, resists. Thankfully, my nature magica altered the channels of the inscriptions, thus weakening the enchantment sufficiently so it gives in a crack. Could I have used fire or air? Sure. If I wanted to risk exploding what's inside. Physical disturbance would be absorbed by the padding and what's left of the enchantment. Magica, not so much.

So much for staying hidden. Clearly, my position is given away as fire begins heading in my general direction. I don't think they know exactly where I am though, as projector fire encompasses my entire general area. Reaching through the hole I made, I pull out a bottle and glance at the label. "Everclear: Fire-Infused Grain Drink (95% alcohol) - WARNING: FLAMMABLE."

Perfect.

CHAPTER 66

While laying out six bottles of one of the strongest drinks made by humans on the stone floor in front of my kneeling form, I work my magica above my head but beneath the top of the crate. Closing my eyes tight and opening my mouth, I point towards the ceiling but above the general area of the enemy group and release my stored lightning magica. A blinding flash of violet light and a cracking sound that shakes the lighter crates and knocks over more than one of the bottles at my feet resounds throughout the room.

Warning! Host has suffered **Deafness.** *Host will be unable to hear for 30 seconds . . .*

Ignoring the ringing in my ears and ozone smell, I blink the spots from my eyes, form magica yet again, and reach forward, grabbing hold of the neck of two bottles. Standing partially from my kneel, I toss one bottle and then the other in an arc. Right as the first passes the location I thought I saw a pair of thugs, I thrust forward with my magica and a flame spear—this time only two inches long—flies forward. Right then, the other bottle's arc reaches its apex, and I fire the other spear I had prepared.

The first spear blasts into the bottle of nearly pure alcohol, resulting in a burst of flame and converting the flammable drink into liquid fire, which splashes to the floor and anything in the area. This is repeated with the second bottle and then a third and fourth, which I started on the instant I released the second spear.

Two final floods of liquified burning death fall the stone floor and nearby tables, chairs, tableware, cutlery, crates, and humans.

Deafness *has been successfully removed. Hearing will return in 5 seconds . . .*

The ringing in my ears fades just in time for me to hear the terrified and agonized wailing of the victims of my savage attack. I knew this would end horribly, but it was that or destroy the room and risk harming the twins. My priorities are clear. They always are. Or were until I agreed to prioritize Aria's safety and training. Thankfully, this time the decision was a simple calculation of value, and I value what the twins offer humanity more than

I value avoiding the agony of burning alive my enemies.

*You have killed a **Gang Thug**. You absorb 119.09 mana essence...*

*You have killed a **Gang Thug**. You absorb 128.54 mana essence...*

Standing, I take out one of Commander Franklin's canteens of water from my [Inventory] and walk closer to the now weakening screams of anguish and harsh smell of burning flesh. I open the canteen and call forth the water inside. As I walk by the blackened and smoking forms, I splash the water onto any wooden crates nearby in an attempt to avoid causing an even greater explosion. As I proceed, the last of the alerts tells me the painful end for these humans finally comes.

*You have killed a **Gang Thug**. You absorb 166.73 mana essence...*

*You have killed a **Gang Thug**. You absorb 178.40 mana essence...*

*You have killed a **Gang Leader**. You absorb 239.97 mana essence...*

By the time I am done soaking the few splashed wooden crates, most of the alcohol is burning away without assistance. The room is silent except for the sound of still sizzling skin and flesh and the footsteps of Theodore and Theodora. I turn to face them and say, "Why this way?"

Theodore answers. "Because you wouldn't have done it otherwise."

I nod, realizing they're right. "Mel is well?"

They nod.

Looking back at the smoking bodies, I say, "We're even." It isn't a question.

They offer me a nod in synchronization, and I turn away from them and walk to the door. When I reach most of the way, I call back over my shoulder. "I'm taking this." The dented crate of 230-year-old elven red wine vanishes as I walk past it and exit the room to be once again surrounded by the thumping bass of music and flashing of multi-colored lights.

***

When I step through the suite entrance, Aria is nowhere to be found. She's likely asleep given the late hour. I walk into my room, remove every piece of clothing, enter my bathroom, throw the sour-smelling things into the incinerator, get the bath water ready, and climb in. Laying my head back, I ask Jo for any skill-up alerts.

Skill updated. Passive skill [Nature Mana Manipulation] has leveled from 4 to 6...

New skill activated. Passive skill [Mana Projectile Weapons (Small)] now avail-

able for use . . .

Skill updated. Passive skill [Mana Projectile Weapons (Small)] has leveled from 0 to 3 . . .

New skill activated. Passive skill [Small Blades] now available for use . . .

[Straight forward enough. I assume you have thoughts?]

I do. You burned them alive, Vic. It was horrible . . .

[Yes and yes.]

Even knowing how awful it is, you still did it . . .

[Yes. Jo, this world is not one of mercy or cleanliness. I live in a dirty, painful, death-filled world, and sometimes I am the cause of the dirt, pain, and death. Someone has to do the things that cause the ugly to show through. I make decisions of life, death, and, worst of all, pain, and I do it because someone else might not be strong enough to.]

And who judges who's deserving of those three things? . . .

[Sometimes others, but the weight of the responsibility and outcome is mine to bear. Mostly alone.]

That's quite a burden to carry alone . . .

[I do what I do for the sake of humanity. That is how I make nearly every decision.]

Until recently . . .

[Well, yes. Until Aria, I suppose. All right, that's enough of that.]

Breathing in and out once slowly, I change the topic.

[So starting tomorrow, we can add range time to our daily routine. I need to sharpen back up. I won't be able to truly practice long-range sniping indoors, but the rest seems feasible.]

Aria as well?

[We'll see.]

CHAPTER 67

The next morning, Aria and I are having our post-workout breakfast sitting in our usual spots at the dining table.

I notice Aria is struggling with something, but I don't know what. I'll give her until we are done eating to say something before I ask. Various expressions cross her perfect elven face, but to me, it just looks like is trying to work herself up to something. I wonder what it is.

She then lets out a breath and says, "Vic, something has to change." I raise an eyebrow at her. "I've been improving. I'm stronger, faster, more flexible, can push longer both magically and physically. But I still can't fight."

I open my mouth to agree when she charges on.

"I understand you wanted me to start at the basics and make my body strong enough, but I'm there now." I open my mouth to agree yet again, but she doesn't stop speaking. "I'm stronger than most humans now, at least those that aren't Specials, and they are all taught to fight. I'm ready. You have to see that."

She is staring at me with a pleading look.

I wait to see if she will continue, but nothing else is coming so I speak. "I do."

"I'm not a . . . wait. What?"

"I see it and agree with you."

The hope and excitement on her face make me smile. "You do?"

I nod. "I do. I was going to propose an addition to our schedule after breakfast this morning. I'm actually quite impressed. You haven't complained about being bored once, even though I know you are with our static routine. Anyone would be. Well done."

Her smile is so bright and honest I struggle to stay focused for a moment. A weird warm tingling works its way into my chest and prickles its way down my body. Touching my chest, I look down and sigh.

Clearing my throat, I refocus on the mission and propose my changes to the daily plan. "There is an arms range on floor twenty. It isn't big enough for sniper work, but it should be good to at least get an introduction and instruction on ranged weapons. I propose we go to the range every evening after dinner. Are you interested?"

She gets up, gives me a hug, and moves quickly into her room to clean up before our daily magica lessons. I can move again after a few seconds and the same tingles pass. Twice in one day. Great.

**

That evening, Aria and I appear in a flash on the twentith floor's infusion pad. The range offers different distances, weapons, training stations, and instructor levels. I walk up to a cryspad and ask for someone who can help a novice start from scratch. I emphasize the need to be exposed to a variety of ranged weapons.

After a minute or two, a female human in a gray camouflage jumpsuit comes out to meet me. She shakes my hand. "Hello, I'm Gina. How can I help? Looking at you, I doubt you are a novice."

She scans me up and down and, frankly, looks a little hungry. I move to stand behind Aria.

Yep . . . I'm brave.

Patting her shoulders from behind I say, "This lady is the novice. Can you teach her as if from nothing? Include everything. Safety, disassembly and assembly, care and maintenance, stance, good firing habits. I mean everything."

Then I turn Aria by her shoulders, look straight into her golden eyes and say, "You told me you have never been trained in weapons before, so please don't rush. Remember what I said—we do things in the right order over the right time. To be sure, you will be tested on each stage of your training before being allowed to advance to the next." I can see her stubborn face forming so I say, slightly firmer, "That is how I was trained and is how you will be too."

My trainees always learn to be safe, and Aria needs special attention never having even touched a weapon before. Shortsighted, idiotic elves.

Aria nods to me trying to be serious but is clearly excited. I smile back at her motivated face. Turning back to the human and patting Aria's shoulder again, I say, "She is in your hands for the next hour, Ms. Gina. I will be practicing at the longest range this place offers."

**

I spend my hour refamiliarizing myself with various short-range (for me) weapons. Starting with my own recently-used hand-projector, I sit at a padded table set aside for just this purpose. I run through the assembly and disassembly process. There are no moving parts in modern mana projectors, but there are many individual pieces that must be placed in exactly the right places or the various inscriptions won't align, and the mana won't flow properly. 164 seconds later, every piece of the weapon from the pressure trigger to the mana stone are laid out before me. Not bad for the first time with a weapon. Not great, but not bad. At the ten-minute mark, I move to submachine projectors. Ten minutes after that I complete the assembly of my final fully automatic repeating rifle. That last weapon's inscriptions were so precise that assembly actually took me over four minutes. The maintenance and care required for that weapon nearly rival Bertha's. Nearly.

Alright, time to shoot. On my way to a free firing lane, I check on Aria and Ms. Gina. I can tell Aria is fully attentive. She is asking questions and pointing at various pieces and parts of whatever weapon they have disassembled to learn about. Excellent.

I walk to my reserved lane—only fifty meters—take my stance, solidify the hold of my weapon, sight down my target, and depress the trigger once. I'm not a huge fan of firing standing upright, but they do not have a range long enough to make prone-shooting offer any value. The red projectile is loosed down the mana-shielded lane and passes through the projected transparent humanoid-shaped target and explodes on contact with the mana shield behind it. The white projection leaves the area of contact highlighted in red while a smaller exact duplicate is also projected next to the shooter back at the firing line. I glance over and frown. The red blotch on the forehead is nearly a half-inch to the right of center. It is what I expected being my first time firing this particular weapon, but I'm still not pleased.

Like most mana-based projectile weapons, there is little recoil, so staying on target is easy. But the first shot is always your guide until gaining familiarity with a weapon. Because a weapon this complicated is uniquely inscribed, there are tiny adjustments and particulars that a shooter will be required to familiarize themselves with. I nod and line back up. Five red mana projectiles fly down the line and explode against the mana shield. When I look at my simulated target, I find I adjusted appropriately. The projection shows one red highlight in each eye, one in the mouth, one in the neck and one in the heart. Nodding, I line back up and let fly.

***

Aria is wrapping up . . .

I haven't made it through even a quarter of the weapons I wanted to, but it is a start and only day one. I meet up with Aria and Ms. Gina and listen as the female human reports she is impressed with Aria's dedication and attentiveness. She agrees to be my inexperienced trainee's personal instructor for one hour every day. She also asks me to get a coffee, but I decline with an apology saying my schedule doesn't allow for it. Aria watches the exchange with a weird expression I can't pinpoint.

When we get back to the suite and start getting ready for bed, Jo interrupts my mental train of thought about a weapons training regimen. I have just reached scattershot projector weight comparisons when Jo lets me know someone is looking for me.

You have a message from Mr. Whyatt. He says he would like to meet at your convenience.

[Ask him if tomorrow evening is acceptable.]

Confirmed for 1730 tomorrow . . .

CHAPTER 68

"I have an ice affinity beast for you." Mr. Whyatt jumps right to the point as soon as I enter his office.

"Excellent. What are the next steps?" I ask.

"Would you like to slay it yourself?"

"That would be preferable if operational security can be maintained." As great as the essence would be, it is more important that as few people as possible know what I can do.

"Please follow me."

He guides me down a few hallways to a pad that leads to a room I can only describe as a prison for beasts. It is rows upon rows of beasts in large mana-shielded boxes. I notice almost all are carnivores and stare at me like I'm an after-dinner snack. Most are not native to the Sea Saddle City area and must have been imported. A few are clearly not from this world at all.

I am looking around when he must notice my curiosity and answer my unspoken question. "This is our holding pen for the training and fighting arena."

I look at him questioningly.

"Ah, you didn't know we have an arena. Forgive me. Floors 140 to 145 are set aside as a large combat area where battles against beasts and other people take place. They can be simple training bouts, or combat for the purpose of entertainment."

The first thing that passes through my mind is that Aria isn't getting anywhere near that place.

He continues. "Let me know if you are interested in using the arena for training. It can be booked so it will be private or by invite only."

No, thank you; opsec is too critical to risk it, and I am absolutely convinced it would be monitored, despite his calling it "private."

"Of course, you are welcome to make a few wagers if you like." He says with a grin.

Yeah . . . not happening. In my line of work, there are measured odds and operations decisions based on gathered intel. A "gamble" without preparation is a near guarantee leading to mission failure and a horrifying death. I say nothing out loud, nor change my facial expression, giving him nothing.

After passing nearly thirty boxes, we come to an unshielded but barred cage that is separated by a five-meter empty square with an enormous white bear with six legs and ears that stick up at least ten inches. The creature appears heavily sedated. I kind of feel bad for it, but just for a moment; this ursine is a killer and, as always, humanity comes first with me.

"This creature came through a rift into this world's northern continent. Proceed with whatever method you feel is best. I ask that you attempt to minimize damage to the body so I can keep my losses on this venture to a minimum."

I nod. That is a fair request. How can I kill it without damaging its body? I walk up to the bear and for the first time send mana through the newly created pathway to my death rune. I found it a few days ago; I was right that it is on my back but not where. It sits against my lower spine, two inches above the tailbone.

[Jo, why are the runes where they are? I don't see any particular purpose or reason behind their placement.]

According to both my available information as well as MilNet, locations differ between individuals and nobody understands why. The same is true for other species as well, by the way, from what they have shared. NanoNet likely has additional information on this topic if you are still interested when you eventually connect to it. Now stop procrastinating and get to it . . .

She's right; I have (completely reasonable in my opinion) concerns because just about everything, including the outcome, is unknown. Not sure what will happen, I send a trickle of mana down the new pathway. A disgust for creation and disdain for life raises in me. I immediately release the mana, and the feeling fades. Gasping and breathing deeply, I try to get a grip on my emotions. I was not prepared for that; death affinity clearly affects my emotions in a profound and disturbing way.

Sitting down next to the bear's cage, I take a few deep breaths and center myself. After a minute, I try once again, sending mana to the death rune. The feeling of wanting to absorb all life hits me. I reach out and touch the bear's soft white fur through the bars. Nothing happens. I send that feeling of absorbing life towards my hand and into the bear. I can see my skin getting pale.

Then I feel it, the bear's vitality; it is glowing with life . . . and I want it. I want to suck it out and extinguish it. Closing my eyes, I feel black ooze reaching for that glow and drinking from it. All that life is anathema to me, and I want it gone. That blazing glow starts to dim and I reach for more. It gets dimmer and dimmer until I smother it and crow in the victory of ending the energy of life.

And then the euphoria of triumph is gone and the search for more is all I know. I drive forward, searching for vitality nearby so I can snuff it out.

VIC! WAKE UP! . . .

Blinking, I fight the emotions and cut off mana to the rune. Looking around while panting, I see myself surrounded by black oozing smoke that slowly fades away.

You have killed an **Ice Mana-Mutated Burrow Direbear**. *You absorb 3,791.03 mana essence . . .*

I shudder and take a huge calming breath. I look at the bear and see it looks a little smaller like something inside of it was removed. It is clearly dead, as its mouth is open and its light blue tongue is sticking out. There is no breath in its body, nor light in its open ice blue eyes.

"Vic?" I jump slightly as Mr. Whyatt speaks. I look over at him; he has one hand in his pocket and the other out to me.

"Mr. Wyhatt. I'm sorry." I stand up and look around. Nobody is here. Despite the black smoke, there is no damage to the floor or the cage nor any non-living object. Only the bear.

Nobody is around, so I continue. "That was my first time using death magica, and it was a little overwhelming. I apologize. I was trying to think of a way to kill the bear without harming the body, and my control of air magica is not good enough to smother it without ripping it apart. If I can even do that."

He stands there frozen. Then he mutters, "I would not have believed it if I didn't see it for myself."

Clearing my throat, I ask, "Not that I am ungrateful, but wasn't the whole point of this to get the stone in that beast?"

The gnome nearly jumps from forgetting. "Of course. Yes." He holds two fingers to his ear and says, "Come in now, please."

Three gnomes arrive in a few minutes, pushing a large, double-stacked grav cart covered with butchery instruments. Mr. Whyatt says, "Prioritize the mana core, please. And hurry."

The cage is opened and, like professionals who do this every day, the three gnomes completely disassemble the massive bear in just minutes. After another moment, I am handed a light, almost blue-white crystal the shape of my forearm and about a third of the size.

"Follow me, Vic, and we can get you home."

CHAPTER 69

Aria and I are sitting across from each other on the couch again. She whispers "Cold" as she runs her hand along the smooth light blue, almost white crystalline surface.

I chuckle at her. "Well, it *is* supposed to be ice mana essence."

Her response is just "Right."

I look at it and think [Inspect.]

Name:	Mana Stone (Ice)
Description:	Mana stones are highly concentrated sources of elemental mana essence and can only be found in one of two ways. First, by mining. Given that mana stone lodes are rare, companies who specialize in mana stone mining will usually purchase the rights from the founder at a high price and then sell the stones at a substantial markup. The second method to find mana stones is by taking them from the carcasses of mana-infused beasts. Only non-humanoid species have ever been found to have mana stones (with the exception of the death affinity); it is unknown why. The element of the mana stone coincides with either the environment or the creature. For example, water mana stones are generally found in lakes, oceans, or other bodies of water or from creatures who live in or near them.
Condition:	Excellent
Risk Assessment:	N/A

Value:	This ice-based mana stone is nearly full, which is exceptionally rare. Essence count: 3,887/3,890

"Dinner and a show?" I ask Aria. In response, she reaches over and bops me on the head. I wince, not because it hurt, but because that is not what I was expecting. "What was that for?"

"Vic, stop wasting time. Absorb the stone," she says, glaring at me.

"Slow down. We have to go through preparations and think about the emotional requirements. Let's wait until tomorrow."

"No. Let's talk through the preparations now. Stop excluding me from the before and after stuff."

I look at her. "It isn't that I was excluding you intentionally, I just . . ." I slow to a stop, thinking of my reasoning.

She finishes for me. "Don't think I can add anything because you view me as an inexperienced trainee?"

Then she reaches over and bops me on the head again. I wonder if she learned that from watching Shen beat Grun so often. At the time I thought it was funny watching that thin woman pound the burly dwarf. Now I have sympathy for the poor grumpy man. And of course, I also now know why she always won these kinds of arguments over Grun's objections.

"Okay, Aria, you win. Let's do it together. The correct terms for the 'before and after stuff' is pre-op and post-op or pre-mission and post-mission. This is an operation, so you and I, together with Jo, will do pre-op planning."

Once again, her smile is bright and excited. And distracting. Aria always loves learning new things. She's like me in that way.

[Hey, Jo, is there a Mental Fortitude attribute or ability?]

No. All non-magica mental checks use the Intelligence attribute as their primary calculation variable. There are various resistances to various mental attacks or manipulations but you don't have any of those. Just give up. You haven't realized it yet, but she has you wrapped around her finger . . .

[She's the student. I'm the trainer. Nobody is wrapped around anybody.]

If you say so . . .

Breaking into my argument with Jo, Aria starts dictating to me what she thinks the operations plan should be. "This is ice, right? So we need to prepare warm things. I think you should do this op or whatever by the tub, filled and heated. That way when it's over you can either dive in or I can push you in if it is going bad. What do you think?"

I smile at her. Not wanting to hurt her feelings, I start with, "I think your premise is absolutely correct. We need to do this in a way where we are prepared to heat my body. That being said, I think the bathroom and tub idea has some planning holes.

"First, what happens if the cold isn't contained in my body but expands beyond into the environment? The moisture in the air from the steam will condense on me and you and the floor, potentially making me and you even colder. And what if it is cold enough to freeze the water? The tub crystal may be able to keep up and stop the water from freezing, but it also may not. And even if it does, the water may not stay warm enough to do any good. It may actually be harmful if at the wrong temperature."

Aria starts deflating.

"Second, the bathroom floor will possibly also freeze and become slippery, putting myself and anyone with me at risk." The poor elf is practically hunched over. "I am not saying these things to be hurtful. You said you wanted to go through pre-op planning, and this is how it works. Ideas are tossed around and the good parts of each plan are taken and used. The less effective parts are put to the side for perhaps use at another time. I'm pleased you were thinking that way and you gave me the basics of an idea. That's how this is supposed to work. You are doing fine. Okay?"

She nods in a subdued way, still upset, either because I declined her idea or because her idea wasn't perfect. I hope I don't end up stopping her from sharing in the future. Was she raised by people who never told her she was wrong? Was she really that sheltered? I get she's an elf and all the human conventions don't apply, but she still has had fifty-three years to grow up. What the hell were these people doing to her? Thinking about all the lost opportunities to advance such a gifted child and then adult (at least in human years) makes me furious with her family once again. Maybe I'll understand one day, but I doubt a mortal like me will ever fully comprehend time the way near-immortals do.

Returning to the lesson, I smile gently at Aria. "When we create an op plan, we are looking at three things. Location, method, and reaction. So how about I take your idea and turn it around a little? I agree we need to be prepared to provide me warmth. What locations would be good for that? The bathroom was an interesting idea, but contains too many risks. Where else?"

Accepting the challenge like she always does, Aria slowly scans the hotel suite. She asks quietly, "Next to the fireplace?"

I smile widely. "Excellent starting idea. Tell me, does the fireplace feel hot enough to you?"

She holds her hands up to it and says, "Not really."

"Good, so what can we do about it?"

She looks at it and asks, "Ask Jo for help?"

"Wonderful idea. Go ahead."

Aria holds her two fingers to her ear and asks out loud with a glance at me and a half-grin. "Jo, can we turn the heat up in the fireplace so Vic won't freeze to death?"

I laugh at the phrasing as I hear Jo's response in my head.

Yes. I can raise the temperature of the fire to the point that it will not put the hotel at risk . . .

"Well done. I think we have part of the location worked out. Where should I sit near the fireplace?"

Again she looks around. This time she doesn't ask the answer, but gives it. Progress. "How about we move a stuffy chair closer. You won't fall out of it, and maybe the cushioning can help keep you insulated."

"Good thinking. Anything else you can think of in regards to location?" Aria looks around and blushes lightly but says, "No."

I smile. "That's okay. Me neither."

She smiles at me and asks, "Do we talk about method or reaction next?"

"I would like to discuss the reaction. Method will be the most difficult, so let's put it off for the purposes of your training."

She just nods, likely not having a preference.

"So tell me. What kinds of reactions should we be prepared to take? Since we already know that I may be an iceman, what can we do about that?"

Her face becomes pensive. Elves don't get wrinkles, but if she were a human I'd say it was scrunched in thought.

"I guess first is the fireplace. Jo should be ready to turn it all the way up," she proposes.

I nod once but say nothing. You can do this, keep thinking.

"We need to find a way to heat you if the fireplace isn't enough. Since water isn't right, do we have warm blankets?"

I nod a few times, smiling. "Well reasoned. Look in your medical kit and see if anything we have might work."

She taps her ring, and the large, gold-colored metal box appears and sinks into the couch in front of her. It has the words "Magica Medical Technologies Large Medical Aid and Preparedness Kit" in white on the front next to a white crystal. Aria touches the crystal, and moments later a holographic screen appears in front of her, listing the contents. She looks at the screen and then looks at me and asks, "Infused thermal blanket?"

I smile at her and nod. "Anything else?"

She keeps looking and starts listing a couple of things. "General-use life-infused restoration cream. Frostbite recovery crystal. Infused warmers specifically for feet and hands. Um . . . I don't think anything else here will help."

"Excellent reasoning, I'm impressed with this being your first cold-mission analysis." Once again I am hit with her blinding smile. I continue. "Can you think of anything else from a reaction perspective we should prepare for?"

Thinking face on again, she looks around. I smile and point directly at her face.

She stares at my finger and blinks once. "Life magica?"

"Yes. Planners are not immune to being used as tools in the operation. You cannot forget your own ability to directly participate."

Looking thoughtful, she says, "You too then, right?"

I smile again. "That's right. Assuming I can physically function, I can add both fire and life magica to the operation. I think we have it all but one little thing. I propose we have Jo prepare me a hot drink. Warming from the inside is just as good as the outside."

She smiles, liking the idea.

"Now that leaves the method. Let's have dinner and think about what emotions ice might require to activate."

We have a nice dinner of meat and potatoes and Aria offers an idea. "What if we have a frozen dessert and think about ice over that?"

"That is genius, Aria."

She blushes and says, "It was Jo's idea. She wanted me to take credit though."

[Bad girl.]

"Well, I appreciate your honesty. It's genius either way."

Over some sort of frozen red fruit mixed with a thick orange sauce, we think out loud about the concept of ice.

Aria says, "Cold always meant slowness or sleepiness to Mom. She said nature tends to slow down or go to sleep when it's cold."

"Hmm. That's good. What else?" Taking another bite and thinking, I say, "I think of it as solid. Unbending. Whenever I was on a mission in the winter or a wintery landscape, I had to either break or cut through ice. It is either solid or broken in my mind."

Aria nods. "That's true." Quiet for a second, she says, "Hey, Vic, why didn't you do the 'method, location, reaction' with the death stone?"

Looking up at her in surprise, I ask, "What makes you think I didn't?" She blinks silently at me. "Tell me, what is the difference between death and ice from the perspective of absorbing it to gain the affinity? Use the knowledge you just learned to answer the question."

She looks at me and then at the remains of her dessert. "You didn't know what the method would be. Thinking back, I guess you did do pre-op. You had me there and told me how to react. We were together in a place where we could do something even if we didn't know what. I get it. Sorry."

I lift my hand and place it on her shoulder. "I know that was scary. I won't pretend I wasn't terrified." Taking my hand back, I sit back in my seat. "Believe me, Jo already gave me a lecture. I am sorry about that. I am not confident I could have changed the outcome no matter what, but scaring you in such a way is not okay with me. Can you forgive me for it?"

She stands up, walks over leans down, and looks me directly in my azure eyes with her golden. "I do." She stands up and says, "You're my protector, and you need to get stronger. I get that comes with risks sometimes."

Then she leaves for her room calling, "I'm taking a hot bath to prep for your next crazy."

Chuckling, I think of another past experience.

[Did you tell her about my [Inventory] crazy?]

I did. She was impressed with your level of lunacy ...

[Me too. She's right though, a hot bath is the correct prep. Can you get a warm drink ready at the right time?]

Affirmative . . .

CHAPTER 70

We are as prepared as we can be with all the supplies laid out, and the foolhardy-but-necessary risks ready to be taken.

"Okay. Op start. Are you fully prepared and good to go? The correct answers are either 'Confirmed' or 'Hold.'"

Aria smiles, rolls her eyes, and says, "Confirmed."

I smile back and stick my tongue out at her.

I close my eyes to a soft, bell-like laugh.

Focus, children...

"Yes, dear."

I get comfortable in the puffy chair near the fireplace, and the chilly crystal appears in my hands.

I close my eyes, send mana into it, and withdraw it from the crystal. I shiver with the cold and appear next to my river.

As usual, I see a stream of mana approaching. This one is so light blue to almost be white, and it is not gaseous, but crystalline. Every motion has a slight cracking sound. It is beautiful and terrifying at once. I don't need to do anything to feel its emotions. Somewhat similar to death mana's desire to end life, the ice crystals go further and emulate the need to stop everything. Motion means heat and is the antithesis of ice. Everything must be frozen still. No motion, no life, no death. Simply stopped.

I find myself frozen without even noticing how. I cannot move, I can barely think.

*Warning! Host has suffered **Freeze**. All movement reduced by 99% for 10 minutes...*

The crystalline structure immediately moves to my raging river and, with a fury, attacks it to stop its motion. There must be stillness in all things. My river immediately starts freezing over.

Warning! Host has received 1 elemental (Ice) damage...

Warning! Host has received 1 elemental (Ice) damage...

Warning! Host has received 1 elemental (Ice) damage . . .

. . .

. . .

. . .

. . .

Pain! All I know is pain as my entire body begins freezing solid. First, my skin, then my muscles, ligaments, and tendons. Then my bones, veins, arteries, capillaries.

Warning! Host has 10% remaining health . . .

Warning! Host has received 1 elemental (Ice) damage . . .

Warning! Host has received 1 elemental (Ice) damage . . .

. . .

. . .

My blood freezes, and the cells floating inside become solid with it. I would cry out if I could. Somehow I feel my nerves and brain freeze.

Warning! Host has 5% remaining health . . .

Warning! Host has received 1 elemental (Ice) damage . . .

Warning! Host has received 1 elemental (Ice) damage . . .

. . .

. . .

The very atoms that make up life become fixed in space and time. Echoing through my mind is the single thought, Everything. Must. Stop. Then I black out.

***

Host has absorbed 2,129.14 mana essence from **Mana Stone (Ice)**

New rune activated. Ice Rune is now available for use . . .

New affinity activated. Ice Affinity is now available for use . . .

Host has been healed for 41 damage . . .

Host has been healed for 41 damage . . .

Host has been healed for 41 damage . . .

Freeze *has been successfully removed. All movement has returned to normal . . .*

I come to in the real world shivering without the ability to control it. I can feel the heat of the fireplace blazing next to me, but it doesn't want to warm me. I can feel the blanket on me, but the heat is too much about motion, and my body rejects it.

A voice in my ear says, "Drink this, Vic." And something is put to my chattering mouth. A drop of liquid enters my mouth, and my mind can sort of feel it. It drips down my tongue to my throat and inside me. Then another. And another.

Finally, I feel an explosion of warmth and motion starting to manifest in my center as more of the liquid enters me. I can finally feel an effect from the fireplace and blanket and barely move my head to look around. Aria is close and pulls the glass back.

Still chattering, I move my mouth barely enough to say, "Ttttthankkkkkks."

She smiles and nods. I am able to move a little more and curl the blanket closer around me. Soon I can reach out and take the glass. I notice I have a mitten on. They radiate a glowing red light and, now that I am thinking about it, I can feel the heat on my fingers.

"That wasn't great," I say through still chattering teeth after taking another sip of the warm liquid.

I hear an exasperated sigh. "Really? Not great?"

[At least I got the rune.]

Yes, you got the rune. I think you came closer to death this time than you did with the death stone. I find that ironic and am hoping you can enlighten us as to why . . .

Finding it difficult to speak, I think to both of them instead.

[Ice is scary. More scary than death in some ways. Ice wants to end all motion. It will not stand for any warmth or motion at all. Time stopped completely. It's hard to explain, but that was pretty humbling.]

Aria says, "If you can get there, go take a bath. I have the water ready for you."

I offer a relieved smile. "Thank you. I think I'd like that."

I require a little help to stay standing and walk so Aria lets me lean on her as I work my way to my bathroom. She leaves as I strip and climb into the tub. That bath is the warmest, most soothing bath I have taken in years.

CHAPTER 71

Lying in bed that night, I go through my alerts with Jo.

New skill activated. Passive skill [Death Mana Manipulation] now available for use...

Skill updated. Passive skill [Death Mana Manipulation] has leveled from 0 to 3...

[Excellent. Death is a fascinating and addictive affinity. I'm interested in its capabilities.]

I know you don't like seeing the damage alerts, but I want you to see how your damage works when using death magica...

*You have struck an **Ice Mana-Mutated Greater Burrow Direbear** for 112.41 death damage...*

*You have struck an **Ice Mana-Mutated Greater Burrow Direbear** for 219.09 death damage...*

*You have struck an **Ice Mana-Mutated Greater Burrow Direbear** for 335.18 death damage...*

*You have struck an **Ice Mana-Mutated Greater Burrow Direbear** for 451.30 death damage...*

*You have struck an **Ice Mana-Mutated Greater Burrow Direbear** for 565.51 death damage...*

*You have struck an **Ice Mana-Mutated Greater Burrow Direbear** for 680.12 death damage...*

*You have struck an **Ice Mana-Mutated Greater Burrow Direbear** for 793.84 death damage...*

*You have struck an **Ice Mana-Mutated Greater Burrow Direbear** for 844.79 death damage...*

[That is a crap ton of damage. What a scary weapon we've added to my arsenal.]

Agreed. The only problem is the speed. It took minutes to do that damage, which is what I wanted to show you...

[Good point and thank you. Everything has balance, I suppose. Can you show me the essence gain again? I was a little too out of it to notice at the moment of award.]

You have killed an **Ice Mana-Mutated Burrow Direbear**. *You absorb 3,791.03 mana essence . . .*

[The . . . direbear was quite strong to give as much essence as it did. Probably like my last bear experience, I would have been squished had it not been sedated.]

I agree again. That was a very strong beast. I wonder how they captured it . . .

[Speaking of getting my ass kicked, why haven't I seen any skill activation from my sparring in the dojo or from the range?]

I've been suppressing them. We agreed you were going to wait on your profile for the end of the four weeks, so all I have been showing are affinity and essence alerts. Was that an incorrect presumption? . . .

I'm silent. That is a fascinating path of deduction for a system consciousness to take. I said nothing specifically about alerts, all I said was I wished to hold off on my profile so I could be surprised and hopefully pleased at the progress. Jo is definitely advancing.

[No, Jo. I'm just surprised by it all.]

For what it is worth, activating ice affinity took all your health but 1 point . . .

[I'm not surprised. The way ice works, it needed to 'stop' me. I'm just thankful it allowed me one. So far none of these affinities seem intent on leaving me dead.]

We can be thankful for that, I suppose. You should absorb the rest of the essence from the stone . . .

I take out the stone. It creates a soft blue-white glow in the dark room.

I place the now-empty box from Mr. Whyatt in my lap.

Host has absorbed 1,756.86 mana essence from **Mana Stone (Ice)** *. . .*

I [Inventory] the dust and put the box back.

[How much essence do I have now?]

Enough for level 6 . . .

[I wonder how leveling will change me.]

I have no idea, Vic. But knowing you, whatever it is, will be completely unexpected . . .

[Goodnight, Jo.]

Night . . .

***

Another six days pass with Aria and me following our training plans and improving our capabilities every day. During our morning stretches, Mr. Whyatt pops into the exercise center and hands me a data crystal.

All he says is "I have a pilot ready. You can join our research team."

Vic, this crystal is directing you to a previously inactive volcano that appears to have reawakened recently. It includes credentials as a member of a research team leaving tomorrow at 08:30, recommended additional equipment, and a primer on volcanic lifeforms. When I compare the location to Commander Franklin's maps, the specific location is titled "Mount Saint Helens." . . .

[I wonder who Saint Helens was. Unusual name for a human, but pre-Invasion people were odd.]

True. Shall I order the recommended additional equipment to be ready tomorrow morning? . . .

Thinking about it, I withdraw the medical kit like Aria did earlier and check what it has for burns and other heat-based injuries. It seems well equipped with numerous cooling salves, healing creams, water-based crystals, and the like. Considering what I paid for these kits, they had *better* be provisioned for just about any injury.

[Yes. Is Aria awake?]

She is reading human entertainment content . . .

Really? I wonder if she enjoys that sort of thing. Or maybe she just wants to try to understand humanity better. Good for her if that is the case.

I get up and knock on our shared door.

I hear a muffled "Come in."

I step inside and walk around her bed to the chair near her room's large window wall which is currently not dimmed. She is sitting atop her covers, her back against the headboard and legs straight out but crossed at the ankes and follows me with her eyes, a curious look on her face. I also notice her face is a little red.

Putting the cryspad face down on her legs, she looks me up and down, flushes deeper, and asks, "What's up, Vic?"

I look down and notice I forgot to put a shirt on. Damn. I always sleep without a shirt when not on a mission but otherwise try to not be unclothed around her as it seems to make her uncomfortable. Shirts get tangled around me during sleep and make me feel trapped so I just don't wear them. Aria on the other hand sleeps clothed in shorts and a tank top which is made of only slightly more material than what she wears while working out.

Clearing my throat, I let her know of my plan. "I have a mission tomorrow." She opens her mouth, but I cut her off with a raised hand. "A solo mission. Sorry." She slumps and looks depressed. I sigh. "Aria, this one really is incredibly dangerous. I am not sure I would go if I had a choice."

This seems to mollify her somewhat, and she nods. I nod back and am about to stand when it's her turn to clear her throat. I sit back and look curiously at her.

She looks down and runs her thin fingers along the back of the cryspad in her lap. "Ummm. Vic. Can I ask you a question?"

I blink at her. "You ask me questions all the time. Why would you ask if you can ask?"

She clears her throat again and says, "This is different. It's . . . Um . . . a personal question."

Personal? What does she want to know? I can't tell her much, given the nature of my work. And my life before that is too . . . no. She doesn't need that in her life, and I can protect her from those sorts of horrors for a little longer.

I say slowly, "I suppose."

Aria looks up at me, her face a bright red. "You know what? Never mind."

I let out a breath I didn't know I was holding and slump slightly. "Okay. Maybe we can talk about whatever it is later."

"Okay. Night, Vic."

"Night."

CHAPTER 72

Stepping from the unarmed Totem Vehicles transport with the six other Whyatt researchers is certainly different from my usual approach to missions, but my identity is hidden, so I can make it work. The masks we all wear are enchanted specifically to prevent toxic fumes from poisoning our lungs. To keep costs down, they were created for the sole purpose of filtering gasses only related to volcanic activity. Of course, there are many ways to prevent airborne toxins, but the more protection provided, the more cost. And it raises exponentially due to how complicated inscriptions can become. So the human, dwarf, four gnome scientists, and myself in our effective-but-cost-effective cloth masks and fully enclosed heat resistant cloaks and boots tromp forward to the UFH cordon.

Motion sensors, mana shields, mobile turrets, and crystal projectors dot the landscape. Blinking WARNING and UFH CORDON in glowing transparent white alerts potential trespassers that the area has been blocked for everyone's safety. An active volcano within a hundred kilometers of a city of half a million humanoids under UFH's protection requires action by the authorities. Thankfully, this is not that uncommon of an occurrence given that both mana spikes and larger creatures have a tendency to make environs dependably undependable. Humans are nothing if not adaptable when it comes to our survival. We learned after the loss of cities to "natural disasters" that special protections and actions would be required to survive not just the Invaders, but the mana itself. As such, numerous UFH teams have been trained specifically for the prevention, protection, and (now rarely used, thankfully) evacuation of cities from nearby environmental crises.

As one would expect of a professional force with expertise, this particular deployment appears polished and choreographed. The troopers in their mottled black and gray MiliMech isolation armor, many times more expensive than our research team's gear, are distributed along the ten-kilometer circled area. A single trooper holds up a hand as we approach one of the four entrances to the cordoned disaster zone. On the top right of her chest is the standard UFH logo, a shield under a globe with the letters UFH inside and a pair of swords crossing both diagonally, and in the center are the acronym ECR, short for Environmental Crisis Response, in common. Only the dwarves seem to love acronyms as much as the human military—probably because of their desire to speak quickly.

A mechanized woman's voice reverberates from the sealed helmet. "Authorization?"

A gnome, our team lead, steps forward and taps his wrist.

The soldier's head tilts to the side as if listening to something in her ear, and then she straightens and speaks. "Whyatt research team, yes." She gestures at another fully armored marine to her left. "Corporal Manendez will escort you to your research site." After a tap of the pad, she continues. "Please inform us if you find the cause. At last report, we will be required to take action to drain this volcano in eleven hours at the current rate of instability growth. Please let us know if your research shows any changes, but our seismic activity detection is likely superior so I do not expect that." Another tap of the pad and her voice changes to become more bland and rote. "You have all received our local comms. If evacuation is ordered, you will follow those orders or be left to die. My team is not responsible for your safety once you pass the cordon. Any injury or death is no longer the responsibility or liability of the UFH military or government. Do you accept these terms? Failure to do so will result in your access past the cordon being denied."

Confirmed receipt of communication authorization and I have sent confirmation of your agreement . . .

[Thanks.]

The marine looks down at the pad and nods, all members of the Whyatt team having agreed to the legal and bureaucratic inanity. She steps aside, and I follow the rest of the team, who are following the corporal. As we climb, I notice clear signs of instability in the area. Whole swaths of the forest are filled with trees leaning or broken.

Mask filtering is sufficient to protect your breathing needs for another six hours at current rate before a mask change is required. However, the toxicity is increasing as you approach the source . . .

Not only is the air getting more difficult to breathe in, but the closer we get to the center, the more evidence we find of quakes ripping apart the ground. Fissures spewing ash and fumes become more common, thus further reducing our masks' effectiveness.

The panting voice of our team lead sounds in my ear. "We are approaching our research area. While it is shielded to offer breathable air, I recommend you not remove your masks in case of a breach. I am sending you your assignments. If you are assigned a search area, please stay in comms and check in every ten minutes at the longest."

You have received orders for a search grid that includes a closely packed group of fissures which are marked as "unusual and required further investigation." . . .

[Excellent. Remind me to thank Mr. Whyatt for setting all this up. Now guide me so we can get the hell out of here.]

I recommend you check-in at the local camp to avoid suspicion . . .

I let out a sigh muffled by the breathing mask. Hiding from my own government and military is becoming a pain. I need to finish detailing out my plans for exposure, willing or not.

A few minutes later we approach a dome of clear gray mana fifty meters in diameter shielding a bustling area filled with various devices no doubt in search of ways to monetize the volcano. I wonder if endeavors like this are even profitable. And then I drop the thought because I don't give a troll's shit.

You are checked in. Search gear has been assigned; I will direct you to it and then to your targeted search location . . .

***

[It's too bad my skin doesn't protect against heat the way it does cold.]

Yes. That would certainly make your already ridiculously overpowered self more capable. And have fewer reasons to complain about said status . . .

Climbing over another massive fallen fir tree two hours from the basecamp, I roll my eyes at the sarcastic tone. I wasn't complaining. Seriously. I was reviewing my tactical advantages and, in this case, disadvantages. If I were in an icy landscape, in the middle of a blizzard, surrounded by a nearly frozen ocean in the nude, and searching for a cold-based creature, I would be in less of a vulnerable state than I am now. Nothing in my supposedly powerful form protects me from toxic fumes, burning trees, spewing steam, or molten lava. I wasn't lying to Aria when I said I wouldn't be here if I could find another way.

Another rumble and vibration beneath my feet cause me to pause and steady myself. Quakes are happening regularly now, occasionally opening new fissures.

[Has Crisis Response updated their timeline? It feels like this isn't going to hold as long as the original eleven hours.]

Not at this time. The magica volcanologists have not updated their findings although I too wonder if perhaps they have simply not communicated it out yet . . .

Well, either way, we need to be out well before they deal with the situation. I have no intention of being around when they fire up the inscriptions they've been drawing to drain the volcano of its energy. After the effectiveness of this method was exposed by the dwarves, humanity immediately began asking about its wartime applications. Unfortunately, that went nowhere, as it takes more than an hour to power up, depending on the area, and is immediately detectable to any creature inside. Oh, yeah. And it can fail and cause feedback if inscribed incorrectly or interrupted. So instead of draining energy from, say, a supermassive volatile volcano, it would push the entry back into it, creating a loop of energy recycling until, eventually, it stored more than both it and the inscriptions would hold, resulting in an explosion many times worse than the original would have been. It is also the reason why all these expeditions are "allowed" inside; if anything that could interrupt the process can be found, it will be by the dozens of teams exploring for their own reasons. Obviously, the ECR team explores to find anything obvious as well.

An unfortunate incident where an Invader force was hidden and attacked during this very process resulted in a tidal wave wiping out the entire population of numerous islands and two, thankfully small, coastal cities in the Pacific. Only cities protected by massive, enchanted fort walls and mana shields survived. This world is filled with hard lessons. On the other side of the copper, there was a spark of good news; it also wiped out an Invader-held city, which allowed UFH forces to regain control of Kong City Island. The mega-corporation Hyoto Engineering now uses that isolated area as one of its major production facilities.

Another quake, this one strong enough to launch me a half-meter into the air, interrupts my musing on this foolishness. I land on my ass and roll downhill for a few meters before another shake throws my prone body back up only to come crashing down onto a fallen tree. After an "oof" of air exiting my lungs and a break in the rocking of earth, do I manage to get a hold of myself and stand.

[For fuck's sake. This is ridiculous.]

You could always leave and forget about magma affinity . . .

We both know I won't do that; the benefit of extending my magica is simply too high.

***

Forty-five minutes later, I am standing at the edge of a hundred-meter-wide, ash-covered crater peppered with perfectly circular holes ranging from one to five meters wide. Each of the holes glows the bright orange of superheated stone, steam, and other poisonous fumes visibly belching from them.

[No wonder this was marked as requiring investigation. There is no way this is natural.]

I concur. The chances of so many perfect circles forming without external assistance exceeds credulity . . .

[Good thing we beat the ECR here. Looks like we are going to have to take some risks.]

Finding a location that will allow me to enter without falling into a glowing hole, I sit at the edge of the crater.

[I'm going to swap out for a clean mask before heading in. The toxicity will be higher near the fissures, and it may not be safe to do so that close . . .]

I learned that from my other missions in similar conditions near toxic land. While this may be my first foray onto a quaking volcano, I've navigated poisonous areas before.

Sensible. Even though it is not required, you may wish to use your air magica. While it cannot create air, it can circulate it enough for the different weights to separate, allowing you to quickly swap out masks, reducing risk . . .

[Great idea. Thanks.]

Creating a bubble, I take a deep breath of purified air, circulate it quickly, causing different densities of gas to separate, duck below the visible fumes from the environs, disconnect the soiled cloth mask, reattach one of my four clean ones, and reactivate the enchantments. Was all that necessary? Probably not. But I'll take any advantage I can get.

Back on my butt at the edge, I begin a slow controlled slide into the crater. This had better be worth it.

Communication of UFH forces has informed personnel that the timeline for evacuation is six hours from now . . .

[Good to know.]

At about halfway, I begin shifting my legs and torso to adjust the slide to the right. I'm a bit closer to one of the strange, circular fissures that I would like. Just as I lighten up on my rightward push, having made it past, the ground begins shaking again. The already-glowing circles brighten visibly from yellow to nearly white, and I lose control of my slide. Shit.

I'm shoved upwards with a lurch from below. It's barely a few inches, but that is enough to remove my limited control, and I land almost sideways. I begin to roll but manage to stop myself from a fully uncontrolled spinning descent by stiffening my left leg and arm. Now I am sliding down three times faster than before, escorted by stones and ash, and unable to stop. My eyes widen, as a glowing hot fissure three meters wide is five meters in front of me and closing fast. With a jerk, I roll onto my front and slam my left hand into the ground. Within my gripped fingers is the same twelve-inch knife I used at the club to kill the tigerkin woman. The blade is jammed into the ground almost all the way to the hilt, dragging at the stony ground and attempting to pull free. The friction of the knife and my body combine to slow my descent until, finally, I come to a halt with my supposedly heat-resistant boots inches from the circle of glowing stone and steaming.

I pull my legs away and then jerk my hand away from my knife. Looking at the handle, the leather grip is bubbling and the visible steel glowing a gentle red. Looks like I'll need a new knife; even if I manage to get it out, its temper will be ruined.

[All right, I'm down. Time to see what we find in here.]

Just like you planned . . .

Ignoring the snark, I crawl farther from the fissure, wait for the shaking to stop, stand, and pat my cloak and pants down. I walk around, attempting an [Inspect] here or there but finding nothing of consequence. It is as expected, but still disappointing.

Seems like I'm stuck doing this the hard way.

CHAPTER 73

A crystal one inch in diameter appears in my hand as I make my way around the crater, keeping some distance from the fissures. I'm looking for a specific one or this may not work. There it is. My target is not the biggest, only being two meters in diameter, but it is the brightest and hottest I can find. Getting as close as I can without ruining my protective gear, I toss the blue orb into the glowing circle and then turn and jog back so I am at least ten meters from any fissure.

Sixty seconds after it hits the white-hot stone, the crystal shines brightly, and a deep blue flash lights the area, followed by the sizzling and crackling sounds of stone being cooled too quickly for its molecular structure to support. I take out the new rifle I purchased for this single purpose—crazy expensive as it was—and prepare for what I believe is next.

Nothing else happens.

Well, that's boring.

I change my rifle to a one-handed grip and withdraw an equally expensive identical crystal from my [Inventory.] Just as I take a step to try again with another fissure, another quake hits. It starts at a rumble, but the volume increases until, with a massive lurching upwards, I slam onto the raised ground. Before I can even think about a reaction, the ground beneath my butt vanishes as the earth sinks a full two meters and I am left floating until I drop and slam into the stony ground once again. The rifle and crystal, which I managed to hold onto during the first hit, slide from my hands as I open my fingers in an attempt to absorb some of the force from the blow.

Thankfully, the earth stops thrusting up and down long enough for me to gather my wits and scan for the threat I believe is nearby. I reach and grab the rifle, but the crystal is rolling away in the rumbling ground. Letting it go for now, I rise to my knees but stop as a new sound resonates from the center of the crater. Lifting my head, I witness the splitting of the earth as many-ton slabs of superheated stone and earth rise and fall outward. The accompanying cracking and crumbling sounds are overwhelmed by an earthshaking screech as two terrifying four-meter-long, serrated, sickle-like protrusions rise from the fissure, followed closely by a creature six meters long and three meters wide that crawls through the massive fissure on six thin legs. Glowing hot magma drips in great splashing clumps from its bulbous form as it frees itself from the surrounding earth.

Huh. So that's what's here.

Name:	**Magma-Engorged and Mutated Antlion Larva**
Description:	Infused antlion larva are voracious eaters and usually found in areas surrounded by other insect life. These creatures tend to dig into the earth, create pit traps for other creatures to fall into, and then snap them up with their massive scything jaws. Ambush predators, antlion larva are not known for chasing or actively hunting prey, preferring to wait in their pit traps. However, there are reports of them chasing down creatures that provoke them, usually other antlions, but occasionally other carnivorous insects. This particular antlion larva was exposed to an influx of mana from an unknown source while submerged in ash on the side of a volcano, causing it to mutate into a magma-based creature and grow many times its normal size.
Condition:	Furious, Hungry
Risk Assessment:	Very High
Value:	Magma-Infused creatures are rare and highly sought after. This creature's shell, mandibles, and mana stone would bring a high price in almost any market.

Excellent.

[Send the signal.]

Sent . . .

The key to the success of this mission is twofold. First, the requirement of threats to the draining operation being exposed and dealt with by the ECR team. Second, the agreement between corporations and the UFH that any creature found and killed, whether by UFH forces or not, belongs to the group that reports it. Decades ago, it was negotiated that when companies respond to an ECR sanctioned emergency by sending research, discovery, collection, or hunting teams, the "generosity" of the groups is reciprocated with the reward of any resources they identify. The UFH agreed because of the gains they make through the energy drain process, which is a substantial amount of power stored in various crystal storage containers similar to mana stones. The dwarves get a twenty-five percent cut as a "licensing fee," but everything else belongs to the UFH military for use in the war.

ECR acknowledges receipt and will send forces to subdue the creature . . .

This is the whole purpose of my solo jaunt. It was critical that a Whyatt team be the one to find what he and I believed to be here, a magma-affinity creature. Thus the need to expose it, report it, and now survive long enough for the ECR team to come kill it. Speaking of which, it is at this point that I should be running at high speed away from the ginormous murder beetle.

Another deafening screech echoes throughout the crater as the antlion's six legs rotate its massive body in an attempt to locate whatever bothered it.

It is unlikely you have any weapons or skills capable of harming such a creature . . .

I entirely agree and sprint to the side of the crater, [Inventory]ing my rifle. Noticing a familiar globe, I lean over and grab the blue crystal with my left hand as I run by, only having to slow slightly. A crashing sound from behind—followed by the stony ground shifting again—causes me to stumble, but I regain my momentum and continue to sprint with a glance backward. I see the massive insect has fully extricated itself from the fissure it burst through and has spotted me. Well, that's not great.

I change my course to the nearest safe path out of the antlion's trap. Not pleased with my attempted escape, the ungainly monstrosity slides its orange glowing carapace down the mountain of steaming lava, stone, and earth, unknowingly mimicking my entrance to its territory. I'm halfway to a crater wall by the time the furious antlion reaches the floor of the crater. Another bellowing screech and the chase is on. Sparing another glance at its closing form, I feel like the creature's six spindly legs seem too fragile to move such a massive creature so damn quickly. Fuck.

[Where's the ECR?]

No ETA is available . . .

Wonderful.

By the time I reach the crater's wall and start to climb, the antlion is only twenty meters behind. Scrambling up the loose stone isn't easy, but in the time it takes the antlion to catch up, I manage to reach ten meters, which I hope is far enough. The insect stops after climbing only enough so it is angled at me. The orange glow of the creature brightens and pulses. Three seconds later, it opens its massive scythe-like jaws and screams. The earth beneath me shakes again, and I slam into the ground and begin to slide backward. My chin makes contact with the stoney ground and I bite my tongue hard enough that I taste the copper of blood. Shaking my head, I grit my teeth, straighten my fingers, and knife my hands directly through the stones and into the earth.

*Warning! Host has suffered **broken fingers (left hand).** All hand motions are reduced in dexterity by 75% for 30 hours . . .*

*Warning! Host has suffered **broken fingers (right hand).** All hand motions are reduced in dexterity by 75% for 30 hours . . .*

My body continues to fall, but my now broken hands and still-pumping legs manage to stop my downward motion. I feel another snap as the weight on my wrists breaks another bone.

*Warning! Host has suffered a broken **wrist (left).** All wrist and hand motions are reduced in dexterity by 90% for 60 hours . . .*

A scream of pain and frustration makes it past my gritted teeth, along with spit and specks of sparkling blood. I hold on for what feels like hours of pain but is less than ten seconds, and then the shaking stops. Glancing down, I notice the antlion's glow has dimmed dramatically. Looking up and forward again, I withdraw my broken hands from the crater wall and, ignoring the worst of the pain, scramble up farther.

Less than a minute later, I climb over the lip and roll unto my back, holding my aching arms up. Tilting my head, I look down and see the creature has stopped climbing only a third of the way up. Surprisingly, it begins to turn its body around. Using my elbows to sit up, I look down, curious. Is it retreating back into its hole? That would be bad. I need that thing.

Thinking of how to prevent it from fleeing underground, it distracts me by doing something completely unexpected. Instead of climbing back down now that it is facing towards the crater, the insect rams its bulbous backside into the stone and dirt of the side of the crater. In seconds, it has disappeared underground.

"Drake shit!"

Scrambling to my feet, I start considering my options. Looking at my gloved hands, I find two fingers on the right hand and three on the left are bent in unnatural ways. Damnit. I think I lost it.

[What the fuck is taking them so damn long?]

While I have no evidence other than the lack of competing priorities, it is possible they are intentionally delaying. The agreement about beast carcasses is void if the original reporter is killed prior to validation of a target...

"Fuck!" I scream with all the air in my lungs.

I can't even fix my fingers because both hands have problems and the bones need to be set before being healed with magica. I'm so furious at myself and the ECR that I stomp around the crater, trying to find another angle to see where it went. It is at this point that the ground starts shaking again. I wobble and find myself directly above an area that has started steaming. This actually gives me hope, and a smile forms under the cloth covering my face when I begin to feel some intense heat coming from directly below me. I leap in the air and as I land, I stomp my feet down hard. Further vibrations happen beneath me, and I have to move away from the area, the heat gets so intense. In fact, the earth starts to glow slightly. Yes! Murder beetle is back!

I stomp again and again as I slowly move farther from the crater. Suddenly, the glowing earth starts to bulge again. This time I turn around and run away.

[Direct me to the nearest ECR team.]

Looking over my shoulder briefly, I grin as I find the glowing bulge following me, creating a long furrow in the ground as the displaced dirt and glowing stone causes it to sink in. Just to make sure the mutated antlion keeps following, I fire occasional air blades at the dirt and clomp loudly while following Jo's green line.

Support incoming. I have updated your location...

The green line makes a sudden shift left, and I turn that way, making extra noise and firing a cluster of air blades in the ground behind me. And then I hear them openly comming each other.

"Target confirmed, open fire."

Three flyers and six armed troop vehicles all begin firing in my direction. Straight ahead of me, I find one of the three-inch cannon barrels on the back of a vehicle discharge a fist-sized gray mana projectile that streaks in my direction.

I skid to a stop and leap backward and to the right. Those fucking trolls' asses!

[Record and connect me to them.]

Throwing myself to the side and covering my head, I manage to dodging exploding earth, shattering trees, and flying shards of solidified air. I scramble to my feet and sprint diagonally away from the soldiers and towards the creatures.

Connection established . . .

Panting, I say, "This is a member of the Whyatt Research team. I'm the one who reported the beast."

One last explosion next to me sends me careening sideways through the air where my ribs make first contact with some sort of solid object, followed by my already-broken hands and wrist.

Warning! Host has suffered a **Broken Rib.** All activity involving moving the body is reduced by 25% and causes pain for 90 hours . . .

Warning! Host has suffered a **Broken Rib.** All activity involving moving the body is reduced by 25% and causes pain for 90 hours . . .

Warning! Host has suffered a **Broken Rib.** All activity involving moving the body is reduced by 25% and causes pain for 90 hours . . .

I collapse to the ground, my vision fuzzy from the pain. I think I hear voices in my ears, but my brain isn't working quite right, and I can't make it out.

Slowly, the blurriness fades, and I recognize the familiar misery of breathing with broken ribs. *Very* slowly, I stand and tuck my arms across my body in an attempt to reduce the pressure. It doesn't help. In the background, I hear the screeching and booms of combat between the military and a powerful beast.

[Status?]

You are out of the line of fire now and beyond the range of any reasonable accidental friendly fire incident. The ECR team attempted to reach you after they launched you ten meters into a tree and allege your failure to respond absolves them of your claim on the creature . . .

[That's not happening. Can you reach Mr. Whyatt?]

Not until the combat is over. All comms are blocked . . .

[Convenient. Guide me back to the battle.]

I hobble through the mountainside towards the fading sounds of battle. It seems like they almost have it down.

By the time I get there, the flyers are gone, but the six vehicles have made a circular cordon around the creature. It's movements are sluggish and it is wobbling, exhausted from both injury and combat. In less than a minute, the antlion collapses onto the ground in a squeak that sounds more like a whimper. I walk up behind one of the vehicles, ask Jo to start recording, and call out, "Thanks, guys."

Twelve projector rifles immediately target me, and I wince from the pain in my ribs as I hold up my wreck of a pair of hands. "Whoa, whoa. I'm a civilian. I'm the one that called you about the creature."

The barrels lower and I drop my arms with relief.

Walking forward past them, I move towards the creature.

A modulated but obviously male voice behind me calls out, "Your claim is lost. You failed to respond when asked and have forfeited any rights to that carcass."

I continue walking and say in a pleading tone, "But Whyatt has an active claim; it is dated upon entry."

The voice states, "That's not—"

"And I identified myself as soon as I saw your team."

I stop two meters from the creature. An [Inspect] tells me what I am looking at is a lifeless corpse. I stare at it for a moment, and the body jiggles slightly.

"I don't think it's dead," I say hurredly as I step back.

Two more shots into its face end the charade. An armored ECR soldier drops the ground from atop his transport and stalks towards me. He is carrying his weapon but it is aimed at the ground. "Your claim is revoked. If you attempt to touch that carcass, you will be shot for attempted theft of government property."

I back away with my hands up and wincing again. "All right, all right. I get the hint. I haven't touched the damn thing. I didn't even touch it before you killed it. I was just trying to survive."

Dropping my hands and sighing, I say, "Look, I'm just a researcher and I'm injured. Can I get a ride out of here please? The body is all yours."

The armored body turns away and says, "Cramer, you and your squad escort this civilian to med center four."

I hear a "Yes, sir" from my right and painfully shift my body in the direction.

[Let the Whyatt team know I have been injured and am heading to med center four. Do not tell them anything else.]

Sent. Will you inform Mr. Whyatt of the incident details? . . .

[Still deciding. For now, I just want my ribs and fingers fixed. Let Aria know I'll be home in a few hours.]

The troop vehicle I'm stuffed in is designed for a specified number of troopers in armor. I am neither in armor, nor designated my own seat, and as such am painfully crammed between two armored troopers, wincing as my ribs and hands get jostled repeatedly.

I also receive black faceplated helmets aimed in my direction. It is a subtle reminder about my now-defunct claim on the creature. I just continue to try ignoring the pain and wishing I was home soaking in a hot bath. To distract myself, I begin making plans for what to do with the new object in my [Inventory].

As my mask is still on and my face is down, the troopers can't see the wide smile on my face when I read the words above the last filled slot in my HUD: **Mana Stone (Magma)**.

CHAPTER 74

The bath is as luscious as I hoped. I might have stayed in here for a bit too long and fallen asleep because water splashes wildly as I'm surprised awake by a knock and the faint voice of Aria.

"Vic, are you okay?"

I call out, "Yep. Thanks for checking. I fell asleep."

"All right."

[She could have just asked you.]

That's true. Ask yourself why she didn't . . .

Thinking about it, I cannot figure out a reason that calling through a door is better than talking with Jo or comming me and finding out first hand.

[I have no idea.]

It will come to you eventually. Have you decided what to tell Mr. Whyatt? . . .

[Yes. Thank him for the opportunity he gave me and provide a recording of the events surrounding the creature. Ask him to handle it discreetly. The ECR teams, corrupt or not, poor aim or not, provide a critical service to humanity and the UFH. And all things considered, a single carcass isn't going to make or break anyone involved, even if it is a rare magma-affinity beast.]

Poor aim? . . .

[They had me in a direct line of fire and missed repeatedly despite their numbers and armaments. An experienced orc-kin would have never even been hit, never mind injured. Hell, I was unarmed, unarmored, without the use of my hands, and unable to cast magica without risking harming them, and I still lived through it. They should be ashamed of themselves. If I were officially alive, I'd send through channels a demand they all go through retraining. How the fuck is humanity supposed to win if we can't even kill a practically naked and crippled level zero?]

I find myself getting worked up again, so I wash up and head out to find Aria eating dinner at the table. I join her and receive a brilliant smile in exchange. Blinking at her, I wonder what the deal is. I mean, I'm thrilled she's happy, of course.

"What?"

She just smiles slyly and says, "Nothing. Just glad you're back."

"Oh. Um. Thanks." Whatever. We have other priorities now. "So, I managed to come away with another mana stone. This time you are going to manage the pre-op and post-op. I'll act as support."

Aria looks excited and nervous. Both are good.

After dinner, she walks me through her plan and does very well. She almost gets it all. I am guessing she finds it easier because it is basically the opposite of ice, which we have already gone through. Then it's time, and I take it on.

***

Host has absorbed 2,044.89 mana essence from **Mana Stone (Magma)** *. . .*

New rune activated. Magama Rune is now available for use . . .

New affinity activated. Magma Affinity is now available for use . . .

Activating the magma affinity is . . . rough. Magma is a weird mix of the destructive desires of fire and the blasé attitude of earth. How can something want to burn everything into ash at the same as not wanting to go anywhere to do it? In the end, the emotion sort of felt like a craving to "return everything to its source," ashes and dust and such. Either way, I nearly die . . . again. Melting to death is not okay, and I decide not to go into more detail than that with Aria. She doesn't need that kind of negativity in her life.

Wanting some alone time from that one, I ask Jo for the alerts as I mentally recover on the balcony with some wine.

Warning! Host has received 75 burning damage . . .

Warning! Host has received 75 burning damage . . .

Warning! Host has suffered **Catastrophic Burns.** *All attributes, abilities and skills reduced by 99% until healed.*

Host has been healed for 75 damage.

Host has been healed for 75 damage.

Catastrophic Burns *has been successfully removed. All movement has returned to normal . . .*

Thankfully, the permanent physical changes to your body are limited in the

inner world. You can burn yourself out with mana, but not melt yourself with magma. That is an important distinction . . .

[You are not wrong. I can't even tell you. It was horrible. I'd take death over ice or magma any day.]

Trying to take my mind off of it, I take a large gulp of the wine. I look at the drops of liquid remaining in my glass and reflect on the UFH's priorities. Humanity had lost thousands to defend the world's wine vineyards and hops farms, but only sent token forces to take back the city of Chigo Town.

Four or five years ago, the defenders had been taken by surprise from the north using a water assault, and now the city is a prison camp and slave hub for the enemy. I know little of it, having been something of a rookie and beyond my pay grade at the time. But I still find it astonishing we haven't even attempted to retake the city. I gulp the rest of the wine.

[I need a plate please, Jo]

Putting it on the chair in between my legs, I empty the rest of the mana stone. As far as I'm concerned the sooner it's dust the better.

*Host has absorbed 1,574.03 mana essence from **Mana Stone (Magma)** . . .*

As always, I [Inventory] the dust.

[Hey, Jo, I don't think we're going to get light and dark by the deadline. And I'm kind of okay with that. To be honest, I'm tired. My mind and body have been under a lot of strain from these affinities. I'm ready for other things.]

I know you're tired, Vic. If anyone deserves a break, you do. Why don't you and Aria take a day off? No mission plan, no stress, no research. Just a fun day for the family . . .

[You know what, that isn't a bad idea. While the operator part of me cringes at the thought of an unproductive day, I think I will take that idea and go with it.]

Any ideas what to do for your first day off in, well, a long fucking time? Or ever? . . .

[How would I know? Let's ask Aria.]

I stick my head in to see her watching a show about some ranger who goes into the wildlands and attempts to track, trap, and teach about wild beasts. Seems interesting and actually useful; I might watch that too.

Interrupting her, I say, "Hey, Aria." She blinks and turns her head to me. "What do you say to us taking a day off tomorrow? Just you and me and Jo off doing anything other than what we've been doing."

I honestly am not sure how she'll react, but what she says is definitely not anywhere near what I had in mind.

"Sure, as long as I make it back in time to do range time with Gina, I'm all for a day off."

You've created a monster, Vic. Nice job . . .

#I concur. Aria used to be such a nice girl . . .

[Oh, please. She found something she likes. Why deny it?]

I think she likes ranged weapons more than magica. Sound like someone you know? . . .

"Sure, Aria. What do you think is a good idea for a day off? I'm not exactly experienced in this sort of thing."

Smiling at me, she says, "I'll take the lead on this operation, Vic."

A monster, Vic . . .

#How could you, Host Vic?

[Enough from both of you. She's my trainee, and it makes me proud.]

CHAPTER 75

Aria arranges for a guided tour of the highlights of Sea Saddle City. She says, "We only have to get out of the grav trolley at certain stops—otherwise there is no walking. And lunch is at a restaurant center with dozens of different places to choose from."

I stop her right there and tell her I'm sold.

Aria and I spend a quality day together. There are a total of five stops on the tour. The first is a museum dedicated to pre-Invasion history. I'm impressed by what the proprietors have managed to save. There are sections dedicated to shows on things called "TelVision." I have a good laugh at an area that has a show about "magical creatures." In another exhibit, they have even managed to save a few pieces of plastic. Somehow, the pieces are sealed, and no mana can get to them to break them down. The crystal display claims they long ago had some processed aluminum and something called gasoline, but those are fantasy materials as far as I'm concerned.

Aria finds human history interesting and asks me all kinds of questions that I cannot answer. I mean, why would the planet's residents do so much to destroy their only home? How would I know the thinking of those trolls' asses? Maybe they were bored without living in constant fear of imminent death.

The second stop is a historic monument called a "space needle." I have no idea why as it doesn't have anything to do with the spatial affinity. The projection says quite a bit of it had to be replaced when mana dissolved all the processed components, but it survived. Barely. We take an inscription pad to port to the top, and I'll admit the view is amazing. Aria's fear of heights strikes, so she is gripping my arm hard.

"If you open your eyes, you can see the city, bridge, fort, and ocean. It's an unusually clear day today." She shakes her head vigorously and hides her face in my arm. "You know I would never let you actually fall to death, right?" She nods but doesn't stop hiding her face. In fact, she moves closer and hides her face in my shoulder. I sigh. "We'll work on your acrophobia when we get to wilderness training."

She just nods into me again.

The third, and my favorite, stop on the tour is a market that claims to have existed pre-Invasion called the Pike. I'm not sure I believe that, given that it is almost entirely underground, but I also don't care. It is filled with places to get different kinds of food, and I get a bit of six different kinds. There is one called "curry" which has a delectable burn. Aria gets the same as me except she adds a dessert. Well, two desserts, but she says she needs it to get over the trauma from the last stop. Either way, the food is delicious.

The fourth is a place we have already been, the Botanical Gardens. What I refer to now as "my" flower looks great.

The final stop is a monument. In the middle of a round area of well-trimmed red grass, a stone statue stands in front of a dome. The large statue, carved from some local gray stone and enchanted to prevent decay, is of three individuals: a female human, a male dwarf, and a male elf. The crystal display reads, "This monument stands as a remembrance of the sacrifice made by our three races to defend this city. Sea Saddle City stands as a joint human-allied territory thanks to the 14,420 humans, elves, and dwarves who died to keep it and its residents free."

There are fourteen trees in a circle that surround the dome, each in remembrance of a thousand martyred defenders. Aria and I walk shoulder to shoulder, circling with the trees in silence and absorbing the feelings of hope and sacrifice that permeate the air. I'm thinking inwardly of the sacrifices I've seen in my years fighting for humanity. The faces of people I've seen die and those I've killed for the greater good are on my mind when Aria speaks.

"Vic?" Aria taps my arm. I wake from my reminiscence and look down at her to find her pointing. "Look at that tree. Doesn't it look unwell to you?"

We are standing next to a "small" western red cedar less than a meter across. She's right. This tree doesn't look right. Its trunk is paler, its fern-like foliage is thin and partially brown, and its branches are more wilted. My botany skill tells me something is wrong, but to verify, I glance around and find the other trees with vibrant colors and clearly full of life. Everything about it says something is wrong. It does not look sick per se, as I can find no rot; it looks . . . weak, maybe? Like it hasn't been receiving as much air, rain, and sun as the others.

I look around for someone official and wave an elven lady over. She moves quickly and with a bright smile, which means young for an elf. Probably under two hundred.

Glancing at Aria then our touching arms, she faces me and says, "Can I help you, sir?"

I point at the tree and say, "Something isn't right with this tree. Has anyone looked into it?"

She looks at the tree and with a frown says, "We have an earth and nature magica service that cares for all the life on the grounds. I'm sure if they felt there was a risk, they would have done something."

A service? Not an individual, but a service.

"I don't suppose this company also offers its services to the Botanical Gardens?" She smiles brightly. "Yes. That location is lovely. The company is quite well known and has an excellent record. Why do you ask?"

I glance at Aria, and she looks at me with her eyebrows raised. I look back at the monument employee and say, "I am a nature magica. Why don't I take a look at it? Maybe I can help."

Frowning, she says, "I don't think I can let you do that. What if you damage something? We appreciate your concern though, and I will bring the condition of the tree up to the service on their next visit."

There is nothing I can do right now. I'll need to come back another time. "That's fine. I just thought I'd offer. I hope they can help the poor tree; this monument deserves the best care."

She beams at me and walks us to another part of the monument explaining some history of how the stone was gathered. I'm oblivious though, only hearing a soft sigh from Aria.

[Jo, you get the same impression right? Is there any way you can find out about this service company?]

I agree and will conduct both a public and MilNet search . . .

[Thanks.]

CHAPTER 76

Except for the bit at the end, the day off is lovely, but we are both tired by the time we get home. After a light dinner of vegetables and dip, we agree to call it an early night.

[How far on foot is the monument from the hotel?]

If you jog the entire time, approximately thirty-five minutes each way . . .

[I'm tempted. Thoughts?]

You would leave Aria? . . .

[First, if I do this, it will be a late-night operation. 02:00 or so. Second, she has no night infiltration training. Third, we can communicate with her or visa versa if there is an emergency. I expect it to be a two-hour op at the most. Hopefully less. And fourth, it would not be tonight. I need to procure the correct operational gear first.]

Are you planning on hiding it from her? . . .

[I don't know. Maybe. I can tell she is getting fed up with me leaving her behind, and I can also tell she is going to push. Or worse, sneak out and do something stupid.]

I lie there in the bed just thinking. Jo was right those weeks ago when she told me I have to reflect before taking action. But the more I think about it, the more my instincts are telling me I have to do this. My mind just won't let it go. There is something wrong and I need to figure it out or . . . I can't tell. But it scares me thinking of Aria or humanity facing the consequences of my inaction.

[Place an urgent order with the armory. I need a night tactical infiltration suite. If you can get it as a full enchanted armor set in less than two days, do it. Cost is no barrier. It needs to be silent and invisible in the dark. I would like both lethal and non-lethal arms for range and melee. You know what weapons I use. Grav lifters for the boots as well as climbing and repelling assistors. Please provide me with an estimate as soon as possible.]

Confirmed . . .

[Is the shield around this hotel a mono or bi-directional protection layer?]

I cannot say for sure without a test. However, the power requirements for a shield of this size being bi-directional would be staggering. And most shields aren't by default. The only logic to preventing exit through the shield would be to counter theft from the armory. However, there are many far less expensive and nearly as effective approaches to avoid loss . . .

[I have a preliminary mission plan in my head. Do some research on remote surveillance. I want to see what this service company does at the site post-mission. I will want to place one at the Botanical Gardens as well as potentially all their other customers. I doubt it is just those two.]

Affirmative. I have a response to your equipment request. Mr. Whyatt has directly responded and requests an urgent meeting . . .

[Urgent as in right now?]

Yes . . .

[Wow. Confirm the meet and tell him I am on my way immediately. Let Aria know if she wakes up.]

Confirmed . . .

***

Sitting across from Mr. Whyatt just five minutes later, he starts by asking, "Will you tell me what you have found that such an order passed my desk at such a time at night?"

Should I bring him to speed? How much trust has he earned so far?

"Can you tell me what you will do with this intel?"

Rubbing his chin, he says, "Fair question. I suppose it depends on the intel. Does it offer an immediate threat to me or my company?"

"I do not believe so. I see no connection at this time," I respond with a shake of my head.

He nods. "If it offers no threat, then I will do nothing other than use it to help until that changes."

"I suppose that is good enough. I assume your surveillance of me has alerted you to travels throughout the city? You are aware I went to the Botanical Gardens?" I ask with a sigh.

He simply nods.

"Have you been told what happened there?"

He places his hands on the table and folds them together in between us. "I know that you used nature magica on a sick plant or some such. Is that what you are referring to?"

I nod. "It is. I used nature magica to heal that flower because it was poisoned."

His eyebrows raise. "Oh?"

"By this." I tap the table. The head-sized mana stone of death essence appears on the table.

He jerks back, calling out something in Gnomish.

He just swore. Something in the mindset of "Sprocket Crack." . . .

[Seriously? That's a Gnomish swear? I am totally prioritizing that language. No more focusing on Elven.]

"Put it away, please. Death is disturbing to have around for most."

It vanishes. "I removed it and was able to help the plant."

He looks confused. "What does that have to do with tonight's request?"

"I found another sick plant." I describe the condition of the tree at the monument. "Here is the key, Mr. Whyatt. Both the monument and the gardens use the same earthcare company. I can tell you with near certainty that I did not just happen to come upon those plants between when they became ill and their facility was cared for by the company."

He looks at me and says simply, "I see."

"Mr. Whyatt, my instincts are glowing like dragon fire on this. Something is not right, and the more my mind focuses on it, the more worried I become. If I leave this be, something will happen."

"You plan to infiltrate the monument and conduct a similar search to what you did with the flower?" he asks.

"Yes. And I am going to tell you something else. This is speculation on my part, but once again my instincts are being set off. While I was on the run in the rainforest, I ran into a diseased tree and diseased bear together. A single bear and a single tree both diseased in the middle of a healthy area of the rainforest. My gut says something is there, and when I am strong enough I intend to return."

Once again, he says, "I see."

Then he starts tapping the table and staring off into nothing.

Focusing back on me after a minute, he taps his wrist and says, "I have approved your rush order. You will have it in twenty-four hours. You should know that set is exceptionally difficult to create, which accounts for the expense. We happen to have one close to your size which we can alter and provide. Otherwise, you are looking at weeks at absolute best."

Confirmation received. 822 silver has been deducted from the Whyatt account...

I nod, saying, "Thank you, Mr. Whyatt. Was there anything else? I wanted to thank you in person for the magma lead. I apologize if you lost the carcass."

He waves it away as if a rare magma affinity creature means nothing.

He clears his throat and says, "Actually, yes." Straightening his jacket, he continues. "I want to make an offer, but I have a concern. I have possibly found you a light magica."

CHAPTER 77

"She does not know the details. She only knows that a large-scale effort is taking place and the help of a light magica is required, or at least highly desired. She also understands the, as you call it, operational security aspect of this." Taking a breath, he continues. "She is an incredibly stubborn and forthright individual. She has, to my knowledge, never betrayed a confidence of importance. I trust her implicitly and ask if you would do the same. I know and understand your beliefs on betrayal. I even applaud them. However, in this case, I wonder if, after I have described her, you will grant her the opportunity to help while not terminating her."

Understanding his meaning, I ask, "She is family?"

He nods once. "She is."

I nod in return. "Then I offer this. I will meet with her. If I feel she can be trusted, I will read her in. If she does not betray me, I will not only not terminate her, I will provide assistance to her in a single time of need."

A smile breaks out on his face. "Thank you. She will be here in four days."

One more down, potentially at least. I'm glad it is almost over.

"Mr. Whyatt, can I ask your assistance on something?"

A surprised look appears on his face. "Certainly, Vic."

"Do you have any advice on how to . . . manage the emotions brought on by an affinity?"

His eyebrows raise so high as to almost split his forehead. "What a fascinating question. To my knowledge, affinities do not have nor exude emotions. Have you observed this?"

Shit!

"I suppose not. Thank you for your time, Mr. Whyatt."

I stand and offer my hand to shake. He stands and shakes it. "I will contact you in four days with the details. And forget about the antlion—it is no longer your problem."

***

The next day is a normal one for Aria and me. We are back in our routine. After dinner, we decide to sit together and watch that show with the ranger. Some of it seems a little silly and for entertainment, but some of it seems on point and widens my view of beast actions and reactions. I will watch this show more.

Your armory order is prepared and available for delivery upon request . . .

[Hold it until after Aria falls asleep.]

So you are planning to not tell her? . . .

[I will tell her tomorrow. I understand you don't agree with me, but I can't worry about her doing something foolish and be on the mission at the same time.]

It is your choice, Vic . . .

The show ends and we call it a night. For the first time when we split up to our rooms, she gives me a hug. "Good night." Then she wanders into the room tiredly and closes the door.

I'm still staring at the closed door. Um . . .

Clearing my head with a shake, I decide I can think about that later. Washing up, I climb into bed.

[Wake me at 01:00.]

Confirmed . . .

***

Jo wakes me, and my order is sitting on the infusion pad. I quietly examine every piece of gear from top to bottom for quality and any potential faults. Finding none, I look at the solid black, single-piece, skin tight under armor and the matte black plates that sit atop it. It will cover my entire body except my face.

[Inspect.]

Name:	**Darkness Enchanted Under Armor Sublayer (1 of 10 of Set)**
Description:	This is the first and most crucial piece of the specialized darkness enchanted Cloaked Infiltrator Set. This set is a specialized armor for use during night actions or any other under-lit conditions.
	Due to its focus on the darkness affinity, this set loses

	nearly all its properties when exposed to light. The Under Armor Sublayer is responsible for the coordination and function of the other nine pieces of the set. This piece also acts as a layer of light protection from piercing and slashing weapons as well as all magica affinities except light.
	The hands and feet have the ability to allow the passage of all magica except light magica. This can be enabled and disabled through the controller.
Condition:	Excellent
Risk Assessment:	N/A
Value:	This piece and set are extremely expensive due to the extreme rarity of darkness affinity in both stone and humanoids. Retail exceeds 600 silver for the set.
Special:	The Cloaked Infiltrator Set bonuses stack for each piece added and start at 5 pieces. 5 Pieces: Offers noise cancellation when any piece of the set contacts another. 6 Pieces: Cloaks the user in a black fog, reducing hard edges and the likelihood of being seen. 7 Pieces: Increases jumping strength by 20%. 8 PIeces: Reduces falling speed by 20%. 9 Pieces: Allows the wearer to stick to any dark surface for up to 5 minutes. With the direct infusion of darkness mana, the 5 minutes can be extended indefinitely. 10 Pieces: Allows the wearer to sink into shadow for 10 seconds. Has a 10-second cooldown. With the direct infusion of darkness mana, the 10-second duration can be extended indefinitely.

[That is the best gold I have spent so far. Sure, it's limited to night operations, but that's fine.]

This is certainly a high-quality set. Without having to [Inspect] every piece, I can tell you that the boots offer noise suppression, and the mask allows for darkvision and provides limited breathing assistance. The armor pieces include a mask, boots (which are more a hardened outer layer), shin guards, greaves, seamless spatial belt, upper arm guards, chestguard, and under armor. It comes with two weapons: a knife with forearm grav sheath and a forearm mana projector. Either of those can be placed on the top or bottom of your forearms.

I find them and [Inspect] each.

Name:	Darkness Enchanted Assassin Blade (1 of 10 of Set)
Description:	This 12-inch knife has an 8-inch blade made of darkness-infused rhodium. The blade reflects no light and has 100% repulsion of any material attempting to stick to the blade. The knife makes no sound during sheathing or unsheathing and will cut through most light armor with ease and medium armor with some effort. The knife will never unintentionally fall off of the sheath, even when hanging upside down. The sheath is a grav plate, allowing for it to snap directly to and from the user's hand. Note: The blade's abilities are reduced in light. The reduction rate is based on the amount of light it is exposed to.
Condition:	Excellent
Risk Assessment:	N/A
Value:	This piece and set are extremely expensive due to the extreme rarity of darkness affinity in both stone and humanoids. Retail exceeds 600 silver for the set.
Special:	The Cloaked Infiltrator Set bonuses stack for each piece added and start at 5 pieces. 5 Pieces: Offers noise cancellation when any piece of the set contacts another. 6 Pieces: Cloaks the user in a black fog reducing hard edges and likelihood of being seen. 7 Pieces: Increases jumping strength by 20%. 8 PIeces: Reduces falling speed by 20%.

	9 Pieces: Allows the wearer to stick to any dark surface for up to 5 minutes. With the direct infusion of darkness mana, the 5 minutes can be extended indefinitely. 10 Pieces: Allows the wearer to sink into shadow for 10 seconds. Has a 10-second cooldown. With the direct infusion of darkness mana, the 10-second duration can be extended indefinitely.

Name:	Darkness Enchanted Assassin Mana Projector (1 of 10 of Set)
Description:	This projector sits on either the top or bottom of the forearm. It fires a chargeable darkness mana projectile which will incapacitate at lower levels of power and kill at higher. The projector will produce no visual or audible clue it has been fired but, as a result, has a maximum range of 15 meters. Note: The projector's abilities are reduced in light. The reduction rate is based on the amount of light it is exposed to.
Condition:	Excellent
Risk Assessment:	N/A
Value:	This piece and set are extremely expensive due to the extreme rarity of darkness affinity in both stone and humanoids. Retail exceeds 600 silver for the set.
Special:	The Cloaked Infiltrator Set bonuses stack for each piece added and start at 5 pieces. 5 Pieces: Offers noise cancellation when any piece of the set contacts another. 6 Pieces: Cloaks the user in a black fog reducing hard edges and likelihood of being seen. 7 Pieces: Increases jumping strength by 20%. 8 PIeces: Reduces falling speed by 20%. 9 Pieces: Allows the wearer to stick to any dark surface

> for up to 5 minutes with a cooldown of 1 minute. With the direct infusion of darkness mana, the 5 minutes can be extended indefinitely.
> 10 Pieces: Allows the wearer to sink into shadow for 10 seconds. Has a 10-second cooldown. With the direct infusion of darkness mana, the 10-second duration can be extended indefinitely.

[This is outstanding. Did you manage to find surveillance gear that could work?]

Yes, provided at no cost by Mr. Whyatt. I believe it is part of the new product line we were shown. You will find it as a box of small black crystals to the right of the knife...

I [Inventory] all the climbing and other assistance gear. The surveillance gear is as Jo described.

[How do I watch it?]

I will show you either during or when we return from the mission. Time is of the essence. It is already close to 02:30...

[Gryphon shit. Thank you for the time check. It took longer than I thought to verify the equipment.]

I immediately strip and then dress myself in the under armor. As described, it covers me completely, including each individual toe and finger, except for my face, and makes slight adjustments to be a perfect fit. I place each piece of armor on, followed by the knife on the bottom of my left forearm and the projector on the top of my right forearm. Finally, the mask, which is a solid black visor with no way to see out of.

[This will be interesting.]

The mask adheres the under armor around my face with a barely audible hiss.

Connection established...

I then see everything normally. Weird.

[This is the best thing I have ever owned except Bertha.]

The inscription, enchantment, and magica to make this set must have been extraordinary. No wonder it cost as much as a fully equipped MilSpec vehicle...

#*I will be that soon...*

[Yes, Grace, you will. And you will look sexy in matte black. We'll be a perfect match in this armor.]

#I agree, Host Vic. If we wanted to be seen, everyone would assume we are together . . .

Stop. Just stop, both of you . . .

[Is there a barrier on my balcony?]

It is only engaged if it senses a presence . . .

[Perfect. Terminate all lights. Activate cloaking fog, and all visual and sound suppression.]

Activated. You are essentially cloaked . . .

[Open the balcony door.]

She does, and I silently walk out.

[Close it.]

You are clear. Mana shield is not active . . .

[Here goes.]

Good luck, Vic . . .

I walk back to the glass and take a silent sprinting leap off the balcony. After clearing the building, I create an air bubble around myself and guide it to float away from the lit hotel to a dark side street. I land at a run.

[Direct me.]

A green line forms, and I follow it on the run for just over thirty-three minutes until I arrive at the monument park. Sometimes I marvel at the nanomachines; despite being on an intense mission just two days ago, I am barely breathing hard after a thirty-minute fast run.

The monument itself and the statue are brightly glowing, but everything else is dark. Most importantly, the trees are far enough away to offer cover. I approach the green mana shield surrounding the entire park, which stops three meters high.

[That is taller than I thought it would be. It looks like the shield projector raises at night. Can I make that with jump assist?]

Jump assist plus a little grav pulse from the boots. Yes . . .

[Let's do it.]

I back up and sprint at the mana shield. At a meter away I couch and leap with all my strength. Jo activates my armor's various augmentations, and

I fly over the shield spread out like a giant osprey. After the shield passes below me, I tuck and land with a silent roll and immediately sprint to the trees.

Moving silently from tree to tree, I reach the center and the tree which is ill.

Staying in shadow, I dig my hands and feet in the hard soil at the foot of the tree.

[Ready?]

Proceed . . .

I can feel the resistance in my hands and feet fade as the mana blockers are disabled. I pass my magica down into the dirt and start to feel around for the wrongness of death. I don't feel it. Or anything out of the ordinary. Could I have been wrong?

[Shit. Am I just paranoid? Could this have been for nothing?]

Try asking the tree for help. I recommend you keep the green glow to a minimum if possible . . .

[Good advice on both fronts. Thanks.]

Leaving my feet how they are, I move my hands to the roots of the tree and try to talk to it. I start a slight rhythm with my mana. It can't hear my hum so I try to sing with my mana. It is a steady rhythmic pulse that slowly increases in pace. The tree feels very sluggish, like it does not have the energy to respond. I try to flow some of my mana to it through the song, to comfort it and let it know I am here to help it. I will help it get strong if it will just tell me what's wrong.

It tries; it is just so tired. I feed more mana and speed up the song. The tree responds a little. I can feel it reaching for the strength from the roots. Pulling from the earth isn't the problem. It needs energy from the sky as well. It needs the sun and every time it tries, it is stopped by that thing.

Feeling the frustration of the tree, I offer to help get rid of that thing if it just directs me. I beg of it to allow me to help. My song is one of pleading, and I need it to guide me so I can offer it succor and allow it sustenance. It tries. It gives me the feeling of blackness at its center. Something right at its heart that makes the food from the sky stop coming. I trace that feeling of starvation right to the center of the tree. An old warren of some animal sits there, and the creature's bones and a mana stone are there. I send out mana and tug it back hard. I feel a pull and a slightly sharp pain in my core. Then the crystal and bones are in my [Inventory].

I slowly back away from the center of the tree and send it feelings of reassurance. It should be able to eat from the sky now. Pure relief and thanks come from the tree. A root raises from the ground and splits the ground, reaching for me. I touch it and send comfort and happiness that it is well. Then the tree sends a feeling of offering and hope. Another smaller root comes from deeper under the ground. It appears to have grown around something. It is a round stone with a circular crisscross pattern. I get a feeling of hope and pleading from the tree. I take it and send appreciation and assurance back. Then I slowly back away from the tree's consciousness, and its roots return to the earth.

You cannot [Inventory] that. It is alive...

[We'll explore living rocks later. I need to clean this up.]

The disturbance will be obvious so, holding the rock in my right hand and touching the earth with my left, I give the earth the equivalent of a bonk to wake it up. I use it to compact and return things as closely as possible to their previous condition. It isn't perfect, but should be good enough.

Warning! Host has 10% remaining mana...

I'm pretty drained at this point. Using mana quickly is always more draining than a slower more moderated burn. I take a few calming breaths and ask Jo a question.

[What is the range of the surveillance gear?]

Eight meters at best. I was warned it is an early release product...

[Great. What is the level of color and shape change?]

Unknown...

[Not great mission prep. Okay. Let's try putting it on the next tree over. That's as close as we can get.]

I use [Inventory] to withdraw one crystal and walk up to the nearest tree. I place the crystal in a branching joint facing the tree I just helped save.

[See what you can do to blend it in.]

Connection confirmed...

Activating camouflage...

The black crystal, which is obvious against the red wood, slowly takes on the same color and stringy texture of the surrounding tree material. It disappears to the naked eye and would take a rather precise angle and direct look to locate it.

[Excellent. Let's hope we can see something. Time to go. This is a very well-done memorial for an honorable purpose. I am not pleased it is being desecrated.]

I start running back the way I came.

You sound angry about it. I don't hear that from you very often...

[I *am* angry. So much sacrifice for the greater humanity deserves to be remembered.]

But not your own?...

[I'm different. If I do my job, the public will ever know I even existed.]

I approach the mana shield when the lights of an approaching grav vehicle shine onto me. Fuck.

I toss a crystal on the ground near the gate and immediately spring to the nearest tree and stand behind it.

[All cloaking is at max, right? Engage camouflage on the crystal I just placed.]

Connection confirmed...

Activating camouflage...

Yes. This facility should not have visitors or facilities support right now...

[Can you let me see the camera?]

A window appears in the middle of my vision. Two humans walk away from the vehicle, carrying a large bag half as big as a person. It looks heavy, based on the grunting of the men.

Why are they carrying a bag and not a storage item? I feel my hand clenching and unclenching the rock.

[Can we hear them?]

They are not speaking...

They reach the mana shield, and the larger of the humans reaches out with his hand not holding the bag and taps the mana shield with his index finger. The shield brightens then fades.

[What the fuck was that?]

Unknown...

[Maybe he has an access key? I have no idea how that happened otherwise.]

Carrying the bag between them, they walk through the gate and towards the memorial.

They pass my tree, so I glance over and watch them walk by the statue and towards the dome. After reaching the dome, once again the man taps on it. Nothing happens.

[What the fuck is going on?]

I hear the one not doing the tapping say, "Open it, you dumb fuck. This fucking dwarf is heavy."

[Shit. Well, that settles that.]

Will you take action?

[If I can. The problem is the light.]

The memorial is so well lit—how can I approach it without being seen?

The big one responds. "I'm trying, but the passkey isn't working."

I move to the closest tree I can while staying behind the duo. They aren't looking anywhere except at the dome and I take a chance. I sprint to the statue.

"Well, try again. We have to do what the boss says. I'll fucking throw you under the grav cart if you fuck this up for me."

Making it to the statue, I stick a small part of my head around the side to look over.

Suit is functioning at ten percent capability due to the light . . .

I wince.

The tapper taps again, and this time a piece of the memorial dome slides down into the ground.

"About fucking time. I swear, you are completely useless," complains the shorter of the two.

They start walking and are clearly moving downward and not straight forward. Luckily, the doorway stays open.

[Is there a record of the memorial having an underground level in the dome?]

Not on the public record . . .

As soon as I don't hear them anymore, I sprint for the doorway. I was right; it is a stairway down. There are no lights, so it is lit from behind only. I start down the stairs, and after about ten meters, the stairs change into a hallway with a slight curve. I hear voices again and stop to listen.

ACTIVATION

"Didn't I tell you people to bring the merchandise to me with minimal damage? Now I have to expend time, effort, mana, and coin to keep it from dying so I can sell it."

[Please tell me you've been recording this.]

Affirmative, since you dropped the crystal on the ground.

[Thank you for taking the initiative; I should have asked. I cannot keep carrying this stone, are you sure I cannot [Inventory] it?]

If you inventory it, whatever is alive in it will die . . .

[Damnit.]

Well, it will just have to be in my shooting hand then. Using my left hand, I flick my wrist, and the knife snaps into it, blade backward.

I move forwards, knife in one hand and projector ready to fire in the other. Slowly and quietly stepping forward, I get the message I've been waiting for.

Suit restored to full capability . . .

CHAPTER 78

Thirty meters further, peeking around the curve, I see the two men from above talking to a third one standing in front of a stone archway. That one is wearing an expensive, ocean-blue suit with a thin rounded rapier at his waist. The bagged dwarf is at their feet.

[Are the crystals traceable from a distance? Can I use them to track these folks if I place one on them?]

Possibly. Clever idea . . .

I put the rock down on the ground and return the knife to the sheath.

[Activate climbing.]

Activated. Five minutes and counting . . .

[Give me a timer.]

4:57 appears in the top right of my HUD and counts down.

Pressing my hands firmly, I begin climbing the smooth vertical surface. Once I reach the top, I transfer my hands and ignore gravity even more outrageously as I become inverted. Hanging upside down, I silently crawl towards the trio until I am directly above them.

3:40 remaining.

Clinging with my two feet and left hand, I point my right arm down at the head of the complainer guy. Taking careful aim at the crown of his head, I charge the first shot with enough mana to kill. As promised, there is no light and the only sound is that of his body crumpling onto the ground.

*You have killed a **Thug**. You absorb 355.97 mana essence . . .*

"What the fuck?" yells the guy in the blue suit. He immediately reaches for his rapier while looking up the hallway to the stairs.

I aim at the finger-tapper guy and charge the projector with only enough strength to knock him out. He kneels over the fallen guy, and I fire into the back of his neck. He collapses on top of the dead complainer.

*You have rendered **Thug** unconscious with a stunning blow. **Thug** will remain unconscious for 60 minutes . . .*

The blue suit guy slides his rapier out of its sheath and backs past my vision into the room.

1:50 left.

I hear a yell from inside the room. "Whoever you are, come out!"

[Really? Does that ever work?]

I believe we have established that humans do things that make no sense . . .

[Fair enough.]

I start climbing down the wall until I am right above the archway. I hear fast footsteps inside. He is clearly running around. I stick my head down to glance inside. The room is huge for being an underground "secret," at least thirty meters long and ten meters wide.

How is this under the monument?

"Whoever you are, you're fucking dead. Do you know who I work for?"

[Modulate voice please.]

Done . . .

"No. Who do you work for?" The voice that comes out isn't mine. It is a vibrating neutral one, completely impossible to identify.

1:20 remaining. Now I wish I had darkness mana.

"You're so fucking dead. My boss owns this city. You are going to die a painful . . ."

He keeps blabbing on while I search the room with my eyes trying to find him. It is filled with cages, but I don't let myself get distracted. Focus, Vic. Mission first.

0:59 remaining. Down to the final minute.

After a few seconds, I see him sticking his head out from behind an overturned table. He has his rapier in one hand and a single-handled crossbow in the other. It looks like a single shot from what I can see.

He is still ranting about all the horrible ways I am going to die from his boss. Asshole still hasn't given me a name. I stick my head all the way down. He sees me, jerks the crossbow at me, and fires all in one smooth motion. He's clearly not a normal thug.

I quickly bring my head back up, and the bolt flies by exactly where my head was. Yep, he's trained.

Thirty-eight seconds.

I bring my head back down and see him reloading. He's efficient at it. I reach down and point my arm at him. Okay, so maybe not that well trained if he isn't fully covering. Setting it to high stun, I take aim and fire. The soundless black projectile splatters against a blue mana shield that flashes into existence in front of the table and disappears.

Ahh, no wonder he wasn't hiding during his reload.

Gripping the archway's edge, I flip to land on my feet. I sprint left and slide behind an unmade bed. A thump sounds as a crossbow bolt embeds into the stone wall to my left, its feathered tail visibly vibrating. There is no doubt this man will be difficult to bring in alive with a mana shield and both a ranged and melee weapon. But if I want to figure out what is going on, I'll have to.

I crawl to the head of the bed, reach above the edge and pull down the two pillows, and [Inventory] them. I call out in my still hidden voice. "I don't suppose you are willing to surrender. I won't kill you." Of course I'm lying. What I really meant was "I won't kill you *immediately*."

His response is immediate. "Fuck you!"

I look around the room and once again struggle to remain focused. I also have to avoid collateral damage. Man, I really want to kill this guy. I take a deep breath and remind myself he can't tell me anything if I kill him. I stick my head up once again and jerk it back down followed once again by a bolt flying through where my eye would have been.

Listening carefully, I can confirm his reload speed is approximately six seconds. That is enough time, with a little support, to—

His next words cut off my thoughts and change every aspect of my plan. "Do you think I'm some senseless brute like those fools you've killed out there? I've been in this business for two decades, and I'll enjoy collaring you just as much as that dwarf on the floor. I bet I could get a good price too! And then I'll make you tell me about everyone you love and collar them too. You have a woman? I'll collar her and take her body right in front of you. You'll . . ."

His ranting voice fades as old memories long ago buried work their way across my mind. The cages. The collars. Faces flash across my vision, ending in a beautiful golden-haired elf smiling at me. Rage like I haven't felt in years thrums through me. A growl emanates from my throat as I lean forward with black smoke streaked with azure drifting from my armored form.

Species ability Mana Rage is now active...

With a roar, I thrust down with my legs and soar through the air, assisted by the grav boots. A thin steel bolt flies at my soaring form and embeds into my thigh. I don't even notice as I land in a roll, and the bolt bends, twists, and then tears free.

*Warning! Host has suffered **moderate bleeding (right leg)**. Host will suffer 4 damage per second for 10 minutes...*

Rising from my roll, I sprint across the long room, leaving behind a trail of black smoke. Six seconds later, the reloaded crossbow is aimed at me. Behind it, I see a smirk on the lightly wrinkled face of this man who will die. The reverberating growl from my throat increases in volume but lowers in pitch. Just as he fires his crossbow, I thrust my hand forward and two white pillows appear in front of me. Their forward momentum comes to a sudden stop as they fold over in the middle and fly backwards at me. My upper torso twists sideways and down, and I pass by the pillows which are penetrating by a bolt.

Losing only a single stride from the dodge, I snap the knife from my sheath from my left arm while charging the projector in my right. The smugness is gone from this deadman's face, replaced with wide-eyed fear. Hidden behind my mask, he can't see the teeth showing from the feral grin. He *can* hear the growl now loud enough to cause vibrations in the smoke leaking everywhere from my form.

His hands shake slightly now as he reloads the crossbow, causing the bolt to drop with a clatter. Finally, I'm close enough. The growl turns into a roar as I leap once again, this time over the overturned table and whatever shield he laid. I push the air around me and spin to face downward and back at him. My right arm points straight at the future corpse's face just as he rises with the dropped bolt in his hand. He straightens and looks up at me, his eyes wide and mouth fallen open. An oblong black ball of mana flies between us, and the back of his neck explodes just after it enters his gaping mouth.

*You have killed a **Slave Trader**. You absorb 686.15 mana essence...*

Species ability Mana Rage is now inactive...

*Warning! Host has suffered **Mana Overload**. All of the host's attributes will be reduced by 95% for 320 seconds...*

My form lands on its feet, but the momentum carries me backward as I weakly tumble onto my back and roll to a slapping stop against the rear wall of the room.

I barely remain conscious and aware. After however long, the blurred vision clears to just be filled with soft edges.

Mana Overload has been successfully removed. All attributes are restored . . .

A few seconds later that sharpens too and I can hear a familiar voice in my head.

Warning! Host has 10% remaining health . . .

Vic, you need to heal yourself. Quickly . . .

Blinking, I look down and see my leg is bleeding, and glittering blood is covering the ground under me. I'm a little confused, but as I don't want to bleed to death, I reflect on my training with Aria and send mana to my life rune. Asking it for help, I call on life magica to examine my leg. I see the various tissue tears and ask it to help seal those wounds and heal my body. The glory of healing and the desire to help floods the wound and it quickly closes. I cut off the mana and stand.

[Jo?]

You activated Mana Rage. I warned you that control might be an issue when you first activated it . . .

[Right. Okay, back to work then.]

Still ignoring what pulls at my attention along the walls, I walk to the dead blue guy and search him. He has multiple storage devices. One is only for coin, so I have Jo do her take-coin-and-absorb thing. The others I take and set on the floor. I turn the table upright and place everything on it. Don't look yet, Vic. Mission first.

Jogging back to the two guys who unwittingly guided me here, I place one crystal in the back pants pocket and another in the inside lining of tapper guy's waist after I make a small slice with my knife. I also do the same to the dead complainer. You never know. I search them both and find a storage container each. While I'm here, I go back and grab the stone from the stairs.

Staying focused on the best way to help, I walk to the bag the dwarf is supposedly in. Using my knife, I cut it open. I verify that inside is indeed an ancient dwarf, bloody and unconscious. I place my hand on him and send him the healing of life magica. He has seven fractured bones (although none are fully broken thankfully), a dozen cuts, and more bruises than I want to count.

I start with the bones and then move to the cuts. I leave the bruises because, based on what I saw inside, I will need my mana. More black smoke rises from my body, but I take a breath and it fades.

The dwarf groans and stirs.

[Call Mr. Whyatt and tell him we have a huge ginormous fucking problem. And that he needs to get his ass to the memorial park right the fuck now with hill giant-sized medical help. Tell him to keep it quiet or we risk compromising everything.]

Sent ...

My voice still modulated, I say, "Sir dwarf. Are you all right? I know you're sore, but I have others to heal, and I need your help. Can you stand?"

The dwarf is trying to focus. He looks at me and jerks backward.

I hold my hands up and say, "I'm here to help, not hurt you. Sir, there are a lot of people in that room who require aid. Will you assist?"

He looks at me with an angry face and nods. I turn around and head into the room full of caged and collared humanoids.

CHAPTER 79

Finally taking a detailed look at these poor people nearly makes me sick with fury, sadness, and betrayal. Two walls are lined with cages, stacked three high. These are old-style cages with steel bars and manual locks. Apparently, the "goods" don't rate mana shields.

[I cannot believe I am seeing this. In human territory.]

I get no response from Jo. I assume she is also trying to determine what the best course of action is.

I look back towards the dwarf, who is staring at the cages with fury.

I say to him, "You go around opening the cages and helping them get out. Bring any that are mortally injured to that bed in the corner." I point to it.

In a gruff and gravelly voice, he asks, "Key?"

"Shit. One sec." I walk to the table and place the two devices from the thugs in the pile.

[Jo?]

I touch each of the storage devices.

I have it. And the collar release . . .

I see both in my [Inventory], withdraw them, and hand them to the dwarf.

Mr. Whyatt affirms he is on his way with help. ETA ten minutes . . .

[That's something, I suppose.]

I go to the blue suit and place his body and weapons in my inventory.

[Do I have a physical bag or something I can keep all the storage devices and the rock in?]

A black bag appears in my hand.

That used to have a rappelling rope in it . . .

[Perfect.]

I load everything into the bag and tie it around my shoulder and armpit. The set belt is seamless to the under armor so it will not tie there.

Then I walk to the dwarf who is helping a young elf male from a cage. I go to the other side of the boy and give him a small amount of life magica to grant him a boost. He is mostly suffering dehydration and starvation. I help him to a clear area.

With a raspy voice, he tries to speak but nothing comes out. The collars must be silencing them, which explains the lack of noise. I look at him and ask, "Say that again."

His lips say "My parents" with a hopeful look on his face.

"Do you see them?"

He looks at the wall of cages and, with a shaking hand, points at one with an emaciated male elf who is kneeling, looking down at us through the bars with a hopeful expression. And then he moves his hand to the right with a female human who is lying prone in the cage.

[How do they get up to the second and third levels? Is there a grav plate? Never mind.]

Not waiting for an answer, I run up and leap to the second-level cage with the woman and grab the bars with my hands. Finding the latch, I grip with the two hands while my feet are against the bars of the cage next door. I pull with all my might but it won't budge.

Use magica, Vic. Don't panic. Stay in control . . .

Taking a breath I think, [Right. Thanks. Release magic in my hands.]

Already done . . .

Pointing at the cage lock, I aim a white-hot beam of fire. The lock turns red then yellow and then white. I release the magica and grip a different bar and pull again. The superheated metal of the lock bends and, with a screech of steel, the door bursts open. I can't smell it because of my isolation mask, but the filth in the cage tells me more than enough about the condition these people were kept in.

I rush into the cage and place my hands on the woman. I can feel she is alive but barely. She is very sick, and her dehydration and starvation are not helping. I send her the healing life of my golden mana and plead with it to help her. Why would they let her get this sick? What use is she this way? It finds joy in helping life flourish and leaps into the woman's body. The golden flood finds the source of her sickness; her kidneys are not working properly. The life energy floods her organs and works to repair them. There is severe damage and strain, and the energy can only stabilize her. I do not know how to direct healing to that level of detail, never having been trained. I only know what Aria knows, which is rather minimal.

Picking her up in a princess carry, I gently walk to the door of the cage, sit down with my legs dangling over, and leap down. I try to make it as soft a landing as possible. With the assistance of Jo and the armor, I barely jostle her. I place her on the floor next to the boy. Then I repeat the door opening for the boy's father. I also drop my large Magica Medical healing kit on the floor and tell the dwarf to use whatever he sees fit in it.

For the next ten minutes, the dwarf and I work to release as many of these poor victims as we can. Between the kit and my magica, we are able to prevent any deaths, I think. Suddenly, a human in maroon steel and beast leather battle armor enters the room, sword in hand. He stops dead when he sees what is going on.

He holds his hand to his ear and literally yells, "Send the fucking medics down here right fucking now. Anyone who isn't sprinting is fired." He puts his sword in some spatial device, walks up to me, and asks, "How can I help?"

In my hidden voice, I respond, "You just did. If you are willing to help more, keep opening these cages and helping people down. I am trying to stabilize the dying, but I have very little mana left." I point at the dwarf who hasn't stopped opening cages or using the healing tools I offered. "He can give you further instructions. That kit was pretty much used up a few minutes ago as well."

The man just nods and moves towards the dwarf. Then I hear the rapid stomping of multiple feet on the stairs coming closer. Four medics, two humans and two gnomes, come flying into the room and skid to halt, seeing the horrible scene.

The second says, "Dear Lord." He must be one of those religious humans.

I jog over to them, saying, "I have stabilized the dying to the best of my ability, but I am not a very good life magica. Please help them."

They look a little surprised at my voice but immediately take action, spreading out and starting to help people.

Still standing by the door, I turn around and look at the room. I am so tired. I really need to see Aria.

[Aria's okay, right?]

Yes Vic, she is asleep and healthy . . .

Nodding to myself, I hear another pair of footsteps coming down the stairwell and hall. I turn to see Mr. Whyatt arriving at the doorway and, just like all the others, he is frozen for a moment by what he sees.

"I don't know what to say. This is not why I came here, but . . ."

He holds up his hand. "Do not say any more. You have saved these people from a fate beyond imagining."

"There are two bodies just over there to the right." I point at the dead and unconscious guys. "Please have them placed in their car outside the monument park entrance. Do nothing else, just place their bodies inside. Please."

He looks back at them and nods. "As you say."

He touches his wrist. "It will be taken care of shortly. You cannot help here anymore. Did you accomplish your original mission purpose?"

I nod. "I did."

"Excellent. Then go home. We have it here."

I sigh and nod. "Affirmative."

I pass the exit, briefly slowing to shoot the unconscious guy one more time to make sure he stays down for a while longer.

You have rendered **Thug** *unconscious with a stunning blow.* **Thug** *will remain unconscious for 60 minutes . . .*

I slowly walk up the steps and look out the entrance. There are several armed guards moving around, but it is relatively low-key considering it could be a madhouse.

I sneak off to the side and blend in with the shadows. With the mana shield down, I have no problem getting past the wall and heading home using alleys. When I approach the hotel, I look up at where I leaped from only hours before. Deciding I can be seen entering the hotel, I step into an empty alley and send all my gear except the bag now hanging at my elbow into my inventory. In the nude, I drop that bag at my feet and make my sweats, t-shirt, socks, and shoes appear on me. I pick the bag back up and walk out of the alley towards the hotel and wave at Mr. Stuffy, who simply nods at me neutrally as I walk to the lobby. I enter the suite and hear the doors slide shut behind me with a quiet hiss. Heading into my room, I drop the bag on my bed, strip again and take a bath.

I soak in my usual spot with my head back. The image of those poor people and faces of the past keep flashing across my vision and I can't sleep.

Can't sleep? . . .

[No.]

Want your alerts? . . .

[No.]

Okay. Can I help? . . .

[No.]

I wash myself, dry with the crystal, put on my full PJs and slowly enter Aria's room. I quietly walk over to the side she sleeps on and feel under her nose to make sure she is breathing. A tear falls down my face as I touch her wrist and feel a strong pulse.

[It could have been her in one of those cages.]

But it wasn't. She is here safe in front of you now . . .

[I'm going to destroy them.]

I understand. Just be careful how many enemies you have to battle at one time . . .

I let out a sigh. [I know.]

I look back at Aria, and her eyes are open, looking at me.

She groggily asks, "You okay, Vic?"

It could have been her.

Another tear falls. "No," is all I say.

She scoots backward and holds the blanket up. I get up and climb in. She leans her head on my shoulder and wraps her hands around my arm.

I eventually fall asleep with tears still falling down my face.

CHAPTER 80

[Is this what family is, Jo? Would I know if I had one?]

I don't know, Vic. You know what I am . . .

[I wish Shen were here. She had such an insight into things. I bet she'd know.]

I bet you're right . . .

I'm lying in Aria's bed with her leaning against me with a leg over my waist. Crap. Blushing, I climb out of the bed, causing Aria to wake.

Looking down at her, I say, "Time to start the day."

***

Aria and I have a normal day. She doesn't push me to explain, and I'm not sure how to start. Over dinner, I finally stop putting it off and begin.

"Thank you for last night. I'm sorry I woke you up."

I notice her face is a little red as she wipes her hands and mouth and looks at me. "Any time, Vic. Want to talk about it?"

Letting out a sigh, I say, "I went on a mission last night." She says nothing, so I continue. "The objective was to find out what happened to the tree at Monument Park and try to resolve it. The mission was a success, but that isn't really when the night ended. I was ready to end the evening and return home, but . . ."

And so I tell her everything I can remember, except the parts involving my past; the mana rage part is blurry, but I do my best. By the time I get to the point of returning home, my voice is cracking.

"I couldn't sleep. I kept seeing you in one of those cages in my mind. I went to your room because I think I needed to see that you were safe. I keep hearing in my mind, 'It could have been you.'"

My voice fades at the end.

I have tears in my eyes again. Aria wipes her own eyes and comes over and takes my hand and pulls me up. I follow without resistance. She pulls me to the couch, where she guides me to sit. She sits a little bit away and then reaches over and pulls my head down into her lap. Then she gently starts stroking my head and hair. I close my eyes and just lie there, feeling her presence.

I hear her humming like her mom and I revel in it. She's here, she's safe, I haven't failed. I repeat that mantra in my mind.

"Vic?" Her bell-like voice is a little hard when she calls my name.

"Yes?"

"Are you going to kill them?"

I hear the bite of anger in that question.

"All of them," I growl. "Every. Single. One."

"Good. I think we should go to bed."

She stops running her hands through my long hair and I sit up. "Thank you."

We split up and move to our bathrooms to wash up and head to our beds.

Vic, I didn't want to interrupt, but you have a message from Mr. Whyatt. He was hoping to meet with you and the light magica tomorrow evening . . .

[Confirm it. We are almost done with affinities.]

I think we are closer than you think. Check your inventory from last night . . .

Climbing into bed, I do. I see the weapons, the body of Mr. Blue Suit. And I see the mana stone. It says, **Mana Stone (Darkness)**.

[What the fuck, Jo? How many coincidences are there? I suppose it makes sense that the tree seemed to feel starved of light from the sun. I just cannot fathom how I keep finding exactly what I need exactly when I need it. What the fuck is going on?]

I wish I knew, Vic. Mathematically speaking, the chances of you actually gathering all the elements is nearly infinitesimally small. Our goal was just that, a goal. A completely unrealistic and unreachable goal . . .

I reflect on the last months silently for a few minutes.

[Actually, upon reflection there is some level of logic. If you break it down, it isn't all coincidences. The ice stone was easy to acquire once we built that business relationship, and using that connection to locate the magma isn't unreasonable. The death stone is much more effective against a flower garden than a tree. Death would have hurt it, but a grown "adult" tree is more robust because it has a huge root system. Using darkness to starve it is completely logical from that perspective. If I am conducting weird experiments to see how elemental stones affect plant life for whatever reason, I definitely follow the same approach as this lunatic.]

That is all true, Vic...

[Moreover, finding a light magica using the same connection used to find the ice and magma stones is not even a reach. It is almost assured to at least be attempted.]

I agree with that premise as well. I'm sorry to interrupt your musings, but you have something of a bizarre message. It says, "Boy, I'm the old dwarf you rescued last night. I got your info from the uppity rich gnome. I want to meet you when the shitter isn't exploding. How about it? If you want to keep hiding your face, I'm fine with that."

[Well, that's interesting. Agree to meet him after dinner the day after tomorrow.]

Vic, there's something else. The message came from a Master Glurmaon Steeltamer...

[A Steeltamer? Like Grun?]

I do not know for sure, but that seems likely...

[I wonder if all Steeltamers are grumpy as their default emotion.]

It does seem to be a family trait. Do you want your alerts from yesterday?...

[I suppose I shouldn't hold it off forever.]

Skill updated. Passive skill [Earth Mana Manipulation] is now level 5...

Skill updated. Passive skill [Nature Mana Manipulation] is now level 5...

New skill activated. Passive skill [Life Mana Manipulation] now available for use...

Skill updated. Passive skill [Life Mana Manipulation] has leveled from 0 to 5...

[It's critical to raise healing. I should really find a way to get professionally trained. Unfortunately, that likely means I'll be found out, so I have to hold off. And Mr. Whyatt doesn't have anyone he trusts sufficiently, so we're stuck.]

Agreed. There is one more thing though. I'll skip the alerts, but from the three humans, you looted two platinum, seventy-nine gold, 5,488 silver, and 3,314 coppers. Most of that is from the slave trader...

[Good! Less money floating around the slave trade. I'll deal with the mana stone, storage devices, and living rock another day.]

D.I. FREED

I think that is a good idea. Get some sleep . . .

CHAPTER 81

I work extra hard during my physical activities the next day. I need to get as much emotion outside of myself as possible. It sort of works. While I certainly feel better, I am still not fully myself. Once again, I find myself struggling to compartmentalize my emotions. I think Aria can tell because she makes much more physical contact with me throughout the day. Just a hand on my arm or pat on my shoulder. Nothing major, but it helps me remember she's safe. I wonder how she knows what I need.

By the evening, I am nearly normal. Over dinner, I tell Aria the plan for the evening. "I have a meeting with a light magica tonight. So you okay being on your own?"

"Are you going to activate light?"

I shake my head. "That is not my plan. We are just doing a meet and greet to see if we can trust each other. She is family of Mr. Whyatt."

She nods. "I want to be there when you awaken it."

Thinking about it, I see no reason for her not to and many for to be there. "Sure. I'd like that."

Smiling, she says, "Enjoy meeting her. Don't fall for her charms."

I let out a single barking laugh at that as I stand up and walk to the pad. We both know the chances of that happening.

***

Upon entering Mr. Whyatt's office, I nearly stagger as I am immediately assaulted with a high-pitched female voice making demands. "Are you the human my buffoon of a brother says I need to work with? Why anyone would want to work closely with him is beyond me. I am here to introduce you to light magica, and you better not be as thick-headed as the last troll's ass I taught. If you are, I can assure you I'll be—"

She stops mid-sentence.

I gather myself a bit from the verbal onslaught and look down at a meter-tall young gnome lady in tan overalls and red pigtails only two feet away, who is looking up staring at me open-mouthed. How did she get so close?

Was I in shock from her "words?"

I clear my throat and say, "Hello. I'm Vic. It is nice to meet you."

I get no response, and I wonder if something is wrong as she's just staring. I check myself out. Usual black sweats with a tight white t-shirt. This is my relaxed outfit I wear around Aria. I feel my face in case I have anything still on it from dinner. Don't think so. My hair is down 'cause I forgot to put it back in a ponytail, but whatever. It was just supposed to be a meet and greet.

Mr. Whyatt is in the back of the room clearly trying quite hard not to laugh out loud.

"Miss?"

Suddenly she takes another step forward and asks, "Are you married?"

Mr. Whyatt can't hold it in anymore and lets out a bellowing laugh.

I look between the two and say slowly, "Nooooo."

"Why not? Do you have any mental challenges? Do you have any diseases or illnesses? Are you able to get an erection? Can you last more than five minutes in the bedchamber? Are you able to make a woman orgasm?"

Mr. Whyatt is quite literally on the floor rolling around, having trouble breathing, he is laughing so hard.

I am once again overwhelmed. "Um, Miss . . . what is your name again?"

"Oh, right. My name is Felindra. It is a pleasure to meet you. Or at least I hope it will be."

"I see. Um. Miss Felindra, I am going to assume that none of those questions have anything to do with the purpose of today's meeting."

She gives me a sultry smile and says, "They can, Mr. Vic. I'm quite skilled between the sheets. If you are inexperienced that's okay. I can teach that along with light magica."

Mr. Whyatt, who had just been recovering, is back on the ground trying to breathe again.

"Miss Felindra, I am very flattered. Honestly. But I really just wanted to meet you and determine if we could trust each other enough to work on a highly secretive and risky project."

She pouts. "If it's my size, don't be intimidated. I can handle a big man."

I hear a thump from the back of the office. Mr. Whyatt just cracked his head on his grav desk as he tried to get up when she said that last line.

We both look over and Felindra says, "Really, brother, you are embarrassing me in front of our guest. Can't you even sit at your desk without falling out of your chair?" Looking back at me, she continues. "Don't let his deficiencies sour you. We are a good family that can be trusted to do sensitive things. And in exchange, maybe you can do sensitive things to me."

I sigh and rub my face. "Miss Felindra. I am not asking about Mr. Whyatt or your family. I am asking about you personally. What we are talking about doing can literally not be spoken about for the rest of your life. This is non-negotiable. You, myself, Mr. Whyatt, and one other whom you haven't met are the only people that can know about this. Ever. Any breach of trust on your part will result in dire consequences for yourself and your entire family. Can you accept those terms? I am happy to meet again in two days if you want time to think it over."

She shudders slightly, but I swear it looks like it's from excitement. "Oh, my. You are firm and controlling. Stop trying to distract me from the important topics."

Looking at Mr. Whyatt, I say, "I'll come with my other assistant in two days. Same time."

Mr. Whyatt nods, back to trying not to laugh.

"Miss Felindra, it was nice meeting you. Take the two days to think about what is being asked of you. If you have questions about the consequences of the decision, I recommend you speak to your brother there." I nod at him. "Good night to you both."

I turn to leave and when I am at the door I swear I hear a moan from her.

CHAPTER 82

All I tell Aria is that the meeting went fine and that Miss Felindra is very forthright and speaks her mind. I'm pretty sure she knows I am holding back somewhat given the skeptical look on her face.

The next day is normal until the meeting with Master Steeltamer. I ask Jo what kind of place dwarves like to meet. She gives multiple answers, and they all revolve around places to get alcohol. So I reserve a private corner room as far from anything as possible in the hotel restaurant's bar.

I wait for him at the entrance to the hotel. When he arrives, I introduce myself without a mask, welcome him with a handshake, and guide him to the bar room I had them set aside for us. As we walk, he looks around. His face is one of disgust, but I think he looked like that when he was saving people and before he met me this evening, so he might always be grumpy. Like I said, maybe it's a family thing.

His face actually changes when we get to the automated bar. Well, slightly. His eyebrows twitch a little. I'll take that as a form of excitement. Or maybe annoyance. Whatever.

We sit down, and I tap the crystal with the drinks menu. I tell him, "Master Steeltamer, feel free to order whatever you want. It is on me tonight."

This causes another eyebrow twitch. He orders—I don't see what—and begins speaking.

"I be Glurmaon Steeltamer, a master of the arts of metal." He stops.

Taking the cue, I say, "Good evening, Master Steeltamer. I am Vic, an agent serving to benefit humanity and its allies."

He nods once, very firmly. "I asked to meet ya because I want ta know what yer business was with those lugs who tainted me mead and knocked me about."

Surprised, I ask to make sure I understand the question. "My business with them?"

He nods once again.

I say quietly, "Master Steeltamer, my business with those lugs was to kill one, knock out the other, and hopefully trace them back to their headquarters and kill every single one of those slaving fuckers."

He stares at me. "Why?"

I respond at a normal volume. "Slavery is an abomination against nature and humanity. With the exception of a few very rare and nearly extinct parasites, there is no slavery in nature. Only we sentient, supposedly advanced, species could come up with something so repugnant. Can I ask why you are asking? I hope you do not believe that I was a party to any of that filth."

"I apologize. I can see ya are earnest in yer feelings to saving those poor folks. Ya gave of yerself to save others, and I want ta understand why. You did na just do it cause ya hate slavery."

I understand now. Once again whispering, I say, "I saved them because they were there and needed saving. If they were held captive by something other than slavers, I would still have saved them."

He stares at me silently, clearly feeling I have to say more.

I sigh. I don't really have anything to hide on this topic, so I continue in a low voice. "I will tell you something else, Master Steeltamer. When I saw those poor people in those cages, you know what else I saw? A young woman's face. Many floors above us is a young elf barely in her fifties, and she is the only living creature on this world or any other I have ever considered family. I spent the night thinking, 'That could have been her.' So no, Master Steeltamer, it was not just because of the slavers."

The drinks appear on our table. The dwarf has ordered something inside of a steel mug the size of his head. I simply ordered a glass of white wine. I hate beer in all its forms.

He picks it up, drinks deeply, and stares at me for a full minute without moving. Finally his eyebrow twitches again,' and he speaks. "Mr. Vic. I thank ya fir bein honest, fir I sense ya are."

When he picks up the mug to take another drink, I ask him a question. "Master Steeltamer, can I ask you a question?"

He drunks, licks his lips and nods. "Go ahead, boy."

"Do you know the name Grundlan Steeltamer?"

The dwarf freezes. "Where did you hear that name boy?"

"I promise I will answer. But please tell me what you know of him."

Still looking at me with his grumpy face for twenty seconds, he says, "He be me great grandson. He was recruited as a Guardian Protector fir the princess and future queen a' the leading elven kingdom at da time. I not be knowing what, but some'n happen, and he fled with his charge. That be all I know. So tell me. How do ya know that name?"

"I met him and his charges. We became somewhat close before, I'm sorry to tell you, he and the princess died. It is something of a long story. Would you like to hear it?" You always ask a dwarf if there is a long story. Time is money to them.

Taking another drink, he says, "Aye boy, I would."

So I tell him.

First I tell him what Shen told me about how they were together for seventy plus years then fled, about Aria, how they were recaptured and how they were betrayed and met me. And then I tell him the sanitary version of our sojourn through the rainforest and into Sea Saddle City. It ends in Grun and Shen's death and how I have taken the charge of guarding and training Aria.

I take a drink of my wine and say one last thing. "He served his charges until the end and sacrificed himself protecting what was most important to him. He died smiling, knowing he took his final enemy down with him. I have nothing but the deepest admiration for Grun. And as time passes, I find I miss his grumpy ass more and more."

I take another sip of my wine and wait silently. He takes another drink. "Thank ya, boy. That be a story me clan can pass down and will make us proud ta share over mead and flame."

Not knowing how to respond, I simply nod. We sit drinking quietly together for another few minutes. From a dwarven perspective, I cannot initiate the end of this session. He needs to be the first to propose we are done for the night. So I just wait for him to drink. It has something to do with seeing who can drink more. Obviously it is more tradition and politeness outside of the dwarven culture.

Tilting his head back, he finally finishes whatever is in that massive mug and looks at me again. "Boy, you saved me, saved my people, saved innocents, and saved my blood until he could choose his death along with his foe. I owe you, boy, and I would repay that debt."

[Jo, are dwarves uptight about debt?] My research on dwarves was about their basic customs for social interaction only. I'm severely lacking in cultural etiquette.

Very. It is not just a matter of personal honor, but an entire clan can be shamed for failing to provide what is owed. Generally, that is referring to crafting, but in this case, I'm sure he feels it applies . . .

[Thanks.]

"Master Steeltamer, are you going to be in town long enough to meet me again in two days?"

"I would, boy, but I lost me place to stay, and those lugs stole me coin."

I had prepped for that eventuality and figured I'd return his coin, but it turns out he would take that as a dishonor. He lost it; I killed those that stole it. It is now mine by dwarven law. Weird, but true.

[Jo, book Master Steeltamer a room and charge it to my account. Just a normal room. It's probably all I will be able to get him to accept.]

Done. I need him to touch the crystal so he can enter . . .

I wave away the dwarf's concern. "That's easy. You'll stay here. Can you touch this crystal please?"

Another eyebrow twitch. "Listen, boy, I will na owe ya further."

I nod. "On that we agree. In two days we will be speaking business, and this is a business expense. Let us speak frankly, Master Steeltamer. In two days, we are going to meet in my suite in this insanely fancy hotel, where you are going to be introduced to your adopted great-great-granddaughter for the first time. And after that, I am going to show you something that I one hundred percent guarantee you will be shocked by and interested in."

His eyebrows *and* nose twitch. Oh-ho! He must be freaking out now.

"Are ye willing to make a wager on that boy?"

[Is the common dwarf thing?]

Yes . . .

"What are the stakes, and what do I get when I win?"

Look at that, a mouth twitch! I'm winning him over with my amazing wit. Or I'm giving him gas. Either is fine.

"If any of what you say be untrue when we next meet, my debt to you be gone."

"Agreed, and if all of it happens as I say, you will teach me one element of metalwork of my choosing. I agree in advance never to share my gained knowledge with anyone for as long as I live. At the same time, you will agree to never speak of what I show you nor of Aria for the rest of your days."

Oh, Vic, you clever little shit . . .

#I concur, Host Vic is a little shit . . .

After some eyebrow and mouth twitching, he says, "I agree ta the terms of our wager." He holds his hand out, and I shake it. He touches the crystal and then stands, denoting the meeting is over.

I do as well and say, "I will see you in my room in two days at the same time as we met tonight."

He nods once and walks away.

Wait till Aria finds out she has a sort of great-great-grandfather . . .

CHAPTER 83

Aria is quietly pensive at the news. Shit. Maybe I went too far without speaking to her first.

"I'm sorry if I overstepped. It never occurred to me you wouldn't want to meet potential family." Her pensive look moves to me, and now I'm really nervous as I continue, explaining my motivation. "I'm sorry. I was thinking it would be great creating this connection now. You will both outlive me by centuries, and it can give you the opportunity to at least be a part of their clan long after I'm gone. It seemed like the right choice at the time."

Her pensive look softens, and I receive a small smile. It is actually a little bit of a weird look, and I can't quite pinpoint it.

She finally speaks. "It's okay, Vic. Thank you for doing that for me. I forget sometimes that you are short-lived and I won't have you around for much longer. Well, much longer for my kind."

I smile and nod, relieved both that she isn't angry and at having figured out what she is thinking.

"Okay. Back into planning. Tomorrow night, you will join me in hopefully activating light magica." Her smile widens even further. She really does want to be involved, which is great as far as I'm concerned. "And the day after, you meet Grun's great grandfather." She nods at that. "But that is all a day away. Tonight and tomorrow we stick to our routine."

Given the time, that means range time, Ranger Bob, and bed.

**

The next day is completely normal. For Aria, at least. I spend the day thinking about the night's plan with the light magica. As the day progresses, I get more and more nervous about letting Aria interact with Felindra. She may be in her fifties, but as an elf who was brought up basically as an isolated healing slave, she likely wasn't taught much about the adult physicality side of things. What if Aria thinks that stuff is normal? Even for an elf, Felindra is a lunatic that could throw off Aria's perspective and expectations. As we finish dinner I have gotten myself so worked up, I am ready to call the whole thing off. I won't let that nutty gnome corrupt her.

I open my mouth to tell her I'm calling it off when Jo interrupts.

Vic, you have received a request from Mr. Whyatt. He asks that you delay your arrival by ten minutes due his attempt to force Miss Felindra to change attire. I have alerted Aria to the delay . . .

Oh, shit. This is bad.

[That's it. There is no way I am letting Aria anywhere near that crazy woman.]

Vic, please be cautious . . .

[That is what I am doing.]

I call to her room. "Hey, Aria! I think we should maybe talk about a change of plans."

A minute later, Aria stalks out of her room with an aggressive look on her face. "Don't try to change your mind. I have every right to participate and am the only person who knows what it does to you. You cut me out of enough. Don't try to do it with awakening affinities."

Her hands are on her hips, and she looks like a smaller golden-haired version of her mother.

"But you see, Felindra is a really . . . forthright person. She is very forward with her thoughts and . . . um . . . desires. I am concerned that you will be . . ." Don't say corrupted. What is the right word? "Overwhelmed."

She lets her stubborn face go a little. "I appreciate your role as my protector. But in this case, I'll be fine. Don't forget I was brought up around many powerful people."

"I know that. It's just . . ." My voice fades at the end when her face returns to its stubborn form.

I sigh.

[A little help? Are there any emergency missions? Can we blow something up? Start a war? Anything?]

I think you are just going to have to play this as things come, Vic . . .

[Damnit. This is going to be horrible, I just know it. Kill me. I can't watch.]

I proceed to repeatedly bang my head on the dining room table and with each thump, I receive the alert:

Warning! Host has received 1 bludgeoning damage . . .

I feel a hand on the back of my neck and turn to see Aria smiling behind me.

"It will be fine. Just relax. Now come on." She grabs my sleeve, and I am dragged to the infusion pad.

***

I make sure Aria is behind me before we enter the office. Stopping a few steps before the door, I take a really deep breath and proceed.

The door opens, and I hear a conversation already taking place. Actually, maybe conversation isn't the right word. Mr. Whyatt is in his normal dark suit. Felindra, on the other hand, is wearing a black dress with a low cut at the chest and a skirt that stops above her short knees. It looks painted on. Her red hair is down and wavy behind her. She is gesticulating with her hands, trying to fend off her brother.

"...you dunce. I can wear whatever I want. Did you see him? How does he not have a wife? Stop screwing with my clothes, Clinky. You are going to ruin my chances. Did you see his ass when he left? I need to—"

Mr. Whyatt interrupts loudly, "Feli, stop! He is not a piece of meat. He is a..."

At the ass comment, I look down and back at Aria. Her eyes are wide, staring open-mouthed at the pair. Looking back, I clear my throat loudly. The verbal war pauses as they both whip their heads over.

Mr. Whyatt starts to say "Welco—" but his sister immediately rolls right over him.

"Oh. Hello, Vic." She starts a sultry walk over. Then she freezes, seeing Aria behind me. "Who is that? Is that your girlfriend? You like them young, huh? I'll have you know I'm not even 175. And I have a lot more meat on my bones than that scrawny little thing. Why is she here? Are you trying to make me jealous? Well, it's working. Give me a few minutes, and I'll have you begging for more. If you just..."

"Feli, stop!" Mr. Whyatt practically bellows to interrupt. I have unconsciously shifted my body to be completely in front of Aria. "Vic is not here for that. Are you Vic?"

I very quickly call out, "No!"

I clear my throat again and glance down at Aria, who has shifted to my right from behind me. She has an interesting look on her face while looking the tiny Felindra up and down.

Shit, shit, shit. I knew it! Okay, stay on mission, Vic. You can salvage this.

Looking at Mr. Whyatt only, I say, "No. We are here to see if you both are willing to take on the project or if you have any questions about the risks."

Mr Whyatt opens his mouth again only to once again be cut off by his sister. "Of course I am taking it on. I know all about secrets. Actually, I have some I'd like to share personally. We can do either the magica or physical first. I'm good with either order." She looks me up and down and licks her lips. "Personally, I'd prefer the physical, but with your other little thing here I can wait. Or maybe she can join. I'm open to it if both of you are. She's just the right size to—"

"Stop!" I scream out. Once again I have stepped in front of Aria, and once again she has stepped to the side. I still cannot fathom her look, but this time she is glancing between Felindra and me.

This is my worst nightmare. Why can't I be in a jungle, buried in sludge, being eaten alive by bugs, taking on an army of orcs? Is there an infusion pad I can use to escape?

Mr. Whyatt thankfully comes to my rescue. "Feli, please! Vic needs your help and not the physical kind. This operation is time-sensitive, and he needs your word you will not speak about what is about to happen."

I take the lifeline and yank hard. "Yes. Please. We need to be clear. This silence is a lifetime commitment. If word leaks, it will be deadly. To everyone involved. Are you clear on the agreement and consequences?"

She just shrugs her bare shoulders. "Yes, yes, I agree. I don't understand why we can't have some fun first, but I'm patient. What is this big secret?"

Aria of all people pipes up. "Let's sit. Vic will sit next to me and Mr. Whyatt. Miss Felindra will sit at the other side so they can reach out and hold hands. And nothing else." That last sentence is said with snap.

[Wow. Aria is defending me from the crazy gnome.]

Vic, you're . . . never mind. Just focus on the operation. Let Aria take care of herself; she clearly can . . .

[Clearly. That's a good idea.]

Felindra looks straight at Aria. "Well, look at that. The scrawny girlfriend has some bite."

Mr. Whyatt speaks up again. "Yes, well. Aria is correct. Let's sit so we can proceed. I think her seating arrangements are quite adequate."

Mr. Whyatt pulls up a seat at his small round table and I hurriedly sit next to him. Aria and Felindra share a quick glare, and then Aria quickly sits next to me. Felindra slowly sits down opposite me, slightly leaning forward, ensuring that I can see her cleavage.

Aria says forcefully, "Mr. Whyatt, why don't you start?"

"Yes, perhaps that is wise." Mr. Whyatt says as he takes Aria up on her offer. "Feli, Vic approached the Whyatt Armory in hopes of purchasing a communicator for young miss Aria here. Vic's record in the UFH is quite extraordinary, so I took up his account."

Felindra interrupts while looking between her brother and me. "Record? What record?"

In answer, Mr. Whyatt looks at me and asks, "How many enemy lives would you say you are directly or indirectly responsible for taking?"

That's an interesting question. I'm silent for a moment.

[Does MilNet have the figure?]

Accessing . . . Ironically, you do not have clearance for all the data. What is available states in excess of one hundred twenty-five thousand . . .

Hmm. Well, I suppose that's an okay start.

"Something in excess of a hundred twenty-five thousand. Any counts above that are classified."

I hear an intake of breath from both Felindra and Aria.

The suited gnome continues. "And how old are you, Vic?"

"Twenty-four."

"Sprocket crack! There is no sparking way!"

Ahh, Gnomish swearing. Like a rainfall in spring.

Mr. Whyatt nods. "It is true, sister. And this is only the tip of the iceberg. To continue the story, I took on Mr. Vic's account and decided to reach out to him in an attempt to determine his condition, mental state, and disposition towards working together in the war. The first two were as expected. The latter was a surprise, however. When he approached me in return he made me an offer. He asked if *I*" —he points at himself— "would be willing to participate in a partnership if I understood that any betrayal would result in my death. And if the business or family did the same in a way that harmed Aria, he would destroy us and every building and business we owned."

Felindra looks at me with a fire of desire and . . . ownership? Fuck! I feel Aria's hand on mine, and then it's gone.

"Well, as you have surmised by your presence here, I spoke with our other brothers, and we have agreed."

Felindra snaps her head at her brother, and she asks, "Even Blinky?"

He coughs lightly and says, "Well, no, not him. But he and his cronies were outvoted."

[You started recording upon entry?]

Yes...

[That bit is valuable intel. There may be some risk of leakage from their end of the partnership.]

Agreed. There is nothing we can do about it now, other than be aware...

Mr. Whyatt proceeds to say, "Let's reach the last line of the inscription quickly then. Mr. Vic also agreed to our partnership and asked me for some things. They were mana stones for ice, magma, light, and darkness."

Felindra snorts at that last part. "Why in the orc's bunghole would you need..."

The last part of her sentence fades from her voice as she begins putting it together. She stares at me wide-eyed.

"Yes, sister, I think you have just realized it."

Looking directly at me, he says, "Vic, I have secured this office from eavesdropping, as best as can be managed."

I nod and say, "Thank you, Mr. Whyatt."

The gnome continues quietly. "As of today, how many affinities do you have access to?"

Looking directly at Felindra, I answer in the order I activated them. "Fire, air, water, earth, nature, lightning, ice, magma, life, and death."

Felindra is frozen solid. Mr. Whyatt continues. "And why have you asked me to bring my sister here?"

Still not taking my eyes off her, I say, "In hopes she will send me her light affinity mana so I can activate it."

Nobody speaks for at least twenty seconds. Felindra's mouth is moving, and I think I see it form the word "son" but I can't be sure.

I decide to proceed. "Aria is here for two reasons. First, because she is the only person in the world I trust without reservation. And second, she has been with me while opening many affinities and understands what to do and how to help. You see, Felindra, activating affinities the way I do is quite traumatic. I have been sucked of life until I am pale white, frozen solid at the molecular level, and melted alive in a pool of lava. Aria is calm and collected and aware of what to do. Frankly, I have high hopes that the light affinity will be less . . . straining. I am not looking forward to using the darkness mana stone I currently carry in my [Inventory]."

And I stop there again.

Turning back to Mr. Whyatt, I ask, "Would it be possible to get some water for myself and Aria?"

Smiling, Mr. Whatty shakes his head. "Unfortunately, that is the downside of having the room sealed. It is quite literally sealed. And, of course, you knew that and were testing me."

I smile at him, nod, and look at Aria. She holds her hand over the table and taps the ring on her finger. Four glasses of water appear.

Felindra is, watching all of this in complete silence. That is until the water appears. She grabs one, gulps it down in two seconds, and slams the glass on the table. I choose one, take a sip, and put it aside. Aria, watching me, does the same. Mr. Whyatt just takes the last glass and lets it sit between his hands.

Looking at her brother, Felindra finally speaks. "Clinky, I'm impressed. I didn't think you had this in you. I'll tell Mother that you are not a completely useless giant's ass."

Mr. Whyatt actually blushes slightly. Interesting.

She turns back to me and says, "Vic, I won't hesitate to say that I want you even more now. Like a drained inscription craves mana and will suck it through a copper tube if it has to."

Now it's my turn to blush.

Aria clears her throat, and Felindra glances at her and, without any of her usual flirtiness or innuendo, she continues. "But I can see the urgency. And what you offer our family and our entire people is worth far more than a tumble. I have a feeling my brother will be approaching you in the future with a few other offers. But we can deal with that another day. What do I do?"

I'm relieved she can be professional. I was close to having to make a hard decision about risk and reward. Sure, I could always terminate her, but I need the Whyatts. At least for now.

I bow my head slightly to her and say, "It is quite simple on your end. You simply hold my hand and send your light mana into me. I cannot communicate while in my inner world, so Aria will be my mouth. Please follow her instructions."

She reaches her hand out to me, and I reach out mine.

We clasp and she whispers, "So soft." Then out loud, she says with a hint of suspicion, "I thought you are a warrior. How do you have soft hands?"

I smile at her and say, "My skin is somewhat special. Anything more than that will be provided at a later time. All secrets come at a price, and this one neither your family nor your business are prepared to pay for."

Talking about how my skin magically merged with a product we all hate made by a company we don't trust during a unique nanomachine activation is definitely something that will come with a high price. For me and them.

"Oh. Well, now I'm intrigued. So I just send you mana?"

I nod. "Yes. Ready when you are."

Then I feel a pressure push into me, close my eyes, and enter my inner world.

CHAPTER 84

The visual representation of light is unlike any of the others. There is no mist or smoke. What it is a solid beam of pure white and it is streaking across the sky. It sweeps everywhere like it cannot miss anything. When it makes contact with me, I feel . . . I don't know how to describe it. A presence, I suppose. I am given the impression of the knowledge of existence. It is both simple and not. Light recognizes the need for everything to exist everywhere. Anywhere there is existence, there must be light. Moreover, it needs to be everywhere at once, and it moves so quickly that it feels it can and should be. The beam finally makes contact with my river, and I focus on it, creating its own existence in the river.

[Have Felindra stop.]

I send my mana with a feeling of emptiness into the river. The beam abhors the lack of itself anywhere and nearly attacks the river with the pure existence of light. It *must* exist at all times in all places. My river blazes with light, and I have to cover my eyes with my arms. Just my eyelids don't help. Then my arms don't help, and my entire body glows with existence too. I'm ablaze with light and form and want, no *need*, to be everywhere. Then it ends and all is normal in my world.

I open my eyes to the real world, feeling a tingle fading from the right side of my neck and look toward Aria first. I smile at her to assure that all is fine. Then I turn and see the astonished gazes of the two gnomes.

New rune activated. Light Rune is now available for use . . .

New affinity activated. Light Affinity is now available for use . . .

[Let's put on a show.]

I quickly create a path to the new rune and send mana to it and back into myself. I start to glow with a white light. My hand brightens to almost the point of not being able to look at it as I raise it above the table.

I stop the mana and smile.

"Thank you both. Light is an interesting affinity."

Aria asks, "You ready to head home, Vic?"

I nod at her and turn towards my left and ask, "Is there anything else, Mr. Whyatt?"

He just shakes his head with a smile.

I say one more thing before we are ready to head out. "Please remember our agreement. Nobody outside this room. Please do not betray my trust."

I turn back to Aria and nod. We both stand and leave the office.

***

As soon as we enter our suite, Aria pulls me to the couch. She pushes me to sit down, sits next to me, and leans against my side.

Speaking out loud, I ask, "Jo, can you put on that ranger show?" After it turns on, I say, "Aria, you were amazing tonight. Thank you for . . . well . . . being amazing."

Her only response is to lay her head on my shoulder. Odd reaction.

The ranger show today is about desert species, especially a few species of infused scorpions. Creepy but educational. Aria gets up and comes back a minute later with a bowl of ice cream. She is enjoying it while watching Ranger Bob do his insect thing. Although apparently scorpions aren't insects. I can't believe they're arachnids. As if they weren't creepy enough. I think about Mr. Stinky and shudder.

When it's over, she gets up, turns around, and looks down at me. "You know, Vic, I'm young for an elf, but not for a human."

Then she wanders off to wash and go to bed.

[Well, that's obvious.]

Your idiocy is annoying me. Do you want your alerts? . . .

[Fine, I guess. Why is everyone mad at me tonight? I thought everything went okay. I didn't have trouble with the affinity.]

Shut up . . .

New skill activated. Passive skill [Light Mana Manipulation] now available for use . . .

Skill updated. Passive skill [Light Mana Manipulation] is now level 1 . . .

[Pretty much what I expected.]

Now how about inspecting that weird living stone?

Right, I completely forgot about that thing. I go to the bag on the table in my room and take it out.

[We should go through those storage devices too.]

I look at the supposedly living stone and tap it with a finger. That's weird. I tap it against the table and it clinks, not like stone, but like metal. Odd. It appears to be ovoid, slightly fatter on the bottom, and has a symmetrical, rounded hatch pattern. Finally interested, I think [Inspect].

Wait, it's an egg?

Name:	Metal/Air Mana-Mutated Peregrine Falcon Egg
Description:	Normal mana-fused falcons are large and very aggressive hunters. They hunt mostly other birds but sometimes will hunt smaller mammals. Their favorite method is to climb high into the sky and then stoop, or dive downwards at 300 kph or more and knock prey out of the sky. This egg contains a still-viable peregrine falcon fetus. Unfortunately, this egg was exposed to a massive influx of metal mana during a particularly vulnerable part of its growth. The mother abandoned this egg when its home, the tree under which it was found, was moved from the rainforest. The egg fell to the ground, and due to the metal mutation, it did not break. The tree had been inadvertently protecting, feeding, and keeping alive this creature for over 15 years when an illness caused the tree to eject the egg for the safety of both. The condition of the fetus is failing, due to lack of nutrition which started from the failing of the tree. Provided the correct care, the fetus could mature and potentially hatch. Countdown to fetus death: 00:00:05:20:17:40
Condition:	Alive but failing
Risk Assessment:	N/A
Value:	At its current health, the value of this egg is very low.

> If it can be revived, the value will likely be high. Such a rare mutation is an excellent object of bonding or study.

[Shitballs, Jo! Did you see that?]

Of course I saw it, Vic. What would you like to do? . . .

[Is Aria still awake? Just to be sure, that is from right to left, seconds, minutes, hours, days, months, years, right?]

No, she is asleep, and yes that is correct . . .

[Conduct an immediate search on caring for peregrine falcon eggs. And what the fuck is the metal element?]

Searching. Based on prior research, if there is any data on a metal affinity, it is not in your currently available access level . . .

[A bird with metal. That might cause a weight issue during flight. Sounds like it might be tough. Still, I know drake shit about eggs. We have less than six days to figure this out. Do you think life mana would help? Shit, I don't want to do anything wrong and fuck this up.]

Calm down, Vic. Let the search results come up first. Then we can take it from there . . .

[Right. Thanks. Oh, I have an idea. Can you do a search for any air or metal-infused cloth in the armory? The effect doesn't matter, I suppose. But the higher the mana saturation, the better.]

Walking over to the corner of my room where nothing else is, I place a meter and a half wide nest on the ground.

[I'm glad I kept deprioritizing dealing with this thing.]

I acquired this nest the first night Shen, Grun, Arial, and I met.

I lean the egg in the corner against a wall of the nest. It looks funny having this massive nest with a single egg the size of my fist in it.

[I'm thinking maybe I can surround it with its own elements if possible.]

I have more than a hundred possible selections. Please provide a way to narrow it down . . .

[Did you find the metal element on any items?]

No. Everything I found is a variety of air . . .

I think about it. It's a bird, hopefully I can do something to offset the weight of the metal.

[What do you think about searching for things that involve lightening weight, anti-grav, flight? That sort of thing.]

Search refined. That narrows it down to twenty-two items. Do you wish to refine further?

[It needs to be of sufficient size and flex to wrap most or all the way around the egg. Oh, go back to the last search and find anything that encourages growth.]

Search refined. Thirteen items. Do you wish to refine further?

So formal.

[Do any of the materials have metal inside, either woven in or through particles?]

Search refined. five items. Do you wish to refine further?

[Relax with the formal stuff. Can that material be purchased by the square meter?]

If you like, and yes, it can . . .

[Buy three square meters of each and the best full tailoring set for under five gold. No spatial storage since it's going in my [Inventory].]

Confirmed. Awaiting response . . .

[Thank you. Keep me apprised. And please set a reminder for me to check the egg every four hours.]

Delivery estimated in forty-eight hours . . .

[Let's see. What else?] My mind is moving, and I cannot really process everything going on inside. Jo is right; I need to calm down. I take a breath and then another. Okay. Think.

I go back to the nest and place all the liquid steel shards around the egg. They almost bury it.

[Price out the cost of five pounds of rhodium powder.]

Confirmed . . .

I cannot think of anything else.

[Am I missing anything?]

The storage devices . . .

[Right. Let's see what we have.]

I settle at the dinner table with the bag and hold one at a time asking for the contents. Most are garbage, and I store those in the "absorb pile" from the bling shop. There are three items of interest from what I assume was the slave trader. Well, four—one is a slave collar, but I won't even touch that. Its foul stench won't leave that storage space until I can figure out what to do with it.

The first is a crystal pad I suspect has the slave trader's notes and records. It's encrypted, and Jo doesn't have the protocols to get through it. I figure this goes to Mr. Whyatt.

The second is a data crystal like the language ones Mr. Whyatt gave us.

[Jo, you can protect us?]

I believe so, Vic. There are, of course, risks . . .

I take it out and let it fall into my hand.

Accessing . . .

Contained in this data crystal is a map with two highlighted locations and a message. The first mapping location is on the western shore of the rainforest peninsula. The other is to the east northeast of Sea Saddle City and in an area that is currently contested . . .

[And the message?]

The message reads, "You paid for these so they are yours. Per our magica contract, I will not release them until you authorize it or five years has passed. I certainly hope they are worth the price you paid. I know I'll be enjoying my retirement on your coin. Asshole."

[Well, that is quite rude. And helpful. I don't suppose it is dated?]

According to the data crystal's first access, it is dated fourteen months five days ago . . .

[You know what, Jo? I am seriously being overwhelmed by all this crap I have to do. Can we keep a log or something so I have a list of my larger missions?]

Affirmative. Mission log created. I hope you like it . . .

Why does she seem so snarky tonight?

On my HUD in the middle top, there is a small quadrilateral with the word "Missions" on it.

I open it with my mind, and I have a list.

Mission Log for Vic (because he can't keep track of his own shit)

Name	Description	Timeframe	Perceived Difficulty
Save Humanity	Your personal goal in life is to eliminate all invaders from this planet. This is an impossible mission, and you need to lower your expectations.	The end of time	Good fucking luck!
Quirky Quicksilver	Because you are one lucky little shit, you have come by Quicksilver ore and a lot of it. However, you have no way to smelt it into pure Quicksilver. You need to either learn to do it and do it yourself, or have people do it for you. Either way, only a handful of people know how.	Whenever	Really fucking hard
Guard and Protect	You have been selected as the Guardian Protector of Arialla Frystera Livera Riverwing. Your role is to protect, mentor, guide, and train her as required for the duration of your agreement.	Duration of Protectorate Agreement	Unknown
Flora Friend	Figure out who is conducting crazy experiments on innocent plant life, why the lunatic is doing so, and make them stop using whatever violent means you choose.	Unknown	Unknown

Slavery Shutdown	Slavery is an abomination that must be ended in Sea Saddle City. You will trace the thugs back to the slavers and terminate them. With prejudice.	As soon as fucking possible	Unknown
Hopeful Hatchery	You found an egg of a mutated peregrine falcon. Do whatever it takes to help the egg return to health, grow, and then hatch. Maybe if you don't screw that up you can bond. Maybe. You do smell.	00:00:06:20:08:22	Low if you aren't your usual idiotic self
Map Highlights	You have "procured" a map from a less than benevolent source with two highlighted areas on it. Explore those areas, figure out what they are, why they are highlighted, and do something about it.	03:10:25:44:18:24	Unknown

[Really, Jo? Is all that attitude necessary?]

Yes . . .

What the fuck did I do? She is usually sassy, but she seems just mad right now.

Rhodium is unavailable in powder form . . .

Looks like I'm Aria's Guardian Protector. Not that it changes anything for me. It is all stuff I am already doing. Looking at the hatchery mission, I sniff myself. Do I smell? Maybe. I'll shower and go to bed.

Wait. I'm an idiot. I go back to the egg and place a "stick" of quicksilver ore in with the pile of liquid metal. It isn't refined, but maybe it can help.

CHAPTER 85

I try to give Jo her space the next day, asking for as little assistance as possible. Aria seems pretty curt with me too. Not rude or mean, just not pleased. I don't understand what is going on.

During lunch, I remind Aria about tonight's meeting. That seems to perk her up a little.

Later that day at the range, she moves from background, introduction, safety, and the basics onto crossbows. There are so many varieties of those it will take a while to get through to mana shooters. It also reminds me of the crossbow and rapier in my inventory. I suppose I should do something with those.

Taking a breath and wincing, I whisper in my mind.

[Hey, Jo. Are you okay enough for me to ask you something?] I hear a sigh.

Yes, Vic. I'm sorry. I am here to serve you and cannot do that if my attitude is so bad you won't talk to me . . .

[Stop there. You are not a servant. You are a partner. The best partner. I know I am not sort of the smartest when it comes to relationship stuff, so if you could tell me how I can do better, it would help us both I think.]

That's very sweet, Vic. But I cannot tell you this time. It is not for me to interfere. You and . . . you need to work it out. But yes, I will try to help as much as I can . . .

[Thanks. I'm not sure what you mean about working it out, but I trust you.]

What did you need to ask? . . .

[Oh, right. Can you price out the rapier and crossbow if I resell to Whyatt? Not sure I will, just asking.]

Well, two things. First, have you thought about giving them to Aria? And second you need to [Inspect] them for me to price them out. And you have received a notice from Master Steeltamer confirming a meeting at 19:00 . . .

[Great, we'll deal with the blue guys' garbage later. For now, we need to have dinner and prep for the meeting.]

***

Aria is nearly vibrating with a mix of nervousness and excitement. I remind her I'm here for her, whatever happens. She thanks me and gets dressed a little nicer than normal. When Master Steeltamer arrives at our suite entrance, I escort him to the dining table and tell him to once again order whatever he wants. I order fruit juice for myself and Aria.

Aria comes out in a skirt and nice blouse. She walks up to my side.

"Master Steeltamer, may I introduce you to Arialla Frystera Livera Riverwing, Grun's adopted daughter. Aria, this is Master Steeltamer, Grun's great-grandfather."

She takes a deep breath and steps in front me. "Hello, Master Steeltamer. Grun was a good man, and he loved my mother and me with all his heart."

I lightly place my hand on her shoulder. Like she did with me, I'm simply reminding her that I am here.

"Hello, lass." I think the sky may open and end all life on the planet; the wrinkly old grump just smiled! And I swear I see his eyes a little watery. "Come sit with me, girl. Tell me about me boy and how you and he spent time together."

I step back and say, "I'll give you two a little time. Aria, come get me if you need anything. Your juice is right there. Master Steeltamer, I'll be back after a bit and we can proceed with the evening."

I turn around and walk onto the balcony. It's raining out, and the sound of it hitting the mana shield is a nice rhythm to relax to. It sounds like drops landing on green leaves; it almost smells that way too. I keep an ear out, but I don't expect anything to go wrong. Now's my chance to look at the slaver's crap. I take out the rapier and hold it before me. It's different shades of blue from blade to hilt. The blade looks like it might have different shades of blue just by itself. At the bottom of the handle, the pommel is a glowing blue mana stone of some sort. Did he have water affinity? Well, time to take a look. I have to admit, it is the perfect size for Aria. Damnit.

[Inspect.]

Name:	Water-Enchanted Damascus Steel Rapier
Description:	This piercing sword's blade is made of three different steels, creating a flowing pattern that resembles waves. Once forged, it was enchanted with water mana, which increases its flexibility, spring, and tip sharpness.

	Injecting mana into this sword will surround it with highly compressed water that can puncture medium armor with ease. However, the thin tip is designed to fit between armor plates. When struck, an opponent will receive piercing damage, water damage equaling 50% of piercing damage, and bleed damage equaling the water damage over 15 seconds.
Condition:	Excellent
Risk Assessment:	N/A
Value:	This weapon was well crafted and is quite beautiful to look at. Weapons such as this are something of a niche item being only piercing, but the look and enchantments give it a very high value in appropriate markets.

[This is a really nice weapon. However, it isn't for Aria. She can't be limited to just piercing. I'll get rid of it. The question is can I sell it to the armory and not have it traced back to me?]

You might want to ask Mr. Whyatt for assistance on that front . . .

[That reminds me. Set something up in a few days to do a debrief on the slavery mission. Oh, add a request to him to gather intel on the metal affinity and bring it if possible. Emphasize this is for research purposes only.]

Confirmed . . .

I swap the rapier for the hand crossbow. It is a nice weapon but standard. No enchantments or inscriptions. I put it back.

[Junk. Aria seems to really enjoy crossbows. Let's start looking for one in case she sticks with it. She's earned it.]

When do you want to take on the darkness stone? That is the last before you are ready to level up . . .

[I cannot believe how close we are. It feels like forever ago we put this crazy plan together to gain all the affinities possible. It's almost over. To answer your question, I don't know. I'm afraid of it, to be honest.]

You expect it to be that bad? . . .

[I do.]

You'll have Aria and me there. You aren't alone . . .

[That's the thing—this time I will be. Anyway, I don't want to think about it right now. What is the status of the egg?]

All I can tell you is the countdown is still counting down. [Inspect] the egg for a detailed analysis . . .

Drinking my juice in peace and quiet is an enjoyable bit of downtime. After thirty minutes, I stand and go back inside.

"Master Steeltamer, Aria. I hope you both are enjoying your time together."

Aria smiles. All the dwarf says is "Aye, boy."

"Master Steeltamer, if you are willing to stick around the city, I'm sure you and Aria can continue to meet. I'd be happy to keep your accommodations available."

"Aye, boy. I wou' like tha'."

I look at Aria, and she nods.

Turning back to the dwarf, I say, "Excellent. So, have I met the first half of our agreement?"

The dwarf nods once. "You have, lad. Now the second half is what I be waiting for."

"Aria, would mind giving us some space?" She nods, grabs her cryspad from the couch, and heads into her room.

I sit across from him and smile. "I'm pleased you were able to help Aria remember Grun. He was a good man, and her memories of him should not fade."

"The pleasure be mine, boy. I learn abou' 'im too."

I put my hands on the table. "Glad to hear it. Okay, enough of that. Let's talk business." I pause. His eyebrow twitches, and he nods once.

"Good. So I believe I promised to impress you. And I intend to try. I simply want to reiterate that everything we discuss here will not be discussed with anyone. Ever. Your clan, your family, your pets. Nobody and nothing can know. Do you agree?"

Another eyebrow twitch. This time there is a nose twitch thrown in for good measure. "Aye, boy, I agree. Not that I believe what you say is worth the secrets."

"Oh. I don't know."

CHAPTER 86

I smile at him and say, "I wonder, Master Steeltamer, what do you think of this?"

I tap the table, and the smallest piece of quicksilver in my [Inventory] clatters on it. I push it towards him, and he huffs and picks it up. He looks at it closely and is in the process of turning it over when he freezes.

[He just figured out what it is.]

Yes...

"I see you figured out what that is. I wonder if that quicksilver ore is impressive enough for you."

He humphs again. "Impressive and unusual, yes. But it take more tha' this boy."

I nod, frowning, and say, "I see. I wonder if this might change your mind."

I tap the table again, and the largest piece of quicksilver I have cracks onto the table, shaking it. It is just about as big as me. I don't need to push it to him as it is currently two inches from his nose.

"What do you think, Master Steeltamer?"

The dwarf is looking at it and is frozen except for his eyes roaming up and down the massive piece.

Then I tap the table again and another piece thumps down. Tap, thump. Tap, thump.

"What do you think, Master Steeltamer? Have I met the terms of our bet?"

The table is creaking, so I store them all back in my [Inventory] except for the first small piece. The poor old dwarf's face is bright red and getting redder. I hope I didn't surprise him to death. Shit, that would be just like me. I really do only try to kill people on purpose.

"Master Steeltamer, are you all right? Do you require medical assistance?"

A poof of air exists from his mouth, and he falls against the backrest of the chair.

He snaps at me. "Boy. Where di' ya ge' tha'?"

I nod at him and say, "That is a fair question, but I am not willing to share it at this time."

"Do you know what you have there, boy? That much quicksilver could—"

"Yes, it could. So Master Steeltamer, I need to hear you say it. Did I meet the terms of our bet?"

The dwarf slams his fist on the table and says, "Ya know damn well ya did, boy. Now tell me what ya planning."

"Thank you. As you said, that much quicksilver could . . . well . . . do many things. Except right now it can do nothing, can it? Because it is still simply quicksilver ore, not quicksilver. You see, Grun told me something interesting when I showed him a piece after I asked him what it was. He said only two clans know how to correctly smelt quicksilver to keep its properties intact."

I stop there. He twitches his mouth and nose. No eyebrows that time. Why don't I have the primer for hairy dwarf code?

Seeing he isn't speaking, I continue. He is clearly going to make me say it.

"I won our bet, and you agreed to teach me any one thing about metalworking that I want as long as I agree to never share it for the rest of my life. The one thing I want from the Steeltamer clan is to learn how to smelt quicksilver in the proper way to make mighty arms and armor that will kill the orcs and their kin in the thousands."

The dwarf shoots to his feet and slams his hand on the table. "Are ya mad, boy?"

[Order me a full mining, smelting, smithing, and anything-else-I-need set. You know what, hold up. Let's just buy a smithy and upgrade all their older shit. See what you can find in the city limits. The closer to the hotel the better, but a better facility is more important. The facility needs to be able to process ore into metal ingots as well as the smithing stuff. I still want the full mining kit. No rush on that, get the best.]

Search started . . .

"Please, Master Steeltamer. Calm down. All I am doing is fulfilling the terms of our bet. And it will end any debt owed as well."

"This be me clan's secret for thousands o' years. It took me clan half as long ta figure it out."

I nod. "I understand and believe you. It will stay your clan's secret. As I said, it will be me, and only me for the rest of my days. Now before you take action on that glint I see in your eye, I can assure you, any attempt to take *my* quicksilver ore by force will result in its immediate destruction. And the location of where I mined it, and where there is likely more, dies with me. I will not have something of mine fall into the hands of those that betray my trust."

The old dwarf is huffing and puffing now. He is pacing and starts mumbling to himself in Dwarvish.

Now here is the tricky part. The dwarven culture—which I have had a crash course in since our last meeting—says he has to initiate the next step. And he has to do it in a very particular way. So I sit and wait for him to figure out how he wants to do it.

"Boy. I do owe ya. And ya won the bet, and that means I owe ya the knowledge ya seek. And I will na dishonor meself or me clan by not fulfilling the bargain. But that there metal could save lives. Many lives. And it deserves ta be crafted by the masters who ca make it into mighty weapons and armor."

I smile. "Master Steeltamer, please sit."

He humphs yet again and sits. He really is a quality humpher.

"It may surprise you to hear that I actually agree to a point. This material is a mighty weapon against the orcs and their kin, and I wish to see it used to remove them from my world. And the experts who make these weapons will make mighty ones indeed. However, the masters did not start as masters, did they? Did you? We all have to learn, grow and become better. You see, through several fortuitous events, I was in a position to attempt to craft. Would you allow me to take some time to tell you the story?"

He nods. The irony is he has to say yes. But I also have to ask. Dwarven societal norms and politics are particular.

I tell him about my liquid steel armor that malfunctioned all the way through to being granted fire affinity. I avoid anything that could be construed as a location or hint at the acid. He is watching me carefully, and when I finish the story his whole beard twitches. That's new. What the fuck does that mean?

"Master Steeltamer, I was in a position where I was forced to create armor out of leftover pieces of shattered metal and some dead lichen using nothing but a hammer with a rock on top as the head and the flames that I could produce from my hand. Would you permit me to show you my very first armor?"

He nods again. I tap the table, and the last quicksilver ore disappears to be replaced with my old armor set, wound from the bear and all.

"This armor set was the first thing I crafted in those circumstances with only general knowledge, a strong arm, and the determination to survive. The damage to the breastplate is from a rather large diseased bear. But that is another story."

The older dwarf takes his time examining each piece and spending particular time messing about with the lichen joints.

"Obviously it is only barely passable to someone of your experience, but keep in mind that I made this set, yes *set*, at the age of twenty-four with basically nothing but scaps and rocks and a wall plant. I'll grant you, I had an advantage with the rather special liquid metal product."

The dwarf looks up from running his hands along my armor and glares at me. "You're tellin' me ya craft this with garbage as the first thing ya ever made?"

I nod. "That is correct. Are you familiar with human Specials and their professions?"

He snorts and says, "Aye."

I nod. "Well, for whatever it means to you, I can take armorsmith as a profession from the nanos if I choose to do so. And I also have a skill called Set Crafting, which I currently have to level two from what you see in front of you."

He just stares at me. I don't know what he wants to see, but after a good two minutes he says, "Boy, I believe you. I canna deny what I see. This armor has your soul in it. I canna believe it, but I see it."

"Thank you for your trust. Back to the original premise. I will be making things just like you and yours will be. I am in the process of acquiring a smithy and smeltery in Sea Saddle City. As I said, I intend to use it to craft myself and my future team things that will kill orcs and their kin. Many of them."

He is really getting expressive now. Lots of twitching and scrunching.

"To be clear, I will not be selling what I create with quicksilver. Honestly, I don't need the coin. I will be using it or breaking it down for use again. Or perhaps storing it for future use. I don't know yet." Leaning forward, I say, "Let me make this clear. I will not allow what I nearly died for multiple times to be wasted on those who I do not trust. Do you understand what I am saying?"

Not letting him answer, I continue. "I intend to craft. I will craft with iron and steel and other metals that I will purchase or smelt. And I *will* craft with *my* quicksilver. Now, Master Steeltamer, will you and the Steeltamer clan be a part of that? Will you and they be partners that want to share in the destruction of our enemies? Or will I simply take what I am owed and do the rest myself?"

For the first time speaking to me, I see a smile. "Boy, do you have any dwarven blood in you?"

I chuckle and say, "I am an orphan, sir. I have no idea."

His face contorts a bit. "Ya have no clan other than that there girl?"

I nod. "That is correct."

An odd expression passes his face as he rubs his beard for a while. "Boy, I canna make this decision meself. But to take it to me clan, I have to say some things you may not want be said."

I smile at him. "Let's talk about what can be said and what cannot."

We spend the next twenty-five minutes talking through what he is permitted to say and negotiating the future. I make my point clear that no matter what happens, the knowledge of how to smelt quicksilver ore is non-negotiable. That is not a bargaining chip nor something to be traded for; it is a given as if I already own it. He is not pleased but eventually acquiesces on the point.

In the end, we come to an agreement about how much ore I will give the dwarves in exchange for them coming to my new facility and teaching me all there is to know about metalwork. And they are free to use my facility as long as I am not, with the caveat that profit from anything sold there is split down the middle.

That whole back-and-forth is what I was waiting for him to initiate. He is not allowed to ask for a bribe, and I am not allowed to offer one. What he and I can do is business. And the result is a bargain that neither party is thrilled but both are accepting of. Actually, I'm ecstatic, but I cannot say that. I have to look all negative and upset.

After we wrap it up, he asks me about something I said earlier. "Boy, you said you were crafting for your team? That be you and your girl?"

I nod. "For now. As I'm sure you know, finding trustworthy people is hard."

He snorts.

Smiling, I continue. "My team will grow, and I expect to have a small strike force to do precision operations that will cause extreme impact in a small area causing maximum death toll, directly or indirectly, to the enemy."

"That be a mighty mine to dig, boy."

"I agree. Can I share something with you in the deepest of confidence? Aria will be at risk if this gets out, so I guard this secret with terminal force."

He smiles back and says, "I swear on me honor and clan, boy. I'd not put my granddaughter at risk. And I'd not betray you either way."

Dwarves and elves don't focus on all the "greats" the way humans do. When you live that long, who cares if it's two or seven greats, especially when all seven are still alive?

I nod and ask, "How many affinities do you have?"

"Fire and earth like most a me kind."

"I see. What is the most a dwarf has ever had?"

Not sure where I am going with this he says with a question in his voice, "There be a story 'bout a dwarf tha' had four one time."

I nod slowly. "That makes sense." Settling my hands flat on the table between us, I say, "Master Steeltamer, I have affinities in fire, air, water, earth, nature, ice, magma, lightning, life, death, light, and later tonight, I will gain darkness."

He proceeds to swear in Dwarvish for a good thirty seconds.

[Never mind, Jo, I got the gist of it.] I hear a chuckle in my mind.

Taking a deep breath, he once again watches for a few moments before saying, "Boy, that be impossible, but I know you aren't lying. Tell me, would you accept a dwarf on your team?"

"Absolutely. A Steeltamer like Grun would make my team all the more dangerous. Of course, I will need some time both to build up my infrastructure and trust the individual. As with any potential team member. Your recommendation would go a long way, of course."

I grin while saying the last sentence. He lets out a bellow of a laugh at that.

"Boy, I think we gunna kill a lot o' orcs together."

A predatory grin crosses my face. "Yes. But first there is something sour in this city, and I intend to clean it up."

VOLUME 6 - NEW BEGINNINGS

CHAPTER 87

Name:	**Mana Stone (Darkness)**
Description:	Mana stones are highly concentrated sources of elemental mana essence and can only be found in one of two ways. First, by mining. Given that mana stone lodes are rare, companies who specialize in mana stone mining will usually purchase the rights from the founder at a high price and then sell the stones at a substantial markup. The second method to find mana stones is by taking them from the carcasses of mana-infused beasts. Only non-humanoid species have ever been found to have mana stones (with the exception of the death affinity); it is unknown why. The element of the mana stone coincides with either the environment or the creature. For example, water mana stones are generally found in lakes, oceans, or other bodies of water or from creatures who live in or near them.
Condition:	Excellent
Risk Assessment:	N/A
Value:	This darkness-based mana stone is average and has a decent reserve of essence. The extreme rarity of the darkness affinity raises the value of this stone materially. Essence count: 2845/3448.

When I am ready to take on the darkness affinity, I fully admit I'm terrified. I think I know what to expect, and I don't want to lose my mind from it. I try to explain what I need for this as we are in our usual working spot, facing each other on the green couch.

"Aria, there is no prep or materials or anything like that for this. I will admit that I am really scared of this one. I think when I come out I will be a mess. And what will I need most is probably comfort. Is that okay?"

Her flawless elven face looks scared at my words. "Darkness can do that?"

I nod. "If what I expect to happen happens, I'm pretty sure it will be harder on me than ice and magma combined."

Her facial expression morphs a few times. It's fast but I think I see fear, curiosity, and sadness. The rest I miss. "All right. What do you recommend?"

I blush a little. "So I think I am going to need to be inundated by the senses." I clear my throat. "All five."

She blinks at me, figures it out, and then blushes too. "Oh. All right, then. I'll make sure I am right in front of you so you can see me as soon as you open your eyes. I'll talk to you so you can hear me. Oh."

She runs off to her room and returns just seconds later holding a cryspad. I raise an eyebrow, and she says, "So I can read to you. I'll have Jo order some strongly flavored and scented food." She shifts a little while looking down and says, "I think you should take off some of your clothes. At least your shirt. And if you think it will be really bad, then your pants too."

I was thinking the same in regards to the shirt, but the pants didn't occur to me.

I open my mouth to object to that last part, but she cuts me off with a lopsided smile. "You can wear underwear or shorts or something. I understand your human sensitivities."

I let out a sigh and nod. "Fine."

Five minutes later, everything is prepared. I am sitting in front of Aria crosslegged on the couch in nothing but a pair of boxers. She is in her light workout clothes.

When I ask why, she says, "It's only fair. And skin contact will be better."

Normally, I might be a bit distracted, but my terror of what is about to come occupies all my thoughts. I look down at my hands and find them shaking. Aria reaches over and places her hands on them.

All she says is, "I'm here."

I let out a deep breath and close my eyes, spending the next few minutes centering myself. The touch of Aria's hands is surprisingly helpful in bringing my mind into focus. When I feel as prepared as I can be, the darkness stone appears in my lap, and I enter my inner world.

***

It is as awful as I feared. Complete and total sensory deprivation. Absolute nothingness. The lack of all things and the need to stop anything from ever being. I cannot tell how long the terrifying feeling of complete emptiness and being alone in the universe lasts. It brings back nightmares that I believed I moved past.

Host has absorbed 2,008.98 mana essence from **Mana Stone (Darkness)**

New rune activated. Darkness Rune is now available for use . . .

New affinity activated. Darkness Affinity is now available for use . . .

When I come to, Aria is right there inches from my face like she said she would be. She starts talking to me, making sure to stay in front of my eyes. She touches me on my face and chest and sides and arms. She moves her entire body into my lap and speaks softly of a story she is reading about an elf and a human. Against her skin, I can tell my body is quivering in terror, but the contact helps me work through it.

Vic, are you okay? . . .

[Not yet, but thanks to Aria and you, I will be.]

Aria turns her head, which sweeps her hair across my face and places hers only an inch away. She asks, "Vic, how about the food?"

I nod, shuddering as the memories surface again.

She has Jo order bright-colored, smelly fruit, and Aria sits in my lap in my line of sight the whole time while feeding me that orange fruit she likes. Of course, she occasionally steals one while telling me about it, and that helps me break my mind out of the hellish loop.

After I feel myself enough, I take a slow deep breath and let it out, relaxing my muscles and mind. I lean my head forward onto hers, causing her hair to tickle my nose. "Thank you."

She responds while chewing an orange fruit, which makes her voice sound odd.

"A' cerse." I hear her swallow, and she speaks clearly this time. "We're here for each other."

I chuckle into her hair and then lean my head back. I am surprised to find my arms wrapped around her waist and cough. I release them and say, "Sorry."

"It's fine. If you need to hold me, you can. I don't mind."

I see my exposed tan skin turn red and lift her off me from the waist. I quickly stand and head into my room, calling, "I'm taking a shower, and then we'll reconvene on the couch."

Yeah. No need for her to see that.

***

"So, tomorrow is a big day. I'm going to level up, and once again I am going to depend on you. But we'll go over that tomorrow. Okay?"

She nods. "We are a team."

I smile and we watch an old episode of Ranger Bob that involves desert birds. While watching, the—thankfully, clothed—Aria is leaning against me.

This episode reminds me of a few missions I had in desolate areas. The wilds of a desert are difficult for any life, but those creatures that do thrive there are exceptionally robust and aggressive. I used that once when I drew the ire of a nest of infused rattlesnakes onto a small Invader encampment. Only the trolls survived to tell the tale, and nobody even knew I was there. I smile at the memory. That was prior to my days with MagiTech. That thought tempers my humor a bit, and I refocus on the show. After it ends, Aria asks for a few minutes of just sitting quietly before we head to our rooms. She leans her head on my shoulder, and I put my arm across her shoulders. This family thing is pretty nice, I suppose.

***

On my way to bed, I stop and look in the nest.

[Jo, does the egg look bigger to you?]

Yes, it does. Quick, [Inspect] it . . .

I do.

Name:	Metal/Air Mana-Mutated Peregrine Falcon Egg
Description:	Normal mana-fused falcons are large and very aggressive hunters. They hunt mostly other birds but sometimes will hunt smaller mammals. Their favorite

method is to climb high into the sky and then stoop, or dive downwards at 300 kph or more and knock prey out of the sky.

This egg contains a still-viable peregrine falcon fetus. Unfortunately, this egg was exposed to a massive influx of metal mana during a particularly vulnerable part of its growth. The mother abandoned this egg when its home, the tree under which it was found, was moved from the rainforest. The egg fell to the ground and due to the metal mutation it did not break. The tree had been inadvertently protecting, feeding, and keeping alive this creature for over 15 years when an illness caused the tree to eject the egg for the safety of both.

The egg's condition has stabilized thanks to the influx of mana-rich metals. However, it cannot grow or hatch with what is available to it now. Further materials are required to increase viability.

Note: There is the possibility of enhancing the abilities of the fetus if fed the correct mana-rich materials.

Countdown to fetus death: N/A

Condition:	Stable
Risk Assessment:	N/A
Value:	At its current health, the value of this egg is low. If it can be enhanced or offer assured viability, the value will likely be high. Such a rare mutation is an excellent object of bonding or study.

[It didn't grow; the metal shrank as it absorbed it. We need those materials. Can you ask for a rush order?]

Request sent . . .

I pet the egg lightly. Thinking for a second with my hand on the egg, I figure it might be worth a shot. I send a tiny trickle of air mana into it. The egg absorbs it, but nothing else happens. I send more. It absorbs it. I keep sending, and it keeps absorbing. Then it pushes back, and I immediately stop.

[I wonder what that did.]

Response is for an additional fifteen silver—which is double the price—it will arrive tomorrow early afternoon...

[I don't care. Do it.]

Confirmed. While you were busy with Master Steeltamer, you received a response from Mr. Whyatt. He confirms we can meet at the end of the week. He has no specific response to the request regarding the metal affinity...

I lean another small stick of quicksilver ore against the egg and then climb into bed.

[Anything else outstanding?]

Just your alerts. Of which one is a biggie...

[Okay. Let me have it. I have no idea where the rune is again. But I'm not interested in it right now. Tomorrow before anything else, I'll activate the mana manipulation.]

Before you decide that, here are your last few alerts. I think you'll like what you see...

*New Achievement activated. For activating all advanced magica runes, the Achievement **Rowdy Runic** is now available. This Achievement grants you 30% increased mana flow rate. Do you wish to show or hide your Achievement?*

*New Achievement activated. For activating all advanced magica affinities, the Achievement **Affinity Absorbed** is now available. This Achievement grants you 30% increased mana flow rate. Do you wish to show or hide your Achievement?*

[Wow. I'll what, be able to use mana instantly or something? I guess the standard runes and affinities aren't special or something.]

Not instantly of course, but much faster. Hold your thoughts on that last bit; there's more. Title incoming...

I'm excited. Titles always offer the best rewards.

*New Title activated. For activating all standard and advanced runes and affinities for the first time in the history of the system, the Title **Magical Machine** is now available. This Title grants you a 50% increase to maximum mana. Do you wish to show or hide your Title?*

[Shitballs, Jo! That is fucking huge.]

Yes, Vic. All the awards for first-time stuff are usually higher. The quantum nanomachine hive may actually be growing because of you . . .

[I wonder if there is an achievement for mana manipulation for each affinity. Would that push the nanos even further?]

I thought you might ask that. There is only one way to find out . . .

I activated ice and magma during daily magica exercise with Aria, so the only one left is darkness.

[You know what, I don't want to wait. Where is that fucking rune?]

When I don't know the location of a rune, the only way I have found to locate it is to send non-affinity mana to every part of my body. It sets off all the runes, but there's nothing I can do about it. It's not like there is anyone that can teach me, so I just do the best I can with what I have.

The darkness rune is twoish inches below my belly button. Weird spot, but whatever. I create the pathway, which is practically instantaneous. I walk to the balcony, equip the entire Cloaked Infiltrator set, and send darkness mana into it. It loads up to its maximum—which is three hundred percent standard—and then I create darkness around the balcony. The blackness spreads, and the sounds fade along with the light. I push it out and form a bubble so nothing comes in.

Then I release it, [Inventory] the set, put my PJ pants back on, and go back to bed.

[Well?]

Congratulations. You did it, Vic . . .

New skill activated. Passive skill [Darkness Mana Manipulation] now available for use . . .

Skill updated. Passive skill [Darkness Mana Manipulation] is now level 1 . . .

New Achievement activated. For activating all the advanced mana manipulation skills, the Achievement **Masterful Mana Manipulator** *is now available. This Achievement grants you +30% to mana flow rate. Do you wish to show or hide your Achievement?*

New Title activated. For activating all standard and advanced runes, affinities, and mana manipulation skills for the first time in the history of the system, the Title **Magnicarum Maximus** *is now available. This Title grants you a 100% increase to maximum mana. This bonus will always be the final calculator and will stack with ALL other bonuses. NOTE: This Title requires highly impactful* *changes to the host's nanomachine system. As a result, this Title's effects will not take place until the next level up. Do you wish to show or hide your Title?*

[I'm kind of in shock.]

Imagine the restructuring the nanomachine system has to do for this one. You totally broke the quantum hive . . .

[Tomorrow is going to be a very big day.]

For all of us . . .

CHAPTER 88

I wake to Aria having leapt and landed on my bed, throwing me a few inches in the air.

"Gah! What is it?"

She crawls up, sits on my chest, and cups my face.

"It's your big day. Leveling up. Waffles and bacon for breakfast!"

Ordered . . .

I smile into her hands. Well, I am a fan of waffles. And bacon.

I laugh. "Okay, okay! I need to breathe!"

Of course, I have no problem breathing, but she still needs to get off so I can eat bacon. And as usual I am wearing only my PJ pants, so . . . yeah. She needs to get off. As always, I remind myself I am her trainer and guardian. And going to die long before she even feels time pass.

Breakfast is a fine affair with Aria asking questions about leveling up that surprise me. They are quite professional and about the process, what changes can come about, how it might alter our training, what she can do to supplement it, et cetera. When did she become such a quality operator? Not that I am displeased; this will make her training that much faster and more effective.

We just hang out and start doing pre-op for leveling up. We talk about what should be at hand and what to do in case assistance may become required. The problem is, of course, nobody has a clue what will happen, so we are making several assumptions that may or may not turn out to be of quality or use.

***

All the stuff I ordered for the egg arrives just after lunch. I take my tailoring kit and a piece from all five materials and lay them out.

[Jo, I can't believe I didn't think of this yesterday. What is the price for an air mana stone? It doesn't have to be big. Three hundred to five hundre, maybe?]

Searching...

While Jo is shopping, I show Aria what my plan is, and she proceeds to tell me how horrible that will look. I try to explain that I don't care how it looks, only how it functions. She lets me know that I am a complete dunderhead and that the bird is not going to be forced into my fashion sense pre-hatching. I just sigh and let her tell me the "right" way to organize the fabric. Of course, it takes twice as long, but if it makes her happy, I guess I don't care that much. None of this has any negative impact on anything, so why not? What's funny is she runs this like an operation, and I follow orders like it is and she is the commander in the field. Perhaps crafting could act as an alternative form of training when done properly. It's worth considering.

I was able to locate a 375ish essence air stone for five gold that can be here in thirty minutes. Mana stones are expensive, but that is absolutely outrageous...

[Don't care. Do it. Getting a long-term pet, mount, ally, whatever is well worth the coin outlay. And if it ages well, it could be Aria's after I'm too old or dead.]

Morbid, but fine. Ordered...

Aria and I then add a mana stone pocket so it will be touching the egg. Aria acts like a drill sergeant, speaking to me as a young recruit as she tries to explain to me that the stone is the "heart of the outfit" and needs to stand out.

I didn't even know we were making an outfit, nor that outfits have hearts. Again, I am just following orders. The stone arrives, and Aria basically shoves me out of the way and gets working to put the little egg in the right position and assure that the air stone is all aligned right and reflects the light in the right way. Maybe I'm training her in the wrong field or at least using the wrong method. I'll reflect on it. Anyway, the "outfit" finally meets her standards, and she stands back, gives me a side hug, and states that the operation was successful. If she's happy, I'm happy, I suppose. Her effort makes her happy and costs me nothing but a few minutes.

Vic, even if you turned her into a mini-you, I agree with Aria. That is beautiful. Well done...

Aria beams like both statements are the biggest compliments in the world. "Thanks, Jo. All right, Vic. Time to level up. Strip and climb into bed. I'll go get all the medical gear and such while you're doing that and talking everything over with Jo."

She wanders off, and I do as told.

[Did Aria just take over this operation?]

Pretty sure she did. Ready for your profile? We're early, but that's okay. This way you get a "before and after" of the level up . . .

Feeling like I relinquished control of myself to the two ladies in my life, I just think, [Sure, Jo.]

Before we proceed though . . .

New skill activated. Passive skill [Clothworking] now available for use . . .

Skill updated. Passive skill [Clothworking] has leveled from 0 to 3 . . .

Skill updated. Passive skill [Sewing] is now level 6 . . .

Skill updated. Passive skill [Tailoring] is now level 5 . . .

[I wonder why Tailor isn't a profession choice.]

There must be some prerequisite missing. You have more to catch up on that we have been suppressing. Enjoy . . .

New skill activated. Passive skill [Boxing] now available for use . . .

Skill updated. Passive skill [Boxing] has leveled from 0 to 4 . . .

New skill activated. Passive skill [Kickboxing] now available for use . . .

Skill updated. Passive skill [Kickboxing] has leveled from 0 to 2 . . .

New skill activated. Passive skill [Wing-Chun] now available for use . . .

Skill updated. Passive skill [Wing-Chun] has leveled from 0 to 2 . . .

New skill activated. Passive skill [Taekwondo] now available for use . . .

Skill updated. Passive skill [Taekwondo] has leveled from 0 to 2 . . .

New skill activated. Passive skill [Jiu Jitsu] now available for use . . .

Skill updated. Passive skill [Jiu Jitsu] has leveled from 0 to 3 . . .

New skill activated. Passive skill [Karate] now available for use . . .

Skill updated. Passive skill [Karate] has leveled from 0 to 2 . . .

[Were the creators experts in hand-to-hand? It's fascinating that they would list each martial art as a different skill. Not that I disagree; they are all completely different.]

Based on all the limited information available, I believe they were individuals who wanted to be experts and decided to enter their fantasies into the system. That is only my supposition, however. As far as the details of each art are con-

nected, I imagine the hive took what they did and made it effectively useful...

[Well, given their naming talent, maybe you're right about the creators. I mean really, Nuking Knockout? And given the precise movements of each martial form, I imagine the hive would have had to make advancements to make any adjustments to the body related to movements, strikes, et cetera.]

All that makes sense. Now shut it and focus. Let's close the inscription loop...

[Yes, dear.]

Skill updated. Passive skill [Mana Projectile Weapons (Small)] has leveled from 3 to 5...

New skill activated. Passive skill [Mana Projectile Weapons (Medium)] now available for use...

Skill updated. Passive skill [Mana Projectile Weapons (Medium)] has leveled from 0 to 2...

New skill activated. Passive skill [Mana Projectile Weapons (Large)] now available for use...

New skill activated. Passive skill [Projectile Mana Weapons Maintenance] now available for use...

Skill updated. Passive skill [Projectile Mana Weapons Maintenance] has leveled from 0 to 3...

New skill activated. Passive skill [Crossbows] now available for use...

New skill activated. Passive skill [First Aid] now available for use...

Skill updated. Passive skill [Sprinting] has leveled from 1 to 3...

[It's too bad I couldn't activate explosives, traps, sniping, woodcraft, or anything of other skills I use on an assassination mission.]

Really, Vic? How many Specials do you think have so many skills activated before their first level evolution? Shut up and stop being greedy...

[Ouch. Sorry.]

If you are done being an idiot, I was going to say you are now caught up on alerts. Here is the last look at yourself pre-level up...

Name:	Michael Uriel Victory	**Nickname:**	Vic	Titles: Scorching Magica (Hidden)
Age:	24	**Evolution**	0	

		Level (Essence):	(28,093.16 /1,000)	First of Your Kind (Hidden) Mana Born (Hidden) Mana Master (Hidden) Magical Machine (Hidden) Magnicarum Maximus (Inactive, Hidden)
Species:	Magnicarum	**Class:**	Unassigned	
Professions:	Primary: Unassigned Secondary: Unassigned	Available: Armorsmith		
Health:	167/167 (+9)	**Mana:**	732/732 (+353)	
Physical Attributes:	Strength:	16.3 (+2.2)	Constitution:	16.7 (+0.9)
	Agility:	13.1 (0.8)		
Magical Attributes:	Intelligence:	16.2 (+2.1)	Magica:	48.8 (+10.9)
Miscellaneous Attributes:	Absorption:	20.1 (+0.5)	Regeneration:	.97/second (+0.22)
Abilities:	Species Bonus:	Mana Lifeline, Mana Manipulator, Emergency Regeneration, Mana Rage		
	Density Bonus:	Affinity Aficionado		
	Activation Bonus:	Liquid Steel Skin		

Skills:	Active Skills:	Kickboxing: 2
	Inspect: 2	Life Mana Manipulation: 5
	Inventory: <10>	Light Mana Manipulation: 1
	Passive Skills:	Lightning Mana Manipulation: 3
	Air Mana Manipulation: 6	Magma Mana Manipulation: 1
	Armorcrafting: 5	Mana Compression: 5
	Botany: 2	Mana Infusion: 3
	Boxing: 4	Mana Manipulation: <10>
	Butchering: 1	Mana Projectile Weapons (Small): 5
	Cartography: 2	Mana Projectile Weapons (Medium): 2
	Climbing: 2	Mana Projectile Weapons (Large): 0
	Clothworking: 3	Mana Splitting: 5
	Cooking: 0	Metalworking: 5
	Crossbows: 0	Mining: 3
	Cycle Driving: 1	Nature Mana Manipulation: 6
	Darkness Mana Manipulation: 1	Projectile Mana Weapons Maintenance: 3
	Death Mana Manipulation: 3	Sewing: 6
	Diving: 0	Set Crafting: 2
	Earth Mana Manipulation: 5	Skinning: 0
	Elemental Absorption: 4	Small Blades: 0
	Fire Mana Manipulation: <10>	Sprinting: 3
	*Projectile Fire Mana Manipulation: 5 First Aid: 0	Swimming: 2
	Herbology: 2	Taekwondo: 2
	Ice Mana Manipulation: 1	Tailoring: 5
	Jiu Jitsu: 3	Water Mana Manipulation: 7
	Karate: 2	Wing-Chun: 2
Runes:	Fire Rune, Air Rune, Water Rune, Earth Rune, Nature Rune, Lightning Rune, Ice Rune, Magma Rune, Life Rune, Death Rune, Light Rune, Darkness Rune	

Resist-ances:	Basic Elemental:	1.0	Adv. Elemental:	1.9 (+0.9)
	Pain:	5.3 (+0.2)		
Achieve-ments:	Brave, Bold, and Boneheaded (3, Hidden) Beast Basher (3, Hidden) Nuking Knockout (2, Hidden) Mighty Mana Mastery (Hidden) Rowdy Runic (Hidden) Affinity Absorbed (Hidden) Masterful Mana Manipulator (Hidden)			

[That feels like good improvement. I wonder how it will change.]

That is quite impressive, Vic. You worked diligently over the last month and more to get to this point. You don't know because we have been hiding your profile changes, but the diminishing returns are starting to become very impactful. You have had little growth the last week. A level up is basically required at this point; your saturation level is about as high as it can get . . .

[Saturation being how much change my nanos can support?]

Change and learning, yes. There is a ceiling before they must evolve . . .

[What is my density now?]

738 . . .

[Why isn't my density shown on the profile by the way? That seems an obvious thing to have there.]

I concur. Unfortunately, the system does not allow it to show until level five. That is a hard block for the nanomachine system, so I cannot modify it. I do not know why . . .

[This system's creators make no sense to me. I guess when you're in a rush to save your species, you make some bad choices, though.]

Possibly . . .

Aria comes in then, sits on the edge of my bed by my waist and says, "Okay, Vic. I think I am ready. How about you?"

I ask out loud, "How long does a level zero to one usually take?"

Based on my available—yet outdated—information, anywhere from a few hours to a day . . .

Aria nods in response. I also tell Jo to make sure Aria eats healthily and has what she needs. They are free to buy food and clothes and such. I figure it could be two or three days with everything I've been through, so better to be prepared.

Aria pats my cheek. "Vic, we are as prepared as we can be for this operation. Go ahead and become stronger."

I nod at her.

[Jo, are we ready?]

I believe so, Vic . . .

I take a deep slow breath and say, "Jo, ask the question."

Host has reached sufficient mana essence to reach the next level. Do you wish to convert 1,000 mana essence into nanomachine growth? . . .

"See you on the other side . . ."

[Confirm]

Congratulations! Host has reached level 1. Essence conversion and nanomachines evolution under way in 5 seconds. Please stand by . . .

"Good luck, Vic."

Three seconds . . .

Two seconds . . .

One second . . .

Essence conversion and nanomachines evolution under way . . .

I black out.

CHAPTER 89 - INTERLUDE

A secure communication from two undisclosed locations:

Male voice: "You mean you found him?"

Female voice: "I think so. He activated his nanos."

Silence . . .

Male voice: "If he's hiding, there's a reason."

Female voice: "Of course."

Male voice: "Do nothing."

Female voice: "Understood."

***

Whyatt Hotel, Floor 50:

I wonder if I will ever understand humans. Is it possible for someone like me who will live for thousands of this world's years to possibly understand the mindset of mortals who die after a short century or less? How the fuck did they live without mana? I dry my face with a towel and swap from a run to a grav strengthening machine. This one works the muscles in my legs. As always, I start with my calves and then work to my thighs. Follow the plan.

Grunting from the effort, I reflect on how humanity has supposedly battled the orcs to a standstill. What is most ironic is the humans have much more in common with the orcs than the allied species. Both use combat as a measure of superiority and force as their first solution to a problem. In some ways, humanity is worse. According to the museum my Guardian Protector and I visited, before mana came, they nearly destroyed their own homeworld. Can you imagine if a species this barbarous had mana as long as the orcs and their filthy kin? They would have become like swarms across worlds and made the orc wars look like a battle between children with sticks. Hell, if the orcs had gone about it differently, they could have recruited the humans. Not that they would have. Humans are too weak. For now, at least. With mana flooding this world, their strength will grow. Assuming they survive, my mother felt the humans have maybe ten generations before the power of mana truly begins to show in the species. They reproduce quickly enough.

Another male is approaching to proposition me. These fools have no idea. I ignore him and move to another machine; this one uses the grav plates to work the back of my thighs, stomach, and lower back. I am so far above these "suitors" they truly do not know. It is not their fault. And Vic is trying to teach me patience. Vic . . .

According to my mother, he will be my future. I don't understand how that can be. He has what, ten or twenty years before he ages to the point of being too weak to protect me? Being a human Special might buy him a little more, but it's all just a good night's sleep to my people. Then why do I feel a pain inside when I think of him dying?

I wonder if Vic knows what love is. I don't think so. He doesn't know it, but I'm almost positive he loves Jo and me. In his own way. Maybe I can get him to admit it. Wait, did I just think that? Ugh.

What was mother thinking? If I didn't know better, I'd say she had to have heard the words of the world wrong. There is no way. Okay, yes. At his young age, he is more dedicated, courageous, talented, brilliant (at anything that does not involve affection), and gifted beyond measure than any other human alive and many longer-lived species. I shudder to imagine what he might have become if only if he had the time. And then I feel a pleasant chill at the thought of having so much time with him, pointless as it is.

Sometimes I wonder if he truly is human. He just seems so beyond the rest of the species. How is he able to use all the elemental affinities plus the greater ones like my own life and Feli's light? It's just not possible. Nobody can do that. And yet he can and does. I've seen it in our training. My mother's warning echoes through my mind, but he's human and won't live long enough to fulfill that future, with or without me.

Adding to my skepticism of his species, on top of all his gifts and his utter lack of restraint in killing anyone who he feels is harmful to what he views as his, is his body. Stunning and sexy to the eye. And touch, which I discovered only recently. His skin is so smooth and completely flawless. More perfect than even an elf's. Despite the workout already flooding my body with blood, I find my skin flushing an even deeper red. Was it my introduction to Feli that allowed me to realize how attracted to him I was? No, I knew; I just denied it. He's human, after all.

Humans in general are a rather average race in regards to appearance. My people are, of course, the superior species when it comes to charisma and appearance. And magica. And agelessness. And most things, actually. It is simply fact; we've had hundreds of millennia, after all. But Vic . . . I feel another flush as I remember our last time together before he fell asleep so long ago. I admit I may have taken the opportunity to explore his exposed body a little before I realized what was going on.

I've supported him when he recovered from the death, cold, and heat of awakenings. I didn't believe him when he said it would be the worst. And yet I was there when he woke from whatever horror he experienced while awakening darkness. That was scary. I've seen Vic sad, angry, hurting, stubborn, even needy, and affectionate. I had never seen Vic scared before. The bear, the orcs, the bastards who killed my mother and Grun; he kept staring death in the face, and yet I never saw fear. But what I recognized in his amazing crystalline eyes . . . that was unadulterated terror. Something in the darkness broke him for a little while, and it scared me more than I thought possible. I thought he might not recover, it was so bad. Again, with that pain in my middle thinking of my world without him.

I didn't realize how much I have come to depend on Vic and his constant presence. Normally I'd figure this is a huge mistake, or even temporary, given how soon he will be dust, but I could not stop being scared for him. And for myself. How did that happen? And how did it happen so fast? How does awakening an affinity of darkness allow you to see?

And darkness! The rarest of all the greater elements. I know barely anything of it, and seeing how terrified the bravest man I know was of it, I don't think I want to. I'll stick to my crossbows and healing, thank you.

And now, after all this time without him I find myself longing for his company. He's been there sleeping for how long? Jo used another word, but he's sleeping. I thought being without him would make it easier. But instead, I find myself drawn to him even more. How did this happen? Why? Mom, why a human? He'll be dead so soon, and it will hurt so much. How can I hope and fear equally and at the same time?

I jerk slightly and drop my legs when Jo's voice finally returns to me. I miss her nearly as much. How long has it been this time?

Aria, I'm sorry I've been gone so long, but I believe Vic will be awakening soon. If everything is as it appears, I would give him between two and four hours . . .

ACTIVATION

My entire body tingles with excitement. Finally! I stand and stumble slightly not realizing how hard I've been pushing myself. Wow, I'm tired. I had better not tell him.

Wiping myself off, I walk over the floor pads and stretch. I smile remembering Vic's lessons on stretching. Anyone who doesn't stretch is bad and should be shot. A tired chuckle escapes from my lips.

When I'm done, I head up to our home and soak. Huh. Our home.

Luxuriating in a steaming bath after an exhausting workout is lovely. Vic got me into this, and he was right.

I have just completed processing the alerts, and I think we need to talk while you're washing yourself up. There have been some changes, and you should be prepared . . .

I sit up in the tub with a splash, and with my fingers to my ear I ask, "Is he all right? You're scaring me."

Oh, he's fine. His level up is not what any of us expected. I won't share most things because they would break his confidence, but you deserve to know this. I'm not sure how he will react, but from what I can tell . . .

CHAPTER 90

Returning to awareness with my face staring at a golden blonde head is something I was not expecting. Blinking, I look around. I am still in my bed, and Aria is lying next to me on top of the covers with her head on my chest and shoulder and arm draped over my torso.

[Jo?]

Welcome back, Vic...

[Are you okay? Am I? Is Aria? What happened? How did we do?]

It's all right. Relax and let me tell you what happened. Don't wake up Aria or she won't give you a minute of peace to catch up...

[Catch up? What do you mean?]

Let me tell you about what happened after you went into hibernation...

[What? Hibernation? What the fuck is going on, Jo?]

My body stiffens.

Calm down, Vic. Relax your body or you'll wake Aria up...

I close my eyes again, take a few breaths and relax. I'm still nervous, but I have control of my body again.

Thank you. So here is what happened. When you blacked out, I was alerted that the system had to do an assessment on your nanomachine structure, density, usage statistics, available functions, activated capabilities, and so on. You get the picture. This is a completely normal process. I kept Aria up to speed on the process.

[So far so good. I'd hate for her to lose the training time. What's the problem?]

It is at that point that things started going a bit . . . different. I received messages that your various nanomachine system assessments failed due to "density of mana particles causing oversaturation of nanomachine mana engines." What followed was the message: "Corrective action required. Hibernation mode activated" at which point your entire body started glowing your special azure blue, your hair included. In fact, you glowed so brightly that we could see it through your bed covers. I told Aria that I had it under control and she should stay calm . . .

[Thank you for helping Aria. I assume you were lying.]

You glowed for six days, Vic. Of course I was lying! . . .

[Six days? Damn.]

Shut up and let me finish; that is just the beginning . . .

This cannot be good. How bad is it? It's bad. Fuck.

During the six days of glowy Vic, Aria continued following the mission plan. Thankfully, you gave me authorization in advance to purchase daily necessities or she would have been in a bind. Aria graduated from crossbows, by the way. I think she really likes them though and may come back to them. We had several nice discussions, and I think we are becoming friends . . .

That relaxes my racing heart a little.

[I'm really happy to hear that. Thank you.]

Of course. Anyway, after six days and five hours, the system gave an alert that it found a solution to the system fault. It was doing a reconfiguration and to please stand by. It was at that point you stopped glowing and everything looked okay. But nothing happened; you just lay there. Another day went by and there was no change until the system gave another alert that reconfiguration was complete and a system restart was required. Thankfully, the system gave its usual five-second timer for major corrective action, which gave me time to send a message to Aria. I told her I would be gone for a bit but I would return and she should continue on the mission plan . . .

[That means Aria was alone for a good portion of my sleep.] Looking down at her sleeping form, I think, [Clearly she needed to know I'm okay.]

Let me finish. I reactivated just six hours later, so it wasn't too bad for Aria. The alerts were mostly having to do with a system restart and reassessing your nanos. The system then stated that the fault resolution was complete, at which point you received an unexpected notice . . .

Her voice in my mind fades slowly. [What? What happened? It broke, didn't it? I fucking broke it. Great. I'm going to be crippled for life or something. How am I going to do my job or train and protect Aria if I'm crippled?]

Vic, calm the fuck down. Stop jumping to conclusions. What it said was that your class assignment was initiated to resolve the fault . . .

[Oh.]

Articulate as ever...

I'm so distracted, I miss her snark. [Isn't that a level five thing?]

Yes. Which is why the next alert stated there was yet another *system fault. Class assignment cannot happen before level five so the system stated it was initiating a resolution and your level up process started again. Thankfully, this time each assessment was listed as successful. I won't get too much into the details here, but the system said a lot of stuff about your density, abilities, and on and on. Basically confirming that even the nanomachine system finds you a freak...*

[Can't really make an argument against. Go on.]

The system stated that its nanomachine evolution was underway, and you started glowing again. This time it flashed between all the colors of your affinities...

[Light show. Wonderful. Just give it to me Jo. I want the bad news. Am I dying?]

No. But let's come back to that. There is more. It turns out that the system isn't allowed to expend essence on leveling up without explicit host authorization. That is another hard block. So instead, the system just disposed of five levels worth of mana essence in an instant. Now, you recall we did something similar at a smaller scale in the cave?...

[Yeah. We removed that debuff.]

Correct. If you recall you received something of a small benefit, the species ability Emergency Regeneration? Well, that happened from 1,250 mana. So this time your channels and nanomachines were flooded with just over thirteen thousand mana essence...

I wince. [Shit.]

Yes. To avoid damaging your mana channels, the system kept having to reboot you. You rebooted, did the flashing lights, and rebooted again. And each time took longer. Until the fifth and final reboot took twelve days...

[Twelve days.]

Yes...

I don't respond for a while, thinking about the consequences of that.

[Jo... how long?]

I'll answer, but will you let me finish?...

[Yes. How long?]

A little under two and a half months . . .

CHAPTER 91

Jo gives me a few moments to absorb and choose to respond or not. My mind is blank and in shock, so I am silent.

At some point, she continues.

After that last restart took twelve days, you received a number of alerts noting changes in your system and body. They are almost all good news. One I think is good, but you need to decide. The last you will not be pleased with. What order do you want them in? . . .

[Backwards from what you listed. Always bad news first—good news is easier to adapt to. And I trust you. Just go ahead and let's work through it together.]

Thank you for your trust. Here is the first . . .

Warning! Host nanomachine system has undergone strategic reconfiguration. Available data is insufficient to support evolution. Connection to the Nanomachine Network is required . . .

Connection to nanomachine network underway. Data sharing commencing . . .

Nanomachine system update complete . . .

[Well, fuck. There goes our cover and anonymity.]

I'm sorry, Vic, there was nothing I could do . . .

[It's not your fault. And the gryphon's out the roost now, anyway. Nothing we can do but move forward.]

Thanks, Vic. Here is the one I think is good, but you need to decide . . .

New Species ability activated. Mana Feeding is now available for use . . .

[Mana Feeding? I eat it or something?]

Remember when you started having a freakout and asked if you were going to die? . . .

[Thanks for rubbing that in.]

Well, the answer is no. You are not dying . . .

[Umm. Well, that's good. Why do I need an alert telling me I'm not dying?]

What I am saying Vic, is that you are no longer dying. At all. Your body is feeding off the ambient mana and not dying. Your body and its cells are now fueled by a pristine source so your negative cell mutations have ceased. You are no longer aging. You are effectively immortal as long as you have mana around to feed your cells and nano. You no longer need to eat or drink, or remove waste. Your body is one hundred percent efficient in its absorption, usage, and excretion of matter . . .

I'm completely silent. I just noticed that without realizing it, my arm has curled around Aria's form and started rubbing her blonde head.

[Are you sure?]

Yes . . .

[I assume I can still die from the physical stuff. Like getting shot or stabbed or whatnot?]

Correct. However, one of your alerts will help with that. You can be killed, of course. But it isn't as easy anymore. We'll get to that . . .

[Does that mean I will look exactly as I do for the rest of time unless I die by someone else's hand?]

That is what my current data suggests, yes . . .

I'm not sure what to think about that. I look down at Aria's blonde head and find my hand there.

[I need time to process. Keep going.]

The rest I believe you will like. Although your assigned class is a bit . . . odd . . .

Congratulations! Host has completed evolution and reached level 1. The following changes have taken place in the nanomachine system . . .

Congratulations! Host has been assigned a class. Evaluation for class commencing. Note: Class evaluation criteria are cumulative. Good luck, Host . . .

Default selection for host is a Basic Class . . .

Due to the host's elevated and balanced growth of both physical and magical attributes and activations, host will be assigned an Intermediate Class . . .

Due to the host's basic affinity activations, host will be assigned an Advanced Class . . .

Due to the host's advanced affinity activations, host will be assigned a High Class . . .

Due to the host's basic and advanced mana manipulation activations, host will be assigned a Grand Class . . .

Due to the host's total and complete basic and advanced Magica activations, host will be assigned a Globally Unique Class . . .

##Error Found. External mana influence detected##

Due to the host's cumulative activations and unique species, host will be assigned a Singularity Class . . .

Congratulations! Host has been assigned the Singularity Class, **Inquisitor Magnicarum** *. . .*

Class:	Inquisitor Magnicarum	
Description:	There will only ever be a single Inquisitor Magnicarum at one time across all worlds. This singular individual acts on behalf of the greater purpose of *{Redacted}*. The Inquisitor Magnicarum is an investigator, diplomat, protector, and executioner of and for all beings. The key to the Inquisitor's ability to successfully complete its missions is anonymity. The Inquisitor will be in plain sight among victims, or hidden in shadows among the guilty as required to complete his mission. The Inquisitor Magnicarum is a figure of tremendous fear and hope and thus is only seen as such in exceptionally rare circumstances. Sometimes a world can be witness to an Inquisition less than once every 500 years. The Inquisitor will be working to find the truth in all things and provide support or exact punishment as it sees fit. The greater *{Redacted}* will be the final assessor of the Inquisitor's judgements as none other has the rank or privilege. The Inquisitor will be rewarded or punished according to meeting his mission and the greater purpose of *{Redacted}*.	
Class Abilities:	Mask of the Inquisitor	The Inquisitor Magnicarum calls upon this item of power only when acting publicly. When called upon, this mask has the appearance of liquid smoke of any color of the Inquisitor's choosing. It will be atop any other mask or helm worn. The Mask of the Inquisitor prevents the

		identity of the Inquisitor from being discovered in any way that involves mana and cannot be physically removed by another.
		When looking through the eyes of the mask, the inquisitor will see through any deception and illusion to find the truth.
		Duration: 60 minutes, Mana: 100, Cooldown: 90 days
	Cloak of the Inquisitor	The Inquisitor Magnicarum calls upon this item of power only when acting publicly. When called upon, this cloak appears like a layer of liquid smoke over the Inquisitor's body and can appear in any color of the Inquisitor's choosing. It will be atop any other armor or clothing worn.
		The Cloak of the Inquisitor prevents the identity of the Inquisitor from being discovered in any way that involves mana and cannot be physically removed by another.
		When wearing the cloak, the Inquisitor's defenses will never be pierced by an attack, physical or Magica, that does less damage than 2x the mana invested in its creation. Once all the mana is used, the cloak will dissipate and cooldown will begin.
		Duration: 60 minutes, Mana: variable, Cooldown: 90 days
	Staff of the Inquisitor	The Inquisitor Magnicarum calls upon this item of power only when acting publicly. When called upon, this staff appears as a streak of liquid smoke the exact height of the Inquisitor with a large, smokey orb head that is constantly in a circular motion. It will be atop the Inquisitor's existing staff if

		one is equipped no matter its size.
		When wielding the staff, the Inquisitor is the supreme judge of all truth and lies. Any individual exposed through the Mask of the Inquisitor as deceiving the staff's wielder may be struck by a blow equal to 2x the mana invested in its creation. This blow bypasses all armor and protections to strike at the true core of the deceiver. Once all mana is used, the staff will dissipate and cooldown will begin.
		Note: This ability also removes any level cap for the Staff Combat skill. Duration: 60 minutes, Mana: variable, Cooldown: 90 days
	Concealing Smoke	This ability protects the Inquisitor when he is not wearing his cloak and mask. The class of the inquisitor will never be exposed by any method using mana. Permanent passive effect
	{Redacted}	{Redacted}
	{Redacted}	{Redacted}
Bonuses:	Attribute Bonus:	Physical Attributes: +0.5 per Inquisitor level Magical Attributes: +1.0 per Inquisitor level Regeneration: +0.25 per Inquisitor level Mana: +100 per Inquisitor level Note: For classes of "High" rarity or above, the attribute bonuses are retroactive to any prior level gains.
	Skill Bonus:	Inspect: +1 per Inquisitor level Staff Combat: +3 per Inquisitor level
	Resistance	Illusion: +1 per Inquisitor level

	Bonus:	{Redacted}: +1 per Inquisitor level

[Um. Jo?]

Yes, Vic? . . .

[What the fuck! What is with this class? I'm an assassin. A sniper. A killer. Not whatever the fuck this is. And what the fuck is with the external interference? And the redactions? What the fuck, Jo?]

Calm down, Vic. Please remember I had nothing to do with it. I have no influence over the nanomachine system's class analysis. And the external interference is unknown. I can offer you nothing on either front. I'm sorry . . .

I close my eyes and just try to breathe. I am no spy or diplomat. Did I get a useless class? I mean, sure, the bonuses are nice. And it looks like there are two hidden class abilities, so maybe there's potential. But I assumed I would reach level five and be assigned an assassin or covert operative class or the like. Right now I feel like what I received is just a big pile of drake shit.

Do you mind if I share my thoughts on your class? . . .

[Of course you can, Jo. Please do. I need you to help me keep this all straight. Right now I am pretty disappointed.]

I understand your feelings. That being said, I don't see this class being all that different from what you normally do. Where does the class prevent you from using your infiltration skills to take down an enemy fortress? Does your class stop you from using a sniper rifle? Aren't you currently investigating a slavery ring and an individual who is corrupting the city? Don't you want to find the enemy and punish them? Moreover, aren't you Aria's protector and the rescuer of all those poor captives? Sure, there is something of a showman's aspect here, but it sounds like that is really, really *rare. And the attribute and skill boosts are quite impressive compared to the basic or intermediate classes most receive. What do you think? . . .*

I think about what she is saying, and I reread the description. And the deeper I read into it, the more I wonder if I overreacted. She's right. Nothing in it stops me from doing what I do. In fact, in some ways it gives me something of a license to do it.

[Thanks for that smack, Jo. I needed it. You are completely right. It actually fits moderately well if not perfectly; I was just in too much of a rush to judge against my expectations to see it.]

D.I. FREED

Of course, Vic. Do you want me to continue with your alerts? . . .

[Give me a few seconds to clear my mind and then go ahead.]

CHAPTER 92

Activation ability Liquid Steel Skin has evolved. It is now Density ability Condensed Liquid Steel Skin . . .

[Oh. That's an interesting change.]

Agreed. This one is an ability that encourages your physical side rather than magical side for once. There are two things to know in regards to this evolution. First, your skin can be infused with mana to increase its armor efficacy. The more mana the more protection. Its default state is the same as before. Second, your skin's sensitivity can be increased or decreased through the nanomachine system control. You can either direct me or set it using your HUD . . .

[Added protection is always valuable, and sensitivity could be handy for precision work. Like feeling for traps or faults in metal. Great evolution.]

There could be other benefits as well. But Aria will help you explore those. The next set of alerts are just updates to existing skills . . .

[Aria hasn't been training in traps or crafting, has she? Those can be dangerous. I know she's a life magica, but what if something happens that renders her unable to control mana?]

No, and that is not what I mean. Here are your alerts . . .

I can nearly taste my relief while looking down at her and my hand's location again.

Skill updated. Active skill [Inspect] has leveled from 3 to 5 . . .

That last alert is a notification after your new class took effect. So you went under with [Inspect] at two—you got to three from your class. And now your nanomachine evolution has refined how you use the skill and it increased it further. I will remind you that [Inspect] has a ceiling of fifty, not ten, so don't expect a world of difference. It is worth noting that this is a very common update for leveling up . . .

[Common or not, I like it. Maybe I can see the details of armor protection or even the level of people or objects. It has got to be at least something. I'm pleased with it either way. Anything that makes us stronger is a win.]

Agreed . . .

Skill updated. Passive skill [Air Mana Manipulation] is now level 7 . . .

Skill updated. Passive skill [Darkness Mana Manipulation] is now level 2 . . .

Skill updated. Passive skill [Death Mana Manipulation] is now level 4 . . .

Skill updated. Passive skill [Earth Mana Manipulation] is now level 6 . . .

Skill updated. Passive skill [Ice Mana Manipulation] is now level 2 . . .

Skill updated. Passive skill [Life Mana Manipulation] is now level 6 . . .

Skill updated. Passive skill [Light Mana Manipulation] is now level 2 . . .

Skill updated. Passive skill [Lightning Mana Manipulation] is now level 4 . . .

Skill updated. Passive skill [Magma Mana Manipulation] is now level 2 . . .

Skill updated. Passive skill [Nature Mana Manipulation] is now level 7 . . .

Skill updated. Passive skill [Projectile Fire Mana Manipulation] is now level 6 . . .

Skill updated. Passive skill [Water Mana Manipulation] is now level 8 . . .

[Well, that's an unexpected boost. Excellent.]

Actually, it isn't that unexpected. Remember that a nanomachine system evolution enhances what you do and are. While your attributes are balanced, your skills are not. You are incredibly magica-heavy in skill levels, and specifically mana manipulation . . .

[That makes sense. Is there anything else? I feel like when I was opening presents and saw Bertha for the first time.]

Vic. Will you please let go of your obsession with that gun? . . .

[Unlikely.] I hear a sigh.

Anyway, you have two more alerts in the vein of above . . .

[Mana Manipulation] has evolved . . .

New skill activated. Active skill [Mana Sight] now available for use . . .

I know you are a dense, brutish, crazed lunatic, but even you have to be able to figure this one out . . .

[You say the sweetest things. I assume I will have the ability to see mana when active. What is the mana draw?]

I'd applaud your cleverness if I could. As for your draw question, we will have to test it. This is an uncommon but not rare skill according to NanoNet, and the draw varies based on the Special. The formula has yet to be discovered . . .

[Okay. I don't suppose [Inventory] evolved?]

No. However, we have a plan for that, don't we?...

[True. Okay. Is there anything else?]

A few things.

Host has reached sufficient mana essence to reach the next level. Do you wish to convert 1,500 mana essence into nanomachine growth?...

You still have over 13,000 mana essence. You are technically able to level from one to five with what you have remaining.

[What will happen when I reach five? I already have a class.]

Unknown. However, I strongly recommend we hold off until you absorb all the spatial treasures. That will raise saturation and could help cause an evolution when you level up again. With the exception of your class and ... um, immortality ... your level up was quite standard. You received great bonuses by being so saturated, and I think we should continue doing that ...

[Putting that ability aside, I agree about the spatial containers. Please add that to the mission log. I also agree with your saturation recommendation; that could be a great advantage for humanity. I'll think about it. Anything else?]

Added to log. And yes. But it isn't about your level up ...

[Why do you sound nervous?]

The first is that your egg is in good shape, but not hatched. It has grown slightly. We did receive a small amount of information on the metal affinity, but nothing that helps. The only beings that can use it are beasts. There is no record of a humanoid with it ...

[Good news on the egg. If we can find a metal element beast, maybe we can use it to provide sustenance. Can you start to research if there are any in this general area?]

Confirmed ...

[What else?]

I'm sorry, but I told Aria about your mana feeding ability and what it means. I know it was breaking your confidence, but you have to know what it could mean ...

Once again, I stare at the golden blonde head and my tanned hand rubbing it gently.

[How is she? It had to be tough being alone for that long.]

She wasn't alone the whole time. As I said, I was able to speak with her regularly.

And she rather deeply engrossed herself into training to occupy time. She moved to strength on floor fifty. She is also quite proficient in several projectile weapons. As predicted, crossbows seem to be an area of focus for her . . .

[Now that her body is balanced and her coordination is passable, we can start her hand-to-hand and then wilderness training. Order two full camping and wilderness survival sets; armor is separate, so skip that. Make sure they are not spatially blocked.]

Should I order one large tent or two smaller individual tents? . . .

[Order both.]

Vic . . .

[Stop.] I hear a sigh.

You can't delay it forever . . .

[What else do you have?] Another sigh.

I have been holding a number of people off from a communication perspective saying you had an emergency mission and would contact them upon return.

[That would be the Steeltamer clan, Mr. Whyatt, and who else?]

The individual you wanted to acquire the crafting facility from . . .

[Another thing to add to the mission log. Set up a headquarters facility.]

Added to log . . .

[Set up meetings with both no sooner than two days from now. I've apparently returned from my "mission." Anything else before I get out of bed?]

Do you want your updated profile? . . .

[Yes!]

I'm excited about seeing it after the level up and it will take my mind off . . . other things.

Name:	Michael Uriel Victory	Nickname:	Vic	Titles: Scorching Magica (Hidden) First of your Kind (Hidden) Mana Born (Hidden) Mana Master
Age:	{24}	Evolution Level (Essence):	1 (14,905.66 /1,500)	
Species:	Magnicarum	Class:	Inquisitor Magnica-	

			rum	(Hidden) Magical Machine (Hidden) Magnicarum Maximus (Hidden)
Professions:	Primary: Unassigned Secondary: Unassigned		Available: Armorsmith	
Health:	232/232 (+65)	**Mana:**	2242/2242 (+1510)	
Physical Attributes:	Strength:	16.8 (+0.5)	Constitution:	18.2 (+0.5)
	Agility:	13.6 (+0.5)		
Magical Attributes:	Intelligence:	17.2 (+1.0)	Magica:	49.8 (+1.0)
Miscellaneous Attributes:	Absorption:	22.3 (+2.2)	Regeneration:	1.24/second (+.28)
Abilities:	Class Abilities:	Mask of the Inquisitor, Cloak of the Inquisitor, Staff of the Inquisitor, Concealing Smoke, *{Redacted}*, *{Redacted}*		
	Species Bonus:	Mana Lifeline, Mana Manipulator, Emergency Regeneration, Mana Rage, Mana Feeding		
	Density Bonus:	Affinity Aficionado, Condensed Liquid Steel Skin		
Skills:	<u>Active Skills:</u> Inspect: 5 Inventory: <10> <u>Passive Skills:</u> Air Mana Manipulation: 7		Kickboxing: 2 Life Mana Manipulation: 6 Light Mana Manipulation: 2 Lightning Mana Manipulation: 4	

	Armorcrafting: 5 Botany: 2 Boxing: 4 Butchering: 1 Cartography: 2 Climbing: 2 Clothworking: 3 Cooking: 0 Crossbows: 0 Cycle Driving: 1 Darkness Mana Manipulation: 2 Death Mana Manipulation: 4 Diving: 0 Earth Mana Manipulation: 6 Elemental Absorption: 4 Fire Mana Manipulation: <10> *Projectile Fire Mana Manipulation: 6 First Aid: 0 Herbology: 2 Ice Mana Manipulation: 2 Jiu Jitsu: 3 Karate: 2 Kickboxing: 2		Magma Mana Manipulation: 2 Mana Compression: 5 Mana Infusion: 3 Mana Manipulation: <10> *Mana Sight: 0 Mana Projectile Weapons (Small): 5 Mana Projectile Weapons (Medium): 2 Mana Projectile Weapons (Large): 0 Mana Splitting: 5 Metalworking: 5 Mining: 3 Nature Mana Manipulation: 7 Projectile Mana Weapons Maintenance: 3 Sewing: 6 Set Crafting: 2 Skinning: 0 Small Blades: 0 Sprinting: 1 Staff Combat: 3 Swimming: 2 Taekwondo: 2 Tailoring: 5 Water Mana Manipulation: 8 Wing-Chun: 2	
Runes:	Fire Rune, Air Rune, Water Rune, Earth Rune, Nature Rune, Lightning Rune, Ice Rune, Magma Rune, Life Rune, Death Rune, Light Rune, Darkness Rune			
Resistances:	Basic Elemental:	1.0	Adv. Elemental:	1.9
	Pain:	5.3	Illusion	1.0 (+1.0)

	{Redacted}	1.0 (+1.0)	
Achievements:	Brave, Bold, and Boneheaded (3, Hidden) Beast Basher (3, Hidden) Nuking Knockout (2, Hidden) Mighty Mana Mastery (Hidden) Rowdy Runic (Hidden) Affinity Absorbed (Hidden) Masterful Mana Manipulator (Hidden)		

Congratulations, Vic. You are a real Special now. How does it feel to be all growed up? . . .

[I could shed a tear. Both for the gains and your wit.] I hear a laugh.

[Oh, I almost forgot. Grace, dear, how are you? You slick and shiny on the outside and in? Ready for a ride?]

#*I am slick and ready to rumble, Host Vic. Thank you for asking. My new upgrades make me all tingly inside. I can't wait to show you my stuff . . .*

You two are going to drive me to drink . . .

I just laugh in my head.

All right, Vic. When you wake up Aria, please just . . .

[I'm her trainer and protector. That is my priority.]

And what if she wants more? . . .

[It is too much of a risk.]

Shaking my head, I look down at the top of the blonde head and give it a gentle shake. "Time to get up, Aria." All I get are grumbles. Grinning, I shake harder. "C'mon. Time to get up."

She stirs and bends her head up to look at me. Her smile is huge.

I smile back at her and say, "I'm sorry I was gone for so long."

"Welcome back, Vic. I missed you. Are you okay? Jo won't tell me what happened beyond that you are doing great, that the level up worked in the end, and that other thing." Blushing bright, she asks, "She told you, right?"

I nod at her. "Jo says you have been advancing your training and are doing very well. I'm really happy and proud of you to hear that."

"Thanks."

"It means we can advance your training. Are you ready to start hand-to-hand?"

Aria climbs off me and is kneeling on the bed. I see she is wearing an extra-large white t-shirt that says, "I'm the boss." And that's all I can see of her clothes. Her legs are curled under her, but they have nothing covering them.

Oh, shit.

I hear her bell-like laughter. "Relax, Vic. I can see the panic on your face. Take a breath. Everything is okay."

I nod slightly and let out a breath. Was I holding it before?

"Vic. How do you feel? Do you need a shower or anything?"

"I think a shower would be a good idea." Yeah, a cold shower. I can feel my body reacting to her.

She giggles and stands up. It turns out I was right. The shirt ends at the bottom of her rear and, yes, she had nothing but the shirt on. What is she trying to do? As she walks to her room I can see her figure is more muscular than when I fell asleep, but otherwise it looks the same. Curves and such in all the right places and proportions. Her more muscular legs are smooth and tanned.

Closing my eyes and breathing deeply, I remember that I am her trainer. This is going to be a problem. Potentially a big one. Cold shower. Now.

I forgot about my skin. The cold shower isn't cold to me. Yep. A problem.

I eventually come out of the shower after getting a hold of my emotions and throw on my normal sweats and t-shirt. Feeling like I can focus, I ponder how much I have to do and I start to feel overwhelmed.

First, I look at the egg as I walk by it. It looks mostly the same, just a little bigger, and Aria has made a few changes to the wrappings and metals. [Inspect] provides no new information—I mean, it's an egg, so no real surprise there. We need to get a metal element beast skin and dress it. I'll figure something out from there.

[Anything on the metal element beast?]

There are numerous options actually. However, I recommend we focus on the spatial items first . . .

[Fair enough.]

I bring the basket of all my shitty spatial containers out into the main room and find it empty. I call to Aria that I will be on the balcony and hear a muffled acknowledgment in reply.

On the balcony, I sit in my usual loveseat and put the basket on my lap. I am about to order a wine when I remember my new species ability.

[Jo, can I eat and drink if I want to?]

If you like, yes. You just don't have to . . .

[Good to know. Will I have to pee if I drink?]

We will see, but I do not believe so. Your body is simply too efficient; as such, it will break down anything and everything that is not extremely saturated with mana. And even then, I doubt it . . .

[Well, no time like the present. Can I have a glass of white wine?]

You have meetings set up in two days with Master Steeltamer and Mr. Whyatt. You also have an appointment to meet a Realtor in four days . . .

[Thanks, Jo. Can you bring up the mission log and highlight the changes?]

Mission Log for Vic (because he can't track of his own shit)			
Name	Description	Timeframe	Perceived Difficulty
Save Humanity	Your personal goal in life is to eliminate all invaders from this planet. This is an impossible mission and you need to lower your expectations.	The end of time	Good fucking luck!
Guard and Protect	You have been selected as the Guardian and Protector of Arialla Frystera Livera Riverwing. Your role is to protect, mentor, guide, and comfort her as required for the duration of your agreement.	Duration of Protectorate Agreement	Unknown
Flora Friend	Figure out who is conducting craze experiments on	Unknown	Unknown

	innocent plant life, why the lunatic is doing so, and make them stop using whatever violent means you choose.		
Slavery Shutdown	Slavery is an abomination that must be ended in Sea Saddle City. You will trace the thugs back to the slavers and terminate them. With prejudice.	As soon as fucking possible	Unknown
Hopeful Hatchery	You found an egg of a mutated peregrine falcon. Do whatever it takes to help the egg return to health, grow, and then hatch. Maybe if you don't screw that up, you can bond. Maybe. You do smell.	N/A	Low if you aren't your usual idiotic self
Map Highlights	You have "procured" a map from a less than benevolent source with two highlighted areas on it. Explore those areas, figure out what they are, why they are highlighted, and do something about it.	03:08:13:22:09:54	Unknown
Evolve [Inventory]	**Through an act of monumental idiocy, you have reached level 10 in the [Inventory] active skill. It is time for you to evolve it, and your plan on doing so, under the guidance of your dashing and bril-**	**Before next level up**	**This should be easy, even for you**

	liant nano consciousness, is to absorb as many different types of spatial containers as possible.		
Buy a Base	You are planning to set up your own little group of fellow lunatics. To do this, you need a facility. Go buy one that has all the crafting and shit your fellow lunatics need.	Whenever you find a place	Just spend coin. You can do it, Vic!
Perfect Pupil	You need to train Aria how to survive and thrive on her own. Start with hand-to-hand instruction and then add wilderness training. Her limit of only life magica will be a challenge to overcome for both of you. *Note: This mission is a sub-element of the Guard and Protect mission.*	Starts soon, and ends when she is ready to do dangerous missions on her own	She is a willing pupil. Don't screw this up.
Anonymous No More	You are likely found out. You need to do something about it. What, is up to you.	Really soon, before they come get you	Unknown

[Thanks, Jo. So what do I do with all this junk?]

Just touch each of them, and you will see them disappear. I will be instructing your nanos to absorb them. Remember to not attempt to absorb the jade ring...

I take a sip of wine.

[Okay. Here goes.]

I start touching a bunch of rings, bracelets, anklets, earrings, toe rings, other rings I don't want to think about, pins, hair accessories, and whatever else sparkles.

[You know. A storage device in the hair doesn't seem like a horrible idea for someone like Aria who does more than just a ponytail.]

No bad, Vic. Propose the idea to her . . .

I am proven right when, as I am almost all the way through, Aria joins me on the balcony with her hair in a braid. She sits in the seat next to me, holding her own wine glass. A red. Is that the one I . . . err, "acquired" from the twins and gave to the hotel for storage? I decide not to ask.

Smiling at her, I say, "Hey. I'm making the world a less glittery place."

I keep touching, and they keep disappearing.

She giggles. And finally, it is just the jade ring.

[How did we do?]

Not bad. Saturation is moderate to high. We can do better. Let's get more . . .

[Okay.]

I look at Aria. She is in sweats and t-shirt like me, but her braid somehow starts at the top of her head but is still attached. How does she do that? It draws attention to her and is kind of distracting. Shaking my head, I ask, "What do you think of a storage device for your hair? I only wear a ponytail and I have my own way. But it might give you a bit of easy space and can hold a few hidden weapons too. Not a lot of people think about a hair tie as threatening, for example."

She offers me a huge smile as a response. My mind hangs for a sec. I hear in my foggy brain, "Sounds like a plan."

Fuck. I clear my throat and say, "Feel like a trip to the armory? Let's go spend some coin."

She beams at me and leaps up before running inside. I'm frozen mid-drink because that leap caused her loose shirt to also leap up. Fuck.

CHAPTER 93

We head back to floor five with the miscellaneous items. Immediately upon appearance on the pad, we are assisted but a human woman in the usual Whyatt black and white. I ask, "Can you please take us to your spatial storage containers?"

She bows and says, "Of course, sir and madam. Please come this way."

She turns to lead us away when Aria and I look at each other.

Aria mouths to me, "Sir and madam?" I just smile as we follow to an area twelve by six meters.

The very posh and proper helper asks, "Is there a particular kind you are looking for?"

I point at Aria and say, "She is looking for something for the hair and possible others. I'm going to start walking around and touching things."

Aria laughs and asks the women a specific question about concealed weapons inside inconspicuous hair accessories.

And I, like the shitty customer I am, go around literally touch every fucking thing in sight.

[Gryphon shit, Jo. Tell me it won't always be like this.]

Well, if you had an [Inspect] higher than twenty-five, we might have a chance of simply walking close . . .

[That's not happening for a long fucking time. Touchy-touch it is.]

There are far more objects in this section than in that smaller store, but the ratio of choosing things is lower. Unlike the prior time when I walked out with at least forty shiny baubles, this time I am stuck with only twenty-six pieces of useless garbage. Win.

Aria has long since picked her stuff and is keeping the woman busy now. I walk over, and we check out. Six gold poorer, she and I head back to our suite.

"Thanks, Vic. What do you think?" She tilts her head and shows me a completely plain and totally unthreatening hair clip amid her braid.

"It's perfect. But didn't you get two things?"

"Yep!" And then she bounces into her room. Okay, then.

Back on the balcony, Jo and I keep up the ridiculous absorption routine until the last one is gone.

[Please tell me we are done?]

Your saturation level on this is high, and the nanos have processed an incredible variety of spatial mana layouts. It's time for the jade ring . . .

[Oh, thank you! This was the most annoying operation we've done together.]

Really? The cave wasn't worse? . . .

[Definitely not. This is even worse than the shit we did in the cave. At least that had an element of risk and excitement. This is so boring.]

I think you're delirious from the pain of shopping. Either way, get the ring and place it on your palm. Let's do this slowly . . .

I do and feel a tingle in my palm.

This mana pocket is quite bizarre. I am detecting affinities other than spatial, which should not be possible . . .

[Can we absorb it?]

We can. The question is, should we? I cannot seem to get inside. No wonder it was in the bargain bin. They probably thought it was a single sub-pocket item and broken . . .

[Want me to try to access it?]

I'm not sure . . .

[Jo, I'm done with this operation. My plate is incredibly full, and this is taking up brain power I cannot spare. Can you just absorb it and then we level up?]

Vic, why are you so upset about this? . . .

[I don't know . . .]

Seriously? What's really bothering you? . . .

I let out a sigh. [I am not great at telling these things, but I think Aria wants to be intimate.]

Congratulations for stating the obvious. Why does that make you upset? . . .

['Cause she's Aria, not just some girl. She is my trainee and charge and I her trainer and her guardian. There is a serious conflict there. And what's worse, wouldn't it be betraying the trust she has in me? Would I be betraying Shen and Grun, whose deaths I am responsible for, by the way? And what if I screw this up and she goes back to hating me? How can I do my job if she despises me? Or if I don't and we become so close I cannot see past my feelings and I fail at teaching or, in the worst case, protecting her?]

Now that my verbal explosion happened, I am limp in my chair and afraid to even open my eyes.

[Jo. You know me. I know shit about women, relationships, love, affection, being a boyfriend, or what's expected of me. I've known what family is for what, a few months? I'm . . .]

Scared . . .

[Try panicking. Terrified.]

Oh, Vic. I think you should talk to her about it. Please talk to her about it . . .

I take a deep breath.

[Okay. I will.]

I sit up. Thinking about protecting Aria makes me think of her protecting herself.

[Can you please find the best crossbows the armory has access to that will fit Aria? Show me the list when compiled.]

Search initiated . . .

[And you might as well do a search for staves while you are at it. If I am what I am, I should procure and learn to fight with a staff. Can you find out if the dojo has a staff instructor?]

Confirmed . . .

I open my clenched fist and hold out the jade ring.

[I think we should just absorb it.]

Okay. Want to try to access it first? . . .

[Sure, I can do that. I just wear it and what?]

Send your mana into it . . .

[Non-affinity mana?]

Good question. Let me do a few more scans . . .

This results in more tingles from my palm.

I don't know. Sending non-affinity mana may damage it. Or not. I have no recommendation on this. There are too many unknown variables to make a proper recommendation . . .

I sigh. Other complications aside, I really am getting fed up with the whole thing.

[Just absorb it. After all this, if I break it, I'll be too angry to speak.]

Understood. Absorbing . . .

The ring in my palm flashes gold, then green, then brown, then white, then gray, then dark blue, then silver, then my azure blue. Then it disappears.

[Jo what the fuck hap—]

I'm cut off as my entire body seizes. I feel a shocking pain in my body and start shaking and thrashing in the chair. My mind can see what is going on but not participate. I am just watching. I can't think messages to Jo. I can't call for help. I can do nothing but lie there and shake as my body falls from the seat onto the steel balcony floor.

Warning! Host has suffered **Severe Electric Shock.** *Host has completely lost body and mind control until &%^$(%*

My HUD flickers and vanishes as I witness purple sparks begin to crackle and spark all over my body. I feel electricity—my own lightning element—launching attacks on my body. Over and over I flash as sparks roll up and down my body. On my skin, over my locked open eyes and in between my snapping teeth . . . everywhere. I smell burning. In my mind, I am howling in pain, but I just shake on the floor, occasionally smashing my head or back into the chair or table. After a spark causes my body to curl upon itself, there is a massive blinding purple light, a deafening crack, a burst of pure agony, and I am finally released from the pain into unconsciousness.

CHAPTER 94

"Vic! Vic! Talk to me. Are you okay? Vic!"

I groan. Where am I? What is going on? I try to move and find it impossible.

"Vic! Can you hear me?"

I hear words but nothing makes sense. My attempt to speak fails, and all I can manage is a groan. Am I on a mission? Did I get injured? Captured? Shit, am I a prisoner?

"Vic, try to use your life magica. I can't touch you."

Life magica? How would I use magica? I have gear. If only I could reach my collar for the healing crystal.

"Vic, please. Try to focus. You're scaring me."

Then I hear static in my ear. Is my earcomm malfunctioning? How can I have a comm if I am a prisoner?

The static becomes louder and starts to clear slightly.

"Jo? Jo? What is going on? Why won't he respond?"

The static is clear enough to barely hear a voice.

Vic? Stay calm, Vic. Everything is okay. Stay calm. You aren't alone. Aria is here. I'm here . . .

"What do you mean, Jo? He's fucking sparking and steaming! He's not fucking okay!"

Vic, don't try to move. Just stay calm. Can you talk to me? . . .

I know that voice. Can I talk to it?

[Hello?]

Vic! . . .

Do I recall that voice?

It's me, Jo . . .

[Jo?]

Yes, Vic. I'm here. I'm Jo and I'm here. Just stay calm. Your nanos are trying to repair the damage . . .

My brain starts to engage slightly. I remember Jo. Jo's always in my head. Is she the blonde I have in my mind? Wait, no. That's not Jo. Why do I feel so weird when I think of her?

Aria is here with you too. Don't move. Try to relax your body if you can . . .

"Vic, can you speak?"

[Aria?]

Yes, that was Aria. You can talk to us both this way okay? . . .

"Vic. I'm here."

[I remember Aria. Blonde. Mine.]

"Sure, Vic. Can you talk to me?"

[Scrambled. Can't move.]

Things are clearing up. Somewhat at least.

I have this, Aria. Vic, do you remember the jade ring? . . .

Do I?

[Think so?]

C'mon. Focus. The ring.

[I think I didn't like it. It was so annoying.]

I hear light bell-like laughter in my ears, not my head. I know that laugh.

[Aria? I can hear you.]

"I know, Vic. I'm here. You're almost done pretending to be a thunderbird. Then I can touch you and help."

Things are almost clear now.

[Oh, good. 'Cause this sucks. What happened, Jo? Things are clearing up a little. What happened with the ring?]

Things getting clearer is good . . .

Even in my current state, I can make out the relief in those words.

We need to get you inside and into bed where you can rest and recover. I'll explain there . . .

[Okay. I think I can feel my body again. Sort of. I feel the wind. Are we still on the balcony?]

Yes. Feeling the wind is good. Aria, give touching him a shot. If it works, send a very tiny amount of life mana. Just a drop. We can't overwhelm his system with more magica. Just enough so he can help you get him to bed . . .

"Okay."

I can feel a soft hand on my chest followed by a tiny trickle of warmth. It warms my insides and chases away a sliver of the pain and exhaustion.

"It worked, Jo."

I see, Aria. Vic, can you try to move? Help Aria help you to bed . . .

I open my eyes for the first time, and it's blurry at first. I don't really understand the passing of time right now, but it eventually starts to clear up. I see Aria's beautiful face over me. I try to move. I can. Sort of. I can shift and roll over. I see myself and I'm a bit surprised. And embarrassed.

[Why am I naked? And steaming?]

I hear Aria laughing softly followed by whispered words, "You have nothing to be ashamed about. Believe me."

Vic, your clothes were vaporized, and you are steaming because of what destroyed your clothes. We'll get to it all, but you need to get to bed so you can sleep and heal. Help Aria get you up . . .

With monumental effort, I am able to move myself. After another few minutes I can even sit up and—get this—stand. I'm a champion.

Aria and I shuffle inside to my bedroom, and she does what she can to throw the covers over and then lay me down into bed. Well, it's more of a flop. She adjusts me so I am facing up and in the middle of the mattress, throws the covers back over me, and heads into her room.

[Jo?]

Rest. Close your eyes and try to sleep if you can. Give your body and nanos a chance. I know you are confused and don't understand. Please have patience and trust me. I have asked Aria to keep you company in hopes it will help calm and relax you enough to sleep . . .

She's right; I am completely confused and overwhelmed. I close my eyes and just try to breathe. I hear Aria lightly padding back into my room and feel her lifting the covers and crawling in next to me. I can feel a shirt and bare legs as they pressed against me. She lays her head on my shoulder and arm across my torso just like when I woke earlier today. It's soothing. I welcome the darkness to the rhythm of Aria's breaths on my bare chest.

***

I blink myself awake, fully aware and relieved to see my HUD again. Then I notice the sound of water running in the bathroom. It stops, and Aria exits the bathroom wearing that same shirt as before. She crawls back in bed next to me, kisses my chest, and lays her head down on my heart.

[Jo?]

I'm so sorry, Vic. I didn't know that would happen . . .

[I'm pretty sure nobody could have predicted that. Whatever that was.]

That ring was more special than we understood. How do you want me to do this? Bad news first like usual? . . .

[Always bad news first. Good news is easy to adapt to.]

My left arm starts rubbing Aria's back over her shirt. She starts tracing the contours of my chest and stomach with her left-hand fingers.

"Jo is catching me up." Aria just nods on my chest.

That ring was an impossibility. It contained the affinities of life, nature, earth, light, water, air, and spatial. All of these together were infused into the mana pocket, I have no idea how, and created what the nanomachine system is referring to as "Living Inventory." There was a small pocket that had the ability to support life in it . . .

[Everyone knows that spatial storage cannot support life. That makes no sense.]

And that is the reason it never occurred to me that would be the reason I could not access inside of it. Only natural things could enter it. So when you absorbed it and your nanomachine system tried to learn its spatial structure . . . well, it kind of freaked out. Do you remember the flashing of the different colors before it all went back? . . .

[I think so.]

That was your system trying to figure it out. In order to determine how to evaluate the spatial structure, it had to analyze each of the pieces. So it broke down every affinity, one a time, and started examining them and their relationship to each other. Well, your highly saturated nanos were able to figure out how the spatial structure works. It turns out that lightning mana is used to combine them in a global form so each is connected and dependent upon one another. And the lightning mana is both the connector as well as the adhesive that makes it all work . . .

[So my nanos figured, "Hey, let's try that?"]

Actually, yes. That is exactly what happened. They decided to combine all of your affinities except lightning, use what it learned from your first crazy experience with creating spatial affinity, and combined that with the high-level saturation caused by absorbing so many spatial pockets, and zap. It attempted to create a living inventory mana pocket. At first, it wasn't working because there wasn't enough throughput...

[So the nanos freaked and tried to get more.]

Yes. And this is where your HUD failed, by the way. As a solution to the lack of mana, they engaged your species abilities, Emergency Regeneration, Mana Rage, and finally Mana Lifeline. We'll get to that last one in a bit. Your body had a bit of a fit at the sudden influx and outflow of energy. That, apparently, was not sufficient, so they put the full thrust of all of that mana into a single "joining." In essence, it poured all the built-up mana into an electromagnetic connection structure. The result is something of a larger spatial globe made of thousands of tiny globes of your different mana affinities all held together by your lightning mana. The good news is, it worked. The bad news is your body sort of... failed...

[My body failed?]

Yes. You kind of died a little...

[Uh-huh... How can I kind of die a little?]

Well, you see, your system still had Emergency Regeneration and Mana Rage going at the height of the rest of the magica pressure. Which means the strain on your body was incredibly high. Too high, so your body kind of failed. Fortunately for you, the nanos seemed to have a plan. Hence we now know what Mana Lifeline does. It allows the conversion of mana into health and visa versa at a two-to-one ratio. So what your nanomachine system did was use your Emergency Regeneration and Mana Rage to funnel mana into health using Mana Lifeline. It was sufficient to sustain you and prevent your health from reaching 0.00...

[Ouch.]

Of course you then went into Mana Overload as the debuff hit you from Mana Rage ending. You were barely alive, so losing ninety-five percent of your attributes nearly killed you again and turned you into the complete mess you woke up as. With a little help from Aria, you survived. She was able to stabilize your health drop despite getting shocked repeatedly and, well, you know the rest...

[Wow.]

I reach over and hug Aria tight to me.

I whisper, "Thank you."

She hugs back as best she can from her position. "Of course."

[Well, I have no interest in seeing the alerts from the disastrous portion of that experience. Can we skip to the good stuff?]

Absolutely. Congratulations, you have evolved skills...

Skill updated. Passive skill [Lightning Mana Manipulation] has leveled from 4 to 10...

No further progress is available for [Lightning Mana Manipulation] until an advanced version of this skill is activated. All mana used to advance nanomachines for skill [Lightning Mana Manipulation] is now directed to overall nanomachine advancement...

[Lightning Mana Manipulation] has evolved...

New skill activated. Passive skill [Electromagnetic Mana Manipulation] now available for use...

Skill updated. Passive skill [Electromagnetic Mana Manipulation] has leveled from 0 to 2...

[Inventory] has evolved...

New skill activated. Active skill [Living Inventory] now available for use...

Skill updated. Active skill [Living Inventory] is now level 1...

[Wow. I'm thrilled, of course. But isn't lightning already electromagnetic?]

The nanomachine system breaks down both mana and skills in different ways. Lightning is by itself not magnetic. Ions need to be changed, charged, and discharged, so yes and no. In the case of the system, the two are different. On top of that, the lightning manipulation skill is viewed as "offense" while electromagnetic manipulation is considered "support."...

Whatever, I'll just accept it 'cause it's a great addition to my arsenal. But seriously, why does this shit always happen to me?]

Vic, I am going to answer without snark. Because you are overwhelmingly powerful and are completely incapable of supporting it...

I'm silent while reflecting on that statement. A minute or two later, I respond.

[I suppose that's true.]

I look down at Aria and rub the back of my fingers on her cheek.

[I can explore the [Living Inventory] later. Was there anything else?]

Something this momentous deserves an Achievement, don't you think?...

New Achievement activated. For creating an unknown and original skill, the Achievement **Clever Creator** *is now available. This Achievement grants you +5% growth in the skill you created. All future original skill creations will add an additional +5% to the growth of each. Do you wish to show or hide your Achievement? . . .*

New Title activated. For creating an original skill using all basic and advanced mana types that is not pre-built into or developed by the system itself, the Title **Visionary Eminence** *is now available. This Title grants you +30% effectiveness towards crafting all original pieces. If the craft is using a primary profession, it is +50%. If using a secondary profession, +40%. Do you wish to show or hide your Title? . . .*

Aria's fingers begin to wander a little too low, so I gently cup her cheek with my hand, and she stops.

[Those are good. Nothing mindblowing, but good nonetheless. Anything else?]

No. That is all from that. I have details on the procurements you wanted for yourself and Aria. But they can wait until tomorrow . . .

[Excellent. Good night, Jo.]

Good night, Vic. I'll give you two some space to talk . . .

CHAPTER 95

"Hey, you. Come up here so we can talk." Looking down at Aria, I see she is blushing a bright red and moves herself so her chin is on her hands, which are on my chest. She is facing me and just a lovely sight.

"I want to talk about . . . well, this." And I make a gesture at the two of us with my right hand. My left is on the skin of her lower back.

"Okay, Vic. I know. You're scared, right?"

I nod. "Petrified."

"Can you tell me why?"

I do. Just like I did with Jo, I tell her my fears about how she is a trainee and those sorts of relationships rarely work out due to conflicts during training. How I am concerned this is disrespecting her and her parents, who I'm already suffering guilt about and who were my friends and family too. About how I'll screw this up, she'll hate me, and I won't be able to protect her. About if I don't and it's wonderful and I let my feelings get in the way of doing my duty—if she gets hurt because of my failure, I probably won't be able to live with myself.

"And above all, Aria, you know who I am. What I am. I am not a good person. I am a killer. A murderer. I have done things that you might consider heartless. Even evil, although I personally do not believe myself to *be* evil. I have put the survival of the human race above my own, and I will again. I am absolutely certain I will. I can't stop but think you deserve a better man. A good man. I'm happy to train you and teach you and prepare you. But love you? Do I even know how? I've never known love; how would I know how to share it with someone?"

A tear falls from the corner of Aria's golden eye and leaves a wet streak on her perfect cheek. "Vic, you view us as family already, right?"

I nod. "I do. As much as someone like me can."

"Do you know what family is?"

I sigh and shake my head. "Not really."

"You do. You just don't know it. It's trust and love."

I blink at that. Is it that simple?

"I see that look on your face. Yes, everything about family starts with those two emotions. So, yes. You know love because you already feel it. You just didn't realize. You love Jo. And you love me."

Oh. Could I, of all people, feel love?

"As for the future, ask yourself what you believe. You witnessed a little bit of my mother's power. She could see things through the natural world sometimes. She was an incredibly gifted nature magica and had the ability to know things that the world knows. She hid this from you, but she knew we were going to die before the betrayal that led us to the orcs. She saw it coming. She also saw a . . ." I can tell she is struggling with the right word. "A *helper* but that he could only save one of us. When we ran into you, she said it was like the world shone again. There was hope, and it was you."

Once again tears are flowing, and I reach forward to wipe them with my thumb. She smiles sadly but continues.

"She said that you and I would be together and it would be for a reason that wouldn't become known right away. My mom told me you'd be a perfect protector, and partner, and eventually lover. She said you would be the perfect one for me. Of course, you were human so I figured she meant it to be temporary until you died of old age. But now . . ."

I complete the thought. "I'm not mortal anymore."

"Yes. You're not big into the fate thing, and I don't blame you. But sometimes the world around us can sense things we can't. I don't think that is fate. It's power, and I know you believe in that." She pauses for me to think about what she said.

I reflect on it and nod. She is correct; I do believe in power, in its various levels and forms. And have experienced enough to know for a fact I have only witnessed a fragment of the types and strengths of power wielded.

"Vic, I am one hundred percent confident that you will screw up. Just like I will. We both will. But I trust you and you do me. Maybe I will die, maybe you will."

She lowers her head again and so her wet cheek lies against my skin. Her next words are softer.

"Your change to agelessness . . . I wonder if maybe it is this world's gift to me. An immortal guardian, teacher, confidant, and lover. I wonder what I did to deserve it."

I rub her head again and answer even though the question isn't directed at me. It reminds me of something—a sentence said to me long ago by someone when I asked the simple word: "why?"

I speak her answer out loud to Aria. "Sometimes we are given gifts not for what we have done, but what we will do."

She nods. "That is a heavy responsibility you and I both bear, don't you think? What do you say we share it together? You already trust and love me. How about risking making it deeper and sharing this burden? I think you could use it, and I know I could. However long we live, a thousand years or a hundred or ten, we'll share ourselves, and I think it will be wonderful. What do you say?"

I'm absolutely still. Thinking it through. "Is it that simple?"

She smiles big at me. "I think so. I love you. You love me. And you didn't answer my question. Will you give us a try?"

I'm silent for a minute thinking.

"You know, that is the first time anyone has said those words to me."

She tilts her head up to look at my face. "Which?"

"I love you."

I watch as another tear falls from her eye, down her cheek and onto my chest. She says through the emotion, "You are probably the person who deserves it the most. Will you welcome it?"

Will I?

"Yes" is my only response.

Her smile grows, and she pushes her body up and kisses me on the mouth. I don't know how to describe it. My whole body tingles with adrenaline. The kiss breaks, and Aria backs up a few inches.

I'm breathing a little heavy when I say a little nervously, "Um. You know I've never been intimate with anyone, right? Like anything. That was my first kiss."

"That's okay. You did great." A half grin forms on her beautiful face. "We'll learn together, and maybe in this case I can teach you a thing or two."

My voice comes out nervously. "I have a fear that I am going to suck at this 'cause I've had no experience, education, or preparation."

Her bell-like laughter rings through my room. "Then I'll lead. I can teach some, and we'll gain experience. I know we can figure it out together, just like we'll do everything else together. And frankly, I can feel you're pretty prepared."

And she kisses me again.

She is an excellent leader. Just like she said, we explore each other and learn and explode with feeling and love and affection and joy. She is a giving lover, and I try to reciprocate as best I can. It is beyond anything I have ever imagined, and we spend the night giving and accepting to and from each other.

CHAPTER 96

The morning of the following day, I wake still lying in my bed with Aria on my chest, arm and leg draped over me. I look up at the ceiling and wonder if some greater purpose or whatever really did guide us together. Or is it simply the power of the world like Aria said. Something even greater?

I let out a shaky breath and compartmentalize that fear and focus on what I can control.

[Thanks for giving us space, Jo. I'm sorry if that was awkward for you.]

Thank you for thinking of me, but no. Remember what I am, Vic. I am the consciousness of your nanomachine interface. In other words, I am you from the other side of the copper. A version of you made of mana, per se. We share the same goals, wants, desires, and affections. I feel for Aria because you do. Thank you for saying it, but you didn't have to . . .

[Well, thank you anyway. For everything.]

You are welcome, Vic. It has been my pleasure to serve . . .

[Okay.] I let out a breath. [Did you say you have some equipment that might meet our specs?]

Yes. The crossbow and then the staff. I have eleven that could meet the need. Can you refine the criteria? . . .

[I don't know. Aria is a life magica so any affinity except death will work the same for her. Are there any repeating crossbows? Obviously, skip anything liquid metal.]

Yes. Eliminating death affinity and non-repeating leaves three. I do not include liquid metal in any searches for obvious reasons. Would you like to see them? . . .

[I would.] Aria stirs a little but settles back down.

Displaying. Enchanted ammunition is a separate purchase for each . . .

Product:	Description:	Affinities:
HyperWare "Shiv" Compact	This mini crossbow has limited range and damage, but is extremely sleek	Air

Wrist Crossbow	and easy to miss. It is worn on the wrist using a specialized and custom joint handle and quiver. The device hides in plain sight, appearing as a bracelet that holds the crossbow and as many mini bolts as can be attached surrounding the wrist. After each shot, the crossbow automatically reloads and shifts the loader to the next bolt. A clever and well-hidden—if low damage—self-defense weapon.	
HyperWare "Mac" Repeating Hand Crossbow	This repeating hand crossbow is a larger version of the "shiv" except the autoloader cartridge is inside the device itself. The Mac is an open-carry vehicle of death with damage and range highly conducive to both distance and close-range use. The earth enhancements and inscriptions allow for impact damage as well as piercing with bolts that have an unusually wide but thin head.	Air, Earth
MagiTech CR231 Repeating Hand Crossbow	This MagiTech creation is the largest hand crossbow available on the commercial market. The crossbow was developed using particularly lightweight and flexible proprietary MagiTech materials. The CR231 is a long-range weapon with the fastest reload speed on the market, reaching almost that of mana projector weapons. The lightning inscriptions allow for high-speed action as well as possibly stunning the target. While this weapon is less durable than its counterparts, its speed and output	Lightning

are well worth the risk and expense.

They cost one, two, and four gold, respectively . . .

[These are great finds Jo. Well done. Order four Shivs and two CR231s.]

That many? . . .

[Absolutely, why not? We each have two wrists after all. Or they'll just be backups for Aria.]

Of course. Why didn't I think of that? . . .

[Next time, maybe. How about my new staff?]

Before I respond, I have received a hit on a search for the metal element . . .

[Oh, tell me!] I practically shout in my head.

Calm down! I have found a hide from an individual claiming to have slain a metal-element herbivore . . .

[Is it credible? How much?]

I give it fifty-fifty whether it is a fraud. It is five gold. Remember Vic, that is a fortune for most of the populace. In short, it is outrageously expensive . . .

[Whatever. It's worth a shot. Buy it. And remind me I have the feathers when we eventually use this hide to make a nice blankie for our little egg.]

Aria will almost certainly want to participate in that exercise . . .

I sigh. [Agreed. Buy a few air stones while you're at it; just buy them if it seems good. I don't want to bother. Now, let's proceed with my staff, please.]

I have found twelve options that I believe will be a good fit. How would you like me to narrow the search? . . .

[Fuck if I know. I know drake shit about staves.]

I think for a few minutes.

[Um. How about any that have multiple affinities?]

All my selections have at least two . . .

[Damn you for being so on top of things. Can any of them change shape?]

All but one . . .

[For fuck's sake, Jo, stop being such a dashing and brilliant nano consciousness. I have nothing to work with here.] Is that a snort in my head? Did my nanomachine consciousness just snort?

It is quite difficult being me at times . . .

[I'm sure. What if we add a lightning requirement?]

Well-chosen. I knew you could do it. Here is your search result . . .

Smiling, I read the only remaining choice. I like Jo when she is being sassy.

Product:	**Description:**	**Affinities:**
Hyoto Engineering "Twister" Spearstaff	The highlight of Hyoto Engineering's staff and spear lines, this staff can shift shape into a single or double-sided spear. When a staff or double-sided spear, it has the ability to break into two equal portions, creating fighting sticks or dual mini spears. When full size, the spear is also weighted for throwing. It is said this spearstaff has inscriptions on literally every portion including the center joint. This weapon is truly deadly as it can stun, burn, and shield with its three affinities. A well-trained wielder is needed to avoid self-damage.	Lightning, Air, Fire

This selection is fourteen gold and likely the most expensive weapon you will purchase for a long time if ever . . .

[Stop there. No further discussion needed. I want it. It's fucking brilliant.]

Ordered. Updated body measurements are required for delivery in fifteen days . . .

[That means I have to get up.]

Yes.

I slide out the bed slowly enough to not wake up Aria and go to the cryspad for measurement.

Measurements confirmed. Your physical size and weight have increased. In case you are curious, since your last measurement pre-level up, you are 0.77 inches taller, have 8.39 percent more muscle mass, and your bones have increased in density by 6.91 percent...

[No wonder Aria has such a hard time helping me walk. Not sure about the height, but increased muscle mass and bone density are great.]

I believe your height will grow no more than one or two inches in total, no matter your level. The nanomachines are attempting to perfect you, not turn you into a giant. That being said, your muscle mass and bone density will continue to change for quite a while as they are adapting to your changing physical attributes...

I go to do my morning thing when I remember I no longer have to pee. Or sweat. Weird. Well, I still want a quick shower. So I go take one. Halfway through, Aria joins me, and the shower turns from quick to a few hours including a move to the bath. Not helpful for my aim to be productive, but it makes Aria happy, so I am willing to make the sacrifice. I'm super generous that way.

***

Sitting in the hot bath with Aria on my lap, I play with the tiny gold ring on her left small toe. That was the mysterious second spatial container she purchased. I'm not sure why it was a secret, but I also don't care. While twiddling with it, I reflect on how this all started. That reminds me I still have to deal with being outed.

"I need to check in with my HQ now that my presence is known."

I don't say it out loud, but I am well aware I can't check in with HQ without MagiTech's involvement.

Aria reaches over to get the shampoo. Somehow during the hours-long cleaning, we never actually got clean. "You could always just quit."

I blink. That thought never crossed my mind. An entire field of possibilities runs through my mind. That could work for so many reasons. Aria has no idea just how clever that off-handed idea is.

Aria is correct. Your required service years are long past. You can retire at any time...

"Thanks, Jo."

I need to think for a minute. This opens a whole set of unexpected dimensional tears.

Aria starts washing my long hair. Interestingly, it has stayed that exact same length since my activation. She uses her nails on my scalp, and I close my eyes in bliss.

"That's amazing." Was I really missing out on all this? No wonder people are so into relationships.

"Weren't you planning on starting your own team to be under your own control? Doing what you think is right when you can rather than being ordered to was your aim, yes?"

"Yes. You are, of course, right."

I can start on the bureaucratic end if you like. If you file to create a corporate structure the right way, you have a chance of getting a MilSpec procurement license . . .

"Start the documentation on that, but don't file anything."

Confirmed . . .

"And do the retirement too. But don't file it."

I speak the last two commands out loud so Aria can hear.

I just sit there and let Aria wash my hair. I hear "I love your hair." She changes from scrubbing my scalp to running her hands from top to bottom all the way through my long strands. "To be honest, I've kind of found it distracting the entire time we've been together. Even when I thought you were just an annoying human."

I chuckle at that, recalling her various conflicting looks and comments during our long trip through the rainforest.

She picks up a tall glass Jo arranged for us and rinses me off and washes the rest of me with no funny business. While doing the same for her, I say, "We need to get you started on martial training in the dojo. It is a long and painful process, but the number one best way to train. You should also start thinking about the kind of melee weapon you like, although there is no rush there. I have already taken the initiative to procure a few crossbows I think you will like quite a bit."

She kisses me, and my face is covered with soap again.

Shaking my head, I say, "After sufficient progress there, we will start our wilderness training. You should be prepared that it is quite challenging, both mentally and physically; you will likely struggle some. At the rate you pick things up, I figure three months on hand-to-hand, three more on weapons, and then we head out and go back to the rainforest. What do you think?"

"You won't teach me hand-to-hand?"

I laugh. "That kind of *combat* training is not my area of expertise. The other kind, we'll definitely be one on one, although you're doing more of the training than me."

She giggles as I rinse her off and then myself.

"Jo, can you please set up a dojo routine for Aria? Start with general boxing, kickboxing, then Wing-Chun and Taekwondo." Looking at Aria, I explain my choices. "Based on your body type, strengths and weaknesses, I think those are the best for you to start with."

Confirmed...

Walking out of the bathroom following Aria, I am admiring her fine body when I say, "If you struggle with those, we can look at something else which may fit you better."

See, I can mix business and pleasure. Right? Maybe?

[Did you set up my staff training?]

I did, but I asked them to add spearstaff, fighting sticks, and dual small spear training. There is a delay in finding the correct instructors...

[Tell them I'll pay well. Maybe we can reserve or rent some time from someone from Hyoto Engineering? I wager they have experts who test the products.]

That is an excellent idea. Request sent...

"Aria, Jo found us a potential metal-affinity hide for Eggy."

She looks over her shoulder and smiles. "Thanks, Jo. I'll help you make something nice for it."

Of course. It should arrive in a few hours...

I stop at the egg and inject air mana into it until it's full again.

[Can you set me a twice-daily reminder to do that?]

Confirmed. All the documentation you requested has been completed but not filed. Retirement requires a reason for the request. Corporate requires a corporation name and business purpose...

After getting dressed, Aria and I head to the table for some breakfast.

[The business stuff can wait. As for the reasons...] I look at Aria across the table and think, [I am going into business on my own and am starting a family.]

Aria beams at me.

Completed...

I take a deep breath and say this next part out loud. "Jo, request a remote meeting with Command at UFH SF HQ. The armory must have a secure communication facility for rent. Find it and arrange it for whatever meeting time HQ demands."

Aria reaches over and holds my hand with a sympathetic smile.

[Jo, what does the NanoNet have regarding my date of activation?]

Checking your records on NanoNet . . . It appears that your activation is listed as two days ago. All of your hidden data remains hidden, including your class. Fortunately, NanoNet never shows species publicly as all Specials are human. On the other hand, your level is showing as one so they will likely inquire how you leveled up so fast . . .

It's weird watching Aria eat and not being hungry.

[Well, there is no reason to hide anymore, so go ahead and use NanoNet as you see fit. If at any time our confidential information is put at risk, shut it down.]

Confirmed . . .

"After breakfast, we'll do the gym and then the dojo. That appointment set up for Aria, Jo?"

Confirmed . . .

"Thank you," Aria says with a smile.

Returning it, I ask, "I assume you wish to continue at the range in the evenings?"

"Definitely," she says with a firm nod.

You have a meeting with UFH SF HQ at 10:00 in Whyatt Armory's secure facility room eight . . .

[Thanks, Jo.]

Aria says, "You'll do fine, Vic."

The gym helps me focus my mind and prepare for the meeting. I think I know how it is going to go, but if Nicci is there, this could be even more complicated. I need a plan, and I am struggling to come up with one I am happy with. I will need to at least partially play this as it comes, especially with some of the information I will be sharing and requests I will be making. And to whom.

CHAPTER 97

10:00 hours arrives, and I actually feel mostly prepared. And somewhat relieved. There are people I trust, at least as much as I trust anyone, Aria excluded. If I stay focused, this can be more beneficial than risky.

I am escorted through the armory's security facilities until a door with the number eight next to it is waiting.

[Once inside, do nothing and say nothing, Jo. Please.]

Okay, Vic . . .

I take a breath, touch the crystal pad, and enter.

The secure room is three-meters cubed with dark gray walls, a square metal table with a dim white crystal in the center, four chairs, a small crystal pad both near the door to exit, and a large one on the wall for display. As soon as the doors close, the privacy inscriptions flash along the walls. The room that is supposed to be empty has Nicci in one chair and my KH commander in the other. So much for a remote crystal meeting.

The short-but-burly man sitting to the left says, "Good morning, Lieutenant Commander Victory. Thank you for reaching out to us. Please sit." Nicci is smiling at me the whole time. I used to find it friendly and cute. Now I wonder how real it is. I still don't see any deception, but she could simply be better at hiding it than I am at finding it.

"Thank you, sir." I walk all the way around the table and sit at the seat opposite the table. There is no way I am sitting with my back to the door.

"Hey, Vic. Nice hair," Nicci says in her usual friendly manner. I have it up in a ponytail for this "meeting."

I simply nod and say, "Thank you, Nicci."

"Lieutenant Commander Victory, you have returned to us after some absence. Can you tell me why you took so long to report in and why you haven't filed an AAR?" AAR is military speak for After Action Report. In short, an AAR is me saying what happened. No hyperbole or bullshit. Just a listing of the events and facts.

I am looking at him and not at Nicci. "I was concerned about operational security, sir."

"I see. We know that you failed in your mission—a first for you for as long I have been the KH commander. The troll mercenary and his company have been causing quite a bit of trouble. Did you know they attacked the peninsula-side bridge fort?"

That surprises me. That place is, well, a fortress.

"I did not, sir. That is quite surprising given the fort's defenses. It would take a major incursion to even threaten that facility."

Nicci pipes up now. "Normally, you'd be right, but someone interfered with or disabled all the MagiTech liquid steel equipment on the base. Including that worn by its defenders."

Commander Braskins continues. "Thankfully, we had several non-MagiTech defensive measures at the facility. With those, and support from the fort on the other side of the bridge, we were able to fight off the invading raiders with relative ease."

"That is excellent, sir. The UFH should never put all its coins in one spatial bag, after all."

"MagiTech has provided quality technology to the UFH for many decades, as you know. You helped us test a number of them after all."

A warning. "True enough, Nicci."

"You said you were concerned about operational security, Lieutenant Commander Victory. Please explain." He refuses to call me Vic. Commander Louise Braskins came from the UFH forces in old Europe. His somewhat nasally accent and pretentious tone help affirm his very by-the-book approach to command. Everything as it should be, lined up just right. As I have "secretly" shared with Nicci, that is just fine as far as I'm concerned, as long as he keeps that rod up his ass away from actual operations. Someone like that is great as the face of the KH to report up. Especially since KH doesn't exist publicly. As an added benefit, that kind of "sharing" can build closer relationships which can be exploited later.

"No, sir."

His precisely trimmed eyebrows raise. "No? Lieutenant Commander Victory, explain why not."

"Not while a MagiTech representative is in the room, sir."

"Vic?" Nicci sounds exasperated. I understand. When I first started being loaned to them, I put her and her team through quite a struggle with what I was and was not allowed to say in their presence. I always erred on the side of less. Of course, that was all intentional and laid the groundwork for an event such as this and what is about to come.

"I see." The commander is no fool, as Nicci knows. Stuffy, strict, and a precisionist, sure. But unintelligent he is not. "Is there any preliminary report you can share?"

"I could not determine the efficacy of the new munition" is all I say.

"Why not, Vic?" Nicci asked.

"Because I never fired it."

"Why didn't you fire it, Vic?" She is getting frustrated with me.

"That is classified."

Nicci lets out an exasperated sigh. "Commander, can you please order Vic to report?"

Commander Braskins is staring at me without even giving Nicci a glance. "I am afraid I cannot do that, Miss Purle. I need to see the report before I can authorize declassification. I assure you, *Lieutenant* Commander Victory will provide all the details MagiTech requires. Like you, I am not pleased with the outcome of this mission, and we will make sure that the record shows the mission failure is not due to MagiTech equipment. Now if you could excuse us" —he is glaring at me hard— "I have some personal debriefing to do."

"Of course, commander," Nicci says as she gets up, puts her hand on the pad, and leaves the room. When the door closes, the walls flash again and Braskins leans back in his chair.

"What the fuck happened, Vic?" And the stuffy, uptight asshat is gone.

CHAPTER 98

Those of us in the Knight Hunters are specialists. My specialty is infiltration, assassination, and targeted destruction. I am the Knight's Sword. Braskins is the Knight's Tabard. He is the face that everyone sees and recognizes and shows those in the know what they expect to see. He is also a quality strategist. Additionally, we have a Shield in charge of intelligence and counterintelligence, a Steed in charge of procurement, equipment, and transportation, an Armor in charge of defensive action missions, and one other. Actually, there is another in addition to that, but it has been empty for a while.

To the commander's question, I answer simply with, "Noctis Venandi."

Braskins become still. A few seconds later, he slowly reaches and touches the crystal on the table. I move to sit opposite Brasknins as it flashes white, and we wait in silence for about ninety seconds. Then a man appears on the crystal display pad.

Baskins and I both jump to our feet, salute, and say "Admiral."

Admiral Josia Michial Drunchen III is the last of the current Knight Hunters. Yes, Michial. He is the true commander and one whom only a handful know exists. He lives full-time in some hidden location somewhere and is the Knight's Honor.

"Sit down, you two. And quit it with all that pomp and shit." Of course, we never will and he knows it. But he likes to complain about it anyway.

"Thank you, admiral," Braskins and I say. We say "admiral," but he has never worn a military uniform in my presence once.

Admiral Drunchen asks, "What the fuck happened, Sword?"

I find it funny that what he asked is, word for word with the exception of my name, the same question Braskins asked. "I believe we have a security breach, sir. I believe someone or someones at Magitech are attempting to sell out humanity."

"Fuck!" yells the admiral. "We've fucking suspected something is going on with that fucking company." I don't think I have ever heard anyone swear as much as I do Drunchen. It's impressive. It is also a KH-only thing. The rest of the military leadership is pretty much like Braskin's public persona. But not the admiral. As we say, Honor runs his shop how he fucking sees fit. "Shield has been looking into them for a fucking while and is very suspicious. I fucking knew she was fucking right but we cannot fucking find anything hard. Their shit is fucking everywhere in the UFH. Fuck!" That last word is exclaimed quite loudly.

I pop into his profanity-riddled rant. "Admiral. If you bring her in, I can file my report verbally now. This is Kraken-level and includes personal matters."

"Fucking fuck! Are you fucking calling for a Kraken-level action?"

"Not yet. But admiral . . ." I pause for a few seconds. "Noctis Venandi" is how I finish.

"Shitballs, Sword! Shit fuck shit asshole fucker . . ."

Oh, he's on a roll now. I side-eye Braskins, and he takes the hint.

Interrupting the foul-mouthed tirade, Braskins says, "Admiral. Perhaps we should call Shield?"

"Fucking fine." The admiral looks down and touches something.

A moment later, the visual on the pad splits, and the mana crystal starts to share a signal with two mana pathways. So far, the highest we've been able to effectively create is four secure mana connections. Something to do with crystal mana density blah, blah technobabble blah, blah. The meaning is, high-security calls cannot include more than four source mana connections. It is a pain for secure communication and action planning.

On the new half is a screen with a woman who is blurry but clearly wearing a mask and hood. None of KH except Honor has seen everyone's face. Braskins knows mine and Armor's. We all know the admiral and Braskins. In fairness, we think we're seeing the admiral's face, but who knows. What they see from my end is a blurry picture that is only in grays. No long blue hair, which is too bad. Shield has a good fashion sense, and I'd like her to take on how to do something other than a ponytail.

Like all of us on the call, the voice is modulated for secrecy. "Sword, how nice to see you again."

"Shield, a pleasure." We give each other shit whenever we meet. It's a friend thing. Or at least as much as people like us have friends.

The admiral pipes up. "Shut the fuck up, you two. Shield, Sword has called for you. He claims to have information to share regarding a potential Kraken-level event."

"Oh, fuck. Sword, what the fuck did you do this time?" Yeah, we Knights are a foul-mouthed bunch.

"Shield, I have a verbal report to file. It contains personal information as well. Please be discreet in your inquiries."

"Affirmative, Sword. I'm curious now. You never have anything personal to report. Ever. What the shit is going on?"

I take a breath and say, "I activated my nanos."

Shield waves her hand and says, "We know that, Sword, we're not amateurs. Stop dragging it out and tell us the real news."

I glance at the admiral and say, "I have the highest nanomachine density in recorded history. I activated at 728 parts per million."

The admiral, who was in the middle of drinking what I assumed was his usual tea with a splash of something, spits it out and starts coughing.

After getting his breathing under control, he yells, "Fucking shit, Sword! You fucking waited until I was mid-fucking-drink to fucking drop that on me, didn't you, you little fucking shit?"

Smiling slightly, I say, "Of course not, admiral."

Shield interrupts. "Are you serious Sword? 728? That isn't just the fucking highest. That is at least four fucking times as high as the highest recorded."

"Confirmed, Shield. It's at 738 now, but that isn't what matters. Here is what happened. And you won't fucking believe at least half of it."

I tell the story from the beginning. The only parts I leave out are my species, that I have a class, my immortality, my visits with the twins, how advanced Jo's personality is, and the details of Aria and my intimacy. Some things are to be shared only in the right circumstances. Everything else is on the table for information gathering by Shield. She needs it all to provide the right recommendations.

The admiral starts swearing up a storm again. Shield interrupts and says, "This is really fucking huge, Sword. I am going to be researching this for quite a while to make recommendations. This plus other intel gathered points directly at MagiTech. But not where within it."

Braskins pipes up. "I have concerns about the slavery ring and experiments happening in this city. Shield, see what you can find about instances in other cities."

I interrupt and say, "I agree with Tabard. Admiral, I request freedom protocols."

The admiral asks, "Oh? To what level?"

"I'm going to retire publicly. MagiTech will know I cannot be trusted, so infiltration there is pointless. I will start my own private company for front-facing actions. They will consider me a non-entity and pay little if any attention. I can use that to figure out what is going on. I will absolutely terminate the abomination that is the slavery ring in Sea Saddle City and use that to trace wherever that takes me. My instincts are telling me there are connections between that and our eventual target. I simply need to follow the trail.

"I also have deep concerns about that attempt on the fort. Why would the troll king's group launch that attack? Everyone knows we have MiliMech defenses all over the fortifications throughout UFH. So why attack? Did the raiders do it unilaterally, were they misinformed, or is something going to happen to MiliMech? And I also suspect that the elven Riverwing clan events that led that family to me are connected somehow. Something is going on here, and it is fucking huge. Kraken-level. And if we don't do something about it, humanity may not survive it."

There is silence for a few seconds when Shield asks me, "Your gut is guiding you again, isn't it, Sword?"

"It is. When I focus on the outcome, I get a feeling of deep dread, conflict, and death on a global scale. I cannot get more specific, as you know."

The admiral says only "Well, shit."

I continue as if he hasn't spoken. "I need to share something else, but you may not ask questions. This is one-direction information flow."

Shield says, "Sword?"

"I am level one. As you know." I see Braskins, the admiral, and blurry Shield nod.

"I have a class. And it is singularity level." Absolute silence. I continue. "Something is coming. I know it."

The admiral says, "All resources on this, Shield. Hold nothing back. We need information more than any action right now. Sword, what do you need?"

"I need six things. Leviathan-level clearance to MilNet at a minimum. I need my retirement approved. I need my business application with MilSpec access approved to the same level clearance. I need authorization to call on my account at BoGH. I need authorization to grant my nanomachine system consciousness auth codes to connect to Noctis Venandi. And I need authorization to bring in some specific individuals up to wyvern level so I can build my team."

I stop and let the admiral think through my requests. He always takes time on requests.

I glance at Braskins then back at the display and say, "Also, sir, I'd like authorization to evaluate someone for Knight's Aura."

Braskins clenches his fists on the table and says, "Sword..."

"Be careful, Sword. Are you sure?"

"I am. This is an evaluation only. I admit I am somewhat compromised on this individual, so I will simply make a recommendation, document my observations, and turn it over to Shield and Honor."

The admiral asks, "Sword, are these your emotions speaking or is it something else?"

I lean forward and say, "I believe it to be something else but, as I said, I am compromised, so I could be wrong."

The admiral sits back in his chair and drinks what is left of his tea. He touches something. "All your requests are approved except the last. Let me get back to you. Tabard, you will stay please when we are done."

I say, "Thank you, admiral."

He nods and says, "Shield, what do you need?"

After a head tilt, her response is "Clear the way for me, admiral. This will cause a shitstorm, and I will have to push some folks. Including two mutual associates of ours in the UFH leadership who are attached at the hip to MagiTech. I also may need access to Sword in person for a leviathan-level discussion."

"Done and approved. Once Tabard leaves their location, you are free to visit. Use Steed to avoid notice."

"Thank you, admiral."

"Tabard, you need to handle MagiTech. If those fuckers get a scent, we're blown."

Braskins, with his usually strategic mind, says, "I have an idea. Why don't we paint Sword's retirement as less than voluntary due to this mission failure? His service and reputation would allow us the freedom to give him a parting gift of sorts, hence the MilSpec business license. This will also reinforce that he is not a threat to MagiTech."

Smiling, the admiral says, "Well done, Tabard. Do it. Sword, you are being thrown under the grav cart again. Sorry."

I couldn't care less.

"Affirmative, admiral. Shield, what level of trust do you have in the Whyatts? Specifically Filckerson Clinkerforth Whyatt and his sister Felindra?"

She responds with "I'll get back to you. We can discuss in detail when I arrive."

I nod. "Thank you. That is all for me, admiral."

The admiral says, "I will bring Armor and Steed up to speed. This is why we exist. Don't fuck it up. Noctis Venandi."

"Noctis Venandi," we all say in response.

Braskins touches the crystal, and Shield vanishes. I stand, salute, and move to the door. The screen goes black, but not off, when I touch the pad and exit.

CHAPTER 99

May I speak? . . .

I am being walked away from room eight and out of the secure floor.

[Yes. Thank you for staying quiet.]

Of course. That explains so much, Vic . . .

[Does it?]

Don't be a dunderhead . . .

I smile. Reaching the pad, I touch the orb and return to our suite.

[Is Aria still at the dojo?]

Yes. She is struggling on her first day and not pleased with it.

[I would imagine not. I remember when I started. I was five or six maybe? I sucked at it and was very upset. Of course, I wasn't in a dojo, and it was definitely not for practice.]

What can you tell me about what just happened? . . .

[Did you receive the auth to Noctis Venandi? If so, do you have updated clearance to MilNet?]

I did and I do . . .

[I do not want to bias your information, so use the new clearance. You should have copy clearance now too so conduct a full data set update as resources are available. While you're in there, rerun your research on metal and other affinities. And quicksilver too.]

Starting search . . .

[I'll ask Aria's help on naming our new company. I have no idea what to call it.]

How about something with Knight and/or Sword in it? . . .

[Oh. That is an interesting idea. It has certain implications but it's a place to start.]

You do realize that pre-Invasion, Noctis meant night as the opposite of day, not like the warrior...

I chuckle. "Yes. It was something of a joke to the founder I think. Everyone knows it's wrong, but it is so ingrained now, nobody cares. In fact, I think some of the teams like the pun."

What about you?...

[Does it affect any mission in any way?]

I see. In other words, you couldn't give gryphon shit what it's called. The hide arrived while you were gone...

[Excellent.]

I walk quickly to the pad and check it out. It is a piece of folded, silvery leather and quite large. I pick it up and unfold it onto the dinner table. It is so big the edges are hanging off all the sides onto the floor. Looking at the shiny material, I think [Inspect].

Name:	Earth/Metal Mana-Infused Mountain Goat Hide
Description:	The tough hide from an infused mountain goat can be used to craft armor and accessories particularly effective defending against piercing and bludgeoning attacks. The herbivores from which this type of hide was taken spend most of their lives climbing up and down steep mountains and ravines. The particular goat from which this hide was taken rubbed against the stone of the mountain as well as the many metal deposits at that location. This unfortunate goat took a bad step and fell to its death at which point it was found and skinned.
Condition:	Excellent
Risk Assessment:	N/A
Value:	Metal-infused hides are rare and valuable to any with the ability to work leather. This will find an excellent price on the market in any location.

[I find what the system decides to share and when fascinating. Can you send a note to the seller asking if we can buy the location from them? I doubt we'll get an affirmative, but it is worth a shot. If they refuse, run a search for likely nearby locations of mountain goat herds.]

They claimed to have killed it in the sales advert...

[I don't care in the least. I want more goats and possibly access to those metal deposits. Did my mining set arrive? And does leatherworking require its own sewing tools or does my tailoring kit meet the need.]

Yes on the mining kit. Normal sewing kits do not include a set of leatherworking tools. However, yours is a premium kit that came at a premium price...

[Set up a meeting with a local BoGH branch manager about withdrawing substantial funds from a personal account and setting up a business account. Aim for five days.]

I'm sorry, Vic, your involuntary retirement has just been announced...

[Whatever. I don't give a shit about that.]

Aria limps in with an angry look on her face, covered in sweat and bruises. I wince. She doesn't say a word. Just painfully makes her way into her room and the door slides closed behind her.

[That bad?]

Seems so...

Should I go check on her or let her have her space? Sigh. I don't think now is the time to go with how I would manage someone who is only a trainee.

Given what I have learned, I do not believe the facility being scheduled for review this week is appropriate. I would like your permission to cancel and refine the search criteria...

[Do it.]

Confirmed. What level of renovation are you willing to accept?...

[Fuck if I know. Hell, if it is better to build it ourselves, let's just buy the land and do that. But we need the right location.]

What location criteria do you have?...

[Good question. I'm not sure. Let me think about that. For now, use your judgment based on what you know.]

Confirmed. Search commencing...

I don't hear anything from Aria, so I decide to risk it and see if I can help. I knock on the door separating our rooms and say, "Aria?"

Nothing.

[Open the door slowly so she has the chance to tell me to go away.]

It gradually slides aside. There's nobody visible, but I hear a little bit of movement and water in the bathroom. I go to the bathroom door and knock gently. "Aria? Can I help?"

Silence.

"Aria?"

I hear her slightly muffled reply. "Come on in, Vic."

I put my hand on the pad, and the door slides aside. I step in and see Aria in the tub up to her neck in steaming water.

I smile and say, "Hey. I don't mean to disturb you. I just want to know if I can help."

Looking at me, she ducks under and comes back up dripping and swipes her blonde locks out of her face. I notice swollen and bloody knuckles. "Feel like flexing your life magica muscles?"

I smile sympathetically and say, "Sure, I'm happy to."

Exiting the bathroom, I strip down, just leaving my clothes on the chair. I return and climb into the tub. I slowly float to her without touching. Now that I am closer, I see bruises all over her, split lips, and a nice shiner forming. Wow. That was bad.

"Can I touch you?

She offers me a weak, slightly swelling smile and nods. "Please."

I lay my hand on her shoulder, close my eyes, and send my life magica into her. I ask it to help her bruises and pain. She is suffering, and I plead with it to help her heal.

A golden glow suffuses both of us, and after a few seconds, I can hear a sigh from her.

"That is so much better. Thank you."

The mana tells me she still has bruises all over her skin and muscles and one or two pretty bad bone bruises. Nothing hard enough to break anything, but enough to leave the memory and learn for next time. I can recall a number of broken bones and knife wounds that taught me how to fight. The early stages are bad if they are done well. This is combat, not dancing, and certainly not a game. Aria needs to be prepared to fight, kill, and survive, not play at those things. Pain, more than almost anything, teaches.

I keep sending my magica, and I feel Aria press her body against my chest.

Not helping me focus. I try to not get distracted and let the mana tell me what else is injured. She has some contusions on the top of her feet and her knuckles and an eye that will get hard to see out of if it isn't handled. Wow. Bad day. No wonder she was so angry.

I go through each and every single injury and heal them. Then I let the mana go and lean back against the tub wall.

She follows and curls up on my lap. "Thank you. That is so much better."

"Of course. I know that the early weeks are bad. When you learn this way, it is bad at first. Back when I still had scars, I could have shown you some from my early days learning to defend myself. It was to avoid starving to death, so that is different, but in this world, you learn or you die. All I can tell you is that if you hang in there and suffer a bit for the time it takes, you get good enough to give back eventually. And the pleasure of seeing your tormentors on their back or face brings such joy to make it all worthwhile."

"You needed to fight to eat?"

"Yes. When I was young. I don't really like talking about it."

She nods into my neck; that and my head are the only thing not submerged. "Hey, Vic?"

I close my eyes, lie my head back and rub her wet hair. "Hmm?"

She sits up, lifts my head and kisses me quite deeply. She breaks away and says, "You helped me. So now you get my thanks."

And she dunks her head under the water and thanks me.

CHAPTER 100

Over her dinner, Aria asks me, "How did it go with MagiTech and your HQ?"

Right, because of the whole beaten to a pulp and, ahem, aftermath, I never got a chance to catch her up. "Officially, I am being retired for screwing up and such. Unofficially, I have the freedom to start my own company and investigate what is going on."

"Oh. Are you okay with that?" She looks concerned.

"Oh, sure. I have never cared what others thought of me except how it applies to a mission. I believe that is one of the reasons I make a good operator. Mission first." I put my hands on the table and say, "Speaking of which, I need your help naming my . . . err, our company. For reasons that I cannot yet tell you, we should have variations of either the word 'Sword' or 'Knight' in it."

I have an answer from the goat hide seller. He agreed to sell the location for another five gold . . .

"I can't ask why those words?"

[See if you can talk him down to three. Don't give in too easy or he'll ask for more.]

Confirmed . . .

I shake my head. "I'm sorry. Not yet. I'm hoping eventually, but not yet."

She looks down at her plate. "Is that going to happen a lot, you not able to tell me things?"

He agreed to four . . .

[Approved.]

I sigh. "I hope it happens as little as possible. But yes, occasionally I will have to hide some things from you. I'm sorry. All I can say is that I won't lie. If I can't tell you something, I will say I can't tell you."

Procurement complete. Map data acquired and added. Would you like me to add it to your mission log? . . .

[Yes.]

She silently eats for a few minutes.

I say softly, "Aria, this is one of those things being in a relationship with me means." I force myself to choke out "It's not too late to change your mind."

A cold feeling is spreading throughout my body. I look down, angry at myself. I should never have let it get this far. Why is everything blurry? Damnit.

She lets out a breath, stands, walks to my side, leans down, gently lifts my head with her hands and looks directly in my crystal azure eyes with her liquid gold. "Not a chance; I can accept it. I shouldn't have expected that sort of thing to change. Just be patient with me. Okay?"

I slump in relief, close my eyes, and lean my forehead against hers. "Sorry. I didn't realize it would feel this way."

She moves my arms to make room and sits on my lap. "Love isn't easy, Vic."

"I'm getting that. Will it always be like this? So up and down?"

She tilts her head up and kisses me tenderly. When she pulls back, she says, "I hope not. I've experienced some things before, but never a relationship like this. Maybe it gets easier?"

"I hope so."

She kisses me again and then stands and returns to her seat and returns to eating. "So what kind of company?"

I blink at her, trying to figure out what she means, when I recall what we were talking about before.

"Oh. Right. We are going to be a mercenary company with a focus on targeted strikes against the orc and kin. We will also pursue certain other concerns such as slavery, attempts to subvert humanity, and assisting our extraplanar allies as possible. These will be approached in a military manner. In other words, terminal. I have not figured out how we will be making money yet. Maybe we'll be a not-for-profit entity. I have no idea."

She nods as I get to the end. "Human business and laws make no sense to me."

I chuckle and respond. "To be honest, me neither, and I have little interest in it. I'll be hiring people to take care of that side of things."

"What sort of methods will we be using to complete missions?"

I give her a big smile. "That is a great question. I caught that you slipped in a mission prep term. Nicely done." She smiles through her food. "We will primarily be covert operators like me. Infiltration, assassination, precision strikes, that sort of thing. We will also have at least one crafter besides me —if you can call me that—and some medical staff for defense and rescue missions. You'll probably be a part-time participant in that group if you're willing. Additionally, we'll need someone to market us to the various factions, tribes, companies, clans, etc. That is pretty much as far as I have gotten on it."

She nods again, wipes her hands and mouth, and says, "I'll think about it. Let's sit on the balcony and enjoy the evening together. Then we can take care of Eggy."

Happy to do so, I stand and offer her my hand. We walk to the balcony, I sit down on my newly replaced loveseat, and she curls up on my lap. The last loveseat sort of burnt up. She reaches and grabs a loose lock of my azure hair and twirls it around her finger. I rub my hands down her head and into her silky hair. We both just watch the night.

After a few minutes, she asks, "Have you and Jo discussed leveling up again?"

[Jo, go ahead.]

We have, Aria. We can level at any time. In fact, we can go all the way past five with the available essence. The issue is right now Vic has a low saturation rate. He hasn't really been doing anything since the last level. Sure, he could level, but what would it give him? . . .

I speak up then. "My thought is to initiate a new daily plan. Like you have to learn new skills, so do I. I need to learn how to use my new spearstaff when it arrives. And I have a lot of work to do to start a company. You are going to need to get acquainted with your new crossbows. And of course, your hand-to-hand and eventually melee weapons training. Then if you get far enough along, wilderness training. It is going to be a busy six months.

"Morning exercises are a must, but they may be shorter to fit in the weapons training. I expect we will both feel quite drained and overwhelmed by it. Will you take that on with me?" I place my finger under her chin and gently tilt her head up to look at me. "It is completely fine if you don't want to, you know. I'd rather have you happy doing something else than miserable just because you think I want you to. Just because I find that kind of thing fun, doesn't mean you have to."

Sitting up, she straddles my lap and, turning her body to face me, she leans in and gives me a gentle but long kiss. Pulling back, she says, "I'm in. After all, we're both life magica. We heal each other." Grinning, she continues,

"And then thank each other."

I chuckle. "Sounds great."

She returns to curling in my lap, and we sit like that for another hour before going in. In my room I lay the hide on the bed.

[Jo, do I have any meetings tomorrow?]

You do. Tomorrow morning is Master Stonetamer and tomorrow afternoon is Mr. Whyatt . . .

[Right. I have the next day off though, right?]

That is correct . . .

Looking at Aria I ask, "You met Grace, right?"

She nods. "I did. I like her. She has a dirty mouth."

I laugh. "Yes, she does."

To all three of them, I send the message: [The day after tomorrow, we are going to take Grace for a ride in the country to see some mountain goats. Grace, are you ready for your maiden voyage with all your new upgrades? I can't wait to see you.]

#I am very excited, Host Vic. How often does a maiden get to experience her first time twice, after all? . . .

What is it with you two? . . .

Aria starts laughing.

[Jo, pick up two mountain climbing sets so they arrive before we leave on our little trip. And don't let me forget the mining gear in case there is any good ore.]

Confirmed . . .

I kick off our next project. "Okay, let's create a new cocoon for Eggy. Remember, it needs to be able to grow with the egg and have slots for these air crystals that Jo thoughtfully purchased. If you want to bling it up that's fine, I could use the tailoring and sewing. Also . . ." I dump all the feathers from the osprey and a few small pieces of quicksilver ore onto the pile of cloth and hide. "We should incorporate these so they are touching Eggy. Everything we can give helps. Now while you start thinking how you want to boss me around, I'll give Eggy some air mana."

Aria huffs and says, "I am just concerned that Eggy will have your terrible fashion sense if I don't take care of it while young."

I smile while leaning over the egg. "Yes, dear."

Good boy, Vic...

#Miss Aria, I am impressed how well you have trained him in such a short time. Can we talk later?...

Yep. That's me, badass special forces assassin and covert operative sniper, wrapped around the proverbial finger of the three ladies in my life. It's a good thing I thrive on sarcasm and wisassery.

Touching the egg, I inject mana and then head back. Aria has laid everything out. She gives me specific instructions and corrects me when I am doing something wrong. By that I mean, "Stop, you'll make it ugly if you do that and stunt Eggy's growth." I'm smiling the entire time—I enjoy when Aria shows her aggressive side. Don't judge.

When we unwrap Eggy and take it out to give it its new "outfit," I see the chain from those months ago that I completely forgot about. Back when I first emptied the nest, I noticed this thin silvery chain woven into the sticks and branches.

"Well, hello again." Aria looks at me with a question, and I point at the chain. "I totally forgot about this."

She just shrugs. Whatever it is, she cannot be distracted from giving Eggy the perfect little wrapping.

I look at the chain and think [Inspect].

Well, that's odd...

CHAPTER 101

Name:	Totally Normal and Boring Chain
Description:	Yep, this is a totally normal and boring chain. Ignore it completely. It is totally not worth your time. Just move on. Off you go now.
Condition:	Absolutely horrendous
Risk Assessment:	This item is too worthless to have any risk
Value:	Utterly, completely, and totally worthless. You should move onto something nice.

[Um, Jo?]

I see it, Vic. That is . . . unusual . . .

[Is there a projector for Specials so I can share their screens with non-Specials?]

I will research that . . .

"Hey, Aria. Do you have the equivalent to the [Inspect] skill? Some sort of item analysis ability?"

She raises her head from blinging Eggy. "Sort of, but mine is not really effective. Why?"

"Can you come here please?"

She looks confused but comes.

I point. "Use it on that chain."

She looks at the chain and her eyes flash gold almost too fast to notice. Then she shrugs, "It seems to just be some normal and boring chain to me."

Vic . . .

"Normal and boring you say. Okay, thank you. Sorry to interrupt." She sighs and goes back to her egg beautifying project.

[There's no way the words she used were random.]

I agree . . .

[I'm going to poke it. See if you can read anything.]

Don't you remember what happened last time? Is this a good idea? . . .

[Fair point. But what do you recommend then? You know I can't leave an unknown possibly harmful object in my home. With Aria. And it's right next to the egg.]

I understand Vic, but I don't think this is a good idea . . .

[I'm poking it.]

"Aria, I'm just letting you know I'm poking the totally normal and boring chain." And I do. I feel a slight tingle.

[So?]

That was . . . different . . .

[Helpful, Jo.]

Unravel it and put it on Eggy when Aria is done beautifying it . . .

I very carefully unwind the delicate chain from the nest. It takes a good five minutes to just to get it free without damaging it . . .

[Jo?]

Let this one be, Vic . . .

Fascinating. As curious as I am, I know she would say something if she could. Some intricacies of the system are beyond me and I either trust Jo or I don't. I look over at Aria in the midst of her work. I trust Jo more than anyone . . . and with the most precious things in my life.

"How are we doing?"

Smiling to herself and her work, Aria answers, "Just about done."

She has arranged all the cloth, hide, feathers, stones, and quicksilver ore beautifully. The egg almost looks like it could take flight and glow its way to its destination. She really has a gift for this.

"That looks amazing. You did a fantastic job."

She beams at me.

She wipes her hands and goes into my bathroom, stripping on the way. "I'm taking a bath before bed."

ACTIVATION

Once she's gone, I stuff the chain in so all of it touches the egg and do a quick [Inspect].

Name:	Metal/Air Mana-Mutated Peregrine Falcon Egg
Description:	Normal mana-fused falcons are large and very aggressive hunters. They hunt mostly other birds but sometimes will hunt smaller mammals. Their favorite method is to climb high into the sky and then stoop, or dive downwards at 300 kph or more and knock prey out of the sky. This egg contains a still-viable peregrine falcon fetus. This egg was exposed to a massive influx of metal mana during a particularly vulnerable part of its growth. The mother abandoned this egg when its home, the tree under which it was found, was moved from the rainforest. The egg fell to the ground and due to the metal mutation, it did not break. The tree had been inadvertently protecting, feeding, and keeping alive this creature for over 15 years when an illness caused the tree to eject the egg for the safety of both. The egg's condition has improved dramatically thanks to the influx of mana-rich metals, pure air mana, and mana stones. However, it cannot grow or hatch with what is available to it now. Further materials are required to increase viability. Note: There is the possibility of enhancing the abilities of the fetus if fed the correct mana-rich materials. Countdown to fetus death: N/A **Countdown to fetus hatching: N/A**
Condition:	Stable
Risk Assessment:	N/A
Value:	At its current health, the value of this egg is moderate. If it can be enhanced or offer assured viability, the

> value will likely be high. Such a rare mutation is an excellent object of bonding or study.

Definitely better than last time. But it says it still needs more and different materials to grow. Almost certainly that means metal affinity. And that is what the day after tomorrow is for. I strip and head into the bath after Aria to show her how much I appreciate how lovely the egg looks.

CHAPTER 102

The next day, Aria and I start the morning with a strength-heavy workout, which makes us both tired and Aria sweaty. We return, and she washes up to say hello to Master Steeltamer.

He arrives on time, as always, and Aria and I are waiting on him. As soon as he walks in the door, she gives him a hug and kiss on the cheek, which causes him to get all flustered. It takes most of my focus not to laugh.

"Welcome back to our home Master Steeltamer. Please join us at the table. Have you had breakfast?"

He does his usual grump routine with me. "Aye, boy. I ate."

I nod. "I'll give you and Aria a little private time. I have a bit of work to do on the balcony. Feel free to just order any food or drink you like."

He's about to argue when Aria interrupts. "Thanks, Vic."

She drags the dwarf into a seat and sits opposite. Then she starts chattering away about something-or-other. As long as they are happy.

On the balcony with a glass of juice, I ask Jo for some catch-up.

[Did you ever hear back on the Hyoto training request?]

Yes. They have asked for some time to look you up and will get back to me "when they're done"...

[I see. Well, that sucks. I really want to start my training.]

It is a rare toolset with equally rare experts willing to train...

[I suppose if we have to we can just focus on the staff and ignore the rest. Not optimal but better than not training at all. What else we got?]

You have some alerts from your crafting sessions with Aria for Eggy...

[Excellent, let's see.]

New skill activated. Passive skill [Leatherworking] now available for use...

New profession activated. **Tailor** *is now available to be selected. Note: Only a single primary and two secondary professions can be active at one time.*

Skill updated. Passive skill [Leatherworking] has leveled from 0 to 2...

Skill updated. Passive skill [Sewing] is now level 7...

Skill updated. Passive skill [Tailoring] has leveled from 5 to 7...

[Looks like leatherworking was the missing skill. Great news. I wonder why leatherworking is required for tailoring.]

The prerequisites are defined by the system. Anything beyond that is unknown...

[Whatever. What else do we have?]

Everything you ordered for tomorrow's goat hunt should arrive well in advance of your planned departure after breakfast...

#*I'm very excited to get out and about. It's boring down here...*

[I'm sorry you've been stuck there so long, Grace. I promise, now that we are active we'll be traveling a lot more.]

#*Thank you, Host Vic. I look forward to it...*

[Jo, what about the land for the facility?]

Unless you can provide me more criteria, I am working on my own. It is taking a little time...

[How about if I tell you it needs to support multiple underground floors, numerous secret entrances and exits, the ability to support flying vehicles and beast mounts, have enough space for defensive structures that will do as little harm to innocents as possible, and be a facility hardened from a tactical magica strike?]

I see. Well, that certainly will aid me in narrowing down the search...

[The research on MilNet?]

I have located references to numerous additional affinities: space, sound, poison, metal, spirit, and smoke so far...

[Wow. I assume all those are beast-only?]

With one exception. Space is an odd affinity since it seems to be manufactured through compression and injection of mana, forcing the creation of a spatial pocket. You did this yourself. However, there are unconfirmed reports of space being used by creatures to teleport. That last note gives credence to the fact that you have not awakened spatial affinity yet use it. Space and gravity appear directly related, as they are the only ones that can be manufactured at this time, which is why I did not list the latter separately...

As for the others, very little of the data referencing them is credible. I am attempting to filter to find anything usable, but all I see now are references to various creatures. For example, I have discovered numerous references to a creature called a "banshee." It reportedly uses the sound affinity. However, there is no record of one having been killed, nor a mana stone retrieved; thus, this cannot be validated. Its sound attack could simply be air affinity directed in a particular way. The others offer similar scenarios. Our allies are unable or unwilling to share details on what they ironically identify as "Special" affinities . . .

[That's what they call it?]

I can only go by available reports . . .

[Keep battling through it. I trust you to find something credible.]

Thank you. Your business documentation is on hold until you think of a name and determine the details of the business itself. Your meeting with the bank manager is scheduled for four days from now . . .

[Speaking of names, I suck at naming things.]

Bertha would agree . . .

[Hey! Lay off my girl. She was one of a kind!]

Let her go, Vic. She's in the blowy-uppy afterlife . . .

[Oh, Jo, she was such a sweet thing. I hope the artillery doesn't pick on her.]

I will find time for counseling on your calendar . . .

[Probably wise.]

They're wrapping up . . .

[Thanks.]

I get up and slowly make my way inside. Aria is hugging the dwarf and says to me, "I'm going to change and head to the dojo."

She walks up to me, stands on her tiptoes, kisses my cheek, and heads to her room.

I sit with the dwarf at the table and start right away, "I deeply apologize for vanishing so abruptly. I cannot tell you what happened, only that the experience made me capable of fighting the enemy for centuries to come."

Did he catch it?

His bushy eyebrows rise, emphasizing the wrinkles on his forehead. "I see. Well, good. Boy, I look forward to fighting by your side against the damn orcs for at least that long."

He got it, and he knows not to share it based on how I phrased my statement.

I nod. "I do have a few updates to share, although not nearly as much as I had hoped due to my unexpected . . . absence. I am no longer going to procure a pre-built facility. It is likely I will either be buying an empty shell I customize or annexing land and constructing it all myself. I plan on building the place to be an underground fortress with a top facade as the front-facing element of our work. In particular, I plan on having a compact but fully equipped smeltery and crafting facility. Do you think the Steeltamers will wish to be part of that?"

Grinning like a madman, he says, "Aye, boy. I think we can come to an arrangement."

"Excellent. I will inform you when I am ready to take the next step. I assume you heard through your own information network I was retired from the UFH?"

Nodding, he says angrily, "Aye. Word is they threw you on da street after ya got screwed on a mission."

"Yes. While it is not quite that simple, as I am sure you understand, that is the basic truth of it. As such, I am free to start my own business, which we have already discussed. So there is nothing stopping our plan from proceeding."

He nods.

"Due to being unable to follow up, I have made zero progress on our mutual concern regarding slavery in Sea Saddle City and elsewhere. Once I get certain things worked out, I will be taking up that charge again. I am meeting with Mr. Whyatt on that very topic this afternoon, so some progress may have been made in my absence."

He nods again.

"I also might have something for you outside of our original agreement. I possibly have intelligence on a mountain range with some metal veins. It's reliable, but only fifty-fifty so. I will get back to you in less than a week on it. Either way, I wanted you to be prepared in case something comes of it."

As soon I say the words "metal vein," his whole body twitches, and his eyes glow red with fire. Cool and creepy at the same time.

"The next six months for Aria and I will be on training, training, and more training. When not training I will be working to build my new business which takes a lot of bureaucracy and documentation in the human world. I will be keeping you informed as time passes. And that is my final update for you. What do you have for me?"

He shuffles in his seat. "Thank ya, boy. Some of our information overlaps. We be partners with ya on building yer smeltery and smithery. Including the ability to smelt quicksilver. If ya can find more ores of any kind, that will go a long way."

Playing like him, I simply nod.

"I have a few candidates who I am looking into for your team. Would help if ya could tell me what ya need."

"Very fair. I need one crafter who is youngish and talented but not too young to teach me. I also need a front-line shield warrior who will not balk at the dirty work. I will do the covert missions; what I need is someone who can beat the shit out of things while making a racket, getting hit, and keeping beating the shit out of things until I can get into position to wipe them all out. He must be able to follow orders though. That is key. These dwarves will be working with many different species and must be completely okay with that. Does that help?"

"Aye. That be perfect. I ge' back to ya on the folks so ya ca' meet."

I nod.

"The clans be meeting soon, so I be leavin'. Gunna be one er two months."

"Good fortune to you on that. Communicate with me in advance, and I will have your room ready for when you return."

"That be it for me business, boy. I see you and my granddaughter be together now. That right?"

"It is, Master Steeltamer. I am a lucky man."

He nods, "Aye, ya be." He clears his throat. It sounds like mountains falling. "Boy, you said you had no clan or family?"

I nod. "That is correct. I have been alone all my life until now. I brought myself up on the streets of a human city on the east coast of this continent called Bostonia. I joined the military as young as I could get away with and was with them until . . . well, yesterday, I suppose."

He nods. "That be admirable, boy. Dwarves see clan and family as life. And you are with my granddaughter. Our clan meets in three years fir da joining ceremony. I wanted ta let ya know if things go as hope, ya maybe ca' attend 'n ask ta become a Steeltamer."

I'm silent. That is huge. Like ginormously fucking monumentally huge. Dwarves only accept an outsider or two every few centuries.

"Master Steeltamer, I am honored and flattered beyond my ability to express. Thank you so much. If all goes according to plan, I hope we can have this discussion again in three years."

"Aye. All right, boy. I be heading back to me clan now. May the flow of the stone guide you."

We clasp hands. "And you, Master Steeltamer."

CHAPTER 103

Aria's dojo lesson is as bad as last time, but she soldiers through with less healing. She wants to experience it to a point as motivation. I can sympathize with that.

She heads to the range after lunch while I head to Mr. Whyatt's office. Please don't let Felindra be there.

After I am guided into the office, I discover to my relief it is just the male gnome.

"Welcome, Vic. Please sit."

I do and start. "I am terribly sorry, Mr. Whyatt, for my extended absence. It could not be helped, and it was definitely worth it. The mission resulted in my ability to help fight the orcs and their kin for centuries to come." I use the same tack as I did with the dwarf.

He smiles widely. "Then the leveling went even better than I had hoped. I'm pleased to hear that. Well done."

I give him the same updates I did the dwarf, and he takes them similarly. He offers gnomes to help build the facility as well. And of course wonders if one could join the team.

"The answer is definitely yes. Obviously, trustworthiness and the ability to take orders are the most important. I would be looking for an engraver and/or enchanter that can both do the job and can teach me how. It is critical they be open to working with other races. I am looking to build a small medical team as well for rescue and aid missions like the one you and I had the misfortune of participating in.

"And that leads me to my question for you. Have you made any progress on the slavery ring? Was there an outcome to the crystal devices I placed on the thugs? And were you able to learn anything from the body of the blue-suited asshat?"

Mr. Whyatt shifts in his seat. "Ah, yes. Well, we have been able to track the thugs to a number of places. I will send them to you now." He touches his wrist.

Map data received and updated . . .

"We have made very slight progress on the ledger that you provided. All I have for you is a reference to a creature-breeding program or company. We are not clear which. Here are the details."

Another tap of the wrist.

Received . . .

"I have hope we can read the remaining contents soon, although I expect realistically it will take some time. On another matter, I noticed a particular weaponry purchase that I would like to inquire about, if I may."

I nod.

"The spearstaff. Can you help me understand why you would spend enough coin to equip a battalion on a single weapon?"

I did not expect this line of inquiry, but I should have. That is a miss on my part.

"How secure is this room?" He gets up and walks to the middle of the floor. He depresses a section and says, "In ten seconds, it will be secure."

I wait.

"Clear," he says and sits back down.

"Mr. Whyatt, you are familiar with Specials enough to know we get something called a class, and that class offers specific benefits based on any number of factors, but mostly who we are and what we do."

He nods and responds. "Yes. I believe they are assigned at level five. Did you level to level five? That would be quite impressive."

"No, Mr. Whyatt, I am level one. But I was assigned a class anyway. And it is . . . unique. And I mean that using the true definition of the word 'unique.' Anyway, staves are a key to that class; that is all I can say."

"I see. Do you have any training in staves or spears?"

I sigh. "None. And you have found something of a problem. I reached out to Hyoto to see if their experts would train me. Their response involved investigating and getting back to me at some point. I am stuck, and I don't mind admitting quite frustrated by it."

"I see. I might be able to help. The Whyatts have an excellent relationship with the senior members of the Hyoto family, which is why we are their only reseller. Otherwise, they sell directly. Let me see what I can do and get back to you. What will you permit me to tell them?"

"That is an interesting question. My answer is a question in return. What would be required to get them to teach me? There are certain things which cannot get out, as you are aware. What do you think is the right answer?"

"Can I share some of your record and that you have the three affinities of the staff?"

My record . . . I suppose the non-classified parts will come out now that I have been retired. And having three affinities is rare but not impossible in a human.

"I agree."

"Can I share that the Whyatts are personally investing in you and your future?"

"Yes."

Smiling proudly, he says, "Wonderful. I believe they will agree to at least meet with you."

"Thank you, Mr. Whyatt. That is a hill giant off my shoulders."

"How else can I or Whyatt help?"

"Actually. There is something. I'm going to throw something out there and just see where it lands. I want to level up again. In fact, I could level up several more times. However, I wish to level at incredibly high saturation. If you don't know, saturation is the amount of learning, change, and mana our nanos can absorb before being reset at the leveling evolution. The more saturation, the more the Special has spent helping their nanos grow, learn, be exposed to, and thus the more gained at level evolution. Those Specials who level without high saturation are wasting an opportunity to improve. The reality is level is nothing more than a representation of mana essence gathered and the number of evolutions they have gone through. More is not necessarily better."

The gnome clasps his hands in front of him, looking very interested. "We know some of what you speak, but not much. In fact, we have been quite baffled by the concept of levels for decades now. We always felt there was more potential but could not understand how to get there."

Unsurprised, I nod. "This is likely your answer. When I leveled from zero to one, my immensely high saturation caused some amazing phenomena, one of which we have already discussed. Leveling up without fully saturated nanomachines is an unmitigated waste. I was planning on using my physical training to aid in gaining saturation, but that is long-term. I was hoping you might be able to help provide some advice to saturate sooner. I came to you with this because your people are very intelligent about mana and magica and such. Specifically, you and your family also have connections with individuals with those skills. And I trust you. At least as much as I can."

"Thank you for sharing that and for your trust. I will have to get back to you. Can I call in someone external for assistance? No names or details will be shared. It will all be theoretical."

I nod enthusiastically. "Sure. Thank you. Mr. Whyatt, if you can do this for me and the outcome is impactful, I will give you something. Something huge."

"Oh? Can you give me a hint?"

Grinning like a hunting direcat, I say, "Nope. But it is something nobody thought was possible. Something that makes that collar you gave Aria look like a child's toy."

Mr. Whyatt nearly falls out of his chair, he jerks so hard.

"Vic. I assure you, I will work hard on this. Thank you for your time."

He shakes my hand quickly and runs to his desk to work hard on it.

CHAPTER 104

I get my own dojo and range time that evening followed by Aria and I spending time working with magica. I have decided I need to put focus in three skills. Mana compression and mana splitting are the primary. And I decide to use [Mana Sight] when Aria is working so I can study both it and her and her magica.

[Mana Sight] is a fascinating active skill. I have to actively turn it on and off, which is weird. And when I do enable it, I can see the flows of mana around me. For example, Aria glows golden all the time, but when she is casting magica, she flares with it. Moreover, as she uses her life magica to heal cuts we make on my arm (it doesn't really hurt—it is just a thing we do now), I see the golden particles flowing inside her and then into me. It is quite fascinating, but I get a headache rather quickly. I'll need to practice to get the skill leveled up, according to the NanoNet. Headaches and sometimes nausea are apparently common early on.

Mana compression is self-explanatory. I try to create things with my various magicas and then compress those down as tightly as possible. Mana splitting is when I try to form more than one object at a time with my magica. What I am stuck on—and it makes me furious—is my inability to consciously control two different kinds of magica at once. I can create two fireballs or two windblades. But one windblade and one fireball causes one or the other to fail. Aria can see my frustration and gives me a kiss to calm me down. It works. I know it is a matter of practice and patience, but I am getting upset because it could be such a valuable asset. Imagine using flame and augmenting it with air as a control or enhancement.

Aria interrupts my brooding to say. "Honey, you should also practice your new lightning ability. See what it can do."

Sometimes she calls me honey. I don't know when it started, but I feel nice when she does it. I walk up to her and give her a long, deep kiss.

"Thank you. That is exactly what I need to do. Remind me to thank you properly tonight. It's too important to not deserve a reward." She smiles and bounces a little as she walks away to eat.

On the non-magica front, I decide that after dinner I am going to explore my [Living Inventory]. I don't understand what it is or how it works, but I want Aria there in case something goes wrong. She and Jo can work through any problems.

Once fed, I tell Aria my plan and she, of course, says she is happy to help, but recommends I do it in bed in case there are issues. I'm heavy. So I am naked in bed, and Aria is next to me in her large t-shirt. This one says "My Special is special" in my azure blue. Man, I love her. And she's so hot. And lying practically naked next to me.

Focus, Vic!

[Okay, Jo. How do I do this?]

How the fuck would I know? Just initiate the skill and hope for the best . . .

[You'd make a great scientist. "'Just push the button, Vic. What could go wrong?"]

Vic? . . .

[Yes, Jo?]

Just push the fucking button. Oh, I recommend closing your eyes . . .

"Okay. Here goes."

I think [Living Inventory].

And I open my eyes. Nothing happens.

"Well, that was anticlimactic."

Aria giggles.

Try a different command. Instead of just the name of the skill, try to tell it to do something. Or to look into it . . .

"Attempt number two."

Open [Living Inventory]. Nothing.

Activate [Living Inventory]. Nothing again.

Look in [Living Inventory], Show [Living Inventory], Access [Living Inventory], Initiate, Start, Launch, Move. I keep trying words and actions, and it's all becoming quite disappointing. I'm going to throw in the towel. I'll just fucking find a way to pry it open and dive in some other day. I have Aria here and . . .

I'm a fucking moron. It's a *living* inventory. When Jo tried to open it, she couldn't because she couldn't *enter* it.

I think Enter [Living Inventory]. I feel a tug, open my eyes and I find myself in a whole new world.

My bare feet sink into soft dirt. I feel wind and a cloudless blue sky. There is light but no sun. And that's all, just dirt and sky and air. I kneel down and feel the dirt. It is totally dry.

[Jo, can you hear me?] No response.

I am going to need to experiment. Can I use my magica?

Using my feet and hands, I try to send earth mana into the soil. I can. The soil is just like in the real world, except there is no life to it. It is completely dead. I try to create a bowl in the ground, asking the earth to move. While it does, the dry soil is so soft it quickly collapses back into itself. I think I need to figure out how to bring some life to this place.

Why not? I send life magica into the soil. It simply dissipates, which is what I expected.

So I have to read up on how to create an ecosystem. Awesome. Botany, here I come. Now how do I get out of here?

I close my eyes and think Exit [Living Inventory].

I open my eyes back in my bed, and Aria is looking at me with concern.

"That was interesting."

[Jo?]

I lost you there, Vic . . .

[I'm pretty sure you're not allowed in. At least at the current level.]

Aria is touching my face, looking relieved.

I smile at her and say, "I'm fine. Let me tell you and Jo what is going on. The [Living Inventory] is an entire world just sitting there. There is a sky and air but no clouds or sun. It's quite amazing. The ground is a soft dry dirt, nice to sit in. On the other hand, it is completely dead. There is not a bit of life anywhere. I think I need to start an ecosystem. Which of course, I have absolutely no idea how to do. Jo, new research project. How to build an ecosystem from nothing but lifeless dirt."

Confirmed . . .

Aria says, "Sounds fascinating. I'm glad your body stayed at least. Someday I'll hopefully be able to join you in there."

I jerk to stillness.

Looking concerned, she says, "Vic?"

Shaking myself, I said, "Sorry, love. You just triggered something. We need to advance that world. It's critical."

Aria looks at me and says, "Okay. Do we have to advance it right now?"

Then she crawls on top of me.

Nope. It can wait.

***

The next morning after Aria's breakfast, we gather all of our climbing, mining, and overall mountain-goat-searching gear together.

We are standing at the garage pad waiting our turn. Aria is standing next to me and looking forward to getting out of the city for the first time in quite a while. I can't blame her.

[Almost ready for your ride, Grace?]

#*Absolutely, Host Vic. I've been waiting for months to be ridden by you . . .*

Aria coughs.

It is our turn. I press the orb, and an absolutely beautiful mana cycle with sidecar flashes. It is completely black matte and looks brand new. Not a scratch or stain.

Aria says, "Set all lights except the front and rear to be Vic's azure please, Grace."

Suddenly, along its matte black surface, lights of my azure blue appear along its sides in thin strips and beneath it, giving it an ethereal glow that looks just plain . . .

"Sexy," Aria says.

I nod. "Yes. Grace, you look like sex on a grav plate."

#*Thank you both. This is the best I have felt since I was activated. Now hop on and let me show you how well I can serve beneath you . . .*

Aria just out and out laughs this time as she moves to sit in the sidecar. I take the seat behind the control pads.

[Activate shields and all defensive measures. We're going out of the city, and there could be some danger, so make sure you keep your auto-targeters looking for danger.]

And we are off with the nearly silent hum of the sexiest vehicle I have ever mounted.

CHAPTER 105

[Jo, give me a path to our destination.]

I see the line that Jo always shows me and follow it. After twenty-five minutes, we are out of the city heading southeast. I speed up slowly to test the mechanics, and everything seems fine. Raising our anti-grav, we are twelve inches off the stone-paved earth and with a slight finger movement, I push the reactor. We speed forward, the mana shield protecting us from the wind and debris.

We pass some farms and other smaller buildings, all protected by mana shields and a few auto-turrets. Then we pass the last vestiges of humanity's hold in this area and are in the wilderness.

"Vic, this is amazing. When can I drive her?"

"You only get to mount Grace when I get to watch."

#Host Vic is quite kinky. Miss Aria, I am open to it if you are . . .

"I'm totally into it. Grace, you are the only lady I will share Vic with. Well, Jo, but she is part of Vic, so it is more like she is sharing him with me."

That is both true and sweet. Now stop flirting and start working. We are in danger zones for the rest of our journey . . .

"Hey, Vic, next time let's leave the sidecar and I'll sit behind you."

Of course, I'd love to have her near me the whole time, but there are practical concerns. "Are you sure? It could be a long ride having no back support. And we'd lose the sidecar's armaments."

I don't think she's given up on the idea when she says, "Let's see how it goes."

After two hours of traveling using what little remains of the old roadway system, we have to get off and travel over open land. During our travels, we pass many reminders of the pre-Invasion world. Collapsed piles of scrap that used to be large buildings are scattered around the open area. Aria asks what we are seeing, and I describe the situation that led to it. "All these pre-Invasion constructs used the highly processed materials common to that time, and that dissolved from mana's aggressive disdain for them. This was one of the key causes for the ninety percent die-off of the human race during the Invasion. Well, that and the orcs, of course. But the mana-caused infrastructure failures were responsible for many times more deaths than the Invaders themselves. At least at first."

"Oh" is her only response.

Surprisingly, there are a few buildings with part of their structures still standing. As we pass one I think out loud, "I wonder what it was like to live in the old world. There were no monsters, or orcs, or beasts. Just other humans and the world. It must have been so peaceful. And probably really boring."

Aria laughed. "Honey, unless you are doing something that will lead to the exploding of something or someone, you're bored."

It's true. As I have stated many times, I am a killer. Aria really does not know me well.

We eventually reach our first guideline by the supposed hunter. We arrive at a waterway that—according to the old maps from Commander Franklin—was once called the Carbon River. We are directed to follow it for several kilometers until we are in the mountains. It will cut south and come to a lake. Supposedly, our intrepid goat hunter found the mountain goat just southeast of here against an incredibly steep mountain face. Either way, I'm excited to get out with Aria. We both need a brief break. After all, I've never had a family, and that means I've never had a family vacation before. I'm surprisingly excited, actually.

Another two hours traveling and we find the southern split of the river into a narrow mountain gorge with tall mountain walls on each side. So far, so good. I'm getting hopeful this guy isn't totally full of drake shit. I wonder how he found this place.

I have to raise Grace another six inches (thank you, MilSpec grav plates) to get through this incredibly rocky terrain. The gorge starts to tighten even more, and along with fallen boulders from loose rock faces, we barely make it through. I decide it will be easier and safer without the sidecar. Also, if Aria is next to me, I'll feel she is less vulnerable.

I stop the cycle and sit up.

[Hey, Grace, I wonder if it would be okay with you if we left the sidecar and continued with just the primary.]

#*That would be fine, Vic. Would you like me to disengage? . . .*

"Aria, you get your wish. Climb on behind me."

She climbs out the sidecar, settles herself behind me, wraps her arms around my waist, and snuggles right up. It's nice.

[Disengage.]

There is a click, and the sidecar moves a few into the right and slowly settles to the stony ground.

Location marked...

"Okay. Back at it."

We are able to make much better time with just the primary cycle.

We are approaching the location given to us as the lake. Assuming his distance measurements are correct...

They aren't. He was a good five kliks off. So he's both geospatially impaired and a liar. Whatever, it's still outdoor time with Aria.

#Potentially hostile entities in scanner range...

I immediately stop the cycle and ask out loud so Aria can hear and prepare. "Location and number."

#One kilometer to the south-southwest. Detectable humanoid life forms...

"That is in the direction of where the lake should be. Not a surprise that a lake has life. Let's go slow. Aria, get your scope ready."

I feel a slight shift against my back followed by, "Ready."

We move in our nearly silent cycle about eight hundred meters and can look down into a lake valley. I clearly see a lot of movement. And possibly buildings. That was not in the plan for this trip. I pull my scope and look down into the valley. Aria does the same.

"Shit."

I immediately back us up. Hopefully, none of them happened to look up when we were there. At this distance, it is unlikely but possible to be spotted.

[Jo, can you get a message through to HQ without being detected?]

Affirmative...

"Stay here, Aria. I mean it."

I crawl up to the edge of the valley again and look through my scope for ten minutes, assessing the entire valley. Thankfully, my skin prevents me from being punctured by the jagged, stony ground. My clothes are not so lucky.

[Send the following: Enemy spotted sixty-five kliks southeast of Sea Saddle City. Based on structures, encampment contains approximately sixty orcs, and at least three ogres and two trolls. Night assault viable. Request instructions.]

CHAPTER 106

"I came here for a lovely few days off with my girl in hopes of checking out some goats. But no, I have to run into a fucking raiding band of the enemy. Fuck these guys! Screwing up my vacation." I'm back with Aria and Grace, pacing and clenching my fists.

"Vic, honey. You're ranting."

I sigh but don't stop pacing. "I'm sorry, love. I'm annoyed that our romantic outing is ruined. Now I am going to have to send you back on Grace to the entrance of the gorge and prepare for a night assault mission. Ugh."

"Wait. What do you mean send me back? I'm helping."

I knew this was going to happen eventually. I just wanted a little more time. Be strong, Vic. You can be strong enough for this.

"No Aria, you are not. You are going back."

"Don't do this, Vic. I'm not useless."

I turn to face her but don't approach. "Love. I'm sorry, but in a situation like this, you are. Not only that, you are a liability to me. Please, Aria. Please do this for me."

"Every time. Every mission. You have not involved me once. What have I been doing all this work for if not to help you?" She almost yells that question.

"Aria. You are the first and only living person I have ever loved. You basically taught me what it means. I wish nothing more than to have you with me as I conduct a night assault on a superior force in a defensible position with nothing but a knife and a close-range mana projector. But you can't. You aren't ready."

She opens her mouth to speak, but I continue without letting her. "You have no gear, no preparation, no training, and no experience. Not only will you get yourself killed, you'll get me killed, alert the enemy we are aware of their position, and lose humanity the advantage of surprise when something goes wrong." I let out a breath. "I'm so sorry, Aria. But you and Grace need to go. And go far. Far enough that if something happens to me, they don't find you when they do a large area search, which they will. I only have a few hours to plan this op." The next words are just above a whisper. "Please, love. Just go."

Aria has tears on her face. They almost make me cry too. In fact, my eyes are getting a little misty. Please, Aria. Please.

Instead of yelling, she whispers. "You think you'll die?"

"No, I don't. With my gear, training, and magica I think I can infiltrate, gather intel, conduct a few silent kills. If I'm lucky, terminate the leadership and cause chaos. But if you come, I will be so worried about you I will make a mistake and fail. And yes, die."

Warning! Host has received 1 bludgeoning damage . . .

I saw the slap coming of course. It didn't hurt. Physically, at least. Do I ache this much because we're lovers? Would it be less painful if I still thought of her as I did before?

Her face is angrier than I think I have ever seen it. "Don't you dare blame me! Everything that happened to my mother was my fault—I won't be responsible for your death too. And I. Am not. Weak!"

I open my mouth to tell her I didn't mean it like that, but before I can speak, she turns around, wipes her eyes, runs to Grace, gets on, and drives away, not looking back. Damn.

Now I have to do something I don't want to.

[Grace. Do whatever it takes to make sure she stays on you and is ready to return to the city. If it goes bad, you put everything into shields and grav plates and get home. Turn the shields bi-directionally so she cannot get off. Stun her if you have to. She is not to follow me, get off the bike, or do anything other than wait for word. If something goes wrong and I fall, you leave immediately with her. Grace, confirm your orders.]

#Confirmed, Host Vic. I'll take care of her . . .

[Jo?]

I'm so sorry, Vic . . .

[I don't understand what she meant by everything that happened to her mother was her fault. Shen died because I flashed too much coin. On top of that, she's never been on a mission before, so how could she understand that it isn't about strength or weakness? It's not her fault she doesn't know what she doesn't know.]

You're right, she doesn't understand. But she loves you—just believe in that . . .

[Hopefully, that stays true. For now, we only have a few hours to plan for a night assault.]

Confirmed...

***

I receive authorization to conduct the assault from SF HQ, which means it comes indirectly from Honor. So much for my retirement.

Having darkness magica makes all the difference when it comes to night assaults. Not only can I power my gear, I can attack from angles that were never available before. Then again, still no sniper rifle. I need to resolve that gap.

As I enter the valley after the sun goes down, I equip my darkness armor, knife, and projector. This should be fun. I'm trying hard not to think about Aria. I need to focus.

[Night assault mode. Hold all non-critical alerts.]

Confirmed. All cloaking enabled, all silencing enabled, maximum stealth. Three hundred percent charge on suit...

The orc perimeter is a half-circle. They have put red mana lights every twenty meters or so as a sightline for the roaming sentries. It appears they are planning to make this lake a base of operations. I see sentry towers under construction all along the perimeter. Fortunately for me, only three are completed enough to house a sentry.

#Aria has attempted to return to the gorge...

FUCK!

[Please tell me you stopped her.]

#Affirmative. She claimed a biological need and attempted to return upon completion. I engaged the N14 Omni-directional Stunner and have isolated her inside the mana shield. I cannot lift her, but she is in the shield and will not be able to leave it...

[Did you two make it to the gorge entrance?]

#Affirmative...

[Thank you, Grace. I hope Aria doesn't hate you as much as she will me.]

#I'm sorry, Host Vic...

Vic, sentry approaching. Target in range in ten seconds...

On mission, Vic. Focus.

An orc wearing brown leather armor with metal plates in critical locations is walking just outside the light perimeter. Walking inside will prevent him from seeing out effectively and reduce his night vision. Orcs are not stupid. He has two throwing axes on this belt and a meter-long sword on his back, marking his readiness for melee and ranged combat.

[Inspect.]

Name:	Orc Scout (Sentry)
Description:	Orcs are fighters, plain and simple. They live for combat and use it to determine everything from mates to leadership. This orc is a specialist in sighting and tracking prey. Always prepared to act, scouts generally have exceptionally heightened senses and act as the first line of defense to prevent surprise attacks. As a sentry, this orc is armed for both ranged and melee combat. He has a mana horn to call for reinforcements or send messages very quickly. Note: Mana horns do not require air to blow through them. The air mana infused into them just needs to be activated.
Condition:	Healthy
Risk Assessment:	Moderate
Value:	None beyond its death being good for humanity and its allies.

I send enough mana for a kill shot to my wrist projector and silently creep just outside the line of the light perimeter. He turns to the right, not noticing anything. I pick this location because it is a corner of the semicircle perimeter. For patrollers, corners are always the most vulnerable to night assault, which is why most camps are round. As this one is only partially set up, it is a semicircle and thus has two corners I can and will exploit.

Once the sentry is a quarter of the way between mana lights, I create a bubble of darkness around the mana light at the corner, and it snuffs out. I silently sprint forward, holding my projector steady and aimed at the orc as he turns to see why the light went out. I fire, and the lightning-fast black blur of my mana strikes the orc in his unprotected throat just as he is taking in a breath to call out and reaching for his signal horn. I wrap him in darkness quickly and he falls without a sound.

Target terminated...

This is what I discover is the truly deadly part of darkness magica. It is a complete lack of everything. When inside it, unless you're used to sensory deprivation, it is a very traumatic experience. Not for this guy, though—he's already dead. Maybe he's lucky.

I drag the sentry's body back to the trees, release the darkness magica on him, and stay there awaiting the next sentry. Most orc bands have a tendency to change patrols rarely, once a day or so, which means I should be okay for a little while based on my observations while planning. Well, with three exceptions, but that's next. The reason for the scarce patrol swapping is simple; they don't require nearly as much rest as humans. Orcs sleep for about three hours every human day at the most. It is a distinct advantage in almost every kind of warfare against all other species. Some in the UFH feel it is one of the two reasons they wage war so effectively. The other reason being, they reproduce in mass.

Well, the next five sentries don't have to worry about reproducing anymore, as their bodies are now lying beyond the tree line. Wanting to try something, I touch an orc sentry body and think "Send to [Living Inventory]." It disappears with the exception of a spatial container and the horn. Yes! I send the other corpses and [Inventory] or absorb what won't go. After my mana bar is full again, I head into the camp; now for those three spotters.

CHAPTER 107

The orc subculture is one of combat and strength. The better the fighter, the higher up in the hierarchy. That does not mean a bunch of dumb barbarians are in charge. The top combat experts are just as clever and tactical as any humanoid. Orc leadership is strong, brilliant, and dangerous—especially the few exceptional leaders that run warbands. If they weren't so clever, they would have lost the war tens of thousands of years ago.

The shaman caste is a little different, as they only compete among each other and are rarely challenged outside of the caste. They are few in number and quite powerful so are not considered expendable. From what we understand, shamans are often the voice behind the fighter caste rulers.

And finally, orc-kin such as ogres, goblins, ettins, and trolls have a different set of rules. An orc cannot usually kill an ogre, and almost nothing can kill a troll.

When the leadership of a raiding party like this fails to do something major (such as, say, defend their camp), they are challenged almost immediately. And if a leader is killed, there is usually a power struggle for a replacement. I have used this many times to my and humanity's benefit as a distraction and slowing tactic. It doesn't last long, but minutes can matter.

In this case, my primary targets are going to be the orc leadership as well as the ogres and trolls. If I had known this was going to happen, I would be packing mana explosives. As I don't have any, I have to rely on stealth and magica. I even think I have a plan that just might work for the trolls, but it's a substantial risk. We'll see.

Before any of that, I need to terminate the surveillance of the three sentry towers. They will be the first to see the outer perimeter sentries dead. Again, this whole plan only works because there are just three completed and occupied towers covering a proportionally large area.

Terminating a guard at the sentry tower isn't as challenging as I fear, thanks to darkness magica again. The image of sentry towers covered by lights and seeing everything is nonsense. If there were lights, how the fuck would the sentries see anything not lit? Their night vision would be trashed. Sentry towers are not supposed to look inside the camp, but out. And to see out, they need their night vision or targeted mana lights (which these don't have). The purpose of a tower is to use the advantage height gives the observer. Anyone who attacks is going to be theoretically easy to find thanks to the light perimeter, sentries, and the noise and lights they will make. At larger, more built-out encampments, I've seen some sentry towers with mana spotters or auto-defense crystals, but not in this makeshift dump. And who would possibly expect a human with darkness affinity to just happen to pop by their lovely little camp in a hidden valley surrounded by mountains?

As I silently make my way further in and away from the light perimeter, I cross a few wandering late-night orcs who I have to avoid or kill silently, but that isn't hard with this gear. I [Living Inventory] their bodies—corpses lying about would kind of give me away; missing orcs are explainable in any number of ways. I reach the first tower and watch the sentry until he gives a signal then climb the ladder in silence. The orc is looking out at the perimeter with a crossbow. Over a period of less than two seconds, I place a darkness bubble around the top of the tower, point my projector, and put a kill shot to the back of his neck.

I climb in, put a knife in his brain, and [Living Inventory] him.

Target terminated . . .

I successfully repeat this at the second tower; again a few orcs have to die on the way. Too bad.

The third sentry tower is a close one. I think this sentinel is getting suspicious, having not seen the expected patrol. While he is scanning the area, the orc actually sees me stick my head over the top of the ladder. The surprised look on his face lasts just long enough for me to set up a darkness bubble around his body. I flip on [Mana Sight], thinking it might grant me the ability to see what is going on inside. It does through the particles, and what I see is surprising. He is freaking the fuck out. Thrashing and waving his hands, followed closely by dropping his crossbow, waving his knife frantically, and eventually stabbing himself. I shoot him at that point. After a knife through the brain, the body disappears. What an interesting reaction.

Target terminated . . .

There is some compelling research going on that postulates orcs have heightened senses which help them in combat. Our allies insist it is true but are unable to provide evidence beyond the obvious. I wonder if the sensory deprivation of darkness does more to them because of losing all of their advanced sight, hearing, smell, and touch. Definitely worth experimenting with.

Assuming they follow our understanding of their standard check-in processes, I have approximately an hour and a half. That is why I waited for them to signal. It would be more, but I had to travel between them, after all.

[Show me a timer for eighty-five minutes please.]

I'm now on the clock, and it is time to move onto the bloody slaughter part of the mission.

I sigh. I was supposed to be on vacation.

***

As I reach clusters of tents just inside the outer perimeter, I find them in groups of three to five, and each cluster is spread out farther than I would expect from my previous experiences. I wonder why until I see the clan colors different for each cluster. Ahh. These particular clans don't get along. I can use that. I head to the cluster I believe is the best opportunity, as it lacks sentries and sufficient mana lights. This must be a minor clan.

Thanks to my suit and training, I enter a tent completely silently. A snoring orc is lying on his back on a thin mat. In his sleeping hand is a chain that leads to the corner of the tent. A young female elf is asleep with a metal collar at the end of the chain. I always hate this part. I cannot free them; I simply will not take the risk. Mission first. I made the mistake of freeing slaves once when I was new and naïve; it got all the slaves killed and myself nearly killed. I couldn't sleep for weeks.

I snap out my knife silently, slit the orc's throat, then jam the blade through his jaw into his brain. One to silence, one to kill. Sure, the throat-slitting usually kills, but not always. I once nearly died to a supposedly dead orc who was wearing a healing ring. Always be sure.

Target terminated . . .

I hit the sleeping elf with a stunning strike from my projector; Jo tells me the alert states she will be out for no less than an hour and, given her physical condition, likely longer. If she wakes up and sees her captor gone, she may try to flee and disturb the camp. Sorry, miss. Mission first.

[Lower the timer to sixty minutes.]

One hour and counting.

I think for a moment about sending the elf into my [Living Inventory], but

I just don't know enough about it. I haven't sent anything in there but myself, and I didn't even really go. And candidly, I believe keeping its existence a secret is more important than the lives of these individuals. It has the potential to change the war and, as cruel as it sounds, these poor slaves do not. I have not even reported the unique skill to KH . . . yet. So I decide to just wait and hope I can release her and the rest of the slaves later.

I kill and [Living Inventory] every orc and stun every slave, some male, some female, in this cluster. The next cluster is similar, except one of the slaves wakes up. She tries to call out to me, but I stun her before she can make noise. Poor little thing. She has clearly been a slave for only a short while, given the lack of damage to her neck from the collar. A tiny slip of a girl. For good measure, I stab that orc through the eye instead of the jaw. I feel a little better after that. I don't use the eye for covert ops because it causes seizures in orcs, which equals noise. This time, I make an exception.

Three clusters of dead orcs and unconscious slaves later (the others are empty), I move closer to the center of the camp. Finding the ogres is easy; they don't have tents so much as cloth houses. At nearly four meters tall, ogres sort of stand out. Unfortunately for me, the center area is well lit with mana lights and has its own patrol. On top of that, the center area tents are closer together, meaning any sound will alert them all.

CHAPTER 108

I have to time this exactly. There is a small gap between patrolling orcs that I could sprint through, but I would have to do it without disturbing anything or anyone. Unfortunately, with the mana lights my suit's effectiveness will be nearly null.

When one sentry rounds a corner, the following cannot see each him, so I can slip by at just that moment. In theory, at least. I'll be honest; the plan is a little weak, but it's that or risk a noisy assault and then picking them off one at a time when they are alert. Definitely a worse plan. And if it works, once through, there are plenty of shadows to . . .

Shadows. Ugh. I need to get my head out of my ass and fully utilize my capabilities. Granted, I only had a few hours to plan this op, but still. I expect more of myself, and I should.

I am currently hiding in the shadow of a tent that houses a cook, waiting for my mana bar to be completely full. Never *ever* kill a cook. They are the only orcs visited randomly at all times of the day or night. With a flexing of will, I melt into the shadow.

One of the set abilities of my cloaked infiltrator set gives me this ability:

10 Pieces: Allows the wearer to sink into shadow for 10 seconds. Has a 10-second cooldown. With the direct infusion of darkness mana, the 10-second duration can be extended indefinitely.

Hopefully, this will work. Three seconds later when the sentry turns the corner, his shadow is at its longest from the corner light and just touches a shadow from my tent. I "jump" into that shadow from the cook's tent, and twelve seconds later when his shadow touches a tent's inside the perimeter, I jump again to that one. Thankfully, I have thirty seconds since I charged the suit to three hundred percent, so I use no personal mana as I move from shadow to shadow until I am inside the perimeter enough to be hidden from the sentries. Appearing next to a tent with an ogre, I sneak inside.

Being inside a shadow is interesting. I can see everything clearly, but it all appears oddly angled and stretched. Anyway, it works great, and I can't wait to use it to kill a dragon's hoard worth of Invaders. I exit the shadows and, after letting my mana refill (which was barely used), I blanket the entire inside walls of the tent with darkness and look at the massive creature. This ogre is pale-skinned, fat, and huge, like all its kind. It has a lot of scars and is missing some fingers. Tough life. Oh, well. Time to help him out.

I take aim with my projector and put more than three times the mana I used on any orc. I cannot use the knife on the ogre to silence it; he is just too fucking big. I might as well try to cut down a tree with my fingernails.

Aiming for the temple of its enormous head, I release the shot. The ogre jerks, makes a cracking sound as it crunches something I must have missed, and falls still. It is only then I jam my knife into its eye. I practically have to stick my entire hand up to my wrist to get it in there.

Target terminated . . .

Why do I have Jo keep telling me that? Because they might not be fucking dead!

I [Living Inventory] the massive body to a huge yank on my gut. It hurts. Shit. Need to be careful with that. My skill level is still low on [Living Inventory].

I then see what the cracking sound was. He was sleeping with a female dwarf, and his jerk broke her in an awful lot of places. I nearly vomit. Shit. Sorry, lass. I [Living Inventory] her too, thinking I can maybe return her body to her clan at least.

I search the tent for anything useful. These creatures are considered to have a leadership role, so unlike the peons out there, something of value might actually be here. I find a few bags made of beast skin, of which one is spatial storage which Jo tells me is just its coin. I [Inventory] the coin and absorb that. The others are just [Living Inventory]ed.

Turns out I was right on my count of three ogres, as the last two die the same way as the first. Ogres don't have the same advantages of reduced sleep as orcs. The opposite in fact; it's something about their size. My poor [Living Inventory] is getting filled with just the bodies of my enemies. Shame it's the first thing. I feel like I am dirtying it somehow. Then I think about what Aria would say to my ridiculous thoughts, which causes me to remember the slap and her inevitable anger. Taking the mask off, I wipe my eyes and, putting it back on, admonish myself. All these fucking emotions are going to get me killed. Focus, Vic. Mission first.

Forty-four minutes.

Waiting for my mana bar to refill enough, I move to the next tent, which is an orc of leadership level. I hear two orc voices.

[Translate.]

Orc One: Mithoc, we are being called into the commander's tent. You must attend.

Orc Two: Why? That fool has us here for no reason. The only thing to slaughter here are these four-hoofed herbivores.

They're killing my goats! First, they ruin my vacation and then they kill my goats. Oh, they are so fucking dead.

Orc One: You have received your orders. Follow them or not at your own risk.

I hear shuffling and I see who I presume to be Orc One exiting the tent. I quickly blend into the shadows. He leaves, and I use the shadows to move into the tent of Orc Two—Mithoc, I suppose. Not that I care.

This orc is clearly upset because he is ranting to himself in Orcish, slamming his fists into the desk he must have transported using spatial storage and breaking it into five pieces. His back is turned, and he is panting over what is left of this desk. Darkness surrounds him, and he freaks, just like the other. This is definitely a thing. Pointing my wrist at the bubble, I shoot, followed by the standard slice, stab, and search. I find his spatial storage and divest him of it. His body and everything except his spatial storage goes into my [Living Inventory]. I empty the spatial storage of everything, Jo grabs the coin and absorbs the bag, and I send all the rest to my [Living Inventory]. Two items refuse to go. They are both crystals, and I ask Jo to analyze them.

Accessing . . .

They are both information on orcish clans. There are no maps or tactical information . . .

[Send them to Shield when it is safe to do so.]

I turn around and head to the next tent. No orc. They must be gathering as ordered. I search the tent and nothing is here. Same with the next and the next.

Thirty-six minutes.

A troll's tent follows. I know before I even enter because I see rot on the tent's surface. A side effect of a troll's tremendous regeneration is that it leaches life from its surroundings at times. Not all the time, but usually when it is hurt and needs to heal, and almost always when sleeping. Trolls are nearly impossible to kill because of this. Cut off a troll's leg? It will grow another. And what's worse, there is a small chance the leg will grow into a troll. Super creepy. The only known way to end a troll is to overwhelm its regeneration with fire or acid. Those cause the regeneration to slow to normal mortal levels.

Trolls also tend to be big, strong, and, while not geniuses, are smarter than ogres. The troll king, who started my whole grand adventure, was the smartest and largest male on record. And supposedly able to regenerate acid wounds. I was supposed to test an incredibly high-temperature mana munition on him. Who knows if it would have worked?

I peek my head in and see the troll sleeping. Looks like he's not welcome into the big gathering. I sneak in and blanket the tent with darkness. Here is the tricky part. I am gambling that I can do enough damage to cause mass regeneration and make him vulnerable enough for me to use fire. I hope. I put half my mana into the projector. I'd put more but I still need to use fire. If this experiment works, I can go on a troll-killing spree. Fun!

Using the set's climbing ability, I am hanging by my feet and left hand from the top of the post in the center of the tent. I take precise aim for the eye of the troll. Please work. My hand steady, I fire. The troll jerks and lets out a bellow then falls back. He tries to move and is stirring as his regeneration kicks in and is pulling energy from the environs. He is just groaning now. Thankfully, I put up the darkness barrier, which I now have to release to use other magica.

Knowing acting quickly is the key, I jump down directly onto the troll's chest, engaging the climbing so I stick. In one motion, I create a ten-inch-long beam of white-hot flame and thrust it into the center of his throat. He tries to bellow, but I've burned his larynx to a crisp. His arms reach for me, and I quickly disengage the climbing and leap off his body and flip in the air to be above his head. As I land, I jam the flame right into the top of his head. I hear sizzling, and the troll tries to bellow again, but no sound comes out. I leave the flame in there to completely melt his brain. The troll starts to jerk, and the entire area three meters around the troll becomes a dead zone. It keeps expanding as all life is sucked into the troll. I keep my flame in his head and up the mana and increase its length to reach through his torso.

Warning! Host has 10% remaining mana . . .

More sizzling and twitching, and the dead zone widens for a short time then slows and stops growing. C'mon. Die already!

Warning! Host has 5% remaining mana . . .

I keep the flame going until I hear what I have been waiting for.

Target terminated . . .

CHAPTER 109

I drop all mana use to help it rise faster from the nearly empty bar it is. After [Living Inventory]ing the body, I search the room. There is nothing of note but two ratty spatial storage bags. One is its coin, which Jo handles, and the other contains complete crap like clothing and food I wouldn't touch even if offered coin. I empty it, have Jo absorb the container, and send the rest to [Living Inventory]. The food could make possible compost material. Some of it had maggots. Yuck. Trolls are so nasty.

Speaking of, I can't believe that worked. If I could just hold darkness and another magica at the same time, I could really be dangerous—to orc-kin in particular with their apparent aversion.

[Once it's safe and everything is calm, we need to do some research on the darkness affinity.]

Agreed. Its value is both surprising and undocumented . . .

The next troll tent is empty. I wonder if she's important enough to be at the big meeting. The tent has bones and bone jewelry, as well as a half-eaten gnome male. This tells me our important troll is a female. Possibly a matriarch. That is seriously bad news. Matriarchs use magica. Fuck. I search the tent and find a storage container with . . . what the fuck? What the fuck is she doing with bars of metal? That is all this bag contains. Hundreds of bars of metals. What. The. Fuck.

[[Inventory] its contents and absorb the bag, Jo.]

Complete. You have acquired 950 bars of damascus steel . . .

[Trolls don't make steel. Shit, only their elites even use it. And this is fucking damascus. The orcs I killed in the rainforest used damascus weapons. This is really bad.]

Agreed. While we have insufficient evidence to trace to its source, its existence raises many questions . . .

[I need to hear what is going on in that meeting. And maybe offer some mass destruction if possible.]

I concur . . .

Twenty-two minutes.

I see the largest tent in the middle and I sneak towards it, occasionally entering tents which are mostly empty of orcs. The ones that aren't, I terminate their inhabitants. Sure, orcs don't sleep much, but when they do, they tend to sleep in shifts. Hence why only three of the five clusters were sleeping in the outer region of the encampment. And here, only about one-third of the tents house sleeping orcs. Not that I am complaining about my kill count. I'll kill every Invader I can find, given the opportunity.

The last tent I enter before the large one is clearly a shaman's. All kinds of totems, amulets, and other spooky shamany stuff is hanging throughout. The shaman has a wooden chest in one corner, and by the other corner is a female elf asleep or unconscious in a vine cage.

Looking back at the chest, I step closer but do not touch. This is another one of those things learned from experience. I use [Mana Sight] and see it glowing with green and silver mana. Nature and spatial. Likely the green is the trap. I stop an arm's length away to try to see how the mana is laid out.

I am in no way proficient in magical traps, but normal traps I know. Every trap has a trigger, an attack vector, and an enabler/disabler. Seeing the mana flowing and moving, I start to discern a pattern. My head is aching. Gah. Fucking annoying. I want this trunk; something important is inside.

"You need the shaman's amulet to open it," a raspy voice says in Common. In reaction, I leap back and aim my projector at the source of the voice. The female elf is sitting up in the natural cage, leaning against the vine bars and looking at me. Shit.

[Voice modulation.]

I approach the cage and, very quietly, I whisper, "Please remain silent."

Returning to the chest, I re-engage [Mana Sight] and see the lines of green mana flowing. There are three obvious and bright vertical lines that cross where the chest mouth opens. Those would be the triggers. Following the lines, I trace one to the right side of the chest, and one to the left. At each side, the mana swirls in a circle. The one on the right swirls to the left and the one on left swirls to the right.

I walk back to the elf and ask in a whisper, "When the shaman touches the chest with his amulet, does he unlock it on the right or left?"

Opening her eyes wide, she says, "How did you know—"

I interrupt. "Please, miss. Time is short. I still have to strike at the large tent."

"You're mad. They have a troll matriarch, this shaman, and a commander with two personal guards."

That is way too much for a raiding party. Who are these fuckers?

"Miss, please. I need to know."

She looks at me through the vine bars for a few moments and finally says, "Opens using the left and closes using the right."

I bow my head and say, "Thank you, miss. What is your name?"

"Brinettera. You may call me Brin."

"Brin, please be patient and wait silently."

I go back to the tent and, with [Mana Sight] on, I examine the left "opening" side. The swirling pattern is completely consistent. No variation at all. In fact, that is the complete opposite of the right "locking" side. I bet the amulet is an exact match in mana flow to the locking side and thus an exact opposite on the unlocking. Clever lock and trap.

I go to the locking side and send a small amount of nature mana into my hand. A vaporous ball appears above my palm, which I begin swirling around with a flex of my will. I manipulate it a bit here and there to get it the exact size and perfectly circular shape of the "lock." After thirty precious seconds, I am able to also duplicate the swirl. Now it is a duplicate in size, shape, and speed of the lock. My head is pounding. I carefully take that to the unlocking side and press it against the lock. The green flickers and dies.

I drop my [Mana Sight] with a sigh of relief. Returning to the front of the chest, I break the vine and wooden lock with my knife and lift the lid. Old fashioned . . . weird.

Inside is a massive spatial zone with mounds of coins, clothes, rolled parchments, a ton of amulets and totems, bones, and bodies.

[Do we have room for all of this in [Inventory]?

I recommend placing all the bodies and bones in [Living Inventory]. The rest can be placed in your standard [Inventory].

I do that. After it is empty, I ask Jo to absorb the chest, and after a few seconds and tingles, it vanishes.

That was an impressive gain. A very powerful spatial container. And likely very expensive . . .

So I'm taking his coin, his stuff, and his expensive chest. Ah, well. Win some, lose some.

When the chest vanishes, something remains behind. Under what would have been the chest is a hole with a bag the size of a gnome in it.

[That clever fuck.]

Indeed. Nobody would dare move it for fear of the trap and the shaman himself...

I touch the bag and nothing happens.

It is not a spatial container...

I open the bag, and inside are mana crystals of all shapes and sizes; the colors are red, blue, gray, and brown. All the basic affinities.

The bag vanishes a moment later. Time for the big meeting.

Thirteen minutes.

I walk to the elf, whisper one word ("patience"), and walk out.

CHAPTER 110

There are two orc guards at the main entrance to the large tent and many shadows are available around the well-lit circular structure. Unfortunately, there is a large open area to the opposite side of the tent entrance and no cover there—so the front door it is. I melt into a shadow on a nearby tent and shift to a shadow of the entrance guard, then again right at the tent entrance.

Moving to a shadow on the inside of the tent, I observe a large area with a table. Five burly orcs, one troll, and a smaller and stooped orc shaman holding a gnarled wooden staff sit around it. The commander is easy to spot at the head of the table and flanked by two guards. The shaman looks confused for a moment, scans the tent, then looks back at the group arguing at the table.

[Translate with clan color as an identifier. Record.]

Red-blue Orc: . . . not be working with humans. They cannot be trusted.

Black-red Orc: K'thok clan agrees. We should kill them and steal what they wished to sell.

Blue-black Orc: The K'thok clan are as stupid as they are lazy. We are going to use what they are selling us to kill the dwarves.

The commander is watching the back and forth with a sneer. His guards have no facial expressions at all.

Blue-white Orc: The Rithick clan can kill the dwarves without these abominations. Humans affront the great mother and our ancestors with their creations. We should kill them, destroy the filthy things, and return to planning for the dwarves.

Red-blue Orc: The Rithick clan only cares about their failing ancient traditions and rotting ancestors. We should kill the humans and use their weapons, not destroy them.

My mana bar is at half.

Red-Black Orc: You are both fools. Why would we kill them when we can study and improve their creations like we've done before? We will use their weapons against their disgusting allies and then against them; then those too will be beneath our feet and chained in our beds.

The commander speaks up then.

Commander: Culthork is correct. We are using these humans' greed and killing their allies.

It does not miss my notice that the commander is also wearing red on black.

Black-red Orc: Of course the commander sides with his clan. The N'graks are always manipulating the situation to take advantage.

Matriarch: Humans are nothing but food and barely that. Your feeble struggles against these mortals are petty and weak.

The shaman bangs his staff on the ground, and it makes a cracking thunderous noise. All the orcs except the commander and his guards wince. The matriarch ignores it just as easily. Thankfully, my mask and armor filter it for me.

Shaman: The argument is pointless. Our master has ordered us, and we will follow his commands. And I sense the approach of our . . . allies in their flying abominations.

All the orcs and the troll stand and exit the tent. I drop one of my surveillance crystals, tell Jo to camouflage it, and quickly flow through the shadows out of the tent. Shadow jumping to a tent that is the last one next to the large central command tent, I can see the group move to the opposite side of the large tent and into the cleared area. I leave the shadows and duck to refill mana and observe what is to come.

The group lines up in two groups with the commander, matriarch, and shaman a large step in the front. A few moments later, I can make out red and white lights in the sky approaching. My mask has excellent darkvision (as you would expect from a night assault set), and I can see it is a gray grav transport with four projectors in the front and two in the back.

I have grav jumped out of many just like that. In fact, I dropped out of one from fifteen kilometers to start the mission in the rainforest those months ago. It has the word "MagiTech" on the side door and nose. The traitors' vehicle approaches and slowly lowers to float three inches above the ground in the center of the clearing with a hum.

The loading door on the side slides open, and two humans step down and take two steps forward. They are wearing black combat suits of plated liquid steel and are armed with large fully automatic mana projectors. A third human, a woman wearing a black suit with a white shirt, follows them out, walks a few steps past the guards, and stops. The orcs, not changing their formation, approach.

The human speaks. "I am here for the sale. Commander N'grak?"

The commander steps forward and speaks in growling Common. "Human, you are late. If I was so inclined, I would kill your men here and now, take your cargo and the vehicle, and chain you to pleasure me."

The woman scoffs. "You and your barbaric filth would die before you drew your arms. The vehicle would destroy itself before you could capture it, and I would kill you in your sleep."

The matriarch takes a step forward and speaks up. "I wonder how your bones taste, human. Should I rip off your arms and have a lick?"

This is likely posturing to demonstrate neither side is weak or afraid of the other . . .

[Really? I was expecting a make-out session shortly.]

Nobody likes a wiseass . . .

The human speaks again. "I could melt you into a puddle of goo at my feet, troll. Now are we here to trade or threaten?"

The commander huffs, takes off a ring, and throws it to the woman. She catches it, puts it on, nods, looks back at the transport, and calls out, "Bring it."

Two other humans exit the transport carrying a steel box one meter wide and half a meter deep and tall. They drop it at the feet of the woman and head back into the transport.

The human says, "Remember our deal. Those are not something we can produce again. For you, at least." Then she turns around and walks back into the transport. The two guards climb aboard, and the transport raises into the air and flies off.

The orc commander walks up to the box and opens it. Unfortunately, I cannot see what is inside from here. A minute of looking inside later he speaks in Orcish.

Commander: Bring it back into the command tent. We must discuss our attack on the dwarven clan meet and agree which of your clans split which spoils.

The commander waves, and two orcs approach from the side, pick up the box, and carry it around the tent. All the orcs follow and head back in.

[This is really bad.]

I agree, Vic. A dwarven clan meet has the leaders of the largest clans in attendance. It will be a catastrophic blow to the entire dwarven race if there is great loss of life . . .

[It also has to be incredibly heavily guarded. Whatever they received has to be devastatingly powerful.]

#Host Vic, Aria is awakening . . .

[Is she all right?]

Yes . . .

[Hold her there.]

#Affirmative . . .

I have informed her I am blocking her communications. She is quite angry at being stunned and trapped . . .

[I understand. I'm trying to protect her. And everyone.]

I'm sorry, Vic . . .

Mission first, Vic. Focus. Deep breath.

[I am tempted to just launch a large-scale strike on the tent. If it destroys the weapons, that would be victory enough.]

Agreed. Prior planning did not account for these variables. Destruction of the weapons has been prioritized . . .

[I need to see where that case is in the tent.]

The surveillance crystal cannot see it . . .

[Back with the fun kids, then.]

Using the shadows, I sneak back to the entrance and scan the tent layout. Everyone is back exactly where they were except that the steel box is to the left of the commander at the opposite corner of the tent from the shaman and matriarch.

[Is the tent protected?]

I need you to touch it to be sure, but I do not believe so. Your entry was not barred, and there is obvious damage to the cloth walls . . .

[We are going to go with no, then. I'm calling an objective change. I need to destroy that box at a minimum and the tent if possible. And you might as well turn off the timer.]

Change recorded . . .

That sort of thing is valuable for the AAR. Recording changes to an unofficial but authorized mission is a very military thing to do and a habit I follow because there is no downside.

The timer vanishes off my HUD just as it passes under the four-minute mark. I exit from the large tent and look around. There is nowhere I can see that shows me the box from the entrance. So I am attacking from the side. Okay. In that case, I need a good angle and possibly some height. Moving to the side of the tent with the box, I look around.

[There!]

CHAPTER 111

I agree, Vic. An excellent find...

I move towards my target, killing and [Living Inventory]ing orcs along the way. I cannot even express how much of an advantage it is to store the bodies. If I had to use a regular spatial item, each individual body would take its own slot, never mind all the gear and other miscellaneous items. And of course, missing orcs and dead bodies result in two very different outcomes. Needless to say, I've had a tremendous advantage over any of my previous encampment or facility assaults.

Having reached my target, I climb up and kneel inside the partially completed sentry tower. It only has two walls and no roof, but it offers height, the right angle of attack, and it is adjacent to the perimeter for a more direct route for evac.

[I need mass destruction here. The biggest boom I can produce.]

I recommend using high compression. It is likely the large-scale absence of orcs will be noticed shortly if it has not already. That the bodies are gone has bought you some time, but that cannot last...

I agree completely. Kneeling behind the wall and facing the corner to produce as little light as possible, I create a ten-inch ball of fire. I heat it to white-hot and push down to compress it to two inches.

[Hopefully not leaving bodies bought us time.]

I add more to the outside of the two-inch ball, and it is ten inches again. And I compress again, this time to three inches. And again. I repeat the process until my head is aching with the pressure of holding so much compressed mana. The most compact I can achieve before it becomes unstable is nine inches. My mana bar is at twelve percent and shrinking.

[I need to improve my Mana Compression skill. I hope this is enough; that box looked reinforced with enchantments.]

Sticking my head up, I look around and see a good amount of motion.

[Looks like some orcs are missing from the camp and nobody can find them. That's a shame.]

Quite...

Keeping the ball in the corner, I line up my body for a targeted strike on the spot where the box hopefully still is. I bring the ball over and its light gives away my location to everyone in the area. I hear calls in Orcish.

Warning! Host has 10% remaining mana...

I point, and the ball streaks towards the tent. After it launches, I leap out of the tower, ready to run for the perimeter as soon as I land. Then a massive white flash appears behind me. It lights up the entire valley enough that it appears to be day. I land and sprint for the trees.

I can feel a vibration from the earth beneath my feet as I run with all my enhanced strength. I see the wind whipping around me as dirt and dust flies by. And then I am struck from behind by the shockwave. [Flood my skin] is all I can think to say as my body is kicked into the air and hit from behind by a stone that knocks my body rotating horizontally. I can barely understand what is going on when I feel a massive collision to my legs followed by spinning until my back hits a tree trunk followed closely by my head and I know only blackness.

***

When I come to, I look up at a dark blue sky.

[Oh, shit. Is it dawn?]

Actually, it's dusk of the next day. You were concussed, and your regeneration took a while to heal your wounds. I managed to harden your skin at the last moment as you requested so your wounds were not fatal, which they would have been. That explosion was... extraordinary...

[There is no way my blast did that.]

I agree. The likely cause was inside that box. Alerts report that you slew all but the matriarch and shaman. Likely the matriarch managed to regenerate sufficiently; it is also likely her resistance to fire is higher than most of her kind. I show no damage to the shaman, so he either ported out or had a powerful shield. By the way, the shaman's elf slave is not shown as slain as well. Unfortunately, every other slave died along with the orcs...

Damn. I had hoped I could do something for them.

[What are my debuffs?]

None at present. You are a hundred percent. Aria is a mess. She saw the explosion all the way at the gorge entrance and has been hysterical with worry for you...

[Can you tell her I'm fine and will be on my way to her shortly and she is to stay there? And that I'm sorry I worried her and that I love her. Grace, has she remounted you?]

#She has, Host Vic. She is crying all over my seat . . .

I sigh. My poor elf is probably feeling alone and trapped. Again.

[Time to go back and see the damage.]

It was clever of you to think of your skin at the last second, Vic. It saved you . . .

If I was really clever, I would have thought of the possibility of setting off whatever they "purchased" from MagiTech. Even though modern mana explosives generally don't work that way, I should have been more prepared. That being said, even if I did expect it, I never would have been prepared for an explosion of that magnitude. What was MagiTech thinking?

My mana and health bars are full. So I stand up and walk back to the encampment.

CHAPTER 112

As I step out of the tree line, I see a crater 150 meters in diameter in the middle of where the encampment used to be. Dragonballs on a plate!

[There is no way something small enough to fit in that box should have been able to produce that much heat and force. Sure, I've seen a sixteen-inch projector do it, but that takes so many mana stones to fire and has such a long cooldown it isn't worth the expense and risk. What the fuck is MagiTech doing giving this to the enemy? Can you imagine the impact it would have on the war if I was able plant one of these in the various encampments throughout the globe? And are they building those in a human city?]

Recall the MagiTech operative's statement of not being able to easily produce more . . .

[I suppose, but this level of betrayal just doesn't make sense. They are humans too and would fall under the orcs the same as the rest.]

We need more information to understand the motivation. For now, you should focus on the updated mission objectives which you successfully achieved . . .

[I was trying to destroy the box and maybe the tent and leadership, not the whole fucking camp. And think about all the storage containers and intel lost . . . and the poor slaves.]

Harsh as it may seem, your original aims are no longer relevant. You already know this to be true. As for the spatial containers, intel, and slaves, it is likely you would have fled before acquiring any of them either way. At least this way they do not serve the enemy, and the slaves are free from torment . . .

Still not pleased with myself, I say nothing. She's right. I know she's right. That doesn't make me feel like we had a victory though—objectives achieved or not.

I walk to the edge and look down. The crater is completely empty. There is nothing representing life in sight.

[Can you imagine what would happen if this went off in a dwarven cavern complex?]

The damage would be apocalyptic...

I wonder where the matriarch and shaman are. Did they port out? They are certainly not here. Nobody and nothing is here. It's a fucking dead zone.

I climb into the crater and slowly work my way down and towards the center.

[Can you get a signal to Noctis Venandi?]

Not without Grace seeing it too. She is my repeater. I can send to SF HQ, but the codes will be seen if not understood...

[Damn. That's a no, then.]

As I move closer to the center, I hear cracking beneath my feet. Looking down, I find the top layer has superheated to a thin solid. Kneeling, I pick a piece up and look at it. It is a glossy black sheet that, when I hold it up to the nearly set sun, I can see is filled with bubbles of various sizes. How the fuck did this happen? Mana explosives are supposed to be specifically designed to not go off unless triggered intentionally.

What a fucking waste.

Eventually reaching the center of the crater, I clear out a small area of the glass-like crust and put my hands in the ground. I plan to send my mana down into the earth and see if there is anything worth salvaging. There is little hope, but I figure it's worth a try. Just as I am pushing my mana down, a wrinkled green hand and arm breaks through the dirt and latches onto my throat. I try to scramble back, but the hold is firm. As I grab my knife the arm jerks sideways and smashes me into the ground, headfirst. All I see are lights and sparkling colors, and all I hear is a ringing that won't allow me to focus.

*Warning! Host has suffered a **stunning blow**. Host is unable to take any action for 10 seconds...*

When I can think again, I see the matriarch climbing out the dirt of the crater, still holding my neck. Looking around, I see my knife was lost out of reach by the jerking motion and blow to my head. The matriarch excavates herself from the ground and lifts me up. I am hanging by my neck six inches off the ground, but she is not choking me dead for some reason.

Her voice is like scratches in my ear. In Common, she says, "Well, hello there. Did you do this, human? Do the humans believe they can sell to us weapons and then use them to kill us? You did not think I would survive, did you?" She gives off a dry crackling laugh.

I notice half of her other arm is missing. Creepily, I see it slowly growing back. Fucking trolls.

"I have been living and eating and growing stronger for longer than your species could make cohesive sentences. You can't kill me. And once I share your betrayal, you won't have anyone to trade with."

Leaning in, she says quietly, "Your bones will help me recover, and I will enjoy hearing your screams as I pull them from you."

Sending a massive flood of mana into my lightning rune, I throw a blast at her. She screeches loud enough to deafen if it wasn't blocked by my armor. She drops me, and I scramble away on my backside.

I throw a darkness bubble on her and engage [Mana Sight] and focus on what is going inside it. I find her twitching on the ground and can tell if she weren't in the silence of darkness the screams would be louder still. Returning to normal sight, I begin to stand when I am launched into the air by a massive thrust from below. My body slams back into the hardened ground and rolls towards her. Then I am launched again. This time when I land, I my knee collapses out from under me with a crack. Screaming, I grab at it. She is clearly still screaming as well, but neither Jo nor I can hear it through the darkness. All I know is my knee is fucked, and she can control earth magica. I have managed to keep focus sufficiently, so the darkness has kept her crippled. Unfortunately, I need to heal my knee, but I'll have to let go of the darkness magica to do it.

Deciding against it, I start to crawl towards where her head is in the black cloud. What I see through my just reengaged [Mana Sight] is that she is ablaze with green and brown mana. What appears to be tentacles of brown are whipping and waving around in the ground with her at the center. As one is about to touch me, I roll away from it. Just as I roll, a section of earth jolts up where it would have contacted me. So that is how she did it.

The green glow outlines her body perfectly; I can see it entirely internal to her body and she is using it to eject the purple lightning. In fact, it's almost gone. There is a substantial portion of the green going to her left arm, likely to heal and regrow it. However, what stands out the most is a blazing element of green in her center where a human's naval would be. What the fuck is that? Humanoid creatures do not have mana cores.

I have to roll again to avoid another blow from below, which brings me back to my current predicament. There is no way I can get close with those earth tentacles waving about randomly. Shit, I'm going to have to release the darkness so I can heal and regain mobility. I do and immediately flood my knee with directed life magica. As the dark smoke fades around her, I feel the pain and swelling drop and the ligaments and tendons knit back into place.

Able to move again, she looks around and sees me. Both of us stand. I reactivate [Mana Sight] and start to raise my hand. She quickly raises and stomps her foot, and I see the glowing brown of earth mana shoot towards me. I leap to the side, and a sharp spike as long as I am tall launches out of the ground where I was standing. I roll and point at her, and she is once again covered by darkness. She screeches again, and I drop [Mana Sight] as I sprint towards the edge of the crater.

Massive spikes of earth start driving from the ground all over the crater. I have a split second notice before a spike lances into my right leg from behind. As I am sprinting forward, I fly off the spike rather than stay impaled, but blood flies everywhere, and I scream in pain yet again. Damn, that hurts!

Lying on the ground, I flood my projector with mana. Fuck this shit. Pointing it at her, I use [Mana Sight] again and try to keep my hand steady. Specifically, I aim for the bright light in her center. Putting two-thirds of my remaining mana into the shot, I fire the projector. The dark mana strikes true, and she screeches even louder than before, doubling over. I drop darkness and heal my leg.

In my [Mana Sight] I can see the light in her core dimming. What the fuck? Additionally, with that bright green fading, I can see slight silver lights in her thighs. Spatial inside her body?

She screams words in Troll that I skip completely because Jo doesn't speak Troll, and I don't give a fuck what she's saying. My leg is strong enough for me to stand and I haltingly do so. I create a blue flame spear and launch it at her. She sees it coming and glows brown. A pillar of dirt lifts from the earth and takes the hit of the spear. It drops, and I create another and launch it. And another and another. I launch spear after spear. At the same time, I have a single fireball forming, white-hot like the last one but not nearly as compressed. After the sixth fire spear is blocked, I fire another and simultaneously send the flaming ball.

Warning! Host has 10% remaining health . . .

The white-hot mass is not headed directly at her like all the spears before. The troll matriarch sees it at the last second and glows brown, but it is too late as the compressed globe makes contact with the ground a few inches to the right of her foot and explodes. There is a flash, and a blazing white explosion lights the valley for the second time today.

CHAPTER 113

I crouch down with my head between my legs and my arms over top. The shockwave hits me and, while it is certainly nothing even close to the MagiTech-assisted one, it still sends my exhausted body rolling a short ways. I send life magica to my prone form and look over at the matriarch. She is covered in white flames, rolling on the ground, whacking at herself with her one complete hand and arm stump. I use my [Mana Sight] and can see the matriarch's brown mana fading. Unfortunately, I also see the green in her center very slowly lighting up again.

What is that? I prep and launch a blue flame spear at her. It strikes her right shoulder, and she screams again. I throw another and hit her in the hip.

Warning! Host has 5% remaining mana ...

Damnit.

I stop spending any mana and release [Mana Sight]. The white and blue flames are still burning all over the matriarch's body, and I get up and exhaustedly walk the long way around to her head. She cannot seem to focus on anything but putting the fire out.

[Activate mana lifeline with fifty percent of my health.]

I suddenly feel a little weaker as my health bar drops to a little less than half, but I see my mana bar rise a bit.

I create a white flame spear, walk up to her thrashing form, and thrust it into the top of her head. She screeches again, but the screeching fades slowly as her thrashing halts. I find it interesting that the area does not rot like other trolls. Are matriarchs different?

I activate [Mana Sight] again and see the blazing green back where it was. Not quite as bright but close and getting brighter.

Warning! Host has 10% remaining mana ...

Releasing the flame spear, I stand back up and walk to her side, kneel next to her, and, focusing, create another fire construct. This time it is only red hot, and I mold it to be shaped like a hand. I put my real hand inside like it is a glove and drive it into her center. Using [Mana Sight], I can see where that bright green glow is. I surround it with my hand, close my flame-gloved fingers, and yank.

With a squelch and sizzle, I pull out a glowing green crystal. The instant that happens, the green fades from her in my [Mana Sight]. I disable it, and I can see her body start to shrivel and darken from green to brown. Dismissing the flame glove, I press my hand on her chest and release an aura of death. I find the remaining dimming life from her and suck it out.

Target Terminated . . .

I fall on my butt and just pant for a few minutes.

[Jo, tell Aria to leave the sidecar and she can come get me in the valley if she still wants to.]

I will. You just killed an immortal . . .

[We all have bad days.]

I send her body into [Living Inventory], but after it disappears, I hear two clinks and see two small round pins.

[Are those the silver lights I saw? She stored spatial containers inside her body?]

It appears so. Touch them and let's see what we have . . .

[That is so unsanitary.]

I touch one and then the other.

One is a substantial cache of coins—which I have taken—and enchanted objects of much variety. You do not currently have sufficient spatial subpockets to store them. The other is another four thousand bars of damascus steel. I have moved those into the spatial subpocket with your prior stack . . .

[Absorb the empty one.]

It vanishes. I stand and scan the area. Nothing. As that wasn't exactly a quiet battle, I can assume I am alone.

I take my travel clothes out of my [Inventory] and send my armor in its place. Naked, I pick up my clothes and walk to the lake.

[Make sure we get that armor repaired. And let Aria know I'll be in the lake.]

Affirmative . . .

I put my clothes on the lakeshore with the pin and green crystal on top, slowly walk in, and just submerge myself. Not saying or thinking anything particular, I swim around in the lake. I am floating on my back on the surface when I hear Grace approaching, I assume with Aria driving.

She drives right up to the shore. Looking over, I see Aria getting off Grace and walking to the edge of the water. I stop floating and swim closer, but not all the way. Everything except my head is submerged.

She sits at the edge of the water and says, "Hey."

I look at her.

"Jo walked me through your entire mission while I was driving here."

I just keep looking.

"I'm sorry, Vic. I didn't realize." Then in a near whisper, I hear, "I didn't know."

She looks down and puts her hand in the water slowly moving it in a circle.

"You don't understand what it is like to be responsible for the death of family. What you said brought back memories and guilt. I know you weren't, but I thought you were blaming me for being too weak and getting you hurt. Like I was for my mom." That last part is a whisper. "Being too weak to help and watching those you love die in front of you is the greatest torture I know."

She sighs as tears fall from her eyes to mix into the lake. "None of that was your fault. You did the right thing—protecting me and yourself. But I couldn't see it past my anger and sadness, and I hurt you."

She had been looking down at the water with her hand in it this whole time. Now she looks directly at me.

"I'm sorry, Vic. I betrayed your trust and your love. I know how hard those things are for you and I . . ." She chokes. "I'm so sorry."

The lakewater running down my face stops Aria from seeing my matching tears. With a glance, I find my mana full again. I create a ball of fire under the water near me. It starts to bubble and seethe. I push the ball a little deeper and send more mana into it. It glows brighter, and the water around it heats. Then the area starts to steam.

"Come in before I run out of mana. The lake water is clean and pure."

She giggles and wipes her tears away then strips and joins me. We swim around just holding each other; our closeness representing her apology and my forgiveness. A fish flops to the surface. And then another.

I cut off the mana and say, "How about we camp out? I think I found us a late dinner."

She hugs me so tight I think she wants to squish me inside of her. I hug back, and we stay that way until there are a dozen fish on the surface of the lake and the water cools again.

CHAPTER 114

We are lying in the tent together at the edge of the lake in a single large sleeping bag.

Aria is snuggling close to me when she says, "So you kind of blew all the orcs up. A lot."

"Well, they killed my goats."

She snorts and then stuffs her face in my chest in embarrassment.

Chuckling, I say, "I'd still like to see if I can still find any. This gorge is a perfect habitat for them with food around the various bodies of water and mountains for defense and housing. In the morning we'll try again."

"Whatever you say" is her response.

[Jo, can you move any appointments and send a message to Master Steeltamer? Tell him his clan meet is compromised and give him a sanitized summary of the orc's conversation as well as the events.]

Sent...

[Also, send a message to Gunny saying: "I'll be starting my own fishing company soon. You interested in a career change?"]

Sent...

[So. Alerts?]

I feel the plethora would not meet your current needs...

[I feel that too. Advice?]

How about I just give you the death toll and essence total to start?...

[Sounds like a quality plan.]

Total kills:

57 orcs - 40,844.73 mana essence

3 ogres - 12,988.01 mana essence

2 trolls - 31,436.90 mana essence

31 elves - 24,512.08 mana essence

12 dwarves - 11,947.33 mana essence

3 gnomes - 3,810.30 mana essence

7 beastkin - 11,877.21 mana essence

4 humans - 441.01 mana essence

Total mana essence - 137,861.57

[I feel sick.]

Vic, I will say it again - there is nothing you could have done for them. They were going to be slaves for the rest of their tortured lives. You gave them a quick death and an escape they could not have dreamed of. Contrary to what you desired, you were never going to be able to save them. Any of them . . .

I still feel disgusted with myself.

Would you like to stop or keep going? . . .

[I can't keep focusing on my failures, so let's push on. I know we got a lot of stuff. How about coin?]

Platinum - 41

Gold - 1,239

Silver - 13,311

Copper - 9,845

[Ummm. What the fuck were they doing with so much coin?]

Unknown. Most of that is from the matriarch and the shaman's chest . . .

[This is way off, Jo. This feels wrong to not just me, right?]

It is indeed quite suspicious. Trolls are not known for spending coin in great swaths. It is a mystery why such an amount would be the matriarch's possession. You also need to include the near five thousand bars of damascus steel. This is definitely not what one would expect to find . . .

Reaching over with my left hand, I push my pants out of the way and grab the glowing green crystal from the matriarch.

I've distubed Aria in my stretching, so she is looking and sees it. "I've always thought mana crystals are pretty."

I nod. They are, in their own way. But that is not what this is.

[Inspect.]

| Name: | **Marsh Troll Matriarch's Regeneration Core (Nature)** |

Description:	Troll females are not born strong or with the ability to regenerate like their male counterparts. Instead, they can use magica. For marsh trolls, it can be earth, nature, or water. As troll females age and eat a diet high on meat and bones, they become stronger and grow physically. Eventually, they will reach the same size as males. When this happens is unknown, but at some point in the female's aging, she grows a mana core in her lower torso. It is always one of her primary affinities, usually but not always the same as her first. This core acts as a mana and regeneration engine for her and makes matriarchs exceptionally difficult to kill. Once a matriarch ages beyond 5,000 years, she is able to regenerate limbs and cast Magica at a near-constant rate. Once a matriarch ages beyond 10,000 years, she becomes strong enough to cast wide-ranging area-of-effect Magica and is nearly impossible to kill due to the strength of her regeneration core. Once a matriarch ages beyond 20,000 years, she is considered *immortal* as her core will regenerate her as long as it is still inside her body, no matter the body's condition. Regeneration cores are different from normal mana stones in that they offer mana essence and regeneration essence. While not an affinity, regeneration essence is still beneficial as it grants the host the ability to regenerate a limited amount of health without using mana.
Condition:	Excellent
Risk Assessment:	N/A
Value:	This is the first recovered core from a matriarch over

	20,000 years old. The item is quite literally priceless.
Special:	Nature essence count: 8,221/15,988 Regeneration essence count: 10,274/17,103

Repeating the matriarch's first words to him, I think [Well, hello there.]

I concur...

[Can I only absorb the regeneration essence?]

Yes. I can take care of that for you, but you shouldn't. And why just that essence?...

[What do you mean I shouldn't? Regeneration sounds amazing. And as for the nature essence, I suspect someone else is going to be able to use it soon.]

I see. That will help her quite a bit. You have an alert that will make regeneration essence moot. But I'll hold off on that, as I believe you are about to be occupied...

Good enough. Turning on [Mana Sight] I look down at Aria. I see her blazing gold like always. But this time I see a tiny flickering of green in there too. I thought I was mistaken in the past as my skill level was low and I was just not used to [Mana Sight], but now that I know what to look for, I can confirm it is definitely there.

Turning it off, I try to get my elf's attention. "Hey, love?"

"Mmm?"

"Have you ever tried nature magica? I have no idea how elves activate or whatever their affinities."

She shakes her head against my chest. "No. My life magica is so strong it will overwhelm any other magica I might have had. Remember we talked about this?"

I cough slightly. "Ummm. Would you believe me if I told you I could see nature mana in you?"

She's silent for a full minute and then asks, "Are you serious?"

"Totally. When I look at you with [Mana Sight], I see the green of nature. It is very dim, but definitely there."

She's silent again.

"Are you sure? It can hurt me if you're wrong."

"I'm nearly positive. But now you've made me nervous," I respond hesitantly.

She kisses my chest and makes a request. "Can you inject some nature magica into me?"

Taking a nervous breath, I re-enable [Mana Sight] and send the loving partnership of the green nature mana into Aria. I see the green flood her body and direct it at the minuscule sparks in her heart, head, and just below her navel. It is welcomed by the dim green already there, and her green merges with mine and flares bright. I disable [Mana Sight] and see Aria glowing green as she is looking at her hand and seeing the evidence for herself.

The green glow doesn't fade as she looks at me, absolutely beaming. She hugs me and kisses me and says "Thank you" a few times in between kisses. Then she thanks me the only other way she can, still glowing green the whole time. I also glow green as we hear the song of nature, our bodies are in perfect rhythm with the humming of the natural world around us and our love.

CHAPTER 115 - INTERLUDE

<u>Somewhere:</u>

"Our slaves failed."

"Failed."

"We will succeed."

"It must die."

"It's kind must die."

"It will die."

"It will be wary now."

"Yes, wary."

"We are hidden."

"Hidden enough?"

"It will die."

"We will continue."

"We will continue."

"It will die and we will continue."

"Another opportunity approaches."

"Opportunity?"

"It will come to us."

"It wants power."

"We will give it power."

"And it will be ours."

"And we will continue."

To Be Continued . . .

AFTERWORD

Before anything else, I want to thank my readers from Royal Road for helping make this a better story. THANK YOU! THANK YOU! THANK YOU!

Indie authors depend on reviews and word of mouth for advertising, so if you would be willing to write a review that would help me a lot. I especially love the 4 and 5-star ones :-)

***

I want to apologize if you experienced struggles with the tables. Kindle as a platform is terrible at them. I did the best I could to keep it legible and hope you will be tolerant. In the end, the layouts are out of my control. Thank you for your understanding.

***

As with all LitRPG works, it is important to recognize the experts, sources and public faces of this relatively new genre.

First and foremost I want to recognize the awesome authors that make me want to keep reading and make this genre what it is (this is by no means an encompassing list. Just the ones that make me want to read and write):

- Aleron Kong
- Tony Corden
- Daniel Schinhofen
- Johnathan Brooks
- Xander Boyce
- Jay Boyce
- Tao Wong
- M.H. Johnson
- Jonathan Smidt
- Blaise Corvin
- Alexey Osadchuk

- Roman Prokofiev
- Shemer Kuznits
- R.A. Mejia

And about a bajillion more! Thank you all so much for inspiring me to write, even through you had no idea you were doing it :-)

I REALLY REALLY want to thank and encourage you all to watch to the LitRPG Podcast on YouTube. It's amazing.

https://litrpgpodcast.com/lit-rpg-novels/
Ramon is wonderful I listen just about every week.

Also, you should think about joining these Facebook Groups:
- GameLit Society
- LitRPG Book
- LitRPG Adventures: Reviews & Discussions
- LitRPG Daily

And for you fellow authors:
- LitRPG Author's Guild (Admined by the incomperable Ian Mitchell)

Printed in Great Britain
by Amazon